They're at It Again

Stories from Twenty Years of Open City

D0879570

They're at It Again

Stories from Twenty Years of Open City

Edited by

Thomas Beller and Joanna Yas

 OPEN CITY BOOKS

All stories were originally published in *Open City* magazine; where applicable, further acknowledgements appear on the first page of the piece.

Printed in the United States of America

Book and cover design by Nick Stone

Library of Congress Control Number: 2011905947

OPEN CITY BOOKS
270 Lafayette Street
New York, NY 10012
www.opencity.org

ISBN-13: 978-1890447-59-5

11 12 13 14 15 16 17   10 9 8 7 6 5 4 3 2 1

For our readers and writers

Contents

Introduction

Thomas Beller

1.

A LITERARY MAGAZINE'S RELATIONSHIP TO TIME IS A strange thing. A newspaper is pegged to news of the day; a weekly magazine can be dated by the content and style of the ads—the more cutting edge the product (a computer, a car), the more absurd and enjoyable the ad in hindsight. A glossy magazine has the fashions of the day in the ads and in the photo shoots, exaggerated and immediately identifiable. Even web sites become visually dated and of their time. You can distinguish a page that is current from one made five years ago or even two years ago; my own personal site has a 2001 feel, and like someone who holds onto clothes or drives an old car, I harbor the vague wish that it will shortly become aglow with a retro appeal that will rescue it from its current dowdiness.

Magazines that publish literature, on the other hand, are trying to publish news that stays news. Should good writing date? Yes and no. Pick up the best literary journals and the writing is still fresh even if the magazine itself seems totally of its time: this is true of almost every issue of the *New American Review*. If you stumble onto Philip Roth's first published story in *The Paris Review* from 1958, will it still seem to be a fresh piece of writing? Yes. But you will read it differently knowing what he went on to do. This is also true of *Grand Street, Antaeus, Granta, Threepenny Review, Story,* and so on. The old issues are snapshots of a world. The assembled writers and their work are the visible part of that world. If you have been involved with putting the issue out, however, they are also markers in your own personal life, with a whole cosmology attached, rooms full of people, some dead, and some changed beyond recognition, old loves, old arguments.

2.

At around the same time we decided to close *Open City*, we had a party for issue 30. I waded into it with this dark secret, which made the party more intense and in a strange way heightened the joy.

Open City has always had amazing parties. We do this for fun, and to promote the magazine. But I would argue that the people involved at the center of it—Daniel Pinchbeck and I, at first, then Robert Bingham, then Joanna Yas—have all had a very deep need for extended family. To compare a party to a family is too much. But a magazine is like a club, and the parties were, in some odd way, indoctrinations.

The party was in a narrow bar on the Lower East side (we did one party in Brooklyn and it wasn't so great; in this way *Open City* is a bit of a dinosaur, a Manhattan-based literary scene). Ed Park, editor and writer, read a droll short story. Alissa Quart, a whip smart cultural critic who did a Nieman Fellowship at Harvard and returned to New York with the stunned, almost wounded look of a poet, and a manuscript of what she described to me as "nineties poems," read her poetry. The bartender, a bear of a man, screamed at everyone to shut up and then eloquently chastised the chatterers for not respecting literature. Everyone shut up, for a minute.

I stood at the front door greeting people as they came in and making sure they forked over their ten dollars for the issue and free drink. Way back in the beginning, Daniel and I, and then Rob, too, would stand at the door at our parties and try and collect five or ten dollars, try to sell the magazine. We treated it like a hustle. The money was small time, petty cash, but the feeling was enormous.

In our earliest days, 1991 or so, Daniel and I ran a reading series atop a bar called Flamingo East on Second Avenue and Thirteenth Street for which we somehow got people to pay five bucks. I remember the pleasure of splitting the cash afterward. Martha McPhee read at that series, a story we later published; her first. An agent rushed her after her reading.

This would be the last party for the magazine. People of many different ages were crammed into the bar. This wasn't a generic crowd, not a passive herd grazing the great plains of art galleries, nibbling cheese, but rather people who were excited and on a mission—a mission to be part of something, a passion for writing, self-promotion, and everything else that happens when people dress up, go out, see and be seen. A mission to talk.

I took particular pleasure, that night, from a number of conversations I had with people in their early or mid-thirties, who seemed totally amazed and psyched to be at an *Open City* party, with great issue just out, ten years after they had first discovered the magazine. They spoke with that back-in-the-day nostalgia that is tinged with self-congratulation. I was there! I was there at the start!

What I loved about these exchanges was that these people were all referring to a period around 1999, 2000, 2001. We had just started to publish books at that time, an incredible run right out of the gate: David Berman, Sam Lipsyte, Meghan Daum.

They were recalling a moment of contact, when they came into the world of letters, the world of writers and publishers, suddenly animated from something distant to something they were part of, something they could aspire to and enter. And they did enter that world! The people talking to me had jobs, they were surviving, writing, editing.

For them ten years was an incredible span of time. It *is* an incredible span. During that time, Open City Books published authors including Jason Brown, Rachel Sherman, Jerry Stahl, Sam Brumaugh, Leni Zumas, Steve Tesich, and Edward St. Aubyn. But as they spoke, I was thinking that by 2000 the magazine had already existed for ten years. The time they harkened back to as a kind of golden age was a time when the magazine had been rocked by tragedy in the form of Robert Bingham's sudden death. The whole scene was so awful: both Bingham and I had books coming out that spring. He had just gotten married. It's terrible to talk about it, both for the facts recalled, but also because of how insufficient the talk is to live up to the moment.

At the time of Bingham's death we were preparing an "editor's issue." For some reason that was never thought through but everyone seemed to agree on, we hadn't previously published ourselves in the magazine. The editor's issue would be the exception to that rule.

The issue was about to go to press. How to handle it? Not publish the issue? Publish it without comment? And what kind of comment should there be? And who could provide guidance on this matter? It seemed absurd to go to press without comment, but what to say?

I had written an editor's note for issue one, and I wrote another for issue ten, trying to juggle grief and a wish to not be funereal, to honor Bingham by going forward. It was a ridiculous wish but that was how I felt. We ran a gloomy photograph by Ken Schles, who did our first two covers, on the cover. "No one told us adulthood would get so complicated," my editor's note began.

As David Berman said recently in an article about the magazine's closing, it is amazing that *Open City* continued for another decade at all. A large part of that is owed to Joanna Yas. It took a little while for Daniel to formally leave. It was a difficult transition. Our ideas about literature, contentious but fun in the past, melted into something unrecognizable. I was interested in writing; his interests had begun to encompass the religious and the apocalyptic. This was an unhappy, delicate time—we had started the magazine together, then become part of a trio, and were now left with each other again. I started a web site devoted to location specific essays set in New York. It was like a solo project.

For Daniel and me, the magic, the thrill, the compassion and empathy, whatever we had as friends and co-editors, was gone. We bashed each other over the head in various ways. Then Daniel sailed off to other adventures and Joanna and I went about the business of putting out the magazine and finding books to publish. I scanned the horizon and acted on whims, reached out, delved now and then into the slush pile, all the work of an editor. I attended to fundraising.

Joanna also worked as an editor, and in addition she more or less did everything else. She was a one-woman publishing house. Her editorial skills and organization were only part of what powered the magazine forward, though. Another part was that Bingham had hired her. She knew him. She knew Daniel, had witnessed our interactions. She had seen a lot of crazy stuff in the year she worked for the magazine before everything blew up. She had seen it blow up. And so even if she hadn't been around for the first decade, she understood it, somehow. She embodied it, became its archivist. On a spiritual level, this was crucial and wonderful. It was continuity. It was a way forward. So we went forward.

3.

This anthology is a punctuation mark on *Open City*'s two decades and marks the end of the magazine's run. Why did we close? We decided to close the magazine the way Hemingway described bankruptcy—gradually, then all at once. Our last issue was so good, I thought, and the party for it was so good. Why stop? On the other hand, why not go out in top form, when everyone is still in a good mood?

Now we have arrived at two round numbers: issue number thirty. Year number twenty. We'd often been referred to as a literary quarterly, and over the years have participated in a kind of soft obfuscation—about our circulation, about how often we published. To have these bold round numbers, twenty and thirty, seemed almost funny in their plain truth.

4.

Some of the stories in this book appear in their entirety. Quite a few are excerpted. In one case (James Hannaham), the author revised the version we published and asked us to print the rewrite, which we have done. We were going to print the whole thing; his rewrite came in half as long as the original.

"Excerpt," in most of these cases, is a euphemism for reading the first pages until it seems like what the story sounds like. We decided on doing excerpts so that we could get as many voices and styles represented, and to coast on as many coattails as possible. But it was not an easy decision.

Everyone I talked to about the idea of excerpting pieces, all of whom had been in the magazine, was in favor of doing a book full of complete stories. But, after expressing this opinion there was, often, a brief pause. Something clicked, and they said (actually it was Vince Passaro who said this, but Vince contains multitudes), "On the other hand I'd rather be in there as an excerpt than not at all."
His story, "Cathedral Parkway," appears here in its entirety, but I felt the sentiment would be widely shared. Better something than nothing. This imperfectionist credo is what, in part, made doing *Open City* seem possible to me.

5.

For a long time I prided myself in being able to hustle a living while doing the magazine as a patrician gesture. By patrician I partly mean in the social sense—grand, beneficent, Plimptonian. But I also mean it in the sense of patronage, of patronizing, which is surely one of the most ambivalent words. On one hand it means to condescend to, and on the other it means to support, to respect and admire.

Doing *Open City* was an opportunity to assume the patrician position: to grant favors. To create something for which there is no explicit need, only a desire. The patrician position is where you get to be a "Yes!" in an ocean of "No's."

Open City was always edited by more than one person. We always emphasized the yes. Everyone got to publish what he or she loved. We were not about consensus. We were about enthusiasm and intensity.

It's good for your health to say yes. But the irony of running a literary magazine is that after a while it also becomes an exercise in saying no. It's a no machine. Every day envelopes pile in, to which you have to say no.

New literary magazines are always about a circle of friends as much as an expression of any literary aesthetic, though the two can be hard to distinguish sometimes. Personal affinity often leads to literary affinity, and vice versa. It's common, though so is the pain that is felt when one does not lead to the other.

If a magazine exists long enough, it comes to be seen as a kind of public utility and one's slowness in responding to the slush pile is greeted with the same irritation as a blackout or lack of hot water. As an aside, where did the phrase slush pile come from, and what does it mean? Bingham, with his typical knack for ingenious mispronunciation, always called it the sludge pile, which in many ways seemed accurate. We would launch occasional attacks on it, but it always seemed to grow larger, like primordial ooze which threatened to overtake the whole operation.

Any new magazine dedicated to new writing will inevitably be focused on new writers, but not all new writing is by new writers. In fact, not all new writing is by living writers. There is an archival component to most of our issues—we liked excavations and reclamations, and posthumously published such writers as Richard Yates, Cyrill Connolly, Ford Madox Ford, Jerome Badanes, Alfred Chester, Charles Bukowksi, and Paul Bowles.

Inevitably, our early years involved a lot of hero worship—Bingham and I staking out Robert Stone at the 92nd Street Y. Daniel summoned an Allen Ginsberg photograph of Paul Bowles lying on his deathbed to illustrate Alfred Chester's letters to Bowles in Tangier. We landed a David Foster Wallace story and nonfiction from Denis Johnson; I reached out to Mary Gaitskill, who published short stories in issues number 1 and 7.

The second decade's energies tended more towards discovery. We published ten issues in our first decade, and twenty in our second. A list of writers who had their debuts in *Open City* could fill it's own volume: Lara Vapnyar, Amine Wefali, Sam Brumbaugh, Vestal McIntyre, Martha McPhee, Alba Arikha, Sylvia Foley, Josh Gilbert, C. I. Shelton, Ish Goldstein, Cannon Thomas, Nico Baumbach, Malerie Willens, Ryan Kenealy, Sam Lipsyte, and many more.

6.

Of all these yes's one stands out for me.

Vestal McIntyre's story "Octo" was discovered at a group reading party at contributing editor Laura Hoffman's apartment in 2000. Betsey Schmidt, editor at large, who was pregnant at the time, stood up and said, "maybe it's hormones but I think this story is amazing."

I read it and, not pregnant, concurred. I was really excited about it. I went kind of nuts about that story. Part of my excitement may have been the result of reading unsolicited manuscripts which, done in large quantities, are not good for the soul, or any sense of literary perspective. But there was more to it than that. This evening was at that awful juncture when the whole enterprise was fraying and its future seemed unclear, not least of all because it now had so much emotional baggage. I needed a cause, and here it was.

The manuscript, it turned out, had been sent eight months earlier. The phone number no longer worked. A terrible sense of anxiety, of missed opportunity shot through me. It had started to snow. The party was breaking up. I got in my car with some other people, including Vanessa Lilly, and we went to the apartment building of the writer and rang his buzzer. There was no answer.

Just then the building's front door opened and out walked a college friend of Vanessa's. This was fortunate. There was a flurry of explanation. We went in, found the author's front door, and knocked loudly. McIntyre's roommate opened. I don't know what happened to the buzzer, if it didn't work, or if he was asleep, or avoiding someone. We didn't ask. We just explained that it was urgent we speak to Vestal McIntyre. He was at work at Florent, the roommate said, and was there now.

By now it was snowing hard. The ground was all white. It was now nearly midnight. The sense of urgency derived in part because I loved the story, in part because it had been in the slush pile for nearly a year, and in part because it had been sent to the old office at Robert Bingham's place, and so it was a link in a way between what *Open City* had been and whatever it could be, which was a magazine that might publish this amazing story, if it was still available. The Meat Packing District was still defined, in part, but the string of Christmas lights outside Florent. It was still a place where you could pull up and park more or less in front of your destination. It still felt lost, a strange baroque secret inside the city. The setting for a mystery, which was about to be solved.

"Where is Vestal McIntyre?!" we yelled upon entering. I'd had to fight my way through sheets of heavy plastic to keep the wind out. The place was empty. A man with menus clutched to his chest, rather slight and gentle looking, approached. He was a little guarded, understandably.

"That's me," he said.

We explained ourselves. He said the story was not yet published or accepted anywhere else. It was accepted on the spot and we toasted with glasses of champagne. Throughout I was delighted but also felt I had made too much of it, the guy had written a lot of stories surely and I was projecting my own urgency onto this one. So it was gratifying, and shocking, when he pulled up the back of his shirt and showed us a giant tattoo of an octopus that covered his whole back, a sign of his dedication to his material.

7.

The last decade of editing *Open City* has felt in some ways like having custody of a child. The other parents are either dead, their absence both total and impossible to grasp, or I am on such bad terms with them that we never, ever speak, until we're not even on bad terms, just no terms. But I have the kid. And the kid, one way or another, always brings me back to that lost world, the early days, and also the disturbing time when everything exploded. But, to persist with the custody thing, the kid was a lot of hard work but also an incredible source of joy. Like children do, *Open City*, by sheer force of the life, energy, and good feeling it generated, lifted my spirits, lifted me into a state of pleasure and curiosity and life. It's a magazine, it's over, life will go on. But there was a lot of life in it. A lot of death, too. Thirty issues in twenty years. A lot of life pressed into those pages.

The Long Ride Back Home

Mohammed Naseehu Ali

Mohammed Naseehu Ali, a native of Ghana, is a writer and musician. He is the author of The Prophet of Zongo Street, *a short story collection. Ali's fiction and essays have been published in* The New Yorker, The New York Times, Mississippi Review, Bomb, A Gathering of Tribes, *and* Essence. *A graduate of Bennington College, he lives in Brooklyn.*

 BEFORE THEIR DEPARTURE FROM BOLGATANGA'S lorry station Abure had told his son, Sando, that they would be on the road for only two days. But the journey was now in its third day, and from hushed conversations Sando overheard between the driver's mate and other disgruntled passengers, they still had at least another day of travel before they reached Kumasi, the big city down south.

The M.A.N. Diesel-headed lorry was packed with sheep, yams, goats, guinea fowl, cows, bags of millet, bales of hand-woven *fugu* fabric, and about two dozen humans. The lorry's long rectangular hull, divided in two sections contained the beasts in one, while the food, human, and merchandize cargos were held in the other. With little room below, about half of the passengers had to perch on the food cargo—their heads extending beyond the lorry's wooden frame, in danger of being tossed to the ground any time the driver dodged a pot hole.

The lorry traveled at donkey-trot pace. To make matters worse, the driver stopped at every village along the Bolgatanga-Kumasi highway, to either off-load or replenish his human and animal cargos. Sometimes the driver would disappear for hours, visiting a relative or a mistress, as some of the passengers insinuated. Some of the passengers would roam about the town or village to buy food. Others would bring down their animals, so they could graze in roadside bushes and to also defecate before they loaded them back onto the vehicle. There were three other boys and a girl in the lorry who were about Sando's age, and Sando had hoped he and they would perhaps form a friendship and play together; but all the kids acted as if they had sworn a vow of silence.

I

Between his chest and his raised knee Sando clutched a rubber bag that contained his only possessions: two worn out *obroniwawu* T-shirts, a sleep cloth, a pair of hole-in-the-knee khaki trousers, a straw hat, and a cache of creative, handmade playthings that included his favorite and most valuable belonging—the catapult he used for hunting small rodents and birds. The catapult, a gift from his maternal grandfather when Sando turned nine, was a testament of the old man's confidence in Sando's hunting ability. Sando's marksmanship, the accuracy with which he nailed grass cutters was so superb the grandfather nicknamed Sando "the shooting wonder of the savannah." Many times during the trip, Sando fingered the contents one by one, to make sure the catapult was exactly where he had put it when he had packed up the bag.

The air in the lorry was laden with the putrid smell of cow dung, the incessant high-pitched quack of guinea fowl, the odor of unwashed human bodies, the acrid, sustained stench of oozes from open, untreated cutlass wounds the passengers had suffered back on their village farms, and finally, the odious and murderous reek of hunger. Shortly after the lorry had left the station, a bitter, sour, and nauseating taste rose from the linings of Sando's colicky intestines. It made its way up his throat and then to his tongue, where it lodged throughout the journey.

Barely two years before this, Abure had taken Alaraba, Sando's older sister by three years, to Kumasi, where she worked in the household of one of the city's richest men. At least that was Abure's claim. Abure had also told Sando and his mother that the rich man Alaraba worked for had been so impressed by her diligence that he had enrolled her in a night school, to learn how to read and write. Whether this was true or not, Sando had no means of knowing, as both he and his mother had not heard from Alaraba herself since she was taken away.

Sando was one of thirteen children Abure had sired among five women. Like his father, Sando was short and wiry, though where the boy was as perky and nimble as a gazelle, the father was as slow as a tortoise, and when in conversation blinked slowly, like one who had seen a witch in broad daylight. Sando, as if to make up for not inheriting his father's blinking-eye syndrome, stammered when he spoke.

Sando's father had never married any of his children's mothers. The tradition of his Frafra people, a largely animist population with few Christians and Muslims among them, demanded from a potential suitor a dowry of four hefty cows and a lump sum of money before one was given a wife. A perpetual lazy bone to begin with, Abure certainly didn't have the means to afford even a cow's leg, let alone four bulls. He, like many men in the Frafra north, relied on the alternative, concubine arrangement, which conveniently suited Abure's amorphous lifestyle. He came to the women, impregnated them, and left. But as soon as the children reached the ages of ten or eleven, Abure returned and snatched them from their mothers. He took them down south, to work as house servants. With the monthly wages Abure collected for the children's labor, he purchased mosquito coils and bicycle spare parts, which he sold up north for much bigger profits. With such neat arrangement Abure couldn't have asked for more from the god of his ancestors, to whom he now and then offered libations for lifting him out of the perpetual destitution in the north.

Five days after Sando and his father had set off from Bolgatanga, the lorry crawled into a parking slot at the infamous Kumasi Kejetia Lorry Park. As Sando and his father meandered their way through the city's humongous central market—where they delivered Abure's guinea fowls to his customers—the young boy fantasized about living in one of the multistory buildings he had seen from the lorry's top when they drove into the city. *A real concrete and block house with real aluminum roofing sheets and glass windows and real doors and a mattress for me to sleep on.*

Sando imagined his first three days in this sequence: Day One—take a bath, eat, and sleep; Day Two—visit his sister; Day Three—go with his father to find a placement for him at the local elementary school, a promise Abure had made to the boy and his mother. What both mother and son didn't know was that Abure had months ago made a promise to a Kumasi Muslim man named Abdul, that he would get him a good workerboy next time he traveled up north. "Babu Shakka," Abure had sworn. "In Allah's name, I will bring you a veryvery obedient and hardworking boy. And this one is my very own son."

Like most men on Zongo Street, Abdul had multiple wives. Though Islamic shari'ah allowed Muslim men to take up to four wives, Abdul, cognizant of his limited means, had married just three. With as many as a dozen and a half children from his three wives and with no real vocation—other than being a *dillali* for pawned goods transactions on the street—Abdul himself was desperate for a householp that could serve the dual purpose of servant and income-generator in one. Moreover, Abdul's second wife, Asanata, had been nagging him for a servant, to help with the family's increasing chores.

"Thank you, thank you, thank you!" Abdul beamed when Abure appeared at his door mouth with Sando. "This must be the son you promised me, ko?"

"*Babu shakka*," answered Abure in the affirmative. He inhaled his perpetual smoke pipe as deeply as if his very life depended on it.

"He looks like you, ko?" said Abdul.

"*Babu Shakka*. And I promise you he will work wellwell for you and your wife and your family."

After a period of sustained bargaining for Sando's services, the two men agreed on seventy cedis per month, and Abure demanded that Abdul paid the first three months upfront. The haggling was carried out in Hausa, a tongue in which the father spoke only in adulterated pidgin, and of which Sando understood just a handful. Abure looked at his son and grinned, exposing his tobacco-stained teeth. Though confused, Sando bowed his head, unwittingly acquiescing to the deal between the men. In less than five hours of Sando's arrival in Kumasi, the transaction of leasing him into bondage had concluded. Sando was further confused, saddened even; the whole transaction reminded him of another that had transpired just an hour ago in the market, in which his father and his customers had haggled for the price of his guinea fowl.

Perhaps Abure had sensed that Sando was no fool after all, and that the son may have understood what was unraveling. He drew Sando aside and whispered to him: "You will start school in a few months, boy, when school reopens. But first you have to work to raise the money for the fees, you hear me so?" Sando did what was expected of an obedient son and nodded, though by now he had begun to develop a deep mistrust of his father. Abure left a few minutes later, promising he would take Sando to see his sister "when I return in two months time."

Barely seconds after Abure had left the vizier's house, Asanata, Abdul's second wife, handed Sando a sleeping mat, and guided him to one of the two rooms in the *zaure*—a long and narrow passageway that led to the house's open courtyard. Aside from being used for storage, the zaure room assigned to Sando also served as the mess hall for boys in the compound. It was there they took naps in the afternoon, played games, and took refuge at night when they ran afoul of their parents.

Sando looked around the darkly lit room in apprehensive fear. He untied the rubber bag and pulled out his catapult. He did a thorough inspection of the contraption, then slid it in the front pocket of his khaki trousers. He tied the bag, which later became his pillow, and placed it next to the mat. As Sando sat still on the floor, he heard Asanata screaming, "Sando! Hey, Sando! Saaandooo!" Sando answered, "A, A, Anti," and dashed out of the room into the courtyard, responding to the call for what was the first of a million errands he would run for the Abduls and other families in the compound.

The vizier's house was a rectangular behemoth with more than thirty rooms, three open kitchens, and half a dozen chicken coops. Not counting the Abduls, the house contained eleven other nuclear families, and a total of eighty-three inhabitants. And very soon after Sando's arrival, his name was on everybody's lips. "Go buy me this, Sando." "Sando, go and wash my clothes." "Here, Sando, take these shoes and polish them." "Sando go climb the tree and fetch us some mangoes." He was ordered left and right by the old and the young alike. "Sando, you bastard, didn't you hear me call you?" the rascals would bark. Poor Sando would dash toward his commander with a "Sosososorry, Papa" or "Sosososorry, Anti." As his father had instructed, Sando called every female "Anti" and every male "Papa", no matter their age.

Sando's day started as early as the first cock crow. His immediate set of tasks included sweeping Asanata's verandah, filling up the hundred-gallon drum in front of her quarters with water he fetched from the public tap outside the house, washing and sanitizing the sheep's pen, and finally feeding the animals their breakfast of salted plantain peel and water. Then it was time for Sando to start a charcoal fire, boil bathwater for Asanata and her three children, before he set off to buy *koko da kose* for the family's breakfast. No porridge and beancake for Sando; he was given the surplus, hardened *tuo* from the previous night. And on the many occasions that Asanata didn't have any suppie for him, she would casually say, "There is no food for you this morning." To this, Sando would nod and bow his head.

At mid-morning Sando washed the family's dirty linens, polished their dusty shoes, and ironed their wrinkled garments. By the time he was done with these chores, around one o'clock, Asanata had already bottled her *biyan-tankwa* for Sando to take to the market square, where he hawked the ginger brew until sundown. This business brought in a decent income to Asanata—enough to buy food ingredients for the family's supper and to pay for Sando's monthly wage.

Sando's only free time came after *lissha*, when the families had completed the final obligatory Muslim worship, and had gathered in little clusters in front of their verandahs to eat supper. Sando and the other worker boys and worker girls in the compound ate only after their masters and mistresses had finished eating. Sando accepted whatever portion was given to him with gratitude and retreated to the zaure, where he ate in silence. The food was never enough for him, so he topped it with lots of water, and also with the crumbs he sometimes got from other families—their way of compensation for the many errands Sando ran for them.

Sando worked all day and every day, and was unofficially allowed only two free days in a year: the day of the Feast of Ramadan and the day of the Feast of Sacrifice, the two major Muslim holidays. And only on those days was Sando left in relative peace. He would sit in the zaure room as the streetfolks began the festival of eating, dancing, and gift-giving that marked the end of the monthlong Ramadan fasting, and would also do the same during the Feast of Sacrifice, when the city's Muslim residents slaughtered thousands of cattle, sheep, and goats to mark the end of the pilgrimage to Mecca. When would his own eternal fast and sacrifice end? Sando wondered during those festive days, as music and laughter poured in through the window.

Sando was lying in the zaure room on the day of his third Feast of Sacrifice at the vizier's house when three boys barged in and quickly locked the door behind them.

"Bend down," said Asim, the oldest of the gang.

"Whawhawha . . . what now?" asked Sando. He was accustomed to all sorts of pranks and bullying from the compound boys, especially when he returned late from their errands. But Sando didn't remember running afoul of any of the boys lately. He asked again, "Whawhawha, what have I done, now?"

"I say bend down," came Asim's menacing response, followed by a knuckle to Sando's head.

Confused, Sando laughed, but still refused to do Asim's bidding.

"Habahaba . . . haba, whawhawhat . . . what have I done thithithi . . . this time, hah, hah?" asked Sando, who tried to laugh his way out of his predicament.

"I say bend down!" Asim said, and slapped Sando on the head again. He instructed the other boys to hold Sando's arms, and before the poor worker boy knew what was happening, the boys had pulled his half-torn knickers down to his knees. Sando put up a struggle and managed to free himself from their grip.

"Whawhawha . . . what is allall, all this now? I don't like this o!" sputtered Sando. The boys suddenly burst into laughter. But it took Sando a few seconds to realize that they were mocking his *koteboto*, which was an object of derision and even contempt on Zongo Street. "He is koteboto, he is koteboto," they hissed and giggled. Sando quickly covered his nakedness with his open palms.

"Now turn," Asim said angrily, as if the discovery of Sando's uncircumcised penis had further incensed his ire. He grabbed Sando's arm, then twisted it violently. Sando succumbed and lay on his belly. With his nose touching the floor, Sando blew dust into the air, only for him to inhale it again.

Asim quickly climbed on top of the servant boy, his erection blindly seeking the mouth of Sando's anus. Sando tried to move his body sideways, to thwart Asim's efforts, but he was overwhelmed by the other boys' grip on his arms and legs. Powerless, Sando gave up and could only imagine himself a lamb being sacrificed to Allah. A violent pain shot through Sando's body as Asim forced his way through. Sando screamed wildly, but nobody outside heard his cry. A commotion much more important to the compound of the vizier's house was taking place then: a cow being led to the slaughter pit had somehow managed to set itself free. The beast ran amok, knocking down everything and everyone in its path, while the hysterical housefolks ran helter skelter for their lives. The compound was filled with the moos and bleating of the other soon-to-be-sacrificed animals who—in their exclamations—appeared to encourage the aberrant cow to elude its pursuers.

Though Asim and his cohorts were oblivious to what was exactly taking place outside, the loud noises certainly encouraged them to carry on.

"Haba, haba, please. Whawha, what have I done? I bebe, beg you, now," Sando pleaded, as the pain exploded. Asim continued, gasping with each stroke, while the two boys—amid suppressed laughter—hissed, "*I-mishi! I-mishi!*", urging him to give Sando some more.

Who Sando had been before this encounter was now light years in the past. Personally, Sando had hardly thought about sex. He would sit and listen quietly whenever the boys in the compound chatted about their adolescent fantasies and boasted the number of girls they had bedded. In his present agony he wondered if women, when penetrated by men, suffered the same pain he was experiencing. Sando had heard that Kokobiro, the transvestite chop bar owner on Yalwa Street, slept with men at night, and Sando had often wondered how a man could sleep with a fellow man. *How could anybody enjoy this ordeal? Why are they doing this to me?* Though Sando's body convulsed in shock, he feared he might put himself in even worse trouble if he shouted for help. Master would likely take the boys' words over mine, he thought. And, besides, wasn't a servant to obey? Always. He thought of his father's whip and of the distant possibility of school.

After a couple of minutes or so, Asim pulled away from Sando's rear. He was all sweaty and gasping for breath. Calm had also been restored to the vizier's house's compound. The defiant cow had been apprehended, but not until it had dragged its chasers all the way to Zerikyi Road and had triumphantly knocked over the tables and food trays of many vendors and hawkers along its way. The captors flogged the crazy cow as they dragged it back to the house, in blind retaliation of the pain it had put them through. Also, the two dozen or so cattle, goats, and sheep slated for sacrifice had all been silenced by the fawa's blade. The zaure and the large porch outside were smeared with blood as young adults carried the animals into the courtyard, where they were skinned and hanged out to dry in the sun.

With little noise coming from outside, the boys thought it wise to leave, lest they be caught if Sando screamed again. They snuck out of the room, and left Sando curled up on the dusty straw mat. Sweat poured from every pore. His breathing, short and irregular, prevented him from crying. He made an attempt to get up, but his backside hurt so badly he slumped back onto the floor. The sharp, burning sensation around his anus was followed by an oozing down his thighs. He rubbed his fingers on his skin and lifted his hands to the light. What Sando saw was a mixture of blood and a watery, milky fluid, which dripped from him the way water escapes a faulty tap. With a rag he found on the floor, Sando wiped off the mess, and with his backside still on the floor, he slowly managed to put on his knickers.

The following day was the festival's "meat distributing day," when the dried meat of the sacrificed animals was shared among family members and friends and poor folks in the community. Sando was given a few pieces of beef and the innards of a goat, which he spent hours cleaning, to get rid of the feces hidden in the animal's intestines. Later that day, as Sando joyfully made himself a pot of stew with his share, Asim and the two boys approached him. "Let me tell you," said Asim. "If you dare open your mouth about what we did, the whole street would know about your koteboto." Sando swore he would not say a word to anybody. But the boys, assured that Sando would keep his word, raped him several times more, taking turns with each encounter. They stopped only when Asim, who was sixteen, got his first girlfriend. At one point, Sando considered waylaying his assailants near the football park and attacking them with his catapult. But he backed out in the end, afraid that his most-prized possession may be confiscated if he used it in that manner.

Then in the eighth year of Sando's arrival in Kumasi, a group of military officers toppled the country's government. The revolt that ensued after the coup d'état was very popular among the nation's poor masses, who chanted: LET THE BLOOD FLOW! The blood of the small elite class that had oppressed, and made destitute of, the nation's majority. Sando, nineteen at the time, took advantage of the four-month-long chaotic and "freedom for the masses" euphoria that swept the nation. He fled the vizier's house.

Sando relocated to the Asawasi market, to the east of the city. There he found work as *kayaye* and also as errand boy for the rich cola-nut merchants. Very soon Sando was making four times more than his father had made on his behalf. But freedom, as they say, has its perils. Before long, Sando fell into bad company at the market, where he slept in big storage rooms with other migrant workers, in whose midst existed many miscreants. He took to drinking pito, a favorite among his fellow northerners. This locally produced brandy heralded an ecstatic, if delusional, period for "the worker boy from the vizier's house," as he was sometimes called. Sando truly felt that the revolution that followed the coup d'état, for better or for worse, and for all the killings and public floggings of citizens, was waged to free people like him, to give them back their lives—to restore their collective dignity.

Yet, for all of Sando's newly acquired autonomy, sex eluded him to his grave. Apart from what happened at the vizier's house, Sando never had any real sexual encounter—not even the prostitutes on whom he wasted some of his hard earned income. He came very close to fulfilling this desire, once, when Suraju—Zongo Street's notorious swindler and *drinkard*, connected him with a woman at Efie Nkwanta, the old whorehouse on Bompata Road. But, the girl fled the room naked on seeing Sando's koteboto, considered ill omen by the city's prostitutes.

When Sando turned twenty-one, he developed a peculiar, if mysterious disease. It started with a few boils on his left thigh, but within ten days of the appearance of the first boil, Sando looked like a giant boil himself; the affliction now covered his buttocks, legs, and upper body. His face, body, and legs swelled as if he was being pumped daily with a toxic liquid. The boils would break open, releasing a mire that attracted flies to his body. Tormented by this unknown malady, and with no place in the city to call home, Sando headed for the only refuge he knew—the vizier's house. After their initial anger and the curses shot at him for running away from them, Abdul and Assanata, fearful of the karmaic implications of turning away a human in dire need of help, had a change of heart. They pleaded with other folks in the compound to allow Sando the usage of the zaure room. The housefolks agreed, and emptied the room of the bags of maize and konkonti they had in storage. Soon afterward they and their children avoided the room altogether.

A decade after his arrival in Kumasi, Sando had yet to set eyes on his sister. And as for Abure, the last time Sando saw him was when the father trekked to the Asawasi market not long after Sando's escape from the vizier's house. The father tried then to convince Sando to come with him back to Zuarungu, promising to make him partner in a farm he had started. Sando had flatly refused the offer, and had boldly reminded his father of his many deceptions. Powerless against a now grown Sando, Abure had departed in shame. Sando drank himself to stupor that night, a celebration of the fact that for the first time in his life he had mustered enough strength and courage to say "No."

A decade after his arrival in Kumasi, Sando had lost all but only one of the original possessions contained in the little rubber bag he had carried into the city. The catapult. It remained the only surviving link between Sando and his mother and his two sisters and his grandfather and his village. Though Sando never used the catapult in Kumasi, it always imbued him with the hope that he would one day return home to Zuarungu—to the Savannah and its exotic birds; to the lizards he and his childhood friends chased and shot with their catapults; to the nocturnal calls of the black cricket, who at dusk emerges from its hiding place under the logs and burrows to sing and celebrate its mere survival for yet another night. It was in such dreamlike state that Sando's hopes dissipated into the reality of his death as he slept one night in the zaure room. In his final seconds, Sando believed he was embarking on a journey, a rather long one, back to Zuarungu. And unlike the rickety, smelly lorry that had a decade earlier brought him to the city, *he*, this time, traveled in luxury, held aloft by white-feathered angels, who sang the songs of his childhood as they accompanied him, *the shooting wonder of the Savannah*, on his long ride back home.

I Was in Flowers

Jonathan Ames

Jonathan Ames has written three novels, I Pass Like Night, Wake Up, Sir!, *and* The Extra Man, *which was recently adapted for film. His work as a columnist for* The New York Press *was collected in four nonfiction books, most recently* The Double Life Is Twice As Good. *In 2009, he created the HBO television series* Bored to Death, *which stars Jason Schwartzman as a struggling Brooklyn novelist named Jonathan Ames who moonlights as an unlicensed private detective.*

ABOUT FIVE YEARS AGO, I WENT TO SEE THIS MALE prostitute. I'm not gay, but something is wrong with me. Something happened in childhood.

So I saw this guy's ad in the *Village Voice* and called him. All it showed was his muscular torso. But that didn't really matter. I don't care what a man looks like. "I saw your ad," I said on the phone. The rest was pretty easy—price, address, time. He could see me in an hour. If it had been any longer, I probably wouldn't have gone. When you have a self-destructive compulsion you need to act on it fast.

He lived in a five-story walk-up on a busy avenue—bars, delis, restaurants, banks, and drug stores. He buzzed me through the vestibule. I climbed the dirty, anonymous stairs to the third floor and was so nervous I thought I might faint or have some kind of convulsion. I couldn't stop trembling. He opened the door a crack, saw I was harmless, and let me in.

He was wearing an old blue robe and had a glass of whiskey in his hand. He offered to make me a drink, but I only had a glass of water. He had me sit in this old-fashioned, men's-club armchair and he sat on his bed. It took small talk about the weather for me to stop shaking.

"What's it like out?" he said. "I haven't been out all day."

"It's a mild night," I said. It was early May, around eleven o'clock at night.

"I love spring," he said. "I need to get out."

His apartment was crowded and dark. The furniture was too big for a narrow studio. It was the kind of stuff that was supposed to look classy, like some middle-class family's notion of elegance in their living room (with a touch of hysteria or something)—an elaborate mirrored cabinet, gigantic stained-glass lamps, the armchair I was sitting in, and a faux-antique mobile bar with lots of bottles. The wallpaper was a dark, boudoir-crimson.

The guy also added to the crowded feeling in the place. He was a big lug—about 6'4", 230 pounds, large masculine head, blunt American features, about forty-five, and his hair was close-cropped and receding. He looked like a dock worker, but his furniture was definitely a little queer.

He was a nice guy. Sweet. After he finished his whiskey, he gently asked me for the money and said that I should just put it on the desk— a shiny, fake antique thing loaded up with a messy pile of his mail and a large ashtray of change. I put the money down, one hundred and fifty bucks. He didn't want to touch it, like I said he was sweet, and so you could tell he didn't want to sully things by directly taking the money for what we were going to do.

He asked if I was gay or bi or straight. I told him I was straight, that I didn't have much experience, and what I wanted. "Take your clothes off," he said.

I did and he opened his robe and he had a gigantic cock. "Can you put a condom on?" I asked.

"No problem," he said.

He stroked himself to get hard. His body was heavier than his picture in the paper, but not by too much. When he was hard, he put a condom on, and he stayed sitting on the edge of his bed.

The thing was twice the size of mine and most women tell me I have a nice one. I don't know if they're lying or if this guy was unnatural. Once the condom was in place, I got on my knees and sucked it. I could just about get the head in my mouth. It was thrilling for about the first minute and then it got dull. I felt a little ridiculous sucking this big rubbery thing.

We got on the bed. He took the condom off and spooned me. I asked him what his other clients were like. He said they were mostly married men. "Nice guys," he said. "A few regulars." We lay there silently. I felt small in his arms. It sort of reminded me of what I was trying to re-create, which made me feel a little sick, but I tried to get into it, to feel queer and all right with being held by a man. I wondered if this was how girls felt in my arms. I'm six-foot and bigger than all the girls I see.

"How old are you?" he asked.

"Thirty-two," I said.

"Just a baby," he said.

Then he lubed me up, put on a new condom, bent me over the edge of the bed, and somehow got the thing in there. "Please don't move," I said.

It hurt and then I got used to it, but it never felt good. I thought something might go wrong with my bowels, told him as much, and he pulled out. He washed up, put on his third condom of the night, and I sucked him some more, again kneeling on the floor. I masturbated my cock, which never got hard, but I came on a paper towel he had given me so as not to mess up his rug. He didn't come.

I stood up and he let me rinse off in the shower. His bathroom was small and a little cleaner than my own. He hugged me goodbye and gave me a kiss on the cheek.

"You're good looking," he said. "Next time you'll be more relaxed. We can enjoy each other more."

I got the hell out of there. I hated myself for about two hours, took a scalding bath back at my place, and then was able to sleep. The next day my ass was sore, but two days later it wasn't and I forgot about the whole thing.

Three years later I called him again.

It was around ten o'clock at night. I'd just had a date with a nice woman that had ended early and I was walking to the subway. Then I felt the insanity hit me. It's a combination of fierce loneliness and self-hate, and you need to do something to yourself right away to make it go away. It's like a mental cicada. I can go months, even years, without it happening, and then it's there.

So I found a *Village Voice*. I took it from one of the ubiquitous, battered red boxes, and it's a good thing they're all over the place so if you're hit by madness and have to find a prostitute right away to humiliate you it's not a lot of work. I went to the back pages and spotted his ad. I was pretty sure that it was his torso. There were a couple of other pictures of torsos, but I was sure that I remembered his specific ad.

It was a cold night and under a streetlight I was looking at the *Voice*, waiting for the sidewalk to be empty so nobody would know what I was doing (as if they would know or care, but shame makes you self-centered), and then I called his number on my cell phone.

"I saw your ad," I said.

"Oh, yeah . . . When do you want to see me?"

"Now," I said.

He hesitated, then: "Okay. It's a cold night. I could use some warming up. Have I seen you before?"

"Yes," I said. "A few years ago."

"It's one-fifty. That all right?"

"Yeah, that's fine," I said.

"Well, it's freezing out. Let's make it one hundred."

I didn't know why he was lowering his price. Maybe he thought I wouldn't come. "Okay," I said.

"You remember my address?"

"Tell me again," I said.

I went to an ATM and got out two hundred dollars, then took a cab to his place. I remembered the staircase. I was trembling again. He opened the door a crack and then let me in. He was in the same robe and had a whiskey in his hand, but he had changed. His head was shaved and it didn't look good on him. His head was too large and the baldness made his skull look obscene. He had also put on about thirty pounds— now he definitely didn't resemble his ad. That may have been why he lowered the price.

"Do you remember me?" I asked.

He studied me. He seemed drunk. "I do," he said. "I remember your handsome face. But you never came back . . . Want a drink?"

"Just some water."

"Okay, take your clothes off, handsome, get comfortable."

I took off my clothes, except for my underwear, and sat on the edge of his bed. He brought me my water and sat next to me, sipped his whiskey.

"What do you do? What kind of work?" he asked. I hesitated a moment and he jumped in with: "You don't have to tell me. Or you can lie. It doesn't matter. Whatever you want."

He was hungry for conversation, lonely. He had lowered the price to insure I'd come over. I think he must have been drinking hard these last three years.

"I'm an actor," I said.

"You're in the arts," he said. "I love the arts. I wanted to be an artist."

I didn't say anything.

"I took a painting class in college," he continued, he was tipsy, slurring. "I loved it. I wanted to be a painter. I'd stay up all night painting. But this teacher, my first teacher, told me I was no good. He said I should be a hairdresser. I guess he could tell I was gay. It crushed me. I never recovered. But he was right. I was mediocre at best. You have to be great to be an artist. But I love creative things. Opera. Books. Movies. Paintings. I was in flowers. I might do it again. It's never too late. You never know."

"That wasn't fair of that teacher," I said.

"It wasn't meant to be," he said. He was full of clichés, but his story was heartbreaking.

Then he patted my knee. "Okay, good-looking."

He opened his robe. I got on my knees while he sat on the bed. I don't know why but this time I took the thing in my mouth without a condom. His big belly was just above me. I took my penis out of my boxer shorts and touched myself while he grew in my mouth. Again, I didn't get hard and I came almost immediately, maybe a minute after I had started. It was on the carpet. I stopped sucking him and we looked at the little drops on the floor.

"Don't worry about it," he said.

He went and got a paper towel and cleaned it up, which was nice of him, not asking me to do it. He put his robe back on and I started getting dressed. He watched me. He didn't ask but I put the money on his desk. I put one hundred and fifty there. He'd count it after I left.

He hugged me goodbye. He smelled of the whiskey. "I like you," he said. "Don't be a stranger."

I raced down the stairs and went to a deli across the street. I bought a small bottle of green Listerine and then in the shadows of a doorway poured a bunch of it into my mouth and then spit. I repeated this several times, until I had used up the whole bottle. People walked past me as I spit out this green water but I didn't care. I had to make sure I killed all the germs. I did worry about him looking out the window and seeing me and feeling hurt, but I thought it was unlikely that he would spot me.

I got a cab and went home. That was two years ago. I have a feeling that guy is dead. Probably from drinking. But he was a nice guy. I wish that teacher hadn't crushed him.

The Yellow Slippers

Alba Arikha

Alba Arikha was born and raised in Paris. She has an MFA in writing from Columbia University and is the author of Muse, *a novel, and* Walking on Ice, *a collection of stories. She has recently completed a memoir about her teenage years in Paris, and is working on a novel entitled* Goodnight Please. *Also a pianist, she has recently recorded a CD of her own songs,* Dans le rues de Paris. *She is married to the English composer Tom Smail and lives in London with her two children.*

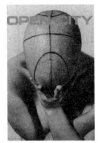

THE MOTHER TOLD THE DAUGHTER TO STOP CRYING. She said, at your age one doesn't cry like that, stop crying like this, you're sixteen years old. The daughter said yes, I know, but I can't stop, it's beyond me. It's him, she said, him. He humiliated me. Who's him the Mother asked, and what did he do to you? And before you tell me, wipe your face, your tears are all over the place. The daughter wiped her face, and as she did so her tears sprang out of her eyes again, a little angry fountain, and they landed on her shirt, leaving a wet stain on the collar.

The Mother had her back turned to her, she was moving her body gracefully, from left to right and right to left, she was preparing an apple pie for that evening, and every now and then she'd lick some apple filling off her fingers. I'm listening, she said, go on, tell me.

The daughter put her hair into a ponytail, blew her nose loudly, and settled more comfortably into the couch. Father and I were walking down Boulevard St. Germain, she said, her voice trembling a little, when I suddenly remembered I had to call Xavier. Who's Xavier, asked the Mother, turning around. Oh, just a guy in my class, the daughter answered, waving her hand brusquely in the air. Why are you making apple pie? she asked, you never make it anymore. That's Father's favorite. Who's coming for dinner? Any guests? I thought Father was busy tonight.

No one is coming for dinner. You know what I told you about boys, the Mother said.

No, what did you say?

Never mind. Go on, she said, turning toward the stove again.

I'm hungry, the daughter said. Well, anyhow, so I was talking to Xavier when I turned around, and I saw these really nice shoes in a shop window. The shop is called Buccelatto. You know it?

No, answered the Mother.

They were very elegant, and very original looking. After I hung up I went to look at them. They were even more beautiful up close. They were Indian looking, you know, kind of pointy, with a gold rim all around them, and little stars around the sides. They were yellow, a pale yellow. I looked for Father but I couldn't find him. I wanted to try them on, but I didn't dare go into the shop without telling him. What if he looked for me and didn't find me? Don't you think that was responsible of me?

Very, answered the Mother.

So anyway after yelling "Father, Father" and making a total fool of myself on Boulevard Saint-Germain— Don't always worry about making a fool out of yourself, interrupted the Mother.

Well whatever, so anyway after that, *and* after walking from the Place Saint-Germain until Rue de l'Université looking for him, I decided forget it, I'm going in anyway. Don't forget to put in some cinnamon. So I went in. I tried them on and they fit me perfectly. And they were not too expensive.

How much? asked the Mother.

Two hundred and fifty francs. Isn't that a good price?

Not for shoes that sound more like slippers to me.

They were not slippers, they were shoes. Anyway, while I was trying them on, I saw Father through the window. He looked very angry, you know the way he looks when he gets angry, his eyes get icy blue, and he gets this nervous twitch, and he walks around in circles. Don't remind me, said the Mother, smiling. So I started to make signs at the window, "Father, Father," I was mouthing through the glass pane, but he didn't see me since he was so angry, so I had to go into the street with my socks on, and the saleswoman, this old hag, shouted "*Mademoiselle, mais que faites-vous, vous ne pouvez pas sortir comme-ça,*" what does she care if I go out with no shoes on. Then Father saw me and came bursting into the store. He started shouting at me in front of the saleswoman and the customers, then he looked at the shoes and he screamed, you really think I'm going to buy you these ridiculous things, why do you always want to look like a clown, do you know I've been looking for you for half an hour, one minute you're in a phone booth then you're not, you think I don't have other things to do than run around looking for you everywhere, *Ah ces jeunes alors!* he said to the saleswoman who made the mistake of asking me if I was taking the shoes. When she said that, he looked at her like she was crazy, and he said, my daughter cannot afford to buy herself these shoes. I pay for my daughter. But I don't pay for just anything. And I'm certainly not going to buy her these stupid shoes. Then, he grabbed me by the arm and he said, Natalia we're leaving this store immediately, thank you Madame, au revoir, and when we were in the street he started yelling at me again. You think you don't have enough shoes, he said, you think you can just walk in to any store like a lady and decide you want something and buy it, just like that, you're only sixteen Natalia, you're certainly not going to start buying things for yourself every week. I am not a rich man. And even if I were, I wouldn't buy you everything you want. Just on principle.

When is the last time I bought something? I asked him, and he said, just last week you and your mother went to the 'Gaieties Lafayette' and bought those bathing suits. Isn't that enough? Then I remembered that it's true, we did buy those bathing suits last week. By the way, I tried the striped one on for Sylvie and she said I look like a model in it. So you see? I was right to pick that one out. It was much nicer than the blue dotted one you liked. Anyway, Father was still yelling at me in front of the store, and all these people in there were talking about us, so I just started crying because I was so embarrassed and then suddenly, who do I see but Betsy Varet, leaning against a tree, and watching us. She was probably standing there the whole time, and I hadn't even noticed her. It was even kind of weird the way she was standing there, as if she had known the whole time that we were there . . .

What do you mean it was weird? the Mother asked quickly.

Oh, I don't know, I mean she didn't really seem surprised to see us there, like it was no big deal, so when she saw Father yelling at me like that she said "Rafael" in her hoarse voice and smiled at me with her big made-up mouth, and Father told her I was acting like a spoiled girl, I wanted to buy these silly shoes, and he pointed them out to her, and she asked me, why on earth would I want to buy such a thing, they looked so much like slippers. Are you listening?

Yes, I am, replied the Mother, calmly, her back still turned toward the stove. Go on, I'm listening. Is it almost finished?

Why, are you getting bored?

No, I'm sorry, go on. Betsy Varet . . .

What? What about Betsy Varet? She's horrible, right?

Actually, yes she is.

Both laughed, Mother and daughter, and the latter squirmed in her seat. When will the apple pie be ready, she asked, Oh, not for a while, she answered. You know that Betsy's husband just died, don't you? asked the Mother. No, I didn't know, answered the daughter. But it makes sense, though. What do you mean? asked the Mother a bit nervously, what do you mean it makes sense? Oh, I don't know, the daughter said, she just looked pretty good, much prettier than she used to. She never liked her husband, isn't that true? Anyway that's what Marion told me. She said Betsy couldn't stand his guts.

Did Marion really tell you such a thing? I'm surprised . . . And I doubt she told you she couldn't stand his guts. That's not a very nice way of talking. You can say she didn't like him. That's enough. We don't need to know more.

Whatever, said the daughter, flinging her hair back. So she really looked that good? the Mother asked quickly, how did she look? Oh I don't know. She was wearing nice clothes and everything. So you want to hear the end?

Yes, sighed the Mother.

It smells good. So after Betsy said that thing about them looking like slippers, Father said, yes, that's so true they look like slippers, ha ha ha, he laughed, were you like that at her age, Betsy, and they both started laughing. I don't know what they found so funny. Then I asked Father very timidly if he was sure I couldn't buy those shoes. He was silent, and he looked at me and then, suddenly, he slapped me. That's it. That's the story. He slapped me in front of that stupid woman and in front of those same people in the store. Then I ran away, very fast, without turning around, and I heard him shout, Natalia, Natalia, and then I took the Metro, still crying, and then I came home. That's it.

Well, said the Mother, her voice trembling a little, I don't know what to tell you. It's true that you shouldn't be so spoiled, but on the other hand I don't understand why your Father got so upset . . . I mean I do but I don't. I mean trying on a pair of shoes is certainly not the end of the world. It's true that we're not rich. I mean we're not poor, that's for sure, but we're not rich either.

Oh really, said the daughter sarcastically, and so what's this then, she said pointing toward the room they were sitting in, a large white living room with contemporary art hanging on the walls, and lots of books everywhere. Oh really, she said again, pointing toward the Louis XV chairs and the antique wooden table. Well, if you want to know the truth, I think we're rich. I mean compared to the other people in my class we certainly are. I mean Father's not a historian for nothing.

The Mother smiled, and then she said, Natalia darling, you should know that historians usually don't make a cent. It just so happens that your Father is a little better known than others. That's all. And he really does not make that much money. It's just that he likes to live well. If you want thoe shoes so badly, then we'll think about it a little more. But I don't think it's right.

What's not right? the daughter shouted, what's so wrong, I mean it's not like I ask for something every day, you know! Anyway, what's the matter with both of you, you've been so strange lately, you never used to be like that with me. So fine, I won't get the shoes, she added angrily.

The phone rang. The daughter picked it up, and dragged the cord into her bedroom. The Mother heard her daughter's voice through the door, she was laughing now, she sounded happier. Then the Mother wiped her hands on the dish towel, took off her apron, and stuck the pie in the oven. She went to the bathroom and looked at herself in the mirror. She noticed she had new wrinkles under her eyes, wrinkles that bulged through her pale skin. Her green eyes had lost their color; they looked washed out, she thought. She noticed some more gray in her wavy black hair. And her once puffy lips looked thinner, too. Could it be, she thought to herself, could it be that I'm getting old? Are men still interested in forty-three-year-old women, she asked herself again. Of course they are, she said out loud, looking at herself one more time in the mirror. Then she raised herself on tiptoe, just to catch a glimpse at her figure. She heard her daughter laugh again, an earnest and fresh laugh, and she felt like going into her room and hugging her. But then, as she was looking at herself in the mirror, she suddenly started crying. Oh my God, she said to herself. She sat down on a little stool in the bathroom, and she kept repeating, Oh my God, I'm alone. She covered her face with her hands. He's already gone, she said in a whisper, he's already gone and she doesn't even know. Every time the image of her daughter came back to her, she cried even more bitterly, and although she knew she was in the next room, she seemed to be very far away.

After a while she got up and splashed some cold water on her face. Then, she put on some powder and some lipstick. She sprayed some perfume on before grabbing her coat, and yelled at her daughter through the door, I'll be back in a half hour, please watch the pie for me. Her daughter called out, Okay, bye Mother, and went on chatting on the phone. The Mother could see her feet sticking out from behind the door. They were moving back and forth gracefully, as she was lying on her stomach, her long black hair falling onto her shoulders. Bye, said the Mother again, too low for her daughter to hear her.

When she got downstairs, she quickly walked toward the metro, sincethe father had taken the car with him. She got off at the Mabillon station, and walked toward the Boulevard St. Germain. When she saw the store she stopped, breathless. The yellow shoes were still in the shop window, and they were just as the daughter had described them. She walked into the store and asked the saleswoman, a nice looking old lady with white hair, if she had any size seven left. The saleswoman said I think we might, I'm not sure though, let me go look. She came back up almost immediately and said, I'm sorry, we just sold the last pair. Would you like to try on another size? The Mother said, no thank you, you see it's not for me, it's for my daughter, she was in here earlier this afternoon, I guess her father got very angry at her in the store, and—

Oh, you're her mother! the saleswoman chuckled. My goodness this is funny! You should be glad you weren't here! Angry is not the word! He was fuming! I mean I know it's none of my business or anything, but I don't think he should have yelled at her like that. Such a pretty girl. Really pretty, and so sweet. Anyway, the funny thing is, after he was done yelling at her, and after he had slapped her, well you know, she added, we all saw it through the shop window, well, after that he looked really sad. His face took on a very sad expression, if you know what I mean. Yes, I know what you mean, the Mother said, nodding her head.

Since he looked so sad, the saleswoman continued, the woman he was with, she looked like she was trying to comfort him or something— the saleswoman paused and blushed—I mean not really comforting him, but you know, she must have asked him what was the matter and everything. The saleswoman cleared her throat nervously. Then, he came back into the store, and he said, where are those stupid-looking shoes my daughter wanted, those yellow slippers, and I told him, excuse me Sir, these are not just stupid shoes, these are fine Italian shoes, and they're not slippers. I mean I know he's your husband and everything, but really you know, this is not a junk store, I just had to tell him, we only sell the best quality here. So anyway, he took the shoes, he paid for them, then on his way out we had to call him back in because he had forgotten his change. Then he left very quickly. I'm surprised he didn't forget the shoes, the saleswoman added, laughing, really, he was so nervous. Well, he's probably home by now, and he probably already gave them to her.

I see, said the Mother. Thank you. Goodbye.

She walked out of the store in a daze. Outside, the sun was very hot. In one month, the daughter would start her summer vacation. She would kiss her parents goodbye one morning, and leave for three weeks or a month, calling once in a while, saying she was having a great time at her friend's house. When she would hang up, the Mother would experience that queasy feeling she always felt when she heard her daughter's voice from far away. Usually, she and the Father would reminisce about her, and look at old baby photographs, especially the one where she stood naked in a plastic swimming pool, a little blue hat on her head, and a red balloon in her hand.

The Mother knew that this summer, she would be looking at the photograph alone.

From Change or Die

Jerome Badanes

Jerome Badanes was a novelist, poet, and screenwriter who died in 1995 at age fifty-eight. A professor at Vassar, Sarah Lawrence, and SUNY Purchase, Badanes was born and raised in Brooklyn. He won an Avery Hopwood Award for Poetry at the University of Michigan, and spent much of the sixties as an antiwar activist, staging street theater. He is the author of The Final Opus of Leon Solomon, *a novel, and the screenplay for the documentary film* Image Before My Eyes. *His poems were published posthumously in the collection,* Long Live a Hunger to Feed Each Other *(Open City Books). The following is an excerpt from* Change or Die, *a novel left unfinished at the time of his death.*

THE BLIK FAMILY WAS A DREAM AND AN EDUCATION. Twelve-year-old Millie introduced me to unbridled playfulness in the face of terror, to say nothing of a love sweeter and more brazen than a teenage boy should ever dream of tasting. Her older brother, the blond muscular Rudy, introduced me to cruelty and to night-marish devotion to a cause. Mr. Blik introduced me to Shakespeare, to Puccini, to softly spoken encourage-ment, to painful reticence, and finally he forced to the forefront of my consciousness an act that as far back as I could remember I had desper-ately kept myself from thinking about: the act of sudden self-oblitera-tion. Mrs. Blik introduced me, above all else, to her day after day pres-ence in her daughter's life, as well as to overpowering womanly beauty, and at one and the same time to the unrelenting progression of wasting away. (At least, I thought, that was one bewildering humiliation my own poor mother had been spared.)

Step by step the Bliks brought me to the very doorway of their inner-most room. I could glimpse into it, enthralled by the impossible fact of their existence—but never was I permitted more than a glimpse. Something hidden, disgraceful, devouring, seemed to live with them in that room, and their close-lipped loyalties to one another excluded me and held me in check. The most I could hope for, I understood quickly enough, was to lure Millie out, to me, and then to hold on desperately, as though both our lives were at stake. And they were.

Could Mr. Blik privately have been on my side in this? Did he see in me a way to rescue his beloved daughter from their innermost room of claustrophobia and shame? Or simply from his eldest son, Rudy? He may even have counted on us to fall in love. He did, after all, encourage us to memorize the lead roles in *Romeo and Juliet.* Didn't he see the danger? The play itself should have given him pause. I was just a boy then, and Millie was still a child. Of course, I hardly needed any encouragement. I was mad for Millie from the very beginning.

Soon, due to certain unsubstantiated accusations against Mr. Blik that even now, so many years after his death, would be an act of treachery on my part to repeat idly, the neighbors started to encircle the four of them with a deadly atmosphere of gossip and intolerance. And only I was their friend.

All four Bliks had survived the holocaust. Not one of my nine relatives who had remained behind in Poland had survived. Two of them—three-year-old twin girls—were posed cheek to cheek in a photograph kept in a small silver frame that stood on the sideboard in the dining room of my aunt's apartment, where I was raised. My aunt told me that when I was an infant my mother could always quiet me, no matter how bitterly I cried, simply by carrying me to the sideboard, where she held me up before the picture as she pointed and whispered the names of my cousins into my ear.

"See, my only little man, the one who is smiling, that's your cousin Gittele, and the other, the one who is frowning, that's your cousin Sorele." Or was it the other way around? I can't even say for sure that I remember my mother saying this to me, though I know that she spoke in a sing-song voice, almost crooning the words—and even now, if I shut my eyes tightly and focus my brain on one such ghostly memory, I can begin to feel the way her warm breath tickled my cheek and soothed my ear. Perhaps what I do remember is no more than a tiny home movie I have made up, based primarily on what my aunt told me, of my mother comforting me so. To this day I don't know which girl was Gittele, and which one Sorele. I am convinced that my aunt doesn't know either. The one time in recent years that I asked her again, she changed the subject. My mother knew Gittele from Sorele, but she took that knowledge with her into the black waters of New York harbor.

In the picture the girls are wearing identical thick coats and woolen hats with puffs on top, looking quite protected from the Polish winter. They are posed cheek to cheek and their four eyes are on a straight line—four large round eyes looking back at the photographer. To me, when I was a boy—and not a single afternoon passed when I didn't turn on the light in our dark dining room and stare at that picture—those four eyes always appeared to be gazing out just past my shoulder, to a world that must have filled them with great apprehension. "Open those pretty eyes, girls, wider, wider . . . that's perfect," the photographer must have cajoled, and then snapped, for their eyes are perfect little full moons. Yet at the same time they seemed to me flooded not with light but with worry—so convincingly that my own eyes would begin to ache. Could my twin cousins already then have had an inkling of what awaited them? One girl is smiling. The other is frowning. Otherwise they are interchangeable. The picture was taken on their third birthday, which was also the day of my birth.

After the war, my aunt managed to locate two eyewitnesses. She had them come to the apartment, a few months apart, to give their accounts of the liquidation of the Vilna ghetto. Each man sat with my aunt at the dining-room table, drinking a glass of hot tea and speaking almost in whispers so that I wouldn't overhear them. Both times my aunt had told me to stay in my room, and both times I managed—without getting caught— to creep along the hall almost to the entranceway to the dining room, where I kept perfectly still and listened. Neither time could I see anything of either of these men, but I was able to hear every word they uttered. I even heard them blowing on the hot tea and sipping intensely as they spoke. Basically they corroborated each other's horrifying accounts. The twins had been shot down a moment before their mother, and right before her eyes, in the Ponari woods outside of Vilna. That they were killed right in front of their mother—each time that stark fact flew like a bat from the tongue of the faceless speaker and dug itself deeply into my chest. From then on—and throughout my childhood—I simply could not keep away from that picture.

Was the frowning girl Sorele, and the smiling girl Gittele? Didn't Gittele, more than Sorele, sound like the name of a girl who smiled? I kept changing my mind. My aunt was of no help. She always told me which one was Gittele and which one was Sorele, but the next time she was just as likely to reverse herself as to repeat herself. She couldn't keep track of her own lies, but I remembered every answer that she gave me. To properly identify my twin cousins seemed to me of life and death importance, and whenever I looked at the picture, my failure to know made me dizzy with a kind of terror. They had been obliterated right before the eyes of their mother, and now no one alive even knew which one was Gittele and which one Sorele. At the same time I felt pervaded by a sense of relief, even of comfort. Didn't I, after all, know who I was, and that my name was Isaiah (and that my aunt knew me by my name), and didn't I know that I existed, in the flesh, in that dark dining room, at that moment? The sight of the picture also filled me with an inexplicable but powerful hunger, and I certainly didn't know for what until the Blik family showed up in my life. There was nothing left of either Gittele or Sorele, except for that small, opaque picture in a silver frame standing on my aunt's antique sideboard—and now upstairs, having traveled to me from that same blackness, there was Millie Blik and her family.

Lost Car

Jonathan Baumbach

Jonathan Baumbach is the author of fourteen books of fiction, including You, or The Invention of Memory; On The Way To My Father's Funeral: New and Selected Stories; B, A Novel; D-Tours; Separate Hours; Chez Charlotte and Emily; The Life and Times of Major Fiction; Reruns; Babble; A Man to Conjure With; *and, most recently,* Dreams of Molly. *He has also published over ninety stories in such places as* Esquire, Best American Short Stories, *and* Boulevard.

IT STARTS WITH MY COMING OUT OF A MOVIE, sometimes with someone—my wife, one of my former wives—and not remembering where exactly I parked the car. I don't panic, I never panic. What I do is try to visualize the various streets I passed through to get to the theater, some memorable landmarks that might help determine the way there and, consequently, the way back. As I tend to be destination-oriented, this method of inquiry inevitably yields a faceless landscape. More potent is the memory of driving around searching for a place to park while sweating the self-induced pressure of arriving at the movie theater on time. I can see the car now, in my mind's eye, parked behind an exceptionally wide van or SUV, black or dark green, the space unlit.

And then walking toward my idea of where the car has been parked, I think I see it in the near distance, not behind a van of uncertain color (that might have been another time altogether) but behind a car very much like it, which may even be the car itself. Closer inspection invites disappointment. My "metallic mist" Honda Civic (perhaps Toyota Corolla) has Massachusetts plates, last I looked, and both the cars I have focused on as potentially mine have New York plates. Reason protects me from despair. The street my car is on is obviously similar to this one and so, as evidence or lack of suggests, is in the same general area. I can remember now finding no spaces on the present street and turning right and then right again and discovering a secreted space between two huge SUVs on this other, parallel street. I hurry over to this other street while

27

the sense memory of my parking there remains fresh. The second street is darker than the first, has only one functioning street lamp.

By this time, I have chased after my parked car on four different streets, each with its own persuasive claim in fickle memory without a whiff of success. In the past when I've been unable to find my car after giving more than sufficient time to the search, I saw no point in destroying myself over the loss of a material object. So I conceded that my car was unrecoverable and I got home by other means. Perhaps the car had been stolen—what other explanation could there be? I had pretty much covered the area looking for it—and so, as I depended on a car, I considered buying a new one or perhaps a previously owned one in near-new condition. Though I'm not a wealthy man and tend to be a cautious consumer, I saw no point in sacrificing my life to a seemingly endless search for something I might never find, my affection for the vehicle notwithstanding. I've been in this situation, I admit, with some reluctance, more than once and I have avoided excessive despair in each case. Sanity, as I see it, is knowing when to move on. In my weaker moments, I tend to believe the world is haunted.

The above is what Joshua tells Clarissa, his dinner companion, a woman he has met through a matchmaking service on the Internet, which promises to bring together potential soulmates. She has asked him to tell her something about himself in the form of an anecdote. They have made a point of sharing embarrassing stories as a way of getting to know the other while easing the awkwardness of what is after all a blind date. The dating service, MatchesMadeinHeaven.com, had told him they were a near perfect match and that Clarissa's personality profile indicated an unusual capacity for empathy. So Josh is warily hopeful of being understood by his date without being judged.

A woman with an interestingly ruined face, Clarissa is, in her own words, a former litigations lawyer who, transforming from the ashes of a midlife crisis, has reinvented herself as a psychotherapist. Josh, on the other hand, has attended medical school without completing the course, has published two books of poems and a mystery novel (under a pseudonym), has taught at different times in his evolving life Renaissance poetry, history, and filmmaking and is currently the book-review editor of a respected journal of opinion with extremely limited financial resources. Since his divorce six months ago, he tends to eat most of his meals out, though at less upscale places than the one she has chosen for their preliminary meeting.

Though he couldn't say why if you put a gun to his head, there is something about her that speaks to his deepest urges. Moments after she sits down across from him, he fantasizes undressing her and burying his face in her slightly protruding belly, sliding his tongue down the incline into the sweet space between her legs.

"You know, I don't think we're all that much alike," she says to him at one point, "and I mean that, I really do, as a positive."

"Not alike in what way exactly?" he asks.

"Well," she says, "for one, if I misplaced something that I valued, I wouldn't give up looking for it until I had it back."

Josh turns his face away, feeling the imprint of her unspoken criticism. "I used to be the same way," he says, "but I've learned to be less absolute."

"Josh, I wasn't being critical of you," she says. "Did you think I was?"

This is when the waiter appears to take their orders and Josh discovers that Clarissa has ordered the very entrée he had in mind for himself. He finds himself in an odd bind and in a quick-witted improvisatory move orders a dish he doesn't much want with a triumphant flourish.

Clarissa laughs. "The Made in Heaven personality profile said we had similar tastes in food. They certainly got that wrong. Interestingly, Herman and I—Herman was my second husband—always used to order the same entreés in restaurants, that is, until I discovered that I really didn't like what we had been ordering."

Without warning—it is an aspect of the haunted thing—his attraction to her takes a 180 degree turn. All of a sudden, he is desperate to get away. "I need to get this off my chest to avoid misunderstanding," he says abruptly. "I have to say I'm not really in the market for a long-term relationship." Listening to himself, he winces at his crudeness, but also resists apologizing for telling the awful transitory truth.

"Good," she says. "It's a relief to have that unnecessary pressure out of the way." She holds out her hand to him across the table, which he takes with gratitude after only a moment's hesitation fraught with internal winds of wonder and trepidation.

Whatever he has agreed to, it is a pact that remains disturbingly elusive.

When the waiter delivers dessert menus, Clarissa rejects them with a wave of her hand. "We can do better than this at my place," she says. "I have two-thirds of a very good pear cobbler at home waiting for appropriate attention. Also, some excellent French roast decaf. How does that sound?"

"Isn't it getting late?" he asks, looking at his watch for confirmation.

A huge raucous laugh assaults them from the table behind, a chorus of near-hysterical discordant amusement. At first glance it appears to be a table of eight women, but then he notices that one of the occupants, the one as it seems amusing the others, is a man with a ponytail.

Clarissa gives him a sympathetic smile punctuated by a charming, perhaps even seductive shrug. "It's not too late for me," she says.

When the check comes she covers it with her hand and edges it over to her side of the table. "This is mine," she says.

"Why don't we just split it," he says, but by the time he extracts his credit card from his wallet, she has already handed the check, trumped with her own plastic, to a passing waiter.

"Then I'll get the next one," he says.

"I'll hold you to it," she says.

More shrill laughter from the table behind them, one of the women falling out of her chair with a thump and an ear-shattering squeal to applause from the others.

On the way out of the restaurant, the oldest looking of the women at the table of eight, not the one who had fallen, winks at him as he passes.

The advertised pear cobbler has some mold at the edges and Clarissa scrapes their plates into the garbage, sighing her apology.

Josh stands up as if it were his cue to leave. "It's all right," he says, more disturbed by Clarissa's abruptness than the loss of dessert. In some pocket of need, he feels as if he has been the one discarded.

"Why don't we go to bed for dessert," she says, "and after, if something else is required, I'll make a pot of coffee."

"Clarissa," he stumbles over the name, "if it's all right with you, I'd prefer having my coffee before dessert."

"Oh my God," she says, "I totally knew you were going to say that. I could have spoken your lines for you."

"Really?" he says. "And what am I going to say now?"

"You were going to ask the very question you just asked," she says, laughing.

He considers his options as if he has several, wondering what he might do that she would not anticipate in advance.

So striving for the unexpected, he opts for sex before coffee and afterward, not unhappy with his choice, rejects the coffee option and goes home before she is ready to part with him.

The next day, almost hourly, he thinks of calling Clarissa—it's the right thing to do, he tells himself—but he keeps finding reasons to postpone, perhaps indefinitely, a decision that had chosen him when he woke that morning.

At about 4:10 in the afternoon when the phone rings, he has no doubt who is on the line. "Have you been thinking of calling me?" she asks before the usual amenities, before identifying herself.

There is not much use lying to someone who appears to know him better than he knows himself. "Well, I have been thinking of calling you," he says.

"And so why didn't you?"

"Why didn't I what?"

"Why didn't you call when you were thinking about it?"

He likes her better when she seems less certain of him and he makes the only answer their dialogue allows. "I didn't call in order to give you the opportunity to call first and ask if I'd been thinking of calling you."

His remark, which he means to be clever, produces a hole in the conversation. "Well," she says after the prolonged silence has begun to threaten him, "if you say so."

The moment he realizes that he is glad she hasn't hung up on him, she has. In echo, he hears her say "pigeon shit," and she is gone before he can register his surprise at what seems a wholly uncharacteristic response.

A former wife used to hang up on him whenever he said something she didn't want to hear (or anticipated not wanting to hear what he hadn't yet said) and the association further fuels his anger at Clarissa. If he calls back, which is his first impulse, he would tell her (though surely she already knows) how intolerable it is to be hung up on. In the end, he decides against calling until, if ever, he is in a position to forgive her dismissal of him.

He imagines Clarissa thinking some version of the same thing and is strangely comforted by the idea that on such short acquaintance they have accomplished a near unbreachable rift.

The next day he calls MatchesMadeinHeaven.Com and tells the counselor assigned him that his match with Clarissa hasn't worked out and that he is open to meeting someone else. "I'll reevaluate your profile," the counselor says, "and get back to you."

Clarissa calls later in the week to tell him of a dream she's had. "In the dream," she says, "we were leaving a movie together—it was a Japanese horror film in which characters transformed according to certain inner qualities—and after walking several blocks, I led you to your missing car.

You seemed displeased and I was sorry in the dream that I had gone to the trouble of finding it for you."

"I see," he says, not seeing at all.

"Josh, the dream was extremely vivid and if you'll trust me to take you there, I have a strong sense that I can find your lost car for you. I won't do it unless you promise in advance that you'll be pleased at getting it back."

"Why did you hang up on me?" he asks.

There are a few beats of silence before she speaks and he wonders if he has inadvertently invited being cut off again.

"When did I hang up on you?" she asks, her tone aggrieved. "Why would I hang up on you?"

"You hung up on me because you didn't like something I said," he says.

"If you knew why I hung up on you, why did you ask me why?"

"Why did you say you didn't hang up on me?"

"Must we have this conversation?" she asks.

"I'm willing to let the subject drop," he says, "whatever the subject."

When they arrive at the movie theater to begin their search, Clarissa corroborates that his local nine-plex, grandiosely called the Pavilion, is indeed much like the theater in her dream.

They set out, hand in hand like two children on a quest, walking slowly, checking out each car they pass for inner secrets, and he feels, and not for the first time, that it is the search itself that matters and not the result. He finds himself hoping that the unlikely, the near impossible, is not going to triumph over what it pleases him to think of as common sense.

At some point they arrive at a nondescript tannish Honda with Massachusetts plates. Her obvious pleasure in the discovery—she does everything but say "ta da"—is almost more than he can bear. He hesitates, not quite looking at the car, before denying that it is his. "Are you sure?" she asks.

The question outrages him. "Don't you think I know my own car?"

"You have to admit the coincidence is impressive," she says, "wouldn't you say?"

"Yes, no, who knows," he says. "All I know, despite certain similarities, this is not my car. Do you ever have the sense—is this crazy, I wonder— that the world is haunted?"

"Of course it is," she says.

Clarissa reluctantly agrees to move on, but after three more blocks in which there has not been another vehicle with Massachusetts plates, she wonders if they might not revisit the Honda Civic he had rejected.

"That's absolutely not my car," he says, which is not actually a denial of her request.

"Even so," she says.

They retrace their steps in no particular hurry, their destination unacknowledged, though find themselves alongside the vehicle in question before either is ready to resume their postponed dispute.

She puts her hands over his eyes to which he makes the smallest of complaints. "What does your lost car look like?" she asks.

It takes awhile for him to evoke a picture in his mind. When he had conceded the car's loss, he had all but erased it from memory. "It's a grayish, tannish color. It's called Metallic Mist. It looks like every other car."

"What's the nameplate?" she asks.

"I don't pay much attention to those kinds of things," he says. "It's a Honda something, a Honda Civic, I think, though it could be a Toyota. No, my previous car was a Toyota."

"When last seen, what kind of condition was the car in?" she asks.

"A few scrapes on the back and on the left side," he said, "which were not my fault. Other than that, and some winter residue, it looked almost immaculate."

"Well," she says, removing her hands from his eyes. "What we have here is a latish-model grayish-tan Honda Civic with a nasty scrape on the left side and some scratches here and there on the back."

"Is that right?"

"Why don't you try your key so there'll be no residual doubts afterward."

He dips his hand in his left pocket to see if the key is still there. It has not gone away, has not forgotten him. In no rush to retrieve it from the depths, he makes a point of walking around the car, going through the motions of noting its disfigurations. "This car has more dings than mine," he says.

She laughs. "I won't say it," she says, "because I don't want you to be angry with me again. If I didn't like you as much as I do, would I be with you on this bizarre errand?"

He felt as if he was standing on his toes in quicksand. "What won't you say?" he says, the words escaping his decision not to ask.

"I won't say what I won't say because you know what it is. Look, I'm sorry, Josh. Really. I am sorry."

"I believe you are," he says, producing the key from his pocket like a magic trick. With grave reluctance, he makes a show of trying to open the passenger door and failing.

She gently takes the key from him and opens the door on the driver's side on first try.

He stares at the ground. "Must be a universal key," he says.

"Must be," she says. "Shall we see if the key is also compatible with the ignition?"

She is one of those women who acts on the likely response to a question—he has intuited this about her from day one—before the answer is ever spoken.

He puts his arms around her, holds her against him for the longest time—people pass in twos and threes, there is cheering, night falls—before he is ready to face the inevitable.

"I didn't know you were going to do that," she says.

Years later, after they are living together, after they have done a scripted TV ad together for MMIH.com in which he has humbly acknowledged her as his soulmate, he still hasn't forgiven her for finding his car.

That she knows he continues to resent her gives him a certain advantage in the relationship. For the first several years, before indifference sets in, Clarissa does whatever she can to make it up to him for having occasioned his humiliation on their second date. With what she thought were the best intentions, the intentions of love, she had willfully done him a favor she had to have known in advance they would both regret.

From Guilty Pleasure

Nico Baumbach

Nico Baumbach holds a PhD in literature from Duke University and is currently an assistant professor in the film program at Columbia University. This was his first published story.

SINCE I WAS A CHILD—AND I NEVER REALLY WAS, which is why I kind of still am—I have always felt that if I wanted to apply myself to a problem, I mean really apply myself, I would invariably be able to conquer it. The catch is *wanting* to apply myself. Because as soon as I approach something that is not clearly within my grasp, I no longer want it. I could of course apply myself to this problem, but do I really want to? Well yes, I do, but in a minute, not right now. Just get off my back and I'll get to it, I swear.

The immediate problem was with my schoolwork. I'll explain. I'll explain this and then I'll get to Cecilia. I was in my junior year of college and I wasn't working and was not doing well and not happy about that. Meanwhile, my two pretty close friends were away—junior year abroad. I'd thought about J.Y.A., seemed like a good opportunity—be in a foreign place, gain distance and perspective, and then change irrevocably, leaving everyone else behind. But somehow I failed to ever commit to a plan. It meant choosing a country and a program and, well, I never did; so here I was, back at school, trying to reassure myself with a new plan. The new plan was that while everyone else was off in foreign lands seeing the world with new eyes, I was going to take advantage of being free from distractions, to bear down, isolate myself, and focus on my work.

But in November, two months after the semester started, the plan seemed not really to have gone into effect. For one thing, the total lack of contact with friends, people calling me, people to make plans with, far from releasing me from distraction, was making me more lonely and restless. The truth is, even when I had friends around, it was more the idea of socializing that often kept me from work, the idea that I should be doing more; my plan should really have been to not complain or worry about the fact that I was always pretty isolated anyway. I lived in a nook in a mostly freshman dorm, called "singles row," a hallway of upper classmen living by themselves. I had imagined it might be an interesting group, others like myself, who have little interest in living in suites with their best buddies and partying every night and so sought silence and concentration, discipline. But, by the looks of things, they were an odd collection of losers, most of whom would probably rather be having parties in suites every night with their best buddies were that option still available. In other words, others like myself.

Then there was the problem of my classes. Part of what discipline means to me is learning things I feel are important. This means history and science. History because I want to be knowledgeable about the world, to have a wealth of facts at my fingertips, to have a sense of scope and the processes of change, and when some reference is made, to be able to know and explain the history and shed new light on the object in question. Science because I want to know how things work, to understand the mechanics of the physical and biological world, and to explain them to those for whom the world is still a shady place of chance and coincidence. The idea was never to become a historian or a scientist, but to be a repository of knowledge, which I would then use for other means, whatever those may be.

But while I had liked the idea of knowing stuff, I'd never wanted to learn it. Or at least, I was proving to have no memory for names, dates, formulas, and theories. This was why I had avoided these subjects before—a possibility since this reputable college wasn't stuffy but enlightened, and prided itself on offering its student body the responsibility that comes with freedom. This allowed you to stick within your comfort zone, while still knowing that you were participating in this great liberal education, as if options not taken were still options. My comfort zone—mostly English classes—of course was never very comfortable, and so I was comforted by not taking what I would have been comfortable taking.

I had fulfilled my plan insofar as I would go to the lectures and discussion groups. I never missed a class. If nothing else, being present could count toward the fulfillment of my regimen. Though I absorbed nothing, I still had some minor sense of accomplishment and secretly I suppose I believed that somehow I was learning against all evidence to the contrary. Like people who buy a tape to increase their vocabulary, and play it while they are sleeping. I hoped that somewhere in the recesses of my mind there was learning taking place that would some day make itself known. So, while as I sat in class, with the hundreds of other students—nothing on the surface separating me from them—furiously scribbling notes, my mind would wander, occasionally picking up on some word or phrase that seemed to be stressed, which I would write in my notebook: "the telophase of meiosis 1." It would offer a key to that knowledge, which I would decipher at a later date—a date that was endlessly deferred.

Okay, stage set, now to get to Cecilia. Well, first I have to start with Jack. I had not liked Jack from the moment I saw him. A guy who lived down the hall who sort of stuck out for me, who came to somehow represent what I didn't like about people who lived in the hall. He was stocky, only about 5' 5", baggy jeans that swallowed up his squat legs, a wallet chain, a hoop earring in each ear, short spiky hair and a pockmarked face. Ugly, I thought—not in a sad lonely way (good), but in a cocky way (bad). I have respect for a restrained sort of coolness, but none for dudes who just want a good time. But as I kept an eye on him—because he irritated me so, he was the guy I paid the most attention to—it seemed that he didn't have so many good times. I'd often see him reading in the lounge on a Friday or Saturday night. And, as it happened, perhaps because he saw me watching him, he developed the habit of nodding Hi to me. And I of course nodding back.

It turned out that I started to at least not dislike Jack. His attitude was far less aggressive than his appearance suggested. When he would nod Hi it wasn't with any necessary expectation of friendship, no eager smile, just matter-of-fact, and I appreciated that. Not a bad guy, Jack, and soon I found myself struggling to repress a smile on my face as I nodded Hi back to him, a smile that might betray the fact that yeah, I might not mind being friends with him.

One day, when I was playing music and had left my door ajar, he peered in.

"Porter, right?"

"Uh-huh."

"Jack. We have a class together. Is that Boulez conducting Schoenberg?"

I had to glance at the jewel box. "Yeah. You want to come in?"

He came in and sat on the bed. "This is the recording where . . ." And then we talked about some other stuff, not much really, not in much detail, and then he left.

But as it turned out it was the first of many similar visits. Jack would come in, always uninvited but not unwanted, flop down on the bed—the narrow room contained a single desk chair and a bed, so the latter was the only place for a visitor to sit—and maybe look through the CDs on the shelf above my bed. "Is this Leon Payne's demo version of 'Lost Highway'?" Jack did a radio show on the college station and he was interested in my willfully esoteric collection of music, endless inevitably failed gestures toward authenticity—oddball regional country western bands from the forties like the Rambling Rangers to avant-garde jazz, a lot of stuff that I knew little to nothing about, but accumulated with the sense that the collection itself counted for something like being an aficionado. Don't think I didn't know that obscurity is its own commodity; there are stores that sell only this stuff.

We'd chat a little about music or maybe movies or books, again not in much detail. "Yeah, I read that, it was good . . ." "Oh yeah? It was good?" "Yeah." "I should read it." Sometimes we wouldn't talk at all, he'd just hang out for a little while, both of us reading different things, until eventually he'd excuse himself and go back to his room. Generally, I welcomed his arrival. A relief, the comfort of another presence to keep me from getting too caught up in my own painfully circular thought process—the endless attempt to distract myself from distraction. But as soon as he settled in, I felt myself getting a little irritated. Here he was taking up my time and space, distracting me from my work. God knows what I could be accomplishing were he not here. But when he would get up to leave I would find myself disappointed and lonely again.

Okay, so Jack and I were in the same class. It was my one English class, my one softball, my one gift to myself in my schedule: The Modern American Novel. And we not only shared the same three-time-a-week lecture in an auditorium, but also the same discussion section once a week. The discussion section, the more intimate ten-person meeting that offered you the opportunity to strut your stuff—not for the professor herself, but for some uncomfortable graduate student who led the discussion. Jack—another reason I liked him—would, like me, sit silently each week, and would take an attitude toward stuff-strutting that seemed to waver between condescension and indifference, but was really about intense fear. Even as Jack's visits to my room became more and more frequent, we would still never share eye contact in section, both sitting nervously, as obscured as we could be in the not unintimate setting, hoping the discussion would never get stalled enough that the grad student would try a new tactic and call on one of us. I'm just assuming this is how Jack felt, he and I, two peas. Anyway there was this one girl in the section who I despised.

Typochondria

Priscilla Becker

Priscilla Becker has published two books of poetry, Internal West *and* Stories That Listen. *Her poems have appeared in journals such as* Boston Review, Fence, *and* Verse, *and have been included in* The Swallow Anthology of New American Poets. *She also writes reviews and essays, some of which have appeared in anthologies put out by Soft Skull Press, Sarabande, and Anchor Books. She teaches poetry all over, and has changed her name to Lørpsliç Bierkegårt.*

IN THE WINTER OF 2004, TWO OF MY POEMS WERE published in this magazine. I went to the party celebrating the release of the issue where I was to receive my free contributor's copies. I had just bought my first pair of big winter boots, I mean gigantic winter boots, the kind modeled after the ones Kiss wore in the seventies. I thought they would change my relationship to winter, and I could stop hating it and get on with my life.

I was meeting a friend at the party who has enough party spirit for two, which was important because my spirit is deficient in that way. I mention this because it was my secret wish to claim my copies and leave, but because I wanted to act normally on account of my friend, when I was handed my copy, I looked for my poem. It is not my habit, when my work is published, to read it.

Early in my publishing career one of my poems was published in *The Paris Review.* I did what I think is the normal thing: I opened the book and looked for my poem. I began to read it. About halfway down, a horrible thing happened: a typo! Rather, an omission—of an entire word! It was a spare poem, with a short line. The missing word made the poem look crippled. I slammed the book shut and never opened it again.

The *Paris Review* editor called to ask how I "liked the poem." I have been asked this strange question by editors since. I know what they mean but I always have the impulse to answer the question they've actually asked: I hate this poem! I don't know what I could have been thinking when I sent you this! I wonder what was wrong with me when I wrote it! In any case, when this editor asked me how I liked the poem, I managed to say that there had been a mistake. "Oh," she said. "I hope it doesn't change the poem." "Well," I said, gathering my courage and reaching for a calm tone, "it changes the appearance of the line." I paused and continued: "It also changes the rhythm of the line." I took a slow breath. "And it changes the meaning." "Oh," she said.

It was the worst sort of omission: the poem still made sense, so no one would know there was a mistake, it just made stupid sense now.

When my book came out, the poem appeared in it with the omitted word restored. I thought seeing the poem as I had written it would rehabilitate the poem for me. It didn't. I flinch whenever that poem comes near. For me the poem is like a child who, once out of my sight, acts like an ass.

A few months before my book came out, *Poets & Writers* magazine published an interview with me. I talked with an intelligent journalist I'd gone to school with. When I was sent my contributor's copies, I read the interview checking for typos. There were none!

But there was something much worse: the article contained many lines of direct quotation—from me. But that was impossible! The journalist hadn't had a tape recorder and took very few notes. Many lines of these "direct quotations" sounded eerily familiar and also quite strange, like the way people's faces can be changed ever-so-slightly in dreams: "It was you but it wasn't you." These quotes were similar to things I said without being things I actually said, off just enough to sound like a bad impersonation. Worst of all, perhaps, was the line the magazine excerpted, enlarged, and bolded: "Right after I finish writing something, I lose interest in it. I'm so through with it."

That "so" stands out like a big pimple on my words. I don't speak like this, but if I were from California I might. The journalist had put my words into dialect.

She also said I'm from a beach town on Long Island. When I called to tell my father this he laughed out loud: "Corey Beach?" he cried, referring to the only part of town in which land and water meet—a yard-wide spit of stones and dirty bay water where I'd spent my summers collecting trash as a depressed employee of the Brookhaven Township.

As an added bonus, the picture of me they printed was off too: they told me it was going to be passport size. The picture is actually much larger. I'd never seen it enlarged. Blown up, it, too, looks like an odd cousin. Worst is my nose, a friend pointed out: "What's with your nose?" she said. It looks pointy in the picture. My nose in real life is not pointy. In the picture I am looking down; my nose seems to point the way.

Oh well, I consoled myself, at least I didn't fare so badly as the cover artist, Li-Young Lee. There's a picture of him inside the magazine sitting in a bathrobe on his curvy sofa with the shades drawn and a long-eared bunny beside him. At least I didn't look like an angry prostitute.

But the repercussions of the near-quotes in *Poets & Writers* were harsh. When my book was reviewed unfavorably in *Parnassus*, the reviewer borrowed liberally from the *Poets & Writers* interview. One of the things he harped on was a "tossed-off" quality in my work ("... I'm so through with it, I'm so through with it, I'm so, so, so ..." I kept hearing). I think this impression of his came more from that excerpted line than from my poems. I felt doubly abused.

Because of these and other incidents, I developed the habit of not reading my work when it's published: I'd rather not know. It may be behaving badly or mocking me from between the covers of a magazine, but I don't care. I'm in a comfortable denial. So, imagine my lack of surprise, my calm state of nonplus, when I opened the pages of issue #18 of this magazine, solely to pretend that I had a normal relationship to the written word for the benefit of my friend, to find the title of my poem, "Blue Statuary," and beneath that my name, Priscilla Becker, and beneath that a poem I'd never before seen! I thought for a moment that *Open City* might be so avant garde, so cutting edge, so open, that they didn't abide by the normal, boring convention of printing the title of the poem on the same page as the poem itself. I looked before and aft my poem. No "Blue Statuary."

The poem that appeared beneath my title and name was about, if I remember correctly, a horse. It had a line in it something like: "Blood. Shit. Piss."

In the days following this new publishing disaster, I puzzled over the sanity of giving over my work to second parties. The editor at *Open City* was mortified, and after some research offered this explanation: the typesetter uses a template to set the type. He then removes the template, substituting the intended poem. But in the case of my poem, he had neglected to remove the dummy-poem. I learned the title of this poem and the name of its author from an apology in the contributors' notes of issue #19 of *Open City*—"Against Witness," by William Wenthe.

At first this error seemed preferable to omitting just one word or changing my words into dialect. This was egregious! No one could think I'd written this poem! As it turns out I was wrong about that. More people have mentioned reading that poem than any other I've published. "I saw your poem in *Open City*," they say, giving me a strange look. I never tell them what happened, I don't know why. Something perverse in me enjoys this confusion. Maybe I am trying to change my relationship to the written word.

The Crossing Guard

Robert Bingham

Robert Bingham (1966–99) is the author of the story collection Pure Slaughter Value *and the novel* Lightning on the Sun, *of which "The Crossing Guard" was originally the opening chapter but was never published. His fiction and nonfiction appeared in* The New Yorker *and* Might. *He was a reporter, contributing editor, and early talent scout for the* Cambodia Daily, *Phnom Penh's first English-language daily, beginning in 1993, shortly after the paper was founded. He was the publisher of* Open City *from 1993 to 1999.*

OH, IF YOU WERE A STUPID, FILTHY NEW YORK pigeon, dulled to its citizens and living off the scraps of the city, you might fly over the government ponds and tennis courts, over the reservoir, through the meadows and softball diamonds and perch yourself on a section of black wall that rings Central Park and marks the beginning of that reliable grid known as the Upper East Side where, sadly, our story begins.

There was a man. There was a man who lived in a constant state of visitation with himself. He was quite unreal. He was a cut-out, a copy, a composite, a great index of anxiety. He lived alone. His wife? Please, for God's sake the woman had left him, and for good reason too. His skill set was his appetite, a very hungry man and a very weak one at that. People invited him to parties out of sympathy. There's old Weatherly, they would say. There's old Weatherly, he looks like shit. And that would be about it. He didn't inspire gossip anymore. His daughter visited him every other weekend in the brownstone he hadn't had the wherewithal to redecorate since his wife had left. He went about in faded khakis that in college had been standard enough fare, but now lent him the air of a flasher. Perhaps it was his skin. He was a very moist man with a disturbingly gray pallor. Most of the time you might as well have been looking at him in his coffin.

Weatherly donned the fluorescent vest of the parental school guard and descended the staircase of his brownstone. His street was built on the highest point of Manhattan. There was a Greek Orthodox seminary at the top and a rehabilitation center at the bottom. Weatherly lived in the middle. It was a crisp, clear day in early December. The air was tonic to his lungs, and for a moment the city seemed wonderfully new. Perhaps it was dry cleaning. Weatherly had spent a good deal of the morning worrying about and then finally getting there, to the dry cleaner. Now that sense of chemical cleanliness and order had somehow carried over to his neighborhood. He passed the deli, passed Karen Cups, a neighborhood shrink walking her dog between sessions, and stopped at a light on Madison Avenue. The sky was a cobalt blue and the runners of the reservoir raised in Weatherly's middle distance rotated with enviable enthusiasm. He wanted a cigarette. The runners, they inspired in him a cigarette. He would give a substantial sum of his unearned fortune for a cigarette if it didn't count as a cigarette, if it didn't mean he was smoking again.

Through the window of the Jackson Hole Hamburger, Weatherly watched the girls of St. Fermin. They were smoking and picking at salads and sodas. Incredible, he was really supposed to protect these girls? And there they were lounging between classes, smoking in the company of their new breasts, exhaling at each other, puffing and laughing away. Oh, why wouldn't they slow the childhood clock down in this town? Most were a few shades older than his daughter, Penny, in what grade he could not tell. But they were expensive little things, weren't they? And imperious too. Since his divorce, Weatherly had taken to eating at the Jackson Hole where he'd witnessed the St. Fermin girls ordering waiters around like servants. They got that from their mothers, no doubt. But premature sophistication had not completely corrupted them, no, not quite yet. There was a yearning, a curiosity in their young eyes hatched widely open by coffee and Diet Coke. No, these girls didn't miss a thing and as they huddled in adolescent conspiracy, Weatherly felt sorry for the boys who might choose to engage them.

Weatherly paused just inside the threshold of the restaurant. The smell of house-blend coffee mingled with that of onions and bell peppers hissing on the grill. From here he had a good view of their trim Caucasian legs jutting out from beneath plaid kilts. He had to force himself to look away. One wore a Guatemalan ankle bracelet. At another table sat a group of zitty boys glaring at the girls. Weatherly was inordinately moved. He took a seat at a corner table near the window and ordered coffee. He had five minutes. An abandoned *New York Times* sat on a chair of a nearby table and Weatherly picked it up and glanced through the international section. Reese was there again. It was a short wire story with a Phnom Penh dateline. Jealousy kept him from reading the story. He and Reese had worked on their college newspaper together. Now look where Reese was, working for the Agence France-Presse. It had a sexy ring to it, the Agence France-Presse. He imagined his friend's erotic life as one of vast sexual plunder interspersed with reportage on political intrigue in exotic hot spots. His old friend would chuckle with disgust if he saw him now, all comfort and ruin, sitting in this fluorescent crossing guard vest.

He peered over the paper and stared at the girls again. A lovely brunette at the tail end of the table locked eyes with him. It was as if she'd thrown a punch. Weatherly's windpipe constricted and his heart skipped. Marsha Dillon came through the door as his coffee arrived. She stood in the doorway in her own fluorescent bib looking at him. Weatherly took a sip of his scalding coffee and stood up. He placed a dollar on the table.

"Just getting the lay of the land," he said.

They passed onto the street.

Marsha Dillon wore an ankle length paisley dress that clashed against her orange vest. A lace collar dipped beneath her collarbone like a doily. On her feet were leather Tretorns over peds. They walked against the wind, against the traffic, downtown on Madison.

"Here," she said reaching into her handbag and passing him a walkie-talkie. "Judith Weintrap has declared the Jackson Hole off limits. Obviously her instructions haven't sunk in yet. Apparently the girls still have their allies on the waitstaff. Most of them are eighth- and ninth-graders. They run on their checks and smoke."

"I see," said Weatherly.

"Also," said Marsha Dillon. "We've been getting reports of stalkers out of the Jackson Hole. Well, stalkers is a strong word, ninety percent of them are fairly harmless. Mostly they just follow the girls a few blocks but some walk with them all the way home. Obviously it can be quite traumatic."

"Obviously," said Weatherly.

Marsha Dillon's husband had written the last of five letters on Weatherly's behalf for the Racquet Club. The two men had never liked each another but their respective wives had grown up in the same insular Pennsylvania town.

"School security is on the same frequency as your walkie-talkie," she explained. "If you see anything suspicious, just call it in. We're supposed to be . . . to be preemptive, or is it proactive?"

Beneath his ridiculous vest and sweater, Weatherly was wearing a brand new button-down shirt that moved laterally as he walked. At first it had been an annoying little scrape but as the two sentinels of Upper East Side security walked on together, his left nipple evolved into a raw agony, a pellet of discontent.

"Whatever happened to flashers?" asked Weatherly. "You know the guys in the smudged raincoats. The 'expose yourself to art' crowd. When Penny was in second grade, she once came home in tears."

"I don't know anything about flashers," said Marsha Dillon.

"I used to think that Kay got some sort of prurient satisfaction out of it. She'd take Penny into her arms and say 'he really showed you his thing-thing? I'm calling the police,' but she never did."

Marsha Dillon shook her head. Already she was having second thoughts about Weatherly and the parent patrol. Like most things when it came to these people, the parental patrol had been organized and scheduled months in advance. Weatherly's now ex-wife, Kay, had thought it a good idea for her now ex-husband to get some exercise. To "get outside and circulate." Now she'd left him. That's what happened when you married early, when you married young for so called love, thought Marsha. That was what happened when you socialized with Democrats who weren't Jews. They were inherently unstable people. She'd always found her friend Kay's husband lazy and superior and now as they turned onto Fifth Avenue, Marsha was visited by a disturbing memory of Weatherly. It had been at a Christmas party. Weatherly had slipped a lit cigarette inside the breast pocket of Tony Blackman's blazer. She hadn't found it funny and neither had Tony.

"I'm going to send you the fucking bill, Weatherly!" Tony had shouted as he shook off his smoking blazer. Weatherly had emitted a disgusting cackle, and later was found by his wife weeping into his cocktail napkin. Kay had ignored the whisperings about the two of them, how Weatherly had aged her, dragged her down with his drinking, with his apathy and persistent unhappiness.

"The plan," said Marsha Dillon, "is to walk a five block by four avenue square. From Eighty-ninth to Ninety-fourth and from Fifth to Lexington. Those are our perimeters."

"That sounds more like a rectangle," said Weatherly.

"It's a square," said Marsha Dillon. "The avenue blocks are longer."

As for Weatherly, he moved up Fifth Avenue wondering what it was about parenthood that calcified lives.

Within his wife's crowd this Marsha Dillon had never been a favorite of his, but at least in their early years there had existed a sense of parity. Now the bipartisan detente engendered by the mutual struggle of giving birth to their respective children had dissipated, and in its place Marsha judged him. She had arrived, quite prematurely, at frumpiness. She was frumpy, and she was a bore.

At Ninety-first Street the girls of St. Fermin sprang from the school doors in a torrent of release, their legs dappled to light orange in the afternoon, their backpacks swinging wildly from side to side. Suddenly a gaggle of them were jostling their way in his direction. Weatherly slowed to take in their onslaught. For God's sake, he thought, these girls didn't need protection. They were the threat. With their budding breasts and Walkmen, with their galvanized strides of undiluted energy sparkling in the fresh winter air, they required only protection from themselves and coming adulthood.

"Keep walking," said Marsha. "What are you doing?"

"Sorry," said Weatherly.

The girls' conversation was a jangle of muted insults and gossip that engulfed Weatherly in a golden pitch of feminine vitriol and then ebbed into softer tones of unarticulated intrigue as they slid past. They hadn't taken the slightest notice of their guardians. Weatherly felt jilted and unduly stimulated. Their presence had rallied his dislike for Marsha Dillon. This was not the first time he had witnessed a pack of well-off teenagers marching through his neighborhood, but to be officially among them, to be guardian and protector was something different altogether. They followed the group of girls from a half a block distance with Marsha Dillon scanning both sides of the street.

How the city had changed, thought Weatherly. Back when he was a boy there had been a sinister grit to the upper reaches of the East Side. He'd gone to school in a respectable neighborhood only a few blocks from Spanish Harlem. But Central Park knew no difference between Ninety-eighth Street and 115th. The neighborhoods bled together in the dust bowls of the park's playing fields. The after-school park of his boyhood. It had been the hour of the warrior, the hour of threat. Weatherly had been a middling member of a gang known as the French Connection. It was an organization born out of hanging around the water fountain, sports, and internal power struggles. The French Connection never beat anyone up but its own members. The double-cross was its ruling principle. A spanking clean MTA bus passed by. New York City in the era of graffiti and great municipal malfeasance. Now the buses sliding downtown on Fifth were spanking clean, and the steel garbage cans dotting the corners were nearly empty. Imagine that when he was a child? If there was one image that rooted Weatherly in childhood, it was the garbage can. That monument to overcapacity teetering, top heavy with waste. The flasher, the streaker, the YMCA rapists, the bus-pass mugger; if there were any sex offenders about today, it was as if Marsha Dillon had erased them.

"Well," said Marsha Dillon, "this is where I get off. I'll see you on Thursday."

"Right," said Weatherly.

"Oh, Weatherly?" said Marsha about to turn into her building. "Are you coming to the fundraiser for the zoo? Sandra Perlbinder needs to know."

"That used to be Kay's department," said Weatherly. "To tell you the truth I don't know. How much is it?"

For a moment Marsha stood by her doorman looking at this slightly stooped, hopeless man. He seemed at once to have aged and regressed to a state of infantile lament. For the first time in her life she felt sorry for him.

"Well, please let me know as soon as you can."

"Who is Sandra Perlbinder?"

"Oh Weatherly," said Marsha Dillon. "I don't have enough fingers on my two hands to count the times you've been introduced."

"Maybe you should cut them off."

A cold blast of winter wind shot off the reservoir chilling his forehead.

"Excuse me?"

"Nothing," said Weatherly. "I'll let you know. The city certainly has changed from when I was a boy."

"I suspect it has," said Marsha Dillon squinting at him, shaking her head in hostile quizzicality. "Why don't you go home now."

"See you at the zoo," said Weatherly.

Perhaps there is no better opportunity for a glimpse into the smudged window of a man's heart than when he sits alone in a pizza parlor. Visited by stress, Weatherly made a habit of seeking sanctuary in a slice. It was his version of tea. There were three pizza parlors within walking distance of his home and he made a habit of rotating between them. He was neither a regular nor a stranger at any. At the particular one in which he found himself, they called him "Boss." Weatherly ordered and paid for his slice and then sat down at a lonely Formica table. He blew on his slice. He watched the men behind the counter do their thing. The oven door opened. The oven door closed. The digits of the cash register covered by a greasy sheet of plastic moved in a slow continuum tallying the sums that fed the strays of the city who sank solo into their slice of solace. This tableaux repeated in every neighborhood in every borough, was it a symptom, thought Weatherly, or was it a cure for a profound and collective loneliness? He blew on his piping hot slice. Two more customers walked through the door, bank tellers and caretakers for the elderly living in high rises, Con Edison workers emerging from the billows of smoking holes of steam to join in the great cross section of the spiritually malnourished. They came in out of the dimming day to console themselves in cheese and toppings, to ruin their dinner.

Weatherly considered using a plastic knife and fork but reneged on the idea as being for tourists. Today he'd opted for the purity of the plain slice, and he would eat it with his hands. He picked the slice up again, gently folded it and plunged in.

"Daddy," came a voice.

The pizza burned the roof of his mouth. He'd been caught.

"Penny," he said. "My God."

His daughter, a fourth grader, was facing him. Was she ashamed to see him here alone? Or . . . Oh Lord, she was with a boy! He was standing just inside the doorway. A red head, clearly a devil now considering giving flight.

"Daddy," said his daughter. "What are you wearing?"

Penny's date had great splotches of freckles and wore no school uniform. She on the other hand was in a St. Fermin gray kilt below a white button-down shirt with a wonderfully rounded collar and blue cardigan sweater. Weatherly was proud of his daughter. She was a splendid girl.

"Well sweetheart, I'm wearing . . . I'm wearing . . ."

"You're wearing one of those weird patrol uniforms."

"Yes," said Weatherly. "Yes, I am."

The barely pubescent red-headed devil with the evil freckles now approached the counter and mumbled his order.

"What's that, Boss?" asked the man behind the counter.

A mumbler, thought Weatherly. Penny's pizza arrived and Weatherly watched his daughter pay for it. Then she paid for his slice. Weatherly couldn't remember ever seeing his daughter pay for anything whatsoever.

"What are you doing here, Daddy?" she asked.

"Well sweetheart I was . . . I was going to ask the same of you."

"I'm hungry," she said.

Difficult to argue with that. The Devil, the little hormonal dervish was now pouring an abundant amount of garlic on his slice. Weatherly had a vision of him sticking a pizza-greasy hand up his daughter's kilt. He wondered if he should force contact with the boy, say something parental to Penny, say something like: I don't think you've properly introduced me to your friend. But they had passed that moment. Randomly, he had met his daughter in the world and she had triumphed.

"You look funny, Daddy," she said and walked with her date to a table in the back of the room. Weatherly looked down at his slice. It had withered and congealed into a face. Within his slice he saw his own wasted face. It was the face of time, a face of age. Tears welled up inside him. He threw the slice in the garbage and walked home.

His brownstone, upon entrance, was an insult. He was greeted by a hallway that undermined him, an alien thoroughfare of despair leading to a living room of fatigue. He walked into that room and threw open the window. A bit better now. Across the street sat in the granite and marble, the Daugherty Rehabilitation Center, a mausoleum to drug and alcohol addiction into which his wife had threatened to admit him. In the spirit of those fights, in the spirit of an old wound, he looked at the grandfather clock his dead grandmother had left him and fixed himself a drink. The gin only increased the whirl, and the sunshine on the living room rug kicked up the headlong promiscuity of his thoughts. The sun made him want to flee, to move, to take some kind of action against his life. Marsha Dillon, could that really be the hand he'd been dealt? Perhaps it was Kay. He was still walking a pantomime of their life together.

When he met another couple at a party and was close enough to smell them, he still viewed these new people from a position of marital distance. Everyone was already formed, busy and befriended. The major roles had already been cast. As for Marsha Dillon, it was the permanence of her that was so ungodly. She seemed destined to play, forever, not for a week, but for the rest of his adult life as it now stood on this planet, she was fated, it seemed, to play a starring role in his life ad infinitum. And it wasn't even as if she was a truly malevolent person or even someone for whom he could openly nourish a hatred. He disliked her, yes, but she had given him no reason to willfully act against her interests. She was a law-abiding citizen of the Upper East Side. One couldn't tie her to the whipping post. The sick part? The really degrading bit about Marsha Dillon: it was he who had positioned himself in her orbit. It was he who had been talked into attending her fundraisers, who'd bowed down to her social schedule. That was what was so insulting. Slowly, gradually, like some kind of terrible erosion caused not by centuries of wind and rain or some other irrefutable force of nature, but through the persistence of his own compromise, she'd insinuated herself into his life. He'd caved in. Slowly and then rather quickly, she'd arrived to direct traffic in his life. And he was not the only one. Other people in this quadrant of the island did her bidding, not out of joy but out of fear. They feared her and walked the line.

Still in his ridiculous apron he sat down on the edge of one of the chaises and took a long sip of his drink. Two months ago he'd quit smoking. Finally he'd done it. Stopped cold turkey, taken the head colds and the misery and all the rest, but now at the bottom of his first drink he knew he hadn't quite made it. He walked over to the wooden box hidden beneath the couch and found an old pack of Parliaments. Parliaments, his mother's brand. He tapped one out and patted himself down for a light. He ripped at the Velcro of his poncho and threw it in the corner. Then he marched around the kitchen counter that separated the living room from kitchen and lit the stove. His hair was on fire. He could hear the sizzle and the smell, and he rushed to the sink and doused himself, ruining his lit cigarette in the process. The miserable filter separated from the body. Then standing in the only room he could now bear due to its functional neutrality, standing alone in his kitchen, he screamed. He really went for it. He dug down deep into the obscenity of his chest and roared.

The Mother of His Children

Paula Bomer

Paula Bomer is the author of Baby and Other Stories. *Her fiction has appeared in dozens of journals and anthologies, including* Fiction, The Mississippi Review, Nerve, *and elsewhere. She grew up in South Bend, Indiana and now lives in New York.*

 THE CAR ARRIVED AND HIS WIFE HELD THE BABY on her hip and waved to him as he trotted down their front steps. "Call me," she said, and he could still smell her coffee-mouth and sour, breast-milk smell as he slipped into the car. She looked old and beat-up, a bit of a double chin resting on her neck. One of her breasts was noticeably larger than the other; this had happened after the birth of their new son, Henry, when her milk came in. He waved back at all of them. Their three-year-old, Jake, bounced around on the sidewalk screaming, "Bye-bye Daddy! Bye-bye Daddy!" He would be gone for only two days. No matter; he was thrilled, thrilled to leave them, stinky, loud, and demanding, all of them. And he didn't feel guilty about it. He loved his family, how they were always waiting for him to arrive in the evening. They needed him. He had framed photographs of them on his desk at work. But they were not always that pleasant to be around.

Ted Stanton was the technology director of a Web site, thirty-five, balding, and with a limp tire of fat around his middle. He played basketball on Sundays in Brooklyn, near his newly purchased house, with other men in their prime who worked in the online world. They played extremely aggressively, turning red and oozing noxious, booze-scented sweat. They never talked business, but every push, grunt, and jump was about whose IPO was fatter than the others. If he wasn't playing ball on Sundays, he sat. He sat on the subway to and from work, he sat at his desk in his office in a sleek loft in downtown Manhattan, and he sat on the couch at home drinking a beer. He sat at the dinner table where Laura served him dinner almost every night. He then sat in front of the TV, and then sat up in bed and leafed through a magazine. Soon he

52

would be fat. He was convinced Laura wanted him to be fat, as she always presented him with a pint of ice cream and a spoon while they watched TV at night. He hated her for this, but he also was relieved that she was there to take the blame, as he would never want to be responsible himself for putting on weight.

He had met Laura five years ago at a party. They discovered that they both lived in studio apartments on Mulberry Street. She was not at all remarkable looking, but her clothes were tight, and her trampy style was unique in his circle of Ivy Leaguers. They slept together that night, at her place. The next morning, deeply hungover, he had to look at a piece of mail on her kitchen counter to get her name. He had forgotten it, or never bothered to ask for it in the first place. They continued to drink a lot and sleep together, and when she accidentally got pregnant, they agreed to go to city hall and get married. Two years earlier, he would have made her get an abortion. But Ted liked her, liked that she was his, and she cooked him dinner all the time. They had fit well together in bed, and while he knew she was no rocket scientist, he found her simplicity comforting. He had been thirty and eager to marry. He never had much confidence with women, and Laura had made him feel slightly good about himself.

She was just fine in every respect, really. Did he love her? This was a subject matter both Ted and Laura found embarrassing. It was something they had in common, this squeamishness about love. Once, after a particularly gymnastic and satisfying lovemaking session, he had blurted out "I love you." She answered him, her face muffled into the pillow, something that sounded like "ditto." This was good enough for him, but thereafter he restrained himself from saying anything in the heat of passion.

And now? Now, he was on his way to San Francisco, to a conference. He flew coach and could barely fit into his designated seat. But the flight left on time and no fat people sat next to him, in fact, no one sat next to him. He had a window seat. A pile of magazines and his laptop occupied the seat next to him. His flight attendant was female and despite the globs of makeup on her face, was relatively attractive and not too miserable seeming. He briefly imagined shoving his dick down her throat. Her tight, navy polyester skirt would rustle loudly as she pulled it up so she could get down on her knees; her shiny, lip-glossed mouth would part as she bent her head back to make room for his erection. It was something he did, imagined violating strange women whom he came in contact with. Once he had even fantasized fucking Larry Worth, the president of his company, in the ass. Larry, chubby, nasty-tempered Larry. Gasping from his smoking habit, the stink of old sweat coming off his dirty boxers as Ted ripped them down and shoved him over his very own desk. The tightness of his asshole, the little pieces of shit clinging to the dark threads of hair. He'd let out one angry scream as Ted stuck him like the pig he was. Larry had been a classmate at Harvard and Ted liked him, but resented him for making more money than he did. He didn't have kids to support. He didn't even have a wife! And definitely not a wife who perhaps defined herself entirely by what she bought.

Besides shopping and minding the children and house, Laura did nothing. In fact, minding the children and house had become a sort of shopping in and of itself. There was new underwear for Jake one day, diapers for the baby the next, and pork chops the day after. Ted knew that taking care of the children and the home was work, regardless of the weekly visits from a Caribbean housekeeper and a part-time babysitter. He wouldn't want to do what Laura was doing. It was thankless, and not only because he didn't really appreciate what she did—which was, in fact, true—but because no one did, not their little children, not the other depressed, defensive, and overeducated mothers she hung out with, not anyone. He was, of course, secretly glad she didn't have a career. But when the sitter came in the morning, Laura went out shopping. And usually, in the afternoon, she strapped the kids in the stroller and shopped some more. She bought nice stuff—Kate Spade diaper bags, Petit Bateau pajamas for the kids, a pair of Gap leather pants for herself. She bought shell steaks, fresh rosemary, organic baby food. She cooked nice dinners with the nice food she bought. But sometimes Ted wondered if there was anyone lurking beneath all that shopping. This kind of thinking made him anxious, and he tried not to go there. He didn't like hyper-intelligent women, but he also liked to think that Laura had a soul.

San Francisco, now there was a nice thought. Ted undid his seatbelt, breathed deeply. Out the airplane window was nothing, a whitish gray, cloudy nothing. Larry was meeting him at what was promised to Ted to be a very happening restaurant. Larry would bring a crowd of fabulously important schmoozers. There would be lots of parties to go to after dinner, lots of drunk, younger women with interesting jobs. But for some reason, despite the fact that Ted was doing quite well, all those loose party girls, all that fresh lemon pussy, the squeaky young recent college grads with their sixty-grand-a-year jobs, never came on to him. It wasn't because he was married. Plenty of his married colleagues had flings.

In the past, his insecurity had made him invisible to women, that he knew. But now he felt as if it were something else. He felt it was because he actually programmed Web sites, was a tech guy. All the young women wanted to fuck the creatives, as they were known. It was as if the nature of his job forced him into a monogamous lifestyle he no longer could bear. No one wanted to talk to him about code. Code was not sexy. He didn't want to talk about code either, frankly. It was just something he had a gift for, something he did for a living. And no women, young or old, did technical work. They all worked in marketing or production.

Did he want to divorce Laura? Hmm. Every day he left for work and she stayed home, he felt them grow apart. They grew eight hours apart every day. He, with adults and computers, participating in the world. She, primarily with young children, sinking into a dull, repetitive existence. Besides shopping, she spent a lot of time picking up. She picked up underwear, dirty dishes, toys, old newspapers. She put away the bath towels, lined up the spices in the spice rack, took the old, bad food out of the refrigerator. Every night she sat cross-legged in front of the refrigerator, perusing its contents. Once, they had sex in common. That, and socializing. Sex, in many ways, was what had brought Laura and he together. Sure, they were both white, educated, and upper-middle class. They both believed in the superiority of all things New York. But it was their fucking that really clinched the deal, the negotiation which was their marriage.

"Something to drink?"

It was early. He knew the flight attendant really meant juice or coffee, but he ordered a Bloody Mary. There she was, with her full cart, leaning over to find a miniature bottle of vodka. She smiled at him. He wanted her to care that he was ordering a drink so early, he wanted her to feel his pain, see him as slightly on the edge. But what did she care if he had a drink first thing in the morning? He was nothing to her. She placed the little plastic cup with the rounded ice cubes onto a napkin, leaning again to do so, this time over his pile of stuff on the seat next to him. She had nice tits. She smiled, revealing a slight overbite. Perhaps the overbite was why he had imagined putting his dick in her mouth. The extra room there, the sexiness of the imperfection. Perhaps she secretly hated men who drank, he thought. Perhaps her father was a drunk who beat her, molested her. He wanted her to care.

The drink tasted good. Slightly horseradishy, very cold. The plastic cup was like a feather in his hand. He felt wild, free. He pushed the little silver button on the armrest and leaned back. Someone behind him coughed in annoyance and Ted looked back. Some guy with a job, like himself. Angry in his little seat, jowly face in his newspaper. Fuck him, Ted thought, and pushed the seat back further, as far as it would go. The back of his seat at this point, he knew, was in the guy's lap. Ted coughed back at him.

An ice cube from his drink fell in his lap. Ted felt it there, felt it cold and hard, making a dark stain on his trousers. He picked it up off of his pants and put it back in his cup. Then he downed his drink.

When they had decided to keep the baby, Laura had been thrilled. She glowed in those first few months, despite her upset stomach, she positively glowed. She quit drinking, smoking, and cut back on her coffee intake. She started watching lots of TV. As she grew larger, they both grew more anxious. Ted worked late at night. Laura began looking for a house in Brooklyn, as the tiny apartment in Manhattan would no longer work for them. She took a prenatal yoga class where she met other expectant moms. She bought baby clothes, researched strollers and car seats. Her life, which once was partying and flirting, turned into obsessive nesting activities. Ted continued to work late and became ambitious in a way he'd never been before. He asked for a huge raise and got it. He wanted a corner office. He, too, became obsessed, obsessed with making more money.

And sex? They continued to have sex, albeit more cautiously, less frequently, and toward the end of her pregnancy, not at all. The last time they had sex during the pregnancy had been late at night, under the covers. Laura's back was facing him as they lay side by side. It took about two seconds before he came. Her pussy had felt so swollen, and so thick with mucous, that it freaked him out. It had felt good, in a way, but alarmingly different and almost completely animal, or something. Like he was fucking a sheep. Overall, it was an unpleasant interaction, regardless of the physical gratification.

As Laura's due date neared, they began attending a birth class. Laura had researched various birth classes—this was one of those things she talked at him about, which class to take, which hospital to have the baby in, to get an epidural or no epidural. Ted did not understand all the hoopla about birth. It was after the birth that things really started to happen, wasn't it? After the baby arrived, that's what really mattered. When he spoke this way to her, Laura would get mad, saying, "It's not your body, so you just don't care. You don't care about me, do you? You don't know how to care about me!" Then she would storm into the living room and turn on the TV. End of discussion.

The birth class met once a week in an elementary public school in the West Village. Ted hated it. The "instructor," Jane, was a beady-eyed, colorless woman in her forties who was relentlessly cheerful about birth despite an incredibly strong hostility that emanated from her person. Sometimes, one of her children attended the class and would sit in a loft in the back of the classroom playing by himself while his mother talked excitedly about vaginas, the uterus, dilation, effacement, placenta, and the like. Ted was disgusted. All the other couples seemed pleased as punch. Then came the practice sessions. Laura would lie on her side and he sat next to her, rubbing her back and talking to her in a soothing voice about oceans and forests. He just didn't get it. Couldn't she just take some drugs and put a sheet over her?

The flight attendant loomed over him suddenly. He ordered another Bloody Mary. She didn't make eye contact with him this time. Good. Maybe she did care, he thought, pouring the vodka into the tomato juice and stirring. His hand shook slightly as he banged the little plastic stirrer around. Bloody Mary. Bloody bloody. At the end of the birth class, they watched videos of births. Ted would close his eyes. Instructor Jane, and sometimes some of the other women, cried and exclaimed, "Isn't it beautiful?" Ted ran off to the bathroom, thinking he might throw up.

He tried to talk to Laura about it. It's not that he didn't want children, he just didn't want to watch them come out of her. Was that so wrong? He admitted, bravely he thought, that he was scared. Laura argued that he would be sad and feel left out if he wasn't there watching.

"What if you don't bond with our son because you're too chicken to see him come into the world?" She'd been sniffly and angry, with only weeks to go before the birth.

"I can't wait to meet this baby," he'd said. "I'm not worried about loving this baby or not. I just am nervous about the whole birth thing. You are too, admit it. You're not so sure it's going to be so beautiful."

"I don't want to be alone, Ted. And I think the immediate bonding thing is real. I want you there in the room with me, helping to deliver this child."

"Instructor Jane is brainwashing you! My dad loved us! He wasn't in the room watching us slither out of my mother's crotch!" He hadn't meant to yell. Laura burst into tears. That was it. He apologized and said he'd do his best. And he did. At the hospital, he held her hand, gave her ice chips, and told her stories of mountains and trickling rain until she screamed at him to shut the fuck up. Jake's head appeared and his wife, huffing, deranged, and drug free, touched Jake's head. The midwife told

Ted to touch Jake's head too, and he did. A wet, hairy little head, stuck in the pelvic bone of his wife. He didn't like it. The room smelled of feces and some weird, thick metallic smell; the smell of fear, the smell of blood and earth. His wife's vagina expanded into something entirely unrecognizable as his son's body emerged. Her vagina was all blood and ooze, as wide as a house, and beet red except for the places where it was a dark, bruised purple; looking at it just made Ted hurt all over. Laura's eyes bulged from her face, black-green veins glistened all over her round stomach and breasts. Dark streaks of shit, poorly wiped off by the nurse, lay smeared on her buttocks, and her once tiny pink rosebud of an asshole was swollen to the size of a small melon. She moaned as if she were dying. He began to fear that she was dying. He had weird thoughts wishing that she would die, just so the damn thing would be over with, and so that he never had to look her in the face again. The midwife yelled, "Take a picture, take a picture!" He had been given a camera by his wife. He didn't want to take a picture. He wanted to curl up in a ball and disappear. Everybody was screaming. Laura was no longer Laura. Her voice came from a place he'd never known was in her. He couldn't stand it. He couldn't stand looking at anyone anymore, and he began backing out of the room, the bitter taste of vomit on the back of his throat. His wife began screaming, "I'm dying! I'm dying! Pull! Pull him out of me!" Minutes later, he held his newborn son. The midwife asked him to take off his shirt first, for some "skin-on-skin contact." He ignored her. Jake, their little boy, their perfect, tiny boy, squeaked and cried. Holding him was, undoubtedly, the most profound experience of his life. Nothing could touch that. But the birth itself rattled him. He had been afraid and now he was, well, traumatized.

The constant whir of the airplane reminded Ted of the computers at work. A soothing, white noise. He was fifteen the first time he touched pussy. A Saturday night, in the graveyard behind Hotchkiss. His first year of boarding school. She was a lovely, bulimic, Greenwich, Connecticut, girl named Mary Todd. They had been drinking vodka mixed with Seven-Up. After fumbling around for a while, Ted, so nervously, put a finger into her panties, searching for it. It was warmer than he thought it would be. No one had told him it would be warm in there. Slippery yes, but with invisible, superfine grains of sand. He let his finger linger there as Mary Todd sighed underneath him. His erection waned as his hand explored, but his curiosity was sated. Like a blind man, he saw with his fingers.

In the year that followed Jake's birth, they went to a marriage counselor, a sex therapist, and finally, a doe-eyed, extremely short woman in Times Square who specialized in post-birth, male sexual trauma. She reminded Ted of Dr. Ruth and he often had to stop himself from breaking into nervous laughter during their sessions with her. He did this by thinking about death. Death, Ted would think, frowning in concentration. We all will die, we all will die, was his mantra. Laura and he spent a lot of time there watching explicit, touchy-feely, sexual-technique videos, while the therapist pointed to a close-up of a penis thrusting in and out of a vagina and said stuff like, "See? It's not a bad thing, the vagina. It's friendly!" Indeed, the vagina had once been his friend. And to a certain extent, the vagina became his friend again. Only on occasion now did he become erectally challenged, so to speak. Only on occasion was he haunted with the specter of Jake's birth. Henry, the new baby, was born while he waited outside. His wife had an epidural and read magazines throughout the labor. The Dr. Ruth lookalike had convinced Laura that Ted needed some boundaries, and that this did not mean he was a bad husband, nor did it mean he was an unloving father. Ted was so thankful for this, so thankful for the support he didn't even know he needed, so thankful that someone had articulated what he felt, that she became a powerful goddess in his dreams. He dreamt of her often, even though he couldn't remember her name. In his dreams, she stroked his head and her voice was the soothing voice of his mother.

The white-gray nothing outside of the tiny window was changing. Bits of land and water became discernible. Ted looked down at his drink. It was gone. At some point, the flight attendant had put a little box with a sandwich, an apple, and a cookie on the tray next to him. Where had he been? He rubbed his eyes. Had he slept? San Francisco was approaching. Suddenly, he felt drunk and sad. He missed Jake, he missed the drooly, gurgly new Henry. And in a lesser way he missed his bossy, aging, somewhat boring wife. She was, after all, the mother of his children. She was a decent, hardworking mother. He picked up the sandwich and started to eat it. He would catch up on sleep in his eco-sensitive hotel. He would drink maybe a little too much at the parties, but not enough to behave inappropriately. He would not get laid, this he knew for certain, because he truly wasn't interested in acquainting himself with the vagina of some strange person. And when he returned home, what to do with Laura's straightforward longings directed toward him? Her foot on his crotch at night, while they lounged on the couch, watching TV? Said or unsaid, he had grown to love this woman. He did not always like her, this was true. He had stared deep into her, watched her produce life, and it had changed him. He knew, like never before, that he would die, Laura too would die, and that even his children were temporary beasts of the Earth themselves. His job, their house, basketball, preschool, and shopping—it was all just waiting, killing time. And while he waited? He would do his best. That's all he could do.

The flight attendant came down the aisle, picking up people's food boxes and accompanying trash. Ted, after wiping up the little drips of boozy tomato juice from the tray, neatly stuck the napkin and the tiny vodka bottle into the empty cup. He was trying to be helpful. He lifted his arms to her with his garbage, to save her the trouble of reaching over for everything. "Thank you," he said, his eyes wet with vodka, and the plane continued to descend.

17 Quai Voltaire

Paul Bowles

Paul Bowles was born in 1910 and studied music with composer Aaron Copland before moving to Tangier, Morocco, with his wife, Jane Bowles. Bowle's prolific career included musical compositions as well as novels, collections of short fiction, books of travel, poetry, and translations. He died in Morocco in 1999. This essay, written in 1993 and published in Open City *for first time, will appear in* Travels: Collected Travel Writing, 1950–1993 *(Ecco Press).*

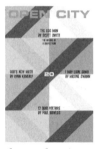

IF I REMEMBER CORRECTLY, THE APARTMENT AT 17 Quai Voltaire consisted of a very high-ceilinged studio with a balcony along one side. I slept up there. Harry Dunham, just out of Princeton, had rented the studio. He had the small bedroom downstairs. It was January, and the mornings were very cold. I could look out of the bathroom window on the balcony at the tracery of branches against the sky, and at the boats going up and down the river at my feet. This was the winter of 1931–1932; there were not many cars passing in the street below. I assume there are more now.

In Marrakech Harry had thought it a good idea to import Abdelkader, a fifteen-year-old Moroccan who worked in the hotel there, and who could, thought Harry, be trained to act as his valet and as a general factotum. This proved to be not a successful venture.

There must have been some sort of heating apparatus in the place, or it would have been untenable and, as a matter of fact, I recall Abdelkader's journeys down the narrow back stairway to the basement in order to fetch fuel. Whether this was wood or coal I have no idea. I know that it was on this staircase where one day he met someone he enthusiastically described as "*comme ma mère, je te jure*," and to whom he subsequently presented me (also on these back stairs). The voluble lady's name was Lucie Delarue-Mardrus. She invited me in to her apartment for a cup of coffee, and introduced me to Dr. Mardrus, who had much less to say than she. I was almost mute, not having read, or even known of the existence of his translation of *The Thousand and One Nights*. It was here that

I first heard of Isabelle Eberhardt, whom Mme. Mardrus described with great relish. They had met in Algeria.

The previous month I had been staying at an Italian ski resort. I was not in the best of health, and I wrote this to Gertrude Stein, who insisted that I return to Paris. But in the meantime someone (there were so many gossip-spreaders on the left bank in those days) went to her and told her that I was with a French girl there in the Alps. The girl and I were merely friends, but Gertrude Stein drew her own conclusions. She disapproved of liaisons between the young men she was interested in and members of the opposite sex. Thus when I returned to Paris and thought I'd go around to the Rue de Fleurus and visit the Misses Stein and Toklas, I telephoned.

There was cold at the other end of the line.

"So you're back in Paris," said Gertrude Stein.

"Yes."

"Why don't you go to Mexico? I think that's where you belong. You'd last about two days."

That was the end of the conversation. She was a Californian: Mexico was her idea of a truly lethal place. I did not see her again until the following summer.

Strange, but it's impossible to remember where I ate my lunches and dinners. I was not interested in gastronomy; I was striving to make a small amount of money last as long as possible, without suffering from indigestion. It seems to me that there was a quite good, medium-priced restaurant in the Rue Bonaparte where I often went.

Two years earlier on my first visit to Paris, I had fallen in love with the Métro. It got one around the city without the rush and roar of the New York subway, which seemed always to be engaged in a race against time. On the subway one compulsively looked at one's watch; on the Métro one looked for DUBO— DUBON— DUBONNET instead. The smell of the New York subway was one of hot metal laced with harbor sewage; the Métro gave off a distinctive odor that escaped from the stations into the street. I had never smelled that particular scent anywhere else, and for me it was a symbol of Paris. Years later in a Tangier *droguerie* I discovered a disinfectant which came in three perfumes: Lavande, Citron, and Parfum du Métro.

Bernárd Faÿ, who lived in the Rue St. Guillaume, occupied a chair in Franco-American relations. What his political ideas were I have no idea, but as a result of having expressed them he was imprisoned for several years after the Second World War. It was at his house that I had met

Virgil Thomson who, inasmuch as he lived at 17 Quai Voltaire, had been responsible for getting the studio there for Harry and me. Virgil also saw to it that I met various people whom he thought I ought to know, such as Marie-Louise Bousquet, Favel Tchelitchew, and Eugène Berman, whom everyone called Génia. He took me one day to see Max Jacob, a strange little man with a head like an egg. Henri Sauguet was there. But I had never read a line of Max Jacob's, nor heard a note of Sauguet's, so that these introductions were somewhat beside the point.

There were two places where I loved to go: the Bal Nègre in the Rue Blomet, and the Théâtre du Grand Guignol. I'd never before seen blacks dancing, and was of course highly impressed by their proficiency and grace. The repertory at the Grand Guignol was necessarily limited, and one had to be careful to choose a program that was not composed entirely of pieces one had already seen. Often during a performance there would be a disturbance among the spectators, and a person would be taken out by nurses in white uniforms. I never believed in the authenticity of these heart attacks and epileptic seizures. The plays did not seem horrible enough to provoke such reactions, although I was assured that the effects were bonafide, since the theatre attracted invalids and neurotics. I thought it was all great fun, including the dramatic removal of the hypersensitive spectators.

Whenever a friend came to Paris and suggested that we eat together, I would choose La Mosquée, not because of its culinary excellence, but simply because the food and the ambiance were Moroccan. (I still dreamed of returning to Fez, which I'd left only a few months earlier.) And now that I recall it, it seems to me that the couscous was not at all bad. Certainly it was better than what one can get nowadays in a restaurant in Morocco. I'm told that now, more than half a century later, La Mosquée's food has deteriorated, but this is not surprising, considering what has happened to everything else.

One day at a friend's flat in Montparnasse I was introduced to Ezra Pound. He and I went out to lunch in the neighborhood. He was tall and had a reddish beard. I recalled a poem of his I'd read in a little magazine several years earlier; it was an excoriation of old people who he apparently thought owed it to society to die before they became senile. It was a cruel little poem. I had shown it to my mother, who said: "Obviously that man doesn't know much about life." Several times during lunch I was on the point of asking Mr. Pound if he still felt the same way about the elderly, but I held my tongue because I thought the question would embarrass him. At the time he was one of three editors of a literary magazine called *The New Review*, the other two being Samuel Putnam and Richard Thoma. He had an appointment with Putnam that afternoon, and suggested I go with him. We boarded a bus and stood on the back platform all the way to Fontenay-aux-Roses. I remembered that Gertrude Stein had said she couldn't have him at her house any more because he was so clumsy and careless. If he went near a table, she said, he knocked over the lamp. If he sat down, the chair broke under him. It cost her too much money to have him as a guest, so she made 27 Rue de Fleurus off-limits to him. I asked her if she thought he minded being excluded. "Oh, no. He has plenty of other people to explain things to." She called him The Village Explainer, which was fine, she said, if you were a village.

My literary activities in Paris that winter were confined to the search for missing issues of certain defunct and moribund magazines of which I wanted to have a complete collection. This took more time and energy than one might expect. The publications of particular interest were *Minotaure*, *Bifur*, and *Documents*, a short-lived review edited by Carl Einstein. These were not to be found at the stalls along the quays, but in small second-hand bookshops scattered across the city, so that in my search for them I was obliged to do a good deal of walking. This, however, suited me perfectly, as there was nothing I enjoyed more than wandering on foot through the less frequented streets of Paris, which I continued to find mysterious and inexhaustible.

The regions which I particularly loved to explore were far from the Opéra, far from the Place de la Concorde or the Arc de Triomphe, all of which seemed too official to be of interest. On a gray winter's day the humble streets of Belleville and Ménilmontant struck me as infinitely more poetic; I could spend hours exploring those quarters, taking snapshots of courtyards piled with ladders and barrels (taking care that no person was included in the picture) and getting temporarily lost, rather as one does in a Moroccan medina. The food in the restaurants of these parts was not much to my liking; I recall the very red and sweetish horsemeat they served, generally with gritty spinach.

But there was one "official" building which delighted me: this was the Trocadéro with its wide staircases going down to the Seine. Am I wrong to associate it with Loutréamont? Surely it was ugly enough to have aroused his admiration, with the two unforgettable life-size rhinoceroses. Apparently these were removed at the time of the building's cosmetic surgery. I can't help wondering what happened to those two enormous animals. Do they still exist somewhere, or have they been destroyed? It seems to me that the French might have cast two more identical statues and placed all four of them at the corners of the Tour Eiffel, with which they had something in common.

Lest I be suspected of harboring perverse tastes in architecture, I should remark that I admired the Palace of Versailles. The openness of the landscape spread out before it, stretching away into the distance, provided an antidote to the occasional feeling of claustrophobia I had in Paris. I assumed that I shared a more or less universal admiration for the place, so that I was really shocked when one afternoon I saw four English tourists stand looking up at the wide façade with an expression of derision on their faces, while one woman said, in a broad Cockney accent: "Talk about *ugly*!"

One night I was invited to dinner at Tristan Tzara's flat. It was somewhere on the way up to Montmartre—perhaps the Rue Lepic. He had a beautiful Swedish wife, his salon was full of African sculptures and masks, and there was a splendid Siamese cat. In spite of (or possibly because of) their generally insane behavior, I'm particularly fond of these animals.

The food seemed excellent to me, but they apologized for it. They had a temporary cook, explained Tzara, since their usual cook had left earlier in the week in a state of great agitation, saying that he would under no circumstances set foot in the Tzara establishment again. It all had to do with the cat, which had never been on good terms with the cook. Perhaps the man had neglected on occasion to feed it. In any case he did not want it in the kitchen when he was working, and thus pushed it out with his foot, an insult which the cat, a huge male, obviously considered unforgivable.

The cook slept in a servant's room at the back of the apartment, and always shut his door upon retiring. But one night he failed to shut it completely, and the cat silently pulled it open. Making certain that the man was asleep, the animal crouched and sprang, landing on the cook's throat, which it began to rip open with its powerful hind feet. Clearly it had every intention of doing away with its enemy. The cook was taken to hospital, and in the morning he appeared at the door of the Tzara flat to deliver his ultimatum: if they wanted to keep him as a servant, the cat had to go immediately. He would not enter the apartment until they had got rid of it. They refused to do this, and the cook went away, threatening to start legal proceedings at once. I asked how the cat got on with the present cook. "Oh, she's a woman," said Tzara. "He doesn't mind women." The cat was sitting on a bookcase next to an African mask, watching us while we ate. Even though I had a strong desire to go over and caress his head and scratch his jowls, I was careful not to approach him at any time during the evening.

The walls of the studio at 17 Quai Voltaire were decorated with several large monochromatic drawings by Foujita. These belonged either to our landlady, Mme. Ovise, or had been left behind by a previous tenant. In spite of the presence of beautifully rendered Siamese cats in certain of the pictures, these works of art seemed unworthy of the studio, which I felt needed something more arresting. Harry was of the same opinion. The Galerie Pierre, which was nearby (probably in the Rue de Siene) was holding an exhibit of "constructions" by Joan Miró. These were made of wood, plaster, and bits of rope, somewhat reminiscent of parts of Kurt Schwitters's *Merzbau*, but conceived with an eye to please. Harry visited the Galerie Pierre and came back with three of these Mirós. They livened up the place, and made me feel that I was really in Paris and that it was the year 1932. The Foujitas had suggested another era—the preceding decade. (When one is twenty years old a decade is a long time.) We put the Foujitas into a closet.

Scarcely a fortnight later I came home one afternoon to find that the studio seemed unusually dim. It took only a few seconds for me to realize that the Foujitas were back in their accustomed places on the wall, and that the Mirós had disappeared. The maid would not have done this; it could only have been the concierge or Mme. Ovise herself. I rushed downstairs to speak with the concierge. At first she had no idea of what I was talking about (or pretended to have none). This was because I described the missing Mirós as pictures.

Eventually she did understand, saying: "Monsieur means those old pieces of wood that someone had put on the wall? I threw them out. I thought monsieur would be glad to be rid of them."

A search of the cellar was undertaken, and the constructions, to which I kept referring as works of art, much to the concierge's bewilderment, were found in a corner with a pile of kindling wood. They were not in prime condition, and had to be taken back to the Galerie Pierre for repairs. It was finally Miró himself who rebuilt them.

North

Jason Brown

Jason Brown is the author of two books of stories, Driving the Heart and Other Stories, *and* Why the Devil Chose New England for His Work *(Open City Books), where this story appeared following its publication in* Open City. *He is working on a novel and a memoir.*

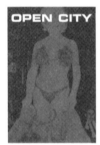

REBECCA SAWYER WAS THE FIRST PERSON FROM Vaughn to score a perfect 1600 on the Scholastic Aptitude Test. When the news hit the *Valley Journal*, Mr. Sumner, her adviser, who had always said she was honors material and who had recommended on more than one occasion that she aim for state college, maybe for elementary education because she seemed to have the patience to work with children, marched her by the arm into his office. She had never been one of the best students in the class, not even in the top ten, but Mr. Sumner was also the boy's basketball coach, and Rebecca knew that in his world, where people were either starters or substitutes she had just been called off the bench. He spoke to her with half-time urgency. He flattened his hands on his desk and shook his head. He called her young lady. He was incredibly excited, he said, about her future.

Rebecca couldn't see how a score a few hundred points one way or another could have much of an affect on anyone's future, when five years before, a girl from Fort Kent, near the border of Quebec, had scored 1550, only to become a veterinarian's assistant.

"That's Fort Kent," Mr. Sumner said, pointing to his right, at a bookcase lined with trophies. "*This*," he said, pointing at his desk, "is Vaughn."

In the hall outside his office, a group of junior girls stopped talking as Rebecca walked by on her way to the bathroom where she stood alone in front of the mirror looking at herself. Next to the morning's article about her scores, the paper had printed a photo of her at her kitchen table. She had large dark eyes, dark hair, and a round face. Some people said she looked Italian or Portuguese; everyone agreed she looked nothing like her parents, grandparents, cousins, or aunts. The bell rang for the beginning of the next period but she kept staring. Some part of her was speaking to some other part of her, deciding something without her permission.

On her way into Mr. Cunningham's U.S. history class, she accidentally slammed the door and felt everyone look up as she crossed the room to her assigned seat by the window. Mr. Cunningham continued talking, referring to the reading from the night before while pointing to the board with yesterday's quizzes held curled in his fist. He asked what had happened in 1865, and looked from Rebecca to the left side of the room and back to her. Mention of the year brought the text before her mind as if onto a screen, the words scrolling down through her thoughts. She rarely spoke in class, but now, she felt, Mr. Cunningham and the other students waited for her to confess that she had always known the answers.

Rebecca's grandmother, Grandmame, was dying very slowly of old age, and every afternoon before dinner Rebecca spent a few minutes in her small room off the kitchen, which smelled of the hall closet and of burnt dust from the electric heater, which Grandmame turned all the way up. According to Rebecca's mother, it would have been cheaper for them to build their own power plant.

Rebecca sat in the green chair and looked with her Grandmame through the window across Central Street to the Methodist church and told her, as she did every day, how school went and what boys she liked. She made up the names of the boys.

"I thought of something to tell you," Grandmame said, "and now I can't remember. Well."

Grandmame removed her hand from Rebecca's and gripped the arm of her chair as if she were about to pull herself up.

"Have you heard anything from your brother?" Grandmame asked, and Rebecca shook her head. Grandmame asked this all the time, and the answer was always no. She dozed off again, her hands folded in her lap.

No one was allowed to speak of her brother in the house, except Grandmame, who did whatever she wanted. Even so, Grandmame always spoke about Jeremy in a whisper. Usually in the same breath she added that Rebecca's mother was cold. Everyone needed someone to blame, Rebecca supposed.

Jeremy's last visit, three months ago, had ended with a scene in the kitchen Rebecca would never forget. She didn't know how it started, or what the argument was about, but suddenly their mother's face turned red and she started screaming obscenities at the top of her voice. Jeremy's face drained for a moment, with his eyes closed, as if he had left his body, and then he flew through the air to punch their mother so hard in the face that her nose exploded with blood. Before Rebecca could even be sure what had happened, Jeremy ran out the door.

When he arrived home from work, her father cursed and threw his bag onto the kitchen table. "He can't keep running," he yelled from the living room where he stood looking out the window toward the river. He said he thought Jeremy had probably hopped the train and gone north, as he had the last time he ran away, to a tiny place called Dennis where he knew people. Her father said he didn't think there was much up there now, or since the end of the seventies when they stopped driving logs down the river. Maybe abandoned logger's camps and old farms. Probably squatters.

"I remember what I wanted to tell you," Grandmame said as Rebecca sat up. Rebecca thought it might be something new this time, even though Grandmame often got worked up over things she had just talked about the previous day. Rebecca was the only one who listened, and the only one Grandmame usually wanted to talk to.

"Not long after I was married to your grandfather, we bought this farm from a family who had seen trouble. I forget what kind now, money trouble. We gave them a good price I think, but they needed to sell in a hurry, so I believe we paid less than we might have."

Rebecca had heard this before and felt annoyed for a moment. The story went along as usual: the family they bought the house from had a daughter who died, and they came to Rebecca's grandparents asking to bury the girl in the graveyard. Their family had lived on the land for a hundred years. But Rebecca's grandfather said no.

Grandmame leaned over as if she believed this was the first time she was telling Rebecca. Each time she told it she reminded Rebecca not to tell anyone, not even her parents.

"One afternoon I was working in the garden when I found a patch of loose ground. I dug deeper with the trowel until I hit something hard. I thought it was a stone. That ground was full of stones when we bought the place. But when I cleared the dirt away, it was a girl's face. There was dirt in her mouth over her teeth, and over her eyelashes. Her skin was half rotted away. The smell was just the most horrible thing I had ever known. I went into the house for a sip of your grandfather's whiskey."

Grandmame paused, shaking her head. It seemed like she was catching her breath to continue. Rebecca tried to think of something to say to stop her from going on.

"I covered her up. I put my garden on top of her. What else could I do? If I told your grandfather, he would have dug her up. I'm the only one who knows she's there." Grandmame's face trembled slightly, and her eyes watered.

Rebecca rested her hand on Grandmame's arm. There was no girl buried in the ground. According to Rebecca's mother, the story had been circulating around the town for a hundred years, made up by the man who once owned the *Valley Journal* at the turn of the century as a Halloween tale for his daughter and her friends. It had been written up several years before to mark the anniversary of the paper.

Rebecca dressed and walked outside carrying her shoes. In the field behind the house, the morning light pinched her eyes and seemed to sap her strength. Wet grass slid between her toes; the sky at dawn had been orange, she could tell, from the white haze still on the horizon. The air held still for a moment over the farm, waiting for the late morning breeze to sweep up from the ocean into the valley. Maybe it would be warm, or the clouds might roll back from the coast. She stood there until the breeze came up, sending the maple and oak leaves into a boil. She was waiting, but for what she didn't know.

The school sat on top of the hill, its windows dark, as if no one were there, though she knew everyone was already in first period, lined up in rooms watching the teachers. Rebecca's friend Kathleen waited for her outside the front doors, in the usual place. Kathleen didn't care about being the smartest girl in school, she didn't even take the SAT, but Rebecca couldn't be sure how much would change between them now.

"I was about to give up on you," Kathleen said. "Smartest girl in school and she doesn't know what time it is." Kathleen shook her head disapprovingly. Rebecca started to apologize, but Kathleen raised her hand. "I always knew you were smart. Nothing you can do about it."

Rebecca was relieved that Kathleen thought being smart was a simple characteristic, like having hideous toes, that shouldn't change anything. And maybe in the past this had been true. Rebecca's father had told her that Grandmame was extremely smart, though you couldn't tell now. He described a time when he was young and his father was lecturing Grandmame on what was true and not true in state politics. She had embarrassed him after church by disagreeing with him in front of his friends. They were walking through the church parking lot, Grandmame yanking Rebecca's father along by the hand as her husband told her what was what. When they reached the end of the parking lot, Grandmame began reciting numbers at the top of her voice. At some point, Rebecca's father realized that Grandmame was listing the license plate numbers of all fifty cars in the church parking lot.

Rebecca's English teacher, Mrs. Lucas, called her up front after class and congratulated her, smiling thinly. Several other teachers did the same thing, but none of the students said anything at all. On the surface nothing changed, but people in the lunchroom seemed quieter when she passed, and when she sat down in the corner next to Kathleen, no one looked over at them. It wasn't what people would say, Rebecca realized, it was what they wouldn't say—even the teachers—as they tried to act naturally. Even Kathleen measured her words as she told a story about her boyfriend David's car breaking down. They were afraid now—of what, she couldn't be sure. Maybe of what she was thinking.

After school, while her mother was out shopping and her father was at work, Rebecca wandered through her parents' bedroom looking at the old pictures of her relatives, most of whom she had never met. She found a portrait of her grandfather standing outside the old barn in his overalls. Frozen in that single moment. She sat down on the edge of her parents' bed and looked at a picture of her brother Jeremy when he was five, leaning over the porch with his face covered in jam. In another picture, at their uncle's wedding, he stood at six years old in a blue blazer and yellow tie, already wearing their father's face. Five years older than her, he had always done things with her rather than make friends with boys his age. It was more of a problem when she started to make friends of her own, and didn't always want him around. She felt guilty about that now, and wanted to take each of those moments back.

She remembered once, she must have been six or a little older, when they were down at Boyton's Market, and Jeremy asked what she thought would happen if their parents both died. She was eating ice cream; it was summer. She didn't answer, had never thought of this before. Jeremy must have seen she looked worried because he told her not to worry. He had it figured out; they would be fine. He knew exactly what they would need and how they would get it.

"You promise?" she said.

He said of course he promised, and then she made him promise again because he had always said that one promise meant nothing but two meant you couldn't get out of it.

The first time her brother ran away was after a shouting match with their mother when he was sixteen. He came into Rebecca's bedroom the night he left and sat on the floor, running his hand down the length of his face. She was afraid to move as he rose on his knees as if he was going to pray.

"I don't know where I'll be," he whispered so lightly she wasn't even sure he wanted her to hear.

Even though he hadn't asked her to, she promised she would come find him, and then she promised him again.

A few hours before dawn, it started pouring outside her window. She had gone to bed early with an upset stomach, without eating dinner. She stood and pressed her forehead against the cold glass, looking into the backyard, and was not surprised that Jeremy wasn't leaning against the well house as the drops thudded against the hollow gutters. She had not wanted to admit for a long time that she knew things others could not know. It wasn't just about facts anyone could look up in a book. Now that the article had come out in the paper, everyone would suspect that she knew too much. When the photo of her grandfather in her parents' bedroom had been taken in 1955, for instance, she knew he was thinking of China Lake where he had grown up swimming with his two brothers. He was thinking of the lake because it was the tenth anniversary of his younger brother's death in the war. She knew this from looking into the photograph, into his dark eyes half-hidden behind his sagging lids. And she knew what her father would never admit, even to himself: that he no longer loved her mother; and she knew that her brother was going to die.

She didn't have the strength to move or say anything when her mother called up the stairs an hour later and then came to sit on the edge of the bed, resting the back of her hand against Rebecca's cheek.

"You're burning up," her mother said. "I'll call."

Rebecca knew she wasn't sick—she just couldn't stop thinking, which was a sickness no one could fix—but she went along to the doctor's office where, in the waiting room, her mother flipped through a *Good Housekeeping*, snapping the pages so fast she could not even have been looking at the pictures. Every time the door to the nurse's area opened, her mother looked up, startled, until finally she slammed the magazine shut and swore. "Jesus." She looked at her watch and folded her hands in her lap. Her mother often spoke to herself. She called it her therapy.

Rebecca stared wearily at her mother until her mother looked up and shuddered.

"What?" her mother said. "What are you looking at?" She stood up officiously and came over to sit next to Rebecca and feel for her temperature again. "You're still burning."

"I'm not sick," Rebecca said.

Rebecca followed the nurse to the examining room. When the doctor arrived, his greeting was hollow, echoing across the distance between his lips and his attention. Rebecca had heard him saying goodbye to the previous patient. She closed her eyes and opened her mouth so he could examine her throat, and every muscle in her body seemed to relax.

"You had a fever last night and this morning," he said. She nodded. His breath brushed her neck as he leaned over to look inside her mouth. He asked her to tilt her neck slightly and she did. He rested a hand next to her leg on the table and pressed his fingers against her neck below her jaw.

He told her she might have a small infection but didn't think she needed antibiotics, at least not yet. In the car her skin seemed to vibrate where the doctor had touched her, like a trivial memory that would not go away, and when her mother asked, Rebecca told her what the doctor had said. For that, her mother replied, we pay him.

Rebecca's father had once said of her mother when no one else was around that she would never let them forget she was from Portland.

Rebecca told herself there was no point in going—she could not change what would happen—yet she had to. She waited until early morning. Her father had said Jeremy jumped the train and rode it all the way up until he reached Dennis, so that's what she would do.

In the hours before dawn, the train moved slowly in the heavy air, the lights from Water Street flashing between boxcars. As she had seen boys from school do, she ran along a granite wall that paralleled the tracks and jumped up on the floor of one of the cars, landing in the cool inside where the clicking of the metal wheels amplified in the empty drum. The train followed the river for ten or twelve miles before crossing over in Gardner and heading north out of the valley into the rich smell of the tidal banks. She leaned against the frame and looked at the black trees in the blue glow of the woods. Only now did she find the tear in the knee of her pants and in the skin underneath, which seemed the only evidence that she had made it this far.

The half-moon passed in and out of the clouds, giving brief glimpses of her white sneakers. The train slowed before each town and sped up as it snaked back into the woods where for several minutes she couldn't see the tops of her hands. The air in her chest seemed to vibrate with the floor of the boxcar, turning each breath into a gasp. She would not be able to scream if she had to, and even if she could, no one would hear her above the scraping of the wheels over the tracks. Jeremy must have felt, as she did now, that he was in the grip of an iron fist that would not let go.

She fell asleep curled up and woke to see the train stretching through a bend in the mist. The sun just struggling through lit up the rust-red boxcars. At one crossing a man standing with a paper bag took off his hat and laughed when he saw her. She hung out of the door by her arm and looked up the track where tree branches arched over the train. Finally, she saw a green sign for DENNIS. The train wasn't moving very fast, but it was frightening to jump and roll in the grass when she didn't know what lay underneath. She rose to her feet and ran for a dirt road, where she turned just in time to see the caboose rocking on its narrow perch.

A half-mile down she thought she saw a gas station and a store on the other side of the road, but there were no people or cars, nothing to suggest a town. Maybe this was the edge of town and she had jumped too soon. She walked in the direction of the gas station, scuffing her sneakers through the dirt. Part of her hoped she did have the wrong place, because if she found him she would have to say something. She never wanted to be the one to speak and hated the feeling of people looking at her, waiting for what she would say, for her thoughts, for what she knew. People were greedy. They pretended not to want things, they pretended not to care, except for Jeremy, who never pretended he didn't need anything from anyone. He needed her to look for him.

A truck approached from behind, sending up a plume of dust as the driver steered with his right hand on top of the wheel, his chin pulled in. Messy clumps of hair stuck out beneath his cap. She expected the truck to drive on to the store, but instead it took a left and crawled over a driveway toward a low farmhouse once painted white and since worn to a rotting gray. She knew Jeremy was inside. It had been this simple for him: jumping off the train, finding an abandoned house. This was the way he did everything, choosing what was in front of him as if there was no other choice.

She stopped walking several times in order to think more clearly, and once almost turned around, though she sensed with resignation that turning around would lead to the same place, in the end, as going through the open front door of the house. A box of rusty tools sat in the front hall and the air felt breathed and rebreathed by the cracked and buckling plaster. A gas can leaned against the wall. In the living room one of two windows was open to the field behind the house where the tall grass bent under a breeze and pushed up again. It seemed impossible that the world outside, where the air moved through the light, was at all connected to the world inside this house, and it wasn't right that she had been able to pass so easily between the two. Jeremy lay on a battered couch with his arms at his sides, his eyes closed. She thought he must be sleeping, but then his eyes snapped open and stared at her as if he didn't know her and she had come to take everything away from him. Small bottles, a plate, and a leather belt sat on an upturned box at his feet. She said his name, but he did not say her name back or change his expression in any way. When he swallowed, a cleft appeared in his chin and the veins of his neck pushed against his translucent skin. His Adam's apple fluttered as his eyes closed, and his chest rose and fell to the timing of heels clomping down the stairs behind her. When no one appeared, she thought the pounding had come from her own head, but the man she had just seen in the truck stepped from around the corner with his hands in his jeans pockets, the leather cap on his head. He quickly removed his glasses to clean them on his T-shirt. He said he was hoping she would come by.

"How do you know who I am?"

"How did you know which house to walk into?" He put the glasses back on and looked at her. He was probably her brother's age or a bit older. He sat in the chair next to the couch, crossed his legs, and put on the face of someone trying to look like a college student, with his chin resting on his hand. His sharp lips chopped off the consonants when he spoke, sounding to her like one of the migrant worker's kids.

"I'm not from around here like my friend," he said, as if this should explain any questions she might have. He leaned back and clasped his hands behind his head with his elbows in the air.

"You're not his friend!" Rebecca shouted in what could not have been her voice.

"Whatever you say." He shrugged one shoulder and glanced over at Jeremy who seemed to see through them. "We've got everything you need here to be happy. We've got food if that's what you need, we've got money, we've got a roof that don't leak—and we've got *business* coming right down from Canada. This here's a stop on the Trans-Canada highway." He looked at her brother for a moment before turning to her and reaching in his jacket pocket to pull out a photo in which she thought she could see her brother and herself when they were younger, but she quickly looked away and shook her head. She couldn't breathe.

"That's my favorite picture," he said, saying it *pi-sure*, while looking away, as if embarrassed. He sighed and dropped his shoulders into the silence that followed and lasted until he seemed smaller than her. "That's at Niagara Falls. I've never been there, but I want to go, I plan to go. In fact, I could go right now if I wanted to. There's nothing stopping me."

"I have to go," she said and then watched him, waiting to see if he would try to stop her.

"Suit yourself." He closed his eyes and slid further down in the chair.

Jeremy turned to face the wall, and she opened her mouth to call out to him—if she just said his name, maybe he would come back with her, though of course he wouldn't. If she said his name, he might explode, as he had that morning at her mother. He didn't want to attack her—the idea would never occur to him—but whatever pushed from the inside against his rising and falling back hated everything, even her.

Outside, she ran across the overgrown field for the road and the tracks, stopping only to catch her breath and look over her shoulder. No one followed. The tracks were empty, running between the fields and into the woods both in the direction from which she had come and where the train was still headed, all the way north, she assumed, to Canada. Everywhere she looked, down either direction of the tracks or across the field into the woods, she saw the starved image of Jeremy's face. She ran for a few more minutes, stopping when she could no longer breathe, to bend over her knees and make a sound in her throat like the wheels of her father's car crunching over the gravel of their driveway.

A train would come eventually, if she kept walking in the direction of home, and if she kept her thoughts straight and parallel to the glinting edge of the rail, which drew her under a canopy of turning leaves. The tips of her sneakers slid forward over the chattering gravel until she was convinced the noise came from Jeremy or the other one following her, and she started to run again until she reached a bridge where the woods opened above a river.

She thought she saw something moving through the trees to the right but instead of going back or freezing (as she told herself to do), she ran toward it, jumping over fallen trees and yelling Jeremy's name. She stopped in a clearing above a stream and looked around, but there was nothing there. The blue sky paled around the edges. Pockets of warmth drifted in the cool air. She looked down the slope, feeling as though she could see inside the wind brushing through the grass. The distant pines leaned together in a sudden gust and were still again. When the breeze returned, it seemed to whistle through her limbs, and she realized that Jeremy had been here, in this clearing, in the grass. He had measured the wind by the movement of the branches.

The train whistle bleated as it passed through Dennis, and she bolted toward the sound. The wheels ground against the rails, ticking off what little time she had left to get home before they knew where she had gone and what she had seen. The boxcars moved through the trees, speeding up as if the forest was rushing south. Some of the Boston-Maine cars were empty, doors slid back on both sides, the sunlight blinking through the openings as she ran to the bridge along a platform from where she leapt half onto the edge of a car. Inside, with her face pressed to the cold metal, she sensed him: Jeremy's face with the stranger's hat and long arms, both of them in the same body standing in one of the dark corners. She looked for their smile, and their eyes, glowing in the shadow, but there was nothing.

The train slowed into each town, the tracks occasionally winding within fifteen feet of backyards and kitchen windows. It was not hard for her to determine the characters and even the thoughts of the people living inside the houses. People wanted you to think things were complicated when they weren't. The train passed close to the window of someone's kitchen where a woman looked up from doing the dishes. She's thinking about her twelve-year-old son, Rebecca thought, who was caught stealing from a corner store. All the information was around her in the air, waiting for her to absorb it. Her own mother was frightened and vain; she always had been and she always would be. Her father was patient and simple near the surface and unhappy underneath. It couldn't be any different than the facts she learned for tests: Pablo Picasso, born October 25, 1881. His first painting *La fillette aux pieds nus*. 1895. A poem she glanced at two weeks before, the "Song of Apollo," with the second stanza, "Then I arise; and climbing Heaven's blue dome, I walk over the mountains and the waves . . . I am the eye with which the Universe Beholds itself, and knows it is divine." The Earth was formed

4.6 billion years ago. The words cesium, curium, erbium, rhodium, argon, osmium, streamed through her head faster than the trees whipping by outside.

She remembered a story her mother told of being a girl in the nineteen fifties and traveling on a freighter across the Atlantic to Europe with her father, who was a merchant marine. There was a storm—a hurricane—her mother had said, and described the ship rising up the mountainous waves, the wind faster than if you put your hand out of the car window on the highway. Her mother had been much younger than Rebecca was now, and as her mother's father helped on the deck of the freighter, she sat alone in the dark cabin. Rebecca had heard her mother tell this story dozens of times over the years, and each time her mother stuck out her chin and wore a blank, put-upon face. Each time, Rebecca mistook her mother's expression for boredom, as if she was being forced to tell the story again even though no one had asked her to. Now Rebecca could see the expression was thinly disguised pride. Rebecca's father realized this, too, which was why he complained every time that it wasn't actually a hurricane. "All right, it *wasn't*," her mother shouted at him one night in front of people from his work who were having dinner at their house. She stood up from the table with tears in her eyes. "It wasn't, okay, it wasn't *officially* a hurricane if that makes you happy. I was ten years old down in a square metal room with no lights or windows and with the boat practically upside down, back and forth for eighteen hours!" Her mother turned and left the table but came back in a moment to apologize and laugh lightly. "My, my," she said when she sat, refolding her napkin. "You'll have to excuse me."

Her mother had been terrified in that room, holding onto the edge of a metal bunk as everything lurched back and forth and the inner workings of the boat groaned. When Rebecca closed her eyes, she could see her mother clinging in the dark compartment with no idea if they would survive or if she would see her father again. The noises of the ship would not have been much different than the noises of the boxcars knocking together as she sped through the woods.

The crossing bells went off one after another as she drew closer to Vaughn, and she expected someone she knew, a friend of her mother or her guidance counselor, to look up from their gardening or their steering wheel to see her face in the open door of the boxcar. When she leapt from the train onto the grass near the town library, she expected the bell at the Catholic church up the street to ring for the six p.m. service or the Baptist church for their seven p.m. service or at least the more distant sound of the town hall clock bell sounding on the hour. But it wasn't Sunday night, there were no services, and it wasn't on the hour. She sat on the grass watching the train pick up speed as it left town, the lights of the caboose fading into the darkening pines, and the crossing bells growing silent, one after another, in the distance.

In the kitchen, the heat from her mother's cooking clung to her cheeks and palms.

"I put all the dish towels in the laundry. Would you grab me one from upstairs?"

Rebecca nodded.

"You're home late," her mother called after her.

"I was at Kathleen's."

"Hurry up and wash your hands and you can help me set the table."

Her mother took the forks and spoons, moving back and forth deftly between the stove and the table with the same urgency she brought to every night's dinner.

"Okay," her mother said after everyone sat, reaching out to take Rebecca's and Grandmame's hands. "Someone say grace, please."

As Rebecca's father started, her mother squeezed Rebecca's hand so hard the bones of her fingers pinched together. Her mother pulled her jaw in and cinched her eyes shut, tears welling up over her bottom lids and washing down her face. She always feels so much, it's as if she feels for all of us, Rebecca thought.

"I think I'm coming down with the flu," her mother said. "I'll go lie down for a while." She plucked her hands away from them and stood up from the table as if from an insult.

"Do you want one of us to come with you, with some food?" her father said. "There is something going around at work. Maybe you have it."

Rebecca knew from the tone of his voice that he didn't think she had the flu, and that he had no intention of comforting her.

"Go ahead and eat," her mother said.

Grandmame stared across the room for a few minutes while her father unfolded his napkin and arranged his silverware in a perfect row.

"Don't let your mother's hard work go to waste," he said as he started cutting into the pork chop. After a few more minutes, after Grandmame had started eating, humming faintly to herself, as she sometimes did, a tune no one recognized and which probably wasn't a real tune at all, her father leaned back and asked Rebecca what she had done at school that day.

"Nothing," she said.

"Nothing?" he said, raising his eyebrows. "Well, that's good. They're getting you used to the working world. You've got three and a half hours—less a coffee break or two—of nothing before lunch, but you don't want to use it all up before lunch because you've got a good four of nothing after lunch. And then you want to be careful to have people see you shove nothing in your briefcase at the end of the day so they think you're doing nothing at home, too." He smiled through this, amused with himself.

Grandmame went back to her room while Rebecca helped her father carry the dishes to the sink. He scraped the plates that she handed to him and stacked them neatly in one side of the double sink with the silverware piled in a basket. She was just turning back to the table for the salad bowl when he started humming a song she didn't recognize. He caught her arm and pulled her toward him, swaying from left to right in a dance he must have learned before she was born—she had never seen him dance. A smile spread up from his chin until his whole face lifted, and he opened his eyes and chuckled before letting go, turning off the water, and picking up the *Valley Journal* from the counter on his way to the living room.

"What about the rest of the dishes?" she asked.

"Leave them, I'll do them later," he said, raising the back of his hand, though she knew he wouldn't. "Go check on your mother."

Her mother lay on top of the covers in the dark bedroom, her arms spread wide, and her eyes closed. Rebecca thought she was asleep.

"Come here," her mother said, holding her hands out like a child wanting to be picked up. Rebecca pulled back at first but then held her hands out. Her mother's crying passed up into her own arms and across the back of her neck.

"He's not coming back, is he?" her mother said. "It's going to be winter soon. It will be so cold up there."

"Of course he's coming back," Rebecca lied, tumbling forward from the weight. Her mother wrapped an arm around her shoulder and squeezed as she buried her face in Rebecca's neck. The smell of her mother's hair was both familiar and distant, like the sight of her brother's face, and the harder her mother squeezed, the more Rebecca felt as if she were far away from this moment, floating over their house and town.

"Please, promise me you won't ever become mixed up with the people your brother did."

"I won't," she said.

"Of course you won't," her mother said. "You're too smart for that."

Her mother rolled onto her back, lifted her hand to her forehead, and sighed. Rebecca waited for what she would say—when her mother lost control, she talked frantically afterward to cover it up.

"I don't know why I was thinking about your brother tonight," her mother said. "Before dinner I was remembering a sailing trip your father and I took right before we were married, when I was already pregnant with your brother. Grandmame didn't even want us to get married, I don't suppose there's any harm in telling you now—because I wasn't Catholic—and she did not approve of taking a trip like that before the wedding, but the wedding was in the fall—it had to be, I forget why, I guess because I was already pregnant. I don't know how we thought we were going to fool that woman. The trip was up the coast on an old tall ship. We sailed for ten days with three other couples. Every evening before dusk the captain and the crew anchored in a small harbor, and while they put everything away and made us supper, we sat on the deck and looked out at the ocean. We had absolutely nothing to do. I knew it would be rare in the life we were starting, but your father, who had worked on the farm from the day he started walking until he started college, couldn't understand why anyone would want to sit still for so long staring at the sky and the water. I think the whole thing was torture for him. One evening before dinner, he stood up beside me, stripped down to his boxers, and dove off the bow. It was as if he just couldn't sit still any longer and he had to make some work for himself. Watching the bottoms of his feet disappear, I just lost it for a moment. It was stupid, but I thought he wouldn't come back up—that he was running away from me. That time on the boat was the longest we had ever spent together, and I felt this desperation of not wanting to lose him. When I saw him crash up a little ways out, shivering and waving with a big smile on his face, I was so happy, I almost jumped in after him, and I probably would have if that water wasn't cold enough to stop your breath forever."

Her mother fell silent with her arms at her sides. Her toes and fingers twitched after a few minutes as her breath settled into the rhythm of sleep. Rebecca listened for her father's footsteps, but she could tell from the distant flutter of a turning page that he was still down in the living room reading the paper.

Rebecca stared at the bedroom ceiling and imagined standing with her mother as her father swam back to the boat and climbed up the ladder. Her father dressed, hopping on one leg, and whispered something in her mother's ear as she bent over, laughing. Rebecca had never seen her mother laugh this way before. Her parents put their arms around each other and walked toward the stern as if Rebecca wasn't there because, of course, she wasn't. Then her father ran back toward Rebecca, but only for his jacket, which lay at her feet, and when he glanced up, there was no look of recognition on his face. Rebecca knew this feeling, had known it all along, of not being seen, but she would also remember the look on her father's face that told of how even this brief moment away from his new wife was too much to bear.

Rebecca went to bed, falling immediately asleep without undressing, and didn't know what time it was when she sat straight up and looked out the dark window. Her clock radio was unplugged, probably from when her mother vacuumed, and her limbs felt heavy as she padded down into the kitchen. The moon hung low in the sky, everything silent except the dormant sounds of the house, the refrigerator, and the furnace in the basement.

"Rebecca, is that you?" Grandmame called from her room. Even though Grandmame rose before dawn, she kept the blinds tightly drawn at night and the room pitch black, so that Rebecca had trouble finding her way to the ratty green chair.

"Is that you?" Grandmame said again. She was only a foot away in her narrow bed, but Rebecca couldn't see her face.

"It's me," she said.

"There was something I wanted to tell you after dinner, but I didn't get the chance."

Instead of going on, though, Grandmame's breathing calmed, and the airless room filled with the musk of her skin and clothes. Rebecca leaned her head back and pictured herself on the train headed north toward Jeremy. She tried to remember his face in that house but could only see the strain of his neck and the cleft where there had not been one before. The harder she tried to remember his face, the more he looked like someone she didn't know. She thought of what her mother had said about winter coming. In one afternoon of snow, everything she had seen up there—the pines, the field, and the low house—would be sheeted white against a white sky. He wouldn't stay in Dennis for long, she guessed, and he wouldn't come back to Vaughn. He would continue north on the train, hundreds of miles through the thick forest until there was nothing but rock covered with ice. She pictured him there, as far up as anyone could go, walking across a blank white plain extending out to the horizon. Her brother, she realized, had gone north not to run away from life, as her father had said, but to know everything. Because he had wanted her to follow, she would have to keep looking for him, even if she would never find him, and even if he was no longer there but somehow everywhere, all around them.

Grandmame shook Rebecca's leg, and Rebecca opened her eyes to the morning light framing the shade.

"An awful, awful thing has happened," Grandmame said in such an urgent voice that Rebecca leaned forward to hear. But then Rebecca realized her Grandmame was about to tell the tale, once again, that she had read in the newspaper of the girl who had been buried in a backyard. There was nothing Rebecca could say to stop her, so she just listened and waited for the story to end.

"I was only six years old when they buried me," Grandmame said as tears soaked the moth wings of her cheeks. "My father wanted to put me next to his mother, but the people who bought the farm from us wouldn't let him, so he dug my grave in their vegetable garden while they were sleeping, and no one knows. No one knows where I am."

The train whistle blew in the distance, the first warning of its approach from the north. Rebecca felt the air shiver from the force of the locomotive against the tracks as the second whistle blew and echoed down the valley, carried on its way south by the tide. The third whistle blew the final warning, though to Rebecca it was less a warning than a cry.

"I don't want to be buried in this place," Grandmame said and squeezed hard on Rebecca's arm. "Promise me you won't let them."

A promise was easy to give, and as Rebecca whispered it, Grandmame sighed as if she had finally been relieved of an unbearable secret.

From Snowed In

Bliss Broyard

Bliss Broyard is the author of a collection of stories, My Father, Dancing, *and*
One Drop: My Father's Hidden Life—A Story of Race and Family Secrets.
Her work has been anthologized in Best American Short Stories, The
Pushcart Prize Anthology, *and* The Art of the Essay. *Her novel,* Happy
House, *is forthcoming in 2012.*

 LILY KNELT ON THE LEATHER COUCH TO LOOK OUT
the window. Seven more inches had accumulated over
the night, erasing any evidence of the snowball fight
from the evening before, and still the snow kept falling.
A thick white blanket was draped over the garden
benches, the boxwood hedge, the lawn jockey at the end
of the front walk—only his lantern held high over his
head could be seen above the drift. A row of evergreens
lined either side of the long driveway, and mounds of snow weighted
down their boughs, prying them back from the trees' black trunks. From
between these trees, a bright red Jeep Wagoneer appeared, sped up the
driveway, and fish-tailed to a stop. Lily recognized it as Bobby Callahan's
car. She dropped out of sight.

None of the other girls sprawled around Cristal Harlow's den had
even glanced up from the television screen. Lily settled against the soft
leather cushions without mentioning the new arrivals. She pictured how
the back of her head was framed by the window, and a small chill ran
through her, making her shiver slightly.

Around the other side of the house, not visible from here, was the
stone wall where Bobby had run up behind Lily the night before. She'd
been scooping snow together, compacting it into balls between her mit-
tened palms when Bobby had rammed his body against hers, pushing
his hips into her, pressing her chest and face forward into the pile she'd
made. She'd known it was him behind her even before he'd whispered
you're mine in her ear and dumped a fistful of snow on her head. Then
he'd pushed off her and run away as quickly as he'd come, Lily's con-

sciousness, it seemed, fleeing with him—she didn't notice the cold wetness against her hot cheeks; she didn't notice the snow working its way inside the collar of her ski jacket until a trickle of icy water ran down her spine, returning her to her body with a start. She'd bolted up and arched backwards, brushing frantically at the snow lodged against her neck. And then outrage jump-started her brain. She gathered up as many snowballs as she could and began running toward the intermittent screams and "gotchas" circling through the darkness, running with the unswerving fury of someone who held her target in her sights.

Of course, all evidence of that encounter was gone as well.

From outside came the sound of car doors slamming and boys' raucous laughter. "Is that Bobby?" Cristal hopped onto her knees to peer out another window. "He's with Eric and Kyle. And they brought more beer. That's so nice. They brought one, two—" she mouthed *three*, then *four* "—wow, five cases."

Lily watched Cristal out of the corner of one eye. Kneeling on the couch as she was, her hands planted atop the sofa's back, her big butt waggling slightly as she spoke, Cristal reminded Lily of a large, plump dog. She would have liked to lay a hand gently on the girl's arm, to tell her to sit down, to . . . contain herself more, but if she did, she knew that she would hurt Cristal's feelings. Lily picked up a copy of *Gourmet* magazine from the coffee table and began flipping through its pages.

Daphne, on the other hand, sat up in the leather recliner she'd commandeered. "Get down, Cristal," she said. "Do you want them to think we've been staring out the window, waiting for them all morning?"

"But she—" Cristal began, glancing at Lily, who was studying a recipe for potato leek soup. Cristal sighed and flopped back down onto the couch. "Well, I'm glad Bobby came back. I knew he would." She turned her head to look out the window again and then stood up. "I better go make some room in the fridge if we're going to fit all that beer in."

Daphne frowned as Cristal headed out of the room, but she kept quiet. In the cavernous leather recliner, Daphne looked even smaller to Lily than her five feet and ninety-seven pounds. But not frail. Even with her pinched little face and wispy short hair, she could never look frail. To be on the safe side, Lily always regarded her as a few degrees short of an explosion.

Courtney and Nicole were also lounging around the den. None of the girls at Cristal's house were particular friends of hers. Lily wasn't close with any of them either, although Courtney sometimes palled around with her at parties. Courtney was pretty with long blonde hair and a full red mouth that was usually fixed into a flirty smile for some guy's benefit. The boys paid attention to Lily, too, which was the reason, she imagined, that Courtney often stuck close by her.

And Lily hardly knew Nicole. She had just arrived at their school at the start of the second term. Some business venture of her father's had brought them here from England. So far, she'd moved among her classmates as distantly and queenly as a Persian cat who had accidentally wandered into a barnyard.

It was spring break, and the thing that brought the group together at Cristal's house was that they were the ones who had been left behind. The rest of the eleventh grade class at Wood-bridge Country Day were off visiting grandparents in Palm Springs or Boca Raton, or helicopter skiing in Utah, or sailing the Caribbean in chartered yachts with their parents. Back home, the snow had been falling on and off for two days now, and Cristal's parents were away—her father on business in Hong Kong and her mother, Cristal said, at a health spa, although it was common knowledge that she was regularly checked into detox.

And so anyone who was around made their way over to the Harlow's house—some of them borrowing a family car and then arranging to stay the night with the explanation that they were snowed in; Lily, who only lived a few miles away, had come on cross country skis. Her parents were happy to be rid of her complaints—there's nothing here to eat; there's nothing to watch on TV; there's nothing to do. She could stay as long as she wanted.

Courtney stood up, saying something about having to use the bathroom, although Lily knew that she was going to brush her hair. At the other end of the couch, Nicole continued to file her nails. Lily wondered if she should go help Cristal, but she didn't want Bobby to think that she was anxious to see him. From the kitchen, rising above the sound of jars clanking and cardboard boxes being torn open, she could hear his voice describing in great detail his daring maneuvers through the snow on the drive over. Lily twisted her hair up into a loose bun atop her head and then teased out a few tendrils of hair to drape along her face. So what if Bobby was the cutest boy in their class or if he was the first thing their basketball and soccer teams ever had that resembled a real athlete. She wasn't interested.

When Lily heard someone coming down the hallway, she bent her head to her *Gourmet*. Filling one whole page was a photograph of a steaming slice of peach pie.

"Oh, please," said Nicole in an exasperated voice, and Lily glanced up to see Bobby holding out a can of Miller Lite. He had planted himself in between Nicole and the television.

"What's the problem? I got Lite especially for you girls."

"I don't care if it's Lite or not. I don't drink beer." "Oh, right, Miss Fancy Pants. Only champagne for you," said Bobby, jutting his nose in the air. Lily lowered her head to hide her smile. " Well," he continued, "I can't help you there. Beer here, beer here," he said in the nasally voice of the beer sellers at Yankee Stadium. He shuffled over until he was facing Lily. She leaned to one side to peer around him and he moved over to block her view. She leaned the other way and there he was in front of her again. He took a step forward and very slightly inclined his hips toward her.

"I know you want it, Lily," he said. She looked down at his feet. The room, it seemed, had abruptly gone silent, but inside, she was pitching wildly, and any possible retort was whisked by these stormy currents from her reach.

Bobby spoke again: "Here you go." A can of Miller Lite appeared in front of his zipper.

She snatched the beer from his hand, and, without thinking about it, found that she could speak after all. "Move Bobby!" Adding more softly, "please." She lifted the can and took a long, deep sip.

"Starting early, aren't we, Lily?" Daphne said.

Courtney walked in, trailed by Eric and Kyle, all carrying cans of beer. "So where's mine?" Daphne demanded. When she received no answer, she yelled to Cristal in the kitchen. Finally she got up and went in there herself.

Bobby plopped down into the leather recliner. "Ah," he said, leaning the chair back, "it's good to be the King."

Kyle sat down in between Lily and Nicole. He bumped his shoulder against Lily's. "Bobby didn't tell me you were going to be here," he said.

Lily raised her eyebrows and took another sip of her beer. Kyle was still looking at her. "Well, here I am," she said finally and turned back to the TV.

The weather man predicted another ten to sixteen inches of snowfall in the next twenty-four hours, and a reporter, his red face peeking out from a large dark hood, appeared on the side of a highway. Over his shoulder a few cars could be seen inching along. He said excitedly, "It's crazy out here folks. The snow just keeps coming down. There's only four to five feet of visibility. So stay home and stay tuned because anything could happen."

"Obviously this bloke has never been to Woodbridge, Connecticut," said Nicole, smirking at her nail file. When she'd arrived last night she made sure that everyone understood that she was *supposed* to be skiing in the Swiss Alps with her boyfriend and some of his friends from University, but two weekends earlier she'd wrenched her knee at Stowe and now had to sit out the rest of the season.

To Lily's mind, the weather lent the day another shot at distinction. Cristal's absent parents. Record accumulations of snow. Not to mention the five cases of beer. Maybe the power would go out, too, she thought happily.

Bit by bit, they advanced their claim on Cristal's house throughout the afternoon. In the back of the fridge Cristal found a bottle of Chardonnay for Nicole that she didn't think her parents would miss. Nicole made some comment about white wine in the cold weather, but eventually she took a sip and pronounced it fine. There was a ping-pong table in the garage, and Lily and Kyle took on Daphne and Eric, beating them four games to three. A lunch of cold cuts and cheese and an assortment of mustards was assembled from the well-stocked fridge. Cristal brought out her mother's large supply of wigs—"she likes to wear them around the house," she explained with a shrug—and all the girls took turns trying them on in front of the large mirror in the entrance hall. Cristal put on a silky shoulder-length one, platinum-colored. "Maybe I should cut my hair. Maybe that's what I should do." She sighed and took off the wig, throwing it on top of the others. "Then my face would look even fatter."

Courtney turned her trained eye on Cristal. "Oh, I don't know," she said, stepping behind Cristal to hold her hair back. "Actually, you've got a pretty face. You should show it more. I could trim your hair for you. I cut my sister's all the time."

Cristal smiled shyly at herself in the mirror, then turned suddenly toward the girls. "I'm so glad we all got snowed in together. I never would have believed that all of you would be sleeping over my house."

"Jesus, Cristal," Courtney said, "the silliest things come out of your mouth."

Lily gathered up as many empty cans as she could carry—the coffee table was littered with them—and brought them into the kitchen. Courtney, Eric, and Kyle were playing quarters at the kitchen table. Lily watched

Courtney bounce the quarter eight times in a row into the drinking glass. After each successful shot, she would slide the quarter out of the glass and, with a nod, designate who had to take a swig of beer. When she got on a roll, she would sometimes single out a person to pick on— usually other girls since they made for easy victories. After a few rounds, the girl would rise unsteadily and stagger off to be sick or lie down.

Lily grabbed another beer from the fridge and stood next to the table for a moment. Kyle wrapped an arm around her hip. "Come play with us. It's your turn to drink for a while."

"I am drinking," Lily said, lifting her beer. She tried to remember how many this was. She lowered her head slowly into her hand and giggled against her palm. She had no idea how many she'd had. She tried to pace herself, only having one beer an hour, but every time someone returned from the kitchen with a new six-pack in hand, asking, "Who needs one?" she'd ripped a can from its plastic yoke, saying, "I sure am thirsty today."

Occasionally she could slip into a mood where she felt she couldn't do anything wrong. There was a dangerous, dislodged feeling to this pleasure, as though she were skidding across the surface of an iceberg.

Kyle squeezed her a little closer. "We made a good team in ping-pong, huh?"

Lily didn't answer, just leaned into him and rested a hand on his shoulder. The weekend before last, at Cindy Alkins's house, they were sitting next to each other, playing quarters then, too, and Kyle reached for Lily's hand under the table. He let go of it whenever his turn came, but after he was finished, he would take her hand up again and stroke his thumb across her knuckles. And he didn't make Lily drink each time he made his shot like some of the boys did when they liked you. He grinned up at her now, frankly meeting her eyes.

"What do we have here?" Bobby said, strolling into the room, and Lily could feel Kyle's fingers settle more firmly on her hip.

Safari Eyes

Sam Brumbaugh

Sam Brumbaugh is the author of the novel Goodbye, Goodness *(Open City Books). His fiction has appeared in* The Southwest Review, Esquire.com, *and* Vice. *He produced the feature documentary* Be Here to Love Me: A Film about Townes Van Zandt. *He works at the Guggenheim Museum.*

 KATE SAT UP, SUDDENLY AWAKE. SHE FELT A STRANGE unease inside her, a sense of her past, or what she could recall, as silver, mercurial droplets falling, falling then splitting off her cupped hands and onto the ground at her feet as she watched. Slipping away like a fallen martini. She touched her mug. It was cold. Bird noises. She looked out the window. Crows, pecking the ground between quick, jerk-necked surveillances. Like those men in Nairobi, she thought. They just don't want anyone unlike them around. She looked farther out over the yellow field, rutted with tire tracks from the Fitzgerald boy's minibike, past the lone black tree, black in any light, past the tire hanging from it, to the fence at the slope of the neighbors.' She looked at their willow tree and rusting jungle gym and soundless dogs. They had dogs there that needed more room, that ran lean and pressing against the fence like caged panthers. One day she'd go cut a hole.

She could hear Ruth moving around downstairs, fixing breakfast. Same old day ahead in the ranch house. Blue outside, blue sky evacuating white clouds. Same old tray coming with the tea, juice, toast and the paper cup of pills. She felt like getting some air. She'd put on her shoes and coat and walk the yard. She'd put on her dress. She sighed, wanting to feel some kind of movement, but the sigh lingered and she felt only stress involving cash outlay.

Down the slope of the pillow she noticed her blue water cup on its side, and then the wet edge of the throw rug. She looked at the chair. It was empty. Ruth, sitting there last night, had knocked over the cup when she'd gotten up to get the novel to read aloud. Ruth hadn't noticed and

Kate hadn't said anything. Kate remembered that as she'd gone to sleep, Ruth had switched to the Bible.

Kate had opened her eyes. "Please go back to the novel, Ruth."

"May I ask you a question?"

"Yes," she'd said.

"Guy, your husband, was he religious?"

"Guy was a pilot. And, well, yes. Yes he was."

Ruth had folded the Bible over her fingers. "Do you hear from him?"

"I get a postcard once in a while, aside from the checks."

Ruth had looked past her.

"He did try."

Ruth had remained silent.

"And besides that," Kate had said, "he pays for you."

"She should hate me," Kate thought. "Did I really say that?" She remembered seeing Guy the day after he'd asked her to marry him. His black hair, black brow, and razor cheeks. He was so stern, and that beautiful, lazy self-content that welled her love for him into envy. They'd gone to the theater near the college to see *McCabe and Mrs. Miller*, and she'd held Guy's hand there in the movie's strange, interior orange hue of preordained separations between people who might even want to be a little in love. But she'd been confused by the plot. McCabe's slow, oddly determined movement through trees and deep snow, and then Julie Christie's opium jar. What had made her go to that? Where was the voice-over with all that had happened to her? She'd asked him these questions afterward and he'd just said he didn't think that it was a good western.

The light of day felt long already. The tray had still not arrived and Kate was already tired from the brief, waking considerations. A bath? It was time to wash her hair, but the red soap gave the bathwater a tan color as if her skin itself was dyeing it. And she needed to buy stamps and to buy stamps she needed to dress right, not in her nightshirt and ratty slippers. And then to buy stamps she had to face the lady with the sad, fat face who chewed her up with politeness within the thirty-second purchase exchange. Above all she had to wait for the will to move, to dress. Did she have money in the drawer? It was the third and Guy's check would come by the fifth. On the fifth she could do all the big errands. She could do the small ones today. The stamps.

"Ruth," she yelled.

"Right Sweetie," came Ruth's voice from downstairs. "Now I've just got your tray going, all right?"

"Of course. Of course that's all right."

The tray came and she swallowed the pills and lay back. She remembered the itchiness of her wedding dress, of the brown August grass. It had been so hot in Ohio, so flat. The town park Guy had chosen for the ceremony had felt as mysterious as a newly mown lawn. He'd been there in his military whites. Going to be a pilot. "Oh his clean, careful motion." His hand around her waist as they'd stood greeting the guests. A brass band in the park rotunda sending them off to a safari honeymoon.

She did miss him. What had she done? It was all right that day. Too hot but all right.

Kate pulled herself up against the headboard and looked around the room. The day had grayed the white walls. She took the sweater from the chair and put it on. It had been her grandmother's and its tight weave was constructed with a patience not usually available anymore. It was a good, bedridden sweater, it made her feel older, done with more of life's comings and goings, and this relaxed her. On the bedside table was a lamp covered by a red silk scarf. She took the scarf and tied it snugly over her hair. She tried to read, but as usual, the words wouldn't settle still on the page, and she lay back. She felt the shape of the pillows around her head and the rough outline of the knit birds on the quilt, felt where she was in bed without opening her eyes. Kate wanted to remember Africa by feel, more than just sight. Sight hadn't been trustworthy there. But nothing, not even Guy, had been trustworthy there. If he had been, she thought, then maybe she wouldn't have brought the illness back with her. But then again, as the admitting doctor had abruptly concluded after listening to her, "It's not the sort of illness you just pick up in Africa. You carry it with you everywhere," he'd said, "like a bad heart."

And then Guy had left without asking the doctor any other questions, and she'd been in that ward for three weeks and had been incapable of asking about herself, or Guy, in any way.

She remembered how it had started, waking up on the plane as the captain announced that they'd just come over the African continent and suddenly feeling, weeks early, as if she were about to have her period. She rested her hands on the coarse stubble of the seat. Her palms were moist and she could feel the upraised black dots in the economy-class material stir, as though they might break off from under her palms. She stood as their descent was announced, and walked down the aisle to the bathroom. She locked herself in. Despite the pounding of the stewardess and Guy, she hid in the small bathroom as the plane touched down and, with its human tube, locked onto the Nairobi terminal.

In their hotel room in Nairobi there was a framed photo of a butchered rhino. Or Kate guessed it was a rhino. It could have been an antelope or a warthog, for that matter. It was a mess of an animal on the dirt around a watering hole. Split, cavernous insides with a curved dome of ribs protruding like the opera house in Sydney. Something kept the vultures at bay, they only stared. Kate was tired from the wedding, the flights, and tried to take a nap, but the photo loomed. A maid came in. Kate pretended to be asleep so that the maid would leave. The maid bustled around a bit, speaking softly to herself. Then the maid was quiet, and she could feel her undulating breath close by. A whiff of rose hand cream and Kate thought she felt a hair being plucked off her head.

The next morning they were heading out of Nairobi on a day safari to a private hunting ranch. The Land Rover driver bobbed hard under his Walkman, harder than any possible rhythm. The city outside seemed silent and unchanging. People walked looking straight ahead. Everything ahead seemed unmapped and it gave her an intimation of fear in the air. She'd initially mistook it for malaise. There was a faint tang of sewage underneath the smells of smoke and exhaust. There were dogs, concrete huts, and muddy slashes of footpath. The ashtray on her side was jammed full with dark-green gum. Guy was reading from the green Michelin guidebook. As the car stopped for pedestrians, Kate glanced out the window. There were two men at a café table who seemed identical. Everybody around them was black, but to her they had no color in their skin, in their clothes. No color at all. It seemed that they weren't really there, and she looked away. She looked at the driver as he inched the car through the crowd. She looked back at the café. One of the men was looking at her, surprised. She was scared and turned to Guy, who was smoking and flipping the guidebook pages. The car began to speed up and she glanced back again. The man was now staring at her openmouthed. He held a palm out as if he wanted to stop her. As she turned around to Guy the man seemed to evaporate in the corner of her eye. "Oh my God, oh my God. Please turn around."

The Land Rover stopped. Guy stared at her. "What is it?"

"Those men."

"Which men?" he asked.

She looked back again. They were there. "At the café, the ones staring at me."

"There's nobody staring at you," Guy said.

"There," she pointed, and began to bang her fists against the window.

"You're making a scene."

"But you see them?" she turned and insisted to Guy.

"The men at the café?"

"Yes. Yes Guy, those two men." But she did not look back.

"There are a lot of men there," he said. "They are all staring at you now because you are making a scene."

Kate asked to go back to the hotel. On the way back she asked the driver to stop again. "I need air," she said. "I need water." And she stepped out of the Land Rover and into the crowd. As she made her way into a crowded market, her head began whizzing, her mouth dry with dust and the market's sudden, choking smells of smoke, manure, and cloves. She saw the African sunlight stretching like caramel, hardening suddenly, and then snapping dizzily into thousands of bright, sharp bits. Then the air cleared and she noticed a man in a tin and plywood stall full of tourist knickknacks looking at her. He wore a purple wrap and a dirty, collared, white oxford. Then, across the street, she saw a group of young men on a roof. They stood around a thin plume of smoke. She walked up to the man in the stall, pointed and asked, "Why? Why does that happen?"

They looked at each other across a counter lined with dozens of wood-carved animals. He said a few words in Swahili, paused when there was no response, then asked politely if she was American.

"Yes."

He adjusted his wool, Rasta-colored cap. "I will go to school there when I finish school here."

"You are a student?"

"I am halfway learning English, but have no more money to study."

"Oh," she said distantly, her eyes looking past him, "I don't have much of that either."

"Please I do not ask that," he said, and went on to tell her it would be a great help to his English studies if he could begin a correspondence with her.

But her eyes were fixed on the plywood wall behind him. Next to some sort of framed manifesto was the photo of the rhino corpse. She stared at the photo, then at him. She told him about the two men in the café as she pulled her eyelids shut with her forefingers.

"I can help you," he said with a quiet seriousness. "I can help you understand these things only African people should see."

She opened her eyes and looked at him. He handed her a pen and two pieces of paper, one with his name and address already written out, and one blank. She scribbled her name and address on the blank one and handed both back to him.

He laughed, and again handed her his address. She took it. He pocketed hers and then, in a sudden, business-like manner, bounced a finger along the heads of the carved animals. "This is the best teak," he said in a bright pitch. "Lion? Zebra? Boar?"

"So you know I saw those two men?" she insisted.

"Kate?" Guy said, coming up behind her.

"Lion? Elephant? Boar? Bird?"

"Kate, where did you go?"

"Fish? Crocodile? Boar? Bird?"

"You know I saw them." She stared at the man, ignoring Guy. "What do they want? What about that photo behind you? I've seen that, too."

Without looking at the photo, he said to her, "That's just another dead rhino." And then he turned his back to her and left the booth. Another man stepped in and took his place.

"Wait," she said, and began to pull bills out of her passport wallet.

Guy's hard blue eyes focused on her with a sudden, confounded suspicion. "Kate," he said.

The man walked swiftly away down a dirt alley. She followed, bills in hand. Guy tugged at her arm as she turned into the dirt alley. The man went up a flight of stairs and into a square, cinder-block building. "Let's stop this right now," Guy said.

She shook her head, shook free of him, and her hair came loose across her eyes as she rushed up the stairs. At the top, she pulled open the door. The man from the stall sat on a low stool between two large, Ethiopian-looking women. He halted their conversation and looked up at her and Guy. The floor was concrete and the room hot and menacingly airless. The wall was lined with stacks of plywood wrapped in wire, plastic bags of charcoal, a shovel, and a large pile of red swaths. The man stood and angrily pointed at her. "You gonna put somebody in big trouble!"

Then he took a step forward and accidentally knocked something metallic across the floor. Looking down, Kate saw that it was a stack of crushed tin cups and spoons which had been tied together with string. The man ripped off his cap and approached her as his dreadlocks tumbled out like snakes. Guy took her arm. Still clenching the bills, Kate looked at the man and began to moan. "Why are you angry? You're angry? You said you'd help me."

He shook his head. "Not supposed to come in here, not supposed to come in."

She wiped tears from her face. "But the men at the café, you said you'd help me."

He reached down to take her hand, unfolded her fingers, and took her money.

Guy grabbed her roughly around the shoulders and pulled her back down the steps. He held her elbow so hard that her arm went numb to the shoulder. He pushed her ahead, back up the alley toward the market square. She felt heavy-legged and drugged, as if she were running on lizards, on snakes, mashing them under her shoes. They pushed through the slow-moving throng. Someone dug a finger into her ear. She wrenched her head free, ducking lower. She felt faint. She could smell the vapid, pine odor of Lysol. It exaggerated the open air stench of sweat and dung. They stopped at a broken fountain in the square's center. Guy looked around. The Land Rover was gone. He grabbed her shoulders. "You just almost got the both of us killed," he said, with more menace than anything she'd seen or heard that day. "One of those women was holding a gun under her dress."

He held her shoulders and stared at her. "What's wrong with you?" Then he looked around again. "Give me that piece of paper he gave you. Where's that piece of paper?"

Guy saw that there were faces in the periphery, watching. Plans were stoking within the slouches of some of the onlookers. "Give me the paper," he repeated.

She shook her head, tucked it in her waistband. "Why did he say he'd help me?"

He turned her to face him. "What are you talking about? What on Earth are you talking about? You went up to him."

"He knew something."

"He knew he had something when he saw you."

"They have a hair of mine, Guy."

"Oh come on."

She stared at him, hair matted on her cheek.

"Look," he said, his voice suddenly low, sensing the crowd receding and an empty space growing around the two of them, "Something's up. Let's get out of here, let's get a taxi back. You need sleep."

"Sleep!" she cried, and stepped back out of his grip. "Sleep's a horse! A goddamned running horse! My hands are full of its hair now." She knelt and scrubbed her palms with the camel-colored dirt. Then she casually lay down on her side in the crowded marketplace, like a local curled up for a nap in the bustle.

Two men, one big and thick-necked with a hand deep in his pocket, stepped forward from the ring around her. Guy stepped back. The crowd was quiet now. The thick-necked man went down on a knee and reached into Kate's waistband for the piece of paper. He knew right where it was. As he withdrew it, she jerked awake and slapped his hand. He stood up, dumbly rubbing his hand, then pocketed the paper. He looked down at her and took a step, over her now.

"Wait," she said.

He stepped forward, straddling her. She brushed her hair away from her face, pulled herself back along the ground. "Wait," she was saying. "Just wait."

There is the smell of Lysol and Kate heard Ruth moving around the room. The Lysol is temporarily shielding all the more durable smells. Despite Ruth, there are still the faint smells of Guy: talc, sweet onion, and wet wool.

She opened her eyes.

Ruth looked up from her dusting. "I let you sleep. No need pushing you if you want to sleep."

"I don't want to sleep anymore," she said. "I didn't want to sleep."

"I'm sorry dear. Do you want some tea?"

"I can't *feel* like doing anything else. It's immoral the amount of time I sleep."

"You need it," Ruth said. "It's the most important thing now. It gives you peace of mind."

"I need a piece for my mind."

Ruth collected her rags and sprays and put them into her pail. "I'll just go and make the tea."

"Oh Ruth, it's a joke." Kate said, breaking into a wide smile. She pushed aside the covers, slid into her slippers, and crossed the room to where Ruth stood, one hand on the broom handle, the other going in small cartwheels in the air between them. Kate put a hand on Ruth's shoulder and gave her a kiss on the cheek.

Flanked by the two men, Guy and she were pressed into a small car, which sped out of the downtown and the tourist zones. They pulled up to a low, white building on a contagiously rowdy slum block. They were led upstairs where there was a bar and two windows with down-turned slots letting dusty rectangles of light onto the floor. The driver stayed at the door. A small, bald, walnut of a man stood behind the bar, watching her. His forehead was large, his eyes messily red and tense, and he seemed to have been waiting for some time. He scared her. The thick-necked man from the square sat in a dark-wood, semicircle booth. He was dressed in a skinny black tie and frayed black suit, the material cheap enough to let the light rest faint and oily on his shoulders. Kate and Guy sat down across from him. His eyes were buttons of tar in yellowed milk. He did not look at Kate.

"Here," he said brightly to Guy. "Here we have a problem."

She looked at the man. "Don't you smile like that."

Surprised, and with a flash of annoyance, the man said to Guy. "You might consider telling your young wife—" And then he stopped, caught himself, and smiled grandly, sympathetically at Guy.

Kate continued to stare at the man. "You're just a big bowl of porridge. Your mouth is full of porridge."

The man laughed, looked at Guy as if appreciative "Here we call it 'ugali.'"

"Your mouth is full of ugali, ugali mush."

He turned and rolled his wrist back toward the bartender. "Let us have some tea and some other items and start again." He looked back at Guy. "Or some beer. Would you like some beer?"

Guy was staring nervously at the tabletop, pinching his bottom lip between his forefinger and thumb as if he couldn't quite catch up to what was happening.

The man looked back again and asked the red-eyed bartender for peanuts. The bartender came over, and without glancing up, set them down, red and shelled. The big man smiled and took a few. For a long moment they all stared at the bowl.

Kate leaned toward him. "You have that smile. Big as can be. What's your mouth really full of? You smile as if you're not a problem for us."

The big man unfolded his thick, gold-ringed fingers and pulled out the piece of paper. "The problem?" he said, still chewing slightly and narrowing a glutinous stare on Guy. "The problem, we think, is hers."

Kate looked past the man. The bartender's eyes were fixed on her. She looked back down at the bowl of red peanuts, withdrew back into the booth.

"What does your wife want with Somali man?" the man said to Guy.

"What Somali man? What are you talking about?"

"My friend, we have fragile borders here in Kenya." He held up the paper he'd found in her waistband, read out loud the name. "Jecko Dube, he a Somali man. His people, with the red bands, those are dangerous people who are your friends and who you are giving the money to."

"Wait, what?" Guy stammered. "We're tourists here."

"Tourists? Yes?"

"Yes."

He pulled out another piece of paper. Held it up for Guy to see. "This your wife's name, yes? Your wife's writing?"

Guy leaned over and looked at it. "Yes."

"Well, they go right to jail now, your friends, and we talk to them in jail so we know soon." He scooped up peanuts, sifted some of the red rind off with his fat fingers, and tossed them into his mouth. "We find this address, see, on Somali man."

He leaned back and smiled at Guy with a hard, cool glee. "You a military man?"

"Are you?"

"You know about jail here? You go to the jail here and people, no matter what your embassy, they don't know where you are."

"Look, we're on a honeymoon. On a safari. You know that."

"Maybe you Agency man."

Guy shook his head. "This is unbelievable."

"What does your wife want with Somali man?"

"What are you selling here? What do you want?"

"What does your wife want with Somali man?"

"What do you want with us?"

The man looked at Kate, then back at Guy. "We sell insulation."

He reached for more peanuts and said in a severe but polite voice, "I cannot ask you to ignore our customs when you go looking for things only African people should see."

"You're not scaring me," she said right back to him. "The red bands are for processions, the tins and spoons are people's things, for their funerals. I saw that in the English newspaper at the hotel." She looked at

Guy. "They weren't Somali, those people. He's not police. Don't you see, Guy?"

Suddenly calm, she studied him for a moment. "What is it you see, Guy?" His face possessed an emotional—moral even—ambivalence that bordered on retardation. Would he still, after all this, see an animal, harbor bland hopes of walking up to an animal and shooting it in the head?

She reached across the table to take Guy's hand but the man took her hand before she could pull back. He pressed his hands around hers. She felt his calloused skin, the warm sweat between the wide creases in his palms. "A funeral," he said, gripping her hand, "passes right before your eyes," and his hands burst open and fluttered upward for mystical emphasis.

Guy leaned over to her and took her hand. "It does not matter," he whispered, "if they are police, secret police, or plain criminals. It's a setup. From the market. It doesn't matter, you understand? The guy in the market stall marked you as soon as he saw you."

Guy reached for his wallet.

"But not the two men at the café, not them," she said. "That was different. That was something else."

The man was rubbing his hands together. "We merely want to insulate you," he said.

Guy drew out a travelers check.

He shook his head. "No, not that."

"It's all I have," Guy said.

"No," he said grimly. "You come with me to the bank now."

"Guy," Kate said, "do not leave me here."

"She has to come too."

"No, " the man said. "She stays."

"Then take the travelers checks." Guy offered.

The man laughed. "She stays. You don't run off. When we withdraw, she can go as she please."

"She comes to the bank."

The bartender had moved around to the front of the bar and was leaning against it. The man reached into his pocket and lay a gun on the table. "Are you ready, military man?"

"Guy," she pleaded, "don't you leave me here. Guy!"

The dinner tray sat on the nightstand; tea, the pills for sleep, a small can of grapefruit juice and a bacon and tomato sandwich. Kate did not hear Ruth downstairs. It was dark outside. Ruth had gone home. It was difficult to keep her eyes open. She'd close them and again the dreams would come. A train leaving a besieged city, a train she could have made if she'd ran. But the airplanes had been crisscrossing the sky all night, nosediving into the city, just ahead of her in big concussion booms and slow-motion balls of fire. Hearty kamikazes, Guy and those young pilots. Going out with the yahoos, the trusted noise. Guy had always talked so loud, the more volume the more truth. Kate opened her eyes but against her will they closed again, closed back into the false heaviness in her veins. Against the dreams that came she said to herself: "These aren't my dreams; these aren't my dreams."

Lying there alone in their newlywed bedroom, the memory of her last day with Guy rose up out of her as if it were a ghost. She watched herself as a ghost go downstairs, her ghost in her cocktail dress. She made herself a drink and walked the halls of their brick ranch house, listening to its sourceless creaks and knocks. She sat on the arm of the sofa with her untouched drink and stared out the front window, down the wide lawn sloping to the road. Across the road was a lawn that sloped up to an exact same brick ranch house. It was a mirror image specter that made her go cold with an instant of unutterable images: a canopy of stretched flesh strewn with chicken bones, clumps of gelatinous blood, and the sucked-clean, white knob of a joint.

She went to the garage, sat in the car with the drink in her hand. She turned on the engine. She was scared, felt as if inside, her determined spirit of solitude had frozen into a blue-nothing sea. The car engine was running but she was waiting, the first push of exhaust coming through the vents. She couldn't bear the McLellons' party, the African honeymoon pictures Guy was no doubt showing despite everything that had happened there. She was scared but she didn't need her drink. If she was at the McLellons' she would need a drink. The engine seemed to rev itself and for an instant the headlights brightened. They were fixed on the lawn mower, the cases of ginger ale and beer, a hoe, and the wedding presents that they hadn't even bothered to open when they'd gotten back. She looked into her glass. What was it, she thought, that made it so she didn't want her drink?

The Key Lounge nagged at her. She'd passed it once a few days before on one of the time-emptying drives she'd been taking every day since Africa. It was familiar, or at least it seemed a place she was supposed to go to. A visit she had overlooked. But it was just a shabby bar in the tumbleweed and trash-strewn part of town and she'd definitely never been in. She should go there now. The exhaust was getting thick, as if a dark, vaporous part of her had escaped and was trying to take her along. Kate rolled down the window. She'd been dreaming up a man at that lounge, a bluesman and a barber, dreaming of running with him under the ice where the water was black and the animals translucent.

When she'd been balled up under that booth after Guy had gone to the bank with the man, her skin outraged and burning where the bartender with the messy red eyes had been groping her, she'd felt that push through something, felt that bluesman's sudden presence there. His judicial, staring presence. "You're there!" she'd said aloud. She thought this must have saved her.

Why else had that bartender, with all his shuddering weight onto her, suddenly stopped and looked into her eyes? Why else had he gotten up looking startled, buckled his pants and left? Why else had she not been raped? She coughed in the exhaust. She felt an odd, uncomfortable rush pass through her. Her eyes burned. That man was at that lounge, she should go there now. She leaned out and pressed the garage door button on the wall. She rolled the window back up and backed out into a velvety orange, suburban dusk. She passed the McLellons'. She stopped, reversed. The McLellons' was a white stucco and glass house on stilts with water nowhere to be found nearby. In the large, central window she could see—the gold and ruby sloped backs of the cocktail guests shifting among bobbing faces like a liquid Klimt painting. She leaned across the passenger seat and tried to spot Guy in the window. A man saw her and waved. She accelerated away, but took a right turn and came back around the block. She parked where Guy could see. She sat in the car and waited.

Guy came out a few minutes later. He paused at the door, the McLellons' patting him on the back, looking at her and then back to him. Then they got on the highway and headed downtown. They exited in the black part of town and she drove around until they'd found the Key Lounge. He'd agreed to go with her but hadn't believed it existed.

They sat in a red booth up front by the window, drinking powdery, acidic whiskey sours. The bar was empty. Guy was talking. "Don't think that it's certain you can trust me about helping you, whatever it is that has been happening to you. I can't understand it, but I want to help you, and I do have an idea."

Kate tried to tell him some of what had happened to her, but the words wouldn't come right and she got flustered. She looked out the window, studying the tattered, piano-key awning, broken and yellowed like teeth.

"Look," he said hesitantly. "Kate. There's a place the McLellon's know of. A charter hospital. It's a good place, they say. It has military coverage. I want to take you there, now maybe, to talk to someone."

She thought she saw a movement outside. "Look," she pointed haltingly.

He looked out the window to the motionless street. He took a deep breath. "Are you all right?" he asked.

She shook her head.

"Are you not all right?"

She shook her head.

He laughed a little, to himself, and looked into his drink. "All right," he said to himself.

They sat there for a moment, silent. Then, reaching down into his briefcase, Guy said with a forced smile, "I want to show you something, it might cheer you up."

She covered her eyes with her hands and smiled. She heard him shuffling through his papers. She slid her hands down off her eyes. The honeymoon photos and various African postcards were fanned out across the table. Amidst photos of the two of them, there was the postcard of the animal corpse.

"Look," he said when he got to it, "of all the things in Africa, the long bones of what's left, the long ears, it looks like a kangaroo."

"It's a rhino," she said. "Don't you even remember?"

"Well, it doesn't say anything on the back."

The bluesman, the barber, she knew, was not there. "Guy," she said. "Would you ask for the check please?"

"You want to go?"

Kate nodded, looking out the window to the moon.

"Good. I don't much like this place. Don't know why on Earth . . ." He shook his head, and then signaled to the bar.

"Look," she said, pointing out the window. The moon was gone.

"There's nothing there," he said without looking up, counting dollars and laying down a tip.

He led her out of the lounge and back to the car. They drove out of the neighborhood, and as the car momentarily glided on one of the last pieces of exposed trolley rail, Kate saw the neighborhood below, the pawn shops, Goodwills, churches, and liquor stores mutate into orange, octagonal lights.

The Silver Christ of Santa Fe

Charles Bukowski

Charles Bukowski (1920–1994) was born in Germany and grew up in Los Angeles. He was the author of more than forty-five books of poetry and prose, including Post Office, South of No North, Hot Water Music, Barfly, *and* Notes of a Dirty Old Man. *After its publication in* Open City, *this piece appeared in* Portions from a Wine-Stained Notebook: Uncollected Poems and Essays, 1944–1990 *(City Lights).*

THEN I GOT A LETTER FROM MARX WHO HAD MOVED to Santa Fe. He said he'd pay trainfare and put me up if I came out for a while. He and his wife had a rent-free situation with this rich psychiatrist. The psychiatrist wanted them to move their printing press in there, but the press was too big to get into any of the doors, so the psychiatrist offered to have one of the walls smashed down to get the press in and then have the wall put back up. I think that's what worried Marx—having his beloved press locked in there like that. So Marx wanted me to come out and look at the psychiatrist and tell him if the psychiatrist was okay. I don't know quite how it got to be that way but I had been corresponding with this rich psychiatrist, who was also a very bad poet, for some time, but had never met him. I had also been corresponding with a poetess, a not very good poetess, Mona, and the next thing I knew the psychiatrist had divorced his wife and Mona had divorced her husband and then Mona had married the psychiatrist and now Mona was down there and Marx and his wife were down there and the psychiatrist's x-wife, Constance, was still on the grounds. And I was supposed to go down there and see if *everything* was all right. Marx thought I knew something. Well, I did. I could tell him that everything wasn't all right, you didn't have to be a sage to smell that one out but I guess Marx was so close to it, plus the rent-free situation, that he couldn't smell it. Jesus Christ. Well, I wasn't writing. I had written some dirty stories for the sex mags and had them accepted. I had a backlog of dirty stories accepted by the sex mags. So it was time for me to gather material for another dirty story and I felt sure there was a dirty story in Santa Fe. So I told Marx to wire the money . . .

The psychaitrist's name was Paul, if it matters.

I was sitting with Marx and his wife—Lorraine—and I was drinking a beer when Paul walked in with a highball. I don't know where he had come from. He had houses all over the hillside. There were four bathrooms with four bathtubs and four toilets to the door from the north. It simply appeared that Paul had walked out from the four bathrooms with four bathtubs and four toilets with the cocktail in his hand. Marx introduced us. There was a silent hostility between Marx and Paul because Marx had allowed some Indians to bathe in one or more of the bathtubs. Paul didn't like Indians.

"Look, Paul," I asked, sucking at my beer, "tell me something?"

"What?"

"Am I crazy?"

"It'll cost you to find out."

"Forget it. I already know."

Then Mona seemed to walk out of the bathrooms. She was holding a boy in her arms from the other marriage, a boy of about three or four. They both had been crying. I was introduced to Mona and the boy. Then they walked away somewhere. Then Paul seemed to walk away with his cocktail glass.

"They hold poetry readings at Paul's place," said Marx. "Each Sunday. I saw the first one last Sunday. He makes them all line up single file outside his door. Then he lets them in one by one and seats them and reads his own stuff first. He has all these bottles all over the place, everybody's tongue is hanging out for a drink but he won't pour one. Whatcha think of a son of a bitch like that?"

"Well, now," I said, "let's not get too hasty. Deep underneath all that crud, Paul might be a very fine man."

Marx stared at me and didn't answer. Lorraine just laughed. I walked out and got another beer, opened it.

"No, no, you see," I said, "it might be his money. All that money is causing some kind of block; his goodness is locked-in there, can't get out, you see? Now maybe if he got rid of some of his money he'd feel better, more human. Maybe everybody would feel better . . ."

"But what about the Indians?" Lorraine asked.

"We'll give them some too."

"No, I mean, I told Paul that I was going to let them keep coming up here and taking baths. And they can crap too."

"Of course they can."

"And I like to talk to the Indians. I like the Indians. But Paul says he doesn't want them around."

"How many Indians come around here everyday to bathe?"

"Oh, eight or nine. The squaws come too."

"Any young squaws?"

"No."

"Well, let's not worry too much about the Indians . . ."

The next night Constance, the ex-wife, came in. She had a cocktail glass in her hand and was a bit high. She was still living in one of Paul's houses. And Paul was still seeing her. In other words, Paul had two wives. Maybe more. She sat next to me and I felt her flank up against mine. She was around twenty-three and looked a hell of a lot better than Mona. She spoke with a mixed French-German accent.

"I just came from a party," she said, "everybody bored me to death. Leetle turds of people, phonies, I *just* couldn't stand it!"

Then Constance turned to me. "Henry Chinaski, you look *just* like what you write!"

"Honey, I don't write *that* badly!"

She laughed and I kissed her. "You're a very beautiful lady," I told her, "you are one of those class bitches that I'll go to my grave without ever possessing. There's such a gap, educational, social, cultural, all that crap—like age. It's sad."

"I could be your granddaughter," she said.

I kissed her again, my hands around her hips.

"I don't need any granddaughters," I said.

"I have something to drink at my place," she said.

"To hell with these people," I said, "let's go to your place."

"Very vell," she said.

I got up and followed her . . .

We sat in the kitchen drinking. Constance had on one of these, well, what could you call it? . . . one of these green peasant dresses . . . a necklace of white pearls that wound around and around and around, and her hips came in at the right place and her breasts came out at the right places and her eyes were green and she was blonde and she danced to music coming over the intercom—classical music—and I sat there drinking, and she danced, whirled, with a drink in her hand and I got up and grabbed her and said, "Jesus Christ Jesus Christ, I CAN'T STAND IT!" I kissed her and felt her all over. Our tongues met. Those green eyes stayed open and looked into mine. She broke off.

"VAIT! I'll be back!"

I sat down and had another drink.

Then I heard her voice. "I'm in here!"

I walked into the other room and there was Constance, naked, stretched on a leather couch, her eyes closed. All the lights were on, which only made it better. She was milk-white and *all* there, only the hairs of her pussy had a rather golden-red tint instead of the blonde like the hair on her head. I began to work on her breasts and the nipples became hard immediately. I put my hand between her legs and worked a finger in. I kissed her all about the throat and ears and as I slipped it in, I found her mouth. I knew I was going to make it at last. It was good and she was responding, she was wiggling like a snake. At last, I had my manhood back. I was going to score. All those misses . . . so many of them . . . at the age of fifty . . . it *could* make a man doubt. And, after all, what was a man if he couldn't? What did poems mean? The ability to screw a lovely woman was Man's greatest Art. Everything else was tinfoil. Immortality was the ability to screw until you died . . .

Then I looked up as I was stroking. There on the wall opposite to my sight hung a life-sized silver Christ nailed to a life-sized silver cross. His eyes appeared to be open and He was watching me.

I missed a stroke.

"Vas?" she asked.

It's just something *manufactured*, I thought, it's just a bunch of silver hanging on the wall. That's all it is, just a bunch of silver. And you're not religious.

His eyes seemed to grow larger, pulsate. Those nails, the thorns. The poor Guy, they'd murdered Him, now He was just a hunk of silver on the wall, watching, watching . . .

My pecker went down and I pulled out.

"Vas iss it? Vas iss it?"

I got back into my clothes.

"I'm leaving!"

I walked out the back door. It clicked locked behind me. Jesus Christ! It was raining! An unbelievable burst of water. It was one of those rains you knew wouldn't stop for hours. *Ice cold!* I ran to Marx's place, which was next door, and beat on the door. I beat and I beat and I beat. They didn't answer. I ran back to Constance's place and I beat and I beat and I beat.

"Constance, it's raining! Constance, my LOVE, it's raining, I'm DYING OUT HERE IN THE COLD RAIN AND MARX WON'T LET ME IN! MARX IS MAD AT ME!"

I heard her voice through the door.

"Go away, you . . . you rotten sune of a bitcher!"

I ran back to Marx's door. I beat and beat. No answer. There were cars parked all around. I tried the doors. Locked. There was a garage but it was just made out of slats; the rain poured through. Paul knew how to save money. Paul would never be poor. Paul would never be locked out in the rain.

"MARX, MERCY! I'VE GOT A LITTLE GIRL! SHE'LL CRY IF I DIE!"

Finally the editor of *Overthrow* opened the door. I walked in. I got a bottle of beer and sat on my couch-bed after taking off my clothes.

"You said, 'To hell with these people!' when you left," said Marx. "You can talk to me that way but you can't talk to Lorraine that way!"

Marx kept on with the same thing, over and over—you can't talk to my wife that way, you can't talk to my wife that way, you can't—I drank three more bottles of beer and he went on and on.

"For Christ's sake," I said, "I'll leave in the morning. You've got my train ticket. There aren't any trains running now."

Marx bitched a while longer and then he was asleep and I had a beer, a nightcap beer, and I thought, I wonder if Constance is asleep? . . . It rained.

Glory Goes and Gets Some

Emily Carter

Emily Carter is the author of Glory Goes and Gets Some, *a short story collection. Her stories have appeared in* The New Yorker *and* Story *magazine. Following its appearance in* Open City, *this story was published in* Best American Short Stories.

HELLO CAMPERS, IT'S ME, LITTLE GLORIA BRONSKI, Campfire girl manque, and your guide through the twisted streets of Glory-town, coming to you live on W-M-E-E. Me, oh Glorious Me, if you want to know where I'm coming from. Tune me out and rest in silence, because I sing no garden variety song of myself. I sing you too, even though it might at first seem somewhat otherwise.

Everyone is very busy denying the last time they were lonely, but trust me, it happens. It isn't just being a solo act, although that contributes; I know women and men who stand in their backyards, safe in the bosom of their family, at the height of their careers and stare up into the old reliable silver-maple tree, mentally testing its capacity to hold their weight. There is that loneliness that other people can't alleviate. And then there's that loneliness that they can, which is what I was dealing with when I put the ad in the personals.

I hate the word horny, redolent as it is of yellowed calluses and pizza crust bunions, but there you go. Sober for eighteen months, I'd been giving up my will to God and practicing the three m's—meetings, meditation, and masturbation. But no matter the electronic reinforcement, it gets old mashing the little pink button all by your lonesome, night after night. Now here's the dilemma I'm staring at: "I AM HIV POSITIVE, WHO WILL HAVE SEX WITH ME?" If I was a guy it might be different, but carrying around the eve of destruction between my creamy white thighs doesn't exactly make me feel like a sex goddess. But I can't possibly be the only positive heterosexual recovering drug addict on huge amounts of Prozac in the universe. And of course, as it turned out, I wasn't. As they tell you in treatment, don't wear yourself out with

Terminal Uniqueness. Another kitchy-koo catch phrase that turns out, finally, to have the distinctly un-sampler-like ring of truth.

The problem was the research. I hate doing it, I hate thinking about doing it, I hate, with every fiber of my being, the process of going to libraries, making phone calls, looking things up, writing them down. Especially on this particular topic, which I'd rather not think about to begin with. But there you go, no stick, no carrot, if you get my drift. I found what I was looking for with very little trouble, as a matter of fact, a magazine called *Positive People*, and I put in my ad: Female, 35, hetero. Permanent graduate student. Red hair, green eyes. You: neither sociopath nor systems analyst. Will consider anything in between.

My first meeting was for coffee with a blue-eyed lanky man who told me that being HIV+ was a small entrance fee to pay to be granted admission into the bosom of Christ. I could see he meant it, because his gaze was flashing out a beam that went all the way into the golden distance of the final judgment. He had come through his trials with one gleaming jewel of truth, and that was all he needed, except maybe a partner to walk through the pearly gates with. "Life is a long joke," he told me, "heaven is when you finally get it." He was smiling, beaming with happiness, bursting out every now and then into relieved laughter, as if he'd just been missed by a truck. "You're sure about that?" I asked him, and he, laughing, held out his hand over the table, as if he was inviting me to run across a meadow toward the horizon. I gave it a friendly squeeze and never called the number he left with me, because I know very well what happens when you run toward the horizon; you get smaller and smaller until you vanish. Was I discouraged? Of course I was discouraged, I was born somewhat discouraged but in terms of action that's neither here nor there. "Pray as if everything depended on God. Act as if everything depended on you" goes the slogan I picked up at either an A.A. meeting or in one of the many pamphlets I'm always being offered by the well meaning souls who infest the Twin City area.

The next call I got was from a man named Jake and he was witty to the point of glibness on the phone, so I thought I'd give him a shot. Over lunch he began to tell me a little bit about himself. While he himself was not HIV+ he had no trouble understanding it—the lifestyle he had once lived, he said, it was a miracle he wasn't. He had picked up *Positive People* because he was looking for a woman who had explored alternative lifestyles and was comfortable enough with herself to be open about it. He had always, he said, loved my type—brainy girls, maybe Jewish, with wild hair and full lips and notions of freedom. Of course he was married, so we couldn't actually have sexual intercourse, but he would love to come all over my beautiful red hair and round breasts, as long as I had a reasonable sense of perspective. He so clearly meant to humiliate and degrade me that it was all I could do not to fall head over heels in love with him, but my vitamin regimen made me strong, and I left him there mid-sentence.

There followed an interlude with an AIDS activist named Garrett, a self-proclaimed Professional Person with Aids. He was always zipping back and forth to Washington, at great cost, he said, to his energy level and serenity. He tried to get me involved in a suit against the NIH for excluding women from early drug studies. And here's me just wanting a simple, frivolous, fuck.

It began to seem to me as if there was simply no hope of finding a little comfort in the world outside my apartment, but just when I had turned my attention elsewhere I stumbled on an uncut jewel, a pretty boy who liked girls, had green eyes and could spell "phlegm" if he had to. Recovering Like Me, answered the ad with great trepidation, feelings of overwhelming shame and geekiness overridden by the normal human imperatives. But here I am to tell you I definitely made it worth his while. His name wass Stefan, and I myself loved that name. Not that it changes much in my life to be, as someone said, getting it regular, but avenues opened that I thought I'd have to detour. Apparently Stefan felt the same because after our second night together, he told me he had never thought this was going to be a part of his life again, and he'd answered my ad out of sheer desperation, which of all human motivations is the only one you can absolutely trust, as far as I'm concerned.

Spring is coming, even to this frozen town, and people here are warming up. This morning on my way home from his house I got out of the car and looked down at the Mississippi River. The sunlight hit the water so it sparkled royal blue and diamond flecked. All winter long it had been the color of frozen iron and here it was now, just like me, babbling away merrily in the sunshine of early spring.

Hannibal Had Elephants with Him

Susan Chamandy

Susan Chamandy lives in Boston, where she directs a college counseling center and continues to write fiction. She has an MFA in fiction writing from the University of Virginia and the Iowa Writers' Workshop. She has also published fiction in Blue Mesa Review *and book reviews in* The Boston Phoenix.

I WAS LYING IN BED THIS MORNING WHEN MY mother came in and told me that Francis Mitchell was coming to her Christmas Eve party. She said he was coming from his daughter's house in New Jersey and he'd arrive about six o'clock, before everybody else got here. She asked me to salt the ice on the walk and reminded me that I'd made and broken three promises about when I'd hang the Christmas lights. "I think I've been reasonable," she said, trying to keep her voice even and positive. She wants things to work between us this time. "I want you to meet me halfway, Jake," she said. "I want you to get up and do the lights. Now. So we can get on with the festivities." She stood in the doorway a minute, her eyes down, but then she went away.

We hadn't seen Francis Mitchell since we left Montreal twenty years ago, after Daddy died. Americans don't know Francis Mitchell. They don't know about hockey. When Francis was interviewed in *Sports Illustrated* last year as one of the legendary Canadiens, my mother sent me the article. In the margin she wrote, "Do you remember Francis? He was Daddy's best friend." Francis played golf with my father almost every weekend. Francis and his wife played bridge with my parents, me locked in Daddy's lap because I was trouble even then. There are pictures of the four of them together—playing golf, skiing, sitting at big round tables with lots of other couples at fancy restaurants. Francis was with Daddy when he died. They were curling and Daddy had his heart attack, and Francis was with him in the ambulance for the five minutes he wrestled with his body.

By noon I was stringing the Christmas lights along the roof of the house. My mother had asked me to do it, so I was doing it. I was earning my keep, up and down the ladder, two feet of lights at a time. It was me and the squirrels out there. I could hear them scratching up the maple behind me, moving around in the frozen pachysandra under the tree. The bulbs clicked as I taped them to the gutter. In places I had them traveling in loops I'd made out of wire hangers. It looked like I'd written something in script about the house, a message.

From up on the ladder I could see my sister at the kitchen table. I knew my mother was in there too because Katie's mouth was going. When Katie first arrives they can't get enough of each other. Last night I heard them from the den, Katie talking about her own nasty self for a while, then both of them talking about love, why it's so rare and painful. Especially in the city, Katie said, and how my mother should still go to singles' parties because she might actually meet somebody nice who's still walking. And then they talked about me, my prospects—personal and professional. Too much college has made Katie a cynical person. She told my mother that my expectations are way out of whack, that I think I'm too smart to have to work. That's not exactly what I said. Before dinner the other night, when I was still feeling good about her being home and it seemed like we were having a conversation, I told her that I knew enough about computers not to have to grind away at some dumb job to make a living. "I don't want to be rude, Jake," she said, "but have you forgotten where you've been for the last three years?"

The gutters were clogged with frozen leaves and I started to throw clumps of them behind me. I watched them drop down onto the snow. Next thing, my mother was standing at the foot of the ladder, wiping her hands on her apron.

"Honey, I wanted them on the bushes. I told you that."

I didn't say anything.

"This is too much," she said, looking up at my loops. "We look like the circus."

"You want me to take them down?"

She laughed and said something quietly, as if she was talking to the snow.

"I can take them down," I said.

Katie came out and stood beside her. She had on her nightgown underneath her parka and my mother's snow boots that are made from pony hair. Her feet looked like paws on the snow.

"Wow, that's ugly," she said.

"Ok, sleep queen, you do it."

Katie started climbing up the ladder, my mother begging her not to, until she was just below me. She leaned into me and reached for one of the loops, but she couldn't get her hands on it. Her shoulders were about where my chest was and I could feel her body struggling to undo my work, as if all her dislike for me was in that struggling.

I put a hand on her shoulder and she said, "Ow." She said, "Get off me."

My mother said, "Katie, sweetie, please come down."

In one quick motion I pulled the loop away from the roof and forced it into a straight line with the Christmas lights dangling from it.

"Lilly's on the phone," she said, her eyes glued to the straight wire between my hands. She was listening to my breath shake.

"Then fucking move," I said. I watched her step down the ladder. I tried to cool off, before I started down myself.

Lilly is thinking about marrying me. She's made a list of pros and cons that she keeps in her panty drawer. I found it one afternoon when she was in the shower. Over the past six months since I've been home she's added all kinds of things to that list. To start with, it was just good sense of humor, smart, romantic, loving (to me, and possibly my own), smokes a pack a day, has been to prison, has explosive temper, talks about computers too much. After she let me touch her again she added, "still good in bed." When I told her that if she got pregnant I'd quit smoking she added, "wants fatherhood very badly" to the pros and "can be manipulative" to the cons.

When Lilly started visiting me in prison, nobody could believe it. She'd been to college, she was married. And when we'd first gone out in high school I was so bad to her even I remember it that way. We were both a little rough with each other, but Lilly was going to class and getting good grades and thinking about going somewhere else the next year, so I guess I was rougher on her.

When I told my mother about Lilly visiting me, she told me to take it easy, not to expect too much, because we just couldn't know how things were going to work out. Even now, with me out of prison and Lilly divorced from her husband and spending time with me, I can tell they still don't believe it. My mother continues to say that we can't know what will happen, and Katie doesn't really look at me when I talk about the house I'm going to build for Lilly and me and our baby. She smiles with only half of her mouth and looks over my shoulder. Yes, I'm still living with my mother. And I know I've got a lot to prove before Lilly stops thinking about "has been to prison," before she'll forget that afternoon years ago out on the driveway when I gave her a bloody nose for saying she was going to leave me. But I'm optimistic about us.

When I first got home from prison, Lilly told me to come up with a word that would calm me when I was about to lose it. I thought "Lilly" until it was Lilly I was losing my temper over. Then she told me to focus on an object, something right in front of me. It should be something neutral, she said, something that has no power over me.

I see things working out with Lilly and me. We are in love with each other. I don't think I'm fooling myself. The only thing that confuses me is how she's turned that feeling into something almost rational. She stores it in a corner of her mind that I can't seem to reach.

I was digging candles out of their holders when Lilly arrived. My mother wanted red candles in the living room. Lilly had so many pine boughs in her arms, I couldn't see her face at first. She dropped her armful on the kitchen table and then sat down and watched me.

"Your mother has the whip on me too," she said. "When she called this morning, she said, take a pair of clippers with you on your run, dear." Lilly gave her little hoot and spread the pine boughs out on the table. She started picking out the thin branches and throwing them into the sink behind her. "She sounded a little hysterical on the phone."

"Not yet," I said. "Wait until her party starts. Then she *really* loses it."

"I don't know if I'm going to make it," Lilly said. I went over and gave her a long kiss. I touched the back of her neck where it disappeared into her red silk blouse. She smiled and said, "Hi." When I sat back down she asked, "Who's coming to this thing anyway?"

"The whole fucking neighborhood."

She threw some more branches into the sink.

"Miss Timmy's coming, right?" she asked. "I love Miss Timmy."

"Miss Timmy and her girlfriend," I said. Lilly looked at me. "Who do you think is the man in *that* relationship?"

She rolled her eyes. Her roommate is a fag so she obviously doesn't think about this stuff. And besides, Miss Timmy was her third grade teacher, so she has kid feelings about her. She's gotten me to say gay person instead of fag—sometimes. When I'm at her house, in case her roommate is listening to us through the wall, or when we're out with her friends. I've overheard my mother telling Lilly not to worry about my ideas about the world. I have some catching up to do, she tells her.

"Remember Hannibal?" Lilly asked. "Carthage? The Punic Wars?" she said when I didn't respond.

"I didn't go to college."

She smiled. "That's your answer for anything that bores you. Come on, you get Hannibal in grade school."

I just looked at her.

"Anyway, there was a show on elephants last night and there was a little bit on Hannibal, how he used elephants when he fought the Romans. You would have loved it. They attached swords to their tusks and built rafts to get them across the Rhone. They were the first tanks! I tried to tape it for you, but something's up with my VCR."

"Hello stranger," my mother said, coming into the kitchen. She hugged Lilly, held the back of her head and kissed her on the cheek. Too much pressure, I thought. I watched Lilly's face over my mother's shoulder and tried to see what she was thinking.

"Lilly, I missed you," my mother said.

"They sent me to Des Moines," Lilly said, and made a face.

"Where it's all happening at," I said. That's from a TV show I like in the afternoons. They both looked at me.

Lilly told my mother about Des Moines and my mother listened for a minute, her face following along, and then she said, "Oh," and went over to the fridge and took out what looked like a cake. She flipped it over onto a plate and it was some kind of loose pink mold. It looked pretty bad up there on the counter as she tried to unify it.

"Francis will be here in about an hour and a half," my mother said. "I want you to be ready when he gets here." She reached up over the stove and took down boxes of crackers. "What are you going to wear, Jake?"

"This."

"I got dressed up," Lilly said.

My mother turned around and looked at me. "Promise me you're not going to hide out in your room," she said. "Francis is dying to see you. And I need your help at the party." When I didn't say anything she said, "How about, you know," her hands at her throat as if she was tightening a tie. What my mother wanted me to wear was out of the question. Just after I got home we went to a men's store in town and bought a suit for me. We decided I needed it for job interviews. But when I got home and put it on and really looked at myself in the mirror, I had to be truthful with myself. I didn't look so hot in it. For three years I'd been eating donuts and potato chips instead of state food, and lying on my bed instead of lifting weights. At least dressed casually I wouldn't look like I was *trying* to look good.

"That was an expensive suit," my mother said.

"I look like a child molester in it," I said. "And I know child molesters."

"You look like a mature, well-adjusted person," my mother said. "What's wrong with that?"

Lilly looked at me and said nothing.

"This matters to Francis, honey. That's all I'm saying. I think he'd like to see you looking like a man."

I glanced at Lilly, but she was looking out the bay window, smiling. My mother saw me trying to catch Lilly's eye and a little doubt came into her expression. "So," she said, clapping her hands together, "let's get organized." She stuck toothpicks in her mold and put a piece of plastic over it. She carried it like a prize over to the fridge and put it inside. "Don't fool around in here," she said from behind the fridge door. "My mousse is balanced on I don't know what." She rummaged around in there for a minute, putting things out on the kitchen table, then putting them back. "There. That'll work." And then she said after a minute, "Oh God, where's the O'Doul's." She let the door close. She thought with her eyes on the door. "I forgot the O'Doul's."

"That's all right, Mrs. K.," Lilly said, "we like Coke."

"Of course not," my mother said. "Let me get my purse and I'm going to send you two. I've still got some cooking to do."

"Let's not do this," Lilly said. "It's not a big deal."

"It's a party, Lilly. I'm going to get my purse."

"*Your* fucking party," I said under my breath, but she didn't hear me and she was walking out the door before I thought of something reasonable to say. "I'll drink the Coke, Mom," I said. But she continued on out the door saying she'd get her purse. "And when those are gone," I yelled, "I'll have a beer."

Lilly shook her head and my mother came back into the kitchen. She stood with one hand on the stove, her eyes down. Scared is how she looked, if you saw through how she was trying not to look scared.

"I'm kidding."

Katie yelled from upstairs, "Francis is lost in New Jersey. He can't find the Tappan Zee."

My mother went over and picked up the phone. "Francis," she said, and laughed. But it wasn't Francis. It was Katie's friend from college. "Jeanie, honey, can I put you on hold," my mother said, clicking over.

Katie has no friends here and she's on the phone most of the time. My mother went to the stairs and yelled, "Did Francis hang up?"

Katie yelled back, "I gave him directions. He'll be fine. Probably."

"Please go get the O'Doul's," my mother said when she came back into the kitchen. "Francis might want some."

"Then what's all the Labatt's for?" I asked. My mother had left a case of Labatt's out in the garage, on the far side, by the back wheel of her car. "I'll go and get some O'Doul's if Francis asks for it," I said. "OK?"

Lilly got up and fished her keys from her coat pocket. She held them up and shook them.

"No," I said.

"You can smoke in the car."

As we drove around the corner and passed the front of the house, I saw my mother moving around in the kitchen. It was getting dark and the bay window was like a yellow bowl of light.

My mother was studying something on the counter—a book or her pink mold.

Lilly looked over at me and shook her head. "That woman's love is pretty hard to take sometimes," she said.

"I have a question for you," Katie said to Lilly when we got back. She was dressed now, putting a cup of coffee into the microwave. She leaned against the kitchen counter with her arms crossed. "Just so you're ready. Is Francis Mitchell an a) famous Canadian hockey player from Alberta, b) famous Canadian painter of favorite winter sports, or c) famous ex-member of the FLQ?"

"You've been on the phone too long," Lilly said.

"I'm excited," Katie said. "Mom says he's kind of a goof, but you know, good hearted."

Lilly never says anything about Katie—maybe that she might have gone to the wrong college or that she's a little young for her age, but nothing I *want* her to say. Whenever she's had enough of Katie, she winks at me and we go to my room.

"Mom wants you to take your shower now," Katie said as we left the kitchen. "She has to run the dishwasher."

My bedroom is on the first floor of the house, which I appreciated as a teenager. It gave me lots of freedom. I slept with a number of girls in that room. At first my mother had trouble with that—yelling at me to unlock my bedroom door in the morning, so the girl had to jump into my closet, making me explain girls' clothes on the floor—but then she left me alone. After a while that room was like a sealed capsule, a satellite off the mother ship, and anything that happened in there was nobody's business.

While I was away, my mother took down my Frank Zappa and Yes posters and had the room painted. Now she has a purple light station set up in the corner for her orchids. That purple light is on all night and I'm almost used to it. When I'd just moved in and was complaining about it, Lilly undressed and stood beside it, to give me new associations.

Lilly sat on the edge of my bed and watched me take off my clothes. "You look nice," she said, leaning back on her arms. "I wish we were at home."

"We are," I said and stood in front of her. I don't know where I get all the confidence. I'm not exactly beautiful. Once, I could have been a magazine model. That's what my mother used to say, along with, I could have gone to MIT and, I could have been a track star, because I had the build for it. But I've seen myself in the mirror—puckered skin between my eyes from when a rocket engine blew up in my face, a welt like a pale caterpillar under my mouth from when I crashed Mrs. Letty's station wagon, a bump at the bridge of my nose where a fragment of buckshot lived until it got dangerous and they had to take me in leg cuffs to a hospital for surgery. I have a face that never quite grew back.

"I see it," Lilly said, looking at my hard-on. "It's very nice, sweetheart, but you know the rules." Our agreement is, not in my mother's house. Lilly is only truly Lilly in her own apartment, and I guess I'm lucky for that much. But I kept standing there because sometimes my wanting to touch her badly is enough to make her come around. Sometimes I just look at her and she smiles and tells me to lie down and it's like there are no limits.

"Go take your shower," she said and flopped back on the bed. I touched her knee and it moved, and her hips tilted a little, but not enough to promise me anything. She waved me away.

On my way to the bathroom, Katie looked up from her newspaper. "Some *woman* called when you were at the grocery store. I thought I'd keep it between you and me," she said crisply.

"Who was it?"

"She said her name was Elaine." Katie looked at me intensely. "Just Elaine. No number and a big attitude. The second time she called, she told me I was lying, that you were really here. I thought, I'll have to ask Jake about *her*. Who's Elaine?" she said when I didn't respond.

I looked at my hand on the counter and that steadied me. I looked at the cuff of my bathrobe where my wrist appeared, where my watch was, where my wrist became my hand. I started to rearrange the glasses set up on the counter, but I still felt it all coming up in me. It was like a column of fire in my throat.

"Who *is* she? Oh, I know," she said, "the latest high priestess of stupid choices."

"What did you tell her?"

She just stared at me.

"What did you tell her, you little cunt?"

"Oh wow," she murmured, the newspaper wilting in her hands. She looked at the ceiling and her face went flat, and then quickly came back bigger than life, and she was crying.

I went to the bathroom and lowered the lid on the toilet and just sat there, my head between my knees. I stared at the bright tiles on the floor until the pattern steadied me.

Elaine had written to me about the kid. At first her letters were friendly, as if we could recapture something we never had. "This is our baby," she wrote on the back of a tiny picture of the kid in front of a silky, pink backdrop. "She's good. And she smells good. You'll want to carry her everywhere." She'd written and asked me to put her on my visitor's list. "I'll bring Robin and you'll fall in love with her," she wrote. She traveled across the state one Sunday and sat for two hours waiting for me to OK her visit, but I never signed the form. At least I could control who visited me. That was when she started calling my mother for money.

"You're going to own up," she wrote in a letter with the blood test results. "Your mother says you're making ten dollars a week cleaning out some guard's closet. But you're going to be a father to Robin. I can promise you that." Her letters must have started coming back to her and that's why she was looking for me here.

I thought of another letter Elaine wrote to me, the first letter a long time ago, the letter that started it all. "Please talk to me, Jake. I'm desperate." That's all it said. A real mystery to everybody but me. She'd taped it to the back door and my mother had found it first. "What's going on?" my mother asked, standing over my bed that night. I got up and tried to look sober. She hadn't confronted me in months. I backed her out of my room with my aggressive good cheer. In my doorway, she wanted to know if I'd done something wrong. I leaned against the doorjamb, which suddenly wasn't there for me. I stood up straight again and said, "She just wants to stay in my pants."

Francis was in a long blue coat and a hat and he looked like he was from an old movie except that he had a gut as big as mine. After he gave Lilly his coat and hat, he stepped into the living room and looked around— at the paintings on the wall with their little lights on, at the bay window with my mother's orchids, at the grand piano and the Christmas tree and the pink sofa. Then he looked at me for a minute. He put his big hand on the back of my neck and rubbed it roughly.

"I knew you in another life," he said. He left his hand on my neck.

"Do you want something to drink?" I asked.

"I'll wait for your mother," he said. He went over and looked at the paintings up close. "That's Quebec," he said, pointing to one of them. "I know that's Quebec. See the guy in the snowshoes? I'll bet that's my buddy Réne Cossard." He laughed and came back over to us.

"You look good," he said to me. He touched my tie, and looked at it for a minute as if it held some deep mystery for him. Then he looked at Lilly. "Jake was a good boy," he said.

"That's what I hear." Lilly slipped her hand into mine.

"You play hockey?" he asked, and I believe he was serious.

"Not really."

"Not really," he repeated. "I remember you out on Morrison Avenue with all your friends, moving the net every time a car came. You loved hockey. I thought Emile had a little Canadien on his hands. What happened to you?"

I waited before I said anything—so that I could rephrase that for myself, so that I could be civil, and part of the community of man, as my mother likes to say. "Who knows," I said finally. Francis looked at me for a long moment, then his eyes dropped down to my tie again.

"And who are you, my dear?" he asked, turning to Lilly.

"She's my fiancée," I said. Lilly smiled at me and squeezed her eyes shut.

"You'd think I'd be ready," my mother said as she came down the stairs with Katie stomping behind her. Katie had changed into another outfit and now she had on high heels. Francis put his arms around my mother and held her, his cheek against her hair. My mother is a small person and Francis had to really stoop over to hug her. When she pulled away, she wiped her cheeks with her hand. And then Katie did the same thing, got all choked up when she was in his arms.

"How about a drink?" my mother said. "I'm going to have sherry. What can I get you, Francis?" Everybody followed her into the kitchen and I sat down on the sofa. I could see Francis's black Cadillac parked out on the street, and I tried to remember what I had expected when my mother told me he was coming.

Lilly came back from the kitchen and sat down next to me. She handed me a tall beer glass filled with O'Doul's. I sniffed it and put it down on the coffee table.

"Francis didn't want O'Doul's after all," she said. She sat back on the sofa and sipped from her glass. She was drinking Coke—for me. Sometimes I want to tell her just to trust me, to have the glass of wine I know she wants. But I avoid that word now. I don't really know what *trust* means to Lilly. Once, when we were arguing she asked, "How can I trust you when I'm the only one you're good to?"

"Ho ho ho," Francis said, carrying his glass of beer against his gut like he was giving it a ride. He sat down on the other side of me. My mother sat on the piano bench and Katie sat on the floor next to her with her legs to her side as if she was a model. There was a chair for her and I don't know what she was trying to prove. She took off her high heels and my mother gave her a look.

"What?" she said.

"Francis," my mother said, "my kids are crazy." She stroked Katie's head that way I've seen her do it. I've gone up to my mother's room at night and she's on the phone and Katie's stretched out on the bed looking at nothing, letting my mother stroke her like she's some kind of house pet.

"*You* look like your father," Francis said to Katie. "It's up here." He pointed to his eyes.

"I agree," Katie said, and my mother laughed to herself.

"Honey," she said.

"She's pretty," Francis said. "There's nothing wrong with looking at yourself in the mirror if you're pretty." Katie leaned against the legs of the piano bench and smiled and I was thinking that I hadn't seen anything like that in a while. Lilly laughed softly and put her hand on my thigh.

"We used to babysit you," Francis said to me. "Sarah called you Wild Animal. You never stopped moving. You moved all over the furniture." He bounced his hand in the air. "You remember that, Jake? You don't remember that. Sarah was my first wife," he said to Lilly. "My first, worst wife," he said, and laughed.

"Oh, Francis," my mother said. She smiled and looked down at her drink on her knee.

"Just a joke," he said. "Sarah and I are actually talking again. She moved to Calgary. She moved out there with her driving instructor, believe it or not."

"That's supposed to be a terrific city," my mother said.

"Calgary's a dump. She can have it," he said. My mother looked at her drink again and Katie walked over to the coffee table on her knees and spread some pink mold onto a cracker.

"You know, I never forgave you for taking these kids away from me," Francis said after a minute.

"I needed to," my mother said.

"I never understood that. It never made any sense to me. Not from the beginning, not ever. Emile would have wanted his kids to grow up real Canadians, and you knew that."

"Francis," my mother said, laughing, but I could see that she was getting angry. "That's not fair."

"What's fair," he said.

"I would have liked living in Montreal," Katie said. "I could speak French all the time."

The phone rang in the kitchen, and my mother told Katie to get it. Katie running for the telephone reminded me of Elaine's phone call, and it wasn't until Katie called my mother that I breathed again. And I didn't listen to what Francis was saying to me until I heard my mother's voice get friendly and excited, thanking someone for that gorgeous package she found on the doorstep this morning. When I heard that, I began to hear Francis. He was saying, "You're Canadian," and he was touching my tie again. "Right there," he said, "no matter what." When he got no reaction from me, he turned to Lilly and started telling her that I was a hyperactive kid. "He was crazy," he said. "You were *crazy*. I remember you tied yourself to the garage door. Me and Sarah come over one afternoon and there's this kid on a rope!"

He reached to rub my neck again and I pulled away a little.

"Hey, *hey*," he said, holding my neck in his big hand. "There's no problem, son. No problem with that." When he finally let go of me, I could feel his hand growing up the back of my neck.

I went into the kitchen to get away from Francis. Katie had left her phone message about Elaine right out on the counter—the top sheet of my mother's towering notepad, a bright yellow square of paper six inches up off the counter as if it was lifting itself, begging to be read.

"ELAINE called," it said. "No number. What have you done to this woman? A hostage we don't know about?" I tore the note from the pad and held it out in front of me. I barely had time to get myself together before the creak of someone crossing the living room turned into Lilly in the doorway. I put the note in my pocket.

"How's it going?" she asked. She had that concerned look I hate.

"Good," I said. "I'm going to cut some of these lemons and limes." I picked up the fruit off the bar, got a knife and a cutting board and sat down at the kitchen table.

Lilly sat across from me. "Are you feeling okay?" she asked.

I nodded and gave her a big smile. The wrong reaction. That big smile goes under "poor communication skills" or "stifled anger" or maybe even "passive aggression" if I keep at it. Lilly has been seeing a therapist for years and she often becomes one when we're alone. It's a real turn on.

"Do you want to go to your room?" she asked.

"Are you going to spank me?"

"Jake, I'm serious."

"About what?"

"This is hard," she said, "Francis coming. For all of you, I think."

I didn't say anything and I was trying not to say anything, but it was all coming up anyway. I tried to focus on Lilly's hair where it started, black and shiny above her eyes, black and sudden against her white forehead.

"Look at me, Jake." She reached for my arm and I pulled away, practically cutting myself with the knife. "Relax," she said.

"You're watching me, Lilly. I fucking hate it when you watch me."

"I just want to understand what's going on. I want to know how you feel about Francis."

"Francis is Francis. Who the fuck cares how I feel about him?"

"I do," she said quietly, looking me squarely in the eye. "But sometimes I don't know why." She got up slowly, almost as if she was tired, pushed her chair under the table and went back into the living room.

It was seven o'clock by the time people started arriving. My mother had put on the *Soul Christmas* CD Lilly gave her, and the Ronettes were singing "I Saw Mommy Kissing Santa Claus" from the stereo in the corner of the living room. Francis had a hard time getting up off the sofa each time my mother introduced him to someone. He'd polished off one of the sixes of Labatt's and was well into a second. When he was introduced, he would shake hands and then sit back down and drink his beer. My mother would stand there and keep the conversation going until somebody moved away or new people were at the front door or she saw that she needed more crackers on her cheese plate.

I was sitting in the den watching TV with somebody's kid when my mother came in and said she needed my help with something. I asked her what, and she said, "Something, honey. Don't be silly," so I followed her into my bedroom.

"Sweetheart," she said, touching her Christmas wreath necklace that blinked on and off. She smiled. "You look nice. I told you that suit looked good on you. You look very handsome. Listen," she said. "I don't want to upset you and I don't want to wreck this party for you, but I think you should know. Elaine called for you. I spoke to her. She threatened me some, but I don't really understand what she wants more than what she's already getting." She let her breath out and shook her head. "Actually, I'm afraid I do, but I don't think we should be into that. I just thought you needed to know all this in case she calls again."

"Is that what you needed help with?"

"Yes," she said, "that was it." And then she looked at me in that way that reminds me I'm the puzzle of her life. "How do you feel, dear?"

"Fine. I feel great, Mom."

She put her hand on my arm. "You need to let go of it, honey," she said. "Tonight, just let go of it."

"I'll do my best."

"Do you remember what I told you about looking people in the eye when you talk to them? You have nothing to be ashamed of, Jake. It's all behind you now."

"You think Lilly would see it that way?" I asked, and immediately I realized that I was not being sarcastic, that I was really asking her. My mother frowned at me, her lips parted. From her expression, I understood that she'd been believing in Lilly and me, more than I'd thought. She'd assumed that I'd told Lilly everything, about Elaine and the kid. She put her arms around my neck and kissed my throat. I could smell perfume in her hair. "I'm very proud of you, son," she said.

"Oh yeah?"

"You've given me a lot of heartache," she said, her voice choking up. "We both know all about that. And maybe that's why I care for you especially. That's true, you know," she said, kissing my throat again. "I think of you all the time, Jake. I want everything for you."

When she pulled away from me her face was all wet. She wiped her cheeks with her hands. "Okay," she said, smiling, "let's party." And when she laughed that makeshift laugh of hers, I felt a sharp twinge in my stomach, like I hadn't eaten for days.

In the kitchen, Katie was standing behind Lilly, helping her put on her Christmas wreath. Everybody had one. "Okay," Katie said, and stepped away. Lilly's wreath came alive on her blouse, a pale light appearing and disappearing under her chin. I wanted her to look my way, to let me know she hadn't given up on me yet. But she turned her back and said, "At your service, Mrs. K.," and went over to my mother, who was taking a tray of little brown cakes out of the oven.

"They're very hot, dear. Please warn everybody," my mother said as she put the cakes onto a platter Lilly was holding.

"What are those?" I asked, standing at Lilly's elbow. She glanced at me.

"Crab cakes," she said, watching my mother's hands as they transferred the cakes from the tray to the platter. I couldn't tell if she was ignoring me. She *could've* been lost in the act of helping my mother. A long time ago I realized that I'm not the only person she enjoys pleasing.

I followed Lilly out into the living room and walked behind her as she offered people the crab cakes. I followed her until it got weird and then sat down in a chair by the Christmas tree. I felt a coin in my jacket pocket and tried to fit it into the slot in one of my loafers. I stopped after a minute because I realized that looked as bad as not looking people in the eye. When I looked up, Francis was watching me from the sofa. He drank from his beer and looked at me with no expression.

"Jake," I heard, and saw Mr. McCarthy on his way across the living room toward me. "How are you?"

"Mr. McCarthy," I said. I got up out of my chair. I stopped shaking hands before he did and it was just my dead hand in his for way too long. He patted me on the back.

"I've been meaning to say hello to you," he said. "I see you out there and of course I'm on my way to the station, or I'm late for dinner, and I can't be late for dinner." He laughed. "But I wanted to say hello."

"It's good to see you, Mr. McCarthy," I said, and reached for his hand. I thought that was going to be it, but I'd forgotten what a sport Mr. McCarthy is.

"Your mother says you're into computers now," he said. "I'm glad to hear it. That's a good place to be." What place, I was thinking, but I nodded and started talking about the new technology. But then that started to feel bad because Mr. McCarthy was looking over my shoulder, even though he was trying very hard to look interested in what I was saying.

"I'm going to get some ham, Mr. McCarthy," I said after a few minutes. "Can I get you some ham?"

"No thanks, Jake. Hey, good luck with things," he said, and shook my hand again. I looked over and Francis was still watching me. He had both hands out to his sides and he looked like a fat kid there on the sofa. I went into the dining room.

My mother had all the food out on the table—smoked ham and turkey, roast beef and mini slices of bread, strips of salmon like pink tongues, a ball of green cheese, and a big bowl of eggnog. I walked around the table filling my plate with food and ended up by the eggnog. I could smell the booze in it. Mrs. Harrison touched my elbow. "So rich," she said. "Your mother is trying to kill us." We talked about my dog Zack, who was run over while I was away. Kenny, her retarded son, was standing beside her the whole time and she kept one hand on him. It was like they were glued together. She said she missed Zack. He was a nice dog, a calm dog. "Sometimes I saw him on the front lawn and he looked positively Zen," she said.

I went back into the living room and sat down in my chair again. My mother was introducing Francis to Miss Timmy, the dyke schoolteacher, who was wearing a patchwork hippie skirt, probably from the days she taught Lilly her multiplication tables. Francis lifted himself off the sofa and took Miss Timmy's hand and kissed it. Miss Timmy's girlfriend just waved when she was introduced to Francis. When the two women left, he sat down and stretched his arms out along the back of the sofa and smiled at the room. Then he saw me and waved me over. I raised my hand and said, "No thanks, I've had too much to eat." He just looked at me, confused. He looked at me that way until I got up and went into the kitchen.

There were a lot of men standing around the bar. I went over to the fridge and put my head inside before anyone noticed me. Francis came into the kitchen and introduced himself to the men around the bar. He patted somebody's back and laughed loudly at nothing. Everybody was quiet for a minute, and Mr. McCarthy looked at Francis, his chin tilted up, happy to listen to anything Francis had to say. But Francis couldn't see that because he was looking at the floor. He just stood there and breathed deeply, as if he was in danger of drowning and that was what he needed to concentrate on if he was going to stay afloat.

The telephone rang and I turned back around and stared into the fridge. It rang again but I didn't move.

"Jake," I heard Francis say. The way he said my name made everyone stop talking. It rang two more times and he said—he was almost shouting—"Pick up the phone, Jake. Your mother's busy."

Mr. McCarthy went over and picked up the phone. He said, "Hello," and then held it out to me.

All she said was, "Jake," and it was like I'd just smoked a bone—that same heavy feeling spreading into my arms and legs.

"Hi," I said. I looked at the men and they were beginning to talk again. Francis was leaning back against the counter, away from everybody, watching me. I turned around so that I was looking into the dining room.

"I want to be friends," Elaine said. I didn't say anything about that and I could hear her getting worked up over my quietness. "I figured you'd be around tonight," she said. "Is that where you're living now?"

"No."

"Where are you living?"

"Around."

"You're like this, aren't you?" she said. "You've always been an asshole to me. I don't know anybody who—"

"I've got to go."

"No way, Jake. You're going to listen to me. I have some things to say," she said—that, and something else I didn't hear because I hung up. I started to leave the kitchen, but Mr. McCarthy was talking to me again and then the phone rang and everybody was looking at me, Francis especially.

"I'm going to put Robin on the phone," she said. "Okay? You go ahead and hang up on her. You hang up on your baby. That's how we think of you anyway."

I listened for a minute and I could hear my own hard breathing coming back at me through the receiver. I listened harder but that was all I heard. I put the phone down on the counter. I picked it up again and I heard a little sound on the other end, not a voice or anything, just like something was brushing up against the receiver. I had tried to picture myself visiting Elaine and the baby, mostly to keep things civil, but that was a pretty fuzzy picture. Just then, though, I had all kinds of things clearly in my head—the kid's little personality, my mother mailing fatherhood checks to Elaine, all the sex and help I'd gotten because I'd been able to make people believe I was working with them, that we were making decisions together.

But then my mind went blank and I felt that heaviness again, that feeling that made everything seem impossible, like if I sat down I'd never get up again. I put the receiver on the counter and went to my room.

I stood at the kitchen sink with a dish towel drying the platters Lilly passed to me and worrying about what she'd said ten minutes earlier. When I'd started to tell her about the subdirectories I could create for her computer at work, she'd said, "I'm exhausted. Can we just wash dishes?" Even though that was something like what she always said to me when I talked about computers, I couldn't seem to turn it off in my head. It kept pouring over me, like the steaming water running over the platters in her hands.

Katie came into the kitchen and said, "I think Mom needs some help out there. Francis is getting belligerent." She sounded almost scared.

"Who's still here?" Lilly asked.

"Nobody. It's just Francis and his big drink."

Lilly dried her hands on my dish towel and went with Katie into the living room. I listened, but I didn't hear any trouble, so I started to wash the other platters that were out on the kitchen table.

"Jake," my mother called from the living room.

"What?"

"Sweetie," she said, and I could hear the strain in her voice. It made me want to run to my room. I finished washing the platters and I wiped down the counter. I was emptying soda cans and beer bottles into the sink and rinsing them for recycling when Lilly came into the kitchen.

"He thinks you're ignoring him," she said. "He says you've been snubbing him all night."

"It was a party, Lilly!" I said, mimicking my mother.

She breathed in. "Can you just come in and sit down with me for a little? Please?"

Francis was sitting at the far end of the sofa, his arms stretched out across the top of the cushions. He watched me cross the living room and sit in the chair over by the Christmas tree. He twirled his big glass in his hand. It was dead quiet for what felt like five minutes until my mother said, looking in her lap, "Francis says he remembers you playing hockey on Morrison Avenue. Do you remember that, dear?"

"Sure."

"I don't think he does," Francis said.

"Why don't people ever believe me when I tell them things?" I said, looking over my shoulder out the window into the dark.

"Okay, Sammy Sincere," Francis said, slurring his s's. "I have my gear in the trunk. Let's see your stuff."

"I think I'm about ready to hit the hay," I said.

"Yeah," Francis said in the back of his throat, "that's more like it."

"Jake, will you help me in the kitchen for a minute," Lilly said.

"I'm so much help tonight," I said, following her out of the living room.

"Do you think you could appease him just a little?" she whispered intensely. "So we can get through this?"

"Are you going to try to control *every*one, Lilly?" I asked. She lowered her eyes and I could see that I'd hurt her feelings, for the first time in a long time. She went back into the living room without saying another word.

"Francis," I said, probably too loudly, as I walked back into the living room, "let's play some hockey."

"That's subtle," Katie said under her breath as I passed her.

"Oh, another time," Francis said, looking at the Christmas tree. "I'm feeling my age all of a sudden."

"No, let's do it, man. I want to show you all the stuff I didn't forget."

He looked at me, trying to gauge how much I meant what I was saying. He decided that I really did want to play hockey, or he'd had too much to drink to really know. When he stood up, my mother's face changed, loosened. In her mind she was already up in her bedroom, sitting in bed, reading the paper.

"You too," he said, standing over Katie. She stood up and they walked ahead of me through the kitchen. Francis was a little unsteady, and with his arm across Katie's shoulders he looked like he was getting some help from her. But as they walked, Katie moved closer and closer in. Because she wanted to, it looked like. "You're a good girl," he said, and she seemed to forget that he reeked of that perfume of beer and whiskey, that he smelled the way I used to smell all the time, as she let him pull her in so close I couldn't see between them.

We stood out on the driveway waiting for Francis to get his gear out of his trunk. The driveway was flooded with light, and as Lilly and Katie talked I could see their breath in the cold.

"I bet he doesn't even remember we're out here," I said. "I bet he's in the bathroom blubbering to himself."

"No," Lilly said quietly, "that man is going to play hockey with you."

"He's *trashed*," I said. "We're lucky if he's passed out on the sofa and not in the fucking street. I don't want to have to carry *that*."

"When are you going to let up?" Katie said. "You've been so unbelievably mean."

I laughed and looked at Lilly, but she had her neutral face on.

I heard Francis crunching through the snow, and then he was coming around the side of the house, his arms loaded with equipment. He put his armful down and started tying a blanket between the two birch trees in the middle of the driveway. Then he put on his goalie pads. Everything: hockey pants over his pants, Lilly holding his arm as he got into them, shoulder pads, shin guards, gloves. When he was finally suited up and his goalie mask was down over his face—just holes in the white plastic for him to see and breathe —Lilly whispered, "God, that's creepy."

Even drunk, Francis was on, and I got only a few shots past him. Each time, I'd move up to the net, I'd let his heavy breathing, his anticipation, get to me and then I'd fire. He'd throw his body at the puck, and Lilly and Katie would cheer, regardless of who won the point.

"That's it?" Francis said when I gave the stick to Katie.

"I'm an old man, too," I said over my shoulder.

Katie got more shots past Francis than I had, but I could tell it was because he'd lost interest.

She ran up and down the driveway, doing figure eights, the puck tied up around her feet. She'd sweep up to the net and swear just before she shot.

"Okay, Jake," Francis said.

He let another one of Katie's shots in and she yelled, "Yes."

"Give the stick back to Jake," he said.

"Not yet," she said. She ran down to the bottom of the driveway and dropped the puck. Then she picked it up and dropped it even farther back, across the street on a neighbor's driveway.

"Give Jake the stick," Francis' voice boomed into the night.

"I don't want it," I said. "I'm done."

"Come on, Jake," he said.

"Yeah, come on, Jake," Katie said. "He's a legend." She threw her hands up over her head, the hockey stick pointing at the sky.

I just stood there beside Lilly.

"What's wrong with this picture?" Francis said, walking toward me. "You're still Canadian, right? Or did your mother take that away from you, too?" He lifted his mask and I could smell the booze again. "What-is-wrong-with-you?" he yelled.

When he didn't get an answer from me, he took the stick from Katie and pushed it into my hands. He walked away from me toward the net. In my imagination, I flipped the puck at his back—hard, so it knocked the wind out of him. But the longer I looked at him, as he readjusted his pads, as he squatted down to retie the blanket, the longer I watched his unprotected back, swollen, and crisscrossed by the elastic from his pads, tired and hunched over with unhappiness, the less I wanted to do that.

Dollar Movies

Bryan Charles

Bryan Charles was raised in Galesburg, Michigan. He is the author of three
books: There's a Road to Everywhere Except Where You Came From: A
Memoir *(Open City Books),* Grab on to Me Tightly as if I Knew the Way, *a*
novel, and Wowee Zowee, *a book about the band Pavement.*

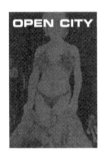

IT'S EARLY SENIOR YEAR, STILL PRETTY MUCH SUMMER,
a Saturday night. The Judy Lumpers have just finished a
set at Dick's Basement, the little club in Quincy, and I'm
sulking in the shadows, agonizing over the usual
botched chords and some of my more embarrassing
unreached vocal high notes, when a girl, a stranger
appearing from nowhere, tells me how much she likes
my band. Here's a first, I'm thinking. If you believe
mythology, or have read the biographies, every guy who picks up a guitar is only trying for the snapper. But really, groupie-fucking is the
province of the more decadent hard rock and hair bands, from Guns N'
Roses, say, all the way down to every aspiring burnout who plays
Peppers, the venue for shitty metal in Kalamazoo. Anyway, the girl introduces herself as Molly and says, "What's that one song, the one about,
like, the tattered tongue of an otter?"

"That's called 'Tongue.' But the line you're thinking is really 'the tender tongue of autumn heat.'"

"Oh," she says. "I like that one."

"Thanks," I say.

"Tongue" is okay, not one of our finest hours, the riff lifted almost
whole cloth from the Sonic Youth song, "Sister." Plus, I never believe anyone except Jake and Wheeler—the Judy Lumpers' bass player and drummer—who says they like our songs.

The only beverage Dick's sells is Faygo Red Pop, so Molly and I tip a
few and shoot the shit while the next band sets up. She goes to Quincy
High, the Gull Lake rival in matters of sport, and she loves the Doors.
She shows me a small tattoo on her ankle, the initials JDM, meaning
James Douglas Morrison.

"I got it last year. My parents don't know yet. This summer I covered it up with Clearasil and my Doc Martens."

"Then what's the point?"

"Well, just to know that Jim's here, that he's a part of me. Do you think that's corny?"

"No, not at all," I say. This is the heart-shaped erection at the center of my brain talking.

The band starts playing and it gets too loud to talk, so we go for a walk on the train tracks that run through Quincy, follow them past the edge of town, out into nothing, out where it's as though Molly and I are the only two people alive, wandering the Earth just because. A breeze rolls in off the cornfields all around us and the air goes from mild and a little muggy to cold and crisp. The temperature drops ten degrees in one second. I've never felt anything like it. Molly stops and crosses her arms. "Where'd that come from?"

"I don't know, but it feels good."

"Do you want to hug for a second, just to warm up?"

"Okay. But I was sweating at the show. A little warning," I tell her.

"That's all right."

I take a deep breath, put my arms around her. The silence that follows makes me self-conscious, so I say, "Like this?"

"Yeah," she says. Then, "Wow, you really do stink."

"I tried to tell you," I say, pulling away. Molly pulls me back.

"But it's not terrible. It smells like, what, like fried onions." She moves her head so she's looking up at me, the eyes saying, Do it, fool, but I can only stare dumbly at her mouth. I need clearance, a guarantee. To go in for a kiss and have the girl pull away is one of my most crippling fears.

"Can I kiss you?" I say.

She smiles and nods, the green light, and I'm grinning back, still as a fucking statue. Molly says, "Were you going to do it tonight or . . . ?"

"Yes, tonight." I lean in and we do it, we kiss. The styles are nice and soft, no forceful probing tongue. Her fingertips brush against my cheeks, my heart stutters, charges faster, like being shocked back to life on the operating table.

Five minutes later we're dry humping in the grass by the train tracks, and I'm picturing gruesome war photos, like piles of bodies in the Nazi death camps, like the Vietnam guy taking a bullet in the brain, to help contain the explosion forming below. When it gets really close, I stop humping and say, "Let's take a little break."

This works okay until we roll over and she's on top. Now I'm help-less, almost a spectator, watching her move against a backdrop of ice-chip stars, the big black sky, the universe expanding around us, her long brown hair falling across my lips, eyes, nose. And then it happens, what feels like every second of human existence charges out of me and into my underwear.

I stop moving again, too embarrassed to say why.

"Are we taking another little break?" she says.

Luckily, a train comes along, a speeding Amtrak, its horn blasting away the question, and I don't have to answer. I get so scared when it roars by that I jump up and sprint into the woods, tripping over a dead branch and falling on my face in the process. It's kind of nice down here among the dirt and the ancient leaves and I contemplate not answering when I hear Molly call my name. But she finds me, she looks down at me and says, "How could you be so afraid of something you knew was com-ing for miles?"

When I stand up she takes my hand.

For our first real date we rent *The Doors*, which Molly says she's seen at least ten times, four on video, six in the theater. She tells me it's the sex-iest movie ever made.

"There's something about Oliver Stone movies. They radiate sexi-ness. With Jim Morrison it's easy, because he's so fucking sexy, but even something like *Platoon* has erotic qualities."

"*Platoon*?" I say. "What are you talking about?"

"I'm talking about the part where Willem Dafoe dies. It's so tragic that it actually ends up being sexy, the way his body shudders when he gets shot. Very orgasmic. Plus there's a little glimpse of Johnny Depp during the village massacre scene."

I think of my anti-coming death fantasies and say, "What about *Born on the Fourth of July*?"

"I know it's not cool to like Tom Cruise, but I think he's really sexy, even in that. He's in a wheelchair, he's got a mustache, he's an alcoholic. But that part where he's screaming the word 'penis' at his mom. Look out."

"*Wall Street*?" I say.

"*Wall Street* is the least sexy Oliver Stone movie, if only because it stars Michael Douglas, who I've found repulsive since *Fatal Attraction*. God, his flat, flabby butt when they're in the kitchen."

Her house is small and her bedroom is between her parents' and little sister's rooms. The make-out options aren't great. There's the basement, but the walls and floors are paper thin and I haven't felt secure there since the time we heard her parents whispering through the vents about what do you think they're doing down there, why are they being so quiet?

So we go to the East-Towne 5, the dollar theatre in Kalamazoo, and we buy tickets to random movies, kissing and groping in the back row like desperate middle-schoolers, hardly glancing at whatever's on the screen. And it hits me at some point that this is where I want to be when the world ends, here with Molly in the dark, dust rising through the projector's beam, listening to some lame comedy or second-run blockbuster while our hands get sweaty from constant holding and I taste her lips, her Junior-Minted lips.

Times are so fine at the East-Towne, our secret haven, that I leave the movies insanely depressed. I cling, sit through every word of the credits to the copyright date, then stumble back into the world like a coma patient who wakes up wishing he'd stayed asleep, or better yet, slipped away forever. Then it's off to the Denny's on Sprinkle Road, for black coffee and french fries with guacamole, and no matter how long we sit there, Molly and I, free associating on caffeine highs, the end is always the same, a little kiss in the driveway, nothing heavy, and she's out the door of the car.

In my secret thoughts, I feel relief. I don't want the pressure of trying to be a top sexual performer, someone like my Uncle Bro, who when I was younger and he lived in our basement, said to me, "Vim, if you ever want a girl to fall in love with you, you better learn to eat a pussy so good it sings back 'The Star-Spangled Banner.'"

We're parked in Molly's driveway after seeing *What About Bob?* for the second time in three days and the goodnight kiss gets longer and longer until the windows fog and our seats are back. I put my hand on her belt buckle, thinking, hoping, she'll stop me, but she doesn't. I undo the buckle and the top button of her jeans.

Down goes the zipper.

"What if your parents are watching?" I whisper.

"They're not," she says.

I stop and clear a little porthole in the fog, look through it to the darkened windows of her house. "How do you know?"

"Because it's midnight, because they're sleeping."

"What about your sister?"

"She's eleven, she's asleep, now come here."

"I can't. I can't get on top of you, there's the gearshift there, I don't think my legs will fit."

"Just stop talking and everything will be fine."

I look at the house again, then back at Molly. I put my hand on her stomach, move it to the edge of her underwear, thinking, What now, will someone please fucking tell me what now?

Her eyes are closed. When I slip my hand under the elastic, she smiles. It's barely there, a Mona Lisa smile.

This is my left hand, my fretting hand. It can form seventh and ninth chords, the jazz chords, can make beautiful noise without me looking or thinking. But it's like there's a mannequin hand on the end of my arm now, some bloodless thing, as I feel, for the very first time, a girl's pubic hair and the dream underneath.

I press into the wetness and rub gently around and for a long minute, forever, nothing happens. Then Molly starts breathing faster. She squeezes the armrest on the passenger door. I watch her hand squeezing the armrest. I move my finger up a fraction of an inch and she gasps.

"Shit, sorry," I say. "Shit. Are you okay?"

She laughs and the sound of her laughter makes me want to pop a suicide capsule. "What? What's so funny?"

"Nothing," she says. "Shhh."

Her hand over mine, guiding me back into the wilderness. I'm concentrating so hard sweat drips into my eyebrows and a mild headache blooms and wild lightning flashes of the past and future ricochet around the inside of my skull. I imagine Molly's parents peering out at the car, feeling helpless and disappointed, imagine being asleep later in my bed and how I'll think of this moment ten, twenty, thirty years from now, imagine my father performing similar acts on my mother in the days before they realized they didn't love each other anymore, imagine almost everything except what's happening now.

Molly releases her grip on the armrest and I panic, try frantically to find whatever I'd found before. Nothing. Her breathing becomes more and more relaxed until it's like she's watching a filmstrip in science class. I pull my hand away, she zips and buttons her jeans. We both move our seats up. "Anyway," she says.

I start the car and turn on the defroster. "I'm sorry," I tell her.

She shifts toward me. "What for?"

"I don't know," I say after a few seconds.

"Sorry is something you shouldn't say unless you know why."

"What if you don't know why but you mean it anyway?"

"Then you've got some kind of a problem."

"Sorry," I say again.

In a single motion she kisses me on the side of the mouth and opens the door. "Call me tomorrow."

On the way home I sniff repeatedly at my finger. I roll down the window, stick my face out, and scream into the early October darkness. I put in an Afghan Whigs tape and sing along with their songs of sexual conquest, trying with all my heart to feel triumphant.

The next day, Saturday, Jake and I go to his brother's apartment in Kalamazoo and spend the afternoon sucking down a case of Old Milwaukee. I was already feeling blue about my lackluster sex abilities, and it only gets worse with a buzz. The more beers I have, the more every thought becomes a picture of Molly's disappointed face, or what I think her face would look like disappointed.

"What the fuck's your problem?" says Gary, Jake's brother, when he sees me sprawled on the living-room floor.

"It's chicks, man, the ladies."

"I know what you need, little soldier." He goes away and comes back holding two shot glasses of brown liquor. "Down the hatch."

After that I take a long walk and end up by Waldo Stadium, where the WMU Broncos play. It's a home-game day and I wander among the big crowds of tailgating students, feeling like something they vomited out of their happy faces.

There should be a pill for when you're with a girl and the lights go out. And I don't mean a contraceptive. I mean something that gives you knowledge of the tender places and dulls the fear.

Just as I'm thinking this, some guy yelling "Go Broncos!" shoves a cold Bud Light into my fist. I drink it down and the world looks stupider.

Back at the house I take the cordless phone into the bathroom and dial Molly's number. "Please," I say when I hear her beautiful voice, "give me one more shit. I mean, chance."

"Who is this?" she says.

I burp into the phone. "It's me, Vim Sweeney."

"Vim? Are you drunk or something?"

"That's right. Just like Jim Morrison, your favorite poet of the darkness." Silence. "I am a dark poet," I say.

"What does that mean?"

"It means I'm not afraid of death or dying," I tell her. "Do you hear me?"

"No. Not really. I'd kind of like to know what the hell you're talking about."

"I'm talking about can I come over?"

"I don't know. I guess so. I mean, my parents are here."

"So let them hear our passion through the vents. I'll just stop off first, at the place, and I'll get that box of rubbers."

She laughs uncertainly. "Vim, this is . . . you're being really weird."

"Ribbed, for her—I mean, your—pleasure," I say.

There's a long pause. I can hear the party noise below, can feel the music going into my feet. I step into the shower. "You should try and get some sleep or something," Molly says. Her voice sounds very far away. "Try and sober up. You're not driving are you?"

"Not yet, but I will be as soon as I get off the phone."

"Don't do that. Stay wherever you are and we can talk some other time."

"Do you love me?" I say. No answer. I slap the tile and ask again.

"Vim, I think I'm gonna go."

I sit all the way down in the tub to stop the spinning. "Great," I say.

"So I'll talk to you later."

"Great."

The line goes dead, the dial tone comes on. It's the loneliest sound I've ever heard in my life and I can't fucking stand it, so I press redial.

"Great," I say when she answers.

"Now you're annoying me," Molly says. "Seriously."

"I lied before," I say.

"About what?"

"I don't really like your tattoo."

"Bye, Vim." She hangs up again.

I pass out for a while, until Gary kicks in the door. "There you are, little soldier," he says over the sound of his piss splashing.

"Where have you been?" Jake says downstairs. "What are you doing?"

"I'm making mistakes. I think Molly and I just broke up."

"Molly? Wow. I didn't even know you were going out," he says.

"We are. We were." I feel like I've been sleeping in that bathtub all night, but when I look at the clock I see it's barely ten.

An hour or so later, somewhat sober after a few cans of Jolt, I get in my car and drive to Meijer's Thrifty Acres, where I pick out a single red rose, the best one I can find, from a cooler in the House and Garden department. Then I take the long way home, Kings Highway, stop off first in Quincy. I circle Molly's block a few times and finally park down the street. There's a long row of pines leading up to her house and I sneak through its shadow, feeling like Ted Bundy, until I'm almost in the yard. All the lights are off except the blue TV glow in the living room. I stand there a long time, staring at the spot where Molly and I parked last night, thinking of the way she breathed during that special little minute when I'd touched her right.

My plan was to knock on her window and give her the rose, an old-school romantic gesture, something I've never tried before, something real, but it's crumbling inside me. All my fake bravery seeps out into the night. The mailbox is just right there, at the edge of the grass. I sprint over and open it, gently lay down the rose, and run back to my car.

Sunday comes and goes. Molly doesn't call and I don't call her. I'm in the middle of failing a geometry test on Monday when I decide to stop by her house after school. I drive around the block again, like last time, going crazy, just like last time. I stand alone on the porch for what seems like an hour. It's cool outside, and very bright, my favorite time of year. I ring the doorbell. Molly answers, but she steps out rather than invite me in.

"There you are," I say. Where else would she be? Her tight, green-and-white striped sweater gives me a little charge, makes me long for the old times of the East-Towne 5, which were just three days ago. I tell her I'm sorry and she rolls her eyes.

"Vim, you say that about everything."

"I do, you're right, but at least now I know why I'm saying it."

"Well, that's just great," she says. "Great, great, great."

"See, I can accept that. I'm trying to be mature." The wind picks up, just like it did in the beginning. "Are we broken up?" I say.

"I believe we are." It hurts me, ruins me, to hear this, but I can't show it. I can't show anything. None of this would have happened if we'd never left the movies, if we'd died there, like I'd wanted to.

"Did you at least get my rose?" I ask her.

"What rose? What are you talking about?"

"I put a rose in your mailbox."

"When?"

"The other night. Saturday. After I called you."

She glances behind me, looking confused. "The mail doesn't come on Sundays."

"That's true."

"And I don't think anyone got it today."

"Maybe you should get it now."

Together we walk to the mailbox. Molly pulls out a thick stack of mail. As she does this, my crushed, dead rose falls to the pavement at her feet. I pick it up and hold it in the air and say, with the sun blinding me and my hand and that stupid rose both shaking, I say, "For you."

Moroccan Letters

Alfred Chester

Alfred Chester (1928–1971) was a Brooklyn-born novelist and literary critic. His most well-known works include Exquisite Corpse, *a novel, and* Behold Goliath, *a story collection. His later works were published posthumously in the collection* Looking for Genet.

Phase 1: The Seduction

 *JANE BOWLES LIKED TO CALL HER HUSBAND, PAUL, A spider. The spider is a dry creature, and she was referring to the spider's thirst to lure its prey into his net and drain its fluids. She herself suffered that fate.*

Bowles met Alfred Chester at a dinner party in New York in the winter of 1962–63 and set out to attract him to Tangier. Brilliant and self-willed like Jane Bowles, Alfred Chester was free in a way a reserved WASP like Bowles could only wonder at. And perhaps Bowles, in an unproductive period during the difficult years coping with his wife's breakdowns, thought Chester could help him break out of his shell.

On his part, Chester was fascinated by the famous writer, author of "Pages from Cold Point," which had held our generation in thrall when it appeared in a New Directions Annual in 1950. When Bowles dangled Morocco before him, with all its exotic attractions, Chester was tempted, but almost immediately fled to Mexico with his lover Extro. The correspondence with Bowles, who had returned to Morocco, reveals the ambivalence of Chester's feelings about Bowles, for he immediately sensed the danger of putting himself in the power of the older writer.

But Chester, who had gained sudden prominence on the New York literary scene as a critic, was even more frightened of what this success would mean to his creative life. Much as he was afraid of any net Bowles might be weaving for him, he saw himself being devoured by the literary scene before he had "arrived" as a writer. Morocco offered an inexpensive escape, the possibilities of a less-complicated sex life, and an oriental culture congenial to his nature.

The letters begin in Veracruz, where Chester is full of complaints, espe-
cially about his hippie boyfriend, whom he uses as an excuse for not com-
ing directly to Tangier. One can sense, in the unpublished other half of the
correspondence, Bowles's first urging Chester to come, then offering him his
house, and, unheard of for the tight-fisted Bowles, money.

—Edward Field

To Paul Bowles
Jan. 31, 1963, Veracruz, Mexico

Dear Paul:

I began a letter to you soon after you left [New York for Morocco],
and am glad now I didn't finish it. I was pretty obsessed [with Extro] at
the time, which is the reason you now find me writing from Veracruz
instead of Tangier, and succumbed to his idea of immediate departure. I
don't like it here. It is hot and humid like New York in August. We spent
two weeks driving up and down the coast (he has to be near the water
for fishing) from Tuxpan to the Yucatan looking for the kind of thing
you find on the Mediterranean, an old cheap house. But nothing, so we
came back to Veracruz and have taken this rather repulsive bungalow
over from a couple of beatniks who look like Jesus Christ and sound like
drugstore cowboys—"Been out on de fuckin street all night lookin to
make a score" or "to score," whatever is the right fuckin grammar. It is a
little moderny tootsy house attached on both sides to identical structures. They called us *maricones* in the little Zocalo last night. Generally
ideal. All I want to do now is write like mad and make enough money to
get to Morocco before it gets much hotter. Though, as I said to Extro
(who is mad for the weather), even if the heat is unendurable we have
our love to keep us cold, which will give you an idea of how things are
going.

My Burroughs review has brought in a gigantic correspondence,
including requests from *Horizon* and the *American Scholar* to write for
them. I'm saying yes to everybody for the money. And I'm going to finish my idiotic novel real fast, not only for money, but also so as not to
have to pay attention to the balmy tropics and my handsome lover, both
of which (whom) irritate the shit out of me. I've asked *Commentary* to
send you tearsheets of the reviews I've done for them, not only because
I want you to read them, but because I'm applying for a Guggenheim to

do a book of essays and would like you to be one of my references. If it is okay with you.

I don't know when was the last time you were in Mexico. I was here in 1950, just before I went to Europe. It is different, and I like it even less than I did the first time. I found only one place that I really like and that's a town up in the mountains halfway between here and Tuxpan. The air and light were like Ibiza, and the people had a dignity that no one but the poorest, furthest out peasants have here. I suppose you know Veracruz, to which: Ugh!

We've been living and screwing in and around the car now for nearly a month, and our bodies have brought endless festivities to hungry mosquitoes, fleas, ticks, and other nameless, winged or unwinged things. I am scabby and itchy and bloody and cranky.

I hope you'll write to me, and more I hope we see each other soon again.

—Greetings from Alfred

To Paul Bowles
March 19, 1963—181 Sullivan St., NYC

Dear Paul:

Je suis de retour et tout seul! Sic transit gloria Extri. We broke up in Veracruz and I left before anyone could change his mind and drove back to New York in four days. Oh it is good to be home. I am a little lonely and spent the day painting the bedroom to get all signs of love affair off the walls. I've nailed his panties to the wall like a trophy, but not in the bedroom. *Eh bien, on recommence.* If I get my Gug or some other money I'll come to Tangier. Meanwhile, I've returned to New York and find myself, if not famous, heavily sought after. Publishers are chasing me. I'm having lunch with Epstein of Random and Haydn of Atheneum this week. But have had special delivery letters and pleas from Knopf, Harpers, and discovered that a story of mine has been included in Faber's anthology of American stories with illustrious names like Capote, K.A. Porter, Saul Bellow, Jean Stafford, etc. Which reminds me. I stopped in at the 8th St. Bookstore yesterday and lo and behold you and I linked in the *Transatlantic Review*, to my great joy. If you correspond with McCrindle you probably knew about this. As I don't, I don't even rate a complimentary copy . . . Next day. Bob Silvers is in the hospital with a mysterious disease that has a name but no explanation: sarcoid. Susan [Sontag] and I are going up to see him this afternoon. You will remember them both (and me) from that evening at Ann Morrisett's . . . I am envious of Marc Schleiffer being sent all over the place. Lasky of *Encounter* wrote and asked me to write something for them and I said (this was in Veracruz), Why don't you send me to Cuba?, and then I never heard from him again. Also I asked him for money. It is a bad habit I have of always needing money, and worse of always letting editors know I do. I think they think it makes me undesirable . . . didn't like Veracruz much. The week of carnival it was a little more interesting because good-looking people descended like gods and also a lot of rich fat Germans who kept giving Extro the eye and getting me nervous. The pot was very strong and I kept falling asleep everytime I smoked it, so it seemed pointless. The last time I fell asleep on it, when I awoke *mon amour avait disparu*. If I'd stayed another day I could have eaten the magic mushrooms, but my grief had killed my appetite. Yes, the cantinas are dull as hell, and the people are not nice. The faggots are just like faggots everywhere, dreary. Mostly I was with beatniks, whom I have learned to loathe, for any number of reasons, but mainly because they are backbiting little bitches. Never mind their Christ uniforms, they all seem to be closet queens and were full of little envies and jealousies about my *menage*. It was disgusting. I accused one of trying to play the other woman and he nearly strangled me on my directness. *Ca se fait pas!* They are like a bunch of Victorian ladies with all their elaborate conventions of what is and isn't done. Ugh! Are you going to get the Formentor prize or something? That would be nice . . . I've just done an article on Albee; it's called "A Woolf in Chic Clothing." Comes out first of April in *Commentary*, and if you would be interested I'll send it. My Miller thing in *Partisan* has been a great success, Phillips tells me (everyone has been telling him so at cocktail parties), and he asked me for anything for the next issue. I'm trying to sell him on a gorgeous story about two men called "From the Phoenix to the Unnamable Impossibly Beautiful Wild Bird." But he will be afraid of it without doubt. I'm also booked for articles on Salinger and Genet, and a review of Rechy whom I deplore. Before I retire from contemporary criticism I want to do an essay on Durrell who is wonderful even if he is fake. I'll review something of yours for the *Tribune* and make it sell a million copies. And also Edward's poems. But the sad thing about all this is that I really can't write a novel. I've been working on one, as you know, and it bores me. Such a long thing to do, and I just don't believe in such long things.

Stories yes. Or plays yes yes. But all these publishers get on my back and scream about novels . . . I just interrupted this letter to read the chapter I wrote in Veracruz and it isn't bad. Perhaps I will go back to it now . . . Did you see Auden's thing on Wilde in *The New Yorker*. Very daring. They seem to have gone mad what with Baldwin's thing and now this. I'm trying to read those Eichmann pieces but they are so dreary . . . It is so strange how full my life gets whenever I am at my emptiest like now. I don't want to live alone ever again. I did it for three years, except for this or that week, and these past five months with Extro, and it is intolerable, but I want someone nice who doesn't need pampering; and can look after my apartment and me and the dogs. Like a servant one screws. The kind of mate men used to have before the opposite sex disappeared with the suffragette movement. Also I think I want a son . . . Our first days in Veracruz we stayed in a hotel called the Campoamor. Isn't that your street? We got ticks, crabs and everything else. Susan is here. So I close with all affectionate greetings.

—Alfred

To Paul Bowles
April 2, 1963—181 Sullivan St, NYC

Dear Paul:

In the same post as yours was a letter from the Gug saying no, so that is that, or anyway for the moment since Jason Epstein has apparently fallen in love with me and thinks I am next on the literary hit parade. I'm trying to induce him to give me a three-book contract and it is more likely than unlikely at the moment. It would be for the stories, this novel (whatever and if it turns out to be) and a collection of literary criticism. It is pretty clear that I'm in a pretty strong position nowadays. Phillips of *Partisan* invited me to a small party of made-its the other night, and everyone including Robert Lowell said, Oh I've heard so much about you. Phillips has also asked me to do a regular theater chronicle for *Partisan*, squeezing into Mary McCarthy's old girdle (which I don't really need, having lost twenty pounds in Veracruz), and I've agreed at least for one issue because he is sending me tickets to all the plays and that will be fun. If my agent can clear a thousand for me on the Random House deal— which may be difficult considering the amount of broken and unpaid contracts I am notorious for having behind me—I shall come to Tangier.

Hooray! It is pretty clear that I can earn reasonable money for these reviews. Enough to keep myself on in any case . . . It took three weeks to miss Extro and then I did something awful, I mean both missed him something awful and did something awful. I wrote and asked him to come back. I don't know whether he will or not. It will depend on whether he has missed me enough to have forgotten that every day for five or six months he hated himself for having succumbed to his homosexuality. I hate living alone and I am really hopeless at finding people unless they throw themselves at me, which is rare. Actually I'm not living alone. Irene [Fornes] is here most of the time, but it isn't the same . . . I had a gigantic fight with Susan over a piece of chicken the other day and all the TRUTH came out. I have hated her for four years. Susan is going to be terribly famous very soon because Roger Strauss, her publisher, is mad about her and is going to make a big thing of her very boring novel . . . I don't think chutzpah is characteristic of beatniks so much as of young people in general nowadays. Oddly enough, the Beats are rather frightened of me usually, maybe because I am so much of a bum myself and am so obviously disapproving of them. We took a couple down from Mexico City to Veracruz in the car and I said not a word for most of the whole eight hours, partly because my stomach was sick but mainly because my heart was sick of them. The dominant one who looked like a pudgy Jesus Christ used the word "fuckin" to modify nearly every one of his phrases and nouns. Finally I asked him why he did it, and while he was dazed by the fact that I evidently didn't find this very *homme revolte*, I added that it was a very rah-rah American boy thing to do. He was utterly humiliated and said he seldom used the word but had smoked too much pot that morning and it brought it on. I usually just accuse them of being middle class when they start getting clever. They are too dumb to question, and it annihilates them. If any of them ever challenge me on why I call them middle class, I don't know what I'll say. But I'm a quick thinker . . . I would answer that letter you got with a postcard saying: Sorry, but I love another. I don't understand what he means by the luxuriousness—sex? money?—of your living, and that bit about congruence of those (who?) who have . . . A man was murdered around the corner on Bleecker St. the other day. He owned the Café Raffio and I knew him vaguely because he used to transport Canadian beatniks over the border during Extro's regime *chez moi*, and I suspected him of drug traffic, and was not surprised to learn he was shot dead in the street. But it turned out an old Italian man who spoke no English murdered him because he had dispossessed him from his little apartment in order to enlarge the coffee shop. The street looked like a Hollywood movie for an hour or so, with the body lying in front of the liquor store and barricades and police and reporters everywhere . . . Someone told me that Girodias has reissued my pornographic novel [*Chariot of Flesh*] and hasn't paid me a cent or told me about it the wretch . . . Oh oh, I have an unsolicited compliment for you from a friend who read *The Sheltering Sky* not too long ago, but I suddenly don't feel like quoting it because I myself hate compliments for old work . . . I have been living on Dexamils and doing with little sleep and less food for a week while writing a review of Natalie Sarraute's essays. I put her down like mad for justifying dullness. I sent it off today and though I am on the edge of collapse, the machine is still running and I simply can't just rest or go for a walk in the park or see a movie or such. Spring, my friends have been telling me over the telephone, has arrived. A week ago at that, and I still have my sweaters on, the heaters burning and the windows shut. The buildings inspector has just arrived with my landlord as two of my ceilings collapsed. They've just gone up on the roof and will be duly shocked and horrified by all the dogshit. Ah yes. Ah yes. You say nothing of your friend. *J'espere que tout va bien quand meme* . . . I'll send the *New Yorker* tearsheets on to you separately. *A Life Full of Holes* is such a beautiful title, and so exact. Greetings and all good things to you.

—Alfred

To Edward Field
June 17,1963—181 Sullivan St., NYC

My last hours on Sullivan St. Nothing left anywhere but a pair of suitcases, one bookcase (for Muriel) and a single straight chair (for Harriet). I have to be out by two p.m. I am very sad, sadder still because Extro went back last night. Four days and three nights together. We went to East Hampton for Saturday and Sunday. I guess I love him. And I guess also he wants to come back. What am I to say when he says to me that I was bad for him because he was living my life and none of his own. How many times have I heard that complaint before? Even recently from Dennis Selby. I told Extro if he were a writer it wouldn't matter and he agreed. The upshot was that we agreed to try again. I told him to come to Morocco in September. I don't know why I didn't ask him to come with me now, right away. Partly out of pride because everyone here thought I surely would.

Partly for his pride—even more so for his pride—so that he could go back to his friends without having given up at my whistling.

He said you were right about the airplane ticket.

Also I didn't ask him to come now because I thought I ought to give myself a chance. I don't know if this is true.

Anyhow, I'm feeling sad as hell because I love having him around and I love looking at him and I love touching him. He looked more beautiful than he ever had before. His face is sharper and he is plumper. (Still skinny, really.) And he has had no one more or less in Ottawa. He was terribly hungry for sex. I don't understand it. And he admitted a boy and a girl up in Ottawa are mad for him. I guess he does want a man really, me.

So I'm sailing Friday. I'd rather have gone back to Canada with him and waited until we could have passage together. But I guess a man has to act like a man. He was surprised at the end when I told him I had missed him and would go on missing him. He said he thought people my age were mainly out of the circle. I said Paul Bowles had told me it happened at forty.

And you are thirty-nine.

He's the only really nice thing that's happened to me in four lousy years in this country. I'm sitting here burning the bed linen with the lousy tears rolling down my face.

I hope like mad you'll both be there at Gibraltar on the twenty-ninth. I wish you were here right now so you could hug me and kiss me on the forehead.

Your review came out yesterday but I forgot to buy it. But I'll bring it to you.

I kiss you both.

—Love from Alfred

Later. Feeling better about leaving the apartment. Feeling good about going to Morocco. Feeling happily anxious and hopeful that Extro is in my future.

To: Harriet Sohmers (Zwerling) July (?) 12(?), 1963
Postcard from Asilah, Morocco

Love it here. Am already married. Big funny thing. Paul dreary and unmiserable. My boy is called Driss, twenty, captain of fishing boat, does everything for me. It worked with the girl [on the ship], and she fell in love, but I guess it isn't for me. I am happy. I am happy. The town is beautiful. The weather is gorgeous. It is cheap. I've nothing more to say on a postcard, *que je t'aime et que tu me manque, et je veux que tu vienne.*

Write xxx A.

To Edward Field
July 11, 1963— B.P. 14, Asilah, Morocco

Edward dyeli—My Edward

I'm here in my ratty little house surrounded by flies and dogs and noises from the street. And I'm tired because I bought a straw mattress to sleep on and it is hard. Driss is all aches and pains from it. I think I'm married to him, but I'm not sure. And I'm too tired and too lazy to think about it. There is one other boy who is courting me, El Hajmi (or something like that), who is gorgeous but unbelievably boring. He banged on the door for hours last night while D. and I were fucking and I think D. has gone off to beat the shit out of him. I feel like Carmen.

It is a relief to be out of Paul's clutches. I felt more and more like a prisoner, especially because he made all sorts of shenanigans so that I couldn't be alone with D. He is an old queen vintage Edwin Denby and I think that his brain has melted from kif. I haven't been smoking much. Driss brought me some mazhoun (hash fudge) the other night and I got higher than ever before. Dreams and hallucinations. Paranoia for a moment when I thought it was poison and that he'd fed it to me to make me paralyzed and impotent. Paul really wants to own me; he is so used to owning people and things here. He keeps saying "they" about the Moroccans, even when he means "he." Like, Larbi [houseman of Bowles] says something and Paul delivers a comment on "they" to me. He is incapable of a conversation. To tell the truth I loathe him. When he says "they" I always feel like vomiting and also when he says anything or when I get a whiff of his sweat or see his flesh. It repels me. He seems so unclean compared to the Moslems. Driss, like Larbi, washes himself five times a day. He is lovely in bed; all the hair on his body is shaved. "They" all do that according to Paul. And you are wrong, "they" have big cocks like the Algerians. We seem to make love more or less continually and he is sensual like a cat and affectionate and won't let me out of his arms all night. It is lovely except he wants to do all the fucking, but I think he will come around because I know he likes it and probably just wants to tell people he fucks me. I took him to Tangier last night, just to get away from Paul really. It was our first time out. And he walked me past every cafe or crowd of boys in Asilah before going to the bus, pushing me around and strutting with his thumbs in his belt, swaggering I mean. (It was ridiculous because he is a pussycat when we're alone and he just dreams.) I felt he was informing the competition that they'd better keep out or off. He brags about being a great drinker etc., but he felt sick on one sip of my martini last night and ordered a Coke for himself. He is really just a baby, twenty years old. But he's captain of his fishing boat, and was a carpenter's apprentice for ten years. It is so nice. He holds my hand in the street and keeps his thigh against mine when we sit together. I'm not paying him in case you're interested. He wants to move in on a permanent basis in two weeks when the fishing season ends and keep house for me. Paul says "they" feel like Moslem women when they go to live with a foreigner. They expect to be taken care of completely and in exchange they take care of you completely. It seems to be true, so far. Shopping in Asilah is lot cheaper when I go with Driss than when I go vith Larbi.

I love Larbi. I love him. Now that I've told him I'm a Jew (and also circumcized) he isn't so worried about me and thinks I can probably take care of myself. Before that he thought I was a helpless imbecile like Paul. Oh, *mon dieu, que j'ai des histoire a te raconter!* About Phedre and everything.

We sat with Ted Joans last night and met the *Newsweek* reporter. He is doing a story on Tangier. I was out when the *Esquire* photographer came to Paul's the other day.

Night. If I wasn't sure if I was married this morning, there is no doubt in my mind anymore nor for that matter in the minds of anyone in town. My house is suddenly furnished and Driss is bringing over a double bed tomorrow as a present. El Hajmi it now appears is working for Driss. In any case, he is back and forth on errands. Driss is cooking supper. We've just spent a couple of hours at the beach café where he showed me off again and made it clear to everyone that we were sleeping together. I'm really in a state of shock. He is working out a budget for us $100 a month. Even Arthur never got me this married this fast or thoroughly. I feel by tomorrow he'll have me wearing a laundry bag and a veil across my face. He says he knows that one day I will be able to afford radios and tape recorders like Paul and a big house and he is content to wait. I know I'm going to wake up any minute and find it was all a dream. In the middle of the room is a tea tray with a pot of mint and three glasses (El Hamji is invited to dinner) and a little disgusting plastic sugar bowl, which delights Driss. Paul is stunned more than I am, I think. He admitted the Moroccans hate going to bed with him and he has to pay more and more to keep them. Can this be true? He said he hadn't spent a whole night with one in thirty years.

El Hamji is back. He looks a movie star version of Julie Perlmutter, only sexy. But boring. D. has just announced dinner.

Love to you both, from your captured (and delighted)
—Alfred

Next morning. Friday.

I'm so fascinated with my new life that I can't imagine you wouldn't be. So I've opened the envelope to continue the letter. I am home alone. Driss will be on his boat until four. He didn't sleep here because of the fucking and the mattress; I mean he got up too late yesterday and missed his boat. Anyway he gave me a lecture in French (so El Hamji wouldn't understand)—and you would be surprised at how much he could say with his twenty or thirty word vocabulary. The point of the lecture was that I musn't appear in public with other boys because then people would talk about me the way they do about the Englishman (who by the way is running a bordello right here in that big house of his). Only with him.

El Hajmi is supposed (D.'s orders) to come and take me and Columbine to the vet's this morning, but I'm going to leave before he comes because I'm beginning to have the feeling that I can't do anything for myself. I'll soon become a dried out old Dr. Schweitzer like Paul. (You were right about him. He never gets fucked.) Columbine bit a little girl the other day. Quite badly, but I don't blame her a bit. The kids bothered the dogs every minute. Now they keep well away. The police came very apologetically. The neighborhood (the whole medina according to Paul) was in an uproar and they wanted to ask the government to throw all the Nisranes (Nazarenes) out of Asilah: me, Paul, the Englishman, and two French queens who teach school. But the police assured me it was all right and just to bring my papers to the medico. That was four days ago, but I haven't been able to find the medico, though Larbi took me there the first time.

I don't feel at all like I'm having a love affair. I'm just married, which is what I wanted and I'm glad. I can't remember Extro. I can't remember anyone really. Even you are a little vague. Maybe Driss fed me a donkey's ear. Larbi has warned me against black magic.

Later still. There's something odd about the tone of this letter. It doesn't sound like there's any me in it. There isn't any me now but I don't mind. A little I do. There is no one thing around to establish my past. Even the dogs seem vague to me. I dreamt Skoura was hit by a car and was bleeding to death in my arms; she was growing grayer but no blood was evident. I woke up thinking I am no one. I am with Dris (he spells it with one *s*) and Hajmi (he spells it this way) and Asilah. Then I thought of all the people in New York looking at each other and being inane and telling each other who they were.

I am not happy or exalted. My cup runneth over and all I can do is sit and look at it. I obviously have to get to work if I intend to support my wife. He promised me a good table this evening.

He just came by for an hour in his fishing clothes to see how I was doing and wanting to cook lunch for me. He says he will find a big house with a kitchen and a toilet for the same amount of money or less, though not on the sea. I said all right because with the two of us here and the dogs we can hardly move around.

Poor Paul. He is pathetic.

Larbi says love affairs between Christians and Moslems are wars, but he doesn't doubt I can win this one since I'm a Jew. It is like my idea of a love affair I guess. The power struggle and all. Perhaps Larbi means I will end up Dris's slave rather than he mine. Though I am, of course, since I do just what he says and I've become almost helpless without him. I couldn't buy Nescafé and light the stove this morning but had to go to a café and a few days ago I bought cloth for sheets and had it cut and sewn all by myself because Larbi was so useless. He's useless because Paul is full of money and Larbi never takes the trouble to haggle. I don't think he cheats. But it is a fact that on large sums the merchant pays 10 percent to the person who brings the client. On the way back from Tangier in the cab the other night Dris gave me his 10 percent of the fare.

I think he is a good boy. I hadn't thought this before. I didn't trust him at all, mainly because of Paul. But then I hadn't entrusted with anything much yet.

Do you want to come back? I will get Dris to find you a good house or if you would live with us, one great huge house. I wouldn't even mind if you each took a turn with him. Now I think of it, I wonder why I don't mind. He'd mind if I did. I think he is probably used to being thrown over. It's so nice not to have to worry for a change. When he isn't around I feel almost as good as when he is around. I mean about him. I mean there doesn't seem to be anything to suffer about.

Will you come back?

—Love, Alfred

I know about a dozen words in Moghrebi and can conjugate "to have"—*andi, andek, andu,* etc.

Next morning. Saturday. Paul brought your letter back from Tangier. He says he never knew anyone who dared throw himself into Moroccan life as fast as I have. Have I done this?

I asked Dris if it was possible he could be as good as he seemed and he said he was. He asked me to be faithful and said he would be.

I'm going to cook supper tonight and attempt to recover my wits today. Already I made tea for myself this morning. Paul and Larbi don't sleep together. They used to for a little while years ago. Will you ask Gait if she will display some of Larbi's jewelry? His book is being published in France. What are you going to do in ridiculous Paris. Dris brought me two pieces of mazhoun as a present yesterday. I wish I could send you one (enough for two) so you could have lovely dreams about me.

I could easily be very happy now, and could love Dris except I am afraid out of pride I think.

Note on envelope: Will you save this letter? It occurs to me I might want to remember what I first felt like. And I can't keep a journal.—xxx

Yes you are right. P. doesn't write anymore.

Epilogue

Almost immediately after this engagement with Paradise, problems arise, and the letters during the next two and a half years relate in full detail Chester's stormy love affair with Dris, the ins and outs of his relations with Paul and Jane, his involvement with Moroccan life as well as with the hippie/beatnik expatriate community. Especially fascinating are his reports of unBowles-like behavior, as the reserved Paul experimented, briefly, with throwing Chester-like tantrums.

It was the high point of Alfred Chester's life. But, perhaps as a result of heavy drug use, Chester suffered several crackups, became increasingly

unstable, especially after a visit by the newly famous Susan Sontag, and was expelled by the Moroccan government in December 1965. From then on his life was madness, wandering from country to country looking for a home, and in 1971, he met his death in Jerusalem, where he had tried to settle down.

—Edward Field

Girl Games

Caitlin O'Connor Creevy

Caitlin O'Connor Creevy lives in Los Angeles and is completing her first novel,
Bad Dad.

I HAVE AN AMPLE RUMP AND LARGE BREASTS, AND MY
hair is red and long and wavy. I am a sexy girl. My face is
a pretty Irish face; when it is made up, it becomes beautiful to strangers—my green eyes, when delicately lined
with black, and gently smudged with gray, have been
called "smoldering"; my cheekbones, brushed with the
slightest wisp of blush—"defined"; my lips, when coated
with a soft mauve, and perhaps, at night, an almost
imperceptible cherry glaze, are indefatigably "kissable." Sometimes, after I
prepare my face, I must stay with the mirror for a little while longer,
because I look so hot I want to touch my boobs and do it with myself.

When I was six, living in a small house in the suburbs of Chicago, I locked
my bedroom door, took all my clothes off, and pretended I was posing for
Oui magazine. I lay on my side propped up by one arm, facing the make-
believe camera, closed my eyes, and arched my back. Then I lay down on
my bed (the "camera" would be above me) and spread my legs—very
slowly, just the action of spreading them was rushing me, making my six-
year-old vagina swell. Then I would matter-of-factly open my small, innocent vagina with my fingers, so that the "camera" could get a close-up.

After my imagination sensed the satisfaction of the invisible photographer, my mind raced ahead to a vision of a forest. I was walking alone,
dark shadows making scary shapes all around, when a strong man came
out of the trees and slammed me to the ground. He pinned me while I
kicked, covered my mouth while I screamed, and pressed my chest to the
ground. He brushed his cheek against my shoulders. His hands were big.
His face was very handsome, and his muscles were strange. He touched my
hair as if he were a curious animal. I was becoming excited, but I snapped
out of it and tried to escape. I wrangled as hard as I could from beneath

his massive body, but, ultimately, he overpowered me. At that point, I put my tiny finger inside my vagina and almost fell off the bed.

Nobody ever tried to rape me. I didn't have weird uncles or a weird dad or stepdad or plumber or violin teacher. I was a nymph developing my sexuality, and I had just seen a pornographic magazine. Pornography had never been in our house before; someone had probably given it to my dad as a gag gift, and he held on to it for a while, in spite of himself. Maybe he actually bought it, for chrissake, I don't know. But who cares. I was six and saw a porno. I don't believe my reaction was cause for psychological alarm. I was a dramatic child.

More than anything else in the world, I wanted to be pregnant. At that time, I didn't understand that I had about 400,000 eggs in my ovaries, and that I needed one to ripen, ripen like a mischievous drupe. I needed cells to multiply around my egg to form a follicle. Then for that follicle-wolli-cle to push its way to the surface of the ovary-bovary. Burst. And release the egg. Poof. Ovulation. Then off to the Fallopian. I needed just one sperm out of a jerk-off's 300,000,000—just one to enter my special place, wriggle through the uterus, into the F-tube. Bang. Fertilization. I didn't know that that was what I wanted. I simply always wanted to be pregnant.

Early on, I took steps toward realizing my goal. At age eight I founded the S.E.X. club. My best friends were my cousins Millie and Bridgette, and I roped them into membership. I was poor and they were rich, but I was oldest and that was the only thing that mattered then. We stole a dusty bottle of rum from the bar in the basement of my grandparents' mansion and sneaked it to the bushes for our inaugural meeting. The rules were:

1) Take a swig of rum.

We passed the bottle between us, none of us having any idea how much it would kill our virgin tongues and throats. But the nubile triumvirate survived the upsetting swig and I soon announced the next phase of S.E.X. hazing.

2) Swear.

This eliminated Millie. She refused.

"Bitch," said Bridgette.

"Asshole," I said.

It was a pretty July day in "Chicagoland," as they say on the radio, maybe even a little too warm; and as Millie dug a hole with a stick and Bridgette looked skeptical, I announced the final test.

3) Run around the yard (landscaped in the Naturalist style) surrounding my grandparents' house, number fourteen, the grandest lot on a very

private drive that was regularly trafficked by service vans of a great variety of service providers—duct cleaners, personal car washers, drapery launderers—anything that extracted dirt for money; and observed by discriminating neighbors walking "Barky," their emotional sponge; and, perhaps most threatening of all, tromped daily by Aunt Snowy, who would soon come out to suntan with a Tab on ice.

Run around the yard—naked.

This eliminated Bridgette. I stripped as B & M became increasingly nervous and giggly. Then I took my thrilling jog—proud and scared—around number fourteen. Only the teenage daughter from number eight drove by, and at that point I was a hair's breadth away from the waterfall, barely visible from the road; I didn't even see the bouncy neighbor pass, but I could hear Millie scream, and was informed about it after I came around the bend, breathless, at that point having experienced dread, power, and orgasm.

I fell into the bushes, my safety. The bushes formed a walled fortress around the property, about six feet high, and inside them was our little forest.

"Oh my God. Oh my God. Jeannie, Jeannie, that girl Jeannie drove by," Millie sputtered.

"I cannot believe you just did that, you are so queer," Bridgette went on, half-laughing, shocked.

"Cover me up! Cover me up!" I said, and the two of them, eight and seven, huddled over me like Chinese wise men. After I had dressed, we loped around the bushes assessing the damage. Did we get away with it? Yes.

Oh, like all kids, we played fishy games—like the spanking game, where Millie pretended she was the mom and I was the bad girl, in which she spanked my bare bottom until it was burning red, then put toothpaste on as a salve. But all in all, childhood was a happy time.

As I got older, I didn't see Bridgette and Millie as much; they were at Ford and I was at Locke, both posh private schools in the city. Ironically, I, the broke kid of the broken branch of the family, was going to the even snobbier school, tuition bills being paid by my dead grandparents, guiding the course of my life from beneath the grass. I couldn't complain. No, I could not complain.

Things in high school weren't as bad as they could have been, although it was strange being the only one in my class who experienced house-shame and difficult assembling deceptive costumes day after day. I did have my best friend, Ann, though, the perfect partner in crime—shockingly beautiful, just shy of six feet, Ann was something of a stoner, but as a Communist puppeteer, she had a duty to get high. Ann has always struggled with the fact that with the development of a slight eating disorder and a smidge of discipline, she could have had a successful modeling career.

Ann and I met our freshman year. We both smoked. After a few rendezvous on the stairs, she started talking. I thought she was a big liar. She told me she was having a relationship with her friend's dad. She said he "looked at her" and she "looked at him." I don't know, maybe it was true. At that point I thought she was weird. Weird for screwing around with people's dads or weird for lying. Our first time alone in the world together, we went to the corner store to get some salt-and-sour potato chips, and when we walked out, she gave me ten candies—Jolly Ranchers, mini Reese's, etc. She had stolen them—which I thought was incredible. I had a hard time with shoplifting. So I didn't like Ann at first. I didn't believe in her, and I thought she was trying to be cool.

The thing was that she *was* cool. She was a bitchy genius and a stone-cold fox. Her hair was jet black and her blue eyes could ice lakes of fire. She looked like a weird Saharan princess who was exquisitely graceful, especially while killing. Ann was going out with Frick, a junior, who had already totaled three BMWs. Ann could deal with that scene; she was schooled. Her dad was a hippie from Florida who made huge cash in self-help. After taking off with the babysitter (he was creative), Mills kept up a decent bank account for Ann, a most amorphous fund that would sometimes vanish, then magically reappear. The ATM was always a bit of a crap shoot. Her mom was a tiny blonde beauty queen who had literally fallen to fucking pieces after her husband took off. Ann was never as stoned as her mom.

My mom, on the other hand, was never stoned. And why would she be? Jeez, I was hard on my mom, as if I wanted her to be stoned. Stoned moms are not so enviable. I wanted to be-pregnant-be-pregnant-be-pregnant, i.e., be a mother. Meanwhile I despised my own mother. Was pregnancy some sort of a contest? That I could succeed where she failed? That I could be loving and real, instead of emotionally shrewd and deceptive? Or maybe I wanted to pass the baton, put myself in charge, believing I could become an authority, physically, by having a belly filled with my own child. Maybe I could diminish her power over me by reaching the same level she had; or understand what her power over me was, and break it.

I could never figure out why my dad married her. Dad was cool. He was funny, the Life of the Party. In eighth grade, he came and took me out of school to go to the Museum of Science and Industry (my brother was too young), and we stared at the geodesic dome on permanent display while he explained that geodesic domes have proved to be the strongest structures ever devised, that earthquakes cannot damage them, that they shelter Arctic radar, and that the best ones are proportionally thinner than a chicken-egg shell is to the egg. He knew what was going on in the world; he read six papers a day. Granted, it was because he was unemployed most of the time, but he maximized his leisure.

I could never spend time the way he did. I spent a lot of time worrying that time was slipping through my fingers. I spent nights staring, wondering how I was going to do the innumerable things I needed to do. It wasn't until I was eighteen that I discovered genuine leisure, not coincidentally when I left home. Freshman year at Columbia was about naps, imported beer, "getting to know" homeless people, drinking Turkish coffee and pretending to like it, et cetera. I returned to the heartland "New Yorked," with a string of intolerable affectations and a distinctly collegiate change in my sensibility about intoxicants and my own sophistication.

Winter break after our first semester at college, Ann and I spent every second together. Ann cooked up numerous schemes, including a very late night in Cicero, a faraway suburb that is deeply Chicagoan and rumored to stay open until 6 a.m. As we shared a $1.99 plate of eggs and link sausage at a booth in one of Cicero's greasier spoons, we reflected upon our brush with death.

"Could you pass the ketchup?" Ann said, pointing at a bottle on the table to my right. I reached over and grabbed the ketchup, taking the opportunity to smile at a police officer sitting at the booth behind us. Being flanked by cops, ironically, was exactly where we wanted to be, as we were trying not to have another run-in with Jerry, the used-car salesman who "liked to party" and with whom we had spent the past hour doing drugs. We had run out on Jerry when he went into his bedroom to grab another bag. It was a mad dash down the Cicero streets, and we were breathless and wild eyed when we arrived at the Dodge. But we figured that if we could just sit tight for a while, after a few hundred cigarettes and two dollars worth of chow, we would have the gusto to make it the necessary blocks to our lost car in the sub-zero early morning.

"Do you remember the name of that street?" I questioned Ann seriously.

"God, no," Ann said, wrapping the last bit of toast around her sausage and stuffing it into her mouth.

"No . . . wait, is it Chaswick? Or Cheswick or something? Some sort of Arkansas subdivision name, like Pembley Arms or something like that."

"Starkey," I blurted.

Desire, our waitress, shuffled over in a housecoat and placed our check under the sugar, then shuffled back out. I could hear the back door swing open and shut, and through the windows I could see her going to sleep on a cot next door.

"Starkey, exactly," Ann said as she patted her napkin to the corners of her lips with her left hand and searched with her right hand for the pack of cigarettes she kept swearing she had put in her jacket pocket.

The table of cops that were in front of us got up to leave.

"Thank God," mumbled Ann.

It was good to be rid of that set of cops; they were beginning to look a little suspicious. The other table of cops behind us was more than enough to ward off Jerry, and furthermore I was developing a crush on the officer I smiled at while smuggling the ketchup. For the sake of vanity, I tried not to scratch my itching head violently—a real sacrifice.

"I can't find my cigarettes," Ann said after she had shuffled through her purse and coat for the fifth or sixth time. Just at that moment the remaining table of four cops got up to leave. I felt a pang of fear and urgency. Two of the four policemen put dollars on the table and left, leaving the cute one and his partner to take care of the final exchange at the cash register. The cute one was eyeing me, clearly stalling as his partner made the moves to go; and when they went to the counter to pay, I caught a glimpse of his badge. On the way out the door, Officer Chris Proscinski fumbled for a cigarette. He stopped to light it and was embarrassed to ask me if I wanted one, although he knew my predicament; it was impossible not to have overheard Ann and me as we lamented our lost Camels. I picked up my cue.

"You don't happen to have an extra smoke, do you?" I asked.

"Sure," said Officer Proscinski, and he handed me a freshly packed cigarette, and then another, as an afterthought. Naturally, he wanted to make sure Ann was taken care of, too.

"Do you know where Starkey Street is?" I asked.

"Starkey Street?"

"I think that's the name of it. Starkey or Starkley or something," I said.

"John, you don't know where Starkey Street is, do you?" Officer Proscinski asked his partner.

The other officer shook his head no, then approached our table in a coppish way.

"What's the problem here, girls?" he said with a scary voice.

"We can't find our car. We don't exactly know what street it's on," Ann said as if she were talking to her stepmother, Buni (pronounced "bunny"), a person she considered her inferior and enemy.

"That is a problem," grumbled the policeman, tilting his head in such a way that his excess neck was forced to bubble over the stiff, starched collar of his uniform. His badge, identifying him as John Zurcher, gleamed in the fluorescence.

The men in blue said that we could come with them, that they would help us find our car. After about an hour of driving around we finally stumbled upon my gold Chrysler LeBaron, nicknamed "The Fiddler" because of a bumper sticker that read "I Fiddled Around at Fiddlesticks" that had been left on the car by its former owner, a sap named Don Kerman who sold a bag factory to my uncle. Ann and I jumped out of the warm Five-0 into our own sweet ride. Officer Proscinski swiftly appeared at the driver's window.

I rolled the window down.

"Thanks so much," I cooed.

"No problem," said Chris.

Chris stood there for a moment.

"Do you want to come in and have a cigarette?" I asked. I could afford to offer, since the group, on our crusade to find the car, had stopped at a 7-Eleven and Chris had bought me a pack.

"Sure," said Chris, and he hopped in the backseat, a little too eagerly. I was slightly grossed out by him because of the couple of unfunny things he said as we drove around, but I was still able to round up some desire for this pig. After we smoked, he began to massage my shoulders by digging his thumbs and forefingers into my tendons so hard I lost my vision. Ann was trying to fake sleep in the front seat, but it became obvious fast that a new arrangement had to be made. Ann got out of the car saying that she had left her gloves somewhere. Once we were alone, Chris promptly got up front and began to maul me.

This grossed me out definitely, and I decided to suck him off and end the thing as quickly as possible.

His professional pants made me edgy, but they came down just like any other. His gun and billy club surrounded me like headphones, and I pretended to hear nothing.

"You better make me come, you dead little baby," he said as I licked his balls. Then he thrust his pelvis and jabbed his dick in my mouth, grunting, "Make . . . Me. . .Come . . ."

As I slid that fucker's spindly dick in and out of my mouth, I had to hold back the vomit. I so desperately wanted it to be over. The little ridges on his penis slid against my tongue as I tried so hard to make him come. I sucked and rammed his cock against the back of my throat. Don't puke, I thought, just a few more seconds, I know he's ready to blast. My need to be successful pushed me to hold out and bob my head faster and faster. For one second I reveled in the humiliation. I felt like a nothing, just a body to be used for this man to get off. I felt like a little worthless slut, and, for one weird dark minute, I liked it.

After I swallowed his bitter load and gagged three times, I sat up and pulled myself together. I whispered, "I'd better rescue Ann."

Chris zipped his fly and followed me, looking from side to side. Ann was asleep in the backseat of the cop car and Zurcher was talking on the CB. I tapped on the glass and Zurcher ignored me, infusing massive doses of condescension into his feigned obliviousness. Ann woke up and hobbled back to my car.

I turned the key and the car commented that "the door is ajar," in its grating, electronic way. The Fiddler is one of the "talking cars" Chrysler manufactured in the 1980s, a model they have since taken off the market.

Twenty minutes into the drive home, Ann broke the silence, "You didn't fuck him, did you?"

"No," I answered.

"Good."

"Why do you ask?"

"The fat cop said he's HIV. You're fine, though."

"Well, what the fuck are you saying to me? Why didn't you come and break in the doors and get me the fuck away from him!"

"Because that fat-ass just grumbled it to me as you were coming to get me out of the goddamn cop car, after I'd been shoved out of our car going *home*, after you were screwing some turd, that's why!"

I didn't know what to say.

"You need to go back to rehab, Annie. You're really showing."

I drove Ann to her mom's apartment and continued on to my own family's home in the suburbs.

As I eased around the bend back onto Lake Shore Drive, I thought about Chris Proscinski's prick, skinny and hard; I could tell what it looked like even before I saw it. It poked me when he rubbed against my legs. That poking prick was one of the incentives for me to opt for a blow job. I sure as hell didn't want to have sex with this guy. But why didn't I say, "Get out of the fucking car now"? Or even "Um, could you please get out of the car now?" Maybe because I was scared he would beg me in a mean way, maybe I felt like he really wanted to get some come out and I was supposed to help him do it. But why was I supposed to help him do it? Why did I feel obligated? I was lazy, yes, I didn't want to hassle with the whiny pleas he would inevitably lay on me, but I felt bad, too. I felt bad for him. He wanted it. I had gotten him hot, I guess. I'd flirted relentlessly. But, God, I didn't want to touch him. Sex stopped being about pregnancy or seeds or any other crap. I didn't want to touch his skin, even by accident.

I was good at being a tease. I found success in it. I could turn guys on— dumb guys who liked sex, yeah, I could turn them on. I could stick out my D-tits, tilt my head and act thirteen. I gave them fake innocence. But then I felt like I had to deliver, and that's when I graduated from a tease to a slut.

The problem now was that this guy had AIDS and called me a "dead little baby." Chances were slim that I had been infected by him, but I had touched the disease and could feel it coming. I curled into a ball every night, convincing myself that I would be punished for all my carelessness and self-disrespect. I tossed and turned, hopelessly trapped in my own skin; I covered my face under the covers and cried, wondering what the fuck I was doing.

Ann's analysis of my promiscuity was that I wanted to screw my dad. I think Ann really did want to screw her dad because she was obsessed with the idea of girls screwing their dads. And what, I wanted to screw my dad more than anyone else? Jesus, I couldn't touch my dad's underwear that were in the laundry room—where they had been fastidiously washed, bleached, and folded by my mother, if not starched and pressed lying there on top of his pile like threadbare pillows for wayward midget hobos— much less envision what went into them. Gross. Ann's proposal unnerved me, of course, and I kept worrying that I was inappropriately repulsed at the thought of doing it with my father.

"I really can't buy that, Ann."

"It's so fucking simple. You hate your mom because you want your dad to love you. He doesn't give you that much attention. You're desperate. You have sex with anyone to replace your dad. On a deeper level, you want to make love with your dad: ultimate proof."

"But he does give me attention."

"No, he used to give you attention. He, like, took you to a museum when you were eight and you're still gaga over it. That was a decade ago. I don't know. Maybe I'm too harsh. My dad's just such an ass, maybe I think all dads are asses. No, your dad is cool."

"I mentioned that thing with the museum, I think once maybe twice, because we were talking about domes. 'Gaga' over my dad taking me to a museum? That's a little . . ." I trailed off, eating another baby carrot from the bag on the kitchen counter.

"The mention of the Astrodome wouldn't really jog my memory about some fucking day trip ten years ago with a man who had nothing better to do, unless I was slightly obsessed."

"Okay, you're a bitch," I said.

Ann stood there staring, then went to the refrigerator and fixed a little dipping bowl of ranch dressing.

"I'm sorry," she said, putting the bowl on the table in front of me.

Then the weirdest thing happened. Tears started falling out of her eyes. She seemed a little shocked by them. I didn't know what to do. God knows she wouldn't want me to hold her.

"Do you want some Kleenex? . . . or. . .some toilet paper? I don't think we have any Kleenex," I said.

"No, no," she said, wiping the stuff away with her hands.

I offered her some of the ranch dip, but she shook her head, and I tried to put the bowl back on the counter discreetly.

"Buni had a baby," she said.

Oh, God, I thought, Her dad really is an ass. How did she find out about this—did he actually call? I had never met Mr. Miller, but I remember the one time he called—from the airport. He called Ann to say that he was in Chicago, but that it was a short stop. He was sorry, he wouldn't be able to see her, but he would be back again some other time. That set her and her mom back about six months. What would this news do?

It was odd. Ann acted like such a little kid about her father—like a ten-year-old whose parents had just divorced. I blithely believed that people our age with faraway dads really were "over it," as they claimed to be. But maybe because her parents split when she was thirteen, at the brink of her sexuality, and maybe because her absentee father was her lifeline, she was not.

"I have a little brother now, isn't that stupid? Isn't it stupid? I don't know her. I don't know him. Fuck. Who cares. Who knows anyone," she said, in a hopeless voice I'd never heard her use before.

Buni had a baby. My God, that was impossible to stomach. Buni, at that point, was sixteen—two years younger than we were. It's no mystery that Ann had complexes; not to mention that she would be eighteen in a month, and Daddy just got a brand new kid. The clock was ticking. Ann had always feared being cut off without a word, but now it was a very real possibility.

Ann gave off a distinct "don't touch me" vibe; her physical self needed nothing, it's true, but she was a tender heart—sometimes, I thought, pathologically so. She was a mad gift giver, giving the most thoughtful presents to anyone with whom she had even the vaguest relationship, and showering those she did know. My mom had a shelf exclusively filled with gifts from Ann. She gave my great-aunt Betsy an antique lemonade pitcher and a matching set of etched glass tumblers for summertime, her driver's-ed teacher a book about Delorean, her boyfriend's best friend's girlfriend a ceramic box shaped like a violin, because the girl mentioned that she had played in high school and wanted to take it up again. The worrisome thing, though, was the homemade candies, her favorite thing to distribute. Ann would slave in the kitchen with paraffin wax and gum paste, pulling taffy or taking the temperature of her nougat to see if it was at the "soft-ball stage"; she could make Newport creams, divinity, rock candy, for God's sake; she knew her way around a penuche and she was working on Hawaiian centers. If she dropped ten pounds, she could make $10,000 a day. She was skinny as it was, but she had to become emaciated to be a professional, and she did not have the discipline. But there was another side to her resistance to modeling—a great part of her soul wanted to be one of "the people," which to her meant nothing less than being an impoverished Cuban.

Her fundamental belief was that life was not fair, but that it should be. That everyone had rights to an innumerable list of things: a doctor's care when dying, running water, not getting shot on the way to school, and so on. Like many nineties leftists she had a great reverence and love for all things Hispanic, à la Che Guevara, and always said "Gracias" (*con acento*) whenever we encountered a Mexican person at a checkout counter; this never failed to embarrass me—it seemed like imposed camaraderie to me. But Ann felt that the fight was on and that the people needed help and organization to make things happen, so she did things like construct a fifty-foot papier-mâché gas pump and drag it in front of the White House to protest the World Bank. She had an unbelievable romance with poverty and agricultural society. Her annual escape to a Marxist puppet farm in Vermont included helping with chores, like gathering wood or pumping water from the well; sleeping on the cold, wet ground protected by nothing but a scratchy wool blanket, and eating basic peasant meals made from the food of the land. To Ann, that was glory—although she could never get enough filet mignon, invariably enjoying the latter with a side of post-consumption anti-rich commentary ("fat preppies, the kill, etc."). Maybe her constant struggle with drug addiction was a way to create a happy medium between the world of total glamour and the revolution.

Sometimes it queered me out to think about the pain behind the Most Popular Girl's pretty face. It wasn't as though I was Ann's bookworm side-kick who secretly wanted to kiss her. I loved her, but our friendship wasn't a case of one idolizing the other, at least not that I could see. Politically, we were polar opposites.

I wanted to follow in the footsteps of Zsa Zsa Gabor. I spent my nineteenth summer in Gabor's native Hungary, where I could never get enough filet mignon—literally. I came away from every fine dining experience with that much more desperation to be swank. I read *Tess* on the banks of the Danube, then cried on a train all the way to Italy. My European stint only encouraged my reproduction obsession. I saw first-rate genes everywhere I looked on that continent. I wanted to establish a chain of cloning kiosks in every town square. On my plane ride back to the USA, I decided to focus on bioethics within my pre-med degree.

Back in New York, school was hardish. I spent Monday through Friday, 5 p.m. to 9 p.m. at the library. My library time evaporated quickly. My brain cooked systematically, following instructions, until my watch beeped, then I could return to my human persona. I did take a five-minute break on each hour, which I spent doodling. As a kid, I had read the Sex section of our old encyclopedia a thousand times. I could never forget the bit about fertilization being introduced into the mammalian body artificially, "with a pipette." Pipette. What an ill plan B. But I considered it. I thought maybe if I could hose the sperm directly into the Fallopian tube using some sort of glass-rod blower . . .

Enough, I would note mentally. I would return to my studies, settling deeper into my cubby and plowing ahead until my watch beeped at 8:55. (I needed five minutes to put my books into my backpack, return materials, take a drink at the water fountain, and so on.)

At nine o'clock, after library time, I would run out into the streets, famished. I might think about going for Indian, but I would end up going to the pizzeria instead, in hopes that the Johnny was there, a loaded pistol of virility who was probably twelve; the Johnny was straight out of Sicily, so he had been having sex for years. I usually ordered a simple cheese slice, and when I did, the Johnny would murmur, "Hot?" I would stare at him as if I didn't understand the question. He would blush, open and close his eyes, which caused a small breeze, pivot to the oven and back, then gently slide the burning triangle onto the paper moon that he placed in my sweaty palms. If he could just jizz on the damn thing, maybe that would expedite things. The Johnny's scorching sperm would be a sure hit; I should move into action phase with him.

At about three o'clock in the morning, I would sleep, and dream again about being pregnant. Dream of a living heart, smaller than an apple seed, beating inside of me. New blood pulsing. Wrists forming to make a place for hands. A brain and spine developing, connecting. Eyelids growing, too young to open. Transparent skin holding together the small body that was twisting and turning with fresh life, kicking against my ribs, and listening to my voice. I would dream of my own skin changing colors, my body changing shape, and my temperature rising. Of everything coming together inside, then my little baby floating out of me into two unknown people's arms. Before I woke up, I would dream that a tree wrapped around me, and the leaves whispered in my ears that I was forgiven.

After graduation, I landed back in Chicago at my parents' house, prepared to "move on." I had been there for about a month; things were okay. I was pretty much just going out with Ann and developing a crop of brain-damaged complexes about my identity and future. Ann finally interrogated me about my longing for pregnancy. "What is your problem?" she asked. She had had her first abortion at fifteen, "snuffed the life out," and could not understand why I wanted to give my freedom away. My mom was bugging me with her attempts to befriend me, and I was bugged at myself for being bugged. There was no reason I shouldn't be kind to my mother; she was a mild-mannered, organized woman who had always been kind to me, not to mention the fact that she created me. But why is it that mild manners suggest a body full of excruciating hate and rage, and organization seems like a symptom of this disease? Mom tried to forge our relationship in her own way. As part of her current friendship plan, she made an appointment for the two of us for a "day of beauty" at a second-rate local salon. I am always up for a manicure, but I didn't want to tell her that I didn't want a facial at this place. There are a number of beauty machines that use electroshock, and it is unwise to undergo questionable versions of such treatments. I didn't want to jump to conclusions, though. Maybe they had a more organic program at Curl Up 'N Dye.

The day arrived, remarkably close to the end of a night, the only trace of which I recall was Ann banging on my next door neighbor's window and demanding breakfast burritos. That was around six, and I was scheduled for a nine o'clock facial with Pam. I wasn't in the mood for a facial. In fact, a blood transfusion would have been much more refreshing. Should I have warned Pam not to touch me? Inform her that the clouds of gin fumes rising from my flesh were not a definite problem but that the pound of marijuana presently rewiring my system was making me a bit sensitive? If she could just concentrate on my eyeballs—just pour some sort of antifreeze, or the exact opposite, or fucking *something* on them, that would be great.

As soon as her hands touched my cheek, I knew I had to get out of there. I put my shirt back on and went into the next room where Mom was getting a makeover. I listened as the makeup artist described the "trendy look" and, through my own pained eyes, watched the misguided application of purple shadow on my mom's haggard lids.

"Mom."

"Hmm."

"I think I have hemorrhoids." Shit, I meant to say cramps but I said hemorrhoids instead. Maybe I did have hemorrhoids.

She looked up at me and surveyed my general appearance: slovenly, green.

"Get out of here," she said.

Ouch. I really was an asshole. Oh, well, I would deal with that problem later. How was I going to get back into bed? I could take a cab, but I had no cash. I guessed I could run into my house, find cash.

My cab ride home was a dream. The cab pulled up in front of my house and I told the driver to hold on. The front door was open, which was odd but not that odd; sometimes it doesn't close all the way. (Maintenance was sort of a non-issue at our pad.) I thought maybe I could find some cash in the front room, but that was not realistic. I was looking, like, in the remote control holder. Ann wasn't on the couch. She must have crawled out the door and gotten a cab—in the a.m. Bravo! I thought, and started walking toward my room when I heard strange sounds. The TV was on, maybe it was the TV.

I stopped midway through the hall. I couldn't decide if I wanted to see and make sure or if I didn't need to make sure. That sick old bed was creaking, Dad was moaning and Ann was grunting, "I'm coming, Daddy. . .I'm coming." I stood frozen on the brown shag, the ugly, battered path between the front room and the backrooms. Then I heard the sound of a hand against skin, followed by Ann's muffled "ugh." A spank, I realized. My dad was fucking and spanking Ann in the bed where I was conceived.

The cabbie laid on the horn.

I walked softly back down the hall into the front room, where I saw Ann's things scattered around. I grabbed her black leather bag and ran back out to the cab and jumped inside.

"What you going to do?" the driver barked.

"Cash machine," I muttered. "Go to 7-Eleven. Go to the cash machine."

Central Park Wet

Adrian Dannatt

*Adrian Dannatt is an English writer and curator living in Paris. His poetry,
fiction, art criticism, and obituaries have been published widely.*

THE APARTMENT BELONGED TO GIORGIO, A GRE-
garious Florentine rock promoter famed for touring
with Iggy Pop in the early seventies and acquiring com-
mensurate habits. By now he had renounced it all and
taken up being fat instead. He drank espresso shots all
day, which gave him an excuse to get away from his
computer and go downstairs, especially as concert
deadlines arose. Despite being famed for making the
best coffee in New York City, a ritual he would perform after dinner for
guests, the promoter still preferred to go and buy a styrofoam cup of
espresso downstairs and bring it back up, especially as B.B. King's Bari
dates approached. With luck he might meet someone he knew, they
could have a "quick" coffee together. In consideration of the man's manic
yo-yo up and down the stairs, precious cup in hand, Sherban had offered
to go for him. It was the least Sherban could do considering he had
already been staying several weeks, unannounced. But Sherban had soon
realized the journey itself was more important than the caffeine.

"Their espresso is really not very good I have to say," the promoter would have to say this every time he paid for another one, approx-
imately five times a day. Meanwhile those Jamaican Blue Mountain
beans creaked and throbbed with loneliness in his freezer.

The advantage was that the fat Florentine was not only the all-time
greatest living Café Roma customer and hence with unlimited credit, but
houseguests, announced or not, were included.

"Giorgio?" asked the portly waiter in fond affinity with a fellow obese
Tuscan. "*Bene,* he's in *Italia,* actually."

Giorgio had returned for a family crisis, the looming and lingering
death of a rich uncle, leaving Sherban to look after the apartment for a
month. Well, he could always get a cleaning woman to come around the
morning Giorgio flew back. Sherban took a couple of almond cookies,

credit being credit after all, and sat pondering the clouds overhead, the metallic-electric atmosphere. It did not look festive.

It was like being alone in Paris on the first of August, the cobbles ringing with silence. Or solitary on Christmas Eve, wandering Trastevere amongst families heading home laden with gifts, the definitive crash of metal shutters slammed shut at every store. A sort of existential loneliness akin to when the airport carousel comes to a halt and your bag still has not appeared, the very last person in the hall and nothing on the automated serpent, just a single unclaimed pram from Zaire. There is no sound more desolate than the silence of that carousel as it jolts to a halt, empty. It was in the spirit of this emptiness, the universal fluorescent gloom of airport baggage claim, that Sherban finished his second espresso. He always ordered two, separated only by a minute. For there seemed something inherently vulgar in a *doppio*, a contravention of the very nature of espresso. A double was cheaper, but of course he was not paying.

He got up taking his copy of *Gazetto dello Sport* that the café owner bought for himself every morning and missed every afternoon. With a nod to the waiter Sherban headed into the streets. This was pleasure. Nothing to do, nowhere in particular to go and no pressures such as telephone calls, U.P.S. vans, postmen, or appointments, a horizon entirely clear of obligation. Sherban walked jauntily, whacking his leg with the altogether satisfying heft of a folded *Gazetto dello Sport*, its print leaving a faint salmon bruise on the trousers he had borrowed from Giorgio. He saw a corner bookstore. Just crossing the road, a rumble and single drop of rain forewarned the storm. By the time he had reached the awning of the shop there was a steady patter of raindrops. On reaching the poetry section, a miserable shelf of Latina Women's anthologies, the downpour began. Panic broken out in the street, people running for cover as if in a Soviet movie, huddling under any available outcrop. The four people in the shop were all secretly relishing the sensation of being trapped by the storm, a couple stood by the open door watching the rain with great seriousness like a meteorological morality play. Sherban also went and stood by the door, under the awning which released a steady jet of water onto the pavement.

"Rain on our parade perhaps," said the woman next to him, addressed with sing-song sadness more to the rain itself and empty street. She was in her early thirties, dressed in a silk blouse, a skirt, and penny loafers, her bare footage more darkly tanned than the rest, he assumed South American.

"Argentinean," she replied. "Yes, of course Buenos Aires. Where else is there?"

"Vast steppes, the pampas, cattle, herds, millions of empty miles . . ."

"You are a romantic?"

"A major storm on the evening of the Fourth of July in an empty city, taking shelter under the awning of a corner bookstore, am I a romantic?"

Naturally her hair was black and there were a few drops of rain on the loose strands. Sherban brushed them, felt the static of these hairs pulled to his fingers against their will by local electricity.

"Mosquitoes?" she asked.

"Rain."

Thunder clapped, and the rain which had been pattering to a close began again, this time in earnest, as if only playing previously. A taxi swished by, sending up a spray of water from the gutter, an arc agleam with oils.

"Thank you."

They stood next to each other in an intimacy that went unstated. Sherban smelled her scent in the wet air.

They tried one bar she claimed was a local favorite but it was shut for the holidays. A couple of blocks further they saw the door ajar at a supposedly modish bar Sherban had been to before because it was nearby and he might find someone who knew him. There was only one other couple in the place and it was darker than the street. Sherban pushed his hand through his soaking hair, smoothing it back and thinking how handsome this made him look. He also saw the wetness of her blouse and the weight of her breasts outlined by it.

She stood proud and self-conscious of their state, feeling the titillating dampness of cloth, enjoying the effect. Sherban led her to a booth, next to the window onto the street. They sat down in silence opposite each other, waiting.

"What's your name?"

"Carmen."

He nodded. When she did not ask him his own name Sherban immediately understood which fantasy they were to play out. Her nipples, though she was wearing a bra, silk also he supposed, stood out through the cloth, hard and dark against her tan.

"Carmen, Carmen." The waiter was nowhere to be seen. Staring into her eyes, not blinking he reached across the table and slowly brushed the backs of his fingers, four fingers, across the surface of her nipples. They moved back and forth under the light, grazing backstroke of his fingers, he could feel the tenderness. Dizzy, short of breath, Sherban actually saw tiny white stars, pricks of light, as if he had performed a sudden, over-athletic act.

Her ears rang as now just the tips of his fingers caressed the extreme point of her nipples. They could not grow harder nor larger, swollen. She was so conscious of them, her hard, ready nipples, his eyes on them, because that consciousness was desire itself.

The waiter came over, they kept their eyes locked a little longer then briefly looked up to order a Sea Breeze apiece. When he left Sherban swallowed hard and reached over the table again. She moved impercep-tibly closer. Fingers slightly trembling he undid the pearl buttons at the top of her blouse, one after the other, a seeming eternity. Then he opened the blouse up, baring her. Carmen felt this, not just the unbut-toning in public but the deliberation, the certainty with which he opened her. She sighed and Sherban stared at her two large breasts high in their silk bra, the depth of her cleavage and freckles upon it. He did nothing but look, that was enough for both of them. Then he put his hands under the table and Carmen laughed, shifting her legs open auto-matically. He reached under the table to stroke her legs, from the knees slowly up along her inner thighs.

"Two Sea Breezes? Thank you." The waiter was bored, barely noticing his customers.

Sherban continued caressing the soft flesh of her innermost legs, stroking with the back of his hands. Carmen sighed, she had let her blouse fall open again, having covered it for the waiter. Now Sherban had reached the juncture of her legs, spread as wide as the banquette would allow. He stroked the edges of her panties, never the middle of them, caressing the limits of the tight cloth. She grabbed his hand under the table and with a tiny groan made to press his fingers against the very middle of her. He pulled his hand away. She whispered "Bastard!" with pleasure.

They left the drinks on the table and caught a taxi. She gave an address up on Central Park West. On the back seat he whispered his command, voice thick. She should hold her skirt up, lift it up. She did so, her legs spread apart on the hot leather of the taxi seat. He began to stroke her inner thighs, higher and higher, till she thrust toward him, whereupon he put his hand back on her knee. She bit her lower lip. As soon as they entered the apartment she put her hand down and grasped his cock, thick and impossibly full. Holding it tightly she went down and kneeling before him unzipped his trousers. His cock was there high in the air, bobbing back and forth with its own mad energy, its tip already agleam with sperm.

"Don't, don't, I'll come." She put her mouth round the tip, opening wide for him, the perfect O.

"I want you to . . . I want you to come, please . . . Sir." She added that last word with a deliberate, delicious flush of embarrassment but by now they were well beyond embarrassment.

"Then wait, wait." She stood up and he fully unbuttoned her blouse, taking it off above her arms. She had the sweetest little stomach, also freckled brown.

"Kneel again."

She obeyed, her mouth already moving to the swollen, throbbing tip.

"Lift up your skirt on either side. Show me your panties." His voice trembled pathetically.

Hesitating for a second, she did as ordered, holding up her skirt so he could see her panties stretched tight where she knelt with legs apart. They were palest blue.

"Wait." He reached down as she maintained the position, legs spread. He touched her panties. They were wet, moist silk, sticky with desire. He pressed harder, feeling her lips wide open, wet. Sherban stood back up and immediately she put her mouth to his cock, licking just the tip, putting her lips over his head, tasting it. Then she began to take the whole cock, as much as she could, into her mouth. Sherban looked down at her kneeling, still obediently holding her skirt up on either side. Then she moved her hands to caress his balls, tight, retracting, pulling up into his scrotum. She was swaying, moving to some inner rhythm, crazy with the lust of the situation, the act.

Sherban could not hold himself, her hands cupping his balls, her mouth up and down his cock, the length of him within her mouth. He staggered, righted himself, as if drunk. His face was as white as if he were about to faint. She knelt there before him, eyes shut in private ecstasy and with a low single groan he came, shooting sperm down her breasts where it ran and gathered in her cleavage.

"I'm a girl who's grateful to swallow," she said later as Sherban lay dazed on the white sheet sofa. He stiffened again as she said it, the outrageous, deliberately submissive small voice.

"Oh my God, how much I love pornographic sex," Sherban croaked ruefully, turning to her.

"So do I." She laughed, slapping him on the stomach. "Mmmh, oh yes."

"Somehow, doesn't that make it less pornographic? I mean if both of us enjoy it equally?"

"You're right, it's the gnawing dissatisfaction at the heart of the perfect sadomasochistic relationship. If the masochist is enjoying it as much as the sadist it can never work," she said.

Sherban ran his fingers lightly down her back, skimming her skin. He could tell her any truth.

"When something turns on a woman and equally turns on a man then in theory it's perfect, pure heterosexuality. Yet I can't help but find it a disappointment. When I first realized a woman could be as aroused by kneeling in front of me sucking my cock, as I was aroused by watching her do it, well, it seemed a cheat somehow."

She snuggled closer on the albino prairie of the sheet-draped sofa, nibbling his neck. How much more pleasing to do all the snuggling and kissing, holding and loving after the sex itself. Both parts were equally important but usually performed in the wrong order. There was no tension, no doubt between them, arms around each other. She had proffered herself, a victory so delicious it could hardly continue. Sherban was paralyzed with that tingling certainty of pure maleness.

"It's hard to tell how much sexual pleasure is just guilt," admitted Carmen, who had longed to enter a Latin American monastic order for years after her Confirmation. "If all guilt or shame were removed, how much desire would be left standing?"

Sherban nodded. Only sex he felt embarrassed about was worth having.

"Hence the tragedy of sex somewhere like Amsterdam or Oslo, all those northern democracies where they don't believe in shame, all those damn guiltless au pairs who say, 'Ooh, yah we must be open about our bodies and desires, it is so natural to have the sex, no?' Really, who would ever want to have 'natural' sex?"

He felt that sudden, illogical urge to express love or entire contentment, but kept his mouth shut.

"Can I have a look around, a quick snoop?" But Sherban was already moving around the apartment, perusing the bookcase, running a finger over the CD collection as if looking for dust rather than taste, closely checking every picture for signature and date, size of the print edition, turning over small tables for identifying marks. There were several things here worth real money.

Sherban's suspicion as to the wealth of his absent hosts was confirmed by the splendor of terrace. "Ye Gods, look at that!" He pulled back the curtains and stood at the French windows, staring in disbelief. Triplicate doors opened onto a marble terrace containing a garden table, pots of flowers, a balcony and a perfect view of Central Park, or rather its tree tops which blustered in the storm.

"The terrace is rather impressive. I wondered how long it would take you to find it."

He stood there with breath misting up the window. She came next to him and he thought she might be reaching for his cock again, currently rather less impressive, but in fact she was just opening the door. The fresh air was intoxicating, a green flurry of leaves blowing in the wind, rain lashing the terrace, sluicing the marble, thunder clouds still over the park. The windows rattled in the tempest.

"Come on out, don't be shy." Carmen led him as they walked across the cold wet tiles barefoot. "Nobody can see us here anyway, the only neighbor is an opera diva and she's traveling the whole time." Water poured down like a cold shower. If Sherban shivered deeply it was because of the level of pleasure, the raw luxury of walking naked on such a balcony in such a storm. "We have tea out here during the summer, but I prefer it when it's raining."

A few leaves were scudding around, blown this way and that, the branches of the trees in the park seemingly close enough to touch. Sherban realized that in fact they could be easily observed, should anyone be interested, from the surrounding high-rises. She was an exhibitionist to boot.

He admired her body again, less taut, less fetishistically constrained without garments but still fit, clearly worked on, her Spanish breasts holding their own proudly on a very adult frame. Carmen was a "real woman," whatever that meant, and naked in the misty downpour she could well have been a classical statue come to life, her body brown rather than marble white. Sherban looked down at his own shriveled seashell sex which had retracted in fear before the sleet. He felt again the embarrassment inherent to being male. Compared to her body, its wide energies, what could we males offer? Violence, of course.

"It's like a penis only smaller," Carmen jested. They laughed, luckily it was one of his favorites.

She put out her arms and they embraced, teeth chattering. Her hands linked behind his back, pulling him close, pressing up against each other.

"Have you been out on this terrace like this before, totally naked I mean?"

"Ah, you are suspicious? How can you tell? Is it obvious I've done this before?"

Carmen seemed beyond guile, there was something in her lack of defensiveness that made him suspicious. She could well be slightly mad. The idea of her potential insanity, it would fit with the exhibitionism and oral fixation, stirred him. Pressed to her nakedness he felt himself getting bigger. Her hips moved to him in response, locking deeper.

"Oh, you find that exciting? You seem to be getting excited by the idea of me out here on the terrace naked, with someone else maybe? Mmm, I know your type."

It was true he found himself increasingly excited, the storm almost an aphrodisiac.

"You want to know all about me out on the terrace? Perhaps you'd like to hear about how I was out here in the middle of summer, a hot day. Maybe you'd like to know how I was bent right over that table there?" And she had done it, his poor little cock was back in action, returning unashamed for more, rubbing back and forth against her stomach. Carmen reached down and put her hand round it.

"With who?"

But she was already taking him back inside, like leading a horse slowly to stable.

"Come along then." And he was of course beyond protest, his hair streaming wet down his face.

Afterwards they were wrapped in robes but it was too late. Sherban had started to sneeze and snuffle. He couldn't remember if the link between sneezing, orgasm, and death was medical fact or medieval superstition. He had definitely caught cold out on the wet terrace and didn't know if several subsequent orgasms, dry, helped or not. Yet it was nice and warm indoors and the thick carpeting, bottle of Irish malt, the towels, and heavy gowns were nursing him. So was Carmen who rubbed his hair dry, gave his back a semi-professional massage, and led him to the master bedroom for clothes.

"Take whatever you want. He hardly wears them anyway, more of a golf type."

Though notoriously hard to please in matters sartorial Sherban could not refrain from being impressed. This was not the standard rich man's wardrobe though there were a few expensive classics, cashmeres and brogues, obligatory basics. Instead there was a most unusual row of suits that hung in darkness like executed collaborators. Sherban checked each one individually, slowly. Something about their soft gray flannel perfection whispered: "Macedonian-Albanian." Sherban could recognize them immediately, this tailoring seemed to boast its national identity. So many displaced, exiled Macedonian-Albanians were beautifully dressed. That tailor who had dressed Proust's chauffeur was a native Macedonian of Albanian descent, he had moved back to Skopje to be close to his family. Thus, improbably, even during Communism some of the best cutting and fitting in Europe came out of the small city of Skopje. President Tito himself would get his suits made over there, he had a whole wardrobe of Skopje three-piecers. In fact "Skopje Man" was slang in Central Europe for a dandy and *flâneur*, who prided himself on perfect attire.

"Who lives here?" It certainly wasn't Carmen, who picked up strange men outside bookstores and loved to call them "Sir" whilst down on her knees.

"You don't think it's me then?" She pulled her black hair back coyly.

"I wish, believe me I wish it were you. You'd make a perfect *châtelaine*. But I don't think you would own quite so unusually male a wardrobe. Who lives here?"

"You already asked me that when we were out on the terrace, just before coming back inside."

What had he asked her on the balcony? He remembered.

"Oh I see." Was she then the professional mistress of whoever owned this place? Or was she perhaps just the unofficial lover, employed in another capacity? Carmen would make an ideal mistress but Sherban suspected that would be too easy, too obvious for her tastes, she would prefer the clandestine and forbidden.

Sherban suddenly tasted a tang of jealousy, like old coins in his mouth. Because he had to admit that living in this apartment with Carmen would not be unpleasant, an astonishing view, high ceilings, quietness, luxury, the occasional hot brutality. He had spent so long convincing himself the rich did not lead better lives and now he was seized with doubt like a teenager hungry for a car.

Now with his bare feet deep in the "master bedroom" shagpile and Carmen next to him waiting to treat him like just such a "master" he felt a pang of self-pity right through his middle like a skewer. Sherban would never own a woman like this, let alone anything approximating this penthouse.

"I don't think I'll wear any of these clothes. I'll let my own dry instead." Sherban turned away from the closet in defeat. He had never been so low before as to refuse someone else's clothes, especially those of such pedigree.

A bitterness seized him that felt metaphysical. And this was what he feared above all else, a bad mood that refused to shift like the weather. He could not afford permanent sadness. He did not have the constitution or cash to sustain it. Sherban knew exactly how much a nervous breakdown cost in this city. He had enough rich friends whose bills he had seen, he knew that it took cabs, champagne and holidays, analysts and spas and ski retreats, sun ray treatment and fresh flowers and very costly, very quiet rooms.

"Don't look like that." Carmen took his arm. They stood at the window watching the rain and the rain and the rain. He would leave. Maybe he would take one tie after all, that fat Cifonelli masterpiece, but he would have to be out of here soon before he lost his only power, that of pride.

Albert Camus

Geoff Dyer

Geoff Dyer is the author of many books including But Beautiful, Out of Sheer Rage, Paris Trance, *and* Jeff in Venice, Death in Varanasi. *His work has appeared in* The Guardian, The Independent, Esquire, *and* The New York Times. *This essay, published in* Open City *for the first time, is now included in* Otherwise Known as the Human Condition, *an essay collection (Graywolf Press). He lives in England.*

I. Algeria

 I'M HERE TOO LATE: IN THE DAY, IN THE YEAR, IN THE century . . .

In the day because all the hotels are full and I end up tramping round in the dark, lugging my pack and money (all of it in cash, a great wad of hard currency), nervous of the hoards of youths who watch me meandering round, concentrating so intently on making it look as though I have lived here all my life and know exactly where I am heading that I soon have no idea where I am on the mapless streets of Algiers.

By the time I find a room it is too late to do anything except drag a chair out on to the balcony and gaze down at the still-warm street, the signs. Arabic: it looks like handwritten water, it flows. The characters have no beginning and no end. Even the sign for the Banque Nationale d'Algiers looks like a line of sacred poetry: elongated, stretched out like a horizon of words. It is strangely comforting, looking at an alphabet that is totally incomprehensible, a liberation from the strain of comprehension. Plus there is nothing else to look at, no neon or bars, and nothing to hear. The only sound is of metal shutters coming down—even though, as far as I can see, all the shutters are already down.

I came here because of Camus. Algiers was his city, the place that formed him and sustained him. During one of his first trips abroad, to Prague, he ended up in a hotel like this and "thought desperately of my own town on the shores of the Mediterranean, of the summer evenings that I love so much, so gentle in the green light and full of young and beautiful women."

In bed, drifting on the edge of sleep, I think of November evenings in my own town that I hate so much, London, with its sky of sagging cloud, where all the beautiful women already have boyfriends.

Too late in the year because the seasons Camus celebrates are spring and summer, when even the poorest men walk like Gods beneath the heat-soaked sky.

It was only a few months ago, when I read the three slim volumes of so-called "Lyrical Essays"—*Betwixt and Between, Nuptials,* and *Summer*—that I realized how essential these Algerian summers were to an understanding of Camus. Before that I'd been happy to think of him vaguely in terms of Sartre, De Beauvoir, Paris cafés, existentialism, absurdity . . .

Everything that is most important about Camus, though, lies less in what identifies him with these names, these ideas, than in what distinguishes him and separates him from them—and that is the experience of growing up poor in Algiers. Everything that happened subsequently is drenched in this early experience of poverty and sunlight.

What for Camus was a source of strength is, for me, a source of neurosis. He grew up rich in beauty; I grew up under a miserly, penny-pinching sky, in the niggardly light of England where, for three months of the year, it gets dark soon after lunch and for three more it doesn't bother getting light at all. For Camus the sky was a source of sustenance that he could draw on at will; for me it is a thwarted promise, something yearned for and glimpsed against the odds. Even in Algiers, on this autumn morning, I opened the shutters with trepidation and find an allotment sky, a sky catarrhed with cloud. A shadowless day of loitering rain.

Too late in the century because nothing of the culture celebrated by Camus survives.

Early in the Algerian War Camus tried to achieve a truce that would spare the civilian populations of both sides (a ludicrous proposal, De Beauvoir felt, since this was a war between civilian communities). After the failure of this initiative, and the disappearance of any middle ground between the FLN-led Muslims and the French pieds noirs Camus maintained a besieged neutrality. With the FLN victory of 1962—two years after Camus's death—there was an immediate exodus of French

Algerians and, as I walk the streets, it seems ridiculous to have expected to find any trace of Camus's Algiers—like an American traveling to England in the hope of finding Dickens's London. But still, with no other guide, I drift around the city, following the very precise advice he offered in 1947:

> The traveler who is still young will also notice that the women there are beautiful. The best place to take full note of this is the Café des Facultés, in the Rue Michelet, in Algiers, on a Sunday morning in April. You can admire them without inhibitions: that is why they are there.

Ten years later the smart cafés of Rue Michelet became prime targets of the FLN's bombing campaign; now, more than forty years later, on a drizzly Friday morning (the Muslim Sunday) in October, I seek out the Rue Didouche Mourad as it is now called. The café itself is crowded with smoke so I sit outside on a bench. Men in jeans and leather jackets go by, men limping, men lighting cigarettes, veiled women, women in flesh-colored tights, lugging shopping, men in leather jackets. And then, at night, the women disappear completely.

For Camus the beauty of the women was just part of his rapturous celebration of the wealth heaped on the senses here. Nowadays, struggling on in the name of Islamic socialism, Algeria is a place of austerity, one of the few countries on Earth where you can't get Coca-Cola. Instead there is a vile soda, so sweet that drinking a couple of glasses is probably only slightly less bad for your teeth than getting hit in the mouth with a bottle of the stuff. In a restaurant that night—womanless, smoky—I order a beer. It comes in a green bottle and that is the major pleasure it affords. The food—chicken, brochettes, couscous—comes on a plate and half of it stays there.

Back in my hotel—disoriented, bloated with starch, tired—I lie in bed and read Camus's journal:

> There is no pleasure in traveling. It is more an occasion for spiritual testing. If we understand by culture the exercise of our most intimate sense—that of eternity—then we travel for culture.

In the morning tattered clouds are flung across the sky; the bay is flooded with sun. Even wind seems a species of light. My balcony rail casts shadows of Arabic script. Even the ants out on the balcony drag a little sidecar of shadow.

Below is a road where cars crawl along on mats of shadow; farther off are two long ranks of primrose-yellow taxis. Standing around, leaning on fenders, smoking and talking, tossing dog-ends into the gutter: this is the real business of a taxi-driver's life; ferrying people around the city is a leisure-consuming distraction. Behind the taxis is a crowded railway station and, beyond that, the port. Still farther off, the bay curls round and vanishes in mist. A few steamers lounge in the blue water. The sea seems vertical, the ships form a pattern as if on wallpaper.

"Nothing of the culture celebrated by Camus survives"—except, I add now, stepping out into the sun-drenched streets, the light. All over the city are huge building sites where the sun pours into vast craters. It is tempting to think that what is being attempted is some sort of solar-containment, trapping the power of the sun and storing it. In fact, slowly and systematically, Algiers is being transformed: from Paris into Stockwell. Necessity is ousting beauty. Indifferent to what it falls on, the light, here and there, snags on the crumbling paintwork of the old French apartment blocks.

Shunting through the blazing streets, a taxi takes me to Belcourt, the area of Algiers where Camus grew up. I get out on the main street and ask a friendly postman—from now on the adjective will be assumed rather than written, everyone here is exhaustingly friendly—if he knows the street which, before the revolution, was called Rue de Lyon.

"*Ici,*" he says, pointing to the ground. "Rue Belouizdad Mohamad."

"*Ici?*"

"*Si.*"

I look up at the numbers and find that I am right outside No. 93. Camus's father was killed in the Great War when Albert was less than a year old and he grew up here with his mother and grandmother. There is no sign or plaque. I ask someone if this is where Albert Camus lived and they do not know who I am talking about.

It is a one-story place with a small balcony overlooking the street, exactly as described in *The Outsider* when Mersault whiles away the Sunday after his mother's funeral. Below are a dry cleaner and a watchmaker. Fig trees line the street. Clothes shops. Boys selling packs of cigarettes. People waiting for buses that stream by, looking and not looking. The sky crosshatched by phone and tramlines.

Almost seventy years ago someone else turned up at this apartment, a teacher from Albert's school, to ask the boy's mother if he could try for a scholarship to attend high school. This was a turning point in Camus's life and, as for many working-class children to whom the world of books is suddenly revealed, he never forgot the debt he owed his teacher.

The course of my own life was changed, similarly and irrevocably, by one of my teachers. The first author I came across who expressed the sense of class-displacement that ensued was D. H. Lawrence in *Sons and Lovers*. A little later I could be heard reciting Jimmy Porter's tirades from *Look Back in Anger* by John Osborne. Then, from Raymond Williams, I learned the political and moral consequences and obligations of being educated away from the life you are born into. Finally, in Camus, who made the most immense journey from his origins, I found someone who stated, in the most affirmative and human terms, the ways in which he remained dependent on them. This understanding did not come painlessly but eventually, in a sentiment that is wholly alien to the likes of Osborne, he achieved "something priceless: a heart free of bitterness."

That is why I came here: to claim kin with him, to be guided by him.

I walk toward the sea and never quite come to it. Always you are separated from the sea by an expanse of one thing or another: docks or roads. No trace of the *plage de l'Arsenal* where Camus glimpsed for the first time the beauty of the Mediterranean. Now there are only the all-consuming docks. Gradually the sky becomes stained with clouds. The call to prayer comes over a loudspeaker, distorted and mechanical, like a factory whistle ordering the next shift to work.

Eventually I come to a stretch of land—I don't know what else to call it—by the sea. It is not part of the port but, although the sea laps against an area of sand, it is not a beach. This is sand in the building-site sense of the word. There is rubble and rubbish everywhere. Rush-hour clouds are queuing across the sky.

Matthew Arnold, staring out at the channel, thought of Sophocles and the sea of faith that had since receded. I think of Camus and the beauty that each year is pushed further and further out into the oil-filmed sea. As the waves lap in I detect a note of weariness in the endlessly repeated motion. Perhaps the sea never crashed vigorously here but it is difficult not to think some vital force has been sucked from it.

Camus concludes his famous study of absurdity by saying we must imagine Sisyphus happy. Easier to imagine him here, thinking "Is it worth it?" for if he rolled his rock up this slope he would come to a heap of rubbish—and when it rolled back it would end up in another even bigger heap. Easier to imagine Sisyphus looking forward to the cigarette that will make his lungs heave under the effort of work and which, when he has tossed away the butt, will add to the rubbish below. But perhaps there is consolation even in this: the higher the mound of rubbish the less distance to heave his rock—until there is no hill to climb, just a level expanse of trash. This is progress.

As I continue walking the sun bursts out again, making the bank of cloud smolder green-black, luminous over the sea. Perched between the road and the sea, between sun and cloud, some boys are playing football in a prairie blaze of light. The pitch glows the color of rust. The ball is kicked high and all the potential of these young lives is concentrated on it. As the ball hangs there, moon-white against the wall of cloud, everything in the world seems briefly up for grabs and I am seized by two contradictory feelings: there is so much beauty in the world it is incredible that we are ever miserable for a moment; there is so much shit in the world that it is incredible we are ever happy for a moment.

For Camus, Oran, the city of *The Plague*, "capital of boredom besieged by innocence and beauty," was the mirror image of Algiers: "a city of dust and stone" that had "turned its back on the sea." After independence two hundred thousand Europeans fled the city and for some time it appeared to be uninhabited, a city decimated by plague. Now, even the dust has gone, but here and there you detect a strange smell: like dry damp or damp dust. Perhaps this persistent whiff of the past is why it actually seems more European—more like the Algiers of Camus's essays—than Algiers itself. Not that Europeans are actually in evidence but there are shops with things in them: clothes, records. There is even that most Parisian of institutions: a lingerie shop.

I take a room on the Rue Larbi Ben M'Hidi, formerly the Rue d'Arzew, a street of arcades and white buildings with yellow ornamentation. Camus lived here for a while—at number 67, above what is now an optician and a record shop that plays music so thin and tinny it sounds like it is coming from the headphones of a Walkman. From there I walk down to one of the main boulevards. It looks like a typical Mediterranean promenade—tiled pavements, palm trees, white buildings to the left, blue sky to the right. Everything tells you that the sea is just below to your right—but you look over and find two expressways, acres of docks and refineries and, beyond all of this, a massive breakwater. "The apparent aim, is to transform the brightest of bays into an enormous port," he wrote in 1939 and that has now been achieved. The sea has been forced out to sea.

A few minutes walk away, the Boulevard Gallieni has been renamed the Boulevard Soummam, but it is still an architectural wedding cake of a street, so wide that the sun congregates here for most of the day, not simply dropping in for an hour as it has to in the canyon streets of Manhattan. Camus watched the young men and women stroll here in the fashions and style of Hollywood stars, but now it is a place where people pace quickly along, not to display themselves but simply to get somewhere else. Women hurry by and then night comes and they vanish: no final blazing sunset of the feminine, just a slow fade into the masculine night.

On my next-to-last day I take a taxi to the Roman ruins at Tipasa, fifty miles along the coast from Algiers. As we begin the long curve and haul out of the city the weather is in the balance, then rain spots the windshield. It is difficult not to take the weather personally and on this day, when it is so important that the sun shines, I think of Camus returning to Tipasa, "walking through the lonely and rain-soaked countryside," trying to find that strength "which helps me to accept what exists once I have recognized that I cannot change it." For me, accepting the fact that it will rain today seems as difficult as coming to terms with the amputation of an arm or leg.

We drive through mountains and then out along a dull coast road. We pass half-finished buildings, the inverted roots of reinforcing rods sprouting from concrete columns: the opposite of ruins. Then, ten minutes from Tipasa, the clouds are rinsed blue and the sky begins to clear. Shadows cast by thin trees yawn and stretch themselves into existence. By the time I enter the ruins the sky is blue-gold, stretched taut over the crouched hump of the Chenoua mountain. The ruins are perched right on the edge of the sea: truncated columns, dusty blueprints of vanished buildings. The sea is sea-colored, the heat is autumnal: heat that has a cold edge to it. I walk through the remnants of ancientness until, close to the cliffs, I come to a brown headstone: shoulder high, two feet wide. On it, in thin letters is scratched:

> JE COMPRENDS ICI CE
> QU'ON APPELLE GLOIRE
> LE DROIT D'AIMER SANS
> MESURE ALBERT CAMUS.

The monument was erected by friends of Camus's after his death. Since then his name has been defaced with a knife or chisel and the weather-worn inscription from "Nuptials at Tipasa" is already difficult to read. Thirty years from now the words will have been wiped clean by the sun and the sea that inspired them.

If my trip had a goal then I have reached it. Every now and again there is a hollow boom of surf as if some massive object has just been chucked into the sea. Flies, impossible to ignore, tickle my face. Waves surf in on themselves. The horizon is a blue extinction of clouds. More than anything else it was the two essays Camus wrote evoking "the great free love of nature and the sea" at Tipasa that made me come to Algeria. Now that I am here I am aware of myself straining toward an intensity of response that I do not feel. The fact that it has been written about so perfectly inhibits my response to the place. What there is to discover here, Camus has already discovered (*re*discovered in the second essay, "Return to Tipasa"). There is nothing left to feel, except "this is the place Camus wrote about in his great essays"; that and the peculiar intimacy of reader and writer.

We read books and sometimes recommend them to friends. Occasionally we may even write to—or about—the author to say what his or her books mean to us. Still more rarely we go to a place simply because of what has been written about it and that journey becomes both an expression of gratitude and a way of filling a need within ourselves. Coming here and sitting by this monument, rereading these great essays, testaments to all that is best in us, is a way of delivering personally my letter of thanks.

On my last morning in Algiers I make my way to the Martyrs' Monument. On a hill overlooking city and bay, the monument—to the million Algerians who lost their lives in the war for independence—takes the form of three gigantic palm fronds leaning against each other. Beneath the apex formed by these fronds is the eternal flame, guarded by two soldiers who stand as if carved from flesh and blood, ripply and dreamlike through the heat haze of the flame. At the base of these fronds are massive statues of guerrillas of the FLN.

If ever a monument aspired to the condition of the tower block, it is here. Of all the war memorials I have visited none has affected me less strongly, more impersonally, than this one. It demands that we become martyrs to an aesthetic edict based solely on scale. It orders us to respond to the scale of the undertaking and we obey—with all the sullenness that obedience compels. What it gives to the memory is not a sense of individual sacrifice but of its own insistent might—the might of engineering, the collective strength of concrete, its imperviousness to the passage of time. It will out-survive everything else in the city, except—and this is all it shares with that other, fading monument in the ruins of Tipasa—the sky that frames it.

II. Rebellion

Albert Camus means something very different to us today than he did at the time of his death thirty years ago. Lesser works like the "Lyrical Essays" speak more intimately to us now than texts like *The Myth of Sisyphus* on which his reputation was based. Two recent books attempt, in very different ways, to relate him to the needs of the present.

Jeffrey C. Isaac's intention in *Arendt, Camus and Modern Rebellion* is to bring the two writers into dialogue, to read them against each other. The somewhat arbitrary nature of this pairing—Orwell and Simon Weil might just as usefully have been brought into the frame—is unimportant, for Albert Camus and Hannah Arendt are, for Isaac, representative of that loose configuration of "resistance intellectuals" whose thought was shaped by—and sought to engage with—totalitarianism and the unparalleled horrors of twentieth-century warfare. Both were incessantly active in politics but essentially non-aligned; both developed a highly personal metaphysics of the human condition, which was grounded in the political realities of the day. Both paid a high price for setting themselves in opposition to erstwhile allies: Camus for his stance on the Algerian war; Arendt for her insistence, in *Eichmann in Jerusalem*, on the part played by "Jewish leaders in the destruction of their own people." Anticipating the postmodernist suspicion of grand ideological narratives, both retained, in spite of everything, a steadfast faith in the human subject that is alien to the characteristic discourse of postmodernity. Hence the need, suggests Isaac, to retrieve their political vision.

In *Culture and Imperialism*, Edward Said positions Camus in such a way as to see how his work "reproduces the pattern of an earlier imperial history." Acknowledging that Conor Cruise O'Brien has shown Camus's work to represent "either a surreptitious or unconscious justification of French rule or an ideological attempt to prettify it," Said purports to go further. He does this by going further *back*, by looking in detail at "earlier and more overtly imperial French narratives," which Camus's books "are connected to, and derive advantages from." This run-up is more impressive than the actual jump. O'Brien is berated for letting Camus "off the hook," but Said's analysis of Camus's texts (as opposed to those that preceded him) falls far short of O'Brien's own persuasive and precise analysis of *The Plague*, for example. The plague in Oran, as we all know, is a symbol of Nazi occupation but, from the point of view of the Arab population, as O'Brien points out, the French who resist this plague are also an occupying force: a symptom of pestilence.

In Said, by contrast, Camus's writings barely feature; he is simply the terminus of an historical process, "an extraordinarily belated, in some ways incapacitated colonial sensibility." Although the purpose of this restorative interpretation is intended neither "vindictively" nor to "blame" Camus. Said soon comes to the conclusion that his "limitations seem unacceptably paralyzing." And while Said disavows any suggestion of authors being mechanically determined by history or ideology, the relative lack of emphasis placed on Camus *vis-à-vis* his predecessors cannot but suggest exactly this.

Let us be clear: there is no refuting the claim that in Camus's fiction the indigenous population of Algeria is, through a sleight of the imagination as casual as Mersault's murder of a nameless faceless Arab, conveniently disposed of. By situating Camus in a history of imperial strategy while studiously ignoring all the details of his life, however, Said similarly and conveniently disposes of Camus as an individual. With his personal anguish over the fate of Algeria thereby rendered irrelevant he becomes, in Sartre's deliberately vindictive phrase, simply an "accomplice of colonialism." In Camus's terms, Said admits sin but refuses grace.

Isaac, on the other hand, is acutely sensitive to Camus's predicament. He judiciously plots his interventions in the Algerian crisis from his doomed attempt at organizing a civilian truce in January 1956 (while a mob of pied-noir militants bayed for his blood) to his eventual "defensive and hollow" opposition to Algerian independence. Neutrality was impossible: his condemnation of FLN terrorism—"which operates blindly" and which "one day might strike my mother or my family"—was seen as implicitly supporting the French army of pacification.

Hence Isaac's exasperated reminder that Camus *was* a pied-noir. As Said would have it, we see Camus either accurately—as the confluence of a history of imperial dominion—or vaguely, inadequately, and ahistorically as a philosopher of the human condition. My own response is to locate him more precisely and more personally.

Camus's father died in the Great War; raised by his illiterate mother and grandmother, he grew up in a working-class district of Algiers where poverty was redeemed by the wealth heaped on his senses by sea and sun.

He recorded these early experiences in three volumes of "Lyrical Essays," which contain some of his best writing. They also make clear why the Camus presented by Isaac is, for all the diligent range of reference, too abstract a figure. "If I can be said to have come from anywhere, it is from the tradition of German philosophy," said Arendt, thereby lending herself perfectly to the kind of academic exegesis at which Isaac excels. But Camus is not at his best in the philosophical works on which Isaac relies. Camus had to stifle himself in order to think his way through *The Rebel*. His, above all, is a *sensual* intelligence. The enduring power of *The Outsider* lies less in the sense of existential absurdity than the glare and heat of the beach and—even more strongly in the "draft version," *A Happy Death*—Camus's evocation of sensual happiness.

In this respect Isaac's contention that the "sentimental vision of the Mediterranean is an important lacuna in Camus's writing" is an important lacuna in his analysis. Camus, whose gaze was always directed from Africa to Europe, from desert to sea, was both formed by this vision of the Mediterranean and gave it its most powerful expression. This vision could only have been articulated by someone in exactly Camus's position, with his peculiar sensibility and with exactly the cultural-imperial legacy of French Algeria to draw on.

Although Camus's vision depends on and is rooted in specific geo-historical circumstances—those of the pieds-noirs—he in no sense *lays claim to* that which he celebrates. On the contrary: "All I know is that this sky will last longer than I shall," he wrote in a characteristic passage. "And what can I call eternity except what will last longer than I shall?"

Of course Camus's claim to greatness cannot rest solely on a kind of pied-noir pantheism. It resides in the manifold ways in which this sensualism was allied with the cause of human solidarity. But this commitment never evolved—because it was inextricably bound up with—a renunciation of the sensual. "If man needs bread and justice, and if we have to do everything essential to serve this need, he also needs pure beauty, which is the bread of his heart."

As we move toward the December of the century, the "unconquerable summer" that Camus found within himself offers more warmth and light than ever before.

OPEN CITY

III. The First Man[1]

In 1958, the year after he won the Nobel Prize, Albert Camus wrote a preface for a new edition of his first book, *Betwixt and Between*. Re-reading these early essays persuaded him that a writer's work was nothing but a "slow trek to rediscover through the detours of art those two or three great and simple images in whose presence his heart first opened." His own writing was nourished by "a single stream," Camus went on, and this stream was "the world of poverty and sunlight" in which he grew up in Algiers.

After years of creative sterility Camus had resolved to trace this stream back to its source in the novel that he was still working on at the time of his death in 1960. According to Herbert Lottman in his excellent biography, Camus referred to the work in progress, in all seriousness, as his *War and Peace*. Even in unfinished form it is a wonderful book. As Camus redrafted and completed it, *The First Man* would have become more of a novel and less of an autobiography; as it stands it is a great attempt to fulfill the ambition announced by Nietzsche's *Ecce Homo*: "how one becomes what one is." Seen in this light it doesn't even matter particularly that the novel is incomplete. "The book *must* be unfinished," Camus noted to himself, conscious that such a project could be realized, definitively, only with the death that curtails its completion.

In the opening pages a husband ("he wore a three-button twill jacket, fastened at the neck in the style of that time") and pregnant wife are traveling in a wagon, "creaking over a road that was fairly well marked but had scarcely any surfacing." Tone and scene are surprisingly Hardyesque but the setting is Algeria, the edge of Africa, and the soon-to-be-born son is not a Jude but a Jacques who, years later, like Camus himself, will try to understand how he emerged from the obscurity to which his family had been condemned by history.

Camus's father was killed at the Battle of the Marne when Albert was less than a year old. Exactly like Camus, Jacques Cormery is raised by his mother and grandmother in extreme poverty. He is a gifted pupil and one of his teachers persuades the mother to let her son try for a scholarship. As the *lycée* reveals the possibility of a life beyond the poverty and ignorance he was born into, so "the silence grew between him and his family." It's a familiar theme but no account of this process is more moving than Camus's. His mother was illiterate (a neighbor had to read the

---

[1]Translated by David Hapgood

192

telegram announcing that Albert had won the Nobel Prize) and the profound feeling aroused by the book comes, partly, from the sense that it is
written for the one person who cannot read it. "What he wanted most in
the world," Camus noted, "was for his mother to read everything that was
his life and his being, that was impossible. His love, his only love, would be
forever speechless."

The urge to bring his past to life, to offer his family the gift of speech,
of words, is therefore inseparable from the desire to achieve a clarity, a
sensual immediacy and intensity that will, as far as possible, transcend
the verbal. The sky, the light, offer supreme, silent expression of this
hope. Words yearn to *be* the light they celebrate. Drenched in the sun
and smells of Algiers, Camus's last novel cries out with the same "famished ardor" that characterized crucial early essays like "Nuptials at
Tipasa." These essays make clear how profoundly Camus's sensibility
was shaped by growing up in Algiers, but *The First Man* aims beyond the
lyrical evocation of times past. In the essays the Sahara is, if you like, a
vast beach; in them Camus is looking north, to the sea. In this book he
looks to the interior, to the heart of a problem skirted in his earlier
books. The Arabs, who, in *The Plague*, were invisible or, in *The Outsider*,
killed unthinkingly, crowd in on *The First Man*. The mere fact of their
visibility is enough to claim the place as their own; by "their sheer numbers" they offer an "invisible menace," an outcome that is premonitory
but not yet inevitable. "We'll kill each other for a little longer and cut off
each other's balls," says one character. "And then we'll go back to living
as men together." A forlorn hope, it turned out, but, as a novelist seeking
to delineate his historical predicament, Camus is less concerned with the
question of who can lay claim to the land than the more profound one:
what claim does the land make on the people born there? Early in the book
a farmer complains that Parisians understand nothing of the situation of
the French Algerians. "You know who're the only ones who can understand?" he asks. "The Arabs," says Jacques.

Camus has a blood-understanding of this psychological bond. It is
dramatically embodied—to take just one example—in the scene
describing the way a crowd would gather if a fight broke out between a
Frenchman and an Arab:

> The Frenchman who was fighting would in backing up find himself
> confronting both his antagonist and a crowd of somber impenetra-
> ble faces, which would have deprived him of what courage he pos-
> sessed had he not been raised in this country and therefore knew that

only with courage could you live here; and so he would face up to the threatening crowd that nonetheless was making no threat except by its presence.

What a book it would have been, what a book it already is! I have itemized some of its themes but the remarkable thing is how, even at so early a stage, these disparate concerns are so intimately entwined. Thirty-five years after their author's death, these draft pages answer the two needs that, as Camus wrote in his "Return to Tipasa," "cannot be long neglected if all our being is not to dry up: I mean loving and admiring."

The Short Story of My Family

Will Eno

Will Eno lives in Brooklyn. His recent play Middletown *won the first-ever Horton Foote Award and his play* Thom Pain (based on nothing) *was a finalist for the 2005 Pulitzer Prize. His work is published by TCG, DPS, Playscripts, and Oberon Books, in London. Other work has also appeared in* Harper's, The Believer, *and* The Quarterly.

BY WAY OF INTRODUCTION, WE WERE ALL BORN IN Eastern Standard Time. To the northeast we came, crying or not, tangled or facing the wrong direction, introduced in breech presentation or like Caesar. We were given the test the hospital gave for newborns and scored highly in the category of self-quieting activity. We weighed less than the phone book of an average city. We were a family with our own gravity, a rural quality, a name, address, and area code. Papers to certify our birth were put in a scrapbook with a newspaper clipping from the day we were born that began, "If you were born on this day," and went on to spell out our destiny and the tendencies of our sign. You could swaddle us in one page of the sports pages.

We needed shelter.

"Here should do," our father said, before a piece of empty land. Papers were offered. He took out his glasses, read to the bottom, nodded, and put his glasses away. The landowner made an X and pointed to it and our father signed his fatherly signature.

From nails and two-by-fours, our house arose. From seeds and roots, trees arose, grass, our yard. We painted our name on the mailbox. We stained the house. We all moved in. We survived the ways you can die when you're a child—playing, sleeping wrong, swallowing funny, or touching something electrical. Our dexterity grew, our grasp of things tightening as time slipped through us and our personalities hardened. We pointed at life. More trees grew. Their leaves fell. We got a dog. Our dog barked. A car drove by, the driver screamed, the car skidded. We got another dog. We dug a hole. There would be yard work in our future. We had a book to identify poison ivy. There was going to be a love of reading with us. Everywhere were the signs, the symbols, the letters, an alphabet. Our blondness faded and our blue eyes browned and words organized themselves around us.

"Berkeley Springs, Berkeley Springs," our mother said, rocking us on every syllable, instilling in us the mystery of Berkeley Springs, about which, later, we would learn nothing.

We recognized faces. We pointed more. We read our lips with our hands and touched whatever we could reach, going over all the Braille stamped into the world. We wet ourselves, got hungry, fought, cried, and drooled, and dealt only in appearances, in accordance with modern philosophy. This is perfectly normal. We made early noises, allusions to contentment or distress, sounds that sounded like things, pre-words, babble, bubbles of saliva, dad, da, ma, mom, mother, or some other regional variant. We achieved immense personal growth, in terms of height and weight. By the age of walking, we learned to crawl, to put anything in our mouths, feel shame, be different, and then walk. Perfecting this, getting nowhere, becoming the same, we learned to sit.

Our father read. We sat across from him, in love with him, within earshot of him being so quiet. Once, he pointed to the words "Santiago, Chile," in the newspaper and said, "This is very sad and faraway." The picture was of a dead-looking cow caught in a tree branch floating down a river. What was a cow in a tree for, we wondered. What was a family doing on the roof? Serene photography of natural catastrophes. We didn't understand and didn't ask and our pretending we knew became our knowing.

If we had to ask our father something, we would go and ask our mother. Where is Santiago, Chile? Or, where was the rake, for instance, or shoes, or a blanket. "Did you look?" was the question she rightly answered the question with, for we asked these last questions rhetorically, lazily having made no effort to locate anything in reality. When the lost noun was found, or a South American capital, or the nonfarming implements of our North American youth, we, our then-photogenic family, got on with life. We, though snow was coming anyway to muzzle our state with snow, would take the rake and a blanket into the yard and rake. Our father sat down with whatever he was always leafing through, books or papers made of trees, possibly bound in the leather of a drowned Chilean cow. He would look out at us and his view of Massachusetts, one of the thirteen original states. We saw him cry at times in parts, reading certain writing, obituaries of past teachers and speeches of the late

Abraham Lincoln. He had a reading sweater, a reading chair, a reading light of which much could be written. Whatever dog we had seemed to know it was a reading dog and would sit next to the chair and light, head on paw, breathing, studious, dog-eared.

He, our good father, would look at us over his glasses when we came in and say, "*Et tu*, Brutus?" We smiled and didn't know how to speak Latin. We looked at the floor and said, "Yeah, Dad, *et tu*."

Our family had a family room. In this, we are not alone. There, by the dog, by the light of the reading light, we talked about literature and writing: Did you read this, Did you read that, Do you know how to read, Why don't you know how to read, Can you use the word "such" by itself, Why don't you ever say anything, How are you supposed to pronounce French?

Other than raking and how to be born, how to lose things and stare and be stung by bees, we didn't know anything. We were never a family before we were a family. There was no way for us to know anything about what to say or do. "There is no textbook," my mother would say, at night, as we stood around smiling in our yard, while our property got dark around us. We lived in a book-lined house on a tree-lined street, beset by sunlight lining our faces, beset by electric light, by the *Encyclopædia Britannica*, and leaves.

We were serious readers before we learned to read, furrowing our brows at simple things, squinting suspiciously at widely known facts, dazed by nightfall as if it were an essay question. When we would learn to write, we would write our names half-backward in our father's best books. We were adding some humanity, some crayon, and entering the only word that we could read, destroying his library from a collector's viewpoint. We were expressing an ancient desire, what cave painters knew, what Adam was after in the Garden, even though we didn't know anything. So began the scribbles, the graffiti, the reams of signatures that we would sign, in hopes of composing our signature. So began the beginning of words cropping up all over.

Ex Libris, our father's books said on the inside cover. We looked through them to see what was not our yard or Massachusetts. Speaking for myself, and for everyone else, there was something in them to be preferred. Maybe it was order, a seeming order, an apparent neatness and meaning on the pages that we could never muster in ourselves or anywhere in our house. Gradually, through our studies, we grew to learn that we did not know how to read.

Nighttimes, in the meantime, we were read to by our mother. Did she want or not want the day or night to come when we could read ourselves, could read ourselves to sleep, when the family would become a book club and the whole house a reading room? Probably, as with all mothers and all questions, yes and no. Probably some nights she was tired, and tired of the story, and she had her own book to read, her own sleep to go read herself to, and was not interested in the destiny of a bunny or a talking steam shovel. Other times, she probably loved to read to us and see our then-unending surprise at the endless repetition. She must have loved how we loved her and looked at the pictures and up at her, mouthing whatever word she said, widening our eyes when the story we had heard the night before took a turn we didn't see coming. We asked for help with things that we didn't understand in the book, despite the completely understandable drawings. She believed our hearing stories about animals facing difficulties and making friends despite them was good for our personalities. Surely, it was. We all went on to become people who were deeply concerned about the animals in children's books and things that can't really talk that could talk. After the story, in bed with an indoor blanket and founded and unfounded fears, kisses were given, childish questions asked, sweet everythings whispered, and she turned out our lights.

Mornings and Saturdays would come.

"Saturday morning is here," our father would explain.

There was our yard for us to tend to and stand apart in. There were little plants and tender trees that were not meant for the climate our house was set in and so would die in the coming winter if they didn't get wrapped in burlap. We wore sweaters with simple wintry narratives knitted into them. We used twine. Afterward, during breakfast, we would use the word "twine," dropping it casually, if children can drop things casually, using the word in a sentence. We did this for our father's sake, to fill him with pride for his little children, for moving so easily between signifier and signified.

"Burlap," we thought, and made plans that would fall through or that we would forget.

One Saturday, our father pointed out the word "mulch" in a flyer we had been sent, altering our future, changing us as people.

One Saturday, he pointed out in the church bulletin that the apse was being repainted. We said the word "apse" to ourselves all day. Nobody liked cats, but we wanted to buy a cat and name him Apse, or Apsey.

During this time, the days of the week were written inside our underwear.

After breakfast, the word Saturday pressing in against us, our mother made us lunch. We were growing more intelligent. There was no evidence of this. We sat down to dinner.

Things continued, and we did, too.

Life flew, changed, fell, rose. We didn't notice life doing anything.

We were distracted from our yard work and the beauty of our home life by our homework. We were learning to read so that one day we could stay inside and read. We would let the leaves fall where they may. Someday, our noses and the rest of our bodies in a book, we would disregard the season, the early dark and dying flowers, our father reading and our beautiful mother motherly, and all of the other things that we, as children, so highly and deeply did not disregard.

Our brother learned to read completely one Halloween. It was quieter in our quiet house. Greenery and weeds lined the walk, ready to die for the year. A pumpkin with the shape of a pumpkin carved into it sat by the door. Our brother always stared at his hands, but now he had a book in them to stare at. We more or less disappeared for him, as each of us would for each of us. He dressed up as Robert Browning. He made a sign that said, "Trick or treat. I am supposed to be Robert Browning. Important poet of a gone age." Our sister said into the kitchen, "John, is there any more corn?" He said back, "Dust and ashes, dead and done with, Venice spent what Venice earned." Our sister asked again. He said, "Dear dead women, with such hair, too—what's become of all the gold." He came back and sat down. Our father said to my sister and me, "We'll make a sign for you two, too."

Our mother was adamant that someone say something during dinner, though nobody usually did. Someone asked somebody to pass something. Somebody said, "What does 'adamant' mean?" Our dining room was like a library. The ones who could read thought about reading. The rest of us waited for the dog to come in and do something funny. For the illiterates in the family, we had a long line of dogs who had scholarly names and came into rooms doing something funny, later to die in some unfunny way. Poor Baron Melchior Grimm, German shorthaired pointer, run over one night by a furniture truck. We dragged Grimmy off the road in a toy sled and buried him in a shower curtain that had the alphabet on it. This nighttime act brought us closer.

Not that we ever fought, ever. When we were little, the word "internecine" was not in our vocabulary. We were quiet. Quiet family, quiet town, Massachusetts, original state. We felt people were to be seen—seen going up stairs, patting the dog, touching their faces, seen staring at books and the trunks of trees—and nothing else. We watched and listened, in the hope of someday understanding, someday correctly reading something into anything.

Someone left a rake in the yard. Our father said, "Doesn't anyone in this house know where anything belongs?" We stood in the yard with the rake. "No," one of us said. "No," said another one of us.

Life went on more. Man went to the moon. Woman did. Presidents were laid into the earth. There were headlines. Years of seasons went by. Snow, the ocean, crocuses, and pails on maple trees. Time was not standing still, but we were, and our faces reflected this. More and more lines appeared, little marks that were not birthmarks, our lips and eyes drying as we stared at our lives.

We readied ourselves for serious things, impossible futures, compelling narratives and prescription glasses. We imagined differences. We craved absolutes. We looked without pointing. Relatives died. We pictured cities. We looked for typos in the Bible, went through the Koran with a Hi-Liter pen, and then gave up on all gods and tried reading new writing from Europe. We studied Latin, to no avail, except to learn where the word "avail" comes from and that the word "dexterity" is more of a mystery than people usually think. Word spread of our speechlessness. We tried changing, made résumés, bought telephones, huge notebooks, typewriters, and tried to grow in ways other than weight. We involved ourselves in marriages and book clubs. We took note of things advertised in language, nonsense, sense, jingles, and slang. We wrote our names forward in our books. We subscribed to anything printed. We proofread our diaries, revised our high school yearbooks. We devised names for dogs and then went to pet stores and animal-rescue leagues in search of the actual dogs who would fit them. We missed our quiet silent dinners together. We missed each other and ate alone, studying cereal boxes and reading milk cartons to see who was missing and what we could send away for. We missed listening to our mother read aloud and to our father to himself. Our underwear made no sense, nor did the days whose names were not written in it. Reduced again to our hands, we read our bodies, our breasts and testicles, for lumps and knots, any sign of some final growth. Things were more behind us than ahead. We longed for things, sappily. We pined and oaked and birched. Every word we traced back to our mother and father, we traced back through their mouths down their throats to their hearts, which were old and beat only halfheartedly. The Autumn Years became all our years, and we did not move gracefully into them. The children got gray and did not have children.

Leaves turned.
We did.

We would have made such a good book, our family. Or such a good cover of a book. We were practically a photograph anyway. Picture us looking at you. Everything is in our yard. Our arms are by our sides. The leaves are red and gold, they are brilliant. We are not. Hold us by the edges. See the tail of our good dog leaving the frame to get food or go into some room and be funny or tragically die. Our yard looks American, the way it is cared for, the dented mailbox, the red flag down, the species of trees, the bicycle, the tricycle. The house behind us is cropped so as to be only one story. One of the children is cropped in half. The father is beautiful, is out-of-focus. The mother, beautiful, is out-of-focus, is holding a rake, is protective, is mindful of her hair, and she is almost smiling. We are open books in our family photo, waiting for the future and the rest of the writing to come. The winter storm-watch advisories, the wills, the diagnoses, prognoses, and obituaries.

Picture the newspaper. A thin column about a local family. It reads, "They are survived by their bookshelves and yard and final dog, Miss Emily Bingo Dickinson, who will be given to the state of Massachusetts and has arthritis." There are other columns about other people. A few pages away: upcoming events, the weather, things that we will never read, a coupon for a haircut, the schedule of a parade.

Troika

Alicia Erian

Alicia Erian is the author of a book of short stories, The Brutal Language of
Love, *and a novel,* Towelhead, *which was made into a film by Alan Ball in
2008. Her memoir,* The Dragon Lies Down, *is forthcoming in 2012.*

 AFTER GARY LOST ON THE QUIZ SHOW, MY FRIEND
Camille, who lived in Los Angeles, drove us back to our
hotel. Gary sat up front—his long legs always winning
him shotgun without ever having to call it—while I sat
in the back of the aged Saab, watching him admire
Camille's thighs. Her short black dress and knee-high
boots conspired to reveal a terrific expanse of toned,
tan flesh that seemed to hold sway over Gary's power-
ful moping. It didn't hurt that she'd been cooing to him ever since we'd
left the television studio: "Don't be so hard on yourself"; "You did your
best"; "Those other guys were just too quick with the buzzer." I, on the
other hand, had barely been able to manage a comforting hug.

"Why the hell did I ring in on that Russian question?" Gary asked, as
Camille merged onto the freeway.

"Even I knew that one," I mumbled.

"You did not!" he yelled. "You have no idea who Zinovyev and
Kamenev are."

"I know who Stalin is. I know how to count to three."

"Friends, please," Camille said nervously, eyeing me through her
rearview mirror. She'd dyed her brown hair a California blonde and I
hated to admit she looked prettier than ever.

I sighed. "Let's don't fight in front of Camille."

"All right," Gary said.

"Did you have fun?" I asked halfheartedly. "Because as long as you
had fun, that's all that matters."

"Just shut up with that crap," he said.

"Sorry."

"Losing is not fun," he said. "Only winning."

"Right," I said. We were stuck in traffic on the 405, which I enjoyed only because we didn't have a car in New York; being in one now, however motionless, felt like something of an amusement-park ride. Gary and I had each taken unpaid leave from our jobs as policy analysts for the Brooklyn borough president to come to Los Angeles. We'd dipped into our savings to cover airfare and hotel. Was that what was bothering me? The money? I hoped not. It sounded so petty, especially since Gary's dream of going on a quiz show was well older than our six-year marriage. I'd never forget his jubilant phone call from the midtown Hyatt after he'd passed the qualifying exam. "The contestant coordinator took my picture *twice*!" he'd exclaimed. "She said the first one didn't do me justice!" It was this—the implication that he might be telegenic—that had led him to believe he'd soon be invited to California. Sure enough, not two months later, we came home from work to find the long-awaited message on our machine.

Looking at the back of his tall head now, I had an urge to touch the short brown hair at the nape of his neck, then didn't. Why *hadn't* he surmised that in a category entitled "On the Count of Three," Stalin, Zinovyev, and Kamenev were nothing short of a troika? Now we were stuck paying out-of-pocket taxes on a fold-up bicycle with tires the size of nickels. Some consolation prize. Meanwhile, the guy who took second place was going to Copenhagen. Mitchell, the name on his podium screen had read. Mitchell with the diffident smile.

Back at the hotel, Gary shut himself in the bathroom and wept. The maid had come and gone in the time it had taken him to lose, and now Camille and I lay side by side on the king-size bed that had been made up in our absence. At the foot of the bed were a dresser and television cabinet, and I thought about opening the latter and turning on CNN. The news tended to have a sobering effect on me and Gary, especially in those moments when we mistakenly thought we had it bad. It was never good to know that others around the globe were suffering, but the reminder always offered perspective.

After listening to his cries for a few minutes, Camille turned to me and whispered, "Maybe you should go talk to him."

I nodded and went to knock on the bathroom door.

"I'll be out in a second!" he called, like he was actually going to the bathroom.

"Okay," I said, adding, "we can hear you out here," just in case he didn't know.

Back on the bed, I suggested to Camille that she give it a go.

"Me?" she asked.

"I'm not very sympathetic," I admitted.

"Sure you are," she said, but we both knew she was lying.

"Go on," I said, "really. I just want him to feel better."

She hesitated only briefly, then got up and smoothed the front of her dress, no doubt borrowed from the fashion photographer she assisted. Hers was the name you saw in the small print of *Vogue* or *Elle*: Camille Lunsford, stylist. She disappeared around the corner and I heard her say, "Gary, it's me. Can I come in for a second?" All at once the crying stopped and voilà: open sesame.

She closed the bathroom door behind her while I lay on the quilted bedspread, listening to the thrum of their voices. In high school, Camille and I had eaten at the same lunch table for nearly a year before it occurred to me to ask her anything about herself. I said, "What are you doing this weekend?" assuming she'd come back with something boring, since she rarely spoke. But she surprised me by answering, "I'm going to my boyfriend's memorial service."

"Oh?" I said. None of us had ever even seen her with a boy. "Who's your boyfriend? I mean, who was he?"

She took a bite of her sandwich, which had been the same every day for the past few months: Branston Pickle on wheat.

"He was English," she said. "You wouldn't have known him."

It turned out that Owen had been a struggling twenty-five-year-old doctoral candidate at USC. Camille had met him at the grocery store where she cashiered, ringing up only half of his cart whenever he came in. With all the money she'd saved him, he'd taken her out to dinner. He was the first person she'd ever had sex with, and the only person she'd ever known who had died. He'd been hit by a car while riding Camille's bicycle, a lavender five-speed with no crossbar. When the police gave it back to her after the accident, all twisted and crunched, she'd thrown up on the front lawn.

The following Monday, for reasons I wasn't completely sure of, I stood waiting for her in front of her locker. "How was the memorial service?" I asked.

"Sad," she said, working her combination. She added, "When it was over, I went back to this hotel with a couple of Owen's friends and had sex with them."

"What?" I said.

"Friends of his," she repeated, "from England."

"Men friends?"

She nodded.

"God," I whispered.

"When you're grieving," she explained matter-of-factly, "all you want to do is be close to people who feel the same way as you."

"Did the men have sex with each other?"

"Not really. They hugged a little, but mostly they had sex with me."

"I think they raped you," I said, feeling terribly frightened.

"No, they didn't."

I looked at her. She was telling me things I wasn't a hundred percent clear on, things I wasn't sure actually happened to real people. Secretly, I remained certain that she had been raped. In any case, I didn't want to be friends with her. She didn't have any rules to live by. She did things that made the world seem too big.

"I don't think you should've done that," I said. "You have to be more careful."

"It was beautiful," she told me sternly.

A month or so later she called to say she was pregnant, and I agreed to go with her to get an abortion. At the clinic, a man and a woman ushered us inside to protect us from a small pro-life demonstration. One of the demonstrators shoved a picture of an aborted fetus in my face and I panicked and said, "It's not me—it's her," pointing ahead to Camille. My usher looked at me, horrified, then dropped my arm and walked away. The demonstrators moved in a little closer to hand me more of their literature, which I accepted. A couple of moist-eyed men said, "Please ask your friend to reconsider." I nodded, terrified.

"Maybe you should reconsider," I said to Camille in the waiting room. There were no good magazines to read, only back issues of *The Smithsonian* with the address labels ripped off, and pamphlets about how not to land yourself in one predicament or another.

"I'm fifteen," she said. "I can't have a baby."

"Do you want to see the pictures from the people outside?" I asked.

"No."

"I guess they're supposed to make you feel guilty," I said, pulling one of them from my pocket.

"Oh my God," Camille said, turning her head.

"If they're so against it," I said, unable to tear my eyes away, "how can they stand to look at this stuff?"

"Are you against it?" Camille asked.

"Yes," I said. "I don't even think you should kill bugs."

"Camille Lunsford," the nurse said then, and Camille got up.

"Will you come with me?" she asked.

"I'd rather not," I told her.

Afterward, at her bedside at home, I asked her whose baby she thought it was. She lay facedown on her floral comforter, the cord of an electric heating pad snaking out from beneath her.

"I don't know," she said. "It could have been either one of them, I guess."

"You should've used protection."

She started to cry. "What if it was Owen's?"

"He's dead," I told her.

"From before he was dead."

"Could it have been?" I asked.

"I don't know."

"Oh, Camille," I said, and without thinking, I laid a hand on her back.

She really started crying then, a torrential wail. Her misery pooled in my palm, then wicked up my arm like the warmth of anesthetic. Except instead of making me numb, I felt too much, and suddenly there I was, crying right along with her. Even then I had a talent for making matters worse.

When the two of them finally came out of the bathroom, Gary seemed a little better. He'd washed off the heavy peach foundation they'd patted onto his face at the studio, and now his skin was its normal ivory. Tiny red spider veins plumed around his hazel irises, but they were only visible close-up. I wondered how long it would be before I saw his straight teeth again.

"Everything okay?" I asked, rising from the bed.

Camille, her own fair skin looking slightly flushed, turned to Gary for confirmation. He nodded, then reached up to loosen his richly striped tie. As he began unbuttoning his shirt, I noticed a heavy ring of makeup around the collar. "Geez," I said, "they make you pay your way out here *and* they ruin your best clothes." I'd meant this as an insult to the television people, but as soon as I said it, I knew it had come out wrong.

"Is that what you're worried about?" Gary asked me. "The money?"

"Of course not," I said, wondering when I'd get this comforting thing right. Suddenly I wished I were back at work, convincing my boss to fund grant-writing classes for nonprofit organizations. That was what I was good at: cold, hard solutions. Any predicament in which one of these did not immediately present itself sent me into a tailspin.

Gary changed into a pair of old Levi's and a T-shirt that advertised his participation in the previous year's New York City Marathon before we headed back out again. Camille was taking us to a place called El Coyote for dinner, but since it was a little early yet, she suggested a detour.

Hancock Park was a beautifully manicured parcel of land encompassing the Page Museum as well as a good-sized research facility, both of which were devoted to the park's main attraction: the La Brea Tar Pits. These were naturally occurring shallows of molten asphalt where creatures through the ages had lost their lives, only to have their well-preserved carcasses fished out thousands of years later by grateful scientists. A series of winding, concrete paths connected pit to pit, all of which were fenced in like zoo animals. Indeed, whether large or small, each pool bubbled up with gassy life.

At five o'clock on a weekday, we arrived to find the grounds nearly deserted, the museum closed. Still, at the far end of the largest pit, an extraordinary scene was taking place. Here, a placard informed, a baby mastodon and its father wailed helplessly from the bank while the mother sat trapped in the black ooze. "She won't drown," Camille said, speaking in the ever present of the diorama. "She'll just become immobilized and starve to death."

"Look over here," Gary called from behind us.

We turned around and he took our picture. "Did you get the elephants?" I asked.

"You mean the mastodons?" he said. "Of course."

Just then, a Russian-speaking couple strode by on the path behind him. His ear turned toward their language as if by remote control; his shoulders succumbed to a hunch. "Here, Hon," I said quickly, holding my hand out for the camera, "let me take your picture with Camille."

He traded places with me robotically, though when Camille slipped an arm around his waist, he seemed to wake up a little. After I snapped the photo, he turned around to look at the diorama, fingers threaded through the wire diamonds of the fence. "Hey," he said, "she's moving."

"Who?" I said.

"Wow," Camille murmured, "I never noticed that before."

I saw what they were talking about then: the doomed mother mastodon swayed ever so slightly on her tether, making her seem vaguely alive and suffering.

"It's kind of funny," Gary said, and Camille giggled in agreement.

"No, it's not," I told them, taking all of it very personally. Surely there was nothing worse than sinking as low as you could possibly go, yet still not being able to raise yourself up out of the muck.

Before he even opened his menu, Gary, who sat across the booth from me and Camille, asked our waiter for a round of margaritas. When he did open it, he didn't read it, just stared down at a red salsa stain on the laminate. El Coyote was packed, the staff dressed in festive, native attire. I imagined their paltry wages and immediately felt embarrassed that we all looked so downtrodden.

"That guy who won today?" Gary said. "I bet he goes on to be a five-time champ."

"Then you would've been beaten by the best," I said, opening my own menu. "Would that make you feel any better?"

He thought about this for a moment and said, "No."

"Are you going to use that bike?" Camille asked.

"What bike?" Gary said.

"Your consolation prize."

"Oh," he said, "that."

"If I had a new bike," she said hopefully, "I'd have to get rid of the one that Owen got killed on, to make room for it."

Gary looked at her. He knew all about the lavender five-speed and how Camille couldn't bring herself to throw it out, coated as it was in Owen's DNA. She'd once told me that she feared it would be like having another abortion, which Gary also knew about, though not the three-some that had led to it. Besides the fact that it was Camille's business, I'd always fretted that it might make her overly attractive to him, or possibly even repel him—neither of which would do. "You don't want a fold-up bike, Camille," he said now, kind of softly. "They're crap."

"I'd pay you for it," she told him. "Then it would be like you won some money."

"We'll see," Gary said.

"Why not?" I said. "At least then we could put a few bucks back in savings."

"Do you think you could forget about the money for just one second?" Gary asked me. "God."

"Sorry."

The waiter arrived with our margaritas and some chips and salsa. After licking salt from the rim of his glass and taking a sip, Gary said, "It was a close game, though, wasn't it? I mean, at least it wasn't a runaway."

Camille and I nodded in unison at this uncharacteristic expression of acceptance. Looking to build on it, I said, "Think about poor Mitchell."

"Mitchell?" Gary said.

"That guy who came in second place," I reminded him. "He's probably feeling way worse than you."

Gary balked at this. "What the hell has he got to feel bad about? He's going to Copenhagen, for God's sake! Me, I'm riding around Brooklyn on a fucking circus bike."

We stopped talking for a while. The waiter came and took our food order, and Gary insisted on more drinks.

"But I'm driving," Camille said.

"Renee will drive," he told her. He turned to me and said, "You don't like margaritas anyway, do you?"

I shrugged. I did.

"Two more," Gary instructed the waiter.

Later, in the car, he dozed beside me while I let the wind from my open window streak hair across my face. Even in the dark I could feel the chalky hills of Los Angeles rising up around us, giving off their dry dust. In a way, I thought this was the most beautiful place on Earth, a strange old ghost town where an endless supply of cars kept people off the city streets.

I glanced at Camille in the rearview mirror, wondering if she'd ever ridden in the backseat of her own car before; if it was unpleasant or lonely; if, through this experience, she'd gained some sense of fleeting exile. "Camille?" I whispered, unsure of whether she was asleep.

"What?"

"Can I ask you something?"

"Sure." She pulled herself up between the two front headrests. Her breath on my neck carried the heat of *ancho* chilies.

"Remember that time after Owen's funeral?" I said, checking to make sure Gary was still asleep. "When you went to the hotel?"

"Yeah."

"Why do you think you did that?"

"Did what?" Gary asked suddenly, startling himself awake.

"Nothing," I said. "It's private."

"It's okay," Camille said. "You can tell him."

"You tell him," I said, irritated now that she would be so forthcoming.

"I had sex with two of Owen's friends," Camille said. "We were grieving."

"You mean—all together?" Gary asked.

"Uh-huh."

He was quiet for a moment.

"What do you think of her now?" I said.

He blinked his eyes a few times, then said, "I think she's very worldly."

Camille sighed. "If I were really worldly, I wouldn't have ended up in an abortion clinic."

"Oh," Gary said, "right."

"Thank God for Renee. She fended off all these pro-life demonstrators on the sidewalk."

"What?" I said, looking through the rearview mirror again. That wasn't the way I remembered things.

Gary, too, was suspicious. "That doesn't sound like Renee."

"It was her," Camille assured him.

I pulled up to the front of the hotel, preparing to surrender the steering wheel, but Camille said she didn't feel ready to drive herself home yet. "Come up to the room," Gary said quickly, craning toward her in the backseat. "We'll make a pot of coffee."

The lobby was pretty quiet when we walked in, save for the night clerk and a bellhop who was eating an apple in the shoeshine chair. A man sat on an antique couch in the small sitting area reading *USA Today*, and when he turned the page, I saw that it was Mitchell. This wasn't much of a coincidence since the hotel offered steep discounts to any guest appearing on the quiz show, but for the first time that day, I felt my spirits lift. It was something to do with the fact that he hadn't changed out of his khaki contestant suit; that his pancake makeup remained intact.

We looked at each other and I instantly remembered the long brown lashes that had turned the whites of his eyes to glitter on the television monitors. His wavy hair sprouted leftward, as if pushed by a nervous hand, and, even at rest, his mouth seemed racked with apology. "Hey!" it yelled suddenly. "Gary!"

At the sound of his name, Gary turned to look at Mitchell, then quickly away again, his eyes fixed on a bank of elevators looming ahead. "Keep walking," he hissed to me and Camille, but Mitchell, who'd begun to jog, was already upon us, right arm extended.

"I thought that was you," he said, squeezing Gary's reluctant hand in his.

"That was me," Gary confirmed.

"Hey, good game today," Mitchell told him.

Gary nodded. "Thanks."

"Hi," Mitchell said, holding his hand out to me. "I'm Mitchell."

"I'm Renee," I said, "Gary's wife. You played very well today, too."

"Thank you," he said.

"And this is our friend Camille."

"Camille," Mitchell said, taking her hand, "nice to meet you."

"Anyways," Gary said, "good night."

"How about a drink?" Mitchell said. "On me. The hotel bar's still open."

"No thanks," Gary said. "We're kind of tired."

I wasn't tired. Plus, I could feel myself becoming very attached to Mitchell. Though he was a bit younger than we were—a graduate student, if I remembered his television introduction correctly—his distress seemed more mature than Gary's, more manageable. At last I sensed an opportunity to be of help, and I blurted out, "Why don't you come up to our room for a nightcap?"

Gary looked at me. "Great!" Mitchell said.

In the elevator up to the tenth floor, he said, "Hey, Gary: You know that guy who beat us today? I stuck around for the rest of the tapings and he actually lost the very next game after ours. Can you believe it? He was just a flash in the pan. A fluke. We got robbed."

Gary didn't say anything.

Back in our room, Mitchell went straight for the phone on the black lacquer desk, ordering an expensive bottle of champagne. He was easy with the person on the other end of the line, laughing over something they said to him, and saying, "Hey, thanks man," when he hung up. He unbuttoned his jacket then, and turned to Gary. "If you think about it, though, it's really just an honor to have been invited on the show."

"No, it's not," Gary snapped. He'd slumped into the black-and-gold striped chair at the farthest end of the rectangular room, by the window. The desk was back there, too, and for a brief moment, I imagined him and Mitchell as a doubles tennis team.

"What's the matter, man?" Mitchell asked, jingling the change in his trouser pockets.

"What do you think is the matter?" Gary said.

Mitchell didn't have an answer.

Camille and I, sitting side by side on the bed, looked to each other for support. "Mitchell," I said finally, "would you mind making some of that coffee on the desk? We need to sober Camille up for the drive home."

She nodded. "I had margaritas for dinner."

"Sure," he said, already ripping into the vacuum-packed grounds.

"Want to watch CNN?" I asked Gary.

"No," he said, "I want to go to bed."

"Just one glass of champagne," Mitchell said, heading for the bathroom with the coffee pot, "then I'll let you guys get some sleep. I promise."

He disappeared and we heard the taps running. Gary gave him the finger in his absence, then looked at me like I was going to hear about it later for having invited him up. I shrugged as if to say *What could I do?*—even though I obviously could've kept my mouth shut.

When Mitchell emerged with the pot of water, I said, "Didn't you bring anyone to cheer you on?"

"Nah," he said, filling the Mr. Coffee. "You know how it is. People have a tough time getting off work."

"I took a week without pay," I offered.

"Oh yeah?" he said.

I nodded. "Going on the show was Gary's dream. I didn't want to miss it."

"Even though I lost?" Gary challenged.

"Of course," I said.

He looked skeptical.

"Mitchell," I said, "did you know the answer to that Russian question?"

He shook his head. "Couldn't think of the word."

"See?" I said to Gary. "You weren't the only one."

"That question was the beginning of the end," he moaned.

Mitchell nodded soberly. "I know what you mean."

"You don't know anything," Gary said. "You're going to fucking Copenhagen."

"Gary," I warned.

He looked at me, then back at Mitchell. "Sorry," he said glumly.

"Don't worry about it," Mitchell said. "Emotions are high. I realize that."

The champagne arrived and we all gathered around the desk as Mitchell popped the cork and proceeded to pour. "Not for Camille," I reminded him.

"Oh, just give me a little," she said.

"A little won't hurt her," Gary added.

"But you have to drive home," I said.

She shrugged. "I could always stay here with you guys."

"We've got plenty of room," Gary put in.

I looked over at the king-size bed. "I guess we could have them bring up a cot."

"A cot?" Gary asked.

"Here's to a good showing," Mitchell said, raising his glass.

"To a good showing," Gary said, clinking it, and suddenly he didn't seem so sullen anymore. In fact, he downed his entire glass in one gulp, then gave himself a refill before returning to his chair.

"God, I love champagne," Camille said, wandering over to him and settling herself on one of the chair's arms. Gary absently laid a hand on her back, much as I'd done that day in her bedroom, after the abortion. It struck me then that comfort was a very mysterious thing; that perhaps, at its most effective, it didn't come from those closest to us.

We were all quieted by the new seating arrangement. Mitchell, who'd finished his glass of champagne, topped off my glass before emptying the rest of the bottle into his own. I had hoped he might sit with me on the bed, but instead he returned to the desk, perching himself on its edge. The coffee percolating beside him filled the room with the smell of morning, despite the fact that we were all still entrenched in the night before.

Meanwhile, Camille had let herself slip off the chair's edge and into Gary's lap. He draped his left arm around her, and all I could think was: that's the same arm that cradles me, the same chest I lean my head against, the same erection I feel when I lower myself onto that lap. And yet, for the moment anyway, he was unrecognizable. Just as he'd been hours earlier, standing behind his podium in the television studio. Yes, he'd botched the Russian question, but there were so many others he'd gotten right—questions I had no idea he knew the answers to. It occurred to me now that I was mourning his loss not only for the immovable sorrow it had brought him, but for the rare glimpse of my husband as a brilliant stranger.

"Well," Mitchell said finally, "I don't want to overstay my welcome."

Camille finished the rest of her champagne and held her glass out crookedly to me. "Will you take this, Renee?"

"Sure," I said, getting up off the bed.

I returned her glass to the desk, where Mitchell remained, despite his threat to leave. When I hopped up next to him, he immediately got down.

"Relax, man," Gary told him.

"Sorry," Mitchell said, and he got back up again.

"And loosen your tie."

Mitchell looked down at his knotted-up self.

"You should probably think about washing off that makeup, too," Gary added, lowering his voice as a parent holding a sleeping baby might. Camille, it seemed, had passed out.

Mitchell turned to look out the window. The heavy curtains were open, framing the 405, where cars now moved easily. Beside the freeway was a billboard for a gentleman's club, flashing a woman's buxom outline in blue neon. Mitchell seemed to be speaking to her when he said, "I just can't bring myself to do it."

Gary sighed. "I know what you mean. You take the suit off, you wash your face, and that's it—the whole thing's over."

Mitchell looked at him. "Yeah," he said. "Exactly."

Gary nodded. "Who knew it would end so soon?"

"You go there," Mitchell said, "thinking you want to win all this money, but that's not it at all. You just want to keep playing."

Gary laid his right arm across Camille's knees, the empty champagne glass still in his hand. "I feel like I'm five years old again," he admitted.

"Christ," Mitchell whispered. He wiped a tear from the corner of his eye.

I smoothed a hand across his back and said, "Try to think about Copenhagen."

He laughed lightly. "Copenhagen? Do you realize that all the trip prizes originate in L.A.? Even though I live in North Carolina, I'll have to fly back here on my way to Denmark."

"I'll trade you a fold-up bicycle," Gary mumbled.

Mitchell thought for a second, then said, "Okay."

"He's just kidding," I said.

"I'm not," Mitchell said. "I don't want to go to Copenhagen."

Gary looked at him. "Are you crazy?"

Mitchell shook his head. "I want a real souvenir. Something that'll last."

Camille woke up and said, "Bikes don't last."

"If you take care of them, they do," Mitchell reasoned.

"Even if you take care of them," she persisted. Then she looked at Gary and said, "Why did you let me fall asleep?"

"Don't worry about it," he told her, but she quickly got off his lap and went straight for the Mr. Coffee machine next to Mitchell.

"Excuse me, please," she said, and he scooted off the desk again. She poured herself a Styrofoam cup of the black stuff and whispered, "I don't know why I did that, Renee. Please forgive me."

"Here," I said, pushing a basket of cream and sugar toward her.

She took two packets of Equal and said, "I'm really sorry," then went for her purse on the bed.

"Hey," Gary said, "where're you going?"

"I'll call you guys tomorrow," she said, tucking the bag beneath her arm. No coffee was spilled as she crossed the threshold of our room into the carpeted hallway.

The door closed and Gary asked, "Is she okay to drive?"

"She's fine," I said.

"I should probably go, too," Mitchell said. He was standing by the window, looking worried.

Gary turned to him. "Were you serious before? About trading?"

"Yeah."

"You'd rather have a bike than a trip to Copenhagen?"

Mitchell sighed and looked down at his dress shoes. "If I knew I had a real souvenir, maybe I could take this tie off."

Gary was quiet for a moment, then got up out of his chair and walked over to the window. He and Mitchell looked at each other in a very sad way, then Gary said, "Here," and reached for the red silk knot at Mitchell's neck. He didn't tug at it as he would've done with one of his own; rather, he undid it slowly and carefully, sliding the ends through this loop and that until eventually the tie draped Mitchell's neck like a tailor's measuring tape. Gary paused for a moment, then unbuttoned the top of Mitchell's starched white shirt. "You've got foundation stains here," he said, running an index finger along the inside of the collar. "Remember what the makeup lady said about getting them out?"

Mitchell nodded. "Baby wipes."

Gary laughed a little at this, but it seemed that Mitchell couldn't. He dropped his head again, then closed his eyes at the soft cuff of Gary's palm against his face. The embrace that followed was a strange, slow collision of two large bodies momentarily drained of happiness. They were comparable enough in height to rest a cheek on the other's shoulder; stricken enough not to concern themselves with the implications of holding on. They wilted against each other so profoundly that I couldn't imagine slipping even a sheet of paper between them. Maybe, I thought, easing off the desk and moving toward them, we'll be going to Copenhagen.

From Drive

David A. Fitschen

David A. Fitschen is a writer and artist living in New York. He no longer tours; you'll understand why. This was his first published piece.

4/18/95 Philadelphia, PA

 DAY ONE. I CAN ALREADY TELL THIS SHIP IS SINKING. Fast. Their road manager is about as useful as wet glue. I get picked up three hours late. Drive all over the city and Brooklyn. Finally Mark and I leave New York after 6 p.m., for a 4 p.m. load in.

4/19/95 Boston, MA

Waiting for the band at this radio station here in Boston. Already one load in today, two songs and load out. Drive five minutes, load in, do the show, end the routine. Two shows in D.C. tomorrow. Four shows, two days. My eye is killing me. Split it wide open taking Dodie's guitar off at sound check.

4/20/95 Washington, D.C.

Ten after five at Omega Studio, waiting for the band to show up. Waiting again. Woke up with blood all over the pillow, dried on my face. Managed to find some coffee and get the fuck going. Can't remember much of the driving. Sunny day out, trucks, broken white lines, driving past the town I was in yesterday and road. Soul Coughing's road manager just showed up. He's the biggest asshole I've met in a long time. That's saying a lot. I should just kick the shit out of him now to get it over with. Hopefully this stupid shit will be over soon.

Here at the 9:30 Club. Loaded in. Had to set the drum kit up in the alley. Just me and the biggest fucking rats I have ever seen, garbage and human defecation. Makes for a nice night. D.C. is a wasteland. Most of the rest of America is close behind. The hotel is not close.

4/21/95 Atlanta, GA

Crushing day on the road. Drove the whole way while Larry drank beer. Could give a fuck at this point. It's only the fourth day.

In the room. No dinner tonight in the hotel where they call you Mr. Fitschen. It's OK. Fancy. On a lake. Talked with Lane today. She was the girl in high school I wanted. But there is no end, there was never a beginning. She crushed my heart then and still does it seven years later. I should have known. I have the world blues in my head thinking of her. How could she know. I never said anything. Standing at a pay phone in the middle of nowhere. She told me she got engaged last night. You figure the irony. I don't know. It would have been nice to see her. Lane Blevins.

4/22/95 Atlanta, GA

Alone in the room. After the 1000's all day at the radio festival. It poured rain for an hour this morning. Soaked to the bone practically all day. Mike Watt was the highlight of the festival. Eddie Vedder, Dave Grohl, Pat Smear, and William. In all sorts of combinations. Spoke with Nate and William, now with the Foo Fighters, for a while today. They seem to be happy with the Foo's. It was good seeing all of them. Don't know how much more of Chris I can deal with before I pound his face through the back of his head. Man, I feel like destroying his world. Another road manager on a total control power trip. Today's joke was a water bottle that rolled around onstage while Soul Coughing played. He told me to get it and I left it. Then he said he wasn't joking. I still left it. Then after the set was over, he tried to tell me something. I chose not to listen. I told him my job was getting the gear from one town to the next. In and out of the club. Dealing with the stage when the band was on, as I saw fit. And if there was a problem with any of that, he could go fuck himself.

It's 10:45 p.m. I think I'll read, beat off, and try to sleep. Somewhere in Tennessee tomorrow. Larry and some fuckhead just came in. Now they are getting high. And this shithead is sitting on my bed. Larry just got off the phone inviting Sebastian and Mark down to get high. So here I am. Naked, writing, and watching this pathetic shit going down.

Had to stop for a few minutes. But now I am back. Dodie came to get high. Now they are leaving. This shit is pathetic. Thought I was going to have some time alone. But didn't happen. Met Jeff Buckley this afternoon. After they finished playing today, I loaded the equipment into their truck and returned mine. They are carrying the gear, which means I ride with the band. This won't be pretty.

4/25/95 Memphis, TN

This town is misery. This shit will swallow you whole in one day.

Can't believe we chose to have a day off here. Nothing to do in this shit-hole. Sun burning holes in me. Went by the Lorraine Hotel where Martin Luther King Jr. was killed. Looking at the balcony where he was shot. Now it has been turned into a state-run Civil Rights Museum. Right in the middle of the most depressed part of town. This state does-n't give back to its people. Went by Graceland. That was a joke. Walked through downtown to try and find dinner. Ten percent closed, ninety percent vacant. There must be a high suicide rate here in Memphis.

Everyone decided to go see Throwing Muses tonight where we played last night. I chose the room. The less time the better. Talked with my girl-friend. Nothing worth saying. New Orleans tomorrow.

4/26/95 New Orleans, LA

Went to Acme with Jeff, Yuval, and Mark. Guess that wasn't smart. Jeff is all right. One of those arty fucks I have nothing in common with, or have anything to say to. The meaningless conversation we had was just that. Had to load out through a maze of people tonight. Have a feeling there might be some fights between some of the crews. These clowns run at high ten-sion. And if they want to bring it to me, here I am. Terri, from Los Angeles, was in town for the Jazz Festival. She and her friend came to the show. No one knew what to do after the show, so we walked around. Terri got drunk, spewing shit I could care less about. It was her birthday, so I let it go. We ended up at Lafit's in the Quarter later. Larry, Mark, and Yuval were there. We all hung out for a while. Everyone pretty well hammered. Last call came. This woman sitting back at the piano bar came and introduced her-self to me. I think her name was Emily. She was from Turkey. You could tell she wasn't from around here. We talked for a few minutes. She was drunk as shit. I decided to leave with her. Larry was left with Terri and her friend. I could imagine what they had to say. I could give a fuck. I was sick of them. Sick of the faces I see and know. We ended up at her hotel. I don't remem-ber what we talked about on the way there. She went to the bathroom and started the shower. I stood in the middle of the room wondering what the fuck I was doing there. She came out. She took off her dress, bra and shorts. She was fucking gorgeous. Straight black hair, perfect small tits with hard nipples, tan lines, all the right curves and her pussy was shaved. I turned to stone. She asked me to join her then disappeared. I stood there for what seemed to be an eternity. Then the thud of her falling over in the shower made me realize where I was and what was going on. I opened the door. She was slouched over puking on herself. I found the door and left. I took the long road back to my room.

Dogfight

Sylvia Foley

Sylvia Foley is the author of the short story collection Life in the Air Ocean. *This story was her debut publication.*

ON THURSDAY CARL BROUGHT HOME THE BRINDLE dog. Moira looked up from the red couch where she sat reading and saw him standing in the kitchen doorway with the brindle on a dirty rope. Carl shrugged and untied the rope. The dog eyed her from behind Carl's legs. "Here," she said to it, "Here, boy." She crooned low in her throat and held out her hand.

"He's scared," Carl said, poking the dog.

The dog went to Moira on shaky legs. There were cuts in his hide. He wasn't a good-looking dog. For Carl's sake, she wanted to like him more than she did. "What hole did you crawl out of?" she asked the dog. When she touched his ears he flinched and growled, and she turned her hand in the air, showing him emptiness.

"I bought him off Troutman," Carl said. "He was hanging around Troutman's runs. The guy was going to shoot him, today or tomorrow."

Troutman raised cocker spaniels in the house behind their house. One or another of his bitches was always in heat. His radio was playing faintly through the trees outside; he kept it on all the time, claimed it soothed his cockers. A stray dog was a weasel to Troutman.

"He made you pay?"

"Troutman for you," Carl said. He curled his fingers into the shape of a pistol. "I gave him ten." The brindle had quit smelling her hand. She let him nose between her legs for a second, knowing he needed to. Then she pushed the dog away.

Carl took off his cap and ran his fingers through his cut-back yellow hair. He washed his hands in the kitchen sink. "I'll put him out with Fred."

"Fred won't like it," Moira said. No dogs ever hung around their own run, since Fred, her old brown dog, was the only one in it.

"It might work," Carl said.

When he came back in she said, "So?"

"Everything went fine."

They ate supper without speaking much. Carl didn't like to eat and talk at the same time. Moira watched him wipe his lips on his napkin. She thought, he is going to be so happy in a minute.

After the dishes were cleared, Moira took out the plastic test kit from the drugstore. She had already performed the test. "This line means I did it right," she said. 'You can't really do it wrong." She showed him the blood-red indicator inside the circle. She watched him, zeroing in on his face so she could spot when that bursting-open moment of joy hit him, but somehow she missed it. Maybe it was too hard to see.

"That's it?" Carl said in disbelief.

Carl used to bet the greyhounds, until Moira put a stop to that. It was in his nature to want some announcer to tell him what he was seeing with his own two eyes. Now, he stared at the little paper circle. "I think I liked it better when a rabbit died." He laughed, nervously.

"No, wait—" She showed him the second line. It was a faint trace, but it was there. "That's the real one."

He leaned across the table and kissed her. Then he laid his flat hand on her forehead. She caught a whiff of fertilizer. She had to jump up for some reason. She milled around in the kitchen, dropping plates into the rack.

"I don't have a fever. It isn't like that," she said, irritated. Carl gazed at her. Tears came out of his eyes in a slow course, and he smiled.

She heard the new dog bleat in the run, and the other dog, Fred, give his odd quavery bark. "They're getting along," she told Carl. She went back toward him and petted his bristly yellow-white hair, and he relaxed against her, his ear to her belly.

The next afternoon they drove out to the trailer park in the Catskills off 9W, where Moira's father was staying. Her father was burning vines when they arrived. He said they were poison ivy vines. Moira could tell her father was already tight.

Carl said, "They better not be poison ivy vines." All of them had breathed the smoke by now.

"It's a joke," Moira's father said. "Trying to get a rise out of her." He jerked his thumb at Moira. "Want a beer, help yourself, Carl."

He fried cheese sandwiches on white bread for them on his sterno stove under the awning. He had learned to cook since his retirement. Moira watched him cut papery slices of cheese with a scalpel. One of the other trailers had a backed-up sewage line, which they could smell as they ate. Her father offered Carl a beer and Carl took it. Carl sighed at the way she was eyeing the both of them, and said it was all right.

"Oh, fine, then," Moira said with some annoyance. She knew when she had been deserted. 'You have to make it easier for him?"

"Come on, the man's still on his feet."

"I can't quite remember why we had you," her father said, gazing at the tops of the poplars. Then he turned and tipped his glass at her as if he were offering her respect.

Moira's father was drinking lime rickeys. It was a drink he had learned to drink in nightclubs, during the war, which he hadn't been to because he was 4-F. Moira remembered him drinking this drink all through her childhood. In spite of everything she liked the sound of its name, rickey. She thought of how, once, he had let her watch him operate on a cat. He claimed a tumor grew the same as a fetus. He had handed her a greasy packet of smelling salts although she was lucid and unafraid. Now she was having a delayed reaction. Her father and Carl were talking in buzzing voices, and she was thinking of that cat's yellow belly fat. Grudgingly she lifted the lid of the cooler and helped herself to a beer. "Have you heard from Mom?" Moira asked, when she hadn't said anything for a while.

Her father turned on the radio and jiggled the tuner. "Her life is too good now. That new guy she's with is taking her to Acapulco, she hasn't got time for me." An announcer gave the time. Moira's father cut back a laugh. "She wants to dive off some hundred-foot cliff. I hope she cracks her skull."

The vine pile had nearly burned down. There were little crackles from it every so often. Carl tried to tell her father about the new dog. "He looks fast. I want to teach him to course a lure." But her father wasn't particularly interested.

After lunch her father started playing around, nudging Carl in the ribs. Moira wished she hadn't brought up her mother. "Ever pay for it?" her father said, patting his belly where the grilled cheese had gone. "Guy like you, had to pay yet?"

Moira shot Carl a look but Carl wouldn't agree to leave that minute.

'Yeah," Carl said, answering her father's question, "But not lately." He ducked his head and winked at Moira, trying to kid her along. It wasn't going to work.

"Let the buyer beware, though, huh," Moira's father said languidly. 'You get what you pay for. Luckily I still have plenty of money."

"Hey, should we tell him?" Carl asked her, to change the topic.

"What? What?" Moira's father had a crust of sugar from the lime rickey on his upper lip.

'You have sugar on you, Dad," Moira said. She pictured her father's swollen fingers clutching a woman's breast as if it were a stone he could throw, a defensive gesture made in fear rather than desire. Had he clutched her mother that way, too, or just some whore? She eyed Carl with glinty eyes. Dad's disgusting, she thought, both of them are. But she leaned over and brushed the sugar from her father's lip with her pinky. His skin was looser on him than she remembered. "Mom shouldn't have left you."

"Damn right," her father said. "I took her to Portland for the A.V.M.A. conference. She learned to ski because of me."

Carl and Moira waited by the rear wheels of the trailer while her father rolled up last night's steak bone in a piece of newspaper for Fred. There was just the one bone. Her father gave it to her and then he took her by the shoulders. "Night-night," he said. The aluminum trailer had turned blue in the twilight. He kissed her cheek with his rimy mouth. His lips stuck a little.

"Carl," Moira said in her clear voice. "Carl."

In the truck she felt the grease from the bone cut through the newspaper and soak her jeans. Now it's two dogs, she thought. She wanted to yell at Carl. She threw the bone out the truck's window. There was nothing to accuse him of. She had no real suspicions. "Not lately," he'd said, which meant "before you." She could smell the tree fertilizer on him, it was in his sweat. When he patted her leg, she pushed him away. "Don't." She put her hands up under her shirt and felt her hot belly.

When they fought at home later, Moira tried to hit Carl, but he caught her arm and held it high above both their heads. She looked sorry until he let her go. Then she hammered herself in the head with her fists, screaming at him, "Pay me, then! Pay me!"

Carl backed up. "That's enough, Moira," he said. He threw his hands up at her and walked away. Neither of them said anything more about it.

She heard the dogs gurgling low in their throats at each other, out in the run.

The sound of one of the dogs throwing itself against the wire fence Monday morning made Moira get up from the couch. Carl had left for work already. She looked out the kitchen window. The brindle was hurling himself at the locked gate, coming from way back in the run. When he leapt, the fence gave, and then bounced back like a spring, throwing him off. She watched the brindle land heavily on the ground, his claws scratching as he righted himself. She could see Fred laying on his side in the cool mud.

The next time the brindle came down, he startled Fred by landing on him. Through the glass Moira saw Fred jump up snarling. Still, Fred blinked; the brindle seized the older dog by the neck, as if he might tear his way free, through wire or flesh, it made no difference.

Sylvia Foley

When she got there with the length of pipe in her hand, though, Fred was leaning back on his haunches, his tongue lathered, and it was Carl's dog gurgling in the bright mud. She couldn't picture what had happened to reverse their order, but there was the brindle dying in front of her. His speckled side heaved and his blood gushed from the main in his throat and he died. Carl was going to be upset, she thought. Am I inhuman? She couldn't seem to feel anything. It was a problem she had sometimes, although it didn't feel like one. She had to depend on herself during emergencies.

She dragged the pipe along the wire to keep Fred back as she opened the gate. It was a gesture; she saw that the old brown dog would not attack her. His hot breath wavered at her shoulder as she knelt. She unbuttoned her shirt and wrapped the brindle's throat with it, knowing it was too late for that. His eyes were glassy. She could hear voices from Troutman's radio coming through the trees. Moira shivered in her bra. A light steam was coming off the body. She felt watched; she thought, well how do people know dogs don't have souls? The brindle's was hovering over her in the morning air. Fred stood by, bleeding patiently from the side of his neck.

Moira rearranged the shirt like a tarp under the dead dog. She dragged the body out of the run and up the slope toward the house. She imagined him following her through the air, mean and scared because he couldn't feel earth under him, so she tried not to hurt him; though it was ridiculous, she pulled as gently as she could. She left his body in the grass beside the garage drainpipe. Then she went back for Fred.

Inside the run the ground was torn and ruined. Wasps were coming from a pile of tires back in the trees between the houses. She crouched and examined the brown dog. "Fred," she said. "Dammit, Fred." Fred's eye rolled back to watch her hands. The gash in his neck had missed the artery. She took him by the collar and led him toward the garage, giving the drainpipe a wide berth. He was caked with raw mud, which stanched the bleeding somewhat. In spite of this her hands turned red and slippery. In the garage she got down a blanket that Carl kept for trips in bad weather. Fred lay on his side for her, and she cleaned him up. Then she got out the last of the penicillin and the suture kit, and stitched the gash with black thread and a curved needle. He was all worn out. His caked fur smelled like almonds. She rubbed his nose for him and let him whine.

When Carl came home he pulled the truck up short in the garage. He came into the house. Moira was sitting on the red couch. "What's with Fred?" Carl said. He slapped his hands on his pants to get the chalky fertilizer off them. He ran his scraped, tarry hands under hot water in the sink. "I brought supper," he said. "White Castle all right?"

Moira didn't want to tell him. She didn't answer. Troutman's radio was keeping those cockers quiet. At the sink Carl peered out the kitchen window. There was a pause and Moira knew he was looking all around the run, as if the brindle might have had anyplace to hide out there. "Where's my dog?" Carl said.

"He's out by the drainpipe. I saved him for you." She met his stare in the best way she could. She wanted to plead but he was against her dog already. "He bit Fred, and Fred had to kill him."

"What?" Carl said.

She said nothing.

"He's dead?"

"Fred couldn't help it."

Carl kept washing his hands, grabbing at his fingers as if they were strange to him. Then he shook off the dirty fertilizer water and went out to the garage. She was afraid for Fred but she didn't follow him. In a little while Carl came back inside. His boots made marks on the kitchen floor. His hands were stained red. He didn't wash them. Silently she cleaned the marks.

They ate slowly, side by side at the kitchen table, their jaws working. They ate the take-out that Carl had brought home. They ate french fries with cold ketchup and burgers with yellow cheese on top. The meat was brown, grey on the inside, but even cold it tasted good to her. Then, gradually, she began to hear Fred whining in the garage. He was weak, and the hollow garage door was made of metal. She knew that Carl heard him too, but he just reached for pie.

They peeled open the square boxes marked 'apple' and ate the pie inside. Carl asked for a glass of lemonade. She wasn't expecting him to want lemonade. When he said he wanted it, Moira got up and took a frozen can from the freezer. The waxy tube of the can soothed her hot hands. While she was making the lemonade she found a smear of blood on her forearm. She had her back to Carl. She put her arm under the tap and watched the blood run off into the pitcher, where it plumed and disappeared. It was nothing he had to see, she thought; it was surprising how much it looked like blood in a toilet. Unexpectedly she felt low, even angry. Should Fred have let himself be torn apart? She stirred the lemonade and watched Carl drink it. Then she cleared away the plates.

After supper she sat with Fred on the garage floor. Carl came and stood over her. His face looked bleached under the harsh overhead light, his scalp showing through his cropped hair. She could not bring herself to move. Fred was breathing heavily, his short ribs rising and falling as she stroked his crisp, small ears. "Are you coming to bed?" Carl said in a voice that was almost normal.

Fred twitched and growled as if he were having a dream.

"He's hurt," Moira said. "I'll be in soon."

Carl turned and went into the house without a word.

Later, when she led Fred back to the run, she saw Carl. He was standing, shirtless, in front of the plate-glass window in the den, his arms spread out flat as if he were attaching himself to the glass. She saw the tubercles of his eyes and nipples. As she looked he dropped his arms and faded back into the house.

She opened the run gate. Fred lay down in the mud. She listened to his slow, gusty breathing. The whites of his eyes showed dull as gravel.

Inside the house, waves of darkness. She bolted shut the garage door by feel. The kitchen wall seemed to buckle slightly as she touched it. She pulled open the refrigerator door and the light went on and she saw her own hand, reaching in. It was many-fingered and bony and stained with mud. Her father had taught her the names for its motions: adducting the fingers, you pinched and grasped. She lifted out a quart of milk. She pinched open the lip and filled her mouth with cold, thin milk, swallowing repeatedly. Only she couldn't get enough of it, so she set the quart down again on the wire rack. The light was leaking over everything. She closed the door. Its form dissolved before her eyes, trace photons shooting away. Gradually she made out the curve of the white sink, the oily window above it. She moved toward the back of the narrow house to the bedroom.

Carl was not asleep. He was watching TV in the dark with the sound off, a pillow stuffed under his head. Moira got undressed, taking off her workboots and jeans and underwear. She took Carl's T-shirt from the back of the chair and put it on. She lay down beside him, the shirt twisting around her ribs. Carl rose on his elbow and rolled toward her. His face loomed. She put her hand out and felt the shape of his mouth as if she were blind. "I know you loved that dog, Carl," she said.

His teeth gleamed in the flickering light. "I thought I was saving him," he said. "Isn't that dumb of me."

She went to stroke his head and he wiped his damp face roughly on the sheet. His leg climbed over hers. She felt his penis harden against her thigh. His hands took her wrists and he held her to the bed. He was climbing her and she said, "Carl, I'm so tired," and he began to cry again.

She felt him enter her, plunging up toward the cold nest of milk in her belly. It was going to be too late now to make him stop. She remembered how he had stood at the plate glass window with his arms spread, his mouth open against the pane. She opened her legs more for him, trying to feel him. He moved faster, grunted and collapsed, letting go her wrists. Then he moved off her and slid away, and she stroked his head because she needed to. He scared her, sometimes; that was what she felt.

After a couple of minutes Carl got up and went into the bathroom and she heard his water running into the bowl. She thought of the blank spot on the test, before the answer had come. When Carl came back he fell asleep almost instantly. She watched him sleep. She extended her fingers, touching his throat at the place where the brindle had torn Fred.

In the morning Moira got up early and went to muck out the run. She had forgotten to leave Fred enough food. He was laying in the mud beside the gate, but when he saw her he stood up unsteadily and shook himself. It was a good sign. She fed him, dumping wet and dry food into separate steel mixing bowls. Then she raked the torn-up ground.

Back in the trees between the houses she cleaned off the rake. There were patches of broken ground near the pile of tires. Moira realized that she didn't know exactly where Carl had buried the brindle. She was sweating heavily. It was still early, but so hot. She looked into the scummy water inside the tire rims. It was only water, she thought, you could not see the harm in it; but it was full of harm anyway. You couldn't drink water like that. She wiped sweat off her face.

She was close enough to Troutman's runs to hear his dogs whimpering, though not his radio. Maybe his radio was out, she thought. She felt her ears prickle as she stood listening between the houses. There wasn't even static. Troutman's radio might have been out for hours, but to Moira it seemed as if all those voices had just now disappeared from the face of the earth. What did that mean, "the face of the earth," she thought.

Carl was a man. This thought occurred to her now over and over, in exactly this language. Carl was a man, her husband; Dad was like a man. She felt a spasm of joy deep inside her. Then it came again, sharper. She had to lean against the tires. She could hear Carl's truck start up in their garage. Carl had loved that dog without trying. This spare life that he had put inside her, could she love it more than necessary? Troutman's door banged, and the radio came on and played through the air between the houses. She sank down to the cool earth under the trees. She let go of the rake. Her hands were empty. She was going to be happy again in a minute.

The Crazy Person

Mary Gaitskill

Mary Gaitskill is the author of novels Two Girls, Fat and Thin *and* Veronica, *which was nominated for a National Book Award. She has published three short story collections:* Bad Behavior, Because They Wanted To, *which was nominated for the PEN/Faulkner Award, and, most recently,* Don't Cry. *She is the recipient of a Guggenheim Fellowship and lives in New York.*

LAURA STOOD IN THE ELEVATOR OF HER APARTMENT building hating the elevator. She kept pushing the number 5 button, but the door wouldn't close. She listened to the soothing babble of the East Indians who ran the front desk; she was comforted by low, unintelligible noise.

The door started to close. "Just a minute!" A tense, blue-veined clutch of fingers followed by a thin arm dangling a big black purse caught the elevator door and made it open. Laura grinned at the tiny, purse-dangling old woman. "Thank you dear." The woman nervously squeezed her purse with one hand and picked lint off her collar with the other. Her lint-picking hand suddenly shot out and stabbed the number 3 light. The elevator stood still. Laura wanted to kick the old lady in the knee. She'd never wanted to kick old ladies before she came to New York.

Her shoes pinched her as she walked down the hall to her room. They'd just put a new carpet in. It was mottled brown and yellow. Every time Laura looked at it, she thought, "cholera." She took her shoes off as she closed the door to her apartment. She went to the fold-out couch and sat down in a sprawl. After five months she had adjusted to the apartment. It no longer made her feel like crying.

Andy had found it during his first week in town, when he had nothing but the suitcase of underwear and suits he'd brought to interview in. When Laura followed him three months later, she found him still drying himself with a single grey dish towel that he draped over the shower curtain, and eating his take-out hamburger dinners on the floor. There had been a fat plastic bottle of Diet Pepsi on the counter, and an open bag of hamburger buns. He only had one frying pan, which was always sitting on the stove with a smooth cake of grease on the bottom of it and a spatula sticking out of it.

"Andy, you're a savage," she'd said, laughing. She'd made him buy towels and pans.

But towels and pans were a small thing. He'd come to New York and gotten a job with the largest advertising agency in the country. He did account work, the most grueling and prestigious position to be hired in right out of school. He often worked until ten at night, and then came home in a cab with a white bag of burgers and French fries, his tie askew like a leash on a runaway pet, his shirt hanging out of his expensive new pants. "I hate to say this, but that woman I work for is a traditional ballbreaker. She made me rewrite the Borax proposal three times today, which was absolute horseshit. It was fine the first time." He'd throw his burgers on the kitchenette counter, and stride into the living room-bedroom, stripping off his jacket and dropping it on the floor. "It's not just me either. Everybody hates her." He'd thump down on the piano bench and pound out ragtime music, which made the opera singer next door start bawling his scales.

Laura couldn't get a job in advertising, although she had the same degree that Andy did. When she went to interviews and heard herself talk, she felt like an aborigine painted and decked with animal claws, shaking rattles and making faces at the sky as she sat before the calm person behind the desk. It was a silly image; she was a small, young woman with a high-forehead and curved cheekbones, wearing lipstick and the cinnamon brown suit she'd shopped for with her mother. She gestured only occasionally with her small hands.

She'd been there six months and none of the people behind any of the desks hired her. So she was a receptionist for an employment agency. She hated that.

She slid across the couch until the back of her head rested against the window ledge. People from the apartment upstairs sometimes threw water down into the street, and it spattered in through their windows and onto their ledge as it passed in a dismal grey comet. Why did they do that? She rolled her lolling body around and tucked one leg under her, her chin resting on her plump, soft arm, her head removed from the filthy ledge. She looked into the body-building gym across the street and saw thick-set young men in shorts standing splay-legged to lift weights, or on their backs on the floor, rapidly curling and uncurling like wounded ants. One was leaning on the window ledge looking pensive, a wave of blond hair across his sulky brow, his squared chin in his big fist. Andy was sure that she loved looking at "those muscle boys" across the street; she actually found them depressing. She dropped her eyes to the street below and imagined what it would be like to be thinking of jumping to her death.

Last night she and Andy leaned out the window and blew bubbles that floated all the way to the corner below, into the crowds of people waiting for the light with their briefcases and bags. They looked up, confused, looked all around for the source of the bubbles, watching in fascination as the shiny circles drifted into the street to be murdered by traffic.

The violinist next door began cranking up and down his scales. Laura felt mild affection for the annoying noise because she had seen the violinist in the hall. He had a pale, beautiful face marred by one pathetic crossed eye and the kind of shy, fumbling manner that Laura always thought was cute. She thought of making a tuna fish sandwich, and felt guilty. She had neglected her exercise program for days. It had been so hot. Sighing, she pulled herself off the couch and took off her brown skirt and her blouse. She peeled off her panty hose in a neat curl and put the blue-flowered towel down on the floor. She took the piece of notebook paper with the penciled chart listing the names of the exercises (Fanny Roll, Flutter Kick), the number of repetitions and little X's marked on the days she had done them. She placed the crumpled paper on the floor where she could see it and got into the Fanny Roll position. She had taken these exercises from a best-selling booklet on thighs. Buying the booklet made her feel like a receptionist. Well who cares? she thought, swinging her naked legs back and forth.

No one at work knew she had a degree in advertising. She had been afraid they wouldn't hire her if they knew. She said she had a degree in English, that she was getting married to Andy in six months and wanted to help out with the bills. They were always asking her about her marriage plans. She'd told them so many stories by now that she'd begun to wish they were true.

She turned on her stomach and put her cheek against the blue-flowered towel. She'd taken the towel from her parent's house. She used to love to dry herself with it when she was a child because she'd thought the flowers were tropical and exotic. She pressed her face against them and kicked her legs up into the air.

"He did it again! That sonofabitch! He's gonna. . . he's gonna, I'll crush him like a bug!"

"Oh, shit," said Laura.

There was thumping from the ceiling and then a crash. Laura heard a muffled roll of placating syllables that was cut off by another burst of ranting. "Oh yeah? Oh yeah? You think I care about those wise guys? Wise guys laughin' at me. Me!"

"I don't care." said Laura. She brought her legs into an upside down V above her bottom and rhythmically pressed her feet together.

Andy opened the door. "Hold that position honey," he said. "I love that exercise."

"The crazy hag upstairs is at it again," said Laura into the towel.

"What is it this time?"

"People are laughing at her."

"Again?"

They paused to listen. They only heard scuffling foot steps and a violently slammed door. Andy walked behind her and put his hands on her ankles.

"Stop staring at me."

"But it's so cute."

"Cute? If you think bondage is cute. I look hog tied. Let go of my ankles."

"Just one more squeeze."

"And another thing! And another thing!"

"Goddamn her," said Andy. He dropped Laura's ankles and went to the piano. He began furiously working his fingers over the keys.

"Now you've done it," said Laura.

A long scream dropped through the ceiling. It was immediately followed by a series of diffuse poundings. Their neighbor was stomping up and down over her floor inch by inch, probably meaning to cover the entire room. Laura pictured the woman in a filthy house coat with hideous red flowers all over it, the hem torn out and the belt dragging the floor. Laura wondered if she'd ever seen this woman in the lobby or the elevator and not realized who she was. There were a lot of weird-looking women in the building.

Andy pounded the piano from one end to the other. Their neighbor stomped. It must be tiring for a woman her age, thought Laura. They knew she was middle-aged, and that she had a teenaged daughter and an old woman living up there with her. Laura rolled on even tempo. "You' re probably making the daughter as miserable as the crazy lady," she said.

"She's probably crazy too. She probably doesn't even care."

She could hear him slowing down though. "Are you kidding?" she said. "I've heard her crying in the bathroom before when her mother was throwing a fit. Can you imagine being fourteen years old and having a mother like that?"

He stopped pounding. "It would be horrible."

"I wonder if she doesn't abuse the kid. The poor thing is always downstairs hanging around with the men at the front desk."

"I know." He moved his fingertips and three sad noises dropped off the keys. "I've heard her screaming things like 'slut.' I've always thought she was talking to the little girl."

Laura lowered her pelvis to the floor, folded her hands across her stomach, and stared at the ceiling. "Even if she's not hurting her physically, she's going to be ruined for life." There was an abrupt silence from the ceiling. Laura pictured the woman sinking into a chair, panting, a fine mist of expelled malice rising from her.

"Oh come on." He got off the piano stool, took off his jacket and dropped it on the floor. "You're being too negative. People go through all kinds of weird horrible experiences and come out okay. What about Bruno Bettleheim?" He took off his tie, draped it on a chair and went into the kitchenette. "I wonder how long she's stopped for?"

"That doesn't make it okay." She rolled over and put herself up on all fours. She began kicking one leg into the air behind her. "I just feel like we should do something."

"Honey, I tried to do something, you know what happened. The kid and the grandmother protected her, wouldn't let me in the door." He pulled his shirt out of his pants and opened the refrigerator. "I'm starving." She heard the rattling and clink of jars and cans being shoved around, heard the soft squish of the sliced bread in his big hand. "Besides, I don't think she's hurting the kid. I've seen that girl and she just doesn't have the gestalt of an abused child. Physically anyway."

"It's sort of frightening the way we've adjusted to it." She rolled into a sitting position and rested her arms on her sweating knees. "When I first came here it upset me so much to even think about that horror show up there, I'd break out in a sweat. Now I can actually listen to it and barely notice it."

"What can you do? Sweating over it doesn't help." He put four pieces of bread on a pink plate on the Formica counter and began piling lunch meat evenly on all of them. "Besides, how can you say you don't notice it? We've been talking about it ever since I walked in. You haven't even asked me how my day was. Or told me about yours."

"How was your day?" She stood and began going through her drawers for a pair of shorts.

"Hairy as usual. But I heard some new dirt. Ives in the office next to me told me that this new guy, Davis, is having an affair with the ball-breaker Miriam. That she's screwing him audibly in her office every lunch hour. That he heard her describing what kind of a lay Davis is on the phone, with her door open."

Laura put on a pair of white shorts and a red T-shirt. It depressed her to hear about the sexual antics of Andy's co-workers. She had always believed that executives screwed underlings astride their desks only in movies, that real people would be embarrassed to do something so corny.

"If it's true, and it seems to be, then Davis is a fool. To publicly put himself in that kind of position! That bitch could totally humiliate him now, and she probably will. I'm thinking of saying something to him, advising him to be more careful."

"I think you should just leave him alone," said Laura. "If everybody didn't react to it in such a lurid way, it wouldn't be so destructive."

"Oh personally, I couldn't care less. I just know other people could ridicule him and him being so new in the company, he doesn't need that." He took a big bite of his lunch-meat sandwich, picked up the plate of sandwiches and walked to the livingroom-bedroom. He sat in the reclining chair and put the sandwiches on his lap. "I just thought you might like to hear about a female in authority doing a stereotypically male power thing. Just so you'll know that it isn't all vice-presidents buggering secretaries."

"Andy, I don't like it any better when women do it. I think they all sound like a bunch of barbarians." She opened the refrigerator and got her dish of tuna fish covered by Saran Wrap, the mayonnaise and the rye bread. She put the stuff on the counter, turned back to the refrigerator and got the big green pitcher of orange juice out. She held the refrigerator door open with her bare foot while she poured herself a glass. "I know you don't think women should be like that," said Andy. "I just thought it would gratify you to know that the option is there. It suggests some kind of equality, don't you think?"

Laura stared at the mayonnaise as she spread it around on the bread. What if she had gotten hired at Bendix and Cohen? What if she had found herself surrounded by people like that? She didn't understand why they wanted to treat each other that way. Life is hard enough, she thought, dumping the tuna on the mayonnaise-smeared bread. "I do think the thing with the secretary was worse though. She's in such a vulnerable position compared to that vice-president turd. And why would he want to do that? Think about it, Andrew. What kind of fantasy is he using her to perpetuate?"

"Yeah." Andy leered as he chewed the lunch meat. "I still haven't gotten him to tell me which one it is. I keep thinking it's the one who's a little overweight."

A slight fear chilled her. She carried her sandwich and orange juice into the livingroom-bedroom, uneasy with the touch of fear that Andy sometimes made her feel. She sat on the edge of the fold-out couch, her plate on her bare knees. "I don't understand why you're trying to find out which one it is. Think how horrible it must be for her working there, worrying about who knows and what they think. How could you persecute a fat girl, Andrew, you who were once a fat boy?"

He laughed his most pleasant laugh. "Don't worry honey, he won't tell me anyway. But if he did, I'd have nothing but admiration for her. Really, I'd think she was wonderful. And she's not fat, just a little overweight. She looks good with those extra pounds."

She slid off the couch to the floor, leaving her half-eaten sandwich on the cushion lump. She put her arm around his leg and squeezed it against her, her face mashed against his scratchy pants; "You're a foolish beast," she said. She felt his hand on her head. It was one of the things she loved about Andy: His reluctance to acknowledge the reality of pain. He didn't see a poor fat girl in a skirt wrinkled across the behind, watching TV and eating too much ice cream, sullenly picking off her nail polish on her desk, desperate for involvement in scandal. He didn't see anything wrong with her at all, just a few extra pounds in a tight skirt. By not seeing the ugliness of her life he helped her ignore it too. He was nice to her, he made her feel pretty. She closed her eyes and held his leg fiercely.

The problem was though, that that didn't change the facts. The secretary was still the victim of a horrible man. Laura opened her eyes, let go of the leg and got back on the couch. Breathing sadly, she picked up her sandwich with both hands and bit it.

"How was your day?" asked Andy.

"Well, Tom Krakowski paid me the supreme compliment of calling me a good receptionist, if that's any indication. I said, 'yeah, I guess so, a monkey could do this,' and he looked unnerved."

Andy laughed like he thought she probably shouldn't have rejected Tom Krakowski's compliment. He doesn't know what it's like, she thought. He's always successful.

"You're probably smarter than him or anyone else there," said Andy. He got up and went to the kitchenette. "Why don't you turn on the TV honey? There might a good movie on."

She put aside her crumb-scattered plate and got up to turn the TV dial. She saw he was taking the bag of potato chips from the cabinet. "Bring the whole bag," she said. She flipped the dial around. On one channel, a dark-haired handsome man was gripping a blonde woman by her shoulders and talking at her furiously, his lips tight against his teeth. "Don't you know what self-respect is?" he snarled. Laura turned the channel. A pale teenaged girl with a high forehead said, "Dad's been acting so strange lately. I'm scared." She turned the channel. A handsome, worried executive was giving a speech at the end of a long table with concerned people in suits seated around it.

"Here you go honey." Andy put a big bowl of potato chips beside her and sat in the reclining chair, a paper towel covered with chips in his lap. "When are you going to send out résumés again?"

"I just did last month."

"Last month! Honey, you've got to have 'em out at all times, you've got to hit the same people over and over again so they'll remember you."

"This is my second bunch of résumés to the same people, Andy."

"Have you called them yet?"

"No. I got reject letters from all of them except Sherwood, Magus and Sloan. They interviewed me last week and I haven't heard from them since." She put as many potato chips into her mouth as she could and crunched loudly.

"How did you feel the interview went? Did you feel anything positive about it?"

"I thought it went all right. I can never tell what those people are thinking."

The executive at the head of the table had begun to melt. His hands bubbled on the table, his face ran down his front. The people around the table rose, covering their mouths. A businesswoman screamed. "My God!" shouted a businessman. "He's an Android!" There was an urgent peal of music.

"What is this thing?" said Andy.

"It might be *Wonder Woman*," said Laura. They chewed their potato chips together.

"I just sometimes get the feeling that you're not projecting as well as you could during these interviews. That you're not really giving them a strong sense of you."

"Andy, we've been through this before. I'm not you, I do things differently than you. I'm not a back-slapper."

He didn't say anything. Angry mumbling began to drip through the ceiling.

"Do you mind if I change the channel?" she asked. She flipped the dial to the channel where the teenager had been worrying. A silver-haired man in a white coat was saying, "Your father's going to need all your strength now, Sara."

"Fuck!" screamed the lady upstairs.

Laura turned the TV up. She said, "Do you know what Natalia told me today? She said that Louie told her last night that he wanted to have kids during the next five years, and that she doesn't even know if she wants them."

"Poor Luigi."

"The really awful thing is that they've been engaged six months and that's the first time they've ever talked about it. And Natalia's an intelligent person."

"I don't give a shit about that!" screamed their neighbor. She said several other things that they couldn't make out.

"It's really frightening to me the way most people just assume that their lives are going to fall into place," said Andy.

"And that goes for you too, Albert!" screamed their neighbor. She began to talk in a furious snarl, the words coming so fast they banged into each other.

"I'll bet I know part of the reason you get so upset about that maniac up there," said Andy.

"I think it's obvious why."

"Well I mean besides the fact that she's upsetting." He paused. "I think she reminds you of your father."

"A nightmare version of my father maybe," said Laura. "He's never been that crazy."

"But picture him in an apartment this size with two other people and nothing to do. I don't think it would take long."

Laura pictured her father in the apartment. She saw him clenching and unclenching his fists in a dramatic dance of fingers. His oily hair stood up on his head. He stared out the window at the muscle boys across the street. He said, "Look at those bastards."

"I wonder if she's as miserable as Daddy," said Laura.

"Probably," said Andy. "Remember the way he yelled and screamed about the dog that barked half way down the block?"

"He didn't just scream and yell. He recorded it and replayed it at two o'clock in the morning on the balcony."

"And what happened on the Fourth of July?"

"You mean the time he waited until everybody was quiet and then ran out in the street with a cap pistol, shooting at everything?"

Andy laughed. They had told these stories before; Andy liked to talk about her father. "Then there was the wash cloth incident. The yard littered with clothes! What provoked that again?"

"All the soggy wash clothes on the bathroom racks."

"He tossed them off the balcony, didn't he?"

"He's really much more imaginative than she is, Andy."

"He's got more resources. She hasn't got a balcony or a yard. What can she do but jump up and down?"

It's so miserable, thought Laura. That poor crazy woman up there, alone with no hope. And us making fun and hating her along with everybody else in the building.

"I've often wondered if she looks perfectly lucid to people she deals with on the outside," said Andy. "Because I never even believed the stories you told me about your dad until the time he went after the caterpillar with the paint-scraper."

Laura curled her legs up to her side and held her toes in her hand. She stared at the TV. "I don't really think you can put them on the same level just because they're both nutty. I mean, Daddy's really intelligent and accomplished, especially when you consider his background."

"Oh, no doubt. I've always thought you got your intellectual nature from your father. He's got an incredible mind for questioning and analyzing. My God, he's actually read all those books lining that living room wall. He impressed me from the first time I talked to him. He didn't just impress me, he inspired me. I changed my major to political science because of your dad."

Laura realized that she was rocking back and forth. The mother of a high school friend once told her that rocking back and forth in silence was a sign of a disturbed personality. She held still.

"It's just too bad that you got all the negativity from him too." He stood and crumpled the paper towel in his big fist. "Although that's really improving. You're a lot more relaxed and positive than you were a few years ago."

"I still can't get a job."

"Don't think like that! You will. You've just got to get on a roll. Put out some energy, some expectation. They'll smell it, I'll guarantee you."

Laura had a sudden mental picture of her older sister, Sherry.

She often did when she and Andy had these discussions. Sherry had told her she was making a big mistake to go into advertising.

All three of them had had a violent argument about it; Sherry had accused Andy of pushing Laura to be like him, of warping her perspective and self-esteem. Laura had wanted to be a writer during her undergraduate years; Sherry had exhorted her to keep writing, to forget about keeping up with Andy. Laura had always pictured herself writing during the evenings, while she was making money at her advertising job. But she hadn't written a story for three years.

Sherry left her alone about it now, probably because it would be embarrassing for her to bring it up. She had had a nervous breakdown two years ago, and had spent four months in a mental hospital. She hadn't done anything since then but wait tables and drink and have short, dull affairs with boys several years younger than she was. She had wanted to be an actress.

There was a roll of angry sound from above, with only one word, "scum!" leaping out in relief.

"There's nothing to watch on TV, Andy."

"As if we could watch with all that shit going on up there." He walked into the kitchenette to drop the wadded paper towel on the counter. He got his giant candy bar out of the refrigerator. "Want a chunk?"

She took a slab of cold chocolate and put it on her thigh to warm. "I don't know how you can say that I get more upset about her than you do. It obviously drives you crazy."

"Yeah, but I just get annoyed at it as an irritation. It doesn't get to me in an emotional way."

"And when I catch him again, I'll . . ."

Laura picked up her chocolate and breathed on it.

"Do you ever wonder," said Andy through his mouthful of candy, "what she's actually saying? I sometimes catch myself straining to hear her words. Sometimes I think she's talking about us. Because of the piano."

"So do I," said Laura. They listened to the cursing rattle of words. Laura lay down, her piece of chocolate resting on her chest. "What do you want to do?" she asked.

"I don't know." He lay down in the reclining chair, working his jaws slowly and heavily as he lay. His arm was slack, the knuckles of one large, black-haired hand grazed the floor. He swallowed. "We could sneak up the stairs and stand outside her door and listen to her."

"Andy, we can't do that. It's childish."

"It might be fun." Laura thought of the little boys who sometimes ran up on to her father's porch, rang his doorbell and ran away giggling. Her father was always threatening to disembowel them. "What if she catches us?"

"Come on, let's do it. Leave the TV on so she'll think we're still here."

The stairwell was dark and primitive, its walls covered with slashes of bright graffiti. It gave Laura the feeling that she was in high school again, skipping class in the boiler room, hiding out from the vice-principal. They crept up the concrete steps slowly, Laura holding Andy's sleeve, both smiling foolishly. Laura had never done things like this when she was a kid, she had always been the one to say, "But that's mean," when everybody else had wanted to go write dirty words on old Mrs. Mirsky's house. But this was different. Old Mrs. Mirsky had never done anything to anyone, while their neighbor had been tormenting them and everyone in the building for months. She felt a thrill of guilt, but it was a strangely pleasant sensation.

"Andy, what are we going to do if she catches us? If she happens to open the door?"

"She can't possibly hear us," he whispered. "Her door isn't that close to the stairwell. Even if she did, what could she do? She's just an old lady."

They opened the stairwell door on her floor and poked their heads out. They saw the crazy lady's door. Laura felt weak with fright; the muttering was quite loud from here.

"Let's go closer," whispered Andy.

"No."

They strained to hear.

"Wise guys," heard Laura, "wise guys eavesdropping on me?"

"Huh? Huh?" The terrible voice was quizzical. "Wise guys laughin' at me?" There was a muffled response from someone else in the room. Andy turned. "Did she say something about behind the door?"

The crazy lady's door swung open. Laura glimpsed a frazzle of stiff grey hair before she turned and ran with Andy down the stairs. They leapt two steps at a time, Laura terrified that one would trip and fall into another, sending them both crashing down the stairs.

They stumbled into their apartment, trembling and giggling. Andy closed and locked the door behind them and Laura saw laughter roll from his face in subsiding expressions of amusement, superiority, and entitlement.

"Andy," she said, giggling. "Andy, you are such an asshole."

A tiny door opened in the center of his eyes and a tiny face peeked out. It was a face that knew what she said was true. She blinked and for a terrible moment she knew it was true too. Then Andy laughed his big easy laugh again.

"Yeah, honey," he said, "and so are you."

He playfully ruffled her hair.

Wild Berry Blue

Rivka Galchen

The author of the debut novel Atmospheric Distrubances, *Rivka Galchen grew up in Norman, Oklahoma, the child of Israeli immigrants. She attended Princeton and went on to get her MD at Mount Sinai School of Medicine. She was a Robert Bingham Fellow and Writing Instructor Fellow at Columbia's MFA program, has been published in* The New Yorker, Zoetrope, *and* Harper's, *and was awarded a 2006 Rona Jaffe Foundation Writers Award. In 2010 Galchen was chosen by* The New Yorker *as one of the top twenty American writers under the age of forty.*

 THIS IS A STORY ABOUT MY LOVE FOR ROY THOUGH first I have to say a few words about my dad, who was there with me at the McDonald's every Saturday letting his little girl—I was maybe eight—swig his extra half and halfs, stack the shells into messy towers. My dad drank from his bottomless cup of coffee and read the paper while I dipped my McDonaldland cookies in milk and pretended to read the paper. He wore gauzy plaid button-ups with pearline snaps. He had girlish wrists, a broad forehead like a Roman, and an absolutely terrifying sneeze.

"How's the coffee?" I'd ask.

"Not good, not bad. How's the milk?"

"Terrific," I'd say. Or maybe, "Exquisite."

My mom was at home cleaning the house; our job there at the McDonald's was to be out of her way.

And that's how it always was on Saturdays. We were Jews, we had our rituals. That's how I think about it. Despite the occasional guiltless cheeseburger, despite being secular Israelis living in the wilds of Oklahoma, the ineluctable Jew part in us still snuck out, like an inherited tic, indulging in habits of repetition. Our form of *davenning.* Our little Shabbat.

Many of the people who worked at the McDonald's were former patients of my dad's: mostly drug addicts and alcoholics in rehab programs. McDonald's hired people no one else would hire; I think it was a policy.

And my dad, in effect, was the McDonald's—Psychiatric Institute liaison. The McDonald's manager, a deeply Christian man, would regularly come over and say hello to us, and thank my dad for many things. Once he thanked him for, as a Jew, having kept safe the word of God during all the dark years.

"I'm not sure I've done *so* much," my dad had answered, not seriously.

"But it's been living there in you," the manager said earnestly. He was basically a nice man, admirably tolerant of the accompanying dramas of his work force, dramas I picked up on peripherally. Absenteeism, petty theft, a worker OD-ing in the bathroom. I had no idea what that meant, to OD, but it sounded spooky. "They slip out from under their own control," I heard the manager say one time, and the phrase stuck with me. I pictured one half of a person lifting up a velvet rope and fleeing the other half.

Sometimes, dipping my McDonaldland cookies—Fryguy, Grimace—I'd hold a cookie in the milk too long and it would saturate and crumble to the bottom of the carton. There, it was something mealy, vulgar. Horrible. I'd lose my appetite. Though the surface of the milk often remained pristine I could feel the cookie's presence down below, lurking, like some ancient bottom-dwelling fish with both eyes on one side of his head.

I'd tip the carton back slowly in order to see what I dreaded seeing, just to feel that queasiness, and also the prequeasiness of knowing the main queasiness was coming, the anticipatory ill.

Beautiful/Horrible—I had a running mental list. Cleaning lint from the screen of the dryer—beautiful. Bright glare on glass—horrible. Mealworms—also horrible. The stubbles of shaved hair in a woman's armpit—beautiful.

The Saturday I was to meet Roy, after dropping a cookie in the milk, I looked up at my dad. "Cookie," I squeaked, turning a sour face at the carton.

He pulled out his worn leather wallet, with its inexplicable rust stain ring on the front. He gave me a dollar. My mom never gave me money and my dad always gave me more than I needed. (He also called me the Queen of Sheba sometimes, like when I'd stand up on a dining room chair to see how things looked from there.) The torn corner of the bill he gave me was held on with yellowed Scotch tape. Someone had written over the treasury seal in blue pen, "I love Becky!!!"

I go up to the counter with the Becky dollar to buy my replacement milk, and what I see is a tattoo, most of which I can't see. A starched white long-sleeve shirt covers most of it. But a little blue-black lattice of it I can see—a fragment like ancient elaborate metalwork, that creeps down all the way, past the wrist, to the back of the hand, kinking up and over a very plump vein. The vein is so distended I imagine laying my cheek on it in order to feel the blood pulse and flow, to maybe even hear it. Beautiful. So beautiful. I don't know why but I'm certain this tattoo reaches all the way up to his shoulder. His skin is deeply tanned but the webbing between his fingers sooty pale.

This beautiful feeling. I haven't had it about a person before. Not in this way.

In a trembling moment I shift my gaze up to the engraved name tag. There's a yellow M emblem, then *Roy.*

I place my dollar down on the counter. I put it down like it's a password I'm unsure of, one told to me by an unreliable source. "Milk," I say, quietly.

Roy, whose face I finally look at, is staring off, up, over past my head, like a bored lifeguard. He hasn't heard or noticed me, little me, the only person on line. Roy is biting his lower lip and one of his teeth, one of the canines, is much whiter than the others. Along his cheekbones his skin looks dry and chalky. His eyes are blue, with beautiful bruisy eyelids.

I try again, a little bit louder. "Milk."

Still he doesn't hear me; I begin to feel as if maybe I am going to cry because of these accumulated moments of being nothing. That's what it feels like standing so close to this type of beauty—like being nothing.

Resolving to give up if I'm not noticed soon I make one last effort and, leaning over on my tiptoes, I push the dollar further along the counter, far enough that it tickles Roy's thigh, which is leaned up against the counter's edge.

He looks down at me, startled, then laughs abruptly. "Hi little sexy," he says. Then he laughs again, too loud, and the other cashier, who has one arm shrunken and paralyzed, turns and looks and then looks away again.

Suddenly these few seconds are everything that has ever happened to me.

My milk somehow purchased I go back to the table wondering if I am green, or emitting a high-pitched whistling sound, or dead.

I realize back at the table that it's not actually the first time I've seen Roy. With great concentration, I dip my Hamburglar cookie into the cool milk. I think that maybe I've seen Roy—that coarse blond hair—every Saturday, for all my Saturdays. I take a bite from my cookie. I have definitely seen him before. Just somehow, not in this way.

My dad appears to be safely immersed in whatever is on the other side of the crossword puzzle and bridge commentary page. I feel—a whole birch tree pressing against my inner walls, its leaves reaching to the top of my throat—the awful sense of wanting some other life. I have thought certain boys in my classes have pretty faces, but I have never before felt like laying my head down on the vein of a man's wrist. (I still think about that vein sometimes.) Almost frantically I wonder if Roy can see me there at my table, there with my dad, where I've been seemingly all my Saturdays.

Attempting to rein in my anxiety I try and think: What makes me feel this way? Possessed like this? Is it a smell in the air? It just smells like beefy grease, which is pleasant enough but nothing new. A little mustard. A small vapor of disinfectant. I wonder obscurely if Roy is Jewish, as if that might make normal this spiraling fated feeling I have. As if really what's struck me is just an unobvious family resemblance. But I know that we're the only Jews in town.

Esther married the gentile king, I think, in a desperate absurd flash.

Since a part of me wants to stay forever I finish my cookies quickly.

"Let's go," I say.

"Already?"

"Can't we just leave? Let's leave."

There's the Medieval Fair, I think to myself in consolation all Sunday. It's two weekends away, a Saturday. You're always happy at the Medieval Fair, I say to myself, as I fail to enjoy sorting my stamps, fail to stand expectantly, joyfully, on the dining room chair. Instead I fantasize about running the French fry fryer in the back of McDonald's. I imagine myself learning to construct Happy Meal boxes in a breath, to fold the papers around the hamburgers *just so*. I envision a stool set out for me to climb atop so that I can reach the apple fritter dispenser; Roy spots me, making sure I don't fall. And I get a tattoo of a bird, or a fish, or a ring of birds and fish, around my ankle.

But there is no happiness in these daydreams, just an overcrowded and feverish empty.

At school on Monday I sit dejectedly in the third row of Mrs. Brown's class, because that is where we are on the weekly seating chart rotation. I suffer through exercises in long division, through bits about Magellan. Since I'm not in the front I'm able to mark most of my time drawing a tremendous maze, one that stretches to the outer edges of the notebook paper. This while the teacher reads to us from something about a girl and her horse. Something. A horse. Who cares! Who cares about a horse! I think, filled, suddenly, with unexpected rage. That extra white tooth. The creeping chain of the tattoo. I try so hard to be dedicated to my maze, pressing my pencil sharply into the paper as if to hold down my focus better.

All superfluous, even my sprawling maze, superfluous. A flurry of pencil shavings from the sharpener—they come out as if in a breath— distracts me. A sudden phantom pain near my elbow consumes my attention.

I crumple up my maze dramatically; do a basketball throw to the wastebasket like the boys do. I miss, of course, but no one seems to notice, which is the nature of my life at school, where I am only noticed in bland embarrassing ways, like when a substitute teacher can't pronounce my last name. The joylessness of my basketball toss—it makes me look over at my once-crush, Josh Deere, and feel sad for him, for the smallness of his life.

One day, I think, it will be Saturday again.

But time seemed to move so slowly. I'd lost my appetite for certain details of life.

"Do you know about that guy at McDonald's with the one really white tooth?" I brave this question to my dad. This during a commercial break from *Kojak*.

"Roy's a recovering heroin addict," my dad says, turning to stare at me. He always said things to me other people wouldn't have said to kids. He'd already told me about the Oedipus complex and I had stared dully back at him. He would defend General Rommel to me, though I had no idea who General Rommel was. He'd make complex points about the straits of Bosporus. It was as if he couldn't distinguish ages.

So he said that to me, about Roy, which obviously he shouldn't have said. (Here, years later, I still think about the mystery of that plump vein, which seems a contradiction. Which occasionally makes me wonder if there were two Roys.)

"I don't know what the story with the tooth is," my dad adds. "Maybe it's false?" And then it's back to the mystery of *Kojak*.

I wander into the kitchen feeling unfulfilled and so start interrogating my mom about my Purim costume for the carnival that is still two Sundays, eons away. The Purim carnival is in Tulsa, over an hour's driving distance; I don't know the kids there, and my costume never measures up. "And the crown," I remind her hollowly. I'm not quite bold enough to bring up that she could buy me one of the beautiful ribbon crowns sold at the Medieval Fair, which we'll be at the day before. "I don't want," I mumble mostly to myself, "one of those paper crowns that everyone has."

Thursday night I am at the Skaggs Alpha Beta grocery with my mom. I am lingering amid all the sugar cereals I know will never come home with me. It's only every minute or so that I am thinking about Roy's hand, about how he called me sexy.

Then I see Roy. He has no cart, no basket. He's holding a gallon of milk and a supersized bag of Twizzlers and he is reaching for, I can't quite see—a big oversized box that looks to be Honeycomb. A beautiful assemblage. Beautiful.

I turn away from Roy but stand still. I feel my whole body, even my ears, blushing. The backs of my hands feel itchy the way they always do in spring. Seeking release I touch the cool metal shelving, run my fingers up and over the plastic slipcovers, over the price labels, hearing every nothing behind me. The price labels make a sandy sliding sound when I push them. He's a monster, Roy. Not looking at him, just feeling that power he has over me, a monster.

My mom in lace-up sandals cruises by the aisle with our shopping cart, unveiling to me my ridiculousness. Able now to turn around I see that Roy is gone. I run after my mom and when finally we're in the car again, backdoor closed on the groceries—I see celery stalks innocently sticking out of a brown paper bag when I turn around—I feel great relief.

I decide to wash my feet in the sink, this always makes me happy. On my dad's shaving mirror in the bathroom, old Scotch tape holding it in place, is a yellowed bit of paper, torn from a magazine. For years it's been there, inscrutable, and suddenly I feel certain that it carries a secret. About love maybe. About the possessed feeling I have because of Roy.

It says *And human speech is but a cracked kettle upon which we tap crude rhythms for bears to dance to, while we long to make music that—*

Next to the scrap is a sticker of mine, of a green apple.

I look again at the quote: the bears, the kettle.

Silly I decide. It's all very silly. I start to dry my feet with a towel.

For the impending McDonald's Saturday I resolve to walk right past my tattooed crush. I'll have nothing to do with him, with his hi little sexys. This denouncement is actually extraordinarily painful since Roy alone is now my whole world. Everything that came before—my coin collection in the Tupperware, the corrugated cardboard trim on school bulletin boards, the terror of the fire pole—now revealed supremely childish and vain. Without even deciding to, I have left all that and now must leave Roy too. I commit to enduring the burden of the universe alone. The universe with its mysterious General Rommels, its heady straits of Bosporus. I resolve to suffer.

Saturday comes again. My mom has already taken the burner covers off the stove and set them in the sink. I'm anxious, like branches shaking in wind, and I'm trying the think-about-the-Medieval-Fair trick. I picture the ducks at the duck pond, the way they waddle right up and snatch the bread slice right out of my hand. I focus on the fair—knowing that time will move forward in that way, eventually waddle forward to the next weekend.

Buckling myself into the front seat of our yellow Pinto, I put an imitation Lifesaver under my tongue, a blue one. When my dad walks in front of the car on the way to the driver's side, I notice that he has slouchy shoulders. Horrible. Not his shoulders, but my noticing them.

"I love you," I say to my dad. He laughs and says that's good. I sit there hating myself a little.

I concentrate on my candy, on letting it be there, letting it do its exquisitely slow melt under my tongue. Beautiful. I keep that same candy the whole car ride over, through stop signs, waiting for a kid on a Bigwheel to cross, past the Conoco, with patience during the long wait for the final left turn. In my pocket I have more candies. Most of a roll of wild berry. When I move my tongue just a tiny bit, the flavor, the sugary slur, assaults my sensations. I choke on a little bit of saliva.

When we enter I sense Roy at our left; I walk on the far side of my dad, hoping to hide in his shadow. In a hoarse whisper I tell my dad that I'll go save our table and that he should order me the milk and the cookies.

"Okay," he whispers back, winking, as if this is some spy game I am playing.

At the table I stare straight ahead at the molded plastic bench, summoning all my meager power to keep from looking feverishly around. I think I sense Roy's blond hair off in the distance to my left. I glimpse to the side, but see just a potted plant.

"How's the coffee?" I ask after my dad has settled in across from me.

He shrugs his ritual shrug but no words except the question of how is your milk. Is he mad at me? As I begin dipping my cookies with a kind of anguish I answer that the milk is delicious.

Why do we say these little things? I wonder. Why do I always want the McDonaldland butter cookies and never the chocolate chip? It seems creepy to me suddenly, all the habits and ways of the heart I have that I didn't choose for myself.

I throw back three half and halfs.

"Will you get me some more half and halfs?" my dad asks.

He asks nicely. And he is really reading the paper while I am not. Of course I'm going to go get creamers. I'm a kid, I remember. He's my dad. All this comes quickly into focus, lines sharp, like feeling the edges of a sticker on paper.

"I don't feel well," I try.

"Really?"

"I mean I feel fine," I say getting out of the chair.

Roy. Taking a wild berry candy from my pocket I resolve again to focus on a candy under my tongue instead of on him. I head first toward the back wall, darting betwixt and between the tables with their attached swiveling chairs. This is the shiniest cleanest place in town, that's what McDonald's was like back then. Even the corners and crevices are clean. Our house—even after my mom cleans it's all still in disarray. I'll unfold a blanket and find a stray sock inside. Behind the toilet there's blue lint. Maybe that's what makes a home, I think, its special type of mess.

And then I'm at the front counter. I don't look up.

I stand off to the side since I'm not really ordering anything, just asking for a favor, not paying for milk but asking for creamers. Waiting to be noticed, I stare down at the brushed steel counter with its flattering hazy reflection and then it appears, he appears. I see first his palm, reflected in the steel. Then I see his knuckles, the hairs on the back of his hand, the lattice tattoo, the starched shirt cuff that is the beginning of hiding all the rest of the tattoo that I can't see.

Beautiful.

A part of me decides I am taking him back into my heart. Even if no room will be left for anything else.

Roy notices me. He leans way down, eyes level with my sweaty curls stuck against my forehead, at the place where I know I have my birthmark—a dark brown mole there above my left eyebrow—and he says, his teeth showing, his strange glowing white canine showing—"Dya need something?" He taps my nose with his finger.

That candy—I had forgotten about it, and I move my tongue and the flavor—it all comes rushing out, overwhelming, and I drool a little bit as I blurt out, "I'm going to the Medieval Fair next weekend." I wipe my wet lips with the back of my hand and see the wild-berry blue saliva staining there.

"Cool," he says, straightening up, and he interlaces his fingers and pushes them outward and they crack deliciously, and I think about macadamias. I think I see him noticing the blue smeared on my right hand. He then says to me: "I love those puppets they sell there—those real plain wood ones."

I just stare at Roy's blue eyes. I love blue eyes. Still to this day I am always telling myself that I don't like them, that I find them lifeless and dull and that I prefer brown eyes, like mine, like my parents', but it's a lie. It's a whole other wilder type of love that I feel for these blue-eyed people of the world. So I look up at him, at those blue eyes, and I'm thinking about those plain wooden puppets—this is all half a second—then the doors open behind me and that invasive heat enters and the world sinks down, mud and mush and the paste left behind by cookies.

"Oh," I say. "Half and half."

He reaches into a tray of much melted ice and bobbing creamers and he hands three to me. My palm burns where he touched me and my vision is blurry; only the grooves on the half and half container keep me from vanishing.

"Are you going to the fair?" I brave. Heat in my face again, the feeling just before a terrible rash. I'm already leaving the counter so as not to see those awful blue eyes and I hear, "Ah I'm workin,'" and I don't even turn around.

I read the back of my dad's newspaper. They have found more fossils at the Spiro mounds. There's no explanation for how I feel.

How can I describe the days of the next week? I'd hope to see Roy when I ran out to check the mail. I'd go drink from the hose in our front yard thinking he might walk or drive by, even though I had no reason to believe he might ever come to our neighborhood. I got detention for not turning in my book report of *The Yellow Wallpaper*. I found myself rummaging around in my father briefcase, as if Roy's files—I imagined the yellow confidential envelope from Clue—might somehow be there. Maybe I don't need to explain this because who hasn't been overtaken by this monstrous shade of love? I remember walking home from school very slowly, anxiously, as if through foreign, unpredictable terrain. I wanted to buy Roy a puppet at the Medieval Fair. One of the wooden ones like he'd mentioned. Only in that thought could I rest. All the clutter of my mind was waiting to come closer to that moment of purchasing a puppet.

So I did manage to wake up in the mornings. I did try to go to sleep at night. Though my heart seemed to be racing to its own obscure rhythm, private, even from me.

Friday night before the fair, hopeless for sleep—my bedroom seemed alien and lurksome—I pulled my maze workbook from the shelf and went into the brightly lit bathroom. I turned on the overhead fan so that it would become noisy enough to overwhelm the sound in my mind of Roy cracking his knuckles, again and again. The whirring fan noise—it was like a quiet. I sat in the empty tub, set the maze book on the rounded ledge and purposely began on a difficult page. I worked cautiously, tracing ahead with my finger before setting pen to paper. This was pleasing, though out of the corner of my eye I saw the yellowed magazine fragment—*cracked kettle*—and through its message it was like a ghost in the room with me. I felt sure—almost too sure considering that I didn't understand it—it had nothing to do with me.

In the morning my mom found me there in the tub, like some passed out drunk, my maze book open on my small chest. I felt like crying, didn't even know why. I must have fallen asleep there. I reached up to my face, wondering if something had gone wrong with it.

"Do you have a fever?" my mom asked.

It must have seemed like there had to be an explanation. When she left, assured, somewhat, I tried out those words—*Human speech is like a cracked kettle*—like they were the coded answer to a riddle.

I was always that kind of kid who crawled into bed with her parents, who felt safe only with them. If my mom came into my classroom because I had forgotten my lunch at home, I wasn't ashamed like other kids were, but proud. For a few years of my life, up until then, my desires hadn't been chased away from me. I wanted to fall asleep on the sofa while my dad watched *The Twilight Zone* and so I did. I wanted couscous with butter and so I had some. Yes, sometimes shopping with my mom I coveted a pair of overalls or a frosted cookie, but the want would be faint and fade as soon as we'd walked away.

I had always loved the Medieval Fair. A woman would dress up in an elaborate mermaid costume and sit under the bridge that spanned the artificial pond. I thought she was beautiful. People tossed quarters down at her. She'd flap her tail, wave coyly. It wasn't until years later that I realized that she was considered trashy.

Further on there was a stacked hay maze that had already become too easy by late elementary school but I liked looking at it from a distance, from up on the small knoll. I think every turn you might take was fine. Whichever way you went you still made it out. I remember it being upsetting, being spat out so soon.

We had left the house uncleaned when we went to the fair that Saturday. I was thinking about the wooden puppet but I felt obligated to hope for a crown; that's what I was supposed to be pining for. I imagined that my mom would think to buy me a crown for my Queen Esther costume. But maybe, I hoped, she would forget all about the crown. It wasn't unlikely. What seemed like the world to me often revealed itself, through her eyes, to be nothing.

We saw the dress-up beggar with the prosthetic nose and warts. We crossed the bridge, saw the mermaid. A pale teenage boy in stonewashed jeans and a tanktop leaned against the bridge's railing, smoking, and looking down at her. Two corseted women farther along sang bawdy ballads in the shade of a willow and while we listened a slouchy man went by with a gigantic foam mallet. The whole world, it seemed, was laughing or fighting or crying or unfolding chairs or blending smoothies and this would go on until time immemorial. Vendors sold wooden flutes, Jacob's ladders. The smell of funnel cakes and sour mystery saturated the air. In an open field two ponies and three sheep were there for the petting and the overseer held a baby pig in his hands. We ate fresh ears of boiled corn, smothered with butter and cracked pepper. My mom didn't mention the price. That really did make it feel like a day in some other me's life.

But I felt so unsettled. Roy's tooth in my mind as I bit into the corn, Roy's fingers on my palm as I thrummed my hand along a low wooden fence. I had so little of Roy and yet he had all of me and the feeling ran deep, deep to the most ancient parts of me. So deep that in some way I felt that my love for Roy shamed my people, whoever my people were, whoever I was queen of, people I had never met, nervous people and sad people and dead people, all clambering for air and space inside of me. I didn't even know what I wanted from Roy. I still don't. All my life love has felt like a croquet mallet to the head. Something absurd, ready for violence. Love.

I remember once years later, in a love fit, stealing cherry Luden's cough drops from a convenience store. I had the money to pay for them but I stole them instead. I wanted a cheap childish cherry flavor on my tongue when I saw my love, who of course isn't my love anymore. That painful pathetic euphoria. Low quality cough drops. That's how I felt looking around anxiously for the wooden puppet stand, how I felt looking twice at every blond man who passed wondering if he might somehow be Roy, there for me, even though he'd said he wouldn't be there. Thinking about that puppet for Roy eclipsed all other thoughts, put a slithery veil over the whole day. How much would the puppet cost? I didn't have my own pocket money, an allowance or savings or anything like that. I wasn't in the habit of asking for things. I never asked for toys. I never asked for sugar cereals. I felt to do so was wrong. I had almost cried that one day just whispering to myself about the crown. But all I wanted was that puppet because that puppet was going to solve everything.

At the puppet stand I lingered. I was hoping that one of my parents would take notice of the puppets, pick one up. My dad, standing a few paces away, stood out from the crowd in his button-up shirt. He looked weak, sunbeaten. My mom was at my side, her arms crossed across an emergency orange tanktop. It struck me, maybe for the first time, that they came to this fair just for me.

"I've never wanted anything this much in my whole life," I confessed in a rush, my hand on the unfinished wood of one of the puppets. "I want this more than a crown."

My mom laughed at me, or at the puppet. "But it's so ugly," she said in Hebrew.

"That's not true," I whispered furiously, feeling as if everything had fallen silent, as if the ground beneath me was shifting. The vendor must surely have understood my mom, by her tone alone. I looked over at him: a fat bearded man talking to a long-haired barefoot princess. He held an end of her dusty hair distractedly; his other hand he had inside the collar of his shirt. He was sweating.

"*Drek*," my mom shrugged. Junk.

"Grouch," I broke out, like a tree root heaving through soil. "You don't like anything," I almost screamed, there in the bright sun. "You never like anything at all." My mother turned her back to me. I sensed the ugly vendor turn our way.

"I'll get it for you," my dad said, suddenly right with us. There followed an awkward argument between my parents, which seemed only to heighten my dad's pleasure in taking out his rust-stained wallet, in standing his ground, in being, irrevocably, on my side.

His alliance struck me as misguided, pathetic, even childish. I felt like a villain. We bought the puppet.

That dumb puppet—I carried it around in its wrinkly green plastic bag. For some reason I found myself haunted by the word leprosy. When we watched the minstrel show in the little outdoor amphitheater I tried to forget the green bag under the bench. We only made it a few steps before my mom noticed it was gone. She went back and fetched it.

At home I noticed that the wood of one of the hands of the puppet was cracked. That wasn't the only reason I couldn't give the puppet to Roy. Looking at that mute piece of wood I saw something. A part of me that I'd never chosen, that I would never control. I went to the bathroom, turned on the loud fan, and cried, feeling angry, useless, silly. An image of Roy came to my mind, particularly of that tooth. I felt my love falling off, dissolving.

He was my first love, my first love in the way that first loves are usually second or third or fourth loves. I still think about a stranger in a green jacket across from me in the waiting room at the DMV. About a blue-eyed man with a singed earlobe who I saw at a Baskin-Robbins with his daughter. My first that kind of love. I never got over him. I never get over anyone.

Hack Wars

Josh Gilbert

*Josh Gilbert is a screenwriter and documentary filmmaker, best known for pro-
ducing and directing a/k/a Tommy Chong. Josh is currently making a documentary about a young autistic man named Jake, who aspires to become a
professional filmmaker. He is a recent recipient of a grant from the Nathan
Cummings Foundation.*

I JUST GOT INTO A SCREAMING FIGHT WITH
Scheinbaum. A huge several block long, multi-act,
mouthy street brawl with Scheinbaum, my fellow tenant, who told me as we were walking from our building
to the bank together that my brand of mediocre, suc-
cess-chasing yuppie-wannabe worthlessness was
responsible for the ass-raping of the Bill of Rights by
the Office of Homeland Security. That all I cared about
was money and being spoon-fed mindless entertainment like a pâté
goose.

"Why are you baiting me, Scheinbaum. You're not making any sense."

"Sense or no sense. It's your brand of money-grubbing and whoring
that leads to the world as we now see it: Fucked!"

"What about you!?!" I shoot back, a bucking bass at the end of
Scheinbaum's line. "What about you? You're stealing cable so you can
watch the Food Channel! What about you, chasing Jimmy Woods
around, trying, to cast him in your stupid cop picture! What's worthwhile
about your lifestyle? WHAT?! You armchair socialist hypocrite!"

"Get away from me, you talentless piece of shit!" he yells. Then, on a
softer note, he adds, "I thought it might sell to support my art."

"Well, news flash. It didn't."

"I had an offer. I turned down the offer. That doesn't mean it didn't
sell. That means I didn't sell it. And it doesn't mean I'm not capable and
eager to write things that matter. I'm not just a hack. Like you."

"Look who's calling me talentless! A HACK! Will the ironies ever
cease!?!"

By this time, we're at the bank. I'm standing near the door, and he's walked over to the cash machine.

"Get outta here," he yells.

"Put your card in the machine!" I volley back, demanding he do what he's doing anyway, forcing a de facto concession.

"GET AWAY!" he screams, his voice weakening with an ascending awareness of the inevitable.

"PUT YOUR CARD IN THE MACHINE!" I demanded confidently.

After a brief pause, he turns around and puts his card in the machine.

Satisfied I've won the round, I go inside the bank to see if the check has cleared. The first installment of the money I'm getting for reworking a rock opera some poor producer optioned and has bags of his personal money sunk into.

Here's a quick run down on the plot: an aging rock star is down on his luck. His benders and drug abuse have ruined his career and driven his wife into heroin addiction and prostitution. The timeless yarn takes a turn into more obscure territory when the rock star's only son, a high school drop out, degenerates into an alienated trench coat Mafioso, grabs an AK-47 and picks off Christmas shoppers at a gigantic mall/amusement park. From here things go down the rabbit hole as Hitler is discovered to be coproducing clone soldiers with the help of an alien staff in the basement of the Pentagon. Ninety-seven hits of acid later, we're in a no-holds-barred bench-clearer between the rock star, his clone, a bunch of school girls, and a Satanic priest who holds the key to time travel. A few shenanigans later, the aging rock star returns to the present and has a nervous breakdown in a parking lot. All of this, naturally, has been observed by a shape-shifting narrator, here manifested as a reflection in a puddle of oil on the surface of the parking lot floor.

Turns out the check hasn't cleared yet.

I head back to the neighborhood deli for a cup of coffee, and who's already inside but Scheinbaum, who sees me coming, opens the door and yells: "GET AWAY FROM HERE!"

I stride right past him to the counter. "I want a cup of coffee, and you can't stop me!"

"Small blek coffee, double da cup?" Sam the Palestinian deli worker asks.

"Thanks, Sam."

Sam knows the daily routines of at least 350 people.

Meanwhile, Scheinbaum starts telling Sam and anyone else who would listen that I'm the hack responsible for the ass-raping of the Bill of Rights.

To which I respond, pointing a thumb at Scheinbaum, "this hack spent all last year changing the world by writing an alien movie."

And it's on again. A couple of Jewish writers screaming at the top of our lungs about who's the bigger hack in front of our neighborhood Palestinian deli workers.

After reaching a natural break in this psychotic debate, Scheinbaum leaves the deli, but not before warning me, with a hefty edge of menace: "You'd better stay away from me! I won't be accountable for what I do."

To which I respond, "You want me to get away from you? Okay. THEN GO AWAY!"

"You guys gotta make peace," Sam advises sagely, as I linger by the counter, watching Scheinbaum stomping across West Fourth Street, past Gwyneth Paltrow's and Lili Taylor's brownstones.

"That ain't so easy when you're neighbors," I say to Sam.

"You're telling me," Sam says with no shortage of irony in his voice, bidding me a pleasant *Salaam Alechem* as I go.

"Shalom, chief." I offer back with a friendly nod. Then I walk back toward my building, past the Paltrow and Taylor mansions and stop at the corner of Eleventh Street to take in the construction progress on Liv Tyler's twenty-five-thousand square foot pied-à-terre, entertaining the idea that if my rock opera project actually takes off, I can cast it on the way to my local deli.

I proceed on toward my building, and who's sitting on the stoop, but Scheinbaum, ready for the final round. "GET AWAY!" he squeals imperiously.

"I LIVE HERE YOU FUCKING MORON!" I snap back, resolving to rise above this idiocy and go upstairs. There's a war going on, for Chrissakes. Human beings are dying in the streets of Baghdad. If ever there were a time to take the high road with Scheinbaum, my favorite person in the world to fight with, it's now. But Scheinbaum's got other plans. He puts a friendly hand on my shoulder, stopping me as I enter the building and says, kindly: "You know you don't have any talent as a writer. You don't have any talent and you never will. All you've ever done with your life as a writer is lay on your back with your legs in the air. Turning tricks. Like a fucking whore. But that's not writing. And it certainly is not talent. So I suggest you give it up now, while there's still time to do something else with your life. I say this as a concerned friend."

"Who are you to talk about success as a writer?" I ask. "Just what do you have to show for all your efforts, oh genius scribe of the ages?"

"I've written plays. Several very good plays."

"Yeah? Sell em?" I ask rhetorically. "At least I've sold something."

"All you've ever done is shovel shit at the circus and suck dick for scraps."

"Fuck you, you commie hypocrite wannabe hack bastard!"

We go back and forth and back and forth like this, like tennis. A small crowd forms and watches on in amusement. I tell him his most recent play, which didn't go anywhere, naturally, was completely derivative of John Patrick Shanley's *Danny and the Deep Blue Sea*. The character choices; the arc of the love story; even stuff like the spelling of "inna" for "in" and "kinna" for "kind"—down to the Goddamned *hand* props!

At which point, he charges me, but this has happened before. He charged me and we almost came to blows a few months ago after I told him I thought Eugene O'Neill's *Iceman Cometh* is a better play than his admittedly well-considered Marxist intellectual rage piece, *Donkey Work*. I know he's bluffing and I stand my ground. But he's all up in my face and I can feel his breath in my eyes and I don't like the feel of it at all and so I say, stepping back, ready to swing, channeling a thousand hackneyed movies: "YOU WANNA DANCE, SCHEINBAUM?!? YOU WANNA FUCK'N DANCE?!? WELL THEN LET'S DANCE!!!"

He reconsiders like I know he will, but I'm so close to blows here, I have to channel my rage. So I pound the fuck out of the community bulletin board. I actually shock myself, because it feels so good. I punch it again. Scheinbaum watches, obviously impressed by the show of animalistic bravado. A monkey beating his chest. Or in this case, a writer beating the community bulletin board.

"Look at you!" Scheinbaum says with a giddy chortle. "You're turning all red. You look like an electrified rabbit!"

"Well congratulations," I say. "You brought me here. I hope you're satisfied!"

"I am."

"I'll bet you are."

I go back upstairs and there's my girl in the hallway, thinking there's gotta be some sort of construction worker brawl going on in the lobby of the building. I bid her good morning, then go to my desk and start writing all this down for future reference.

Moments later, there's a loud banging knock on the door, and of course it's Scheinbaum. Now it's my turn to yell go away.

"Come out here," Scheinbaum yells. "I gotta talk to you. It's important."

So I grab my jacket, put it on and go out into the hallway. Scheinbaum's standing there, suddenly looking flushed and ashen faced.

"I forgot. We can't fight like this any more."

"Why?" I ask.

"On accountta my health."

I know he's been worried about his health lately. He called me in a panic two months ago when I was out whoring in Hollywood. He had a big scare after his long-lost brother Howie called him from Indiana to tell him he was going under the knife—to take care of a heart-related disease that runs inna Scheinbaum family. Scheinbaum just rounded sixty and now: "These fights between us, they gotta stop. It's just too upsetting for my heart."

I say, "Yeah? Well people die at forty of heart attacks too, you know. I ain't exactly calmed by our exchanges. And me wanting to make it as a screenwriter don't have dick to do with that asshole, John Ashcroft. Or Halliburton's contract to rebuild Iraq either, for that matter."

"Let's move on. And don't worry, you're not gonna die of a heart attack. Forty's a kid. Me, I got issues."

"Oh shut up! Your X-rays didn't show a fuck'n thing wrong with you. You're robust as a man of fifty-three. You got more hair than I do."

"It's too upsetting for my heart."

"Well then stop picking fights, Scheinbaum."

"Sometimes I can't help myself. You gotta help me."

"You need some serious meds."

"I'd get those little blue pills, but like most Americans, I don't have health insurance. As if you care."

"Scheinbaum! You're doing it again."

"You're right. Sorry. Shake my hand," Scheinbaum says.

"No, you shake my hand," I say.

Scheinbaum sticks out his hand and we shake on a deal I know he will never keep.

Dance with Me Ish, Like When You Was a Baby

Ish Goldstein

Ish Goldstein shares a birthday with Barry Hannah and lives off the most beautiful train in Brooklyn. This was his first publication.

MY BROTHER CALLS AND TELLS ME TO COME HOME. I drive south along Highway 1 from Oregon, stopping for a nap on a bluff just outside Morro Bay. It is almost sunset and the tide is waning.

I get to my father's in the early morning. It is dark out and the key fumbles in my hands. I open the door to see my brother asleep in a chair beside him. My feet don't make a sound on the wood floor. The moonlight pours over my father's shoulder and I can see how his skin has cascaded on top of itself in layers of decay, cracked and dry, like a creek with no water. The house is stale with heat.

His body is crumpled and creased. I crouch down in front of him and tap my fingers on his knee cap; every six taps he chokes on his breath and snorts. I pat his forehead and comb his hair. Most has fallen but what is left is gray and matted.

"Ish," he says, opening his eyes. "Aren't you cold? It's so cold in here."

"No, I'm not cold Abs," I pull another blanket over him, tucking the ends beneath his toes.

"Did you see the ocean today? The surf is up. South swell. Wintertime," he says nodding his head.

"First Point not Third. I looked through the telescope, but I don't see so well. But you could see it in front, big waves, loud ones. Boom. Boom. How's that cold water in Lincoln City, kill you yet?"

"No, it ain't killed me Abs."

"Would've killed me."

He opens his eyes and they look like clouds.

"I got this pain in my chest, reminds me of when I used to peddle you around on the tandem. You just sat on the back and asked me to tell you stories. But I was working like a dog."

He motions his hand toward mine and I take it. It twitches cold in my palm. Sometimes rotting things are beautiful. The way forms break down, still showing life but in a manner of dying.

"Pick me up," he says. "I been waiting all evening to go for a walk."

I take his feet in my hand, delicately, the way I hold my newborn child, and place them in his slippers.

I layer him in blankets and lock my arms around his lower back, pulling him to his feet with my thighs. He tries to stand and wobbles forward into my chest, his arms branching over my body.

"Let's see, I can do this," he says, shuffling his left foot in front of right. "Twenty paces to the Westmoreland, twelve to the door." He exhales and braces his weight against my shoulder. He moves slow, our breaths counting out time in the dark room. "Maybe we can just go out on the deck," he says, breathing heavy, and I guide him the few steps outside, overlooking the ocean. He leans against the railing and I stand next to him.

We don't speak. My father has always been content staring at the sea and I stare as well. He breathes in deliberate gusts, moving in and out and the cold of his body makes him shiver. The tide laps on the sand, but I cannot hear it. I watch my father watch the ocean, and his eyes are tired sacks and it makes me sick. My stomach tightens. This will be done soon. The ocean is big, the tide is beckoned and pushed by the moon. Swells of saltwater are produced by wind thousands of miles away, and soon my father will be gone and his eyes will shrivel up and turn hard like rocks. Then I will share this with my son. I will get his feet wet and covered in sand.

"Ish," my father says, "you remember?" His eyes are already dead. "Please, my youngest son, you remember?"

And I do. When I was younger while visiting my grandfather in Florida, my father told me if he should ever turn down a walk along the boardwalk as my grandfather did, that I should set my mark and kill him right then.

"Please Ish, please, remember," he says.

My hands throw mad for his face, my fingers digging into his soft cheeks. I cover his mouth and plug his nose shut. He tries to speak but his words muffle in the creases of my hands and I press myself against him. We rest on the railing. It is silent but my body is pushing. Even my violent arms seem hushed in the night sky. His eyes are rolling back now and his skin is translucent with the moonlight on top of his forehead. And why do I have to do this? The flaky skin of his nostrils crack into my fingernails, and he is anxious, his skin sweats cold onto my chest, and my hands want to pull away and pet his hair, to grab his shoulders and shake him to life as if a shock will make him lively. He is going and I will stay.

His breathing slows, it no longer rests in the porous connections of my fingers, and I place my tips at the front of his lips and can feel his air seep out. So I thrust my hands again and smother him. I do not know how long it is until he is all done and gone, but I look at him and swear I can hear him say, "Dance with me Ish, like when you was a baby." And I tackle his dead body and fold his arm over my shoulder, and lead him through a two step, just like when I was younger and we danced the tango outside the house, watching the airplanes fly over the sea.

From Las Vegas Bypass

Benjamin Golliver

Benjamin Golliver was born in Portland, Oregon, and is a graduate of the Johns Hopkins University Writing Seminars. He writes about the National Basketball Association for CBSSports.com and has covered his hometown team, the Portland Trail Blazers, since 2007. He lives in Lake Oswego, Oregon.

I.

PULLING OFF TO THE SIDE OF THE CURVING ROAD to take in the Hoover Dam is a great way to forget that today's high temperature was 106 degrees. It's 8:30 p.m., and it's still pushing ninety outside, and there's a slight breeze coming in over the orange hills above, so that the shirt I'm wearing unsticks itself from uncomfortable skin as a digital camera snaps. The dam, concrete upon concrete, stretches as far as the eye can see, in all directions, provoking all sorts of questions from nearby tourists, none more common than, "Where's all the water?" The canyon walls are marked white by decades of current flow but today the actual water line is at least fifty feet below the white marks. Can an entire river evaporate?

The ride from McCarran Airport to the dam was pleasant and quick, a thirty-mile burst through the desert, pickups with gargantuan off-road tires kicking up dust alongside us. "I always slow down going through Boulder City," says my travel companion as we approach the dam. "The cops here are pretty ambitious." It appears that they are quite successful, too; seconds later, I spot a shiny red SUV with BCPD tattooed on the side pulling out of a driveway, sirens blaring in hot pursuit of a minivan that must have, somehow, exceeded the posted thirty miles per hour speed limit. Boulder City police, and the citizens they protect, don't have many concerns. The small town, with a perfect view of Lake Mead, is dotted with million-dollar residences. It wasn't always this way.

II.

Smoking crack, apparently, is a great way to forget that today's high temperature was 106 degrees. It's 1 a.m., it's still almost ninety degrees, and there is heavy foot traffic in all directions along Swenson and Twain. It's a people potpourri, yes; hookers, tourists, swing shifters, partygoers, cops, and, of course, corner boys and their customers.

The corner boys here sell it all, or so I am told. "Meth for white people, rock for blacks, but everyone seems to agree on one thing," says my travel companion, "the quality of drugs here is shit." I nod, taking in this information slowly, my eyes peeled to three o'clock where two LVPD squad cars have pulled into a gas station, sirens blaring as Young Black Men drop instinctively to their knees, hands in the air, the universal code for "I'm not resisting, please don't shoot." Earlier today, at this same gas station, I saw a woman beating the heat by not wearing any pants. The oversized T-shirt as dress look had been in full effect. She looked like a hurricane evacuee but there was no hurricane. I had tried to laugh it off. I had tried to forget about her.

I look across the street to a concrete strip of check-cashing places and convenience stores and I lock the car doors. We are waiting at a stop light, just trying to get home. At this moment, this isn't where I want to be. It wasn't always this way.

III.

Watching Jerryd Bayless's cesarean section entry into the National Basketball Association is another great way to forget that today's high temperature was 106 degrees. It's about 7 p.m., and it's a cool seventy-two degrees inside the Thomas and Mack gym, and the crowd of thousands are hyped up. Jerryd Bayless cannot be stopped.

Jerryd is the newest Portland Trail Blazer, type A from head to toe: precise haircut, precise wardrobe, precise movement. When he steps into the gym, he glares. When he warms up, he glares. When he cuts to the basket, his body glares at the defense, offended by their weak attempts to stop his advances. When he jumps, his body glares at gravity. He is the best player on the court and he knows it. He glares to let you know that he knows it.

The impact of his entry into the minds of the assembled basketball intelligentsia is forceful and it levitates in the gym air. Ooh. Aah. Scouts, coaches, and general managers are not an excitable bunch, especially not in Las Vegas in July. Usually, they can be picked out of the crowd because they do not react to spectacular plays and they furiously jot notes when the casual observer might wonder, "Did I just miss something?" But the bounce to Jerryd's swag is very real, his dribble is emphatic and effortless, his body control borders on mind control. He is drawing new maps to the basket, he is absorbing contact, and he is brushing his shoulder off. Everyone is taking note. Even the scouts are smirking, which is as close as they get to smiling. Jerryd's parents, both his mother and his father, cheer him on; Jerryd is the younger son, his brother works on Wall Street. An investment banker and a professional basketball player, they couldn't be prouder. One suspects that, in lighter circumstances, his parents get to see a nice young man behind the glare.

His coach for the summer, Monty Williams, former professional player, tall, dark, handsome, bald, still in game shape, stands courtside, arms folded, watching along with the rest of us. Bayless hits an impossible game winner. The gym erupts. It feels like playoff basketball in early June for a moment, not Summer League in the middle of July. Monty, a deep-thinking devout Christian, is old enough to have enjoyed last-second wins before but still young enough to get excited by the thrill of that moment, the pulse of victory. Dressed in his red coach's polo shirt, Monty wipes his brow, trying hard to contain a big smile. He is at ease.

His boss, Blazers head coach, Nate McMillan, former professional player, tall, dark, handsome, bald, not quite in game shape anymore, makes his way down from high in the stands, looking comfortable and serene, but not overjoyed. This is just another buzzer beater for Nate, one of hundreds if not thousands that he has seen in his lifetime. Nate doesn't allow himself to display happiness. Nate knows basketball and he appreciates great shots. Below the hardened exterior, he's probably ecstatic. It wasn't always this way.

Enough About Me

Elizabeth Grove

Elizabeth Grove is a writer and editor living in Brooklyn. She did work in a psychoanalytic training institute, but not in the basement.

EVERY DAY ANYA SEES THE BOY: FRIENDLESS, BESPEC-tacled, husky, a touch, well, spastic. She wonders if spastic is an insult in this case; the school he attends, which Anya passes on her way to work, the Louisa May Alcott School, is supposed to be for children with special needs. But the small number of little men and women who attend it seem not so much to have special needs as they do special appetites, this being their last stop before Hazelden or Betty Ford or someplace where there are euphemisms for "lockdowns."

There they are, congregating before homeroom or whatever it is that begins their day. They have their conversations: fuck fuck fuck fuck fuck. They chain-smoke. They chain-smoke and play hackey-sack. You don't need your hands for hackey-sack—why not keep them busy with something? They make Anya feel old and tired; the small joy she derives from them is that she is not herself a parent staring down the barrel of an adolescence she has helped to create.

Their hair is neon, their clothing doesn't fit—too big, too small— they're pierced in places that seem to Anya to possess a distinct lack of flesh for the task. They take up too much room on the sidewalk where they stage their dramas every morning: clumsy fistfights, some making out, small gestures of collegiality—a shared cigarette, a pat on the back, a general mutant bonding.

Except for the boy. In this palace of losers, the boy is king, which is to say he's in exile even there. He sits on a nearby stoop by himself, making occasional forays to check the bank clock on the corner. His stance is wide and he pitches forward when in motion. His arms swing randomly to keep his balance. But his worst feature, the one that makes Anya turn away and hold her breath as if she were passing a cemetery, is a certain petulance, a certain opaque thickness to his features. Anya knows all too well that this makes one not inclined to like or help him, just two of his special needs among the warehouse of possibilities: like me; help me. It is safe to say the boy's special needs are not being met at the Louisa May Alcott School.

Anya gives him six months before he begins wearing his winter coat throughout summer and completing his conversations with himself out loud.

Everything that Anya has spent her life trying to extinguish, excise, exorcize from herself, burn, cut, bore to death, is in that boy.

When she was in high school on an A Better Chance scholarship, her classmate, Andrew Lumer, fledgling graffiti artist, ran into some boys tougher than he thought he was. They stole his bike, his allowance, knocked him around some. Then they found his fat graffiti marker and drew on Andrew Lumer a black eye, a moustache, and sideburns. They also tried to black out a tooth but Andrew Lumer kept his mouth firmly shut even though or maybe because it kept him from calling out for help.

Indelible, it turned out, was a bit of an overstatement when it came to human skin, but Andrew Lumer's inky bruise and facial hair faded slowly from black to dingy gray before vanishing.

Vengeance, of course, was on Andrew Lumer's mind and on the minds of his friends. That could've been unfortunate, but they went to a Quaker school and were instead encouraged to express themselves in assemblies where they could be guided to a pacifistic point of view, where they could play songs by The Who and talk about anger.

Anya enjoyed The Who and did consider herself a pacifist, mostly because she suspected that in a violent confrontation she would lose and it would be painful. This didn't, however, stop her from imagining a more powerful version of herself beating the living shit out of some real or imagined tormentor.

Still, the boy at Louisa May Alcott keeps her faithful to a non-violent world view. She's a conscientious objector, always.

Anya lives in New York; she's back, running out of money, gaining weight, trying not to weep on the subway in the mornings because if she starts she will have to check in somewhere and that would make her feel even worse. She works at Think, Inc., where she tries to think as little as possible and that is not difficult. Think, Inc., despite its jaunty name, is a loosely organized group of PhDs with more than the usual flair for pretension. They put out *Think Quarterly*, but are so busy thinking that only two issues have appeared annually for the last several years. The editorial board is headed by renowned analyst, Dr. K, who likes Anya because she has a master's degree: she's like Cinderella but not too stupid.

Think, Inc. is housed on one floor of a psychoanalytic training institute: the basement. Anya's office is literally a closet; for the first month she would occasionally walk into the other door on her hallway, momentarily disoriented by the floor-to-ceiling book cases full of patient files where her monastic desk should have been. Aside from Anya, Think, Inc.'s only staff member is Jake, who typesets *Think Quarterly* on inadequate software.

In the absence of completed manuscripts to do anything with, Jake puts his feet up, reads Spinoza and Stephen King, and drinks Mountain Dew by the liter. The extra caffeine almost counteracts the THC he's got stockpiled in his body.

Anya has been at Think, Inc. for two months and has fantasized for about seven weeks that she is not a copy editor at all, but a subject in the institute's latest research project. She taps the walls for evidence of microphones, one-way mirrors, cadavers.

"I think I'm losing my mind," she says to Jake one day.

Jake puts his finger carefully on the place where he's stopped reading *Cujo.* "Want a Xanax?" he says.

Anya sits down heavily. "No," she says.

"Let me know," he says.

"No," she says.

Some evenings she goes out to Sheepshead Bay and sees girls from the old neighborhood. Girls she was in school with. Girls who made no effort at academics but who could wax an eyebrow perfectly in one shot. Anya made an effort, got a scholarship, many of them, in fact. Married a boy with no connection to either motherland— Brooklyn or Russia. Not that that worked. Now she goes to see the girls she can remember; they're all still married, many of them with small children. It doesn't mean they're necessarily happier than Anya is, but she has little patience for their plights and suspects they fabricate their miseries to cheer her up.

"You're so lucky you don't have children," says one. "It really does unspeakable things to the body."

Anya's list of reasons not to have children is long, but bodily damage ranks low on it. It's age, she thinks, not procreation that plays its cruelest joke on form. Age, gravity, and the shrapnel of myriad decisions, all of which include the phrase, "Oh, fuck it . . ."

"So," says Jake sometime during her ninth week at Think, Inc., "you want to smoke a joint?"

"Do you know how old I am?" Anya says. "I'm old enough to be your . . ."

"Sister," Jake says. "You're old enough to be my sister. Maybe my aunt in a nontraditional family."

"Sister," Anya echoes. He's probably right. Think, Inc. has destroyed her mathematical skills, which helps when she looks at her paycheck.

"At least keep me company," Jake says.

In the patient file room she glances around nervously as Jake sloppily inhales next to yellowed onion-skin sheets, the crumbling histories of generations analyzed at the institute. She keeps her hand on the doorknob, imagining the fireball will be sudden and fierce.

Jake stubs the joint out carefully on the metal bookshelves. "Could you watch that?" Anya says. The back of the door is mirrored and she wonders why as she looks at herself become irritable, looks at the silky boyish back of Jake's head. He has a nice neck, too delicate a stem for the rest of him.

"Watch what?" Jake says, looking around. "You have a really cute accent, you know."

"I don't have an accent," Anya says. "I've been here since I was eleven. No accent."

"Uh, okay," Jake says. "Maybe not in the Ukraine." This cracks him up.

"I'm Russian," Anya says.

"What's the difference?" Jake says. He means it.

"I don't have an accent," Anya says again. But she knows it's hopeless. Her ex-husband once told her in exasperation that he couldn't argue with her because when she was angry she stacked up her words with phonetic perfection but no inflection, so that it was impossible to understand what she was saying. She had never believed it was only that.

"You want to go out sometime?" Jake says.

The next day they have a visitor at Think, Inc., an older woman with a bouffant and spike heels who sits herself down at the third empty desk and proceeds to line up prescription bottles wrapped in tinfoil. Anya sees the first one go down and recognizes it: Valium, five milligrams. She looks at Jake, who gestures for her to follow him out into the hallway, and then out a heavily padlocked door into Think, Inc.'s backyard. It is something like freedom.

"That's Dr. K's mistress," Jake says.

"Oh, please," Anya says.

"Really," Jake says. "Okay, she's the executive editor of *Think Quarterly*, but that's because she's Dr. K's mistress. She comes in about once a month to make long-distance calls."

Anya doesn't like these kinds of theories, rejecting them as flabby and misogynistic, but after an hour of listening to the woman chat on the phone, she realizes it's true: fucking. Fucking is the only possible explanation for this woman's presence at Think, Inc.

When Jake gets up again later, Anya follows him out. She likes the backyard he has just shown her. Although the sun is not hitting their scrap of concrete, Anya can see that the sky is a brilliant bright blue. Somewhere not so far from them, the sun is making contact, warming everything in its path. It makes her feel brave and almost happy and when Jake passes her the joint, she shares it with him. From the number of pills the woman inside has swallowed, she figures it's going to be a long day.

Jake looks up and around, the mere movement of his head making Anya feel much more stoned than she is. He scans the buildings above them. "I think," he says, "it's raining snot. Or spit. Or something."

Simultaneously, a beat behind, it's hard to tell, Anya becomes aware of a sound different from the muffled noise of the city. She follows it and high above them she spots the boy sitting on the fire escape of the Louisa May Alcott School.

He's on the stairs, hugging his knees and weeping with no attempt at control. His mouth hangs open and gasps and snorts escape from it. His face is wet from crying; tears drip from his eyes, off the end of his nose, from his chin. The sound is steady: unh-unh-unh.

"Holy shit," says Jake.

"I'll go out with you sometime," Anya says, to fill in the space, to make whatever is happening stop, to keep Jake from being a Good Samaritan, if that's what he has in mind, or maybe it's to keep from having to watch him laugh if that's the other thing he may have done.

When they leave that evening, Dr. K's mistress ahead of them having stumbled toward a cab, Anya sees the boy sitting on the stoop of the school. He seems somewhat recovered, at least he's not sobbing as he rocks and looks through a notebook. A teacher is leaving the school when they walk by, and Anya tries to catch their conversation as the boy starts to speak. "Gotta run, Toby," the teacher says. Anya's sorry she now knows his name.

"Let's go to your place and order a pizza," Jake says. "I live with my parents."

"You do?" Anya says. "Doesn't that interfere? With your lifestyle? With girlfriends? With all the pot you smoke?"

"Not really," Jake says.

It is homey, domestic, this pizza in her small apartment in an outer borough with this man whom she has seen more of than anyone else in months. She started at Think, Inc. in the summer, now they are moving fast through fall. The heat has just started to come up in the apartment, its stale smell reminding her how long it had been dormant.

Anya thinks of the boy and it disturbs her. What is it, she wonders, that separates him from every other zero wandering the city and somehow passing? What lack of style—real or faked, it doesn't matter. What lack of innate grace? What missing ability to convey "fuck you" without even trying? These are microscopic distinctions, it occurrs to her, but the difference is enormous. The leap from that boy to popular bully, that space in between, is so small, she knows. She knows because that space is the scrap of cosmos she happens to occupy, filling it to capacity, feeling it closing in. And now there is Jake, warm and happy and full of pizza, somehow wanting to share it.

Dr. K is on the phone. Anya hasn't spoken to him in a month. "*Exciting news, Anya*," he says. "My book has been accepted for publication. By a mainstream *publishing house*."

"That's *great*, Dr. K," Anya says, in her best Up with People voice, its tone decidedly faded by noon each day, but it's only nine-thirty and she and Jake have just stumbled into work. Outside, it's sleeting.

"I've left it, a copy, on your desk," Dr. K says. "It will have to be proofed, of course."

"Of *course*," Anya says. She watches Jake start in on his first liter of Mountain Dew.

"I'm not much of a typist, I'm afraid," Dr. K chuckles.

"Of course *not*," Anya says, trying to remain cheerful. She locates the manuscript on her desk, on top of the jumble of patient records she and Jake have been reading aloud to each other, killing time. It's typed on onion skin paper, the place seems to have nothing but, the manual typewriter heavier on the r's than on any other key. It gives the impression, of *course*, of being decades old. But with Dr. K. that could be illusory. She wonders if he's an idiot or just affected, but decides with Dr. K. the distinction is probably illusory too.

"Do you see it there?" Dr. K asks.

"*But Enough About Me, What Do You Think of My Narcissism: An Analyst's Memoir*," Anya recites.

"*Exactly*," Dr. K says. Anya wonders suddenly if he's wearing any clothes on the other end of the phone. But enough about her, she thinks, what would Dr. K make of her thoughts?

Some nights Anya and Jake go to Mr. Mezze in Anya's neighborhood. The beer is cheap and olives and miniature grape leaves are free at the bar. Sometimes the owner—Mr. Mezze himself—maybe remembering his humbler origins, maybe just aware of the overage in his kitchen, sends out borek and spanakopita to them. The phyllo, warm and drenched in butter, makes Anya happier than almost anything she can think of.

"What do you want," Jake says one night.

"I want some moussaka," Anya says. "I'm feeling bold."

Jake studies his beer bottle—Latrobe! Anya thinks, it just says Latrobe—and keeps studying it. "I mean, from me," he says finally. "Like, what do you want from me?"

Anya takes a long sip of her own beer while Jake waits for an answer. He has that kind of patience, she's noticed. He seems almost to have forgotten he's asked any question at all. It occurs to her that he is young enough not to know the difficulties what he's asking; in fact, he is so unformed somehow that he wouldn't even know the trouble he would have if she asked him the same.

"I want," she begins, trying to brighten, trying as you would with five year olds, convincing them that washing dishes is a really fun game, "I want you to send me flowers for no good reason."

"Okay," Jake says.

The next morning they arrive at Think, Inc. before he does: a dozen shrieking pink tulips. "For no good reason," the card says. "Jake."

Jake lies in bed, the sheets artfully askew, the sun streaming in the windows: it looks almost like something, this warm sunny winter thaw. He smiles lazily at her, stretches. Mid-stretch he shouts, "Ahh-Ahh-*Ahh*! Ahh-Ahh-*Ahh*!" He collapses and plays a little air guitar. Shaking his head, he wails, "I come from the land of a-ice 'n snow, from the . . ."

"That's 'The Immigrant Song,'" he says.

"That's *your* immigrant song," Anya says from the doorway.

"*I'm* not the immigrant," Jake says. "*I* was born here. My mother . . ."

"I know," Anya says. "Your fresh-off-the-boat mother went into labor watching *Chinatown*. That's why your name is Jake. It's a beautiful story."

Jake pats the bed. "Come here," he says. "The sun is doing really weird things to the dirt on the windows."

As for Anya, she came over—already born—with her parents; some foundations liked her and sent her to college; she left her husband by packing a bag and exiting the apartment; she worked in the basement of a nearly defunct psychoanalytic institute. Was it so wrong to feel the facts of one's existence so tersely, as she often thought while rummaging through other people's files; the patients' minutiae poked, prodded, plundered for every nuance: the impure thoughts about the upstairs neighbor, the upset stomach after the pork chop, the dream about the librarian from fourth grade. Yes, Anna surmised, it was wrong. But what was the other choice? To let it rip, all the Slavic heaviness she carries around, built for tragedy somehow, for opera and expensive brandy and an extravagant bubble bath by candlelight where she opens her veins into the warm water. The capacity is in her, long subdued but not quite dead. It's in the architecture of her genes.

"You've got to love your parents," Jake informs her one night. "At least," he says, "you've got to love that they love the American dream."

"My parents don't love the American dream," Anya says, tossing the day's mail into the recycling bag that hangs by her sink. "They love the Soviet dream, which is to be in America drinking better-quality vodka than they get in Odessa."

Jake stares at her like there are things he might dare say. Then the moment passes. He stares instead into the refrigerator he has opened. "I love the American dream," he says, his back to her.

"Not really," Anya says. "You happen to love the New York dream, and that is to somehow live rent-free in two places. But it's all downhill from there."

"You know," Jake says, "what is so wrong with me? I know you've got a long list, but what happens to be at the top of it right now?"

Anya considers this carefully. "You make love like you're happy," she says.

"I am happy," Jake says.

"You make love and it's like Frisbee, it's like soda pop," Anya says. "It's like puppies and bobbing for apples."

"You're insane," Jake says. This seems to Anya like a good place for him to storm out, but he doesn't. He just walks into her bathroom and takes a bath, and not a melodramatic one either. She can hear the splashing.

Anya goes in and sits on the edge of the tub. He's still not unhappy, she notices, though he does pick distractedly at the grout of the tiles. "How should I make love?" he says. "According to you?"

"I don't know," Anya says. "Maybe with urgency. Like your life depended on it."

Jake slides under the water and taps his fingers along the sides of the tub; she knows he's enjoying the deep rumbling sound that makes. He finally comes up for air. "If my life depended on it," he says, "I would've died somewhere between twenty-two and twenty-four."

Dr. K takes Anya out to lunch when she's finished proofing chapter one. He says he wants to do this on a chapterly basis. "That's so kind, Dr. K," Anya says.

"The least I can do, Anya, the very least," he says.

Chapter one is a reverie of the women who have transferentially desired Dr. K, which seems to have been his entire female patient load. Always the professional, Dr. K declined the invitations, but his imaginings of himself as a more devious psychiatrist are vivid. She's proofed it while reading it out loud to Jake, who's declared it better than *The Stand*. She skims ahead, looking for evidence of the big-haired high-heeled pill-popping mistress, but Dr. K appears to be the model of decorum when it comes to her.

In the slow lunch rush of an Upper West Side diner, Dr. K asks her what her husband does.

"What?" she says.

"Your husband, what does he do?" Dr. K says, sipping his coffee and waiting for her answer.

"I'm not married," she says. "Anymore. I'm not married."

"That's very interesting," Dr. K says. "You look fantastic."

"I'm seeing someone," Anya says.

"You don't say that like you mean it," Dr. K says.

Of all the indignities Anya imagines herself to have suffered, of all the ways that she once thought her life would turn out, ways she can't even remember anymore, she knows this, this present, isn't it, that to be analyzed, unbidden, in a warm and greasy diner on a winter's day by an old and horny shrink. Well, this is a low point, she thinks.

And she figures Dr. K has asked for it, so while he devours a Salisbury steak, mashed potatoes, gray green beans, and several cups of black coffee, Anya unburdens herself. She tells him everything: about coming here with no English, about not wanting to be like the other girls, about not wanting to be herself; she goes on at great length about personal diaspora, a term she figures he will appreciate. About Jake and his unrelenting cheerfulness, a cheerfulness bolstered by lots of reefer and lots of beer and lots of sleep and lots of carbohydrates and maybe lots of her. That he has appeared in her life, all over her life, and this seems not to disturb him at all. That there is a boy she sees every day who rips her heart out of her chest. That he rips everybody's heart out and they all respond as they will. What does it mean, anyway, that there are such people in the world, what does that say about God?

Dr. K signals for more coffee. "Do you want my professional or my personal opinion?" he says.

"Is there a difference?" Anya asks. "I've read chapter one."

Dr. K smirks. "Perhaps not. But suffice to say, there are really only two kinds of people in the world," he says. "Those who find the suffering of the sufferers stupid because they're too stupid to know they shouldn't suffer, and those who find the non-suffering of the non-sufferers stupid because they're too stupid to know they should be suffering."

"Okay," Anya says. "Sure."

"It's a dilemma," Dr. K says. "But what did you think of my book?"

Back at the office, Jake looks up from Dr. K's manuscript. "Did you read chapter seven?" he asks.

"Nah," Anya says. She tries to consider Jake in a new way, as a complicated person in his own right, if not in hers, as a person who has concerns, surely, even if they're invisible to her. She'd spent the walk back to the office along Central Park in its winter starkness telling herself that Dr. K couldn't be right. What kind of analyst tells you there are only two kinds of people in the world? Perhaps, having said all she had said, she had cleared the way for something new, for her and Jake as something, if not romantic, then at least plausible.

"That's good," Jake says. "Chapter seven. I was worried about you."

They smoke a joint right in the office. The mistress won't be back for a month, they decide, her most recent visit having been a few days ago. That they do no work, that they mock confidentiality statutes up and down the line, that they are slowly withering away in a basement is such an open secret that even its openness needs to be hidden from no one.

They decide to leave work, such as it is, early, go back to Anya's apartment and turn up the heat and order Chinese food. They lock up the basement and hit the street with all the school children, walking through the wall of their cigarette smoke.

When Anya peeks down the tunnel to see if the train is coming, she sees instead the boy, one foot in front of the other, on the yellow caution line. She knows he doesn't have the motor control, gross or fine, for that kind of stunt. As soon as it occurs to her—magical thinking, Dr. K would accuse—the boy plops onto the tracks.

He lands on his knees.

His howling begins immediately.

And then he is running sloppily, stumbling away from the direction the train will appear. He shrieks, shrieks that are a long time coming, that go far beyond his immediate circumstances, dire as those might become in a few moments.

Anya watches him, made small by his descent down to the tracks, and feels chilled, sick, and like him, that the world has suddenly gotten much worse in one thoughtless second. She looks at Jake, and he is slightly purple, stoned and stupid, under the fluorescent lights of the station, propped languidly against the blue post. "Oh my God," Anya says. "Do something."

"What?" Jake says. "I'm not going down there."

She takes another look down the long tunnel. There is no train coming. Other passersby are beginning to notice what has happened and they are trying to shush the boy to communicate something, anything, to him. His schoolmates, who have clustered near Anya and Jake, curse and point. "You have to," Anya says. "Get to him. Do something."

"Fuck me," Jake says slowly. "I'm no hero."

Anya moves toward Jake to shake him into some kind of action, but when she grabs his shoulders they feel thin under his thin winter coat. She practically outweighs him, she realizes, she is more substantial, a larger woman than he is a man, stronger. A plan seems to be in action down the tracks but Anya doesn't want to see. She keeps her hold on Jake, buries her head into his thin neck, while they stand, both of them, under Columbus Circle, and wait for braver people to come to the rescue.

Dick

Kirsty Gunn

Kirsty Gunn is the author of five books of fiction including Rain, The Keepsake, *and* The Place You Return to Is Home. *She is a professor of writing at the University of Dundee and lives in Scotland and London with her husband and two daughters.*

 I WAS STILL FRESH FROM MY PARENTS' DIVORCE when my father gave me a car and taught me to drive. It was just before school broke up for the summer and getting hot, and I was too young to be out on the road on my own but my father knew all kinds of people in our small town and he had, as he put it, "conversations." Like he had them with his ladies and his friends, certain conversations about money deals and business debts, so my father could get what he wanted in his life, so he could get his way.

Until that time of the car, though, these kinds of things hadn't occurred to me. I was somewhat held back, you might say, was the reason—made younger than my years by my father and the way he carried on. That's what my brother Michael said. We were both kind of wrecked, him and I, by our old dad and our mother leaving home and moving abroad and it turned out we wouldn't see her again for another fifteen years. So I may be living in the world like everyone else with my own profession and my little tidy flat, but part of me still is that same girl from back then, learning to use the clutch then go first gear, second. Slowly driving on my own down the street where we lived.

There was a boy next door who I used to watch from my bedroom window and dream that one day he might look up as I came carefully past him, practicing in that too-fancy brand new convertible of mine. He had a car of his own, an old lovely car, and would be out in front of his house working on it, an older boy with long blond hair that straggled down his back and the way he stood there in the sun in those beaten up old jeans he wore and T-shirts that hung just anyhow over his body . . . Even now the feelings I have about him mean I could never say his name.

My father didn't know anything about this. I didn't think then he thought of me that way. He just had the driving instructor pick me up after school each day and start the lesson there—as I turned the ignition and put the car in gear. Then we drove back to the house and my father paid him and made me go up and down the streets myself, around the block and over the hill by the shops. Certain times he even came with me, my father, that's how much he wanted me to drive. He'd be sitting right beside me in the tiny seat of the car he'd bought for me as a gift, telling me this way or that, giving instructions on what to do at a set of lights . . . but always looking at his watch, too, and wanting to get back— "to some little chickie he had waiting upstairs" were my brother's words. Or something else he needed to do. Still, those few times with him were times I felt close, when he said "clutch now" or "reverse." And even on the days he didn't come, I thought I could sense his affection in the way he would wave me off goodbye. As if he was pleased to think that soon I'd be in that car forever and I'd be driving away.

So the two weeks passed before school broke up and twice I went out and the boy in the street was waiting, kind of—is how I wanted to believe it was. Hanging around by his car as I drove past him in my own. And twice I saw him look up as I passed, push the yellow hair back clean from his face as I went from second gear into first while time seemed to slow down and then stop, with the blue of that sweet boy's eyes upon me. Thinking, in that moment, how it might be to get someone to love you. To let your mouth go wide open so another person could come in.

But I didn't see the boy in the street again that summer—or if I did, I don't remember. Because something went wrong with the car—something, my father said, that was to do with the engine and that it would need to go in to the garage straight away. "There are often problems" he said "with these little convertibles. You can get a bit of trouble with the braking, stopping suddenly." I remember exactly how he looked at me then, my old handsome dad. He was on his way, I remember, out the kitchen door. "I'll take it in to the garage today," he said, "and you can pick it up later, after school. Dick's a friend of mine. He does the work himself on all my cars. He'll do it in a day and you can drive it home after on your own."

That was a long time ago, that morning when everything changed for me like it had changed for my brother before me but he never talked about it and now he never left his room, just stayed in there in the dark. A lifetime, you might say, and a day with all of my life locked inside it, a secret I would never tell. Even my mother, when I finally saw her, was not someone I could reveal myself to, to show myself that way. When we met, after all that time of her being gone we were both of us strangers. But I do remember how my mother said "You don't surround yourself with certain kinds of people and not feel the consequences," is what she said. "Except your father, well . . . he just found a way of not letting himself feel the effects of anything he did. Or what those so-called 'friends' of his might do."

She was right, of course. For the last time I drove was that day coming back from Dick's garage, and my father, as long as he lived, never did ask me why. Though he was the one who'd fixed it to turn out for me that way. He'd given me the car after all, when I was too young, arranged that it would need to go in to the garage that day, and that the garage would be empty, with no cars at all, no men, no customers around when I walked in to the empty yard. There was the sign RICHARD CLARKE AND CO. LIMITED over the entrance but only one man there in the dark office waiting. *Dick's a friend of mine.* "And I've been waiting for you," he said.

And so I'm left here with the memory of it, fitting in the pieces, all grown up now and old, and my poor brother still in that place where they keep him like he's a child. And my father long dead and the girlfriends gone and my mother, after she spoke with me that day, never did come back . . . And you try to understand, don't you? They say: write down your stories and you'll come to a kind of learning. Write all the way to the ending. Read the story out loud.

But what I'm left with at the end is no different to what I had when I began: a set of keys, a "conversation." A gift. Some kind of start but really with no words to follow. And so you know why there's something wrong with me by now, why the boy in the road is a dream, why my brother stays inside. Why I don't come up to people, don't get close. Something that comes from that mess all over my clothing that day, of oil and other stuff, from that minute of my father walking toward me in the hall when I got home . . . After all that happened, all that he let happen . . . Calling out to me and smiling . . . with some fresh lovely shirt on, and he says "Hi honey, everything gone okay?"

That comes from knowing then what he knew, that he'd given me too, I was one of his "gifts." My old powerful handsome dad. But was never, ever going to say. What had happened. What debt I'd paid. What Dick had done.

Loss Prevention

James Hannaham

James Hannaham's first novel, God Says No, *was a finalist for a Lambda Book Award and named an honor book by the American Library Association's Stonewall Book Awards. His stories have been published in* The Literary Review, One Story, Fence, *and elsewhere. His criticism and journalism have appeared in* The Village Voice, Spin, *and* Salon.com, *where he was on staff, and have been acknowledged in* Best African American Essays, Best Sex Writing, *and* Best American Nonrequired Reading. *He teaches creative writing at Pratt, The New School, and Columbia University.*

THE SAME WEEK HE STARTED WORKING LOSS PRE-vention at Lambert's Department Store, Art spoke to a family member for the first time in twenty-three years. Twenty-five years before, his sister died, and his parents slowly disowned him, a pastime made more challenging by the fact that he lived with them. They cut him off through derision and denial. When he wore a tie to his job at Thrifty Rent-a-Car, they called him a snob. When he got fired for missing a training session, they snickered and called him a low-life. If he confronted them, they refused to admit they were mistreating him, and if he itemized their abuses, they chuckled, called him uptight, and mocked his conviction that their actions amounted to anything real. He delicately asked his mother to help him pay for college and she slammed the kitchen table with both fat hands and hollered, "Since when is you smart, nigra?"

One day the unbearable situation became literally unbearable and he hitchhiked from Jacksonville to New York. At first he wrote and called, but the icy voices of his parents said only "Hm" and "Eh" to his enthusiastic reports from the big city, and they raised no topics themselves. After a time he noticed that they never called, so he decided to return the favor.

Two decades of aimlessness followed: odd service sector jobs, failed relationships, heavy drinking, and at least once, heavy drinking on the job with a future ex-girlfriend. Art ended up living in an attic in Mount

Vernon. Over that time, he had occasionally received a greeting card from his Aunt Virginia—"Wishing you a Joyous Yuletide"—with only a signature and no return address. Sometimes she might write a line or two, sketching a major event like Cousin Walter's funeral or his father's bypass surgery, but she'd wait until long after the fact to send the card, killing his urge to go home, deliberately, he realized after a while. This time, though, Virginia had called him.

She was only eight years older than Art, the love child of his grandfather and a nurse. The family accepted her because she never called attention to that history. She'd gained footing among the Nobles at the same rate Art had lost it, and he sometimes wondered if she kept in touch, just barely, to remind herself of how cruel and absolute their exile could be—"There but for the grace of God," or what have you.

Virginia, her husband Pooka, and their three sons had decided to move closer to Pooka's mom, who had a bad case of rheumatoid arthritis. Art told them about an inexpensive place in a nearby three-family house his landlord owned, and they took it. Now when Art craned his head out of his window, he could see their apartment diagonally across the small parking lot out back.

"It's been too long, Artie," Virginia told him.

"I *tried* to stay in touch," Art began, but the faint untruth of the statement socked him, and dark waters of guilt and rage rose in his blood so he couldn't say more. They never found a suspect in his sister's murder, and Art caught the leading edge of the blame. Mom had caused a legendary scene at the gravesite, berating him with a deluge of tear-soaked religious grief in which she addressed him twice as "Thou," like a priest performing an exorcism. On top of their scorching reproach, he began blaming himself, which kept him drinking, and the drinking kept him shoveling coals of guilt into the hot furnace of self-destruction, as if to keep his parents warm.

Art and Pooka, who was decorated with veiny muscles and a tattoo of his deceased German Shepherd, hauled the family's stuff up the stairs, and Virginia told him the basics about everybody in Jacksonville. So much time had been lost, more time than it even felt like, that once they'd heaved the couch up the staircase, Art was breathless and broken from carrying so much literal and figurative baggage. The sentences he always used to redeem himself had become stale and monotonous now: *I shouldn't have left her at the club. She said she'd be okay. I couldn't have known what would happen.* Angie herself must have forgiven him by now, if forgiveness could come from the grave. The dead didn't hold grudges—well, nothing you could prove. But the *living?* Lord have mercy.

Whenever he saw her, Art scoured Virginia's face as if someone had printed the employment ads on it. If he saw her taking out the trash or pinning clothes on the line, she'd say, "Come for dinner sometime," but she worked at a Tookie's Restaurant, so she never cooked, she just brought home. Nearly every day he gifted her with cleaning supplies or steak marinades, blurted out the number of days since he'd quit drinking, and bragged on his new job.

"Lambert's must be like a Bloomingdale's?" Virginia concluded.

Art nodded enthusiastically. "Yeah! Yeah . . . Just about."

For years he had taught himself not to want a reunion with these tacky, heartless deadbeats; now he hated himself for setting them up in his backyard and then lying about the store just to grasp at his first chance. Comparing Lambert's Department Store to Bloomingdale's, he knew, was like comparing the Hope Diamond to a piece of glassphalt on Gramatan Avenue. Exiled from the rest of the mall, Lambert's sat across two lanes of traffic and a parking lot big enough to land a blimp on. The store carried terrazzo floors that had fault lines everywhere; in many places you could rock back and forth on the loose stones. Shoppers had to trudge up and down the broken escalators for weeks.

On his first day, Art wondered why so many shoplifters bothered with the cheap merch at Lambert's. Did the easy pickings keep them coming on? Were they practicing for Nordstrom's? A week or two in, Art noticed that the boosters weren't doing half the boosting. He saw co-workers slipping lipsticks into pockets, pulling pants on over pants, chucking denim shirts into dumpsters and "finding" them after hours, sneaking sneakers. If he stopped all the employees he'd seen stealing, Art thought, Lambert's would lose three-quarters of its staff. Instead of thinking about blowing the whistle, he wondered if they might make him filch a handful of Hugo Boss neckties as a rite of passage. Bonuses for busting co-workers were five dollars higher than the regular twenty dollars per apprehension, but no one was fool enough to reach out for that poisoned carrot.

Yet the wild west atmosphere at Lambert's inspired Art, and he couldn't keep from sharing the excitement with Virginia one evening on the back stairs. "Lately," Art told her, "some boosters started coming and doing infestations."

Puzzled, she repeated the word.

"This how a infestation go. Some thieves get a group together, okay, but they come in the store at different times. The leader, he'll know who's all the LP agents, and he start taking stuff right out in the open, so that we going after him. He stroll around, all leisurely, loading up his pockets, and the other little minion swipe a lot of merch because the LP force be looking at the main guy who creating that distraction. Then Joe Cool drops his loot in a place where the security camera can't look, like around the corner of a hallway or in a bathroom, and he leave the store with all the LP guys busy, the rest of the gang fly out the front door like the damn roaches do when you turn the light on, and they trip the security gate and whatnot, but they don't care. It's four of them and our attention be on the number one guy, so they get away."

"That's intense, Art, that's like a TV movie of the week," Virginia said, moving her head from side to side. "How do you stop them?"

Art belly-laughed. "Well now, it seem like hasn't nobody figured that part out." He laughed again, and Virginia joined him. He could feel his own eyes sparkle. "But we gonna get 'em. I swear we'll figure it out."

The phone rang and Art answered it. "Connie?" a voice asked. "Is that you?"

"I ain't no Connie," Art laughed, replacing the reciever and turning back to Virginia, who had been lost in thought anyway.

"They don't need more agents, do they?" she asked. "'Cause I have took about all I can from Tookie's." She described how she'd leaned across a customer's space and the woman had blown up, accusing her of creating unsanitary conditions because she didn't wear a hairnet, how the manager sometimes took home half the servers' tips, how the giant bags of popped popcorn in the basement had become party central for vermin. "They couldn't pay me enough to deal with all them rat weddings down in the cellar. But I got to work because Pooka can't get nothing steady on account of his conviction."

"There's a training program to start," Art warned, "and that'll cost you a little. But you could be on the job in a couple of months."

"Thanks so much, Artie."

"That's how family *supposed* to do," he said. Virginia nodded, but the doleful look that passed between them carried a shared memory of how the Nobles had treated him, and when she put her hand on his forearm, even that scrap of sympathy had nearly the effect of a tazer. Art longed for the sweet burn of a neat scotch.

November got underway, and Art improved at making stops. He learned how to read the murky gray TV screens in the surveillance room, how to stay far enough behind a booster to nab him as the alarm sounded, and how to restrain the perp without cuffs or fighting. On the Wednesday when he set his app record, he went home with his bonuses and celebrated by ordering Chinese.

The doorbell rang and Art pulled out a twenty to pay the delivery-man, but when he opened it, Aunt Virginia stood there, scraping her feet against the mat. She tugged at the twenty as a joke that wasn't a joke. He let go of the twenty and she pocketed it. Virginia had applied for an LP job at Lambert's, but they'd dragged their feet, and he'd become suspicious. Sonia in human resources told him that the last quarter had seen record profits, but it sounded fishy. Maybe she meant record lows.

Virginia accepted a beer and arranged her housecoat between her legs on a stool in the kitchen. "You seem happy, Artie," she observed. "What's wrong?"

He told her about all the apps he'd made that day, pausing to describe the oddest experience—he'd stopped a Rastafarian with a box of apricot body scrub stuffed into her knit hat. "Eleven apps got me a two hundred and twenty dollar bonus," he beamed. "You gonna love this job."

"Congratulations," she replied flatly. "I'd love to love that job."

When the moo shoo pork came, Art shared and pretended not to mind that she smoked while they ate. He let her ash in the green cut-glass bowl his ex-wife had left behind. They cleared off the table and lingered at the back screen door. Virginia tied the sash on her robe tighter, carefully balancing a cigarette between her fingers.

"Come back and visit a lonely old man sometime," Art heard himself say, though he realized right then that confessing your loneliness only guarantees additional loneliness.

Virginia held the door between her hands and batted it against the balls of her thumbs. "You know, we're doing Thanksgiving up here this year . . ."

"Oh. Yeah?" Art had a horrifying vision of himself—alone, eating an undercooked microwave turkey entrée suffocated by brown sauce in front of the TV that night, upping the volume to drown out his family's laughter and their music blasting out of Virginia's back window. "And are they coming?"

"Yes, they are."

"And am I coming?"

"You know Artie, they don't view this whole thing same as you. They always say it's you ran out on *them*."

Art scowled. "Give me a damn break. They drove me out! It's like you gotta hold everything they say up to the mirror to make it sound logical."

Art spent the next couple of weeks refining in his head what to say to his parents. For the first two or three days, he considered outbursts like *Why can't you see it wasn't my fault!* but those emotional cries soon gave way to the more self-righteous *I forgave myself a long time ago.* By the end of the first week, the vague, possibly cold *It happened so long ago* had moved to the top of the list. Ten days in, he figured he'd apologize for his indirect responsibility, but then he thought *Why give them more ammunition?* Finally, the night before, he surrendered, deciding to say nothing, as if nothing had ever happened and twenty-five years of estrangement wasn't unusual. *So nice to see you!* No defense works as well as vaporizing the past.

All the mental gum-chewing came to nothing anyway. A late season hurricane, Penelope, climbed up the east coast on Thanksgiving Day, and though the weather service downgraded it to a depression by evening, his parents' plane got canceled until the next morning. "I guess the big reunion's postponed, hm?" Pooka bellowed, sopping a turkey leg in a pond of gravy. His sons Calvin, Roland, and Moke said, "All the more for us," and didn't care when the juice from the swiss chard turned the undersides of their cornbread soggy and greenish.

The delay to a non-holiday made the thought of seeing his parents less intimidating. By the time they arrived at Virginia's, he'd been at work a couple of hours, where all kinds of pandemonium had broken out. Lambert's had announced a blowout sale with an immense banner wrapped around the front of the building like a bow, visible from the highway: HOLIDAY SALES EVENT! 50–75% OFF! The parking lot filled up with dented thirdhand Cadillacs and economy cars with raw, scabby paint jobs and garbage bags duct-taped to their missing passenger windows.

Customers swarmed inside like gypsy moth caterpillars on an oak tree, stripping their host to its branches. In a single morning, whole clothing departments seemed to empty out except for orange and green corduroy pants sized XXL and up. Naked mannequins toppled over everywhere like weaklings swooning at the disorder. Art stumbled over their disconnected legs and torsos on his way to the surveillance room.

Toward late afternoon, the frenzy slowed in comparison to the initial stampede, and a Russian co-worker named Milla pointed out someone she suspected of lifting. She thought he had cut the lining of his coat in a way that allowed him to grab things off the shelves, though it appeared that his hands were stuck in his pockets. Art memorized one or two distinctive things about the coat—you couldn't see faces clearly on the blurry, grayish-blue video screens—and went to the floor.

Keeping his eyes peeled for someone whose coat hat pointed epaulets with large buttons, he entered the chaotic bustle. The song "Cherish" pervaded the store at an almost subliminal level—*You don't know how many times I've wished that I had told you/You don't know how many times I've wished that I could hold you* . . . Art, thinking of Angie, had a vision of himself nabbing perp after perp until eternity and never catching the right one. Just then he passed a woman under a wide-brimmed purple hat who walked like his mother, but he didn't get distracted, as he'd been thinking about her so much lately. After a couple of unsuccessful passes through the Menswear department, he decided to return to the LP room. But as he crossed from the gum-dotted carpet to the stone walkway, kicking hangers aside, he nearly bumped into Pooka, who had a Saks Fifth Avenue bag in one hand and a jacket slung over his forearm.

"I can't talk now, Bro," Art whispered, focusing on the distance. "I'm undercover."

"That's cool, that's cool," Pooka responded.

"You didn't bring nobody else up here, didya? Because I saw a lady who—"

"No man, it's just me and my boys. Virginia an em sleepin' in."

"Give them my name at the register and they'll get you 20 percent off."

Art reentered the suveillance room puzzled and disappointed. Milla had one hand on her hip when he walked in. "What happen? You just give him warning? I see you talk to him."

"Who? No. That was my—Wait." In his memory, Art saw Pooka's coat and then remembered not noticing the epaulets. "That was my uncle."

Milla lowered her chin and raised her eyes. "Uncle? This man is your *uncle*?" She pressed her lips together and raised her index finger into the air. "I am think something would reach out for a poisoned carrot."

"Nah," Art said, wringing his mouth and letting out a bitter laugh. "I most definitely ain't a part." For a moment his mind raced in ten different directions.

Once it had all gone down, he almost wanted to thank his family. They couldn't have given him a better gift—in fact, they wouldn't have. It was almost as if they had made some wacky sacrifice in order to line his pockets and land him a promotion. Art got a sky-high Black Friday bonus, and all he'd had to do was sneak onto the floor and point each of them out. He'd found an LP agent to trail each of them, not just Pooka, and they all got busted—even Calvin, who had only managed to nab one sneaker and a broken videogame. Once he figured out what to do, he'd done it joyfully, and found himself humming along with the muzak when "The Greatest Love of All" came on. *No matter what they take from me, they can't take away my dignity.* Still, he knew they'd sweep aside the tidbit of revenge he had picked up, that it wouldn't transform them, that they would only blame him for ruining their scheme. He wouldn't press charges because he saw them clearly now. He no longer wanted their mercy. How could you want what didn't exist?

They rounded up all the perps on the infestation and brought them into sentencing. Milla notified Art, and he pushed through the ravenous crowd to the back of the second floor. Plastic letters on the door read LOS PREVENTION OF ICE. Art had opened that door at least a hundred times in the past few months to reveal thieving teens and grabby grannies alike. They had all been part of families too, he supposed. But this time he flinched, as if he was about to open a door on a zealous fire. He took a couple of steps back and paced. It occurred to him that he wouldn't be able to use the back entrance at his apartment anymore. With their topsy-turvy perspective, his folks apparently didn't know the difference between organizing a shoplifting crew and trying to reconcile a broken relationship. He imagined the scene as they made the decision to raid the store—sure, Virginia had repeated his story, but someone had said, "Great idea!"? And then they'd *all agreed.* In his mind, when he cast each of them in the stupid plot, their behavior over the years began to make a horrible, nonsensical kind of sense. He held their actions up to the mirror and could see, as if for the first time, the love they'd accidentally shown by attacking him.

Squaring his shoulders, he flung the door open and propped it with his extended arm. Art's mother and father sat at the end of the table, closest to the door; dressed in their loud Florida getups. His shirt was a jumble of leggy girls leaning on cars, hers a lycra zebra number with feathered cuffs. She had on a bobbed copper wig. They turned to him with uncertain smiles, their hands knotted together, and he could see some insane justification for the robbery already forming in his father's oily dimples as he bared his gold front tooth. They were eighty-one and seventy-seven years old, dark and glossy as antique furniture. Nothing would change them now but the soil. It all became hilarious.

Art's face brightened. "So nice to see y'all again!" he said. And it was true for a minute.

Arizona II

Jim Harrison

Jim Harrison is the author of over twenty-five books of fiction, nonfiction, and poetry, including four volumes of novellas. HIs most recent novels are The Famer's Daughter *and* The English Major, *from which this piece is an excerpt. He spends the year in Montana and on the Mexican border.*

WHEN I WAS LOOKING FOR BERT'S PLACE I MOMEN-
tarily regretted drowning my cell phone when I could
have used it for further instructions, but then I was
inattentive at mid-morning feeling a certain warmth
for Viv despite her slanderous letter most of which was
true. I had also been distracted by the idea that I needed
to get rid of all of these personal "issues" (as Marybelle
would have it) in order to proceed with my sacred pro-
ject of renaming the states and most of the birds. For instance, I had no
intention of changing the name of the Godwit. In addition I was having
trouble concentrating because of the alien desert flora that surrounded
me. I had begun at dawn driving toward the fabled Flagstaff then slowly descending five thousand feet in altitude from the forests of the north
to the hellhole of Phoenix, then turning east toward Tucson. When I
found Sandarino Road running through the border of the Saguaro
National Monument I was stunned as if I had suddenly been trans-
planted to Mars. Finally I located the smallish dirt road that led to Bert's
place with its hand painted ominous sign, NO TRESPASSING. SNAKE FARM.

It was the strangest of days, already burning hot by late morning.
Bert was out of sorts as usual and still wore a "Resist Much" T-shirt.
Nothing should come as a surprise with Bert. There was a young woman
named Sandra in her mid-twenties wandering around humming but it
was hard to tell her age because her face was leathery, her teeth bad,
though her body fairly nice. There were tell-tale signs of meth ingestion,
a long time curse even in northern Michigan but only lately noticed by
the authorities who still concentrate on the relatively harmless pot.

Bert showed me all the snake tracks in the sandy property and said
vipers were hiding from the heat, adding that ground temperature

reaches nearly two hundred degrees, enough to start melting the sneakers of the woebegone wetbacks trying to enter our country for work. He ignored Sandra when she took a pee in plain sight near a cactus called a cholla. She was evidently a free spirit or a nitwit.

We ate a nice lunch of garden tomato sandwiches which made my soul quiver because it was my first summer in over thirty-five years without a garden and my very own tomatoes. Bert had heard from his old Lutheran widow friend, now in her eighties, that Vivian had divorced me. While we were drinking quarts of ice tea Bert advised me to stay away from women under the age of fifty because they speak a different language. The words are similar but the meaning is different from what it used to be. Across the table Sandra was petting a tiny rabbit who nibbled a piece of tomato on her plate.

By midafternoon the sun had become reddish from a distant sandstorm and Bert cursed because the monsoons were overdue. Bert left pans of water spread around the yard for the snakes but said they usually traveled to his pond way out back. People in the area would call Bert in alarm and he would remove the rattlers from their yards. He said that the roadrunner bird would eat baby snakes but not the big ones. We were at the kitchen table and now Sandra was licking the rabbit's face as if grooming it. The house was quite bare except for the living room with its walls of books and a desk.

We went out back and Bert began yelling and cussing. A neighbor's cows, mixed-breed Brahmas, had gotten through his fence and were standing in his tiny pond. There were several of them and their feet must have torn up the pond liner because the water was draining away and the fish that Bert said were tilapia were flopping around. Bert beat the cows with his cane and they ran for the back fence breaking it down. Sandra fetched a bushel basket and she and I waded in to gather the fish but we got stuck to mid-thigh in the mud. Bert went for his garden tractor and a rope and pulled us out. "There goes my fish crop," he said.

We walked back to the house and Sandra said her first sentence, "The fish will stink." Bert hosed us off and within fifteen minutes the first Mexican ravens began to arrive. We sat under a tattered awning drinking a cold beer and within an hour I counted seventy-three ravens out at the pond gobbling fish and screeching at each other.

Bert showed me to a spare room that had an old air conditioner in the window buzzing away. I was relieved because the thermometer on the porch said it was a hundred ten degrees. It was siesta time but I had a hard time napping because of the strangeness of it all. I leafed through a picture book on cacti and watched the ravens out the window. They're a bit smaller than our northern ravens but behave the same. It occurred to me that Bert as an independent scientist rather than an academic one lived and acted more like an artist or poet. Such people came up to northern Michigan in the summer and the anthropologists and botanists were often as whacky as painters. While we were watching the ravens and drinking beer and I complained about the heat. Bert sent Sandra for a map and he showed me a mountainous area near the Mexican border about seventy miles away that would be ten degrees cooler and I decided to head that way in the morning. I asked him why he was using a cane and he said that last year after he came home from our class reunion he had gotten nailed by a diamondback out by his mailbox. He had his own anti-venom in the refrigerator but still lost a lot of flesh and the strength of his left calf.

I slept until early evening and when I came downstairs Bert heated up some coffee and set a bottle of tequila on the kitchen table. Bert was always handy at the stove and was stirring a pot of menudo which is tripe stew. We heard a pistol shot from upstairs and Bert yelled, "Sandra cut that shit out," adding to me Sandra was likely shooting at coyotes that were eating the rest of the fish outside the pond. He told me that Sandra was from Uvalde, Texas, and was a bit gun happy. He had rescued her during a drug seizure outside the Congress Hotel in Tucson a few months ago and she showed no signs of leaving.

At dark Bert set up a spotlight and we sat on the porch watching the snakes glide around chasing rodentia. Sandra walked among the snakes but they were bent on rodentia and ignored her.

"You can't keep a dog or cat alive around here but Sandra thrives," Bert said, pushing a snake away from the bottom step of the porch with his cane. The snake struck the cane with a thunk and broke off one of its fangs then crawled away with perhaps a toothache. I picked up the fang for a keepsake and when I turned I was alarmed to see Sandra take off all her clothes and flop into the hammock. She said, "Tequila," and Bert nodded so I went into the kitchen for the bottle, taking a gulp to calm my nerves. When I brought the bottle I looked away in modesty.

"A woman in a hammock is always faithful," said Bert. "It's a question of physics not morals."

The spot and porch light were catching Bert's face just so making him look older than he was, though I supposed this was partly due to nearly forty years of wandering in the desert. He had taught at the local university for a while but then had been "liberated" into being a private scholar by inheritance. It was then that I imagined that I probably also looked old to him. When you spend most of your lifetime outdoors you're not likely to look as smooth as a television newsman. A few years back Viv had bought me some skin care products but I told her I couldn't go to the diner for lunch smelling like a whorehouse. It was hard for me to admit that I had started my little fandango with Babe at the diner well before Vivian's downfall at the class reunion. One day after her lunch shift she asked me to fix her sink trap in her apartment upstairs. It took a full hour and I was there on the kitchen floor yelling out that she shouldn't pour bacon grease in her sink when I turned around and there was Babe in a silly purple nightgown. She put a furry slippered foot on my shoulder and said, "Let's go for it, big boy." All those years of fidelity went out the window. My friend Ad said that marital fidelity is part of the social contract and that the human mind is a cesspool of errant sexuality. Any Lutheran knows what Jimmy Carter meant when he talked about "lust in the heart." Of course civilization would be destroyed if everyone simply followed the smallest cues of lust but then it's also hard to imagine that the God of Abraham and Isaac is keeping a weather eye on our genitals.

It was getting late. I helped Bert set up a fine meshed framed screen along the bottom steps of the porch so when he got up at night he wouldn't be surprised if a snake crawled up the porch steps. Sandra had been singing nonsense syllables in the fashion of my brother Teddy then laughing, then drinking and crying. Finally she slept and Bert sent me into his den to get a sheet off the cot. I covered her and had thoughts about the wondrous physiology of women.

We tried to talk about Iraq but gave up with fatigue. Bert thought that nearly everyone in politics was a chiseler and I had had frequent bad thoughts about our boys being sent over there with bad equipment that doesn't do what it's designed to do. What good is armor if you end up in pieces? We were practically dozing in our seats, and then Bert lifted his pant leg to scratch his wizened calf. We agreed that most politicians were the rattlesnakes of the human race and then we said goodnight.

The Lay-Z-Boy Position

Erik Hedegaard

Erik Hedegaard is contributing editor for Rolling Stone.

 "IT'S JUST THIS SIMPLE. IF I DON'T QUIT SMOKING I'm going to have another heart attack and that'll be it," John Mellencamp said the other day. He leaned forward in his chair, inside his recording studio. "I've got Monday as my target date to stop, but I've had fifty days like that. What a fucking idiot. I've got a wife, a one-year-old son, and a new kid on the way. I've got a twenty-three-year-old daughter, a fourteen-year-old daughter, and a nine-year-old daughter. I've got all these people depending on me, and I'm still smoking. I'm a fucking asshole. I'm a big fucking asshole."

Slipping a pack of Trues out of my coat pocket, I said, "Mind if I smoke?"

John checked out the brand. A Marlboro man since forever, he said, 'Those are girl cigarettes. But lemme have one, man. Lemme have one."

He took the cigarette and placed it between his lips and fired it up with a lighter the size of a Sherman tank. He was down to eight cigarettes a day now (give or take a half-dozen) but during the height of his smoking career, which ended with his heart attack last year, he could put away eighty cigarettes a day, 560 cigarettes a week, 29,200 cigarettes per annum. He was a regular sideshow wonder. "Nobody could smoke like me," he said. 'That's all I did was smoke. Cigarette after cigarette. After cigarette."

John took the True out of his mouth and held it in front of his eyes. Smoke corkscrewed up into the atmosphere and spread out and covered us all. He took another hit. "I just love to fuckin' smoke," he said.

"The difference between you smoking and me smoking?" John said later. "I woke up in the night to smoke. I mean if my eyes opened in the night, I'd smoke. I used to smoke in the shower and just throw the fucking cigarette butts down the drain. My wife Elaine would come in and go, 'John, quit ashing in the shower. And quit ashing on your plate at dinner. And quit smoking in bed. You're going to burn us up.' Yeah. I smoked all the time. When I was fourteen, I'd smoke before school, at lunch break, and after school. I got kicked off the track team for smoking. I got kicked off the football team for smoking — and I was the fastest guy on the fucking team. Now, I'm in Rome, it's 1981. I'm just a fucking kid with a black leather jacket, tattoos, and earrings, and I'm walking around this big fucking place, the Vatican. I pulled out a cigarette and started smoking. This guard came up to me. 'You can't smoke here.' I thought to myself, 'Oh yeah, I guess not. This is where Jesus lives.'"

"I smoked on stage. I smoked while I was eating. I'm smoking in every picture ever taken of me. I smoked on *David Letterman*, although my publicist and managers said it just wasn't cool, like I give a shit."

At the time of his heart attack, John was forty-two years old, no longer young but not really old. He'd been in the music business for twenty years. When he looked in the mirror, he saw a pasty-white, cross-eyed guy with a big fat gut hanging off him. He thought nothing of it. What was there to think about? Then, one night, he woke from his nighttime slumbers feeling like hell. His hands were shaking. He roused Elaine and said, "Man, I'm fucking going to pass out."

Elaine pondered this and said, "You woke up to figure out you're going to pass out?"

Nonetheless, she helped him to the shower, where he smoked the life out of a cigarette and began to feel better. He thought maybe it was the flu. But a few weeks later, while getting a pre-tour physical, his doctor told him the god-awful truth. John didn't believe him at first, calling him a crazy stupid motherfucker; finally, he accepted it and said. "If we're going to continue this conversation. I'm going to smoke. I've got to smoke. If I can't smoke, I'll leave." With one artery closed, he smoked a cigarette in the doctor's office, later checked into a hospital and continued to smoke there.

When he left the hospital, he left knowing he'd lost 8 percent of his heart forever. He left knowing a few other things, too, which he shared with me during our cigarette-smoking time together.

'If you have coronary heart disease like I've got," John was saying, "every time you have a cigarette, it puffs up the cells inside your blood system, as if it was rice or popcorn puffing up. So, if I light up, and I happen to be passing a blood clot, a big blood clot, I could go from being 45 percent blocked to a heart attack just like that."

He snapped his fingers.

"Boom!" he said.

"Jesus," I said, lighting up a smoke.

"Yeah, sure." John said. "I could have a heart attack right now."

He maneuvered my True with certain silky grace, not holding it down toward the hand knuckles, as some smokers do, but somewhere near the tips of his fingers. When the cigarette went into his mouth, it stayed there as the smoke emptied out around his head, occluding it in a kind of ghastly haze.

"Have your various wives and girlfriends been smokers?" I asked him.

He twitched in his seat. "What do you mean various wives and girlfriends? What the fuck does that mean?"

Then he relaxed a little. "Well, oddly enough, none of them smoked until they got married to me, then they all smoked. It was like, if you can't beat 'em, join 'em. And I never ran out. If you were in my house or in my studio, there were these boxes set around all over, literally hundreds of them, and every one of them had forty cigarettes in it and a lighter. It was a very sophisticated way of smoking, but Elaine doesn't smoke now and the boxes are gone."

John had driven a silver BMW 325i convertible to the studio today. He wore blue jeans, a black sweatshirt, white socks, and dark, wraparound shades. He was four songs into the recording of a new album. On some of the walls in the building were awards indicating how his albums had done in the past. They had gone single, double, triple, and quadruple, and quintuple platinum. Because of his success, he's easily been able to find people to take care of his needs. He never has to carry a thing. No paper money or loose change weigh down his front pants pockets, and no wallet bulges from his back pocket. It's all carried for him. "If you and I was to go out to lunch," he likes to say, "you'd have to buy it."

It's a little different for John now. He's in need of the kind of help that's harder to find. Not long ago, in his quest for freedom from the smoke, he went to see a shrink. Right off the bat, the shrink wanted to know if John had ever had any homosexual experiences. He also wanted to know when John had last masturbated.

John hightailed it right out of there.

While we were talking, John said. "To be honest, I've always thought I was Superman. I've done what I wanted and never questioned myself, even when I was wrong. I've never questioned myself about myself. If I felt like doing it, I did it. I've lived like a force of nature. I'm the baddest motherfucker around. But now I'm afraid to walk out of the house, afraid I'm going to run into a cigarette somewhere."

He laughed (bitterly), shook his head, stood up, circled around to the coffee table, and plucked one of my Trues from its package. From the way he talked about smoking, I doubted he'd quit any time soon. It seemed too big a part of him, too much like an animal urge.

"What about sex," I said. "I bet you enjoyed a good smoke after sex." Tipping some ashes into the ash tray, John snorted. "After," he said, "and during."

"Don't tell me!" I said.

"Yeah, fuck yeah," he said, coolly. "The best thing in the world was getting into the Lay-Z-Boy position and smoking. 'Go!' Puff, puff, puff. Yeah, head straight for the Lay-Z-Boy and smoke. I even used to smoke while I ejaculated. Girls didn't like it much but girls that knew me just knew that I was going to smoke. 'You want to have sex? I'll be smoking.'"

John chuckled, thinking about all his years as a smoker. So far, there'd been twenty-nine of them.

"Man," he said, shivering with some kind of pride. "World class."

From *Nightlife*

Rodney Jack

*Rodney Jack served as a yeoman in the United States Navy before earning an
MFA from Warren Wilson College, where he was a Holden Minority Scholar.
He was a Peter Mayer Scholar at the Sewanee Writers' Conference, and
received a writer's grant from the PEN American Center. His poetry appeared
in numerous magazines, including* Agni, Ploughshares, *and* Poetry, *which
awarded him the Eunice Tietjens Memorial Prize. This is an excerpt of a memoir left unfinished at the time of his death in 2008.*

Night of Friday, June 30, 1995

 DREAMED I WAS SWIMMING WITH SOMEONE, SCUBA
diving without diving equipment. We were holding
hands, and our legs were like fins. We admired the
beautiful sea life, the jellyfish. Maybe only I was, or we
both were naked. I was enchanted by a Portuguese
man-of-war overhead, the way its bladder-like cap went
convex then concave. Suddenly it descended, all the
stinging tentacles, although, in the dream, the jellyfish
were the non-stinging kind.

Just before I woke up, I dreamt I went to Oxford Books to find a tarot
deck. It was late and Oxford was the only bookstore open. I couldn't find
the game section. Searched frantically. Went to Oxford wearing a scarf,
bulky material I couldn't leave on my motorbike. Again, I think I came
with someone who had gotten up out of sickbed. His presence was
mostly sensed. I still can't picture the face.

Later in the dream, as the bookstore was closing, I made a last-
minute dash for the tarot cards to no avail. Found myself in a labyrinth,
a classroom or a building where, in a dark stairwell, I was trapped or lost,
afraid of someone climbing the stairs, though that someone was also
frightened.

Saturday, July 1

About 6 a.m. I got out of bed to start the black beans that had been soaking overnight. I was anxious to bake the bread. My hands are proof I have not been in the kitchen for some time. I have several fresh cuts: one made from a paring knife against the index finger while shaving the navel from a Vidalia onion; another cut was made by the "S" blade of the food processor as it slipped off the counter. When I fumbled to catch the appliance, the blade nicked off a bit of skin from the knuckle of my thumb. I also notice other injuries whose origins I have no idea about, except that I probably got them making the meal today, which turned out so delicious.

At about 4 p.m. Dude started getting ready for his weekend evening class. As is his custom, he asks me if his outfit is, or is not, flattering. No matter if I say yes or no, with or without conviction, he hardly takes my word for it. I've learned if I don't exactly prefer his outfit, but say that I do, chances are high he'll go back into the bedroom and change. We were club kids when we met. Nearly five years later, I suppose I fantasize him as club kid still. Maybe because of his amber eyes and olive skin, black is the color I prefer to see him wearing, although he says he's "tired of being Goth." By the time he was ready to leave, having tried on several outfits, we were both exhausted, and it was terribly hot outside.

On the way to GSU, with what I intended to be an earnest attempt at comic relief, I asked Dude if he wanted to make a quick stop at the "Pakistani Burger King." Immediately he started into me with a solemn, didactic tone, asking why I insist on calling it the "Pakistani Burger King," since "those people could be from India or some other Indus nation." I told him I don't think it makes much difference exactly what foreign country they're from, or rather they're immigrants or refugees for that matter. My point being—albeit inane and by that point decidedly needling—wherever they're from, they're not from here.

Then, as Dude can, he called me out for, "trying to get away with blatant indifference weakly disguised as the devil's advocate." He asked why I get so upset when I'm referred to as Latino (a frequent occurrence I mainly attribute to my being, as I was constantly called growing-up, "light-skinned"). "You raise your voice and say you're one hundred percent (blank)!" I'm more than a little concerned by Dude's refusal to say, "Nigger." Apart from any negative associations the word may conjure, I fear, and fear he may eventually come to feel, that it's not only the word, but also the reticence to say it that looms like an imminent fatal blow to our relationship.

At the "Pakistani Burger King," as usual, I requested no mayonnaise on our chicken sandwiches, but, as usual, I got mayonnaise anyway. My subconscious assurance in the rote nature of the exchange, i.e., my request to hold the mayo being answered by receiving extra mayo, lies in my subconscious awareness of the adverse tone of my request. Nonetheless, when we sat on the molded plastic dining bench, and Dude pointed out the heaping servings of mayonnaise extruding from the edges of the sandwiches, I said I was going to take the order back. While swiping napkin after napkin over the drenched half of his sandwich, Dude tried to assure me it was alright.

His meek demeanor of gentle forbearance while swiping the bread fueled either my Libran sensibility, my confrontational attitude, or my overprotective tendencies toward him. At any rate, on occasions such as this (evident in the proceeding account), I attribute my actions to an inability to foresee a union such as ours enduring. Rather valid or invalid, informed by that uncertainty and doubt, I brace myself for inevitable separation. In which case, I imagine Dude may take away at least an understanding of the spirit behind my self-defensive mechanisms, while I attempt to adopt his aptitude for patience and tolerance.

The pretty Pakistani girl who took the order looked at me rolling her eyes when I exclaimed that I distinctly remembered requesting no mayonnaise. Then, using an approach used on me by a white Master Chief Petty Officer in the Navy, I inquired about her proficiency with the English language. I over-enunciated, "Do you know the difference between 'yes' and 'no'?" She turned away and started to shake the fry basket before sprinkling the potatoes generously from a tin of salt kept next to the bubbling grease. This reminded me that I had also asked for fries without salt, but got those crystal-encrusted, lukewarm and heat-lamp dried-out fries anyway. Again, I said "Excuse me" to the pretty Pakistani girl, and when she got around to acknowledging me, I dropped the bag containing the faulty order on the floor next to her leg and demanded a refund. She summoned—I assumed—the manager, a short maroon-colored man in polyester knit slacks and a pinstriped dress shirt with the sleeves rolled up. He muttered something along the lines of a warning against, "throwing dings at my employees." I asked him, "What you gone do about it?"

While waiting in line to return the order, I had surmised my odds with him, and knew that more than likely the situation wouldn't come to blows (although I've been wrong before). He stood at least a foot shorter than me and was slightly smaller framed. Nevertheless, if I happened to have gotten him riled up enough such that he tried something rash, there might have been grounds for a civil suit, which might have served as consolation for both guilty and guilty feeling parties in the event I got my ass properly kicked. So, again I said to him, "What you gone do about it?"

Without blinking, the maroon-colored man leaned in, placed his elbows on the counter and composed his hands to give shape to whatever it was he meant to convey. In what can be possibly described (if there can even be such a thing) as a naive version of "playing the dozens," he proceeded, with sincerity, to relay his exact course of action. "Wellelle," he said, "Fahst, I take you nick, and rrrrrring it! Den, I beat you ast rrrrrrreal goot!" By that time Dude had come up to the counter to say take him home. I was at the ready for a vocal joust, but I turned promptly around and left. Dude drove himself to class from the apartment. As I'm recounting this, I still can't help but smile at being bested in "the dozens" by the manager of the "Pakistani Burger King."

When Dude returned this evening, the bread had risen and the beans were well seasoned.

I'm somewhat surprised at the precision of wind. Last night it thundered and rained fiercely for over an hour. I went out this morning to see about the flower garden. The wind had shot pine straw like arrows through the heart-shaped leaves of the salvias. Our proudest, tallest, fullest celosia had dropped its outer petals into a rosette beneath its thick stem, and I fear for the other celosia, their survival.

Despite the garden's shortcomings, I have noted that where it lacks in depth, it more than makes up for with color. In the back of the garden, the purple impatiens have grown into a bushy impressive showing against the holly. The row of white periwinkle establishes a frontal border for the impatiens and a back border for the coleuses, which are doing quite well there in the sun I thought would overwhelm them. Within the red salvias I dispersed the few fire colored mini snapdragons that were left at the nursery. And, which I like to think of as a testament to summer, surrounding the entire garden are golden marigolds.

Sunday, July 2

Not much private time with Dude lately. Today I began cleanup of the spare bedroom-turned-office. Monumental task. If I apply and get accepted to American College, we'll need extra space where we both can study.

Postponed my scheduled run, because I was exhausted from the cleaning and the other day's weight training when I overdid it with dumbbells. Also entertained a case of hiccups. I cut a thick piece of yesterday's bread, buttered it lightly and tried to swallow down the spasms.

After my run, Dude's buddy from high school, Tyrone, stopped by. He and I were outside talking about being in the service. He reminisced about the Army and I talked about the Navy. Tyrone made an interesting observation, saying that America is so much more littered than overseas. I don't suppose I ever noticed, America being littered that is. I seem to pay more attention to nature, which is what I was doing at the time. The snapdragons and salvias (particularly the snapdragons) appeared to be withering. I've already had to uproot one plant; the rain has been steady, so I can't imagine why they're dying.

Today a nuthatch, wren, cardinal, titmouse, purple finch, and a grackle (which I recognized for the first time as distinguished from the common crow) landed on the feeder. The titmouse, I've noticed, is an aggressive bird that, while feeding, will attack any other bird attempting to feed at the same time. Then again, the titmouse will even threaten me when I'm nearby.

The three of us went to lunch at the Piccadilly. Two guys came in with a tranny who kept looking at me, or vice-versa. I have this fascination with drag queens. They're the quintessential thespians and muses; everyone should have a drag queen in his or her life. Salvador Dali had his International Crisis, and Dude and I have our CeCe Boom. Interesting to me is that I can recognize a drag queen even out of drag. I'm not implying that the ability is such a big feat. It's easy to observe when the gesticulations and the body don't quite jive with the prescribed gender of the costume. I used to think it was just a matter of "acting" like females, when, through CeCe, I realized that there truly is such a person as an androgyne. I think CeCe is one of the bravest people I know.

Over lunch at the Piccadilly, Dude told me that Ms. Marie reported that she is again gainfully employed. Previously, Ms. Marie had quit her job as a collection agent to "get her shit together." She prepaid four months rent and was sitting back enjoying the cathartic rapture of

Montel, *Springer*, and *Oprah*. She told me she realized that her life, and her drinking problem was not so bad, comparatively. That was in early May. By mid June an inebriated Marie came calling to announce that she was moving to Africa at the end of the month. I don't know what spurred that performance, but I had a feeling that Ms. Marie had neither the means nor the intent to leave for Africa, because, when asked, she did not know what part of Africa she intended to visit, nor whether she intended to remain in Africa or return to America. She simply knew or felt that she must "go to the motherland."

When we got back from the Piccadilly, Ms. Marie was sitting on her steps and serving us severe attitude, cutting her eyes, pretending to ignore us and acting appalled when she happened to glance in our direction. When she is perched on her steps, I usually stay clear unless summoned, since, when she assumes that particular position, she seems to prefer solitude while talking on the cordless, or gently shifting her shift while smoking a cigarette.

As yet I have not examined the American College catalog as closely as I've been intending. I must make note to get a grammar checker for the computer. Anyway, I'm looking forward to school, however not getting my adrenaline up, as it is questionable what condition my life will be in when October rolls around.

Monday, July 3

Last night Dude and Tyrone went out. I was having indigestion from the beans and rice we ate for dinner, so I didn't feel up to going. Probably wouldn't have gone anyway.

Purple tinged plants, what appears to be cockscomb seedlings, are sprouting throughout the frontal part of the garden. One side of the impatiens has been damaged. How? I don't know. This week I hope to transplant potted replacements.

Right now, as a result of my spring-cleaning, seven bags of junk— mostly collapsed boxes, newspapers, magazines and what-not— are in the apartment. Six bags are downstairs and one is currently being filled upstairs in the spare bedroom-turned-office. The management has informed us they will be cleaning the windows on Wednesday. Dude says I'm overreacting to think they'd go through the trouble of hiring a crew to clean all the windows in the complex just to spy on the interracial gay couple and find out what they already know, "They're sleeping together. Imagine that!" Of course, I realize the necessity of periodic maintenance. I also understand it's sensible for management to survey rental property. Suspicion and logical explanations aside, I still feel apprehensive.

When evening approached, I went out on my run. As always, I began by walking a block or so down Hermance Drive. The elderly couple that live in the house with the plastic flower adorned yard, were not standing out as usual, and I missed hearing their kind greetings as I passed by their home. They're both so beautiful—gray haired, and with smooth evenly colored brown skin.

Jack and the Rotarians

Luis Jaramillo

Luis Jaramillo's first book of short stories, The Doctor's Wife, *is the winner of the 2009 Dzanc Books Short Story Collection Competition, and will be published by Dzanc Books in 2012. His work has also been published in* Tin House, H.O.W. Journal, *and* Red Line Blues. *He is the associate chair of the writing program at The New School.*

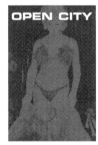

JACK AND THE ROTARIANS WERE NO LONGER SPEAKing. They all sat in the Masonic hall and ate their chicken and baked potatoes grimly, sawing at the dry flesh out of habit even though they weren't hungry. No one had ever invited a Mexican before.

The Mexican was a doctor and he wasn't actually from Mexico. He came from Los Angeles and he was my father, which is why I'm telling this story.

This story is actually the convergence of two events on one day. Nobody talks about coincidence in Salinas. Nobody runs into anybody and thinks, "What a small world." This is only to say that because it was a small town, of course I knew Jack's son.

Jack Jr. and I ran the mile and two mile for the middle-school track team. Jack Sr. coached the long-distance runners and that night, that same Wednesday, the Wednesday that my father attended the Rotary meeting for the first time and the Wednesday of the track meet, Jack Jr. and I kissed.

Kissing is often the point of the story but in this story it isn't. It is the thing that happened that day, but it isn't the point—the kissing was incidental, only one event. There is a Latin term for the assumption that the first action causes the next, just because the two events follow sequentially. My dad said the phrase all the time as a warning against such thinking, *post hoc ergo propter hoc,* after this means because of this. But he meant the opposite. We were supposed to remember it was a fallacy.

At the track meet that afternoon, it was hard for us seventh graders to know what exactly had happened at the lunch meeting and why it mattered. After the dads dropped their kids off, they stood around together, kicking at the grass with their hands in their pockets. We all overheard them talking, "Next thing you know, it'll be all greasers at the meeting." Or, "It had to happen sometime," and, "His son is on the track team, you know."

None of the fathers spoke to Jack Sr.

Jack Sr. didn't care. As a pre-meet warm-up he practiced his favorite activity. While we ran warm-up laps, he ran around the track ahead of us, juggling three tennis balls. He called this joggling.

"Come on you slugs, I could run faster than you even if these tennis balls were axes."

His antics didn't help me. Everybody knew that I was the child of the Mexican who'd gone to the Rotary Club meeting. My teammates looked at me with a kind of awe. I'd never been Mexican before and now I was.

I lived in a house with a pool and my family took trips. I had one sister. My mother didn't push the shopping cart back from the grocery store with all of her children trailing behind. I'd always been brown, but now I was a Mexican.

Nobody said anything to me that day. Maybe they were afraid that I'd stop being a Mexican and that they would look foolish for thinking I was something I wasn't.

Jack Jr. was thin and tall. He had blond hair and very pale skin. He was built like a long-distance runner. He would have been considered good looking, but he often had a worried look on his face. When it was time to pick on the fat kid, or the nerd, he just watched. He didn't defend anybody but he didn't say anything mean either.

This is the same day, the same story. This isn't the day, two weeks in the future when, at the next meet, Jack Jr. elbowed me in the ribs to get around me on his final kick to the finish line, even though we were on the same team. He threw his bony arm into my side, leaving a bruise, and he didn't apologize afterward.

This isn't the time years later, in high school, that we sat on the bus with our bare legs touching on the way back from Monterey, our heads hunched close to the portable video football game.

This is still the Wednesday of that first Rotary meeting my dad attended with Jack Jr.'s dad.

We wore our singlets and the silky shorts that grazed the tops of our thighs, sweat pants and sweat shirts over the racing wear. We ran in our regular running shoes. Our racing flats, tied together around our necks, bounced on our chests. As a team, we long-distance runners ran wide laps around the playing field, jogging slowly to warm up.

I ran just ahead of Jack Jr.

"Hey," Jack Jr. said, covering his mouth so that his father wouldn't see.

"What?"

"Let's not race today. Let's ditch."

"Okay," I said. I didn't know what we would do or where we would go but it seemed that Jack Jr. had a plan. I didn't think past the moment of escape because it was the escape itself that was thrilling. It was danger-ous—I knew we'd be caught—but I liked the idea of hiding. The danger wasn't the attraction, the hiding was. Of course one thing causes another.

We waited until nobody, no adult, was looking. Then we told Jake McInnis and Jeff Wong that we were going to the bathroom. After we made it around the corner, we kept jogging to the bike rack. We unlocked our bikes then climbed on. We pedaled fast.

We rode to Jack Jr.'s grandparent's house. Jack Jr. fished the key out from the birdhouse hanging under the eaves of the front porch. The older Churches had gone down to Cabo San Lucas and we had the house to ourselves.

Jack Jr. showed me a refrigerator in the garage full of Miller Lite. We cracked open beers and sat in lounge chairs on the back deck. The beer tasted like aluminum and it was very cold.

"This beats running around that damn track."

"Yeah. Damn racing."

"Do you want a cigarette?" Jack Jr. motioned me over to his deck chair. He had a pack in the pocket of his sweatpants, as if he smoked all the time. He lit the cigarette with a lighter and blew out the smoke. He waved the pack at me. I took one of the cigarettes and put it in my mouth. He waved the flame of the lighter in front of my cigarette.

"Inhale like your mother just came into the room."

I tried it, gasping in the smoke.

I coughed violently. His trick worked.

"Have you ever kissed a girl?" Jack Jr. asked.

"No, have you?" My eyes watered from the smoke but I kept at it.

"What do you think it's like?"

We got another couple of beers from the garage then sat down next to each other on the same deck chair.

We'd already left the meet, we'd be kicked off the team, and probably suspended too. In the future we wouldn't even live in the same town. I would want to kiss boys and Jack Jr. wouldn't, but that night, that

Wednesday, it didn't matter. We were going to do everything bad all at once.

Jack took a film canister out of his backpack and showed me the marijuana inside. He took out rolling papers and tried to look like he knew what he was doing. His hands shook and the paper made a noise like a leaf. He said curse words under his breath.

When he was done, the joint looked wrong. I didn't know exactly what it should have looked like, but I knew it was too fat on one end and it was kind of loose, so the marijuana dribbled out unless Jack tilted it at a crazy angle. Jack lit it and inhaled. It worked even though it was messy.

I inhaled too. We relaxed against the back of the chair.

"Running sucks," I said. I didn't mean it. I liked running, I just didn't like to race.

"Yeah," Jack said. He put his arms over his head. We sat very close together on the deck chair.

Jack leaned over and kissed me, slipping his tongue in my mouth for a second.

I was horrified and I wanted more. I pulled my mouth away.

"It's probably better with a girl," Jack Jr. said.

That was it.

"Let's have another cigarette," I said. I liked how smoking gave me something to do with my hands.

We shared another cigarette. Neither one of us smoked properly. I felt so happy to be smoking badly next to Jack Jr. We weren't even friends.

We drank another beer each and talked about Dungeons and Dragons. We never knew the other also liked to play. We made a plan to play and smoke a joint before we played. I decided I was a stoner. I'd heard of people getting hooked right off, and I guessed I was one of them.

I'd never had a whole beer to myself before, let alone two. I felt tired and I wanted to close my eyes, so I let them shut. Jack Jr. must have passed out soon after I did.

My father and Jack Sr. found us lying on the one chair. We were so small that we fit, snuggled next to each other like children.

"Let's talk *mi hijo*," my father said, in the car on the way home.

The Miller Lite addled my brain and I thought I might be sick on the floor. Mostly I still felt very tired. I closed my eyes, leaning my head against the glass of the car door.

"I won't do it again," I said. I didn't specify what I meant.

"I know you won't. You are an ethical person."

I pressed more of my face on the cool glass, wishing my dad would stop talking.

"When I was little I used to be able to fly. I flew around the backyard when nobody was there. But then I got scared that somebody would see me, so I stopped."

"That's not true," I said. The story was meant to make me laugh, but it didn't work. It worried me that it might be true. Even then I knew that he was talking about something sexual because the flying was shameful. Something shameful is probably true and this is what worried me. I didn't want my dad to fly.

Later, I pieced together a more complete picture of that day. Jack Sr. had started up a campaign to get my father into the Rotary Club. Step one was to get him to the meeting. He pursued my father like a lover. He called my father every day, "Why don't you want to come to the meeting? It won't hurt you. It'll be good for the community. If you come, I'll teach you how to juggle."

Years before the meeting, Jack Sr. had gone away to college, then came back to this small farming town to go into his father's line of business, insurance. He sold insurance to farmers and lawyers and doctors and made plenty of money at it. The Churches were an old family, old for California, and people trusted them. The Churches might be wild as youngsters—get drunk and flip a car or grow long hair—then they always settled into the family business.

But something happened to Jack Sr. at college. Lots of people pick up a veneer of liberalism, but most of us are lazy. We aren't willing to make our vision real. Jack Sr. saw how the town he came from functioned, and decided to do something about it. He came back to the town with plans. My father was one of Jack Sr.'s projects.

After months of phone calls, my father gave in.

"I'll go to the meeting."

At the meeting that Wednesday, Jack introduced my father around. During the luncheon, the man sitting next to my father, one of the bank vice presidents, leaned over and said, "You speak English good for a Mexican."

My father said, "Thank you. You speak well yourself."

The man looked pleased, but unsure whether or not he'd been insulted. It didn't matter. An insult from a Mexican only meant the Mexican was looking for trouble.

Jack Sr. and my father became friends. The racist old bastards either died or gave up, and Jack stuck around, my father stuck around.

My dad joined Rotary and attended meetings every week, no matter where he was, even when vacationing in Thailand or in Sun Valley for the the annual cardiologists convention. When he was in town, my dad sat next to Jack. Those two never stopped planning or making things happen in the town.

At the last Rotary meeting, the last Wednesday of this story, my father urged Jack to eat the cherry pie served to him even though it wasn't very good.

"You only live once. Waste not want not." And my dad meant both things. He actually knew about wanting.

My father was too intelligent—he was a doctor, after all—to blame himself when the next day Jack clutched his chest and fell to the floor, dead.

Jack was still young. The Churches didn't die young. Everybody came to the funeral.

Even I came. I took an airplane and rented a car and I came home.

At the reception, I saw Jack Jr. standing in a line with the rest of his family, shaking hands. We'd lost touch. He looked like his father. He had the same energy around him, like a suit. Jack Jr. was a little thicker in the middle but still tall, of course, and he was deeply tanned, crows feet around his eyes.

My father whispered to me that Jack Jr. was a doctor now too. He had a wife and a baby girl. He had a clinic and didn't charge people who couldn't pay. My father had told me this before, but I let him tell me again.

Jack Jr. smiled when he saw me. He broke out of the receiving line, "I'm glad you came." He put out his arms to be hugged.

"Your father was a good man. He'll be missed." I said. I felt Jack Jr. shaking like he was crying. He wasn't. He couldn't stop laughing. Maybe we both remembered the same things. Jack laughed so much, tears ran down his face.

"I know," he said. "I loved him so much." We clutched each other like men.

From The Breather

Jeff Johnson

Jeff Johnson lives in lower Manhattan in every sense of the word. Or is it a phrase? Who knows? You may find him lodging complaints at twitter.com/fittedsweats. He's written for the Minus Times, Fence, Jane, ESPN: The Magazine, Vice, The New York Times, The Awl, McSweeney's *and several other publications and lodging-industry newsletters. This is an excerpt of a longer story that appeared in* Open City.

I.

 THE ADMIRAL IS KNOWN AS SUCH BECAUSE HE RAN a pontoon boat full bore into a dock loaded with Cub Scouts ten or fifteen summers ago. It was a humid night, supposedly. Brutally hot. Zero wind. Swarms of mosquitoes. A dense cloud of *something*—I'm terrible at identifying meteorological phenomena—covering the lake.

God only knows what the little pukes were looking for, couldn't have been stars. Some elder stirred them up. Roused them from their tents. Convinced them, possibly, that the willing lips of area trout were puckering for their dangling worms. Rod and reel stuff. I don't have specifics.

What I do know is this: the Admiral had been at McGivern's cottage. Pounding whatever was wet and piney. McGivern's an attorney. The Admiral, something less. The story went he was uninvited. Sweat beading on his forehead. Half the wives repulsed, the other half goading him on. Tiki torches. A punch bowl. The party disbanded. The Admiral pontooning toward a lakeside hamburger stand (closed), or at least attempting to.

Back in the city, before the trial, in one of the Admiral's haunts, a chorus of comrade drunks began cobbling together a defense.

"Why were Cub Scouts on a dock in the first place?"

"That's not scouting. That's fishing."

"On a dock, after dark."

"Doesn't make sense."

"'Course you've heard about the Scouts."

"It's for queers, nowadays."

"I apologize, but *any*thing I've ever done on a dock after dark has not been morally sound."

"A dark dock's where you'd go to, you know, have a kiss, get your penis tugged on or something."

"Or where, if you were a sickening individual, you'd take a group of kids. Who are green about sexual matters. Then you'd talk them. Into letting you. Tug on *their* penises."

"Under the auspices of scouting."

"Or fishing."

"At their age, it doesn't even bring them joy. The Scouts. It brings the penis-tugger. Who is sick in the head. The joy."

"Christ, you're grossing me out."

"It was just probably one big tug session, led by a gay."

"Who lied his way into the scouting game. Moved up the hierarchy. To take overnight field trips. With children."

"And what the *Admiral* did, if we can even call it a crime at this point—"

"Was an intervention. Most likely by a higher figure. A god figure. Along with a pontoon as the vessel. Careening into a dock."

Truth be told, nothing much happened to those Cub Scouts, anyway. Nothing that casts and internal surgical plates couldn't fix. The Admiral got probation. Did the steps. Made the pledges. Raked the library lawn. Proceeded, in due time, to get shithouse drunk again, whenever the impulse struck him. He wound up catching a few more DUIs, sitting in the cooler, walking, eventually, with a few provisions.

We're friends now, sort of. I'll see him out, chugging Windsors and 7-Up. Like none of it ever happened. We all pretend it never happened, even McGivern, sometimes. And when the Admiral's wife calls, he turns to me, and I'll walk out into the parking lot and dutifully blow into the ignition-based sobriety device that will let him start his car, take a stab at driving home. This is what I do. I am a breather.

When my story gets to this point, people have a tendency to grind it right to a halt. Ask if it wouldn't be easier to just call a cab. What I am fairly certain of is, "No." Not with the Admiral, or any of these fuckers. Don't ask me why. They *need* to get in their vehicles. My father was this way, too. Santa Claus could arrive with a sack of authentic moon rocks, and he'd wave him off, throw the car in reverse, and back over a snow hill at the end of the driveway.

Their urge to drive is nothing they can control. Here's an exercise: set a bowl of chocolate pudding down in the middle of a sprawling hardwood floor. Now, set a morbidly obese glutton or a toddler down on that self-same floor. Imagine, momentarily, something else will captivate them beyond that pudding. If you chose Fatty, point to a sack of carrot sticks. If it's Junior—never mind—his face is already in that pudding dish.

That's how bad these people want to drive. Especially when they're wasted.

Now look at me. As much as they want to drive, I want them to drive. Don't tell me what I already know, that I'm just as bad, if not worse. I don't know why I do it. I haven't drank in forever. I have no sympathy for these fellows and their legal woes, nor their health. And no tears, either, for the family in the slow-moving Dodge Caravan that might eventually get sideswiped, and the passengers paralyzed.

Yet something gets me up off my barstool and out into their cars, dome light on, face lowered to my right knee, drunk guy impatiently attempting to balance against the car door as his state-sanctioned sobriety straw finds its way into my mouth. I blow, hop out, watch them make their way out into traffic.

And okay, sometimes I follow.

It's not a sexual fetish. I'm not steering with one hand, pumping my shlong with the other, watching them drift across the yellow line, scuff curbs, decapitate mail boxes. I'm actually seen as a hero to some. To many, in fact. I've had drunks tear up. Do that "We're not worthy" genuflection before sitting down in a bucket seat with a to-go-cup of Myers' Rum and Dr. Pepper cradled between their thighs.

The inevitable: at a certain point, a drunk will plow into something substantial and I'll get a phone call. Have to put on a suit, take the stand, get admonished. Or worse.

2.

I live on what was enthusiastically referred to by my real estate agent as a bluff. The house is actually on a slight incline overlooking a service road that runs parallel to one of the major thoroughfares in my city. There are three public high schools in the area, and my home is in the district of the self-consciously second-rate one. Union families. Speedboats, lawn ornaments, driveway hockey nets, frozen hamburger patties.

I moved here after living across town in a similar home with my wife until one day in the summer of 1989, when she told me that I liked cold cuts. This was meant as an insult. We'd long exhausted everything real to fight about and now our battles consisted of reciting benign facts about each other, issued, of course, with pinch-faced repulsion.

Cold cuts signified bad breath, greasy fingers, clogged veins. Who in their right mind would consume them? I couldn't be bothered to formulate a defense, but I didn't shy away from it, either. After all, if we were bickering about snacks, there was an occasion where I discovered Chex Mix in her pubic hair. I didn't get all sanctimonious about that.

There are worse problems in the world. The Chex Mix could have had tiny legs. Could have only been eradicated via medicated shampoo and a special comb. May have arrived courtesy of a salesman named Reynolds who drifted into town from the Pacific Northwest. But, no, there was no evidence of infidelity. Needless to say, however, we packed it in. I treaded in tidal pools of nurse porn and audio books, Westerns mainly.

She taught aspiring lesbians how to garden (better), be less disappointed. We terrorized no children in custody wars. We liquidated our common assets and ceased all communication, save for death notices in the form of voice mails, left when we're certain the other person will not answer the telephone.

"Aunt Phyllis died. In Pensacola. The bird was eighty-seven."

That was the last one. I'd already left it two months prior. But I was lonely. My ex-wife never called back.

I see her sometimes at stoplights. Her glasses have now grown a necklace, that's how old we've gotten. The chain lets them rest near her bosom, which would sag if it were bigger, but it is delicate and small underneath her immaculate cable-knit sweaters. Sometimes she'll wave and when the light changes, accelerate slowly and drive away.

She's not the reason I do this.

I hear from our friends whose kids are finishing college. I dream momentarily, though not frequently anymore, of the family we never started. Thing is, there's a ceiling on the highs in this community, but I've discovered there's no bottom on lows. Why bring a kid into a city like that?

This was fine when we were young newlyweds having fled Chicago, convinced that all we really needed was each other. Nothing would get us. Not even boredom. For many years, I sat at a desk and said "Jerry Sandini" into the telephone when it rang. I provided answers about the most efficient uses of residential energy, according to customers' bills, as well as their location. Once a month I prepared a report for a large corporate meeting. I rarely got to elaborate on my results and my report was part of a larger file that got boiled into a tiny boxed stat on a newsletter.

This was fine until it led to cold cuts and Chex Mix. And blowing into cars.

Last summer I assisted someone named Kevin. To many, he was known as Sgt. Sucrets—a stocky fellow, late thirties, with an overgrown bleach-blond crew cut. He returned from National Guard duty in Tikrit with an illness that could only be cured by eating cheese curls and washing them down with bar-rail brandy. Sometimes he had visions, sand-blown mind fucks where everyone within earshot could only imagine the original horror that birthed them into existence. Still, despite it all, he had enough sense not to tamper with his Intoxalock. If he did, he'd get jail time.

One night I blow-started his Cressida and crept behind as he ran it along a curb, gently at first, then quickly gaining steam, tires on the passenger side squealing like a duffel bag full of scalded kittens. I tapped my brakes and eased back as he over-corrected and wound up rolling quietly onto a lawn on a sleepy residential street, the car safely bumping up against a tree.

I threw my Civic into park and killed the lights. I left the engine running. I was maybe twenty yards back. I exhaled, mildly relieved for a second. I almost got out of the car, told the sergeant to get the hell out of there. Before we left, I'd made sure he had his seat belt on. He couldn't have been hurt.

I drummed my fingers on the steering wheel for a moment, then decided to go inspect. As I reached to open my door, a light went on inside the house. A figure moved behind a curtain in the kitchen.

Okay, I thought, well, shit.

I waited for the sound of sirens to fill the sky. I shifted into reverse. Sgt. Sucrets's dome light went on. He looked toward the light in the house, then wriggled from his seat belt. Before he could get out, I heard a loud whine. Must be some new cop vehicle, I thought. Then the tree, an ancient elm, toppled onto his car. The windows blew out and rained onto the lawn.

Here was my first real encounter with disaster. I did a Y-turn and floored it.

Resuscitation of the Shih Tzu

Ryan Kenealy

*Ryan Kenealy lives in Chicago where he is working on a colleciton of short sto-
ries about animals in peril. He also runs a horseracing blog called* Chicago
Railbird. *His story "Yellow and Maroon," which appeared in* Open City 7, *was
his first publication.*

I WANTED TO PROJECT A STATE OF INDIFFERENCE TO
Ann's return. I wanted to be smoking on the stoop
when her taxi pulled up. I had to smoke five in a row
lighting one off the other in the half-hour wait for this
effect.

Ann had every right to leave me, then return, on a
sunny day in a taxi. We'd decided that our relationship
should never impede us from further geographic
exploration. We would not strangle one another. So I had no firm
ground for self-pity. I would be indifferent to Ann's return, then try to
fox something else out of her I could legally be angry about, and this
would have worked had the shih tzu's heart not failed.

It was very hot the day Ann returned. The vapors of burning roof tar and
gasoline squiggled the air in the two o'clock sun and the sky looked spattered with grease spots the way a stove looks after bacon's been cooked
on it. In front of the stoop I watched through the vapors a lady in the
passenger seat of a pickup truck fan her naked baby with a *missalette*
from Our Lady of Guadalupe, while her husband sold pork rinds the size
of car mufflers to my neighbors. The shih tzu sat splayed on the stoop
next to me. I cut its hair short the day before so you could see vulgar
patches of pink skin through his shorn salt-and-pepper fur.

Since Ann left, the shih tzu has growled at things like car alarms and
the robotic sound of "The Entertainer" that the ice cream truck loops as
it crawls through the neighborhood. He seemed too proud to need any
consolation from me concerning his absent master. I stopped walking
him weeks ago. I would let him out but sit on the stoop while he mawed
confusedly through the small patch of grass in front, writing some for-

lorn note with his urine. He could wander off at any time and I tried to let him know he could—our relationship had no geographical boundaries.

A jolt ran through me when I saw the taxi turn down our street—taxis normally avoid the neighborhood so I knew it was Ann. The taxi slowed at different points and I could almost hear her in the backseat giving miserable directions. Somehow the shih tzu also knew what the taxi meant and let out a strangely pitched howl as if it were trying to hold back a much stronger howl and the noise let out was the sound of its repression. The taxi rolled to a stop in front of the stoop and with a mechanical click the trunk opened to reveal Ann's canvas bag. The shih tzu began to sprint without direction across the urine-soaked grass, indiscriminately revving a low growl. I was still smoking but the adrenaline from seeing her pay the taxi, seeing her bag pop up before me, numbed me to my crusted lungs. This was when I decided to nub the cigarette and walk to the trunk. The shih tzu growled at me while it ran clipped diagonals around my ankles as if it recognized my resignation, as if it were yelling: *You pussy, don't you remember the plan?*

I plucked her bag from the trunk, then shut it. Ann, still in the seat, turned at the sound of the trunk to see me and smiled. She grabbed her change, exited the taxi, then stutter-stepped quickly toward me in her cork-bottomed heels. I saw the peach fuzz on her arms glistening, as the swarm of vapors intensified with taxi exhaust. I felt her unpainted lips against mine, and her curled brown hair run over my shoulder. I pressed my head far into her and felt trembles spill out of her like laughter; that's when I heard the gurgled noises of the shih tzu. Ann heard them too and through this impossible confluence of emotions that the small sausage body of the shih tzu could not bear, we saw it on the sidewalk—its legs convulsing in the air.

Ann was first to the shih tzu. She reacted by placing her hands on her face like Olive Oyl might. I leaned down to the still-convulsing shih tzu. Our neighbors watched from their card table as I placed my hands on its small hairy chest and without thinking began compression. My hands were flush to its ribcage, with fingers up; most people don't know to do this and end up breaking the victim's ribs. Ann was covering her mouth, trying to keep her shrieks at bay. The shih tzu was no longer breathing and I wondered what it'd be like to have a dead shih tzu in the apartment, to move it around from the couch to the kitchen, to lift its dead head above the water bowl, to ventriloquize growl noises while pulling its black lips above its teeth.

On the third compression the shih tzu coughed out a breath, which meant I didn't need to unseal and blow into its lips where a bit of foam seeped at the corner. We needed to get it to a vet.

Taxis will not pick up a man cradling a lifeless shih tzu. I explained this to Ann with different words, which made her face cringe around the eyes and loosen around the jaw as if she were about to have castor oil spooned into her throat. Our neighbors continued to watch us while breaking apart their pork rinds and splashing them with cayenne powder and lime juice. They own an old pickup truck with tall braces on either side of the bed. At the end of a normal day they'll have ten feet of bent metal stacked in it. But they weren't collecting that day. They were playing dominoes and watching us. Ann walked to their table and appealed to them in frantic hack Spanish for a ride to the vet. She has always been good at doing things like this. They stared at her nervously until a short and wobbly man with a mustache got off his chair and waved us to the brown Dodge pickup that had a dusty pink stuffed animal tied to the grill. I picked up the shih tzu. It was making strange noises and I was afraid to bring it close to Ann. Our neighbor told us his name was Jesús then drove us down the street to North Avenue en route to the vet.

The truck's lame shocks and struts bucked across the grated North Avenue Bridge where prostitutes liked to swagger during the wolfing hours. The river looked uneven and overgrown with nasty life and decrepit fences. Ann talked to the shih tzu in my arms telling it we were almost there, that it would be OK. The shih tzu let out a curdled noise, which made Jesús clench the wheel tightly.

When we reached the vet we offered rushed thank yous to our mustached chauffeur who said, "I wait, I wait." I told him not to and he was quiet, thinking it over. "I wait. I wait."

Like every vet hospital the floors were a shiny laminate. I walked across the reflection of blurred fluorescent lamps, then handed the wilting shih tzu over to a man wearing a white lab coat. He asked a few questions, then walked to another room. Ann and I stood in the hallway not knowing what to do next. We didn't look at each other, we were afraid to. The receptionist put her arm around Ann, then gently led us to seats in the front room that was occupied by a sleeping greyhound and its owner who was reading a magazine.

We sat close to each other. My arm ran the length of her thigh and clasped around her kneecap. She began to cry. Her face was red. I hugged her as tightly as I could, she hugged back with equal intensity. I wasn't worried about the shih tzu, I was worried for Ann, and what I didn't know then was that Ann worried about the same thing.

Three months ago Ann and I answered an ad in the paper calling for manual labor. The ad promised eight dollars an hour, free lunches and a chance to work for the European Circus. The next morning we sat on a curb outside a chain-link fence on Navy Pier with about fifty other people all hoping to work for the circus. At nine a short French-looking man with a cigarette hanging from his lips rolled open the fence, then walked away. We followed him to a trailer and filled out forms. Shortly after we were bona fide circus employees and Ann wearing her tank top, jean shorts, and work boots began to do what she does.

I used to hate people like Ann—people who try so hard to find connections, who concoct bogus ones if none exist, but I got tired of dragging that hatred around. I kind of need people like Ann around me.

The first Eurocarnie she met was a man named Jacques who wasn't European at all—he was from Montreal but insisted Montreal was the same thing as Europe because he, like real Europeans, put a filter in his marijuana cigarette. Ann was mesmerized by this piece of exotica, this filter approach. She told me out loud in front of Jacques in an excited voice about the filter. "Oh, that's cool," I said lamely. And this shared social deviance was the beginning of a bond, something for Ann to snicker about with them. Jacques's purpose for illuminating this detail was different. He wanted to score some weed.

Lunch was a bucket of apples, sodas, and Hostess cupcakes. The scab labor and the lower-echelon Eurocarnies ate around the trailer and tried to talk with one another. I had a shirt on that people liked so people kept saying "that's a cool shirt" with big-toothed grins. I thanked them for the observation, not knowing how to build any conversation out of it. Ann interjected with "that shirt was his grandfather's."

By three we had some of the smaller tents broken down and everyone seemed happy to see the fruit of their work. Jacques decided the time was right to ask Ann if she could procure weed for him and his Eurocarnie cohorts. I was tying down some canvas when she asked if my friend Andrew still sold weed.

We left the pier weary and sundrunk at five-thirty. It felt wonderful to be a part of the rush hour, waiting on the platform for the El with Ann and all the slouched men in suits and women teetering on their pumps. The communal summer weariness made me feel accomplished and proud. On the El I stared out the window, which held a thin reflection of my face shuttling over the blurring brown back porches of apartments filling with post-work television light. I would look at this then at Ann's bare legs. She saw me doing this so she smiled and placed her hand on my thigh. "Can you call Andy when we get home?" she asked.

The Eurocarnies wanted three ounces—apparently they knew not to use the metric system when ordering up weed in the States. I called Andy. I hadn't talked to him in a while, so it was a bit awkward. He lives in the suburbs with his chain-smoking mother and his girlfriend. Because of our conversation's impossibly small radius, whenever I go to visit I spend most of the time looking into an aquarium at his collection of African fish that swim through a plastic skull.

"Three O-Zs—that's a lotta weed, man."

"Whatever you got is fine and feel free to, um, you know, gouge the prices a bit," I explained to Andy, which didn't excite him as much as hearing his future customers work for the European Circus.

That night Ann made us sandwiches and we ate them while watching *Wheel of Fortune* with the sound turned down and listened to a Gene Ammons record.

There's this thing Ann does when she wants to have sex. It's not very subtle. She'll poke with her index finger at my penis then smile. If I wish to do the same I'll also poke myself, then she'll pick it up as if it were a telegraph, and start talking like a machine: "I feel ready to do the devil's work how bout you. Stop." Then I'll volley back: "Armpits may smell corrupt but my hankerin for you is not. Stop." It's a stupid process but it's quick and it works.

I could see the sun setting through the bay window as we rolled around. Her teeth, nose, and elbow made a viscous parallel as we shifted. She had this smile when she saw me acting aggressively. I saw her, the sunset, and Pat Sajak spinning under the slow repetitive hum of Ammons's "Ca' Purange" and I could be no happier.

Andy honked at 9:27 p.m. It was drizzling outside when I pulled the curtains to reveal his van idling on our street. Ann was more anxious than I and did nothing to hide it. When she grabbed her keys her face was all business.

Sliding open the side door of a van produces a scraping sound perfect for an entrance. Ann climbed in and I sat up front next to Andy. He's five foot seven and looked like a Muppet in the plush captain's chair of the van. We shook hands in that cool way you can shake hands with a person you don't know, then took I-90 through the rain while Ann chirped about how wonderful it felt to be in an automobile on the high-way. And it is nice to be on I-90 as it bends before the black steel skyline of Chicago, but it's not *that* nice, and it was obvious Ann was over-nur-turing the conversation.

We turned into the Presidential Towers, which looked like four tall sticks of margarine. There was a guard at the gate reading a bodybuilding magazine. He let us in but his eyes emitted an air of suspicion, perhaps because of the van. This somehow planted the robust seed of paranoia in Andrew. The guard looked like a bodybuilder himself and this is not how Chicago police and security agents are supposed to look. They're sup-posed to be fat "and if you can't outrun them you deserve whatever sen-tence you get" is how a friend of mine explains it. There were more guards in satin jackets with walkie-talkies around the front of the building and Andrew felt that we should leave.

"They're not looking to bust weed-peddlers. They just keep the bums out and administer the lost-and-found department. We're on the same team—servicing the guest. Trust me," I told Andrew.

"What if this is a setup? You don't know these people."

"Andy. You're being ridiculous," I countered.

It took five minutes of this kind of talk to coax Andy out of the van with his backpack chock-full of Mexican red-hair.

Jacques was happy to see us. "Come in, come in," he warmly instructed. Ann led the way. We sat around a television broadcasting *COPS*. The Euorcarnies love this show, they explained, to which I shot Ann a look meant to express how wonderfully small the world really is. We watched intently as long metal Cutlass Cierras and Ford Thunderbirds raced and dipped, shooting sparks over dark pavement until the cops finally smashed them into a barricade, then squeezed what looked like a polyp of a tank-topped human out of the window and onto the ground where it was quickly shackled.

Ann seemed to glow in this company, giggling, and provocatively opening her mouth over their bong. Andy smiled like a father who had just ushered his daughter into the sacrament of first communion, feel-ing a sense of ownership and pride over the dull joy he'd just imparted. I was ready for the evening to end. I've never felt comfortable doing things like this, especially with the TV on to buttress any lulls in the conversation, but I tried to play along because Ann was so intent on impressing these people. At this point I should have made clear to her how stupid she was acting but I didn't, and why she acted this way wasn't revealed until later in the week when she made an announcement over lunch.

"They want me to travel with them to Atlanta and Florida."

"Who?" I asked.

"The European Circus," she said with a smile. "They're taking care of everything. I won't have to pay for food or shelter and they'll be paying me—money that I can save." I said next to nothing in response. As I explained earlier, I had no right to object. I should have brought up rent money and bills and all the other issues that require postage, but I couldn't even do this. She seemed worried I might be hurt that they didn't ask me along as well. She would be gone for three months, she explained, and I was to act as the shih tzu's guardian.

I stared at the silhouette our twisted bodies made on the laminate floor of the vet. For five minutes we held each other until a separate agony seemed to overtake Ann and she broke free of my grasp.

"I deserve this. I deserve this," she said. I reached back for her and she fell into me for a few seconds.

"I'm not a good girlfriend," she said slurping up her tears after she'd broken free of me.

"Stop talking," I said softly, but it didn't work.

"I don't deserve your support."

"Of course you do," I said.

"You don't know. I don't deserve it. I don't . . ."

"Stop talking, Ann," I said.

"No. There's something we need to talk about."

"No. There isn't, Ann. Not right now," I urged her. It was clear to me she'd done something, perhaps fucked an acrobat, and that sucks but she had no right to tell me now. She needed resolve; she needed to stop thinking in this old pattern. The world does not work this way, she is not being punished, the shih tzu's heart is no divine message. The shih tzu's heart failed because it was hot, because I neglected the thing, not for what she's thinking right now. I wanted to tell her this but I didn't, not because it wasn't clear, it was the only thing that was clear. I thought about slapping her, but didn't want to risk waking the greyhound and having it attack me. I tried forcing a stronger hug on her but this made her body recede into itself. "Do you want to tell me more?" I asked not hiding my exasperation.

"Don't you think I should?"

"No," I said, which made her eyes bulge. Then something like laughter hiccuped out of her.

"*No?*" she repeated sobbing and laughing.

"No," I said back. "It doesn't matter right now."

"What matters right now?" She asked.

I guess I should've said the shih tzu, but I never really liked the shih tzu until its heart failed so that didn't seem fair. Before I could respond we turned to the sound of the vet's footsteps along the corridor. He was holding the shih tzu, which was panting and trying to wrestle free. The vet walked over to us, then silently handed it to Ann who flashed a quick smile before walking with it to the counter where she laid down a credit card as if she were buying a loaf of bread. I stood next to her as she pretended I wasn't there. I followed her out to the parking lot where Jesús was waiting in the brown pickup. He opened his mouth wide, unable to hold back the large wave of joy the live shih tzu brought him.

The Girl with No Face

Chuck Kinder

Chuck Kinder's most recent work is his metamemoir The Last Mountain
Dancer: Hard-Earned Lessons in Love, Loss, and Honky-Tonk Outlaw Life.
He has written three novels: Honeymooners: A Cautionary Tale, The Silver
Ghost, *and* Snakhunter, *and is currently working on a book of poems. He is
the director of the writing program at the University of Pittsburgh.*

 I DON'T KNOW HOW MANY FOLKS OUTSIDE OF WEST
Virginia remember Dagmar anymore, but once she was
famous. Back in the early and mid-fifties, Dagmar had
been black-and-white TV's version of Marilyn Monroe,
or, maybe more accurately, of B-movie queen Jayne
Mansfield. Dagmar was the resident dumb blonde with
big breasts on the old *Milton Berle Texaco Star Theater*,
where she cultivated a funny, startled, deceptively stupid look. She also appeared on the TV variety show *Broadway Open
House*, and even had her own short-lived *Dagmar's Canteen* in 1952,
where Frank Sinatra was once a guest.

Dagmar had been my own first hope and inspiration for a future
beyond the ordinary. She had become the source of all my earliest discovery and flight and fame fantasies. But I let Dagmar and her famous
big breasts slip through my fingers.

Dagmar's real name was Virginia Ruth Egnor, and she was born in
1924 in Huntington, West Virginia. When I was a boy, Dagmar's folks had
lived three doors down from us on Waverly Road in Huntington for several years. There were no fences around the small-frame houses on our
road back in those days, and we kids darted in our games like free-range
chickens across that little prairie of backyards. In Dagmar's folks' backyard there was a spreading old oak we often used as homebase, where I
relished the role of being "it" during hide-and-seek. Being "it" meant
that I could hover about that homebase old oak, where it was only a matter of time until one day Dagmar would discover me. Someday Dagmar
would be visiting her folks, maybe sitting out at the kitchen table sipping
coffee one morning with her mom, when through the back window she

would spot a swift, singular, beautiful boy fearless at his play, and with a mere glance Dagmar would recognize the shining of his inner star.

Dagmar would stub out the cigarette she had been languidly smoking, while trying to explain the enigmatic nature of fame to her old mom, and she would rush out the backdoor to that special splendid boy, rush to enfold him in her fame, not to mention extraordinary bosom, her famous nipples fiery red through her filmy clinging negligee (I loved those words: *nipples, negligee, nipples, nipples, nipples*, which were among those magically learned juicy words of my childhood I would roll around on my tongue like holy cherry Life Savers.)

And then it really happened. Dagmar had actually shown up at her folks' home on Waverly Road the summer I was ten. We awakened one August Saturday morning into all the ordinariness of our own lives to discover an enormous car parked in front of Dagmar's folks' little house. It was a CADILLAC! It was a Cadillac CONVERTIBLE! It was YELLOW! I loved that car at first sight. The neighborhood was abuzz. One of Dagmar's prissy little nieces kept sashaying out of the house to preen and prance and keep everybody abreast of the radiant blonde being within. Apparently Dagmar had brought her latest husband home to meet her folks for a real low-key down-home family visit. I skulked and lurked about the little frame house like all the rest of the obscure neighborhood minions that Saturday morning hoping to get at least a peek at the inscrutable face of fame, but to no avail.

Around noon my dad, or Captain as everybody called him, piled as many neighborhood kids as would fit in his old battered green Plymouth station wagon, as was his Saturday afternoon custom, and hauled us down the road to a public swimming pool called Dreamland. Dad was called Captain because he had been the captain of the Second World War, which he had apparently won pretty much single-handedly. He was famous for this. When he had mustered out of the army at the end of the war a hero, some folks had encouraged him to get into politics. Captain was a big, gregarious fellow with an easy booming laugh, a full-blown sort of character folks always declared was a dead ringer for John Wayne, and it was true. Some folks even declared that Captain would be a natural for governor of West Virginia, although he was by nature neither a drunk nor a crook. Captain, who was a generally unemployed hero, hauled all us rowdy kids out of the neighborhood on weekends so that my mom, who was an emergency-room night-shift nurse, and who pretty much brought home the proverbial bacon in our house plus cooked it up, could collapse in peace.

I recall Dreamland as a vast pool of wavy, faintly blue-green water splashing with sunlight, air thick with the pungent puzzling sweetness of chlorine and suntan lotion, joyful screams and squeals strangely echoey, smooth oiled teenage girls parading imperiously with their movie star sunglasses and implicating smiles and the sweet shadowy secrets of their shaved underarms. Music was always blasting from a huge white-stucco two-storied clubhouse trimmed in blue, and blue onion-shaped domes rose above dressing rooms on a knoll at the far end of the long pool. Dreamland was a Taj Mahal of a swimming pool I both loved and feared, a site of excitement and profound failure for me.

Dreamland was where I learned to swim my first spastic strokes, and where I failed repeatedly to muster courage enough to attempt swimming out to the deep end. I was not afraid of drowning in the deep end. It wasn't that. It was, for one thing, my fear of not looking cool and sleek swimming around like the older boys, but dopey as a duck as I thrashed about in the water of the deep end. I was afraid of being embarrassed if I swam out to the huge circular concrete float in the deep end where the older boys hung out as they strutted and flexed their fulsome brown muscled bodies. Mostly, though, my fear of the deep end was because of the bad dreams.

We piled out of Captain's old Plymouth station wagon that Saturday and charged for the ticket counters, bouncing about impatiently as we inched along in one of the two endless lines. And then I spotted her, in the next line, the famous monster girl with no face. I had seen her maybe two or three other times, and it was always a shock. She was a monster girl whose face had no features. It was like looking at a blur of a face. You got the impression of holes here and there for what could have been perhaps nostrils and a mouth maybe, and eyes, like unaligned marbles amid folds and flaps of flesh and hair that looked like fur and feathers. There were rumors that the girl had been born that way, or that her face had burned off in a fire, or been cut to ribbons in a terrible car wreck or by an escaped convict crazy man with a knife. Her blur of a face was at an angle to me, and I stared at it. I couldn't help it. I blinked my eyes trying to somehow adjust them, to get them into focus, to compose something recognizable as the regular human face of a girl amid that pulpy mess of skin. Suddenly the monster girl turned her head in my direction and I jerked my eyes away. But she knew I had been staring. I could feel she knew I had been staring, and my neck burned with shame and embarrassment for her exotic horribleness. I couldn't think of anything worse than being her, a person whose face could never show her sadness, or happiness, if she ever had any, whose only expression would be *horrible-ness*. How could a girl with no face ever leave a dark room? How could a monster girl ever crawl out from under her rock?

Let's head for the deep end, Soldierboy, Captain said to me the minute we laid out our towels on a grassy slope above the pool that Saturday. Let's go kick that deep end's ass, Captain added, laughing that bold confident winner-of-the-Second-World-War laugh of his, and he gave my shoulder a poke with his finger that about knocked me down. I was this boney kid who had, at best, a baffled sense of balance. Then Captain gave me a snappy salute, which meant that I, his little Soldierboy, was supposed to snap him a salute back, a little private father-son camaraderie he had initiated when I was maybe one. I knew what this meant in a heartbeat. This meant that my cowardly ass was grass and the Second World War was the mower. I hated the Second World War. This also meant Mom had ratted me out to Captain about the deep end and my cowardliness and I resolved at that moment to keep my heart hidden from everybody forever.

At noon each day when I came home from playing or school for lunch, there would be two pans heating on the stove. One pan contained simmering Campbell's tomato soup. I loved Campbell's tomato soup. A syringe and needle were being sterilized in the other bubbling water. After I had enjoyed my Campbell's tomato soup, which I slurped with infinitely slow appreciation while nibbling with elegant slowness upon the crumbs of Saltines, Mom would lead me upstairs, and I would trudge forlornly behind her like the proverbial prisoner going to the gallows. I would lie face down on my bed with my butt bared, until such time as I had worked up enough courage to gasp into my pillow a feathered, fluttering little birdy whimper of that word: *now*. Whereupon Mom would deliver into my shivery little boy butt via that needle the approximate size of a harpoon my daily dose of raging male hormones (I had had a little undescended testicle problem that took four visits to the famous Mayo Clinic to eventually make all better). While I was working up the courage to say *now*, Mom would let me jabber my head off, as I stalled. If I sensed Mom growing impatient with me, I would attempt to distract her with entertaining albeit inscrutable stories. Sometimes I would be forced to pretend to confide in Mom, telling her what I hoped would pass as truthful, private things, making my revelations as puzzling and painful as possible to engage her interest and sympathies. Hence I had told her more truthfully than I meant to about my fear of the deep end, and then I had told her about the nightmares I had had for years that as I was swimming along happily, some horrible scary creature who lived on the bottom of the deep end would awake and see me up above on the surface of the water. Whereupon in my nightmares I would feel something grab my feet from below, and pull me screaming down under the water to be eaten raw.

So there was Captain treading water in the shivery blue green water of the deep end, throwing salutes my way and hollering above the pool racket to jump on in, Soldierboy, the water's right. But Soldierboy just stood there looking down his at toes, curled like scared worms over the pool's edge. You can swim like a fish, Soldierboy, just jump on in and swim to your old dad. I'm right here, son, nothing will happen. You won't drown, hollered Captain. But Soldierboy knew he wouldn't drown. That wasn't it. Soldierboy stood there trembling. Like a cowardly leaf. Soldierboy wanted more than anything to be under the water of his beloved shallow end, holding his breath in the currents of uncomplexity at its bottom where nobody could see him. Come on now, Soldierboy, Captain implored, gritting his teeth. I stared at my worried worms. Come on now, Goddamnit, Chuck, jump! Captain encouraged me and slapped the water with a cupped hand. It sounded like a shot. I flinched violently. Why don't you go ahead and jump, chickenshit, a neighborhood boy said from behind me and hooted with laughter. They were all around me, the neighborhood boys and girls, all those creepy kids with their giggles, their laughter. I spun around and ran. I pushed my way relentlessly through hooting human beings who knew me.

I skulked around that lake of a pool and slipped into the shameful shallow end on the far side, among the comforting presence of strangers, where I felt at home. I bobbed about in the shallow water, a floating head, keeping a wary eye out for Captain or any of the evil neighborhood kids, while I plotted my revenge. If only I could transform this once sweet Persian dream of a pool into a lake of acid. Or have schools of gigantic piranha churn the waves into a foam of blood. If only the creature of the deep end awoke while Captain was swimming out there all alone, when suddenly it happened, and with but a shudder of his great muscles Captain would be pulled down into the deep end, and although my old man wrestled heroically with the groping tentacles, for he was such a big brave shit, they slowly entangled him, pulling him into the dark water toward the deep end monster's huge yellow crazy eyes, and great bloody maw.

Then I heard an announcement over the clubhouse's loudspeakers. They announced that we were all honored to have Dagmar, the famous star of screen and television, as a special guest that day at Dreamland. I stood up in the shallow end and looked around wildly. *Dagmar, man oh man!* I saw a crowd passing slowly along the side of the pool by the clubhouse stairs toward the picnic area on the same slope where we had our stuff laid out. In a momentary parting of the excited throng, I was certain I caught a glimpse of utter blondeness. For a moment I considered returning to my site of shame, swallowing my pride in order to see that famous blonde person and her wondrous breasts up close. But I didn't. I had my pride. I turned and dogpaddled with dignity out to the float in the shallow end, where I pulled myself up and sat with my back to Dad and Dagmar and all they meant.

At some point, I began jumping over and over again into the pool. Time and again, I would run and hurl myself belly first from the float painfully into the choppy water. Then I would drag myself back up on the float and do it again. I didn't care. I didn't care if I knocked myself out and drowned shamefully at the bottom of the shallow end. I pictured Captain standing over where they had drug my pitiful drowned body onto the side of the pool, blue-green water draining from my mouth and nose and ears and eyes. I tried to picture Captain crying his heart out, but I couldn't. The only thing I could make come alive in my imagination was Captain carrying my limp dripping body up the clubhouse stairs while some sad song like "Endless Sea" blasted on the loud speakers, and all the evil neighborhood kids were standing around wondering out loud if I would come back from the dead and fuck with them, which, buddy, you can bet I would.

Then I pictured Dagmar swimming toward me underwater. Like a wondrous waterplant's blooming, her beautiful blonde hair floated about her head as her face came toward my own until it filled my vision. Whereupon, in the moment before I lost consciousness, I felt Dagmar's soft white arms enfold me. I was only ten years old, but I imagined myself being deliciously smothered in the immensity of Dagmar's blonde breasts as she delivered the drowning Soldierboy safely to the surface.

So there I stood on the shallow end float trying to catch my breath after a particularly painful bellybuster, when a kid came directly up to me out of the basic blue and excitedly said these exact words: "Dagmar saw you, boy!" *Dagmar saw you, boy!* That kid said exactly that. I swear it! I spun around like an insane top. I looked everywhere. I looked in the water around the float. I scanned the far sides of the pool, and the grassy slopes. *Dagmar saw you, boy.* When I looked back for the kid he was gone. But that boy had been real, and he had said those exact words full of more wonder than any other words of my childhood. I swear it.

Dagmar had spotted me. That much was clear. I believed that with all of my heart. I believe it to this day. Somehow my fierce painful brave bellybusters had caught Dagmar's attention. Perhaps her blue famous eyes were settled upon me at that moment. They could be. They were. I sprang into action. I threw myself from the float like a virgin into a volcano. I exploded into that violence of water and began to swim frantically for the float in the deep end. I thrashed my arms and kicked my feet wildly. I chopped across the rough surface of the deep end, choking, my eyes burning, toward the distant float. The deep end's water strangled into my throat with each ragged stroke and it dawned on me I might never make it. It dawned on me that I might actually drown like a rat. And for what? Fame? Fame wasn't worth it I realized. Fame wasn't worth drowning like a rat.

But at that epiphanal moment I felt strangely calm. I closed my eyes, and simply kept chopping, blindly, but unafraid, trancelike, and then suddenly I touched concrete. I slapped an astonished hand onto the surface of the float in the deep end and held on for dear life. I had not drowned like a rat after all. I had a second chance at everything, including fame. I was coughing and spitting and my sore arms trembled nearly out of control. I wiped water off of my face with my free hand and pushed my hair out of my eyes. I was there. Soldierboy had made it. Soldierboy was at the float in the deep end where he had always really belonged. Soldierboy loved that float. He gripped the edge of the float and looked around to see who had witnessed this amazing feat. He looked for the evil neighborhood kids. He looked for Dad. Soldierboy looked around for Dagmar.

And then suddenly somebody emerged from the water right beside me and grabbed the edge of the float. It was the famous girl with no face. I took one look at her and screamed. I screamed and screamed and fell back into the water, flapping my arms like crazy wings.

Equilibrium

Walter Kirn

Walter Kirn is the author of seven books, including Lost in the Meritocracy: The Undereducation of an Overachiever, Thumbsucker, *and* Up in the Air. *He lives in Livingston, Montana.*

DARLING, YOU WIN. IF YOU REALLY WANT TO KNOW why I don't trust you—not just you, but any of you, particularly if you come from California, slave to stay thin and keep in shape, and call yourself "spiritual, not religious"—then you're going to have to sit there and be quiet, no questions, no interruptions, just drink your tea, and I'm going to have to tell you about Anna, a person I've mentioned a couple times before but only in passing, dismissively, as that girl who I said I dated for a few weeks because I was intrigued by someone who'd introduce herself with a straight face, in public, to a total stranger, me, wearing a halter top without a bra and jeans cut so low I could see her pubic stubble, as "a weight-loss plan before-and-after model" and "the Dalai Lama's former publicist."

But I've quoted those lines before. We've laughed about them. And I've also already told you, as I recall, that the night when this Anna waylaid me, in that vegan café whose profits support a cult, which holds that our leaders have arachnid chromosomes and hail from a planet called Lervish VI, I was actually in the middle of a first date with a young fan (not quite as young as you, though she seemed a bit younger because she didn't sunbathe) whom I'd been told by a mutual acquaintance had been practically stalking me all winter, that's how jazzed she was about my work, especially *Fearmont*, my online graphic novel about white-collar suburban cannibalism.

But we can skip that part too. Old news. You've heard it. How this Anna strode up and plopped down at our table and picked up a cucumber spring roll from my plate and took a slow bite and the juice dripped down her chin, but instead of wiping it dry herself she reached across and took one of my wrists and used my left hand to do the job. And how, after that, she licked my fingers clean right there in front of the other girl, my date, who'd said in an e-mail that she was thirty but seemed to me to be closer to twenty-five because she had no idea who Chairman Mao was (she thought he was the villain in a *Star Trek* film) and believed me when I said I was thirty-six.

But on to my relationship with Anna, which I've always brushed off as a nothing three-week fling, but in fact lasted twice that long and wasn't nothing. It was ruinous. It broke me. It's the reason that I can't give you what you want—or even bother to ask you what you want. Because I suspect I know. I know I know. It's what all of you clever girls want these days: a ride. A ride whose beginning and ending you control but whose middle, the part that costs money, is up to me.

My first week with Anna was fun but nothing riveting, just a few Kubrick movies in my apartment and a day hike up around Point Dume, where the wildflowers we'd been told would blow our minds had disintegrated on their stalks—not that we cared because we had lots to talk about, starting with Anna's bizarre employment history. She explained her modeling work first, clueing me in about those ads for diet aids that purport to show an average American (a woman from some place like Nebraska, usually, who's either a dental hygienist or a teacher) transforming in no time from bloated, pale, and glum to thin and pink and thrilled. These success-story specimens were frauds, said Anna. They were paid professionals like her—individuals with fast metabolisms and enough underlying natural beauty to make the "after" shots appear miraculous. She said she'd done five of these jobs in fifteen months and was just days from finishing her sixth, coming down from a twenty-four pound gain with the help of saline laxatives and a desperate celebrity fasting trick: ingesting cotton balls soaked in maple syrup. These jobs were proving harder each time, she said (the "up cycles" were the nightmare, she informed me, because they distorted the levels of certain hormones, causing bouts of insomnia, amnesia, and even nymphomania), but her rate of twelve thousand dollars hadn't increased, meaning that this loss would probably be her last. She said that her dream, once she retired, was to regain what she called "equilibrium," a state that she feared might be impossible after so many drastic fluctuations.

This led us to the topic of inner peace and Anna's years in service to His Holiness. That's what she called him, not the Dalai Lama, in a voice so meek and overawed that I had to ask her to speak up. She couldn't do it. She adored the man, though he sounded to me, from her stories, like a diva. For example, when he'd appear on *Larry King*—his TV forum of choice when touring America—he'd send her ahead, she said, to check the greenroom for the presence of certain allergens. Peanuts. He had that one. Hair spray. Windex. Microwave popcorn artificial butter. I didn't dare tell her that we who knew him chiefly as the brave, exiled ruler of Tibet and an inspiring spokesman for global harmony might find these sensitivities disillusioning—evidence of a sheltered, coddled life rather than signs of an evolved old soul.

By my second week with Anna I'd formed a rough impression of her past, from her comfortable upbringing in San Francisco as the daughter of an ocular surgeon to her stint at a Philadelphia conservatory where a lesbian clarinet instructor walloped her with a livestock tranquilizer, molested her backstage at a recital, and ended up forking over a hefty settlement that allowed her to work without a salary fawning on the world's top Asian monk. Her six years running errands on his behalf had taken her to all the civilized continents and climaxed with her engagement to a rich young Tibetan aristocrat of a breed that I hadn't known existed. Anna described the fellow as a swank hypocrite, outwardly prayerful and devout but given to ugly dissipations once he was safe inside his London townhouse. She lifted her sweater to show me the plastic surgery that she said he'd demanded she undergo before he'd marry her. The breasts were so rigidly canted, so squarely aimed, that I should have spotted them for bolt-ons when I'd first handled them inside my Acura, after ditching my silly date at the café. Anna called them "my shame" and told a story of fleeing the volatile Tibetan prince (he'd battered her senseless during a cocaine spree) and jetting back home to San Francisco, where her doctor father hugged her close, felt the firm counter pressure of her new chest, stepped back for a look, and fainted to the ground.

"From shock? Because you were flat before?" I asked her.

"Because he'd left me in the care of Buddhists."

By the time Anna told me this story she'd moved in with me. I hadn't invited her. She'd fallen ill. The morning after the fourth time we had sex she complained of a headache, of zapping blue stars of pain, and stayed in my bed while I drove to the pharmacy for a prescription her father had phoned in. She asked me to test the pills before she took them, and once they hit me—soft bombs of sluggish warmth—I wanted more of them. I lost the day. I lost control. My appetite. Perspective. I lost the weekend and the condoms, too.

The headaches persisted and Anna burrowed in. I couldn't blame her. Her place was a crusty old studio in Hollywood with milk-crate bookshelves, a lamp without a shade, a sad little altar of candles and magic bric-a-brac assembled inside an unused fireplace, and a portable massage table. We went there one evening to fetch some muscle relaxants that her softy father had provided to ease her through her hectic diet cycles. When we left, her failure to lock her door—or hunt in her purse for the keys that she'd misplaced—indicated we wouldn't be returning. We took the one item of value, the massage table, so she could repay me in rubdowns for her upkeep until her "after" shot was taken and she received the remainder of her fee.

We passed the week that followed in a condition—companionable, familiar, frictionless—that most couples only experience after eons of mundane proximity. I credited the medications but also Anna's lack of animal needs. Other than the occasional lettuce leaf or carrot shred from a bag of pre-tossed salad, she consumed none of my food that I could see. Nor did she run up my utility bills by watching TV or playing music or turning the lights on after it got dark. If she was reading when the sun went down, she put the book or magazine down, too. Mostly, the magazine. Mostly, the same issue. Her interest in that wrinkled month-old *People* featuring George Clooney on the cover seemed bottomless, inexhaustible. She did brush her teeth, but with baking soda, not toothpaste, and though she sometimes took half-hour showers, she seemed to have mastered some eastern bathing technique that allowed her to keep her thick dark hair clean without applying shampoo. She lived in a manner that barely left a mark, inert and uncomplaining, which made her the ideal roommate. How she'd ever burned off a single pound was impossible to guess.

At bedtime she gave me selfless, long massages lubricated with jasmine scented oil and accompanied by diverting accounts of her PR work for the grand Tibetan. I noticed after a few nights that certain key episodes kept swapping places, about when I asked her to set them on a timeline, to specify their sequence and their dates, she finally lost her geisha cool. "What is this?" she asked. "A cross-examination? I'm not entitled to my private truth? You want me to fill out a time sheet or some shit?"

"I got mixed up, is all." I switched the subject. "When are they going to shoot your 'after' portraits? You must be almost at your goal by now."

"That was *their* goal," Anna said, "not mine. I'm pursuing balance now."

"You quit?"

"I want to be at my best for you. For us. I want to be stable, loving, strong, and whole. I'm redirecting toward the long run."

"I'm assuming this means you won't get paid," I said.

"Nope. Now roll over so I can do your front."

The phone calls to her father began that week, or maybe that's when my tolerance for the sedatives grew to a point that permitted awareness of them. She conducted the calls out of earshot, in my office, sitting in front of the laptop I hadn't touched since *Fearmont* was optioned by Universal, locking in my income for the summer. All I could hear through the doorway of the bedroom were bursts of daughterly, submissive giggling and stretches of soundless listening, as though she was being lectured or taking instructions. I slid in and out of dreams during the calls, some of the dreams so close to what was happening—tree branches scratching at the window, a moth bumping around inside a lamp globe, the guy in the unit under mine cranking Christian rock—that I didn't realize they were dreams until Anna snuggled in beside me and crushed her rubber breasts into my back.

One morning before I knew she was awake she sat down on the mattress, already dressed, and held out a white plastic wand with a pink plus sign visible in a little oval window.

I counted backwards through our days and nights and came up with several more nights than days. Not enough time had passed for this, it seemed. Still, there it was, not a plus sign anymore but a monumental cross. I took the wand and shook it like a thermometer. Nothing changed.

"How incredible is this? More important, how excited are you? I'm in heaven. I think it's fate. It's karma. I think it's what we've wanted since that first night."

"All we did that first night was make out with our clothes on."

"Because we knew there were thousands of nights to come."

I put on my socks. I had to put on something. Then I gazed at the wand again, willing a different outcome. Not a different outcome in factual terms but in my reaction to the facts. Thought is primary. Mind-set has dominion. I kept up the exercise for several days, using the pills to limber up my mind. The effects came slowly, then overtook me. The green began separating from the grass. My head left my neck at moments, my neck my shoulders. I lived on pine nuts and weak green tea and stared for hours at a time at burning artificial logs. I turned forty-four and didn't feel a thing.

"It's my father," Anna said one night. "He wants to talk to you, man to man." She offered her phone in its decal-covered case and I propped it on my pillow, beside one ear. I decided to smile the same way Anna was smiling, hoping for an attitude transfusion. Her father opened with gracious words of welcome, telling me that I was now part of the family and the family was part of me. He discoursed on the futility of planning, praising the forces that do our planning for us and guaranteeing me his full support (including financial help if it were needed) if I embraced "the perfect flame within" and "surrendered wholly to abundance." The speech was so rich in silky abstractions that it eventually turned to music, its sentences melting into melodies. By the time her father let me go, Anna's suggestion that we marry soon—discreetly, without fanfare—felt like a summons from gentle destiny rather than a soft-sell ultimatum.

She must have placed calls to people who made more calls because my computer soon started filling up with congratulatory e-mails from high Tibetan divines whose titles functioned as their names. Some monks sent along pictures of themselves. Their robes were scarlet, their bald heads brown and lustrous, and one of them thanked me for liberating Anna from "the careening wheel of hunger," which I understood to be her modeling work. I didn't reply to the notes, just let them gather, and as they did, I started to find patterns in their terminology. The trendy word "centeredeness" kept popping up as well as the phrase "the perfect flame." Anna's father had used it, too. Was he a Buddhist? She told me that he was.

"I thought he got pissed at them about your implants?"

"Pissed is pissed. The Dharma is the Dharma."

She pestered me daily about our marriage, insisting that she didn't want a ceremony, just the honor of taking my last name and the ability to assure her grandmother (a strict Roman Catholic whom she hadn't mentioned before) of the legitimacy of the child to come. When I pointed out to her that the child to come had only an early, fragile hold on life and might not hang in there to full term, she said we could always try again. I reminded her that we hadn't tried the first time, but Anna took a different view. "If people sleep together without protection, they're definitely behaving with intention." We debated the word "intention." I used its common definition—purpose—but she assigned it a subtler, broader meaning that covered accidents and screw ups whose consequences weren't foreseen but might have been intuited, if the people involved were mediums or shamans.

A view opened up then of all our fights to come and the succession of losses I would face. Her elastic semantics would beat my rigid logic. I'd need a hobby, a refuge, a sanctuary. A basement workshop that locked from the inside.

My mother the telepath called the following morning to ask me, pointedly, what was going on, even though she lived in Michigan and had no way of knowing that anything was. Her timing caused me to wonder yet again if this is a world of women, of women's wills, mingling, negotiating, and skirmishing in a realm inaccessible to men.

"This is total baloney," she responded once I'd burped up all my sour news. "You're sure this speck, this amoeba, is really in there?"

"I saw the test," I said.

"You saw her *take* the test? Or just the outcome?"

"You draw a distinction."

"I draw a vast one."

My mother, a registered nurse employed by a drug rehabilitation center whose patients were virtuoso bullshit artists, laid out a series of possible deceptions. The urine splashed on the test strip wasn't Anna's. The test had been stolen from a pregnant girlfriend or scavenged from a women's clinic trash bin. The character who I knew as Anna's father, who'd rejoiced like a shepherd in the Bible over his daughter's impregnation by a man about town she hardly knew, was an impostor, an accomplice. Also: did diet models in fact exist? As for Anna's extensive travels with His Holiness, could a woman intent on concealing her true history cook up a résumé any harder to verify? "This stinks to hell," my mother said. "This slutball was either knocked up when you met her and couldn't close the deal with the real father—or maybe he was some bankrupt nincompoop—or my little boy has fallen in with gypsies."

"She and the father have the same last name. It's on the prescriptions."

"She *says* it's her last name."

"I saw her ID."

"You saw a plastic card."

"Do I make her retake the test and watch this time?"

"Say it's positive again. Without a reliable paternity test, you still won't know who contributed the sperm."

From your mother, even if she's a nurse and even if you're halfway through your forties, "sperm" is not a word you love to hear. "Meaning I have to wait for eight more months."

"Not going to come to that," my mother said. "It's almost over, this sad fandango. The gypsies are about to pack their wagons. Softer targets, smoother roads."

"Your reasoning, please?"

"Believe this wise old witch."

During my massage that night, lying face down on the sticky vinyl table while Anna knuckled the gristle along my spine, I asked her to list for me again the compounds that made the Dalai Lama sneeze. She remembered the popcorn butter and the hair spray, left out the peanuts, and changed the Windex to Mr. Clean. A twitching in her fingers told me she knew I was trying to set her up. Next I asked about the creepy nobleman: how long, exactly, were they engaged? (Two months, she'd said originally; later five months.) She didn't answer, just grabbed the tube of oil and drizzled an S-shaped stream from the base of my neck down to my butt crack. She spread the oil in circles with flattened palms but without her old geometrical precision. "You're one big spasm in your lumbar. You need a new desk chair. It's cold in here tonight. Did you see on the news those freaky robot girlfriends Japanese bachelors are going nuts for?"

I knew then that my mother was wise indeed. Faith had fled, evasion had replaced it, and Anna would soon be on her way, whether she was guilty or innocent, whether she feared the exposure of her falsity or the ravaging of her sincerity. Verdicts and sentences are petty matters. The trial itself is the ordeal. The inquisition is the annihilation. This insight, once it took shape, felt almost Buddhist. It felt like evidence of inner growth. Not from a book but from experience, from the murk and muddle of real life, I'd derived a noble paradox.

Anna and I didn't part immediately. We circled each other for another week, leveling and deflecting unspoken charges, sidestepping, bluffing, stealing and stashing pills. We grew unnaturally cordial and polite, letting the other use the bathroom first, vying to be the one to brew the coffee. We even had sex a couple of times, me on top, then her on top. I typed on my laptop notebook, she skimmed her *People*. I toasted the English muffins, she buttered them. We stood across from each other beside the bed and tucked in the corners of a fitted sheet.

That weekend at a movie theater Anna patted her bladder area, got up from her seat, took a licorice twist from the carton on my armrest, and slipped down the aisle and out a double door. I missed her instantly. Our last few days together had been a pleasure, orderly, mild, quiet, temperate. I finally was able to picture a life with her, an amiable arrangement that might serve both of us, even with a baby in the mix. When I got home, I thought of calling her, perhaps to apologize. But for what? For rushing things, was all that I could think. I'd pushed for answers, I couldn't just let them come, and now that it appeared they'd never come, it occurred to me I could have done without them.

Then, three months later, I happened across an issue of the magazine I was reading when you marched up to me, obviously upset that I've stopped calling you, clearly disturbed to see me in the booth that used to be our booth, our private romantic nook, ever since we discovered this little place. You demanded that I explain my actions, no fibs and no excuses. I've tried to do that. I'm not quite done though, darling. There's something I need to show you: this advertisement. It's been running in *People* for a year now. MetaSlim. See this young woman who used the product, "Lynn Mathis?" "Fifth grade art teacher from Omaha?" In the first picture she's broad and round, and judging by where she's carrying the weight, it looks like she might be expecting—at least to my eyes. But here in the second picture (yes, it's Anna) she's down, amazingly, to a size four. But she doesn't seem happy about it. Those dull, dead eyes. Those sunken cheeks. That tortured forehead. They usually look delighted by their new figure. Not her. She looks beaten. Desolate. Bereft.

I don't know what to think. I truly don't. Maybe she lost it all naturally. I hope so. It's a rough one, a hard one, not something you just shrug off. I try to keep busy, to stay engaged, be social, to force myself out of the house and meet new people.

I wanted so badly to trust you, to let this grow, to accept you like you accept me, but I just can't.

I meditate sometimes. It doesn't help.

Skate Dogs

Kip Kotzen

Kip Kotzen is the founder and president of neo-utility, a company dedicated to brand building and sales for innovative design companies. He is the co-editor with Thomas Beller of a book of essays on J.D. Salinger, With Love and Squalor, *and has been a contributing editor of* Open City *since 1995.*

I HEARD THAT JACK DIED. I TAKE THAT BACK. I HEARD he was killed. I take that back too. I heard he was put to sleep.

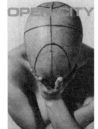

It was one of those pieces of information that had a hell of a lot more resonance for me than for the person who told me. In fact, the person who told me didn't even know Jack. I knew Jack. Not that well really, but I knew him well enough to care about the truth.

When you've saved someone's life, even if that someone is a dog, and then you hear they're dead, it's kind of traumatic. Apparently he OD'd on Advil. Seriously. I guess if you're a dog, that's all it takes, a hundred or so Advil. But that's not how he died, that's how I saved him. I found him at Alison's apartment. He had chewed right through the plastic bottle and was foaming at the mouth. It was about two in the morning and Alison was asleep. We rushed him to the emergency pet clinic. That's one good thing to say about New York, places tend to stay open just about all the time. The vet had to give him an IV of water to dilute the Advil and I had to hold Jack in a bear hug for about an hour with a needle in his vein. Jack was probably up to sixty or seventy pounds by then and was shaking and squirming like mad.

Alison had rescued Jack from the pound, trained him, and cured him of all his bad habits, except chewing through things. Alison loved Jack more than anything. She was entirely devoted to that damn dog.

This is what I heard: Alison didn't have to put Jack to sleep. That's the thing about rumors. They don't have to have anything to do with the truth. Sometimes they're true, but not this time. When they're not true, when they can't be true, people just don't realize the implications. A guy tells me that Alison put her dog to sleep unnecessarily and he just doesn't realize what that means.

I dated Alison. Well, that's optimistically euphemistic. I was sleeping with her. I was walking Jack a lot, even taking care of him for a week here and there, and sleeping with Alison. I really don't know what else to say about Alison or about our relationship. I really can't remember what we ever talked about. In fact, I don't think that we talked about much, but thankfully, most of the time it didn't seem to matter. Jack liked me from the start, which helped. He was wild with everyone else, except Alison and me.

It was an ephemeral relationship and Alison and I both knew it. She had a boyfriend that she would probably get married to (she did), he was away, and when he came back it would all be over. That's not to say that fact didn't depress the hell out of me. She was the kind of slinky blonde they cast in movies as the hit man's girl, the one that by the end you realize is actually the real assassin. I often did feel that some deep meaningful connection was about to happen between the two of us, but our best moments were always purely physical. Making out in the middle of Mulberry Street during the San Gennaro festival. Sex one afternoon in her apartment, with voices of the neighborhood kids filling the room—screams, giggles, wild laughter. The night Jack OD'd, Alison holding onto my hand while I held Jack.

As the day that Alison's boyfriend was returning came closer, she started to slide away from me. The end was unspoken, but it was pretty clear. Our denouement was the trip to Oneonta. Unfortunately, I didn't know that before we left. I don't even know why I went on that trip. My last moment in the sun, I guess that's how I saw it. We were looking for a house for Alison to rent. She had a crazy idea about leaving everything and moving upstate with Jack. She wanted to find a house in the middle of nowhere and spend the winter writing.

A bit of advice: Never take a die-hard baseball fan to within ten miles of the Hall of Fame just to look for houses and go roller-skating. That's what we did. We looked at three houses and went to the roller-skating rink in Oneonta. I wasn't particularly good at skating, and whizzing around the rink in a tightly knit pack was the cream of the Oneonta crop. Fourteen and fifteen-year-old guys who could really skate, hot dogging it through the crowd. Alison thought they were great. She called them Skate Dogs. Every twenty minutes or so the DJ would play some special Skate Dog music and call out for some maneuver that, of course, only the Skate Dogs could do. I honestly thought to myself that if I could skate that well, if I could do those back crossovers, everything would be right between the two of us. When we got back to the hotel room I still had slim hopes, but when Alison came out of the shower and climbed into the other bed, I knew that was that. It was official.

After we got back to New York, I didn't see Alison again. I decided not to call, and I guess she decided the same thing. I missed her, and Jack, but a few weeks later I heard she had rented a place upstate in Margaretville and had left the City. I didn't see Alison again for almost a year until I turned a corner near my house and almost ran right into her. She was with Jack, and when Jack saw me he went absolutely bonkers. It was a good icebreaker because Jack was barking and jumping and licking me like crazy. It took about five minutes before we could get him to calm down. Alison seemed glad to see me, but I think it freaked her out how much Jack seemed to miss me. We talked for just a couple of minutes and that was it. When we said good-bye she really had to drag Jack away. I think this time he knew somehow he wouldn't see me again.

So now Jack is dead and Alison killed him. At least that's the version of the story that made its way out to me in Los Angeles. I don't think it's the truth. It can't be. I can picture Jack perfectly, zipping around the little dog hill in Tompkins Square Park, stealing balls from slower dogs, showing off. Jack was a Skate Dog. Alison loved Skate Dogs and Alison loved Jack. That's my truth. When that guy told me that Alison had put Jack to sleep, I didn't tell him that he was wrong, that it was impossible that she could do anything to harm him, that he must have been suffering terribly. But it wouldn't have mattered to him. He didn't know Jack at all, and to him, the rumor was just as good as the truth. In fact, it was probably better.

From A Little Rock Memoir, Mostly About Other Things

Cynthia Kraman

Cynthia Kraman a.k.a. Cynthia Genser a.k.a. Chinas Comidas is the author of four collections of poetry, most recently The Touch. *Her band's CD,* Chinas Comidas 1977-1980 Live and Studio Recordings, *came out in 2006 on Exquisite Corpse Records. She lives in New York City.*

WHEN I FIRST CAME TO SEATTLE IT WAS A COWBOY town. By that I mean both a town with cowboys and a town going the way of the Old West, toward annihilation. Its fortunes, in the seventies, went boom and bust along with the fortunes of Boeing. When it was bust, as it was when I arrived thanks to the government's whimsical way of awarding contracts, it was full of the emptiness of withdrawing engineers and their families; that exodus made what Ross Perot later colorfully called the great suckin' sound of Americans losing their jobs. The city's older soldiers, those hollow-eyed sailors and out-of-work cowboys who resembled rural versions of Mitchum and Bogart in black-and-white clips, walked down wide vacant streets in staccato silhouette as imaginary dancehall music accompanied their iconic strides. The newest ghosts in town were Alaskan Indians who'd come in with the pipeline and couldn't get back. They drank, and I drank, along the edge of Elliott Bay in bars called IXL and Dew Drop Inn where you got four beers for a dollar and any change was in wooden quarter slugs that got you another beer. I was generally taken for an Indian, which meant that as a woman, I disappeared.

From this position it was easy to see things. One afternoon a white guy was flicked with a knife and blood ran down his forearm. It was exhilarating and repulsive. Just outside the door of the IXL, tumultuous clouds moved out over the bay. I could see where Frank Zappa went fishing from the balcony of the Edgewater hotel. Jimmy's purple haze clung to the horizon. The great drama of water and sky swept any remaining New York cosmopolitan civility out of me in a whipping iodine wave. I went back and used the last slug in my pocket, and settled in.

Seattle was one love, immediately, and Rich Riggins was the other. He was a lean guitar player from Eastern Washington in his mid-twenties when we met. I soon learned that his father had been a drunk, a failed salesman who became a drunk; on his deathbed he imparted a father's wisdom saying, "Richard, get your shit together."

Richard's childhood dreams were to be a car and to disappear, and there was something infinitely, tenderly vaporous in his edgy persona. Richard's brother-in-law came to visit us on Pike Street. His skin was tight and pink like a kid's, his eyes were untouched by strong emotion or any tinge of intellectuality. Over a drink at the Rainbow Tavern he told us he'd become a motivational speaker after running off with his Asian secretary and getting fleeced, then getting punished by his wife. They were now both Christians. He felt he was his own best advertisement for how to improve yourself by telling other people how to do it. He was American in a way I'd never experienced, the American of tentative, ahistorical gesture; he had his back to the Pacific like a scared kid huddled against a fence in an alleyway. For everyone, there was no place to go. The Indians at the IXL, Richard's money hungry evangelical salesman brother-in-law, the SILVA mind melders merchandising the will to power and their kin, the proto-Nazis upstate, and the chicken trade by the Market who were also the kids in the music scene, even Richard with his frayed smile, everyone was part of a desperation that felt strange and flowed into me like a drug. I was never more myself than in Seattle.

From The Natural Order

James Lasdun

James Lasdun is the author of two novels, The Horned Man *and* Seven Lies, *which was longlisted for the 2006 Man Booker Prize for fiction. The title story in his collection* The Siege *was adapted into a film by Bernardo Bertolucci entitled* Besieged. *It's Beginning to Hurt, his latest short story collection, was released in 2010. He has also written four books of poetry.*

 "SO, DO YOU ALWAYS WEAR YOUR WEDDING RING?"

"I do."

"I would never wear one of those things. The way it announces you're someone else's property."

"Shall we go on here or up to the gorge?"

"The gorge."

Abel took the turn that led off to the high part of the gorge. The landscape was thickly wooded, with the granite-walled gash of a nine-mile gorge cutting through the green slopes of the mountains.

"And you've never actually been unfaithful to Antonia in all the time you've been married?"

"No."

"Not even last night, eh?"

"What?"

"Just asking."

They came to the end of the tarmac road and began bumping over a narrow stone trail that climbed through a scrub of yellow flowering broom. Strange rock formations—little citadels of thin, tall, wind-eroded towers—appeared on either side of the road. Stewart asked Abel to stop the car so he could get out and photograph them.

Alone in the car, Abel watched Stewart jump lightly from rock to rock, camera in one hand, tripod in the other. A dull glare of hostility burned in him. He had known Stewart through mutual friends since the Scotsman's first arrival in the States several years earlier, but they'd never been close until these past three weeks on the road together, which had forced them into an intimacy that Abel had quickly found disturbing.

Specifically, it was Stewart's ceaseless and exclusive preoccupation with sex that had unnerved him.

Not that it was entirely a surprise: in a vague way Abel had always known of Stewart's reputation as a ladies' man. And although he'd tended not to believe most of the stories he'd heard—girls accosting Stewart on the street, breaking into his apartment, picked up in cafés and bedded without a word spoken between them—he had certainly noticed that women were drawn to Stewart. He was tall and narrow-hipped, with the rare combination of black hair and blue eyes; the hair curling in thick clusters, the eyes mirthful, with a hint of laconic cruelty. His face, always clean-shaven, looked both angular and polished smooth, like some fine artifact constructed purely for the purpose of making a hand want to caress it. He wore brightly colored silk shirts that must have consumed an inordinate share of his income as a not very successful freelance photographer.

Early on in the trip, Abel had realized that the stories were more likely to have been understatements than exaggerations. He had never been in a position to study the habits of a serious womanizer before, and what he'd observed had been a revelation.

The day after they'd arrived in Athens, a girl in a blue leather jacket had noticed Stewart in the hotel lobby (Abel had observed the brief, involuntary stilling of her glance as she crossed the floor). The next morning Abel saw Stewart handing the leather jacket to the desk clerk.

"Wee thing split before I woke," Stewart had told Abel nonchalantly. "Left her jacket behind."

A few days later, in Meteora, they had both noticed a young Chinese woman leading a tour group up to one of the monasteries. By nightfall Stewart had found the woman, discovered she spoke English, and invited her to join him and Abel for an after-dinner drink. Her manner was almost American in its casual ease, though Abel noticed that she held his eyes longer when she turned to him than most American women did. Not flirtatiousness, he sensed, so much as a remote, dispassionate interest: one empire taking the measure of another. Even so, he found himself trying to make her turn toward him as often as he could. He wasn't aware of competing with Stewart in this regard, but when the girl got up to leave and Stewart offered to walk her back to her hotel, and she accepted without a word of protest as though this had long ago been settled between them, Abel had felt a distinct pang. He and Stewart were sharing a room that night, and in the small hours Abel was woken by the Scotsman's return. Stewart was laughing quietly: not drunk, but lit up in some way.

"Smell that," he'd said, holding out his hand. "Chinese pussy."

A mass of sensations had erupted in Abel as the pungent aroma wafted from Stewart's fingertips: shock, vague anger, and hunger, envy too.

"She wouldn't let me go the whole way though. Can you fucking believe it?" Stewart laughed again. Pacing the room in his vivid shirt and black jeans, he looked coiled and taut, with a wildness about him; an intent, sharp vitality that Abel realized he hadn't fully acknowledged until now.

One night they'd met two English girls—backpackers in their early twenties, up from a month of raves and beach parties on the islands. One had shaven blonde bristles and a stud in her nose. The other was tall and dreamy-eyed, hennaed ringlets falling to her bare midriff. Within a few minutes Stewart had made his characteristic first move on the tall one—a jocular insult carefully calibrated to raise the temperature between them to the point where they became implicated in what, to all intents and purposes, was a lovers' quarrel; one that presupposed the tendernesses that invariably followed.

"I've never met an English girl who wasn't deep down just obsessed with getting married . . ."

"That's so unfair!"

The other girl glanced at Abel. He noticed a sweetness about her face that hadn't been immediately apparent under the bristles and stud. Her cheeks looked soft as a child's, her tawny eyes friendly. He thought of Antonia and the baby. Where would they be now? Outside probably—lazing on the porch or feeding the animals. He tried to picture them. The girl impinged on him, producing a little hip flask and taking a swig from it . . .

"Greek brandy," he heard. "Totally lethal."

There had been a moment a few months ago when he and Antonia had been in the old barn where her father's travel-book business was housed. Winter sunshine was melting the icicles outside the window, and in the sweet gelid light that filled the high-beamed room, Abel had been filled with unexpected euphoria. Watching his wife laying out pages, their swaddled child sleeping in the cradle beside her, he had been visited by stronger feelings of love than he had ever imagined himself capable of feeling. It was as though the full reality of his marriage—its brimming sufficiency—had for the first time been made radiantly apparent to him. The moment had passed, but the revelation had survived untarnished; lit with the gleam of the melting icicles, and filling him with contentment whenever he thought of it.

"Want a hit?" The girl was offering him her flask.

"Oh. No thanks."

"You're the quiet American, aren't you?"

"Excuse me? Oh . . . Not really, just the tired American."

He stood up, catching what appeared to be a brief flash of annoyance in the girl's eye as he made his excuses and left.

Up in his room he thought of her. Was it really possible that she could have been interested in him? He looked in the mirror; felt the familiar jolt at the disparity between his persistently youthful idea of his physical appearance and the image that confronted him. His hair lay thinly over his temples; his torso looked shapeless in the useful light-weight beige anorak he had brought along for the cooler evenings. A *hors de combat* jacket, Stewart had jokingly called it when he first saw Abel sporting it . . . He smiled wanly at himself. He looked middle-aged.

Next morning he discovered that both of the girls had spent the night with Stewart.

Breakfasting with the three of them—him uncomfortable, not wanting to seem either prurient by talking about the night's outcome or priggish by conspicuously not alluding to it; them calm, sated-looking, globed in their mutual contentedness—he had felt both obscurely mocked and, even more obscurely, ashamed.

That was a week ago. Since then there had been a woman in a zip-up dress who worked in the tourist bureau in Thessaloníki, a bespectacled assistant in a camera store, the faded-looking proprietress of a small hotel . . . Not my business what he does, Abel had told himself, but he had begun to feel strangely oppressed. He had never thought of his state of contented monogamy as something unusual or in need of justification, but the effect of Stewart's behavior had been to make him feel as though he had consciously adopted some bizarre, almost freakish approach to life. He wondered for the first time whether his faithfulness as a husband had been a matter of deliberate choice, or passive acquiescence. Had he deliberately suppressed the appetites of a potential philanderer for the sake of a greater happiness, or had his life taken the shape it had because he didn't have those appetites in the first place? Or was it just that his love for Antonia was so strong that faithfulness was simply what came naturally?

Meherangarh

Zachary Lazar

Zachary Lazar is the author of three books, most recently the novel Sway *and the memoir* Evening's Empire: The Story of My Father's Murder. *He is the recipient of a Guggenheim Fellowship and the Hodder Fellowship at Princeton University. He teaches creative writing at Tulane University.*

The Murder Victim

HIS NAME WAS WYATT SUMNERS. WHEN THEY FOUND him, he had just turned fifty—he had seemed younger than that the one time I met him. It was a few months ago, at Vikram and Caroline Aggarwal's house in Jodhpur. The Aggarwals live in an eighteenth-century palace decorated with handmade furniture and textiles, each object specially chosen, resonant with the taste of someone who looks at objects every day as a profession. There must have been forty rooms in the house's new addition, a rectangular court built around the original *haveli* with its intricate screens carved into the sandstone walls.

Sumners sat on a low sofa, dressed in jeans, a zippered leather jacket, and a cotton scarf that looked like it came from the local market. In London, he had been an unsuccesful actor, but now he was a tutor, or as he put it, a "babysitter" for the two children of a movie producer I work for—that's what had brought us together that night, a movie I had cowritten, set in India. Vikram Aggarwal and I were talking about politics and Sumners was sipping his wine, admiring the room. I was speaking about things I knew nothing about, hazarding opinions in the broad way you fall into when you read the paper in foreign countries, even ones you've set a screenplay in. The news that week concerned separatist fighters in the state of Assam. In an act of ethnic cleansing, they had gunned down seventy migrant farm workers from the state of Bihar. The United Liberation Front of Asom. I said if I had not happened to be traveling in India that week I would have never heard of the United Liberation Front of Asom.

Sumners sighed. He had been in the country for three months and was exhausted by it. "All I want is my week on the beach," he said. "Then I'm off to Mallorca with the two brats."

He lit a joint and offered it to me. Unshaven, his hair long enough to be feathery, he had that ironic cheerfulness that people from everywhere have now, like Americans on TV, which like a common language softens the differences between us.

"Where are you going, Goa?" I asked.

"Yes. You've been there?"

"Not for a long time. Maybe twenty years ago. More than that actually. Before it was Goa."

None of the seventy murdered Biharis' names were mentioned in the papers. In ten days, it was Sumners's name that would be mentioned in the papers.

Citadel

The main site to see in Jodhpur is the Meherangarh Fort, which looks like something from a movie. From a distance, it's the beige color of the desert behind it, as are the ancient city walls with their watchtowers. On the ground floor, inside iron gates high enough for elephants to pass through, are rows of women's handprints inscribed on the wall in a rectangular pattern. They're there to commemorate the widows who committed suttee, the ritual of throwing themselves on the pyres of their husbands killed in battle, defending the fortress.

Each ruler built another palace on top of the last. The fort is so tall you take an elevator to the top, and the view from there makes modern skyscrapers seem like the work of barbarians. Along certain ledges you can see the full height of the highest towers, cream-colored, shaped like minarets, and the cubed-shaped buildings of Jodhpur below, all of them painted blue. Someone had to place the carved stones that high up in the air. Someone had to whitewash them each year after the monsoon. The maharaja's wives would lift ornate dumbells to keep themselves slim, or lounge on divans beside marble fountains, their lives spent behind the screened walls of a fortified harem thirty stories high.

Hollywood

For three months—October to December—the actors and crew for the movie I'd helped write had been in Jodhpur, shooting on location at the Bal Samand Palace Hotel. The movie was a sex comedy—there was no special reason it had to be set in India, other than that it would give us an excuse to go there, and without the setting it would be indistinguishable from twenty other movies just like it. Caroline was telling stories about the reaction of the locals, the way everyone knew the names of even the minor stars, the director, the screenwriters—even me, who had not arrived until it was all but over. The merchants had sold the producer and his wife three hundred bed covers. One of the stars, a famous comedian, had bought so much jewelry in one of the shops that the owner had given him the key. He was able to lock it up day and night if he wanted, so no one else could go in.

"How did you settle on Jodhpur?" Wyatt Sumners asked.

"That was Wilentz's idea," I said, passing him back the joint. "I had it set in Khajuraho at first, where they have those temples with the erotic carvings. There were a lot of Kama Sutra jokes we had to cut out."

Sumners took the opportunity to denigrate our boss. "Wilentz must have seen a way to save money," he said. "Probably did a deal with the local council. The mayor."

"It's not the mayor," said Vikram. "The man he would have talked to is called the collector. I always loved that word."

"Sounds like Kafka," said Sumners.

"At least he didn't do a deal with the collector of Assam," I said.

We were still sitting in the large room that opened onto the courtyard. Two great danes lay on their sides on pale green beds trimmed with silk thread. Fires burned in iron bowls, six on either side of the lawn. We had eggplant salad, goat cheese, spring rolls with cilantro and shaved carrots. We drank wine from Caroline's home in Chile. Her five-year-old daughter, Lucinda, came down and spoke to us in Hindi. She could count to thirty in three languages. Her favorite food was macaroni and cheese.

Sumners was going to take the train to Goa that week, rather than fly. In one of the many peculiarities of Indian travel, he reminded us, second class A/C was better than first class. It must have been around this time that I told the story of Veronica and me on the train platform in Udaipur.

The Rani of Mandi

Rajasthan is poor, in spite of all the talk you hear about India's boom. On the road to Jaipur, the capital, you can see almost a mile of ruins on either side of the road where audiences used to watch processions enter the city on elephant back. The elephants would have been caparisoned in red and green and their riders would have been swathed in jewels. Legions of weavers and masons and carvers and musicians had been supported by that way of life, before cars and motorcycles joined the bullock carts and stray dogs on the broken roads. Now the palaces are dilapidated, even a major site like Meherangarh Fort is only partly restored. I remember walking through the empty halls, Veronica and I, through the room of baby cradles, the room of palanquins, the room of Belgian mirrors, the room of arms and armor—daggers, lances, swords. In one of the rooms was an exhibit of antique photographs, portraits of the old royal families. One was of a woman called the Rani of Mandi, on the occasion of her appearance before the court of George V in 1924. She was dressed in a pale sari—I imagined it for some reason as gold—extending one hand behind her hip as if to brush back her veil, the other hand at her breast, clasping a pearl necklace. It may have been that her hair was only pulled back, but it was possible to imagine it as cut short, like a flapper's, like Zelda Fitzgerald's.

On the Platform

We were waiting for a train in Udaipur, Veronica and I, when we had one of those moments you never want to have, moments of revelation, disgust. Udaipur itself is a tourist city, "the Venice of India," built on a lake that encircles one of the world's most famous hotels. Outside the station it had been unusually quiet, almost no one there, but on the platform there was a throng of carts being steered by porters, tea sellers, men with turbans and walking sticks, teenage boys in windbreakers and jeans. It happens all the time in India, the stares of men and boys, an unreadable gaze that is usually nothing more than curiosity. On the streets of a place like Udaipur, it's easy to behave like a child sometimes, smiling and answering when someone asks what country you are from, as if the question is innocent, as if you are glamorous, maybe even a movie star. Your choice in a crowd in India is often to be a child or a hostile intruder.

At first there were maybe fifteen boys, but soon there were more than thirty, moving in closer, like birds, until they had formed a semicircle around us as we stood with our luggage, everything dim on the platform, just a few lights behind the crowd of faces. They began to make longer and longer eye contact, more emboldened as they saw how little there was we could do. They were staring right at Veronica, her long hair coming down over her shoulders, American hair. I waved my hand and said "goodbye," as if being sarcastic, but they knew sarcasm and weren't moved. A small boy in glasses watched me, enthralled, a nervous smile on his lips, waiting to see how I would react. My glance was enough to shame him into averting his eyes, but only a moment later he was staring again, knowing that he was safe within the mob.

I made eye contact with the leader, a tall, lanky boy with a scarf tied around his head like a bandage. I told him to back off.

"This your wife?" he said.

"Move away."

"How many times you make baby with your wife?"

I don't remember a single woman being on the platform. Everyone was a man or a boy, all of them watching now, even those who were by the newsstand twenty yards away. The boy with the scarf on his head was shaking he was so excited, smirking and pacing, knowing that no matter what I did, everyone was on his side.

The Shrinking Globe

The Rani of Mandi grew up in a town called Kapurthala in a palace designed by a French architect who modeled it after Versailles. She was the child of her father's fifth wife—his fourth wife was a dancer from Spain, his sixth an actress from Prague. The Rani's father, the Maharaja of Kapurthala, spent a quarter of his annual income on jewels. The Rani was his only daughter. She was sent to England for her education, spoke several languages, had friends in Hollywood, New York, all over the world. In 1940 she was living in Paris, then the world's most cosmopolitan city, when the Nazis invaded. Some of her closest friends were Jews, and in an effort to save them the Rani bartered all of her jewels to help them gain passage to the United States. The plan was uncovered by the Gestapo, who deported the Rani to Germany. It had taken just a single moment—the moment of her arrest—to strip away everything I have just told you about her. She was detained in a concentration camp, where she died after only two months.

"Did you read that?" Veronica said, showing me the caption at the exhibit.

I hadn't read it. I had walked right by the photograph, seeing just a beautiful woman in lavish clothes, a kind of Indian Zelda Fitzgerald, I'd thought.

The Mob

They call it "Eve teasing" in India—whistling, groping, fits of sexual aggression toward women. The play of gazes, back and forth, becomes distortive, intensifying, compulsive—everyone involved becomes somebody else. At the time, it seemed that anything could have happened, that when the train came the men and boys could have rushed into our compartment and taken turns with Veronica, and in the face of their stares it was hard to decide if the danger was all just imagined. The only thing to do was to decide that it was.

Convivium

We drank many bottles of wine that night at Vikram and Caroline's. They were an easy group of people to talk to, though we came from different places all over the world. At dinner there was Szechuan chicken, prawns in garlic sauce, a salad with beets and greens grown in Vikram and Caroline's garden. Serge and Alain, two Parisians, dealers in antiques, arrived from the airport. Their white shirts and black pants and mustaches reminded me of the cotton brokers in Degas's paintings. Their clothes were so clean they shone.

"We were four days in the Delhi aiport," Serge told us. "Fog for four days. They would keep us on the runway, then back to the gate, then back to the runway."

I felt wrong about telling the story of the station in Udaipur. It had disturbed everyone, raised the specter of xenophobia, not just the men's and the boy's but mine. Everyone agreed that what had happened was rare, so rare it was almost unheard of. It was better to talk about Indian films, as we were now (everyone had seen the films of Deepa Mehta, banned from Indian theaters). We talked about Bollywood, the rival stars

Shahrukh Khan and Amitabh Bachchan, Bachchan's son Abhishek's impending marriage to the superstar Aishwarya Rai. They formed a kind of royalty, these stars. They held stakes in the nation's corporations and could sway the outcome of elections. Like the weather, movie stars were something you could always talk about in India. Even Wyatt Sumners could talk about Aishwarya Rai.

"Stunning," he said.

"The most beautiful woman in the world," said Serge, bored, reaching for the wine.

"Not far from it," Sumners said. He pushed some arugula onto his fork. "You know, they named a tulip after her in Holland."

I thought, if it hadn't been for Sumners, and his trip to Goa, I would not have told the story about the station in Udaipur. I resented him a little for my own lack of tact, knowing I had no justifiable reason for feeling that way. I felt it anyway. When I think about it now, I realize there are no limits to my carelessness, my ignorance. I realize that if I hadn't co-written a screenplay set in India—a sex comedy like twenty others—Sumners never would have been there in the first place. He would presumably still be alive.

The Papers

Sumners was found in a small village outside Goa, hung by his neck from a mango tree. According to the papers, a group of men had either trailed or driven him to that place of huts and cook fires—sixty miles from the beach hotel he'd been staying at—and clubbed him to death, then hung him with a sari from the branches. The police beat confessions out of four suspects, whose stories were garbled, contradictory. One account said that Sumners had made a sexual advance on a local woman. Another that Sumners was buying and selling drugs. As motives reported in a newspaper, these are rational enough to help us stop thinking about the crowbar in the teeth, the feet kicking at the side of the still body. Perhaps the only real explanation is the simple one, that some grievance or misunderstanding had erased the basic assumptions that hold true most of the time, almost anywhere: that people are more or less the same, that kindness or reason will bridge their differences. The suspects who gave confessions were almost certainly innocent themselves. What we know for sure was that Sumners had called home to

England the night before he died. He said he was on his way to Bombay to see a fireworks show.

Cosmopolis

I forgot to mention that there were guards posted inside the gates of Vikram and Caroline's house when we arrived. I don't know if they were armed or not. My first impression was not of the guards but of the lavish grounds—the stone gate high enough for an elephant to pass through, the endless lawn where fires burned in two rows of iron bowls. It looked idyllic (in a way, it was idyllic, all those strangers from everywhere, so easy to talk to). I forgot to mention also that Vikram was part of the local royalty, a nephew of the current Maharaja of Jodhpur. I remember later that night thinking of the Rani of Mandi, of how I had taken her at first for a kind of socialite, someone you might see nowadays in a newspaper or on TV. I think now that in some way this is what prompted me to tell the story of the train platform in Udaipur. In part of my mind, I was carrying the image of the Rani's face at the court of George V, knowing, as I knew by then, what had become of her, of her friends and their world, knowing how defenseless it had turned out to be. Gathered at Vikram and Caroline's house, we seemed in the light of the Rani's story feckless, childlike. The night was beautiful. Its beauty was protected by a gate, and to be on the right side of that gate involved nothing more than luck. Everyone knows this. Everyone knows that luck doesn't last.

Train

When the train pulled into the Udaipur station, there was a decision to be made as to whether or not we should get on. The first few cars were already so full of people that they were hanging out of the doorway, holding onto the frames, the train still advancing. The pack of boys around us dispersed and moved in a scrum toward the tracks, matching the train's pace, luggage clutched to their chests with one arm, their free arms outstretched. It was like watching a sport, or like watching footage from a war. They leapt up into the crowd that was already on the train, a tangle of bodies spilling out of the opened doors—scarves, bundles, rags.

"Let's go," said Veronica.

"You're sure."

"Yes. Hurry up."

In our berths in second-class A/C, the couchettes were made of clean blue vinyl, with a stack of pillows and sheets and blankets and a towel. It was as quiet as the waiting room of an office. I tried to read. The newspaper was full of ads for high-rises in Bombay, luxury apartments with backup power and three tiers of twenty-four hour security. After awhile, the train bumped forward, then slowly moved on into the darkness with a steady, thudding rhythm that invited sleep. Everything seemed far away. Before long it was possible to forget that ahead of us, separated by just a few doors, was the mob of men and boys, crammed into the compartments with bare feet, squatting in the aisles, twisting and hanging from the rails.

Shed

Sam Lipsyte

Sam Lipsyte is the author of the story collection Venus Drive *(Open City Books) and three novels,* The Subject Steve, Home Land, *and* The Ask. *He is the recipient of a Guggenheim Fellowship. This story was his debut publication.*

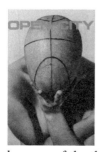

WE STRIPPED BILLY MULLIN BEHIND THE FRENCH Man's shed and Eddie Mullin pulled a hoe down from the hook on the side. Eddie was the one who always wanted a drink from the hose after we did manhunt or home run derby but me and John never let him so he'd walk a half mile for it and me and John used to steal all his army men and do napalm under the garage light but now it was us and Eddie on his own little brother because of the thing Billy said that started it all. Eddie took the hoe handle and dug it in and John held Billy's head and put his hand on his mouth and I lay across the backs of his ankles and bit into his calf Eddie rammed it in harder then popped it out like fixing the toilet and Billy didn't scream but started saying the thing that started it and the wood was smeared with dark thin streaks and John tried to keep his hand on Billy's mouth but Billy bit him so I bit Billy on his leg again and Eddie twisted the stick inside and now Billy's blood sneaking out of his little fat ass and I saw it up over me and I heard the French Man's porch door and I said to John It's the French Man but no one heard because Eddie was yelling You little fuckin' shit wisin' off to me you little fuck and he raised up the hoe and flipped it around and slammed the blade back down on Billy's leg and it sliced clean through and I saw a muscle roll up like a rug under the skin and now Billy screamed and it was like a scream no people have ever done before. You fuck and Eddie kept chopping on his brother and me and John ran back over the gravel hill to the reservoir road and there was a cracking sound so we both looked back. Eddie was walking crazy away from the shed like he was just doing dizzy spins and his hands going red in front of his face and the French Man dropped the crowbar and Billy flopped around like something invisible was holding him down. Me and John ran back home and never talked to each other again and drank from the hose.

Old Soul

Sam Lipsyte

Following its appeareance in Open City, *this story appeared in* Venus Drive.

 YOU COULD TOUCH FOR A COUPLE OF BUCKS. THE window of the booth went up and you stuck out the bills. They might tell you not to pinch, but I was a stroke type anyway. Some guys, I guess they want to leave a mark. Me, I just like the feel.

I went over there on the way to see my sister. There was a lit-up eye with an eyebrow over the door, a guy in front with a change belt, an apron that said Peep City. Peeptown was up the block. They didn't have an eyebrow over the eye over there.

Why do they make these places so dark? I like to cop tit in the light. Guess I have no shame. Maybe I got through shame a long time ago. Somebody said I had an old soul, which I took to mean I'm older than I am, or that I've been places I haven't been.

You could hardly see in there, in Peep City, and all that disco, that ammonia, it made me sick. I looked around for a girl with a good set, one who would maybe tell me I was sweet. Sometimes they asked about handjobs, blowjobs, all the jobs, but I never wanted to go that far. I felt sorry for them. Somebody told me they were exploited. Me, I always paid in full.

This time, just to break habit, I went for what one of them had down below, a few bucks more. She was a giant with plenty on the chest, but I put a fivespot out. She swiveled on the ledge, pushed an ass dusted with glitter out over the sill. I palmed her there, thumbed a pimple near the crack. What am I paying for this for? I thought, thumbing it.

The giant was talking to another girl pressed against her on the ledge. The other girl was a sway of hair that moved like a metronome. The sway took on the color of the strobes.

"What's he doing down there?" said the other girl.

"Jeez, nothing," said the giant.

I dug a knuckle in.

"What the fuck," the giant said. The blind was buzzing shut.

"Prick," she said.

There was a bucket near the door with soapy water in it. I got down like you do for a shoelace, dipped my knuckle in the bucket. The man in the apron came up.

"I got ass germs on it," I said.

I figured it was Peeptown from now on.

There were still a few hours before my sister's visiting hours were over, so I went to visit a friend. This was the guy who explained to me how the girls in Peep City were exploited. The ones in Peeptown, too. He worked the graveyard in the shipping room of a superstore. Another year, he told me, and they might let him come upstairs. He worked mornings in his apartment, stuffing envelopes, selling pot. A guy like that, you hope he has a secret calling, or maybe a guitar. But Gary just wanted to live. Or maybe he thought he wanted to be free. Some do.

When I got there Gary loaded up a pipe and passed it over. I told him all about Peep City, the pimple, the girl.

"You should stay away from that place," said Gary.

"I don't have much choice now," I said.

"All those places, man. Your soul is sick."

"I thought you said I had an old soul," I said. "Now it's sick."

"It's an old sick fuck," said Gary. "Go see your sister. You're going to be sorry you didn't see her."

"I've got time," I said.

Time stops, goes, stops again. When you have an old soul like I do, everything gets old really quick. Nothing is new. An avocado, a glass of beer, it all tastes like it's been sitting out on a table too long.

Gary fell unconscious from all his freedom. I found happy hour somewhere. I knew the bartender, a brush cut from the big one. He was German, the other side. All he had now were a few shelves of New Jersey vodka and a thing about the Jews. I let him rant. I figured with a soul as old as mine, maybe I fragged his brother at the Bulge.

"I'm an old soul," I told him.

"Oslo? Fuck it."

"Not Oslo," I said.

"No souls," he said. "Fuck it. Norway, too. Odin is a yid."

A girl in a tank top got up in my lap. She didn't smell, but her shoulders, her hair, they had a dirt sleep shine.

"You look like that rock star," she said. "Do you get high?"

"I am high," I said.

"No, I mean high."

"Oh," I said. "Sometimes."

"You're buying," she said.

We went someplace, her place, her boyfriend's, her mother's, who could tell? You can't tell from a sofa. Or a couch. You can't tell from a coffee table, or a cross on the wall. She took what we bought and locked herself in the bathroom. I was on old soul time. I lost track of bathroom time.

"Sandy?" I said. She'd know who I meant.

I was getting ready to break down the door. I was getting ready to be the guy who has to tell the whole story to the police, and maybe get punched by them for being the guy who was there on the sofa, the couch. The door opened and Sandy came out, clean and wilted in a towel. Her hair smelled of honey, or hibiscus, one of those. Her eyes were pinned and she handed me a bag, some works.

"There's bleach in there," she said.

"No, thanks," I said. "I just want to take a leak."

I stood over the bowl but I couldn't get flow. When I lie about having to take a piss, I can't piss. I stared at the wallpaper, woodpeckers. On the beaks, or on the breasts of some of them, and on the leaves of trees, was a fine red spray. It was on the rim of the bowl, the tiles, too.

I went back to what I was sitting on and sat with her.

"I guess I should blow you," she said.

"I have to go," I said.

"Don't leave."

"You can keep what we bought," I said.

"You're nice."

"I'm sweet," I put my hand in her tank top, on whatever her habit hadn't eaten off. "Aren't I sweet?"

"You're sweet," she said.

"I have an old soul," I told her.

"What do you mean?"

"I'm advanced," I said.

"I'm intermediate," she said. "I got a badge in camp."

I took a train uptown to where they were tending to my sister. There's a whole block of enormous buildings for people who are running out of luck. My sister was in the Someone-Someone Pavilion. Ventilator, feeding tube, they had everything in her to keep her from going anywhere.

There was a guy in the room I knew from somewhere. High school. Homeroom. Guess he had a name with the same first letter as mine. I once caught him with his finger in my sister under the Ping-Pong table. When he saw me that time he pulled his finger out. Don't be a schmuck, I told him, finish up. Now he had his hands on his knees, a book in his lap.

"Good thing you came," he said.

"How is she?" I asked.

Close to the bed, I saw what a dumb question it was. My sister used to be pretty for her type. She was still pretty, if you like girls who are skulls with a little skin on them, a few strands of cotton for hair. It was hard to believe she was going to live another minute. It had been months this way. I wanted to get in the bed, hold her, but I thought I might knock a tube out.

"Do you mind?" I said to Homeroom.

I locked the door and sat on the chair, the book. It was something about a process, a grief process. I guess the guy had been boning up.

"Hey, you," I said. My sister did a snort through her air mask, this noise like everything that had always been my sister was clotted and wet inside her and we might need a tool to scoop it out. I gathered up the covers, slipped my hand under her gown. I knuckled in down there. Her knees opened in her sleep. Her nipple went up. I pushed the tubes off, bit down.

"Hey, you," I said, into my teeth.

Sometimes when I tell this story to people, I say my sister opened her eyes for a moment and our souls touched, my old soul and her pretty much dead one. I hope they don't believe it. My sister died a few hours later, but I was far away. I went to Peeptown. The place had really gone downhill. Then I found Gary and we went to the Jew-hater's bar. Gary had a bump nose and took the German's theories badly. Gary, I said, shut up and get a guitar. This place needed strummy music and maybe the hate would go away. I'd seen it happen, in other lives. Sandy was there, loaded, doing lap hustles for the dream of a bundle. Turned out Sandy was the bartender's daughter. Deirdre was her true name. We were together for years and years, here and there. I'm sure she was a whore in the time of Bismarck.

Her soul is older than mine.

Fragment No. 17 Mexicói Utca

Giuseppe O. Longo

Giuseppe O. Longo holds degrees in mathematics and electronic engineering and is professor of information theory at the University of Trieste, Italy. He has published three novels, eight collections of short stories, and a collection of plays. His work has received a variety of awards and prizes and has been translated from Italian into several languages. His first story published in the United States, "In Zenoburg," appeared in Open City *in 2001.*

 . . . INSOMNIA, AND IN THIS OLD GROUND FLOOR apartment, insomnia is more obstinate than in Trieste, if for no other reason than the regular passing of trains which shake the whole house, the house of Aunt Margit, they make the old living room chandelier swing, the one I turn on toward 2 a.m. when I wake up and it seems that I really cannot go back to sleep, with all the sleep hard as a fist between the eyes, I go to the window and from below I look up and watch for a long moment the railroad bed, high, thick with acacias and brambles made yellow by the rare lamplights and here is another train dark black fast rumbling in the night and after a few seconds the house begins to tremble and sway, it doesn't tremble immediately, only after a few seconds, when the train has already half passed and it seemed that this time the house would not shake, but no it begins to shake, once the train has passed it returns to silence, at night the street is deserted, in this southernmost suburb of Pest I have seen grassy paths, low little houses, trees in flower, I have breathed that exasperating odor that circulates in the air, lime trees and jasmine, it is almost country, then I leave the window and turn toward the room and in that dim light the furniture watches me, the closets, the cupboards, the upholstered little chairs stained with old excretions and body fluids, Aunt Margit died a few months ago, in April, she was ninety-seven, Gyula told me that they had patched her together with various operations, she had an artificial anus, never a complaint, but she could not retain her body fluids, the emanations godgodgod, that's why the bed, the stained chairs, he told me this yesterday afternoon when we

were visiting the railway museum, she had raised him, that frail little boy, he had become a genius in mathematics, but he was always sad, he had never managed to forget that Russian soldier who had shot his parents in the courtyard, without a reason, he was six years old and his eyes and ears and head were always filled with those shots, the rifle in the arms of the Russian, it seemed like a game to aim the rifle at those two who were walking, but who knows what went through his head, that soldier, to aim and then fire from the high window into the snowy courtyard, and he, little Gyula, Gyuszi, Gyuszika, from the doorway of the apartment on the ground floor looking onto the courtyard, had seen his parents fall who were coming toward him and had already nodded toward him and smiled toward him but they had remained there, on the snow, had fallen and remained there, the Russian soldier had fired from the window, the window had opened and the soldier had appeared, had taken the rifle in his arms and fired, twice, aiming calmly, he didn't remember which of the two had fallen first, it still seemed to him like a game, now his parents would get up, first papa, then mama, first papa would get up and would have helped mama get up, mama would have laughed embarrassed, he would have brushed her coat full of snow a few times, to clean it, then she would have helped papa to clean himself, he already saw papa turn toward him, look at him with his half-closed eyes and laugh silently, with a little breath, a little whistle through his teeth, one of those little jokes he knew how to make, the closed window had opened and the soldier had appeared, he, Gyula, had noticed it because, in opening, the window had sent a flash of sunlight at him, at the ground-level door of the little apartment where he was waiting for his parents, they had passed through the huge door and the very high porch, had entered the courtyard, around the courtyard there were many other doors, homes and offices, there was a blacksmith, a carpenter, there was a shoemaker, the artisans that are usually in the big courtyards, they work in their little shops but now he was not looking at the shops, he was looking at that window which was open there, above, on the wall opposite, at the window there was a soldier, a Russian soldier, he saw his face clearly, a young face, blue eyes, blond mustache, the beret of a Russian soldier, the insignia of a Russian soldier, he had taken the rifle calmly into his arms and then there was the shot and then the other shot, the echo and then again the echo, and after a little a woman had begun to scream in the air in the light in the snow, a continuous howl, slow, which never ended, the Russian soldier had closed the window, another dazzle of light in the eyes and still his parents did not get up and he was uncertain, he understood that the longer they stayed there the more sinister the game became, a few moments before he had seen them from behind the glass of his door window enter through the big door and walk into the courtyard, on an angle, tramping over the dirty snow, full of footprints and tracks black with mud, but how can you remember, I ask him, and he tells me he has everything before his eyes, I have done nothing but think about it all these years, but you can't remember, I say, memories change, change continuously, yes, he says, but certain things can't be forgotten, the Russian at the window, the bodies in the snow, the sounds of the gunshots, I still see all the gutters that pock-marked the wall opposite, the hinges, the exhausts from the stoves, the bumps in the plaster, the closed windows, that one wide open, it is like a movie that goes, stops, backs up, starts again, sometimes it gets stuck on some particular, then stirs again, and in telling this he has bright empty eyes as though he were looking onto another world, now with my family there in the snow I was on the verge of crying, but I knew that I mustn't cry, then there was a lot of confusion, people coming and going, I don't remember anything else, there had been the shot and then the other shot, the dark stain my parents' coats made on the snow, then he is silent for a long time, as if he was about to cry, but he doesn't cry, he looks at me and shakes his head, Aunt Margit had been there to take care of him and had made him study and only after fifteen years had he spoken to his aunt about the shots, the soldier, for fifteen years he hadn't cried, had said nothing, asked nothing, he had closed down, he had studied hard, his parents had been shot like pigs in the snow and he closed down, turned to stone, he had become a great mathematician, I move away from the window, turn toward the bed, but I experience a vague repugnance, that apartment on the ground floor is still inhabited by Aunt Margit, there are her memories, her excretions, her bodily fluids, her smells, they have cleaned, of course, but over here somewhere hides a grayish tangle of her last ruffled hair, over there is a clump of something that has to do with her body, skin, dandruff, scales, I have never seen Aunt Margit, but I see the little glassed-in case with her books, the cabinet with the plates and the glasses lined up, the enormous wall mirror, enclosed in a floral frame decorated with slender feminine figures that change into plants, it is not a physical repugnance that I experience, but a moral disgust, an incomprehension before the facts of life and death, of course there was not the time or place to do an investigation into a soldier who had killed two civilians in an occupied country, the war had just ended, there were plenty of other problems, people had to work, keep warm, eat every day, so Margit had taken him, that baby, who else could have taken him, that sad frail child, black hair hazel eyes, there wasn't even any longer the possibility of making a priest of him, it wasn't done anymore, in fact it was suspect, maybe at night he cried, at first, he was after all only six years old, when the mama is that great and warm thing who hugs us and we feel the tenderness of it, but during the day never a word, never a tear, never a sigh, only that fathomless sadness in the eyes and within all the things he told me yesterday afternoon in the railway museum, they say it is the largest railway museum in the world, acres and acres in open air, under the July sun, locomotives of every kind on the grass, cranes, enormous snow plows, machine rooms, hangars, railroad cars from the nineteenth century, there is even Franz Joseph's imperial train, Gyula insisted that I drive the diesel locomotive of the Hungarian State Railway placed at the disposition of the public for a trial run, and afterward they gave me a certificate, a diploma, *oklevél*, I have my place in the history of this glorious institution, the sense of power that driving a locomotive for a mile gives you, and how could it happen, I ask him when I come down, and he shrugs, I never look at it like that, he says, the how and the why don't interest me, almost sixty years have passed, there's no more pain in him, there is maybe the memory of pain, had there been a trial, I don't think so, had they punished him, transferred him, sent him to Siberia or wherever, I don't know, I know nothing and finally it doesn't interest me, I lived with my aunt, she loved me, then I met my wife, we married, the children, the career, the honors, my travels, all the women I've had who were perhaps one-night stands, he gives himself to sex with profound conviction, made of innocence and integrity, he can't resist the seduction of the beautiful women he meets at conferences, he takes them to bed, it must be a form of compensation, I say, could be, he doesn't like to look into things, he doesn't like history at all, this tells a lot about him, history is useless, he says, for him there is only mathematics, mathematics and the women he takes to bed, this extreme simplification of life has always impressed me, I don't approve, or maybe I simply don't understand, but I hide all this, he has started his two sons in mathematics, I would like to tell him that all that is a retaliation for that ancient assassination, but he wouldn't understand, he wouldn't want to understand, instead I ask him what his father did for a living, he was a clerk somewhere, my mother too, he doesn't know much about it, about his parents, a vast repression, an amputation of the soul, then a functionary of the Museum comes to meet us and begins to show us something, he opens and closes the doors of the train cars, has us climb up and points out details, he speaks in a hurry, I get tired of following the explanations, my mind wanders, when we come out of the hangar the sun beats down on the rusty tracks, on the multicolored masses of wood and metal, beyond the surrounding wall I see scattered blocks of flats, windows and elaborate little balconies, walls with floral patterns flaking from neglect, sloping roofs decorated with wrought-iron spirals and squiggles, clothes hung out to dry, someone appears in the windows, let's go, I say, we look for the car, we walk through the grassy little streets among little yellow houses, ancient villages now swallowed by the big city, cracked sidewalks, elms and locust trees, a few little country restaurants, everything feels old, but fascinating, comfortable, Molnár and *csárda* and my childhood memories, evening radio dramas, when I wasn't suffering from insomnia in my savory half-sleep the voices of the actors mixed with my flickering visions, creating rigorous and incongruous paths that dropped off into sleep, while now, here in Aunt Margit's apartment, something clutches the opening of my stomach, and I don't know if it is the loss of a hope, the sign of suffering, the prelude to a defeat, and another train passes going who knows where into the dark countryside that seems to sleep, whereas probably like me many are stirring now in their rooms, between the corner shelves and the big walnut table, looking for their lost sleep, then I go into the bathroom, turn on the blinding light, the tub and the sink assail me with their whiteness, from the window wide opened onto the courtyard I see the fig tree, the little wall, the wire fence, the house opposite is dark, impenetrable, it is three in the morning, four more hours and upstairs the others will be waking too, we will make breakfast, then we'll bustle around the glamorous streets downtown, then return to Mexicói utca with its torn up sidewalks, the railway beds, the trains that pass continuously, the old house that trembles . . .

Translated from the Italian by James B. Michels.

Tea at the Plaza

Phillip Lopate

Phillip Lopate is the author of the essay collections Bachelorhood, Against Joie de Vivre, Portrait of My Body, Totally Tenderly Tragically, *and, most recently,* Notes on Sontag. *He also has published three novels, two poetry collections, a memoir of his teaching experiences, and a nonfiction book,* Waterfront: A Journey Around Manhattan. *He is a professor of English at Hofstra University.*

WHAT IS IMPORTANT TO AN ADULT AND WHAT matters to a child are so often at variance that it is a wonder the two ever find themselves on the same page. Parents may feel an occasional urge to spend money extravagantly on their offspring, only to discover that it means very little to the children themselves. You buy an expensive antique Raggedy Ann doll for your kid, which she tosses in a corner, thinking it ugly and musty, meanwhile much more enthralled by the shiny plastic action figure they give out free at McDonald's. And yet, if you're like me, you keep falling into the trap of costly, unappreciated presents, perhaps because they're not really for your child but for the child-self in you who never got them when you were growing up.

I remember, when my daughter Lily was four, my wife Cheryl and I sprang for a family carriage ride through Central Park in the snow. We had such an idyllic Currier & Ives image in our heads, and it seemed such an ideal treat for the holidays—all the more special because we were dyed-in-the-wool New Yorkers and usually stayed clear of what the tourists went in for. "Let's just do it!" we cried impulsively, determined to play at being tourists in our own city. Yet I could not help noticing the reluctant, even alarmed expression on Lily's face as she climbed, or was lifted into the barouche, behind the bewhiskered coachman with the tall shamrock hat, stationed across from the Plaza Hotel. We started off at a slow trot; the carriage entered the park, my wife and I entranced by the vista, and Lily starting to whimper and complain that she was cold, until she spotted a merry-go-round, the prospect of which excited her far more than an actual horse giving her a ride. As we neared the merry-go-round, Lily became so insistent that we had to ask the coachman to stop the carriage. I forked over what felt at the time like major dough for a fifteen-minute trot, grumbling as she ran over to the carousel.

I vowed under my breath that I would never be such a patsy again. But we had not yet gotten out of the business, my wife and I, of manufacturing exorbitant "perfect memories" for our daughter to cherish all her days. So we took her to Broadway shows, and to the Nutcracker Ballet (where she fell asleep), and we began—at first very vaguely, then with more urgency—plotting an afternoon's high tea at the Plaza's Palm Court. Somehow that corner at Fifty-ninth Street and Fifth Avenue was the Bermuda Triangle that kept sucking us into fantasies of civilized luxury. You must understand that this was not a case of passing on some proud family tradition: my father did not take me to Brooks Brothers for a fitting of my first suit, but to the backroom of a gypsy shop that probably trafficked in stolen goods. I grew up in working-class Brooklyn, and never entered the Plaza when I was a child, nor did Cheryl, who hailed from hardscrabble upstate New York and might, if she were lucky, get to order a hot chocolate with whipped cream at the local luncheonette. But our child was a middle-class New York child, thanks to our fatiguing efforts to claw our way up the social ladder, and, by God, we were bound and determined to give her all the social graces and sophisticated experiences that befit her, if not our, station in life.

So, with somewhat grim if hearty countenances, we got Lily and ourselves all dressed up, and took her into Manhattan for the thrill of a lifetime. We did not ride the subway from Brooklyn, mind you, as that would have spoiled the general effect, but drove in and, unable to find a parking spot on the street, left our car in a garage a few blocks east of the Plaza, in what must be the most expensive parking area in the planet. But hey! Who cares about the expense? We're treating ourselves! We entered the regal steps of the Plaza, which had powerful electric warmers on (this was winter again), and stood in line at the perimeter of the majestic Palm Court.

I had already called ahead and knew they did not take reservations over the phone; but fortunately the 4 p.m., mid-afternoon line was not that long, and we were assured of seating. In fact, business seemed relatively slow, for a treasured landmark. We oohed and aahed, Cheryl and I, at the fabulous high ceiling, the palm trees, the piano, the marble floor, and the fashionable or laughable costumes of various diners, Ladies Who Lunched. Lily nodded, smiling and looking dutifully about, but seemed a bit cool about it all, as if she were indulging her parents' naïve enthusiasm. Once seated, we took up our menus rather stiffly. The waitress wrote down our orders—three specials with all the trimmings, oh spare not the clotted cream, the crème frâiche, the clabber or what have you, the peach cobblers, the jams, the crustless cucumber sandwiches, the savories, the petit fours, the works! All that centuries of human ingenuity had found to include in this cozy English tradition of High Tea, we wanted.

"Think of it, Lily, Eloise herself ran through this very same room!" I said.

"But she's not real, is she?" said my knowing six-year-old.

"No, but still—"

"Of course she is!" insisted my wife, ever eager to promote and prolong childhood credulity, be it Santa Claus, the Tooth Fairy, or Eloise. She darted me a scolding look: I knew that expression, which warned me that I was in danger of taking away our daughter's childhood with my cynical insistence on realism.

So we kept it Nice; we were all on our best behavior, and commented favorably, when the food came, on the beautiful tea service, the exquisite arrangement of edibles, the deliciousness of everything—in short, it was a dull conversation, but appropriately so, duly dull, you might say. We were proud of ourselves for adhering well to the parts assigned us in this civilized ritual, for coloring within the lines. No one would ever guess we lived in Brooklyn.

We had stuffed ourselves; and now Lily began getting restless, as children will in that post-prandial moment, not yet knowing how to take advantage of a reflective pause. Enough with the talk, she wanted action. I commiserated with her squirminess—more to the point, I felt childishly restless myself, and so I volunteered to take her for a walk about the floor. "Should I come too?" asked Cheryl.

"No, stay and enjoy the last of your tea and a few moments' solitude." (I was already deep in the throes of performing a Good Deed.)

It was fun to walk around with Lily and stick our noses into every corner of the nearby bar, the cloakroom, and the lobby. We pretended to be spies; she picked a person to trail after for a few steps, then darted away madly in the opposite direction and hid, giggling. In our last go-round we came upon a family—a mother and her three young daughters in dresses, the youngest of whom was holding a clutch of balloons. Probably she was celebrating her birthday. Lily was instantly enchanted—not by the birthday girl, by the balloons. They were plump and filled with helium and had stars drawn on them. How she wanted one of those balloons! I could tell it meant everything to her at that moment; so I went over to the mother and asked her if my daughter might have one. The word "borrow" would have been dishonest, as we had no intentions of ever returning it. No, have it for free, just like that, is what we meant; it was a brazen request to ask of a perfect stranger, and fortunately the kind woman understood what was at stake and acquiesced. "Which one would you like?" she asked Lily, bending down. Stalled between the red, the light blue, the orange, and the dark green, Lily finally chose the red. The woman then turned to her daughter and asked ceremoniously, "Would you mind giving this little girl your red balloon?" The girl gravely nodded her willingness to do so, and Lily walked away holding its string, happy—in ecstasies—as happy as I'd ever seen her.

We were both pretty high, delighted with our luck, when we sat back at the table. There is something marvelous in a place like the Plaza about getting something for free, even if it's just a nickel balloon. My wife wanted to know the whole story, and Lily began telling it, with her usual dramatic flair and embellishments. Just as she was gesticulating to make a point, she lost hold of the end of the string and the balloon floated up to the ceiling. How many seconds it took to make its ascent, I could not begin to tell you, but the subjective experience was one of quite extensible duration: just as in a car crash your whole life, they say, flashes through your mind, or just as a glass rolling off the table takes forever when you can do nothing to arrest its fall, so my accumulated past of error, catastrophe, and missed opportunity fluttered before my eyes, while I watched the balloon drift up, up, up, languidly taking its time. Was I passing on my karma of lost illusions to my daughter? It was too horrible to contemplate. What is even more unconscionable is that a part of me wanted to laugh.

This despicable urge to laugh rose in me, in spite of (or maybe because of . . . ?) the fact that Lily has started wailing. Piercing sobs issued from her as she watched her balloon (which had only been *hers* for five minutes) escaping further and further. The diners at nearby tables stopped in mid-fork, perhaps readying themselves to intervene in the event they saw evidence of child abuse; when they satisfied themselves that they were not, they returned to their food, most likely blaming us for not being able to control our brat better. Meanwhile, the captain of the waiters hurried over to see if there was anything he could do. Our waitress began making commiserating faces and noises such as one directs at a little baby. All to no avail. My wife took Lily in her lap and began calming her down.

I attended to the check, handing over my credit card and totaling up the tip, the full amount coming to over two hundred dollars. I could not rid myself of the chagrined feeling that that outlay, plus the garage bill, had been nullified by the loss of a little nothing balloon. "We'll get you another balloon as soon as we leave the hotel," Cheryl promised Lily, who was beginning to decelerate from wrenching sobs to puppy whimpers.

After I had gotten my credit card back and we'd put our coats on and were about to leave, I turned to the simpatico wait-captain and asked him how long it would take for that balloon to come down, thinking it might be possible to retrieve it and give the story of our outing a happy ending.

"Oh, about a week, I'd imagine," he said with a slight accent (Egyptian? Maltese? Cypriot?).

"And is there no way to get it down before then?"

"No way."

For some reason, this report that it would take a week to come down set Lily off on a fresh burst of wailing. Now she was inconsolable. She was like Hecuba, experiencing precociously the fullness of grief. We hastened her out of there, but she kept up her loud sobbing in the street.

"Knock it off!" said Cheryl, suddenly out of patience. "You're making a spectacle of yourself, you're acting like a two-year-old!" While I completely agreed with my wife, I also, in that instantaneous switch of good cop/bad cop roles for which parents are so adept, became entirely sympathetic to Lily's woe: I knew that emotions do not have to be reasonable to shatter us, and that sobs feed uncontrollably on sobs, regardless of our efforts to stop.

"Let her cry," I said. "I'm not embarrassed. Who cares what these people think?"

The truth was, I was strangely happy. The whole incident had struck me as funny, a cosmic comeuppance for our pretensions to being the sort of swells who had tea at the Plaza, though I am prepared to admit that this urge to laugh may have also been a defensive reflex arising from my powerlessness in the face of Lily's anguish. Meanwhile, Lily, as if picking up on my undertone, began to giggle, in-between her sobs—a part of her perhaps recognizing that she *was* being ridiculous, a drama queen, making entirely too much of this. I think, though, that my errant satisfaction issued from a darker source: I felt myself bonding with my daughter in our now-shared discovery that life was composed, at bottom, of loss, futility, and incomprehensible sorrow. There was nothing you could do about it except to laugh.

Years later, that is precisely what we do: whenever we recall the lost balloon, it is always good for a chuckle, and Lily, now ten, is the first to laugh at herself. But we know better than to return to the Palm Court for tea. In fact, speaking of loss, that elegant ballroom, which conjures up Edith Wharton's and F. Scott Fitzgerald's New York, and which we all thought would last forever, regardless of how slow business might be, is hanging by a thread. The new owners of the Plaza have turned a good part of the hotel into condominiums, and have wanted to gut the Oak Room and the Palm Court as well, but the landmarks preservation community prevented them, for the time being. If someday these cherished interiors are demolished, as seems likely, I will be sad but I will not be *only* sad. The Palm Court will have gone the way of Rumpelmayer's, the legendary pink-ensconced ice cream parlor that once stood a block away from the Plaza—both institutions no longer around to torment parents with the chimera of a perfect children's outing.

Twilight at the Equator

Jaime Manrique

Jaime Manrique is a Colombian born novelist, poet, essayist, and translator who has written both in English and Spanish, and whose work has been translated into many languages. Among his publications in English are the novels Colombian Gold, Latin Moon in Manhattan, Twilight at the Equator, *and* Our Lives Are the Rivers. *His honors include Colombia's National Poetry Award, 2007 International Latino Book Award, and a Guggenheim Fellowship. Manrique has just completed* Cervantes Street, *a novel.*

RAMON MADE A LOOPING MOTION WITH HIS CIGArette. He dragged without inhaling, and blew ringlets of smoke that the afternoon breeze wafted in the direction of the street.

I had picked up Ramon after lunch, when my relatives retired to take their siestas. Even though he had his own apartment, he still went to his parents home for lunch, and it was there that I met him. We headed for Barranquilla's shady zoo where we spent the hottest hours of the afternoon strolling under the gigantic rubber trees, meandering from exhibit to exhibit, laughing at the capuchin monkeys gnawing desperately at their tails, grooming and eating each other's ticks, pitching their still moist turds at one another and masturbating gleefully, shooting their come at the zoo visitors. We marvelled at the kaleidoscopic and tuneful tropical birds and at the multiplicity of lethal vipers. All these provided us with plenty of amusement as we reminisced about the main events of our lives in the past decade, when we had been apart.

Now we were having *frosomales* on the terrace of El Mediterráneo, a local Greek coffee shop that is a traditional focal point of Barranquilla's social life.

"Yes, Santiago, all signs of contumacy are being systematically squeezed out," Ramon shuddered, opening wide his tawny eyes. "One runs into death every time one turns a corner. For the people who are marked, it must be like living with a death sentence. You made a salomonic decision to leave for gringo-land when you did; otherwise, you'd probably be pushing daisies. Just last year, I was really afraid for Alejo's life." He paused to check out a young man in tight jeans and T-shirt crossing the street. "For myself," Ramon went on, "I gave up being a controvertist a long time ago. Yes," he seethed, frowning and wringing his hands, "I embrace the mediocrity of it all. If this place was the pits when you lived here, it's much worse now. It's rotting in a million places. This city is like an organism which didn't get vaccinated when it was born, and now it's riddled with monstrous diseases. Barranquilla is a perfect metaphor for the rest of Colombia. But I embrace the collective peristesia of the national soul. And make no apologies for it."

His pretentious choice of words, which would have sounded unbearable in an American or European, rang authentic with him—a perfect example of Caribbean rococo. He was one of the most affected human beings I had ever met, and I pictured him perfectly at home in the court of Louis the XIV. I sat there, agape, grateful that his theatricality remained unchanged, that he lived up to the image of him I had constructed in my recollection over the years. What was a wonder to me was how he had managed to thrive despite the belligerent local machismo.

Like a Balanchine dancer, Ramon sprang up from his chair. "Excuse me for a sec, but I must absolutely inspect that beauty," he said, referring to the young man who now stood at the corner, lighting a cigarette and casting smoldering glances in our direction.

I took a spoonful of *frosomal* as Ramon and the young man made contact. For the past few years I had dreamed of this moment when Ramon and I could meet here in this ice cream parlor, enjoying a *frosomal*, which is a kind of vanilla-chocolate milkshake flavored with cherry and pineapple syrup.

The sun was now in the west, descending, lifting the sluggishness of mid-afternoon. There was considerable traffic; scores of people ambled in and out of the stores, cafés, and restaurants that line Calle 72. A languorous breeze swept down the wide street, and the ungainly bushes of four o'clocks framing the terrace metamorphosed, blooming in one breath, an explosion of scarlet petals and black eyes.

Ramon, looking in my direction, pointed at me with his pinky, as if he were trying to persuade the swarthy young stud to join us. Ramon's maneuvers brought back to me why I had left Barranquilla in the first place. I had realized that as a gay man I could never hope to have a normal relationship with another man here. There was only one kind of known homosexual in Barranquilla, *el marica*, the queen. The others (the vast majority) were the *cacorros*, the "straight" men who went to bed with the queens assuming exclusively the active role. What was considered homosexual was to surrender one's ass. So I left because I wanted an alternative to these clichés. I had returned home ten years later, mortally afraid of sex with strangers, looking upon each new encounter as a potentially reckless flirtation with death. Although Ramon was terrified by the increasing number of AIDS deaths in the city, he still carried on with the promiscuity of the past. He felt fully protected by condoms, and refused to surrender the full expression of his sexuality.

Ramon shook his index finger at the trick, using it like a magic wand to glue the boy to the spot. Then he strutted in my direction.

"*Carino*" he purred sitting down. "Isn't he out of Almodovar? I have to give him a couple thousand pesos, but he'll cooperate. He's shy about meeting you. I'll give you a full report later tonight. Or tomorrow. Or whenever we stop—if we ever stop. I feel almost guilty about leaving you here, but I know that you'd do the same if you were in my heels. We'll have to have a do at my place to celebrate your return to *la Madre Patria*. And please hurry back to Baranquilla. I can't even begin to imagine why you want to go inspect those satanic bananas," he said referring to my father's banana plantation. Ramon kissed me on both cheeks and sashayed down the steps, puffed up like a bird of paradise in heat.

After a while, I decided to go back to the apartment. I paid the check and walked on Calle 72, in a northerly direction. Reaching the corner of Avenue Olaya Herrera I saw, on the grounds of the old soccer stadium, two trucks loaded with armed soldiers.

I went into the park across Calle 72; its grounds were as unkempt as I remembered them, but the leafy almond trees created a cool canopy. A decade ago, the park had become dangerous at night, so few people frequented it around dusk. In my childhood, it was notorious because at night the maids who worked in the neighborhood would use it to rendezvous with their beaus. As a child, I'd come to the park to gather the ripe almonds on the grounds. When I had stuffed my pockets with the yellow fruit, I'd search for a hefty stone to smash the fleshy shells and the porous wrapping underneath that hid the tender, tasty nut. Today I spotted black-coated squirrels looking for ripe fruit, digging on the thick carpet of leaves on the sand. Several homeless people occupied the broken down cement benches of the park, and a bunch of Boy Scouts were practicing some kind of military drill. The children were aggressive and intent; they seemed more like ferocious midget soldiers than regular Scouts.

Arritoquieta opened the door to my family's apartment. She informed me that my uncle was teaching and my aunt was out at a friend's but that they both would be home for dinner, which would be served at 7:30. She offered me a *tinto*, which I declined. I went into the library. Outside, it was still light, but the room was in a semi-penumbra. I sat on the rocking chair by the window. The carmine sun dove in the Caribbean, creating a widespread hemorrhage in the sky. Transfixed, I watched the violent sunset bleed slowly until darkness began to set in. I was relieved I was in the apartment (where I felt safe) and not in the streets. I became absorbed in the process of day turning into night when little squiggles began to appear over the city, darting back and forth at the speed of lightning. At first, I figured it was an optical illusion taking place in my retina, created by the hallucinating palette of the western sky. As the squiggles became more numerous, I realized that they were thousands of bats flying above the red clay roofs of the houses, the tops of the condos, the spires of the churches, the cathedral and the tallest trees. The bats were out for their nocturnal feeding. Out of nowhere, a completely forgotten incident from my childhood came back to me. I must have been five and I still couldn't read.

A frenzy was created in Barranquilla by a woman who died in doctor's office during an abortion. Momentarily losing his sanity, the doctor had hacked the woman's body into many pieces, stuffed them in a bag, and taken a drive all the way to the sea. Every few hundred yards or so, he dumped a chunk of the corpse on the bushes along the road. I remembered the front page photographs: one day her decomposed arm; the next, her eyeless head, maggots crawling out of all the orifices. As a child, this incident filled me with such unspeakable horror I never mentioned it to anyone. In fact, I hadn't thought about it since it had happened thirty-five years earlier. But as night fell from the Caribbean to the equator, over the Amazonian jungle, above the icy peaks of the volcanoes of the Andes, all the way to Patagonia, to the bleak, glacial regions of Tierra del Fuego, this image, this memory, burst through the fortress of denial with such violence, that I sat on the rocking chair in a trance, shivering, sweating a cold sweat.

I could not break the spell until some time later when the tropical sky glowed with shimmering stars the size of planets, and a moon as gigantic and luminous as the midnight sun of arctic summer poised herself in the night sky, not just as a light fixture, but as an object of desire, a deity to be worshipped.

Bees

Thomas McGuane

Thomas McGuane lives on a ranch in McLeod, Montana. He is the author of ten novels, three works of nonfiction, and two collections of stories.

 BILL STOOD WITH THE SMOKE TANK IN HIS HAND, net over his face, and watched the dust cloud from the approaching car. He imagined what he must look like to its driver and felt sheepish. He knew who the driver was. He lifted the bottom of the hive and held the spigot underneath and waited until the smoke speeded heavily though the sides. The day was cloudy, heated and still as he looked within at the gold and varnish chambers, the myriad larval world of bees, a city he could slice into oozing districts or break sweet and heavy between his hands. Bees swarmed around his head, indignant movement swooning piecemeal into the smoke. It was the young lieutenant paying a visit. Yet here he was among the beehives, the place fate had assigned him.

Even if they wanted to sleep in, Aria always got up at five and turned the kitchen light on. If there was no light on by five, the neighbors would get hold of it and it would be all over the valley. Usually Bill and Aria were up by then; but every Wednesday, for no good reason, they slept until seven, after Aria had turned on the kitchen light. It was a bounty rarely surpassed, but especially so in those early years of the war when they were always shorthanded, when you fenced alone and hayed alone, and a night calver was an unimaginable luxury. But today, which was Wednesday, Aria turned the kitchen light on at five, and didn't come back to bed. Bill had had it in mind all day. He had it in mind now. They were supposed to sleep until seven.

This year his hives were out of the flood plain, the hundred-year flood plain that flooded every three years. The soil conservation man told him it was a convulsive river, liable to lateral migrations. So, he moved the hives. He couldn't move his own house or he would move it out of the wind. His dad rode in from western Nebraska a half-century ago and during a long quiet summer, picked his spot and built. Then the wind came up, for fifty years. Everything bent to it, shelter belt, lilacs, the old spruces along the drive.

He was not going to finish this job in time. He was not going to get to centrifuge this honey and get up to the house in time and in any case, he was not going to get there before the lieutenant in his car. He set aside the smoking canister and queerly rearranged the broken combs. He lifted the bee helmet from his head abruptly and then set it down.

Unlike the young lieutenant, he was afoot. The road took a wide curve around the hill between him and the house and the hill was too steep to climb swiftly. Bill was a young man and had to do so much on this place that he no longer felt like a young man. The war had not made him a glamorous stranger that way it did a man in uniform. Why didn't the car slow down? Who else would be out here among these hives? He felt denied a common courtesy.

He would go straight to the house despite that the very distance seemed to be pushing him back, made him aware of his own cloddish footfalls and the glacial emergence of his house from the side of the hill. The car was parked in front, right in the center of the gate so that the two big lilacs stood at either side of the front fenders. It was parked as though no one else needed to use the walk. It was a smart model, slate grey, with rear fender skirts and white walls. The slogan "treasure state" on its license plate seemed to enhance its grandeur.

The lieutenant was sitting at the kitchen table with a cup of coffee. Aria stood next to the stove. The lieutenant shifted his shoulders to look back toward the door as Bill entered. He had coal black hair and an unlit cigarette in the corner of his mouth. The blueness of his eyes gave him a remote quality that Bill thought made him seem here and not here. Aria looked so small just then in her cotton dress and she pressed the finger-tips of both hands against each other as she always did before weighing her words. She removed one hand from this contact and used it to indicate the lieutenant. It was as if there were several lieutenants but that this was the intended one.

"Bill, this is Dan Albright." Her hand moved right. "My husband Bill." They shook hands without Dan Albright getting up. Aria rattled on. She and Dan went to high school together. It was perfect: she was a cheer-leader; he was a quarterback. He went up to the university and joined R.O.T.C. Now he was home on leave from Europe for the first time in three years. There was no mention of their two children, not that they existed, nor that they were in the next room.

"Are you in the infantry?"

"I'm an artillery officer. I'm half deaf. And you're still ranching. I guess that's an essential service."

"So they tell me.""

"What do you do for fuel?"

"I get rations enough for the tractor."

Dan flickered the rim of his coffee cup and made it ring. Aria refilled it. The black stream poured with unusual slowness and when the cup was filled, Aria raised her eyes to Bill's for the first time. He was aware that his mouth was not quite closed.

"I'm going to leave with Dan," she said.

"Oh?" said Bill. He had put all this together and yet he hadn't. The lieutenant stared down at his hands, trying to seem to share Bill's pain. As yet, there was no pain. There was only a sense of caution and watch-fulness about this information. There was a sense of songbirds going on about their business.

"You only live once," said the lieutenant. Bill guessed that this was meant to explain their recklessness but he wasn't sure. He tried to remember how this was different from, "You're only young once," a phrase that disturbed him.

"Have you already been unfaithful to me?" he asked Aria.

"Yes," she said, trying to mix contrition and pride. It wasn't quite working but even Bill understood that this was no time to choose one over the other. Bill's time for wishful thinking had come to an end. He may have still loved her but he certainly hated her. And the thought of carnal turmoil overwhelmed him. He couldn't understand. He was being tossed about. She had loved the land when he hadn't cared. She was the one always finding eternal values in their lives and now she was going off with this uniform. She is leaving me to my bee helmet and my babies; but that hardly worked either. There was a big difference between a slut and someone who was merely more interested in someone else than she was in you. But it was strange: her mouth had become a slash. It was as if she leered about at pots and pans.

One thing he could tell was that they were waiting for him to really say something they could get their teeth into. He felt their need for him to help them get it all out in the air. He felt contemptuous. Forty years later when he saw her on a street corner in Jordan, a withered white-haired crone, he would remember this feeling of contempt for her in her tight little wash dress, next to the stove, waiting for him to fill the air with talk and kill the tension, the uniform leaning heroically against the table and as without an idea as she. Bill would remember the uniform's broad shoulders and olive wool jacket, the battle stripes, the nearly full cup of coffee, when the lieutenant, transformed into a farm-and-ranch insurance salesman, burst his heart and toppled his dead body onto the lobby floor of the Northern Hotel in Billings. Those stirring days came to one who, like all of us, never really changed, the unburied hatchet forever in hand.

But standing next to the relaxed and seated lieutenant in a house filled with a kind of pearly twilight from its small windows Bill was able to escape his pain in a feeling of injustice. This elevated feeling allowed him to elude the earlier sense of a steady and uncompleted physical blow. He was overwhelmed suddenly with hunger. He opened the refrigerator and ate an apple so loudly and so fast that Aria and Dan stared at him. There were dizzying columns of flies at the screen and the distant bawling of a calf that had got under the fence. Bill ate another apple. When he got to the core, he thumbed the small black seeds onto the floor, then looked up.

He walked over to the door that opened between the pie safe and Frigidaire and opened it. He looked in at the two babies, Clay and Karen, two small bumps under a blanket. "What are we going to do with these guys."

"One step at a time," said the lieutenant. The fact that he said this to Aria made it hard to follow. But Bill agreed that this was an ungovernable question that he couldn't ignore. He looked over at Aria but instead of pain, he saw a kind of blank. He knew he couldn't blame her but this look of being stumped on a quiz show was surprising.

Then abruptly, he was dead weary. Apple pulp filled the spaces between his teeth. He felt the individual weight of his eyes. The flies had gotten worse. The lieutenant's uniform, Bill knew, would in time fill with moths.

Bill was trying to understand that Aria was not putting up a fight for the children. The lieutenant was an old boyfriend so that was easier. If it weren't for the children, Bill would be fighting the Japs or the Nazis; but with the imminence of Aria's departure, he thought he might arrange to fight them anyway. These days they seemed to be everywhere; it should be no great task to find and encounter them. He knew that the ranch wouldn't be beautiful anymore. It would be just shapes. She was the one that had found it beautiful; he got that bit from her. And he had believed that the cattle of America were like a big stockholders' company and he had a little share and was part of it. His mother told him she'd had him by herself in the middle of a blue norther while his father jugged a first calf heifer by lantern light. She said she thought she might die. She had seen humble Christ, head down in a desert country, people, strangers, staring at Him. "Who the hell do you think you are, anyhyoo?"

So what did he guess Aria wanted? Fine clothes and a fast auto. Dan stood up, his eyes shining.

"You're being so damned decent," he said and beat his hat against his leg in despair. Bill followed that hat around with his eyes.

"I'm not being decent. I'm just stumped."

"That's true," said Aria. "He's like this when he can't see what to do. He's no hero." This was scarcely an insult. She tried to be realistic. In some ways, their situation was drifting away from them like a rowboat someone forgot to tie up.

"I don't think that's true, Aria," Dan cried. "I don't think I can bear to have this on my hands. I can't be part of this." Dan had lost his looks, his place in time. Without the war, he was sunk. Even now, he wanted circumstances to sort themselves out for him, to sweep him along. One took to gunnery with a sigh of relief.

"You can't be part of this?" said Aria. "You're very much a part of this."

The lieutenant was backing toward the door. Bill was astonished at his lack of conviction. In a way, it depreciated Aria. They all must have sensed it. She was like a woman at the county bake sale sitting at her card table behind a cake no one stopped to look at. If you looked at the ceiling, you seemed crazy. If you looked straight ahead, you stared at people's crotches and buttocks. You had to keep finding a place to hide your eyes. It was the opposite of feeling "at home."

"Maybe you two should go off in Dan's car and try to work this out," Bill ventured. After the war, Dan and Aria actually did marry, a big splashy wedding, much photographed, the uniform making a final appearance. Word had it that she nagged him until he tipped over in the Northern Hotel lobby and Bill wondered if that behavior had begun in the kitchen today. She had never nagged him.

But Dan and Aria didn't want to talk it over. So, Bill saw Dan to the door. Just outside, Dan looked into the middle distance. He was pensive. Bill resented that he thought he had the intimacy to take such a pause.

"What do you think you'll do?" Dan asked. Bill couldn't really tell him to come back when he had a little conviction.

He said, "I was thinking about reinventing the wheel."

With his head hung, Dan left, barely turning back to close the door behind him. Bill thought that that was not an easy thing to do without throwing something out. Bill turned back to Aria and beamed, or tried to. He thought even the attempt might help. Through his pain, he still sensed she was in an awful position. None of the familiar utensils around her could be turned to without awkwardness.

"Let's wake the kids," he said. "You get Clay and I'll get Karen." Bill rubbed his hands together.

They came out of the children's room. Bill had sleepy little Karen under the arms, her bare feet dangling. Aria cradled Clay like a real baby. Bill leaned his face in until the end of his nose touched the end of the little girl's nose

"Want to hear how Daddy put the bees to sleep?"

Octo

Vestal McInytre

Vestal McIntyre is the author of Lake Overturn: A Novel, *which was named Editor's Choice by the* New York Times Book Review, *and a Best Book of 2009 by the* Washington Post. *His collection* You Are Not the One: Stories *was also a* New York Times Book Review *Editors' Choice and won a 2006 Lambda Literary Award for Debut Fiction. "Octo" was his first published story.*

ANGELFISH, BOXFISH, TWO SEA SNAILS, STRIPED grunt, surgeon-fish, hermit crab—Octo ate them all. He outgrew the Sea Monkeys Jamie bought to feed him and he started eating the other fish. So Ma and Daddy say it's time to get rid of Octo.

Angelfish was the first to go. It disappeared. Jamie thought it might've got sucked into the filter and died. I've got to clean the filter, thought Jamie. But the angelfish was under Octo's mantle, being eaten. When Octo moved, a day later, there was wide-eyed angelfish, fins gone, jumbled bones, a strip of skin waving in time with the filter's bubbling. Jamie got the net. He flushed the angelfish. He didn't tell Ma or Daddy.

That stupid fish tank smells, said Rebecca.

Jamie, if you're going to have an aquarium you've got to keep it clean, said Ma.

But that was months ago. Now Octo's eaten everyone else, too. Now it's just Octo, sitting quietly, thinking.

Jamie tries to get Elsie help him make seawater, but she won't. Not in my job description, says Elsie. Elsie's the care provider. She's old and has a limp and can't work. She gets more money from the government if she comes for an hour on the days when everyone else is at work or school. She makes lunch and gives Jamie pills. She's from Queens. Sometimes she stays longer than an hour if Jamie gets her talking. Like the Monday after the weekend when Jamie first got Octo.

Look Elsie! said Jamie. He brought Elsie to the tank.

Whoa! She backed up.

Isn't it cute? Octo was teeny-little, swimming around the tank. He was the size of an umbrella you'd put in a tropical drink. He swam back and forth opening and closing his legs like a tiny umbrella.

I wouldn't say cute, said Elsie getting closer to the tank. But it's somethin. It sure is somethin. You sure you can keep that in a tank?

Jamie told her what the man at the store had told him: that Octo would only survive if the water is kept fresh. Jamie would have to siphon out a little every day and replace it. Otherwise, when Octo squirted ink like he did when Jamie first put him in, he would make the water poison and die.

What do you mean siphon out water? asked Elsie. Jamie tried to show her—he started sucking on the siphon to get it going—but Elsie had turned and walked to the kitchen saying, I can't watch this.

That day Elsie ended up telling Jamie about the giant octopus that was displayed at Coney Island when she was little. You had to pay the guy a quarter, right? And he lets you into this tent, this long, dimly lit tent, and the minute you walk in you can smell the rot. Professor Whoever from Wherever is talkin about how he's traveled the world with this exquisite specimen. And laid out on this big piece of canvas was this dead octopus, half rotted away. Musta been fifty feet long.

Was it real? asked Jamie.

Sure it was. If it was fake it woulda smelled a whole lot better.

It must have been a giant squid, said Jamie.

You going to eat that orange or not? It's good for you.

I'm gonna eat it.

Octopus, squid, what's the difference? said Elsie. Jamie tried to tell her but she just went on. And there was the freakshow with the man with the stretchy skin and the bearded lady and all of that. Of course that's considered cruel nowadays. They don't have that kinda show.

They don't have it any more? said Jamie. He was disappointed.

Of course not, said Elsie.

Do they still have Coney Island?

You never been to Coney Island? What are you talkin, a kid like you?

No.

Elsie shook her head and picked up Jamie's plate. Where they keepin you?

That day Elsie stayed a full two hours. When she pulled on her coat she said, What am I doin, staying so long. You think I get paid extra for this? No sir-ee I do not.

That was when Octo was tiny, when he was still satisfied with tiny brine shrimp. Later, when Octo got sea snail number one, Daddy laughed.

Damn thing's goin after its *own* now, said Daddy. Mean mother. Thinks he's a big shot.

It wasn't a little snail. It was giant. Jamie would follow it around the tank. Its soft part made an oval against the glass, and Jamie would watch it up close, seeing its tiny mouth open and close, littler than a freckle, going wow, wow, wow, eating its way so slow around the tank. One morning snail number one was a bump under the brown web between Octo's two front legs. Octo wasn't moving. The black bars in Octo's eyeballs watched Jamie. You're eating one of the sea snails, aren't you? said Jamie. Octo looked but never blinked. His eyes were always wide open. If my eyes were that wide open, I'd look scared or wondering, thought Jamie. But Octo never looks scared or wondering. He just looks like he knows.

Two days later, in the corner of the tank was a pile of the snail shell in three pieces.

That Octopus eat one of them snails? said Elsie. She never got too close to the tank. She always scowled when she talked about Octo.

Yeah. I think so, said Jamie. Look. He piled up the pieces in the corner. It's like when I eat peanuts.

Ugh! said Elsie. You oughta get rid of that thing. It ate the angelfish, too.

I'm not getting rid of Octo, said Jamie.

That night Daddy said, Damn thing's going after its *own* now.

What's that? said Ma. She was feeding Jacob.

The monster ate one of them snails, said Daddy.

Not a monster, said Jamie.

That thing . . . said Ma.

I hate it! said Rebecca.

Shut up! said Jamie.

You shut up, said Rebecca.

You both shut up and eat, said Daddy.

I don't see why Jamie gets to keep that stinky thing and I don't get to have a dog! said Rebecca.

Yeah! Dog! said Nancy.

Shut up, said Jamie.

Jamie gets the aquarium because he's the oldest, said Ma. When you turn thirteen we'll think about letting you get a dog.

That is so unfair! said Rebecca.

Until then, said Ma, there's no use in whining about it.

That is so unfair! I hate this! He gets whatever he wants!

Do not, said Jamie.

Now listen you two, said Daddy.

Yes*sir*, said Rebecca. You get whatever you want just because you're a boy and you're stupid.

Becca! said Ma.

I am *not* stupid, said Jamie.

All right, said Daddy. He was standing up.

Nancy was crying now.

I hate this place! said Rebecca twisting out of her chair. I *hate* it! The chair fell over and she ran off.

Becca! yelled Daddy walking after her.

Now Jamie, settle down, said Ma moving toward him. Don't cry honey.

Nancy wailed.

Jacob banged his tray.

Jamie hush now, please honey, don't cry. Ma's hands were on Jamie's shoulders.

Judith! Daddy yelled from the other room. Will you shut him up?

Hush sweetheart.

Nancy was crying.

Judith!

I am not stupid, said Jamie.

Shh-shh-shh.

Now that all the others are eaten, Jamie feeds Octo dead shrimp from the store. Ma lets him.

Octo doesn't move much now. For one thing he's too big. His legs are the length of the tank, and then some. They reach the far end then coil against the glass. The coils twitch. He heaves in, stops, then his funnel opens and water billows out, pushing aside the blue gravel till there's a bare spot. Sometimes he gets up and his skin turns into spines and he glides to a different corner. For a few seconds every part of him is flushed pink, coiling and uncoiling, then he's still again.

He's bored, thinks Jamie, plopping a shrimp into the tank. He likes eating live things better. The shrimp flutters down and lands on one of the coils. Octo doesn't move, but his eyes now watch the shrimp from across the tank. Nancy kneels down next to Jamie. Sit still, Nancy. Maybe he'll eat it while we're watching.

Octo breathes in . . . breathes out. Two legs begin to uncoil.

Rebecca passes behind Jamie and Nancy on the way to her room, then comes back and looks into the tank. Jamie can see her reflection in the glass. She puts her hands on her hips, all bratty.

Is that thing eating?

Shhhh! say Jamie and Nancy. Octo has turned the underside of two legs toward the shrimp. Now the shrimp starts to inch up Octo's legs, being passed from one sucker to the next, toward his mouth.

I cannot even *tell* you guys how much that grosses me out, says Rebecca.

Octo freezes.

Shut up! whispers Jamie.

Go on, Becca, says Nancy. You're ruining it.

No problem! says Rebecca and she tosses her hair and marches off to her and Nancy's bedroom and closes the door behind her. Then her music comes on, loud.

Octo begins again, slowly passing the shrimp from sucker to sucker.

I don't think it's gross, whispers Nancy.

Good, whispers Jamie.

I like Octo.

Well I think he likes you, too.

Really? How can you tell?

Well, when he's scared he turns white, and when he's mad he turns red. But now he's his normal color. That means he's comfortable with you. He knows you like him, so he's not afraid.

You mean he can tell me from Rebecca or Ma?

Of course he can, Nancy.

And I'm the only one he likes?

Uh-huh . . . other than me . . . and maybe Elsie.

So can I always watch him eat?

Uh-huh.

Can I feed him?

No. I have to feed him.

Okay.

Without moving too much, Jamie puts his arm around Nancy. Octo freezes for a second, the shrimp already half under his mantle. Then he draws in the rest.

Jamie goes to the bathroom and makes seawater. Before dinner is when he's allowed, because no one else needs the bathtub. He fills the tub half-way, adds a teaspoon from the blue bottle to take away the chlorine, then adds a scoop of sea salt, pushes up his sleeves, and swishes the water with his hands. He drops in the little glass hydrometer to measure the saltiness, and leaves it for a while.

During dinner, Elsie calls and tells Ma she's still sick and won't come tomorrow. Ma will have to leave him his lunch and set out his pills again. Elsie was sick yesterday, too.

She's not quitting, is she? asks Jamie.

No, she's not quitting, says Daddy, she's just sick, right Ma?

I don't think she's quitting, Jamie.

Jamie would be sad if Elsie quit.

Gloria, the caretaker before Elsie, had quit. Jamie had fired Rita, the one before Gloria, because he hated her. She was always late and hardly talked to him and made the same thing every day—macaroni and cheese and an apple. Jamie's proud of this. I fired her, he likes to say. Before Rita, Jamie used to go to school during the mornings at Empire State Developmental Center. He got kicked out because of his Fits of Rage. He's glad, though. He couldn't stand going to school with retards. Now that his Fits of Rage have stopped they might send him back. But he'd rather stay home.

After dinner, he checks the hydrometer in the bathtub. The water is just right so he takes a bucket to the living room. He sucks on the siphon to get it going and accidentally takes in a salty mouthful. He spits it into the empty bucket. Then he gently pours in some new water as old water runs through the siphon, filling the empty bucket.

Octo watches him calmly. He's used to all this.

Late that night, Jamie has a dirty dream. He wakes up, and he's made a mess. This has happened before. The first time Ma said that it was okay. This kind of thing was supposed to happen, and it was nothing to cry about. She said next time he should go to the bathroom, clean up, and go back to bed. No big deal.

But Jamie can't help but feel ashamed. He holds his privates tight with both hands. The digital alarm clock says 12:23. He feels weak and he wants to cry. He wants to fast-forward time until he's clean again and back in bed and about to fall asleep.

He slips out of bed and shuffles into the dark hall, hunched over, still holding himself. He's careful not to make any noise—he doesn't want anyone to find him. Ma and Daddy's light is still on so he's extra-quiet as he passes their door. They're talking.

I'll take him to the docks at Williamsburg and we can dump it in the river. If he thinks it'll survive he won't get that upset.

Ron, there's no way we're going to do this without him throwing a fit. I just don't think it's worth it.

Well it has to happen sometime. The living room smells like shit, the thing is huge. Sure, it was cute for a while, he had somethin to be excited about, he was real responsible about it, but it's gotten way out of hand. You looked at it lately? It's huge! It must be fuckin miserable in that little tank.

I know, I know.

You just explain how sad Mr. Octopus is, Judith. Make him feel bad for keepin it in a tank when it could out in the ocean with its little sea friends . . .

Oh Ron, don't make a joke.

I'm not makin a joke. You explain it to him, and then the three of us will go for a little drive down to the river—Jamie, Pops, and the monster. Simple's that.

That's not going to work! That's not how Jamie thinks. He loves it. He doesn't talk about anything else.

All the more reason . . .

I know, all the more reason to get rid of it. It's not good for him anymore. All I'm saying is . . . I don't know. We just better be ready for a fight.

As Ma says this, her voice is louder and there are footsteps. Jamie runs back to his room and ducks behind the door. Ma opens her bedroom door and the hall is brighter. Then the bathroom door closes and he hears the sink running. Jamie tears off his pajamas, wipes himself with the shirt, and stuffs it under the other clothes in the hamper. He opens the bottom drawer carefully and pulls on clean pajamas. Then he curls up in bed, and pulls the covers over his head, trembling. The bathroom door opens, the light flicks off.

I'm made of rock, thinks Jamie. I'm a statue. He holds his breath. Ma's footsteps come down the hall, past her own door, to his.

Jamie? she whispers from his doorway.

He holds completely still.

She pauses. One onethousand, two onethousand, three onethousand. Then her feet pad away.

You can breathe again but don't cry. Don't cry don't cry don't cry. Four onethousand, five onethousand, six onethousand. Did she close her door?

He hears Ma close her bedroom door.

Don't cry don't cry.

He thinks of the things that usually put him to sleep.

He's in a treasure chest at the bottom of the ocean.

He's a baby chick still in its shell.

There's a secret about Octo that Ma and Daddy don't know. Octo once escaped from the tank.

It happened at about one o'clock on a Tuesday afternoon three weeks ago. Jamie had been looking at a comic book on his bed, waiting for Elsie, when he heard a loud bump come from the living room. Elsie? he called, but she usually buzzed once or twice to be let in before she used her key. Jamie ran to the living room and saw the tank tipped over on its side and water running across the stand and pouring down, turning the orange carpet brown. Octo was heaving himself across the carpet with his back legs, waving his two front legs before him. His body was pale, almost white. He reached the corner between the bookshelf and the wall, stopped, huddled into the corner and reached up, searching the wall with his front legs. He whipped them around the bookshelf and pulled down some books which fell open onto the floor.

Oh no, oh no, said Jamie, stomping the floor, not knowing what to do. He ran to the bathroom, started filling the tub with cool water, threw in a scoop of sea salt, then ran back to the living room. Octo had dragged himself along the wall to the sofa, coiled his legs around the sofa's feet, and was stuffing himself beneath.

Oh no! cried Jamie. He grabbed Octo's body and pulled. Octo turned from white to red at Jamie's touch and black ink dribbled onto the floor. Jamie had never felt Octo before. Octo's skin was sticky, and as Jamie pulled he felt like rubber. Oh please Octo, let go. Jamie quit pulling, knelt, and started unwrapping Octo's legs from the sofa's feet. Another of his legs coiled around Jamie's arm. Please, pleeeease, Jamie was crying now. Finally Octo gave up. His whole body relaxed and Jamie picked him up. He was much heavier than Jamie imagined. His legs dangled and tried to wrap around Jamie as he carried Octo to the bathroom and put him into the tub. Octo rippled red and white and again squirted ink at Jamie. He lunged away from the running water to the far end of the tub and gathered his legs in coils with the white suckers showing. I'm so sorry, Octo. Jamie hated to scare Octo so. Don't move, just sit still. Jamie turned off the water and ran back to the living room. He knew he had to settle himself down and get things cleaned up before Elsie came, but he couldn't stop crying. Stop crying! he said to himself and struck his fist hard against his thigh. Stop! Stop! Stop!

He righted the tank, replaced the cover and light that Octo had pushed onto the floor, and dragged it, stand and all, into the coat closet. He scooped up the gravel that had fallen onto the carpet and threw it in the kitchen trash. He went to the bathroom to get towels and Octo was still curled up, pale now, with dark rings around his eyes, and the water was murky with his ink. Just stay there. Everything's gonna be okay. Jamie grabbed three towels from the shelf, ran back to the living room and started mopping up the water on his hands and knees. It stunk and everything was still blurry even though he had stopped crying and his nose dripped and he didn't wipe it.

The buzzer buzzed.

Oh no. He quickly bunched up the towels and threw them into the closet. Then he went to the bathroom and looked at himself in the mirror. His eyes were red and wet and his hair was a mess. He washed his hands, splashed his face and flattened his hair.

The buzzer buzzed twice more impatiently.

Okay, Octo, just be quiet. Everything's okay.

He went back to the living room, but before he could buzz her in, he heard Elsie coming up the stairs.

Jamie? What's goin on? You okay?

Jamie undid the latches and opened the door for her. Yeah, I was just going to the bathroom.

You sure? You been cryin? She touched his chin and made him look her in the eye.

Nuh-uh.

Phew. Elsie wrinkled her nose and fanned herself with her hand. That pet of yours stinks to high heaven. I don't know why your parents . . . but she didn't finish because she knew it upset Jamie when she talked bad about Octo. She limped to the kitchen, without noticing the dark spot on the carpet in the corner, or that the tank was missing.

She opened the fridge and bent over. Bologna again? Or beans and franks?

Bologna, please, said Jamie sitting down at the kitchen table.

How's your Mom and Dad?

They're all right.

Yeah? They gettin along?

I guess.

You're lucky kid, you know that? To have a family that gets along. You should see my family. Get us all in one room, everybody's either yellin at each other or not speakin to each other. One or the other.

We don't always get along. We fight.

Take my little sis Sarah. She hasn't talked to her daughter for two years, *two years*, and ya know why? Because she married an Italian Roman Catholic. Two years! You know how long that is? It's torture for both of them, but they won't give in and call the other. I tell her, Sarah, you're missing out on your daughter and your beautiful grandson. He's gonna grow up not knowing you. Why do this to yourself? But she won't budge. So stubborn just like our father. Mayonnaise, right?

Right.

And mustard?

Right.

Anyways, so she won't budge. I tell her, you're a Jew livin in Bensonhurst. You run the risk. What do you expect? Now if I could show her your parents, maybe that would do somethin. Your mother's Jewish right?

Yeah.

And your father's an Italian Roman Catholic, right?

He's Italian.

And look, they get along, they live in this nice apartment, they have good-lookin kids . . .

Elsie pinched Jamie's cheek, but he didn't smile.

What's the matter kiddo? You're not talkin to me.

Jamie had only been half-listening to her. He had thought he heard a sloshing sound from the bathroom, then decided it was his imagination.

I don't know, he said. I don't feel good. I'm sick.

Well go lay down then. I'll call you when it's ready. You don't look so good. She put the back of her hand against his forehead. Go lay down. Rest. Go on.

On the way to his bedroom, Jamie peeked into the bathroom. Octo was still in the same position, but he had returned to his normal spotted pinkish-brown. Just a few more minutes, whispered Jamie and closed the door.

He lay on his bed, closed his eyes, and listened. Elsie began to sing in the kitchen. Jamie believed in the power of crossing fingers. He crossed his fingers on both hands and tried to cross his toes in his shoes. *Please don't go to the bathroom,* he said in his mind. *Don't even go in the living room. Just stay in the kitchen.* If she found Octo and saw the mess she would tell Ma and Daddy and they would hate Octo more than they already did. They might even decide he had outgrown the aquarium and make Jamie get rid of him. He imagined taking Octo back to the pet store. The man would be surprised to see how big Octo had gotten and he'd say it'd be easy to sell Octo to a new owner. He'd put Octo in a tiny tank, and Octo's frightened eyes would watch Jamie. He wouldn't understand why he was back there. What if the new owner didn't feed him right or change the water? Now Jamie was crying a little, just imagining it.

Elsie's singing burst through the kitchen door and into the hallway. Jamie crossed his fingers so tight his knuckles popped. The bathroom door slammed. Then Elsie screamed. Jamie screamed too. He ran to his doorway to see Elsie backing into the hall, clutching her chest with one hand and holding up her pants with the other.

Elsie! It's okay! He just got out and I haven't had a chance . . .

What in the hell? Elsie tucked in her big shirt and zipped up her pants. Scared the livin . . . Look at me. I'm shakin like a leaf. What in the hell is that thing doin in there, boy?

Don't tell, Elsie, please! He just got out and I had to put him somewhere till . . .

Got out? Oh God, I have to sit down.

Jamie followed her to the kitchen, tugging on her shirtsleeve. Please, Elsie, don't tell Ma and Daddy. It's nothing really. I just gotta put him back and everything'll be okay.

Quit pullin me, kid. Elsie sat down heavily at the kitchen table and put her palm to her forehead.

You're not gonna tell, are you Elsie?

Settle down. Just give me a second. You said it got out? What do you mean, it got out?

He just pushed the lid off his tank and crawled out.

Oh Jesus.

No, it's okay, Jamie wailed. He never did it before. I'll just stick the lid on tighter. Don't tell! Jamie clutched Elsie's arm and shook her.

Would you get off? Elsie pushed him. I won't tell, just settle down, kid. Quit cryin. I'm the one who just got the pee scared outta me.

So you won't tell?

No I won't tell. None of my business anyways.

Jamie sat down and wiped his eyes. Really?

Yeah. But you better clean it up. And if they ever do find out, I didn't know nothin and had nothin to do with it. You got that?

Yeah.

And you owe me one, kid. Now eat. I'm leavin. This place is too much for an old woman. Damn near gave me a heart attack.

Okay.

And don't go tellin your mother I left early either.

Okay.

Don't get paid to deal with this.

After she left, Jamie cleaned up. He sprayed disinfectant on the carpet. He went to the bathroom, dipped the bucket into the bathtub, and nudged Octo toward it. Octo calmly climbed in. He made all new water for the tank, and took bucketful after bucketful to the living room. It took all afternoon. He tested the water. Then, very carefully, he poured in Octo. He fastened the lid to the top of the tank with a few pieces of black electrical tape.

Since then, Octo has never escaped, though Jamie sometimes finds him snaking one leg up to press against the lid.

Rebecca hasn't talked to Jamie or even looked at him for two days. She goes through these phases, when she's so sick of him she has to pretend he doesn't exist. If he says anything to her she gives him a dirty look or just turns and walks away.

This time she's mad because she's tired of sharing a room with Nancy. Jamie's always had his own room, she complained to Ma. Why can't *he* share for a while? Ma told her that Jamie is a teenager and needs his own space and went on about how he spends the whole day at home while she gets to go to school and to her friends' houses—talking like Jamie wasn't listening even though he was.

Two days went by, Rebecca not saying a word to Jamie. Then, on the third day, Rebecca comes home from school earlier than usual, before Ma and Daddy are home from work. Jamie's watching videos on TV. Rebecca sits down on the far end of the sofa. Jamie looks over. She stares at the TV, scowling.

Hi, says Jamie.

Rebecca looks at him calmly, then turns back to the TV. They sit in silence, then Rebecca says, You know, you could like, volunteer to share a room with Nancy. It's only fair.

Why should I?

'Cause! You've always had your own room, and I've always shared. I never get any privacy. I can't even talk on the phone in private. I'm either out here and everyone can hear me or I'm in there and Nancy's crawling all over my bed wanting me to play with her. I have to shut myself in the hall closet to have a simple conversation!

You can take the phone into my room if you want.

That's not enough! I want to have my own room! Look, we can trade off. I can have your room for a few months then you can have it back for a while, like that.

No. I need to be by myself.

Oh screw you, Jamie! You get everything you want and you just can't share, can you!

Screw *you!*

I hate you, you know that? Rebecca yells and throws a pillow across the sofa at Jamie. Sometimes I wish you'd just die!

Shut up! Shut up or I'll tell!

Screw you, you big baby! You are such a pain in my butt.

How am I a pain in your butt? I leave you alone. I don't even talk to you!

You don't even *know* how miserable you make me, Jamie. You should hear how the kids at school make fun of me! They say I have a retard brother and it must run in the family. I get that all the time because of you!

Jamie lunges at Rebecca, punching aimlessly. Rebecca shrieks, pushes him onto the ground and kicks him hard. He pulls her down, and they roll across the carpet, punching and slapping until Jamie's head strikes the leg of the coffee table. He lets out a hoarse bawl and digs his teeth into Rebecca's arm. She pushes and scratches his face until he lets go and curls into a ball.

I hate you! she screams. Her voice cracks and she bursts into tears. She hits him again and stands up. I hate you so much!

You're gonna feel bad later for saying that, Jamie whimpers.

No I won't! I'll never feel bad 'cause it's the truth and I'll never say I'm sorry! She stumbles away from Jamie.

He feels beneath his eye. There's a little blood.

Look what you did! he cries.

I don't care! She's standing beside Octo's tank, holding her arm where Jamie bit her. You're such a sissy! I can't believe you bit me! She glances down at Octo. You and your stupid ugly pet. She hits the glass with her fist and Octo glides to the opposite corner.

Leave him alone, says Jamie. He jumps to his feet and moves toward her.

Daddy's getting rid of that thing, you know, says Rebecca, backing away from Jamie into the hallway.

He is not!

Yes*sir!* I heard him tell Ma he's gonna pour Lysol in there and kill it.

What?

And she told him not to and he said it was the only way to get rid of it and you'd think it just died.

Liar! Jamie lunges for her but she runs into her bedroom, slams the door and locks it. Jamie pounds on the door. Liar! You're lying!

Am *not*, comes Rebecca's voice and she laughs meanly. Your stupid pet's dead!

Jamie howls and beats the door.

No response.

Rebecca! You're lying, aren't you! When did you hear that?

Rebecca is ignoring him now. She turns on her music, then starts to sing along. He pounds one more time then goes to his room, locks the door, and lays down, trembling. He thinks back to when Octo ate the hermit crab. It was the last one to go and the only one Jamie actually watched Octo eat.

He had been sitting by the tank watching the crab overturning gravel with it's scissor-claws, looking for food algae to eat. It was happier, Jamie thought, now that it didn't have to compete with the snails.

Suddenly, Octo pounced, covering the crab with his legs and quickly drawing it under his mantle. The crab scrambled under Octo for just a second, then it was still.

Wow, Jamie whispered to himself, and he thought, should I have stopped him? But how could I? He was so quick! Jamie had not known Octo could move so quickly.

Now, laying on his bed, Jamie thinks of how Octo fools everyone by being so calm. He spends his life sitting, watching, taking in what's going on, so everybody thinks that's all he can do. Then, when he needs to, he strikes quick like a snake.

Ma knocks on the door. Jamie?

I'm taking a nap, Ma.

Everything okay?

Yes. Go away, please.

Jamie lies on his bed thinking until Ma knocks again and says, Wake up, honey. Dinner's ready.

Okay. Just a minute.

He rolls out of bed, tucks in his shirt, and stands up straight. He walks out, down the hall, and into the dining room.

Jacob is laughing and smearing gravy across his face and kicking the legs of the high chair. Eat right, Jacob, says Ma, who's spooning mashed potatoes onto her plate.

Daddy's cutting Nancy's roast beef for her and telling a story from work about how Johnny Rosso's gonna transfer to the Bronx rather than deal with the district supervisor, who everyone hates.

Mommy, why isn't Rebecca talking? whines Nancy.

Mind your own business, says Rebecca.

Is there something wrong, Rebecca? asks Ma.

No. Tell Nancy to mind her own business.

Jamie! says Ma. What's that on your face?

Everyone looks at Jamie who's standing in the doorway.

Huh?

You have a scratch on your cheek, honey, says Ma standing up. You're hurt.

Oh.

Ma holds his chin and looks close under his eye and says, There's dried blood. Who did this?

Everyone's watching except Rebecca who's frowning down at her plate.

Jamie says, Rebecca.

Rebecca doesn't look up.

You two had a fight? Is that what's wrong? said Ma turning toward Rebecca.

Rebecca shakes her head and quietly says, No.

Ma turns to Jamie, who says, We were just playin, Ma. It was an accident.

Ma licks a napkin and wipes hard under his eye. Too much roughhousing. You two should be careful.

Ow! Easy, Ma.

They sit down. Jamie eats quietly while Daddy goes on with his story. Ma alternates between listening to Daddy and cleaning up Jacob, who has settled down now and is shoving one spoonful of mashed potatoes after another into his mouth. Rebecca doesn't look up. Nancy glances from Jamie to Rebecca, then back to Jamie. She begins to cry quietly. After a minute, Ma notices.

Nancy, what's wrong?

Nancy sobs and big tears fall into her food.

Honey! What is it?

Nancy wipes her nose and between sobs says, Jamie and Becca hate each other.

Nancy, they don't hate each other, says Daddy.

Mind your own business, Nancy, says Rebecca.

Shush, Rebecca! says Ma, then to Nancy, Sweetheart, everything's all right.

Stop crying and eat, says Daddy.

It's okay, Nancy, says Jamie quietly because he's next to her. Shh.

Nancy doesn't stop crying, but wipes her face with her napkin and begins to eat again.

Jamie is surprised the next day when the buzzer buzzes at one o'clock and it's Elsie. She hasn't come since Monday, and it's Friday.

Elsie, you're back!

I'm back? Where'd I go? Just been a little sick.

Are you all better now?

I'm a little better. When you're my age you're never *all* better. How bout you? You been okay by yourself?

Yeah, Ma's been leavin lunch for me, and I just sit around and watch TV. Pretty boring. I thought maybe you'd quit, and Ma just hadn't told me.

Quit? Na. Why would I quit?

I don't know. I thought maybe you just got sick of me.

What are you talkin about? Sick of my little friend? Elsie shakes Jamie by the shoulders and he laughs. No way!

Elsie sits down at the kitchen table and Jamie tells her about how mean Rebecca was to him and about the fight. Telling the story makes his chest tighten and his eyes tear, but he stays calm, even when he gets to the part about Octo.

And she told me Daddy's gonna kill Octo. She said he's gonna poison him and not tell me a thing about it.

Poison him?

Yeah. Pour Lysol in his tank and kill him.

Sounds like your sister's making up stories.

You think so?

Jamie, your sister's havin a hard time. You gotta leave her alone when she wants to be left alone . . .

I *do!*

. . . and sometimes you gotta leave her alone even when she wants your attention, ya see? Once you prove she can't make you laugh or cry just like that, she'll start treatin you like a real person. Things'll be okay, kid. Wait and see. Elsie puts her hand on Jamie's shoulder and heaves herself up out of her chair. She goes to the fridge.

Jamie says, So last night I didn't dream about anything but Daddy killing Octo. I spent all morning checking where all the poisonous stuff is, like Lysol, bleach, fingernail-polish remover . . . sort of memorizing how everything's arranged under all the sinks.

Why?

So if I find Octo dead, and I see that the Lysol's gone or the bleach is in a different place, I'll know Daddy did it.

Jamie, you're dad's not gonna kill it. And if he did, then what? There are more important things . . .

At least I'd know, Elsie. I'd know he did it.

Elsie was quiet. Then she said again, There are more important things, kid. What happens if the octopus dies on its own, eh? I wouldn't be surprised. It's way too big for that tank. It hardly moves anymore. What then? You gonna blame your dad for that?

Not if he doesn't do it.

I'm just afraid you're gonna get all upset and blame him anyways. Just remember, kid, he's your dad. He wants what's best for you and you gotta respect that.

What if he doesn't *know* what's best for me? What if he does what's bad for me?

You gotta respect him still.

That's not fair.

But that's how it works.

Well . . . he doesn't want what's best for Octo. That's for sure.

Ah, what're we arguin over anyways? says Elsie, setting a bowl of soup in front of Jamie. Your dad's not gonna kill Octo.

But Elsie's wrong. Late that night, Jamie is going in and out of sleep. He can't get comfortable. In his dream he's in tentacles and branches and seaweed. He's holding his breath, then he gasps, surprised that he can breathe water. Now he's out of his dream and out of sleep and he kicks off his sheet cause it's hot. Now he's underwater again and the difference between being awake and being asleep doesn't make the same sense. He's at a wall of coral and he touches the surface. It's sticky. His hands stick. Then his nose burns at breathing bleach. Or is it just the thought of breathing bleach?

A bump from the living room yanks him out of sleep. He knows what it is, but he can't believe it—partly because he knew it would happen (and can never believe when those things actually happen), and partly because his head's only halfway out of the dream.

He's out of bed and stumbling down the hall and he hears Daddy's voice. *Shit . . . Shit!*

There's the tank, knocked to the floor, the glass broken like a spiderweb. The lights go dark, then flicker back on. One big and one small spot of wet are growing on the carpet: the smelly tank water that poured against the wall over the socket, and the ammonia that grows out of a plastic bottle. Daddy's coming toward Jamie. Aw . . . now Jamie . . . Lights off again, then on. Octo's white on the orange carpet with all his legs coiled tight to him, polka-dot suckers exposed. Jamie, c'mon . . . back to your room . . . The socket sparks and the lights go off except the hall light. Jamie's mind is crying like a baby and his body is flying into a Fit of Rage.

Daddy grabs his arms and holds him down. Easy Jamie! Settle down!

Ma, in her nightgown, rushes in. Ron! What's going on? she asked. She clutches Jamie from behind and he elbows her, but she holds on. Shhhh, she whispers into his ear.

Between Ma and Daddy, Jamie can't move.

What did you do Ron? asks Ma.

What do you think? he asks. Shoulda done it long ago.

How can you say that?

They think Jamie's too frantic to hear, but he's taking it all in.

Let me go! he says again and again, first screaming, then his voice cracks into a whimper. Please, let me go.

They let him struggle away.

Nancy! yells Daddy, Go back to bed! Nancy, who was standing in the doorway in her nightgown, runs off.

Jamie picks up Octo. His long legs drop limp, almost to the floor. Where are you taking that? asks Daddy. Jamie, sobbing, carries Octo down the hall. Ma follows him to the bathroom and watches him put Octo in the tub and start filling it, adding sea salt bit by bit.

Now Jamie, what are you doin? asks Daddy from the doorway.

He might live! wails Jamie.

Jamie, your pet's dead. And it's not just me that killed it either.

Go away! screams Jamie. I hate you! This is the worst thing that ever happened and you did it!

Don't you talk to me like that, kid.

Daddy steps forward, but Ma stands to stop him. Ron, don't. Just leave him alone.

What, has this place gone nuts, that a kid can talk that way to his dad?

Go away! screams Jamie.

Ron, go. I'll take care of this.

You two are nuts. Ya gonna bring that thing back to life? The thing is dead. And it's happier that way I'm sure.

No he's not, says Jamie. He might live if we keep him in here. We can take him to the ocean and he'll get better.

Take him to the ocean? Daddy laughed. But Ma was already saying, Honey, it's all right. We can take him to the ocean.

What did you say, Judith?

Go, Ron! she yelled.

Nuh-uh, this is crazy. This isn't right. You think a kid could talk to his dad that way when I was a boy? My Pop woulda smacked me upside the head. None of this coulda happened. This is all so fuckin nuts! An octopus livin in my fuckin living room, stinking up the place, and Jamie thinks it's the most important thing on earth. It's all that matters, right? Even though everyone else hates it and the girls are scared to death of it, right? Now Jamie runs the place. We gotta pay good money to feed the ugly thing, so Jamie don't get upset. Fuckin *nuts!* And if it decides to take a stroll around the apartment while we're at work, no problem! Jamie's in charge now and the octopus can do what it likes.

How did you know that Octo got out? cries Jamie.

Elsie. How else?

Ron!

Jamie's head drops and he doesn't move or say anything for a moment. Daddy clenches and unclenches his fists. Then Jamie says in a small voice, so they know he means it, I never want her to come here again.

Oh Honey, says Ma, and puts her arms around him.

I don't want her anymore. I don't want any more care providers.

See? says Daddy. Thinks he runs things now.

Judith waves him away.

Jamie turns his back to Daddy and looks down into the tub.

Don't worry, Jamie, says Ma as she turns off the water. Tomorrow morning we'll take him to the ocean and let him go. He'll be okay.

Daddy stomps down the hall yelling something, but no one's listening now.

Jamie puts the bucket on the floor of the backseat, gets in, and braces it between his knees. Nancy sits in the back too, and Jacob's in his seat between them. Rebecca's in front with Ma.

While Jamie was putting Octo into the bucket, Ma had woken up Nancy and Rebecca and got them excited to go on rides at Coney Island. Jamie knows it's just because Daddy's grumbling and needs to be left alone.

They drive. The avenues are like the alphabet—M, N, O, P—leading to the ocean. They pass housing developments, nice neighborhoods with lawns, Jewish men with hats and beards.

Octo looks smaller, sort of deflated. The water is foggy with bits of brown flesh.

Suddenly the signs aren't in English anymore. Nancy asks what kind of writing it is and Ma says it's Russian and it means we're almost there.

Ma parks and they get out of the car. She puts Jacob in the stroller, and they and walk across the lot. The bucket is heavy so Jamie has to walk slow, squinting in the bright sun, but he doesn't want Ma to help him. They walk down a narrow alley between two old brick apartment buildings the color of sand. They climb stairs to the boardwalk. Rebecca helps Ma with the stroller. Old people sunning on benches open their eyes just a little to watch them cross the boardwalk. The sky is perfectly blue and steam is rising from the sand into the hot morning. The stroller won't go onto the sand, so they all wait on the bottom step while Jamie walks across the beach. Nancy wants to go, too, but Ma says to hush, let Jamie do it alone.

It's hard to walk on the soft sand. Jamie staggers across the beach and climbs onto a jetty made of big rocks extending out into the ocean. He hugs the bucket to his chest. It smells bad, but then ocean air gusts the smell away. Jamie hobbles from stone to stone down the jetty, careful not to slip.

About halfway down, he stops. The water looks deep, with sand churning up from the bottom. He puts the bucket down on a flat stone and sits down beside it. A big wave comes and soaks his foot. The water is freezing cold. Much colder than Octo's tank.

But it's okay, because Jamie knows that Octo is really dead. Daddy killed him. Slowly, he tips the bucket. Water trickles, then pours out, then Octo slides out like a lump of trash. He plunges into the water and sinks out of sight. Bye, Octo, says Jamie.

He imagines Octo coming back to life down there in the dark. Filling back up like a balloon, spreading his legs and crawling to deeper water. He imagines it, but his heart isn't in it. He's just telling himself a story, like Ma and Daddy do, to settle him down.

He leaves the bucket there because he doesn't need it anymore, and returns to the others.

They all walk down the boardwalk toward the amusement park. They stop at an open-air restaurant for fried egg sandwiches and tater tots, and sit on a bench watching the ocean while they eat. Nancy and Rebecca are talking about the rides, but Jamie doesn't listen.

People are jabbing umbrellas into the sand and setting up lawn chairs. Two black women in bathing suits wade in the water up to their knees. They laugh and shift from foot to foot, hugging their arms to their chests.

When they're done eating, Ma gathers the trash and says, Well kids, ready for the rides?

Nancy and Rebecca ride the bumper cars, but Jamie stays with Ma and Jacob. The park is getting crowded. He feels nervous. He's not used to being around people.

Ma laughs at Rebecca speeding around in her tiny car, and at Nancy butting heads with a teenage boy. Look Jamie, she says.

Yeah, I see.

They go to another ride where Nancy and Rebecca spin around in cars shaped like bumble bees. The cars go up and down and Nancy shrieks and giggles. After they get off Rebecca says that she's bored with these kids' rides. She says she wants to ride the roller coaster. Ma says okay, but it's the last ride cause Jamie's tired.

Jamie can't know this but, down on the beach, Octo has washed up onto the sand. He lays in a brown tangle of legs until a wave comes and rearranges him, taking two legs and setting them like clock hands that say three o'clock. Then another takes him further onto the sand and turns him upside down so if you looked, you could see the little beak in the middle where all the legs meet.

Two little girls, twin sisters, are digging with pink plastic shovels. One notices Octo.

What is that thing?

I dunno.

They walk over and look down at him.

It's like a sea animal or something. *¡Mira Mama!* she calls to their mother.

¿Mama, qué es esto? asks her sister. She takes her plastic shovel and gives Octo a shy prod.

Their mother, sitting in a lawn chair, lifts her sunglasses. *¡No lo toques, Mija!* she yells.

Ew, says the first girl. That thing is so gross.

But what is it?

I dunno.

¡No lo toques! calls their mother.

There are two signs at the roller coaster: One has an arrow and says YOU MUST BE THIS TALL TO RIDE THE CYCLONE, the other says NO SINGLE RIDERS.

Oh no! whines Rebecca. Nancy's too little, and I can't go on by myself. She looks up at Ma.

Don't look at me, laughs Ma. I've got Jacob.

Rebecca turns to Jamie. Jamie, will you go with me?

Jamie kicks at the dirt.

It'll be fun, Jamie. Please? Otherwise I can't go at all.

Jamie is silent. He doesn't want to go.

And I *really* want to go, says Rebecca.

All right, he says finally.

They walk between the rails and give the man their tickets. There are only four other people riding. They climb into the middle car, the man locks down the guard rail, and the cars begin ticking slowly forward.

Thanks, Jamie.

Jamie doesn't respond.

Look, I feel really bad. I'm sorry I fought with you and stuff. I'm sorry I scratched you . . . And I didn't mean it when I said I hated you. I was just mad.

The car lurches into an incline.

Jamie says nothing. He isn't mad at her, and wishes she'd just leave him alone. He watches the blue sky as they climb up and up.

And I'm sorry your pet's dead. I really am. I'm sorry about everything. Jamie? Come on. Please say you forgive me.

But suddenly they're roaring down. Their hearts leap into their throats and they both scream. Rebecca's scream has a laugh in it, but Jamie's is pure terror, like he's facing death. He grabs Rebecca's arm tight and doesn't let go the whole ride.

Waiting

Martha McPhee

Martha McPhee is the author of four novels: Bright Angel Time, *which was a* New York Times *Notable Book,* Gorgeous Lies, *a National Book Award Finalist,* L'America, *and* Dear Money. *She currently lives in New York City and teaches at Hofstra University. "Waiting" was her first publication.*

THE DAY THAT THE MEN LANDED ON THE MOON OUR father left us. I was seven. Julia was nine. Jane was eleven.

Hot and overcast. The air was opaque and thick, but soft. A visible heat swelled like waves around us, shimmying up our legs. All the trees were still, the way they are before a storm. Our big white house and the bright green lawns, a small pocket in the woods. The excited voice of a newscaster crackled through static on the radio and Jane kept fidgeting with the dial. She had set the radio up in the kitchen window so that we could hear outside. July 20, 1969. Three-thirty, or four.

Jane, Julia, and I were dizzy with excitement, running through the sprinkler on our front lawn. The water fell in crystals and we leapt through them, catching them on our hot skin. Mine tingled and I was happy.

"By the time we're thirty," Julia said, raising her left eyebrow. She could do that. She said she had double-jointed muscles in her eyebrows. "We'll be going to the moon for vacation in spaceships." She clapped her hands and kissed me and I kissed her back and then we twirled around in circles holding hands. Thirty seemed so far away. But Dad had said that time changed as you grew up, it passed more quickly. Years became months, months became weeks, days turned into minutes. Now I was impatient. Julia said that people were already making reservations to go to the moon and the spaceships were all booked-up for years.

Mom watched us from her garden. She was pulling up weeds just the same as every Sunday, nearly hidden among the columbine and purple delphinium. A card table holding a watermelon stood on the lawn near her. We were waiting for Dad to come back from a tennis match before eating supper. Mom and Dad had made a special supper, southern fried chicken with thick, crusty skin and chocolate wafer ice-box cake. Dad promised that we could bring the television out to the lawn and watch the men on the moon while looking up at the moon. I hoped it wouldn't rain.

"It's getting late, Mom," Jane said. "Where's Dad? The *Eagle*'s gonna land soon."

"Don't whine Jane. He's coming, dear. Just be patient," Mom said. "He'll be here any minute." Mom wiped her brow. Her hair was pulled back with a red bandeau and she was sweating. She looked down the driveway, squinting, straining to hear.

It was a long driveway of red gravel that sliced through the trees to the road. Then we heard a car.

"Jane," she said, "aren't you going to fix that damn radio? I can't hear a thing of what he's saying." She started digging again. A heap of weeds were piling up by the edge of the garden. Day lilies trimmed the house and the shutters were freshly painted.

Then, a pale blue Ford sedan roared up the driveway, screeching to a halt. It was a familiar car but it wasn't Dad's. Maybe Dad had borrowed a car. We always borrowed cars when ours broke down. But Brian Cain stumbled out of the driver's seat, flailing a letter in his hand. Brian Cain was a friend of my father's. He and his wife, Camille, came to cocktail parties at our house and always left before our bedtime because he got so drunk. I wondered why he was here now. His hair was white and thick and he was a big man with a potbelly that spilled over his plaid Bermuda shorts. All his flesh was loose, as if it might fall off like meat off a boiled chicken. He stood at his car door, trying to steady himself. His eyelids were red and swollen and his cheeks puffy. But the hand with the letter kept swatting the air.

He slammed his car door and my stomach jumped.

"They've run away," he screamed. "Ya hear me, Eve. They've run away." he screamed again. His voice echoed through the trees, against the house, louder than everything. Even the radio static vanished. "I'm gonna kill that bastard." He stumbled toward my mother. Her face wavered. We were frozen watching, watching as Mom rose from the dirt, above the flowers to approach him, walking in slow motion toward him.

"Brian," she said, soothing. "Brian." Her legs were long and blotched with dirt. She wore her bathing suit with the short skirt of enormous daisies. Little palm prints of dirt stuck to her cheeks. Dirt was in her fingernails, between her toes. "Calm down. What's happened?" The humidity had curled her hair.

Brian breathed heavily. The three of us stood there solemnly. The sprinkler fanned back and forth spraying us and the water turned suddenly cold and unpleasant, prickers piercing my skin. I wished that Dad would hurry up and get home.

"I gotta shotgun an I'm gonna kill the fuckin' bastard," he screamed. Then he started poking at the letter with his index finger stabbing the letter. "I'm gonna find 'em and kill 'em." He turned over the card table and the watermelon smashed into the grass. Raw pink swarming with black seeds like flies. Water seeped into my ears, clogging them, muffling sounds and everything blurred.

"Go inside, girls!" Mom said quickly and vehemently. "Brian, let's talk about this. Brian." She was talking more quickly now. "Jane, don't just stand there, take them inside."

Jane took us to the laundry room and locked the door. That's where we hid sometimes while playing games. That's where Mom sent us when we misbehaved at the dinner table. I was giddy with that feeling of getting away with something bad, squirming to get hidden.

"What about Mom?" Julia said. "We shouldn't leave her there."

"Yeah, what about Mom?" I asked looking to Jane. I was shivering.

"Shush. She's O.K.," Jane said. Her eyes were wide and remote. She wrapped a towel around me. The laundry room smelled of everything clean: of lemons and ammonia and bleach and detergent. Our clothes were neatly stacked in three piles. Summer jumpers and underpants with pink balloons. But folded you couldn't distinguish whose pile was whose. I started to laugh. White blouses, just pressed, danced on their hangers in a breeze sneaking through the window.

Julia cried and pulled me close to her. Her skin was spongy and wet and I laughed some more. Then Jane began to cry too, wrapping her arms around both me and Julia. But I continued to laugh. My bathing suit was too small. The straps were slicing into my shoulders. I buckled at the waist, wheezing uncontrollably. I couldn't help it. Julia's suit would become mine and Jane's hers. I wondered if Jane would get Mom's suit with the daisies. I loved that suit.

"Stop," Jane yelled into my ear.

"Where's Dad gone?" I demanded. "When is he coming back?" But they couldn't answer me. They just cried.

Dad had fallen in love with Brian Cain's wife and they had run away together. They went on the summer vacation that we'd planned as a family. First to Maine and then to Nova Scotia. At the moment though, we had no idea where he was. We thought he just needed time. I remembered how he would buy time from us. When we cried he gave us crisp dollar bills and pleaded with us to stop. Time and space were money. He knew about time: it's brevity within the larger scheme of things.

He wanted peace.

Later, the vacation would be included in Mom's long list of things that Dad had stolen from us.

Dad could lift me up easily and set me on his shoulders. On his shoulders I became tall and dizzy. I could see and touch the tops of things. I was above everything but the trees. Above my mother and sisters, swirling around in the field behind our house. The air felt different up there, colder, fresher. I would say, "Run Daddy, run." and clasp my hands around his warm neck. His hands were tight around my ankles. "Run Daddy, run." And Dad ran and ran and ran while I felt the wind against my face and kept my eyes wide.

For a long time after my father left, I was afraid of getting big. I was afraid that when Dad came back I'd be too big for shoulders. Jane and Julia were already too big for his shoulders.

At first, we expected Dad would come back. The four of us lay on Mom's bed and waited. The ceiling fan stirred overhead, slowly and rhythmically, cooling us. All the windows were closed. That was the way Mom wanted it.

While we waited, we watched television. Before we hadn't been allowed but now things were different. We watched the *Million Dollar Movies* and the *Late Movies*, and then the *Late Late Show*. We didn't talk much. We didn't want to disturb Mom. She was tired. We just lay there, waiting to fall asleep. Some nights we watched until the station went dead and the bedroom became blue with electric TV light. Glasses half-filled with water and jars of asprin shimmered on the bedside table. The channel purred a magnetic hum. I tried hard to fall asleep before the others. I was afraid of being left awake alone.

In the mornings we slept late and ate breakfast in bed. Jane put Mom's eyelet apron on over her pajamas and cooked enormous amounts of creamed chipped beef and made large pitchers of orange juice. Julia and I arranged a silver tray with doilies and flowers in a vase.

We hung half-moons of oranges from the glass rims and rolled the silverware into napkins. On the creamed chipped beef we sprinkled lots of parsley. When the tray was ready, Julia and Jane carried it together to Mom's bed. Every morning was the same. We wanted to keep it just that way.

After several days, we started trying things.

"Write him letters," Mom said. She sat up abruptly and looked at us across the bed. It was early afternoon. I was lying on my stomach picking at the cold food on the breakfast tray while Julia examined my scalp. She was looking for things, she said. She was always examining me with Q-tips: my belly button, my ears. I don't know what she was hoping to find on my scalp but her fingertips felt good in my hair.

The curtains were drawn and bright light leaked through the seams. Jane was at the foot of the bed making a food shopping list.

"If you tell him how much you miss him and how much you love him, he'll come back." Mom's eyes were red and puffy, but she smiled a wide hopeful smile. My heart started to race. I thought that Dad didn't know how much we missed him.

So we wrote, furiously, on pads of white paper. Crayons and magic markers spilled out of their boxes, getting lost in the folds of snarled sheets. We worked with determination and Mom was pleased. You could hear pens scribbling over the page. Godzilla roared across the television screen in a landscape filled with giant rocks. I wrote "I love you", just "I love you", at least one hundred times all over my blank white page.

"This is stupid," Jane said. "You promised that we'd go food shopping." She stood up and tossed her pad on the bed. She was standing in front of the television and the light made her nightgown transparent. I could see her thin legs and large underwear. Her eyes were big and dark. Mom said she had Dad's eyes.

"Write, Jane," Mom said. "We need you to." She rested her back against the backboard. It was upholstered in lavender fabric printed with large tulips, just the same as the spread, and it seemed to swallow her up.

"He's not coming back," Jane said. Everything clenched inside me. I could feel the crumbs in the bed. I stopped writing. It was so easy for Jane to ruin things. She sat down and started scraping all the left over creamed chipped beef onto one plate. It had turned thick and wobbly like Jell-o. The little flakes of beef had curled, dried up again. But still I wanted her to leave it alone. I was hungry. I was always hungry.

We never did send the letters. They stayed in the bed with us, accumulating beside books and television guides, the newspapers and rubber bands.

Sometimes we had fun in Mom's bed. We fell in love with movie stars. Mom with Laurence Olivier. Jane with Omar Sharif. Julia and I fought over Clark Gable. A week of Cagney turned into a week of Cooper. And then came three with James Dean. The men had long since returned from the moon.

In mid-August we finally heard from Dad. He sent us a package. It sat on the kitchen counter while Jane decided what we should do. Sunlight caught the glossy parcel paper and it shined. The box became a golden box and the bold black letters of Dad's print shouted out our names.

Jane was at the stove in Mom's apron, stirring. Julia stood at the sink, trying to retrieve and wash plates for our breakfast. The sink was piled with pots and pans and glasses and plates.

"Let's just open it," I said. I couldn't understand why Jane wouldn't open the package. My chest pulsed and I could feel my thumbs throb. It seemed the box was throbbing too.

"We shouldn't open the box," Jane said. Her hair was long and out of braids: her face red from the heat of the stove. The spoon in her hand was covered with a thick film of white cream. "Or maybe we should open it and smash whatever is inside and send it back to him."

"That's absurd," Julia said, moving toward the box. She liked big words. She was a show-off. Of the four of us she was the only one with brushed hair and the only one out of her nightgown. She was wearing her pink leotard and toe slippers. I agreed with Julia, though at first I didn't believe that Jane could be serious.

Jane ripped open the package and inside were three presents wrapped in cheerfully colored paper. Jane reached for one of the presents and Julia grabbed her arm and they started to fight. Their faces went red and splotched. They pulled at each other's hair. But all I could think about was the present. It seemed to grow. My impulse was to grab so I grabbed the present marked for me and ran.

"Traitor," Jane screamed after me. "He doesn't love us anymore, Kate."

I ran through the hall, up the stairs to my room and lay on the bed. I held the present in my arms and remembered Dad's hands. They were strong with long slender fingers and not too much hair. Dad and I had a game. I squeezed his hand four times. He then squeezed mine three times. I squeezed his twice. He squeezed mine once, long and hard. Each squeeze was a word. "Do, you, love, me?" "Yes, I, do." "How, much?" And the last squeeze indicated how much. Sometimes he'd squeeze so hard it would hurt.

I got sick. Fever crept beneath my eyes, making it hard to move them. My body turned to aches and my lungs grew sore. It was a familiar feeling. I had had pneumonia seven times since I was born. It was one of those queer things that I was proud of. Julia and Jane were sent away to a college friend of Mom's who lived in the south. Mom couldn't handle more than one sick child and after awhile she couldn't even handle one. She said the doctor said that it would be best if I went to the hospital. She said, not to worry, that going to the hospital didn't mean I was any more sick than I'd been before. She said that he said it would bring my father back.

I spent two weeks in the hospital and Dad did not come.

Early September I went home. My sisters were still away. I crawled into bed next to Mom and her arm wrapped around my stomach pulling me into her chest. The sheets were gentle and smelled of so many things: of Mom's honeysuckle perfume, of detergent, of sweat.

The house was quiet. The television was off. Outside the sun was sinking into the trees and the sky was striped with paths of color turning first orange then violet and then a deep red. Every so often Mom would wake and stare, blankly, listening. A web of creases surrounded her eyes and they were swollen. She'd fall asleep again, pulling me with her, deeper against her chest. I lay there trying to keep my eyes closed. But they were heavy and static seemed to sizzle beneath the lids.

Then, I heard the sound of wheels rolling over gravel, rolling slowly, cautiously. It was already quite dark on that side of the house. Carefully, I slipped away from Mom and went to the window. A car was sneaking up the driveway, my father's white Volkswagon. Instantly, I was flooded with joy. I shoved the window to open it, but it wouldn't budge. I wanted to scream out to him. I could see him. He stepped from his car, rising tall above it. I could see his head of black curly hair.

"Dad's back," I shouted. "He's back." And I clapped, turning to Mom. But she was already at the bedroom door, locking it. I asked her why and my stomach fell.

"Quick. Be quiet. He's just here to get things," she said.

Her voice was abrupt and sharp. She wrapped her arm in mine and we moved close to the door. In her other hand she clutched the phone.

His footsteps pounded into the rug as he climbed the stairs, one after the next, to Mom's bedroom door. The banister creaked. Blood rang in my ears.

"Eve," he said, knocking. "Open the door." His voice was calm and even. It hadn't changed at all. "We need to talk."

"Go away," she said. "Go away or I'll call the police." She started dialing on the phone.

Almost instantly they were fighting. First about Camille, then about us, then about money. Their voices vibrated in waves into my skin. My eyes were wide and stinging.

"I'm going to come in Eve. I'll smash the door down if I have to," Dad said. The room was messy. The drawers of Mom's bureau hung open and clothes streamed out of them. Dangling bras and underwear. Her taffeta dresses. Her purse strap. Her robe. Books and papers and magazines cluttered the floor. The slow air of the ceiling fan made the papers rise and sink as if they were breathing. Mom was a clean person. She loved being clean. She loved washing behind our ears and scrubbing our necks. I felt sorry for Mom.

"She was sick, damn it," Mom said.

"You spend up a storm. What do you think? That money grows on trees? You put the children in the hospital and run up thousands of dollars of doctors' bills. What do you think I'm made of?" Panic electrified his voice. I couldn't breathe properly.

I had to concentrate to breathe. My tongue felt too big for my mouth. "I won't work another day in my life. I'll go to Hawaii and live on the beach. I'm not going to be burdened with all these bills that you run up carelessly."

It was my fault.

"Daddy," I blurted out. I wanted to explain. There was silence, loud silence. Mom and I sank down, into the rug. It was prickly. Little things were in it. It hadn't been vacuumed in weeks.

"Kate?" he asked. "Is that you, sweety?"

"I was sick Daddy," I said. I swallowed. I needed to swallow.

"Oh baby," he said, drawing out the words. "I didn't mean . . ." He stopped. I could hear him on the other side of the door, sinking down as we just had. I pushed my cheek into the hard wood door. Maybe his cheek was pushed into the hard wood door too. "Baby. Open the door for Daddy."

I thought if I just let him in everything would be all right. I could explain. I thought if I opened the door they could work things out. He would come back.

"Kate," he said. Kate. Kate. It rang in my ears. I reached for the knob and as I did Mom grabbed my arm. In her hand my skin was soothed. Her hands were soft and warm and gentle.

"Tell him no, Kate," she whispered in my ear. "Tell him you don't want to see him."

I said, "No, Dad." A thick lump caught in my throat like cotton and my mouth became dry. "No Daddy, we don't want you. We want you to leave Daddy." Then I started screaming it. "Leave Daddy." My face burned. In fact, my whole body burned. I screamed blindly. "Leave Daddy." And then I heard him cry. I wanted him to cry.

The police came discreetly, without flashing lights. Two solid men in blue suits. And I heard them coming up the stairs and I heard the crackling of their walkie-talkies. I heard them ask my crying father to leave. From the window in the late evening light I saw Dad being escorted to his car, a shadow between two solid figures, his arms linked in theirs. Gently they set him in his car. And just as quietly as he came he drove away.

What They Did

David Means

David Means's most recent short story collection is entitled The Spot. *His other collections are* A Quick Kiss of Redemption, Assorted Fire Events, *and* The Secret Goldfish. *He is a professor of English at Vassar College.*

WHAT THEY DID WAS COVER THE STREAM WITH long slabs of reinforced concrete, the kind with steel rods through it. Maybe they started with a web of rods, then concrete poured over, making a sandwich of cement and steel. Perhaps you'd call it more of a creek than a stream, or in some places, depending on the vernacular, a narrow gorge through that land, a kind of small canyon with steep sides. They covered the cement slabs with a few feet of fill, odds and ends, cement chunks, scraps, bits of stump and crap from excavating the foundation of the house on the lot, which was about fifty yards in front of the stream. Then they covered the scraps and crap with a half foot of sandy dirt excavated near Lake Michigan, bad topsoil, the kind of stuff that wiped out the Okies in the dust bowl storms. Over that stuff they put a quarter foot of good topsoil, rich dank humus that costs a bundle, and then over that they put the turf, rolled it out the way you'd roll out sheets of toilet paper; then they watered the hell out of it and let it grow together while the house, being finished, was sided and prepped for the first walkthroughs by potential owners. His nesting instinct, he explained, shaking hands with Ingersol, the real estate guy. Marjorie Howard rested the flat of her hand on her extended belly and thought due in two weeks but didn't say it. A few stray rocks, or boulders, were piled near the edge of the driveway and left there as a reminder of something, maybe the fact that once this had been a natural tide glen with poplars and a few white birch and an easy slope down to the edge, the drop-off to the creek or brook or whatever it is now hidden under slabs of concrete—already sinking slightly but not noticeable to the building inspector who has no idea that the creek is there because it's one of those out of sight of mind things, better left unsaid so as not to worry the future owners who might worry, if that's their nature, over a creek under reinforced concrete. So all one might see from the kitchen, a big one with the little cooking island in the middle with burners and the wide window, is a slope down to the very end of the yard where a tall cedar fence is being installed, a gentle slope with a very slight sag in the center—but no hint, not in the least, of any kind of stream running through there. In the trial the land-scaper guys—or whatever they are—called it a creek, connoting some-thing small and supposedly lessening the stupidity of what they did. The DA called it a river, likened it to River Styx, or the Phlegethon, the boil-ing river of blood, not citing Dante or anything but just using the words to the befuddlement of the jury, four white men and three white women, three black women, two male Hispanics. Slabs were placed over the creek, or river, whatever, on both adjacent lots, too, same deal, bad soil, humus, rolled turf, sprinkled to high hell until it grew together but still had that slightly fake look that that kind of grass has years and years after the initial unrolling, not a hint of chokeweed or bramble or crabgrass to give it a natural texture. And the river turned to the left further up, into the wasted fields and wooded area slated for development soon but held off by a recession (mainly in heavy industry), pegs with slim fluorescent orange tape fluttering the wind, demarcating future "estates" and cul-de-sacs and gated communities once the poplars and white birch on that section were scalped down to the muddy tire-track ruts. What they did was cover another creek up elsewhere in the same manner, and in doing so they noticed that the slabs buckled slightly upward for some reason, the drying constriction of concrete on the steel rods; and therefore, to counterweight, they hung small galvanized garden buckets of cement down from the centers of each slab on short chains, a bucket per slab that allowed a slight downward pucker until the hardening—not drying, an engineer explained in the trial, but setting, a chemical change, molecules rearrang-ing and so on and so forth—evened it out. So when the rescue guy went down twelve feet sashaying the beam of his miner's lamp around, he saw a strange sight, hardly registered it but saw it, a series of dangling buckets fading out into the darkness above the stream until the creek turned slight-ly toward the north and disappeared in shadow. What they could've done instead, the engineer said, was to divert the stream to the north (of course costing big bucks and also involving impinging on a railroad right-of-way owned by Conrail, or Penn Central), a process that involves trenching out a path, diverting the water, and allowing the flow to naturally erode out a new bed. What they could've done, a different guy said, an environmental architect who turned bright pink when he called himself that, ashamed as he was of tooting his own horn with the self-righteousness of his trade—or so it seemed to Mr. Howard, who of the two was the only one able to compose himself enough to bring his eyes forward. Mrs. Howard dabbled her nose with a shredded Kleenex, sniffed, caught tears, sobbed, did what she had to do. She didn't attend all of the trial, avoiding the part when the photos of the body were shown. She avoided the diagrams of the stream and lot, the charts and cutaways, cross sections of the slabs. Nor could she stand the sight of the backyard, the gaping hole, the yellow police tape and orange cones, and now then, bright as lightning, a television news light floating there, a final wrap-up for the eleven o'clock, even CNN coming back days later for a last taste of it. What they could have done is just leave the stream where it was and buffer it up along the sides with a nice-looking, cut-stone retaining wall because according to one expert, the creek, a tributary into the Kalamazoo River, fed mainly by runoff from a local golf course and woods, was drying up slowly anyhow. In the next hundred years or so it would be mostly gone, the guy said, not wanting to contradict the fact that it might have been strong enough to erode the edges of the slab support and pull it away or something, no one was sure, to weaken it enough for the pucker to form. The pucker is what they called it. Not a hole. It's a fucking hole, Mr. Howard said. No one on the defense would admit that it was one of those buckets yanking down in that spot that broke a hole through. Their side of the case was built on erosion, natural forces, an act of God. No one would admit that it had little or nothing to do with the natural forces of erosion. Except silently to himself Ralph Hightower, the site foreman, who came up with the bucket idea in the first place, under great pressure from the guys in Lansing who were funding the project, and his boss, Rob, who was pushing for completion in time for the walkthroughs. Now and then he thought about it, drank a couple of beers and smoked one of his Red Owls and mulled over his guilt the way someone might mull over a very bad ball game, one that lost someone some cash; he didn't like kids a bit, even innocent little girls, but he still felt a small hint of guilt over the rescue guy having to go down there and see her body floating fifteen yards downstream like that and having to wade the shallows in the cramped dark through that spooky water to get her; he'd waded rivers before a couple of times snagging steelhead salmon and knew how slippery it was going over slime-covered rock. Other than Ralph Hightower and his beer, guilt and blame was distributed between ten-odd people until it was a tepid and watered-down thing, like a single droplet of milk in a large tumbler of water—barely visible, a light haze, if even that. All real guilt hung on Marjorie Howard, who saw her girl disappear, vanish, gulped whole by the smooth turf, which was bright green-blue under a clear, absolutely brilliant spring sky. All that rolled turf was just bursting with photosynthetic zest, although you could still tell it was rolled turf by the slightly different gradient hues where the edges met, melded— this after a couple of good years of growth and the sprinkler system going full blast on summer eves and Mr. Howard laying down carefully plotted swaths of Weed & Feed (she'd just read days before her girl vanished in the yard that it was warmth that caused dormant seeds and such to germinate, not light but simply heat). Glancing outside, her point of focus was past the Fisher Price safety gate, which was supposed to mind the deck stairs. She saw Trudy go down them, her half-balanced wobble walk, just able to navigate their awkward width (built way past code, which is almost worse than breaking code and making them too narrow or too tall, stupidly wide and short for no good reason except some blunder the deck guy made, an apprentice deck kid, really). She was just about halfway across the yard, just about halfway to the cedar fence, making a beeline after something—real or imagined, who will ever know?—in her mind's eye or real eye, the small bird bath they had out there, perhaps. What they did was frame the reinforcement rods—web or just long straight ones—in wooden rectangles back in the woods, or what had been woods and then was just a rut filled muddy spot where, in a few months, another house would come. Frames set up, the trucks came in and poured the concrete in and the cement set and then a large rig was brought in to lift the slabs over to the creek, or stream, or whatever, which by this time was no longer the zippy swift-running knife of water but was so full of silt and mud and runoff from the digging it was more of an oozing swath of brown substance. Whatever fish were still there were so befuddled and dazed they'd hardly count as fish. Lifted them up and over, guiding with ropes, and slapped them down across the top of the stream—maybe twenty in all, more or less depending on how large they were. Then more were put down when they moved up to the next lot, approved or not approved by the inspector who never really came around much anyhow. Then the layers of crappy soil stuff and then the humus and then the rolls of turf while the other guys were roofing and putting up the siding, and the interior guys were cranking away slapping drywall up fast as they could with spackling crews coming behind them, then the painters working alongside the carpet crews with guns popping like wild, and behind them, or with them, alongside, whatever, the electricians doing finishing fixtures and the furnace and all that stuff in conjunction with the boss's orders, and the prefab window guys, too, those being slapped into preset frames, double-paned, easy-to-clean and all that, all in order to get ready for the walkthroughs the real estate guys, operating out of Detroit, had lined up. Already the demand was so high on account of the company which was setting up a new international headquarters nearby. This was a rather remote setting for such a venture, but on account of low taxes (an industrial park) and fax machines and all the new technology it didn't matter where your headquarters were so long as they were near enough to one of those branch airports and had a helipad on the roof for CEOs' arrivals and departures. Housing was urgently necessary for the new people. The walkthrough date in the spring because the company up-and-running date was July first. What the ground did that day was to open up in a smooth, neat little gape, perfectly round, just beneath the weight of the girl—which wasn't more than thirty pounds, maybe less but enough to spar forces already at bay, but that doesn't matter, the facts, the physics, are nothing magical, as one engineer testified, and if this tragedy hadn't've happened—his words—certainly the river itself would have Avon out, eroded the edge, caused the whole slab to fall during some outdoor barbecue or something, a whole volleyball or badminton game swallowed up in a big gulp of earth. There one second, gone the next was how someone, best left unsaid who, but most likely CNN, described what Marjorie Howard saw—or sensed, because really the phrase seems like a metaphysical poem or maybe a philosophical precept (bad choices on the part of the contractors, no, not choice, nothing about choice there, or maybe fate of God if that has to do with it, one local news report actually used the phrase Act of God, if it's a phrase). But it was an accurate account because standing in the kitchen it was like that, seeing her go, watching her vanish, and all the disbelief that she had seeing it, the momentary loss of sanity and the rubbing of her eyes in utter, fantastical disbelief, would burgeon outward in big waves and never go away no matter what, so that between that one second she was there and the one where her little girl was gone was a wide opening wound that would never be filled, or maybe finished is the word. What they did was guide the slabs down, doing the whole job in one morning because the crane was slated to be used on a project all the way over in Plainwell, and then think while eating lunch from black lunchtins afterwards, feet up on a stump, Ho Hos and Twinkies at the end, looking at the slabs, the river gone, vanished, the creek gone, vanished, nothing but slabs of still-damp cement swirled with swaths of mud—the buckets hanging beneath them out of view—we did a good morning's work, nothing more, nothing less.

Adhesiveness: There Was This Guy
Albert Mobilio

Albert Mobilio is the recipient of a Whiting Writers' Award. His books of poetry include Bendable Siege, The Geographics, Me with Animal Towering, *and* Touch Wood. *His essays have appeared in* Black Clock, Tin House, Cabinet, *and* Harper's. *An editor of* Bookforum, *he teaches at The New School's Eugene Lang College.*

 THERE WAS THIS GUY I KNEW WHO KNEW THIS GUY who let that guy who played Radar on *M*A*S*H* blow him. The guy I knew said that the other guy, who said he was homo only when it paid, told him that Radar was in town to do some kind of dinner theater where he sang and talked about *M*A*S*H* and Hawkeye and the big-nose guy who wore dresses. This other guy worked as a singing waiter in the restaurant where almost the whole staff was la-di-da. But, like he said, he was just part-time, for cash. Anyway, he gets to talking with Radar because Radar wants to know about nightclubs and bars in town where he could hang out. But the guy is itching to ask about being on TV. He asks Radar if that guy on the show, Honeycutt, wasn't a real pussy, and Radar says to him, "You mean BJ," and he says it like he's asking a question.

So they end up in some queer bar drinking Campari till Radar starts in about an early flight he's gotta catch, and says why doncha come back to my hotel and we can raid the mini-bar. The guy I know tells me he told this other guy, "Shit man, like you don't know he wanted to crawl up your ass," but the other guy told him, "No way, we were just drinking and the TV guy was paying and it was, like, we might as well drink at the hotel." So when they get there, Radar pulls out a couple of tiny bottles of Schnapps and says, "You know if you put this stuff on pressure points like your wrist or the back or your neck it's just like Tiger Balm and Ben Gay. It's a heat massage."

"Surprise, surprise," my guy says to me. Before you know it he's dripping Schnapps over the other guy's belly and mopping it up with his tongue. The not-really-homo guy's got his pants down around his ankles, but Radar stays completely dressed, except for the boner he's got out and he's working on. Your guy Radar does this guy good but doesn't let the guy touch him, which that guy says is okay with him, being part-time and all that, and when Radar's done with the guy he stands up and finishes himself with one hand and gets his wallet out with the other. The other guy said while he is getting blown, he sees Radar's glasses keep sliding down his nose and he uses the guy's cock to poke them up. "Sheesh, why not take the fuckers off?" my guy said. But the other guy said, "Maybe he needed them to see something he wanted to see."

Then the guy said that while he was looking down at his bone in Radar's mouth he was thinking, "This is Radar the TV guy." Only, he's also thinking, Radar's not wearing those wire-rim glasses he wore on *M*A*S*H*. He's wearing horn-rims. Red ones. Somehow, this bugs the guy. He wanted Radar to look more like Radar. Anyway, he got a fifty, which the blown guy said was not so great but the guy I knew said was really gravy on top since he says the other guy is really 100% and it was all Sunday in the park for him. The guy told my guy that Radar auto-graphed some hotel stationary for him and that he wrote, "To a good soldier, from Radar, #4077 M*A*S*H Unit." But the guy put it in his pocket, and left it there when his pants went through the wash. All you could read afterward, was the word "Good," which Radar had written extra dark and underlined a bunch of times. The guy I knew said the guy he knew told everyone for months about getting blown by Radar until all the people he knew told him to shut up about it. "Big shit," the guy I knew said someone said. "You let some TV asshole blow you. Like that doesn't happen to somebody somewhere every day."

Johnny Stinkbait Bears His Soul

Thorpe Moeckel

Thorpe Moeckel is the author of three poetry collections, Venison, Making a Map of the River, *and* Odd Botany. *His work has appeared in* Verse, Orion, Shenandoah, Rivendell, Virginia Quarterly Review, *and* Field. *He teaches in the writing program at Hollins University in Western Virginia.*

YOU KNOW THOSE GUYS THAT SLINK AS IF FROM THE catalogs, glossy with all the finest, talking vectors of cast and other crap, latest Gore-Tex jockstrap clamping their nuts like a vise—they are not me. No, I'm worse.

I'm a gearhead in reverse. I fish in found things. For wading, thrift shop sneaks are best. Reclaimed soccer cleats are crap—trust me. I fish with flies tied with beard hair and milkweed down. Once I tied a muddler with Her pubes thinking it would make me lucky. No luck.

For one thing it's boring shopping in stores stocked with all the latest, some know-it-all pretending he knows it all looking to hook you. And don't think those dinks fish barbless. Hardly ever release you.

Besides fishing, redemption is oatmeal each morning in a small china bowl with white blanch marks where I scraped the barnacles. Each morning this bowl and the oatmeal in it and the coffee, too, is a boat drifting me back to the day in Maine I stepped on it while casting a dog-hair (German Shepherd) Deceiver for stripers in the Presumpscot River on a drain tide.

I caught nothing that day. I casted. I waded. I was happy. I found a bowl. There are days like this. You go about them like you've come unglued from living and maybe you are living for once. I don't know. I don't know shit.

The day was hazy and I was wearing waders found at Goodwill for four dollars. They leaked a little, even though I'd duct taped the slit along the seam. It was nice, really, feeling the water swash around my right foot, the wool sock doing its job. People are always giving people hell about fucking sheep like they never wore wool. Like we aren't all shepherds. What the hell.

I like recycling barns, dumps, second-hand stores, garage sales. There is no junk. There are things nearly new, things with potential. You and I, we have previous lives too. Our souls have inhabited many hosts and many are our compatriots. That fish I caught or that kid caught, I forget his name, in Scarborough Marsh a few weeks after I found the bowl, you see, we knew that fish.

That was a fish!

The kid was one of my clients, as once with a forged degree I counseled teenagers. Truth is, I let places counsel the kids. My office was where I liked it. That day it was an Old Town Tripper I got off an outfitter who used it as a clinic canoe on rivers more rock than water. It was nearly bulletproof with Kevlar where I'd patched it so it would float again. We were paddling around, shooting the breeze, him an orphan living with his sister, the lead-guitarist for a dyke-punkabilly band, Rugged Twat. Once I would have said to myself, poor guy, but not anymore.

I had my nine-weight between my legs with forty feet of line stripped out, trolling a shrimp pattern tied with snips of hyperpink Chia Pet fuzz. Wacky fly but a good one. We were floating awkwardly and rapping the general way. Him testing the waters, me trying to make him feel safe and maybe lift a laugh or two out of him. "What has two eyes and no mouth?" I asked him.

"What?" he said. A heron whispered over us then like some cargo glider loaded with tanks of mystery.

"Mississippi."

My nine-weight is a fiberglass antenna plucked from an Army surplus jeep, then threaded and glassed some eyes to and a grip. It works good, if you know how to work it.

"I thought Mississippi has four i's?" he said.

"It does," said me, clinically. I wrenched a stern pry. The kid paddled like there was no tide, like we were in a park pond, shitfull with swan and geese. "That's the point."

"Was that supposed to be therapeutic?" he asked after a minute. I wanted to flip the boat then, but kiddo was on so many meds it would have been fineable to dump him most likely by the EPA.

That rod I gave two years ago to my pop who bends it for drum now and sea trout in the Lowcountry. Or so he says. Two winters ago, pop's divorce came through with his second wife and then a day later his pop, who I knew as Big Ron, passed on. The Her formerly known as my wife had kicked me out a month prior. It was okay because me and pops were buzzing on a day, ripping the lips of sea trout and knew if nothing there was always sea trout.

I'm a fish, you see. More than a fisherman, I am a fish. I become the fish that I cast for. It so happens that last evening in a stream so anorexic with drought and wasted besides with acid rain from the crap spewing from the coal-fire plants, I stalked brookies. I became a brook trout. Don't ask me to explain it.

In exchange for the nine-weight, Dad gave me a one-weight that bends like a gymnast and is more sensitive than my pecker. I employ it in the quest for brookies near my place in Hurt, Virginia.

By now you've probably guessed that I worked with mixed-up teens so long I am one, again, only now in a man's body, which is not good but kind of fun in a desperate and joyful way at least if you know how to work it.

For instance, I finagled some plastic barrels off a pickle company and made me a houseboat out of scrap lumber I drug from rivers in Virginia where I came after running from the detox. For a time I lay low with a guy who once was a friend but had become too big for his britches with the bucks he made as a full-time prescription med dealer. With fist, bat, and bottle, he gave me retro plastic surgery one night in a blackout, says him, and anointed me Johnny Stinkbait. I am grateful forever. Later I found a surplus library bookmobile, a six wheel, eight cylinder with a rivet-solid Grumman body, and drove it onto the barge I built on the lake here that is brighter this morning than a National Merit Scholar. Plugged in a potbelly and a few sundries, so here we are.

I score oatmeal from the nearby commune that makes and sells hammocks, tofu, and their own Don't Panic It's Organic–brand oats. It's good. My bowl is best. I hold it cupped like a breast. It is not true like a wheel is true. It must have been wave-altered in the tides as it was. I eat from it with my eyes and eat it with my eyes, from its blue paint in bold strokes, the trees and mountains, birds and rooflines. It is white with blue on the white and know that I stepped on it as much as it reached for me, this bowl tossed or swept from some deck and what has been eaten from it and who turned it and who it will be with next are questions that smooch me like any unanswerable.

From this life afloat, a moped when its running scoots me to the hills where I sneak around for brookies with no need to paint my face as years of staring life in its black and blue one has done it for permanent.

Her. Her was good. Sweet wife, Her gave and gave. Wore a mishmash of vintage elegance gleaned from the same wherever junkheaps that I love, Her, and filled those digs like nobody has or ever will, if you want to know. You don't want to know.

Then Her dumped me passed out at the detox. I guess it's like when men had women put away for menopause, menstruation, witchcraft, and such—comeuppance. "Scorned one make the beloved a patient," reads the headline. I blitzed and Her said, "Go on. Be ADD, an every-thingaholic. Take your Intermittent Explosive and Language Processing Disorders, to name a few," Her said, "and go on." On I've been. I mean, why not a little mental hygiene via spiritus of grape, hop, and rye? I'm a sweet tooth, and like my sugar fermented.

I tell you they're wrong who say that matters only you and your woman. The only sanctity ever was fishing.

Knew it when I ripped a snagged treble that came back hungry for my eyelid, pops and pal paddling for my six-year-old screams thinking snakebit. Knew it then and that was Arkansas. Knew it pulling bluegill from golf course ponds with mushrooms and Styrofoam for bait. Knew it learning to swim across the Coolasagea, rod in mouth, catching underwater eddies, losing no ground even in flood. Knew it that year I only fished with corn because dad did with flies. Knew every cast was a metaphor for faith better than scripture. Knew it as a plebe sneaking nights from barracks on Parris Island to throw a mattress-foam crab pattern like pick-up lines for ladyfish in the tidal flats of the Broad. Knew it in blackwater swamp and clearwater glade. Knew it on the Kennebec, the Maury, the Potomac, and the James. Knew it in the Bitterroots, the Alleghenies, the Sangre de Cristos, and the Coast Range. Knew in Cape Breton, Cape Hatteras, and Cape Fear.

Jesus knew so, too. Consider him at the Sea of Tiberius, at Gennesaret—such bounty, henceforth, etc.

But I'm telling you Her, she was this plumpness of good French-Canadian, Lewiston, Maine, breeding who stocked boots at the Salvation Army in Bath—mercy—Her'd hook me up with such fine scores and nice knockers like catfish head, each one of them puckered and few whiskers.

So this kid is quiet and me quiet and the reel starts screaming, I grab it and feel that pull, which could be the Almighty Himself. "Dag," kid says. Kind of whispers it. "What is it?"

"Fish," I say. The marsh is in my hands and the sky on it at once and I say, "Kid take this, take this and keep the tip up and let the fish run but keep the tip up the line tight."

"Dag," the kids says over and over, quieter each time.

I say, "No dag, this is the shit." And kid still won't take the rod like he knows it will hook him harder. "Take it," shouts me. "Keep the tip up."

"Doesn't it hurt the fish?" kid asks.

"Yes, but it hurts you worse. It hurts you best," I say as he takes it and the sun starts blinding me right out his eyeballs so full of the life through the line rod bend grip is kid. "Keep the tip up, kid," I'm panting. "Let it run." That was the best counseling I ever did.

Someday I will come rich and famous writing a book on Piscean Therapy. The kid turned fish. I saw it with my own two bloodshot ones. He evolved, by golly.

I dance now to think of it. There is room to do on the deck I put on the truck-houseboat's roof. And I sing a little jingle. Pluck a slide ukelele one potato two potato three potato four. Heart, I sing, you are a poodle-eating carp with tampon strings where your eyes used to be. You are dace and you are blowfish, heart. You are muskie and lamprey, madtom and sturgeon. You are bloatest grouper and sublimest bonefish.

Kid played it good with me screaming Keep the tip up as love and fear breakdance in our chests and the boat follows the fish running for the rice thick along the tidal mud and some place gillinstinct know and no other. Kid got it next to the boat on that barbless shrimp pattern, and he is watching and breathing heavy. "What now?" he asks after a minute.

"Let it go," I say, reaching to release the hook.

"We're not eating it?" kid asks.

"No," I say. "We're setting it free. Watch it close." It is a lovely striper, mix of bayonet and starlight. "Watch it go."

Now I eat from the bowl. I take my oatmeal with peanuts and goat milk. Someday I'll be a striper. I'll be salt. I'm evolving. I know it. I was chub. I was out of season brown trout heavy with roe. Friends, you've got to be a fish, there is no other way to live.

Hello, this is Bob.

Antonya Nelson

Antonya Nelson's most recent collection of stories is Nothing Right; *her novel,* Bound, *was released in 2010. She teaches creative writing at the University of Houston.*

 WHEN MY FIRST BOOK WAS PUBLISHED, TWENTY years ago, I sent copies to most of my relatives. The feedback was mixed. My younger brother complained that our family's secrets had been exposed; my cousin said the experience of reading the book made him feel as if he was reading my diary, and not in a good way; and my grandma Velma told anyone who noticed the book proudly displayed on her coffee table that it was nothing but smut.

And so ended the massive mailings of copies of my books to relatives.

But in order to write a story, I have to have some personal investment in the material. Oftentimes that investment is solely based on my own exposure (the "diary-like" stuff my cousin mentioned), and I don't shy away from exposing myself. But occasionally the true-life business of my friends or family members ignites in me some desire to write a story.

One such occasion was an overheard cell phone conversation between my son, Noah, then eleven years old, and his best friend, Bob. We had recently moved to Houston, leaving Bob in New Mexico. It was late summer, 2002, and the phone conversation between the boys was uncharacteristically brief. I noted this aloud. Noah said, "Something's wrong. I don't think that was Bob."

Literally, it was indeed Bob. Bob had been calling our house for years, always opening with the endearing deadpan salutation: "Hello, this is Bob." I loved hearing his six-, seven-, eight-, nine-, ten-year-old voice announcing his old man-like name. "Hello, this is Bob. Is Noah there?"

"Or if it was Bob," amended Noah, there in traffic on the cell phone a thousand miles away from his best friend, "he's really depressed."

This moment took root in me. It scared me. It implicated me. It made me profoundly uncomfortable. And so it grew into a story. Bob, and his sadness, was at the center of that story. I named his character Dick, which, like Bob, seems such an improbable little boy's name. I borrowed Bob's basic family structure (an all-male household with conservative political leanings). I was uncomfortably aware of using my son's real-life friendship, yet the despair of that overheard phone conversation would not leave me alone. In the story, the mother protagonist, my own stand-in, worries about her role in breaking up the best friendship between the two boys. The mother feels responsible. I felt responsible for Bob's sudden unhappiness. I was guilty. But of what, exactly? We'd moved after a series of hard experiences: a miscarriage, an extraordinary vandalism of our home, a dire diagnosis of a close family member, and, of course, 9/11. Like the characters in my story, my family relocated. Was I still unsure of whether we were running toward or away from something? I don't think I know the answer to that question yet.

In order to continue writing the story, I had to put away the thought that one day Noah would read it. I couldn't write with that audience sitting on my shoulder. Yet I also did not want him to feel as if I'd betrayed Bob. In my story, Dick runs away. Dick apparently has become a sociopath. The mother, in my story, feels as if she's rescued her own son but somehow sacrificed Dick. My first instinct was to change the locale of the characters' home, to move it from our small New Mexican city to the large and more dangerous and anonymous Los Angeles. This relieved some of the autobiographical pressure; I wasn't imagining Bob's Las Cruces backyard, but a completely different one in L.A. Next, I gave Dick twin brothers (Bob doesn't have twin brothers), and a pair of parents based on some other, actual, parents I know. Then I let them be dog breeders based on the nasty dog breeder I'd recently had occasion to visit. This distortion of realities mimics the process of dreams, in my experience. In dreams, you may occupy the locale of last night (say, the hotel bar) yet in the company of your high school boyfriend (dead) who's trying to convince you to climb under a big mock rock (you saw it in SkyMall, when you finished that book you'd brought and had nothing else to read). It's all autobiography, but it's also all nonsense.

Bob didn't kill small animals or run away from home. Bob was only temporarily depressed. But Dick went ahead and did those things. And when Noah finally did read a draft of the story, he immediately recognized Bob in the character Dick, never mind the scene change or ensemble shake up. It made him sad, and so I began to try to change more of the details. I made the two separated best friends girls instead of boys, but this was impossible. The ache of the original moment was peculiar to

the reticence of young manhood, to the specific hole-in-the-chest sensation that a crying male inspires in me. No two girls I could imagine captured that feeling. Providing fictional Dick with sisters was also a failure.
Changing the boys' ages was not possible—they needed to be younger
than sexual awakening, yet older than childish distractibility. One of
them listening to the other needed to know exactly what it meant to be
"depressed." They needed to be on that eleven-year-old cusp, that year
when the boy suddenly no longer wishes to hold his mother's hand.

I did as much as I could to keep my son from feeling betrayed. Being
true to my own sense of story, and my own need to unpack that charged
moment in the car, is the imperative of art. I was investigating my feeling of guilt: I had somehow made that phone call occur. I was responsible for that boy's misery.

In truth, years later, my son is no longer best friends with Bob.
They're friends, but not close. We moved back to New Mexico, and the
two of them went through high school together; they pass each other
between college classes now, saying hi. The distance between them is
benign, intangible, untragic. The rift in my story is extreme and tragic.
The sources, in each instance, however, are the same. But fiction, in my
experience, distorts by dramatizing, by exaggerating, by pursuing a singular character trait into extremis. An extreme version of Bob, Bob X, is
what produced Dick.

An odder experience, for me, is when people in my life recognize
themselves in my fiction when they haven't been anywhere in my
thoughts while producing it. I had no fewer than a dozen men claim that
it was they who were the model for a character in a story I wrote called
"Or Else." That guy is a liar who breaks into another family's home in
Colorado, pretending to belong there. Not only did people recognize
themselves, they didn't like the person they appeared to be. In other
words, they thought I'd not only written about them, but revealed just
how unsavory they were.

That character, named David, is based on myself: I'm a professional
liar. I even had that confirmed when, earlier this year, I took a polygraph
test. Strapped in and sweating, I watched the instrument register my
responses, the scritching needles jumping and charting my apparent lies
two times: once when I was asked if I was wearing shoes (I was, but they
were Crocs, so maybe when I said "yes" I was sort of thinking "if you can
call them shoes") and next when I was asked if I'd ever pretended to be
somebody I wasn't. "No," I guess I lied. In truth, I guess I pretend it all
the time. My character David, like most of my characters, is based on

some extreme version of myself. It's another version of what I perform on friends and family, pursuing one critical trait to an exaggerated length, letting the chips fall where they may.

The scariest sensation for me, in writing from my real life, is when I find myself pushing a character in an extreme direction, watching the fiction unfold more dramatically than the real-life experience did, and then having that fictional event actually happen in my life. This has happened more than once. For instance, a story I wrote a long time ago featured a suicide. It was pure invention, at the time, and then, in an uncomfortably short space of days, it wasn't. The fictional story didn't inspire the act—the real person never read about my characters—but my own creative uneasiness about the factual personalities inside the fiction turned out to be unsettlingly close to the truth. That is, I knew something without quite knowing I knew it. And maybe this is what makes writing fiction the dangerous activity it is. Not that you're predicting or somehow influencing the future—I don't subscribe to that kind of magical thinking—but that you are in possession of a keen and double-edged sensitivity to the people and possibilities around you. On the one hand, it makes you empathetic. On the other, it makes you overly aware of what might naturally happen next. It makes you usefully cautious as well as hopelessly anxious. It produces both art and insomnia.

I caution students not to write with the idea of revenge. I urge them to consider the ways in which their characters absolutely have to be who they are in the stories: could it be a father instead of a mother? A coach instead of a minister? A Rottweiler instead of a Golden Retriever? Could it be in 1989 instead of 2003? Could it be in Los Angeles instead of Houston? And if it absolutely has to be a mother, and she has to live in Wichita, and she has to have once been a professor, could she at least not have five children? The novel I've just finished writing is set in my hometown and is filled, necessarily, with a lot of my own life. Included in that is the very factual serial killer, the BTK, and some strange overlaps between his era of mayhem and my own adolescence, which occurred at the same time. I wouldn't have thought to write about the BTK if that weren't the case, and the fact that he once took a college class with one of my mother's colleagues is central to a small part of the novel's plot line. I could not change that fact in my fiction; the killer had to have mimicked a folk-song lyric and sent his sick creative ditty to the local newspaper. I debilitated my own professor mother when I fictionalized her; I made her emeritus from women's studies instead of English literature; I made her old colleague African American; I turned her from a warm hostess into a chilly academic; and still I worry that my real mother will be wounded by the character serving as her stand-in. All I can offer in my own defense is that I tried hard to consider other possibilities only to discover that a few essential parts could not be changed unless I wished to abandon my original impulse for caring to write the story. I can only hope that I've interrogated the autobiographical sufficiently and arrived at the ideal: a fiction that can be made of no other configuration. Too much distortion can pull you, the author, away from your initial interest in the material. Too little tweaking can leave you open for losing friends or disappointing your children. Fortunately, my real mother is an avid reader of and believer in fiction; she'll forgive me my mother character if the novel is good enough.

Semiprecious

Mike Newirth

Mike Newirth was fiction editor of Bridge *and* The Baffler *magazines, and a guest fiction editor of the journal* Fifth Wednesday. *His writing received a* Transatlantic Review *award and has appeared in magazines and anthologies including* Another Chicago Magazine (ACM), Other Voices, Chicago Reader, In These Times, Personals, A Fine Excess, Boob Jubilee, *and* Pushcart Prize XXII. *He currently resides in Chicago and teaches at the University of Illinois.*

MACK BOWER BEGAN WORKING RIGHT OUT OF Northwestern for Mercury Trading, first as a runner, then as a trader. While his friends drifted away, immersed in business and law school, extending their educations of enrichment, he was rising at 5 a.m. in his small Wicker Park apartment to hustle downtown on the Blue Line, to jam himself into the index option pit at the Chicago Board of Trade, shout himself hoarse and bang his knees on the rails. He was a mechanical jumping man in an umber polyester blazer. His ID tags jangled when he bid. He revered the idea of this lucrative quick-shot career. No more school for him, but straight into the mix; that love was his juice, his morning alarm.

For some months he stayed lucky and traded well, shepherded the firm's steady profits from scalpings, focused upon the less volatile rice and oat options, fearful of deeper waters. The holidays were a blur of spilled martinis at Magnum Steakhouse, the windshield-sized grins of the bosses, his pals from the floor with shirts opened, doing vulgar karaoke at a disdainful cabaret. He received an outsized bonus, which he put into credit card debt and one toy, a Porsche 924, secondhand and scratched, but still the real deal. Then, approaching his second winter, it was like his cardsharp's hands were turned to mallets. For in fact it was the money of other people, grouchy and exacting puppeteers, that he temporarily held, and it gradually became clear he'd never endure to trade in real commodities, the Middle Western gold of corn and soybean futures, where the permanent money resided, that he wasn't meant to become another of the Board of Trade's swinging dongs. Following his third disastrous margin call in a month, he was brusquely terminated in a management office with walls flypapered by old arid insults.

When that happened, he was only recently involved with Audrey, an older woman, lithe, possessing a hummingbird's shapely nervousness. When she steeled herself to make her own move, the part of him still obsessed with the science of options saw it coming.

Mack enjoyed being jilted, in a hateful sort of way. Once relieved of his job, he'd become aware of Audrey eyeing his fraying wardrobe, his diminishing ego, with calculator eyes. She'd liked the thought of him as an A-list boho, but jobless bohos were easy to come by in that neighborhood of well-to-do hipsters.

So that night in his chilly apartment he could barely resist prodding her on through the drama. After takeout Pad Thai and Panang curry she excused herself to the bathroom. When she returned her mouth was thinned, set in the way he'd seen her brush off intrusive strangers. "How about another beer?" he asked.

"No thanks," she said. "We have to talk."

"Oh. In that case, I'm going to have one."

"I have some bad news for you," Audrey said, raising her voice in the front room as he uncapped an Old Style.

She talked for a while, hitting the high notes: the weariness of relationships, an unforgotten ex-lover calling late at night from faraway, and so forth. She seemed upset. It was heartfelt and rehearsedly spontaneous. Mack held her, body gone inert, heavy now, and looked around at the living room. He willed his own face smooth, already recalling what was: their first night together, when she'd giggled like an easy teen, and blushed with her whole body, which he'd never seen.

Audrey left composed, sobered. Mack watched from the window as her Subaru pulled away, flew off into the unroofed sky of what never happens.

A storm blew into Chicago, walls of gray snow, then freezing rain. Mack paged his old dealer, repeatedly punching the once-magic numbers, but there was no reply. Mack was out of the game, and had no connections. He stood on the fire escape, chaining cigarettes, woozy with Valium and beer, gasping the frigid, splintered air.

In the morning, he walked through the moonscape of frozen slush, gluey on his boots, to the Polish deli across the street, bright and spotless inside.

Mack appeared, a bloody-eyed apparition in a Scissor Girls T-shirt and jeans, a straw man in the snow to the blocky Polish woman and her daughters who froze in the bright white kitchen when he entered. Mack stood before the long refrigerator case, thinking it was the cleanest chrome and glass in Chicago, dazzled.

He purchased food strange to him: beet salad, ham on the bone, neon-orange hunter's stew studded with sausage chunks. A buck-toothed teen with tomboy hair glowered as she assembled his packages. The matriarch watched from the cash register. When Mack fumbled his money across, she touched his hand, and their eyes met. He saw a large plain woman with lacquered curls and a pale face.

"You live there?" the woman asked, tilting her chin to the gray window.

"Yeah."

"Alone?"

"Yes."

She chuckled, a dry click in her throat. "That building used to be filled with hoodlum," she said. "Now is boys like you. But you won't stay. You go on, you get family."

Mack snatched up his pierogi and pickled herring, annoyed to feel himself blush.

"I'm here now," he said. "Don't need no *family*."

The woman and her daughters grinned at him.

It may have been her surety that set him off. She'd amplified the gnawing sense that it was time to double back, to examine his tracks.

With sandwiches and a thermos of coffee, he left for New York that afternoon. The scratched Porsche slid like a drunk dancer on the slushy roads that led south, out of Chicago, but the interstate was smooth as glass. He drove almost without stopping, shot onward by ephedrine and old punk-rock cassettes. He made Pennsylvania by dawn. It was like the sun never quite rose: the sky lightened over I-80, yet remained sepia.

As he crested the George Washington Bridge, a glass shard of happiness stabbed him. It was the spires of Manhattan coming in to view. Mack turned up the Minor Threat, stormed across the peninsula, and headed on toward Long Island.

Yet by the time he rolled into the driveway of the old house, he was exhausted, faced with the fact that he really didn't know why he was here. His mother had passed from cancer years before, and seeing the clean and empty driveway glittering with salt, he could guess where Dr. Bower was: a warm island somewhere, observing the glide of sailboats in a brown horseshoe-shaped cove, never a participant.

Mack still had a house key, he still knew how to defuse the burglar alarm. That house was like a museum to him, full of shining white floors, his father's artifacts, paintings, African sculpture. He paused in his father's study, littered with giveaway loot of drug companies, and breathed in the perfumes of warmth: the strong central heat blowing, his father's pipe smoke and coffee. Old theft fantasies flickered across Mack's mind. He recalled his teen vandal years, vials of Quink ink spilled into the doctor's file cabinet. Only gestures now.

In the narrow bed of his old room, Mack slipped into sleep. He woke up to dark windows, queasy and disoriented as a kid with the flu. He sat on the edge of his bed, and looked around at the low ceiling, the blank white walls. Of course the thumbtacked rock star and halfpipe posters were long gone. What remained was the sense of a confinement amputated from years.

It had been that way in Mack's era of first times, when he had his first girlfriend, a tiny Puerto Rican girl named Beatriz who, like Mack, was in a terrible hurry, and thought sixteen was old enough. Beatriz and Mack walked home after school, up the neighborhood's tree-swollen crescented streets, inured to the tangles of young shriekers about them, the click and pop of their skateboards and mopeds. They'd figured out sex pretty quickly, and for quite a while went a little crazy with it. Beatriz was always flushed and sore, Mack bruised in places once never imagined, and there was never any orange juice left in the fridge.

Mack always kept one ear cocked for Dr. Bower, who arrived quietly as an assassin, but he never said a thing about it. Mack watched sometimes as his father and Beatriz passed each other in the kitchen, regarding one another warily with silent smiling courtesy, Beatriz in her short skirt and short jacket, the doctor's eyes hooded behind half-glasses. In the gleaming room's forced quietude he seemed to weigh Mack's randy good fortune with sad remove. In those moments Mack would follow her outside into the big front yard to kiss her goodbye, lingering in the yard as she set off down Longview Road, and when he returned to the kitchen the doctor had usually vanished, the moment passed.

Every day after school Mack would open his shades to the late light, sit at his desk, and watch Beatriz work on her compositions, cross-legged on the rug with score sheets spread around her, a petite girl with shining dark hair and a permanent smile. She was a prodigy in composition; with no money of her own, she yearned for a scholarship to the Eastman Conservatory. Her worn backpack was stuffed with music texts, and John Cage and Tchaikovsky lived on her crack-hinged Walkman. Mack loved to see her at work, to watch her tiny hands ink each delicate note into place on the blank staffs. He never perceived the obvious, that her talent would steer her away from him. Still, what grew between them in that room endured more than a year. Seven years later, that was amazing to Mack; and the time elapsed, those seven years, seemed merely appalling as he sat on the bed with the same collapsed springs, and thought about those times with her.

He drove into town. The 924 threw up brown ice at the intersection of Main Street and Port Washington Boulevard. He furtively circled the high school parking lot, counting the new cars gifted from parents to seniors as talismans against traffic stops, glistening in the thinned air. Three girls in bright ski parkas huddled in a Lexus, exhaust coiling. The driver held a small silver pipe. The passenger waved at Mack as he cruised past, but when he cranked down his window they drove off, leaving giggles and a Van Morrison song in the air behind them.

On Main Street, Mack saw more stores had gone under, their windows now darkened. Like the Gallery Luncheonette, where his little group hung around: the tall red booths he huddled in with Beatriz, her scores, and cups of coffee were now pulled apart and piled by the windows. He glimpsed the chrome spear of the grill hood. The movie theater was knocked down. In its place was Café America, a resturant owned by the local mob guys, all neon and white paint and Goldtone.

Mack found Beatriz's house. It was a frame duplex with frayed yellow paint. He stood on the sagging common porch and rang what he believed to be the proper bell. After a minute a young, small woman in a dirty robe yanked open the door. They stared at each other through the glass of the storm door. Mack stepped back. She was big in the hips, and had a slack mouth. He flashed upon regret, before realizing this wasn't Beatriz.

"What do you want?" she asked him. "If you looking for Clarence, you supposed to call first."

"No," Mack said. "I was looking for a girl who used to live here—"

A sly smile transformed her face, and she said, "I remember you, oh boy, do I remember what I used to hear about you."

"Who are you?" he said.

She pouted. "Oh, you don't remember me? I'm Angel. Beatriz's my sister."

"Yeah, okay," he said. "You were pretty young then."

"You were pretty young, too," she said, composed and lewd.

A thin man with long hair glided up behind Angel. He put his hands on her shoulders and looked at Mack with cool slitted eyes. "Who's this, babe?" he asked.

Mack looked at him, at the streak of white in his coarse black hair. He pounced upon the name. "Clarence Kang," Mack said.

He moved Angel out of the way and stepped out onto the porch. "Do I know you, man?" he asked. Then recognition stole practiced cool from his face. "Hey, it's—I do know you! It's Mack, right?" Mack nodded. "Goddamn. Come on in, Mack."

Mack stepped inside the house. Clarence shut the door and grabbed Mack in a sloppy, outsized hug. "Damn, man, it's been years since I seen you. Not since high school, right?"

"Just about," Mack said.

"You left town, though. Didn't you, you smart guy."

"I thought I should keep moving," Mack deadpanned.

They moved into the front room. Clarence was grinning, waving his hands around as he talked. Mack inventoried the furniture, all the same, worn down now, slipcovers gone gray. Videotapes with garish color-copied labels were stacked up against the walls. On the coffee table, a tiny baby slept in a bassinet, swaddled in blue blankets, his face pinched and strange. The room smelled of incense and plastics. The heat was up high; Mack began to sweat.

Mack recalled Clarence as one who hung around all day in an alcove behind the high school, burning the hours, Metallica or Mötorhead ruling the boom box. His friends were the crazy ones, the burnouts and aspiring felons. Mack was there on the day a lesser jock called Clarence a slant. Clarence beat him down, then kept punching. The freaks watched and grinned, but Clarence stayed calm and businesslike about it, plunging narrow fists into the jock's mouth until it was torn and bloody.

"He used to go with my sister," Angel said.

Clarence whistled. Angel poked at him. "Pig," she said.

"She was fine, all right," Clarence said, looking at Mack with hooded burlesque admiration.

Mack asked, "Where is she now?"

"L.A.," Angel said, shrugging. "She's getting a doctorate. She don't call home often, we don't talk much. All she cares about is her crazy-ass music. She's my sister, I love her, but she's just self-centered, you know?"

Mack sat down hard on the couch, thumped by the beams and springs. The gray walls and stained stucco ceiling shifted before his eyes, blending into light.

He'd spent time in this room, too, winter days with nothing to do besides a little homework. Making out with Beatriz on this same couch, not going further for fear of her mom. He remembered the piney scent of her hair, stiffened by Aqua Net, and her open eyes, focused elsewhere. She could kiss him long and hard and remain undistracted, thinking of her latest composition all the while.

When Mack looked up, Angel had walked away. Clarence knelt at the coffee table, rolling a joint. He shook the excess pot into a lacquer box which brimmed with it, then lit the joint, inhaled, and held it out. Mack could smell the acrid smoke, and it awoke his old appetite, consistent as a nasal drip.

"You look like you could use a hit," Clarence said.

Mack took the joint and nodded, holding in smoke, then raggedly exhaling. "I just drove in from Chicago."

"Damn, really?" Clarence said. "Just to see me, right? I'm touched."

"That's right."

"Seriously, man, what's the deal? You looking for Angel's sister?"

"I guess so. I don't know," Mack said. "Is that your child?"

"Yeah." The edge dropped from Clarence's voice. He carefully touched the baby's forehead. "This is my little man."

"That's cool."

"Kid costs a lot of money, though," Clarence said. "It's not like a few years ago, when all I did was put in work and then party. Now, every cent I make I have to watch."

"What is it you do?"

Clarence held a finger to his lips, grinning, dropped a merry wink. "Lots of stuff. I move lots of stuff. Are you looking for anything in particular?"

"I don't know."

"I was in furs for a while, and rugs. Imported." Clarence spoke in a conspirator's tone. "These, though, I just move these for the fun of it." He held up a videotape box: a gangster in a white bloodied suit, his face a death snarl, and a machine gun firing from each hand. "Movies from Hong Kong, man. Jet Li, Simon Yam; they're the best. Me and my boys dupe them off the laser discs, move 'em out of Flushing. American movies, they all suck, you know? But you never told me what you were doing back here, anyway."

"I just wanted to get out of Chicago. It seemed like a good quick trip."

Clarence sighed. "Remember Pat Menoli, Cynthia Banks, Rob Gordon? They're all dead. The two overdosed on the same batch of smack, and then Rob hung himself, 'cause he's the one got it for them. You remember Gaudy Gaudioso? He got himself electrocuted, on top of a train."

Mack felt his lips turn heavy, the presence of absence in the room.

"I'll tell you something, Mack," Clarence continued, "I walk around and I hear their voices. This town, it's turning into a graveyard. We're going to get out of here, man, once we fix the house, and sell it. Right now, for me, it's just me and Angel, and Joey here—my boy—and making dollars to live right." He pinched out the roach, frowned at it, then broke it open upon a fresh paper.

"Where is Angel's mother?"

He looked up. "She died, man, two years ago, had a heart attack. Don't ask Angel about it, okay? She'll start crying and all that."

Beatriz's mom was short like her daughters, but heavy, her features grainy from long hours at work. Once Mack perceived a jealousy in her of her daughters, two sassy run-arounds, and a dismay at Beatriz's fierce concentration, dedicated to her frivolous pursuit. She remained reserved with sad eyes downcast around Mack, the white boy from across town, but he heard her through walls and doors, saw the results when Beatriz ran from the house, crying, into the bleak yard where he waited for her. Dead now, and in the ground, leaving her girls alone.

The room's windows were growing dark. The match flare illuminated Clarence's smooth cheek as he lit another number. He looked younger than they were. "You're still hung up on Angel's sister, aren't you?" he said.

"I'm hung up on all of them. Just now there was this girl in Chicago."

"Who was she?"

Mack sat there, wanting to tell, yet bloated with miles and cannabis. Clarence watched him with steady eyes. Mack looked away, leaned over and gazed at Joey's still face. "Her name was Audrey."

"Okay. So what happened with Audrey?"

"Nothing much." Mack frowned and reached for the joint. "She dumped me. It pissed me off, you know. I think I thought something else was due to me, from her." He took a big hit, close to seeing, but the dope stood in the way. He exhaled in ragged coughs. "It's like—let me ask you something: you remember how, when we were younger, we'd be going out with girls, getting jerked around and all that, and we'd think that someday we'd be with, you know, women?"

"No, I don't remember ever thinking that," Clarence said. "Girls, women, what's the diff."

"Forget it."

"Are you sure this isn't just about Angel's sister?"

"I'm just thinking about her now," Mack said.

"You guys hung out for a while, right?"

"Almost two years. But that was a long time ago."

"I'm not seeing that makes much difference," Clarence said. "Maybe I shouldn't say—ah, fuck it. She's engaged, Mack. She's got some smart fella out there who coughed up a ring. A wise-ass from her music school."

Mack heard the words and waited for the pain, the metal kick, but in this cushion of familiar geography he was isolated, as if fortunately so. It would come later, he knew, the melodramatic regret, familiar as a winter coat. He was in no hurry to feel it.

Passing headlights caught Clarence's face, sharpening its angles into feral cuts. Mack saw him illuminated and wondered at all the things he knew. Father, husband, boyfriend, smuggler. Mack looked at his little baby and envied his life.

"I hate to be the one to say," Clarence said, waving the joint, "but gone is gone."

Mack leaned back, and went back to a spring day, in this room. Beatriz was sitting by herself, curled up in the armchair. There was something about her that day that was new to Mack. Her posession of self, her understanding that things stretched on beyond this town, beyond her mother, and beyond him. She'd shut them all down like an endless compositional rest. Outside the air was alive with pollen; they'd been sniffling all day. She was wearing the necklace Mack had given her the previous Christmas, when every moment still promised intimacy, a necklace of white, semiprecious stones. It glinted in the sun, like her glossy hair, with the cheap opaline shine of hoarded memory. And though in a sense she never really looked at Mack again he remained in thrall, dazzled by her resolve.

"Hey, are we two washed up old heshers or what?" Clarence said. He leaned forward, into the smoke. "It's been snowing, Mack!"

Mack turned around. Beyond the narrow window, the air shook with chunky white flakes. It was energetic snow, potent; he saw it smothering New York, blocking the highways back to his cramped Bucktown apartment. Right then he didn't know where he lived, where home was.

"Angel's making dinner," Clarence said. "You hungry?"

"You know I am," Mack said. "I don't know why I drove out. I don't even know where my father is. He could be anywhere. I don't even know if I wanted to see him."

"Let go of what you don't know," Clarence invited. "Hey, you stay here as long as you want. We go back, remember?"

"I remember," Mack said. It was truth, inevitable, and all he had. "We go back."

Smirking, Clarence peeled out another Zig-Zag. His son stayed deep in sleep. Scents seeped in, the food Angel was preparing, an oily sizzle of garlic and serranos, and in the stuffy parlor it smelled better than good. Mack sat back and watched the snow fall and fall.

Curiosity

Sigrid Nunez

Sigrid Nunez is the author of six novels, including A Feather on the Breath of God, Naked Sleeper, *and* Salvation City, Her most recent work is Sempre Susan, *a memoir about Susan Sontag.*

 BACK WHEN I WAS BETWEEN COLLEGE AND LAW school I lived in a tenement building on the Lower East Side. My grandmother had died and left me some money—not a fortune, by any means, but enough for me to pursue my dream of living in New York for a year or two or even longer if I was careful.

I found a part-time job right away: weekend nights, I waited on tables at Phebe's on the Bowery. Coincidence: my name is Phoebe, and I immediately dropped the *o* since obviously that spelling was cooler. (In law school, I changed it back.) I tried to live as cheaply as possible, resisting, for example, the boss-looking vintage motorcycle jacket for sale at Trash & Vaudeville on St. Mark's Place. I bought a lot of other stuff there, though, mostly out of the final-markdown bin: a whole wardrobe for one or two bucks an item.

I didn't know anyone in the city when I got there, but all I had to do to meet people—some of whom are still my friends almost four decades later—was hang out in Washington Square Park. There was also Tompkins Square Park, but I avoided it after a barbaric-looking woman with a tattooed scalp hit me with an empty beer can and a stream of abuse cut off by a belch so fierce I thought I'd see flames shoot from her mouth.

As for my neighbors, I never got to know any of them. It was a run-down, seriously neglected building—a building for poor people ("which is precisely why you have no business there," my parents grumbled). Years of grime had accumulated in the halls, which reeked of what some said was roach killer but others said was the smell of roaches themselves: a smell like peppered roses. There was a sign above the front door:

Please Keep Lock And Not Let In Strang Peoples. But the intercom system usually didn't work, and tenants left the door unlocked and let in strang peoples all the time—a risky practice, for sure, but one which, at least while I lived there, brought no harm.

I lived on the second floor, in a railroad apartment—kitchen, living room, bedroom—with windows facing the street, and no bathroom. The toilet was in a closet behind a curtain, and there was a small tub in the kitchen. (You could only bathe sitting up.) I slept in a loft, which in winter could make me feel like Heidi but in summer was like lying inside a coffin. In the living-room floor was a hole large enough that, if I put my eye to it, I could spy on the Ukrainian family below. I didn't have to put my ear to it to hear them fighting, which they did most days. They also did so much cooking that it was like living above a restaurant. Every hour of the day, it seemed, something was cooking down there; I could have survived on just the fumes. These were not the only immigrants in the building. In fact, the tenants were mostly immigrants, including other Ukrainians and a young Polish couple next door, who were expecting a baby and who fought a lot, too, but savagely, like archenemies. Across the hall lived a pale, skulking young man who always acted nervous, his intense dark eyes rolling in a kind of anguish when you looked him in the face, as if he was guilty of some crime. The whole place made me think of Dostoyevsky, whose work I had skimmed in college.

Also across the hall was a woman who looked to be about my age, and who I thought at first might become a friend. She was very pretty, though she wore too much makeup and too much audible jewelry— you'd think it was the Tambourine Man coming up behind you—and she didn't seem to own a single outfit that didn't make her look like she'd been hosed down. She had, I noted with envy, lots of dates, but she was not friendly. Whenever I said hello to her, she would just barely smile and then immediately drop her gaze as people do when they don't want you to speak to them.

I knew her name because it was on her mailbox (though this was the kind of building where many tenants don't put their names on their buzzers or mailboxes): Viktoriya Tiborovsky. From what I could tell, she had no fixed schedule, which made me think either she was some kind of student or she worked irregular hours—though I also suspected that, like some other able-bodied people in that building, she might be collecting unemployment or scamming welfare. She had a cat, which sometimes darted into the hall when the door was open. A skinny young cat of a startling, refined beauty, with a pointed little muzzle and magnificent eyes: Audrey Hepburn transformed by a spell.

One night just after I had started my shift, she walked into Phebe's and sat down at a table in my station. When I approached she looked at me as if she could not quite place me. "We live on the same floor," I said. "My name's Phebe." With a hesitation that struck me as rude, and without any expression, she said, "I am Inna," before turning her full attention to the menu I'd handed her. She had an accent, as expected, but the name was a total surprise. But whatever the story—and it could have been as simple as that she was subletting from someone named Viktoriya Tiborovksy—I was no longer interested in her. Reserved people have never been my type.

I liked her even less when I saw what a small tip she had left me.

My curiosity revived, though, when I figured out (and this did not take long) that the men I observed on their way to and from her apartment were not really dates. It astonished me that she could be so bold. I wouldn't have expected her to worry about the super since no such person appeared to exist, and, from all evidence, the landlord would not have cared how a tenant came up with the money so long as he or she paid the rent. But what if one of the neighbors reported her to the police? (For that reason alone you'd have thought she'd be nicer to me.) I found it hard to believe I was the only one in the building who knew what she was up to. Not that there was a stream of men coming and going all day long; it was more of a trickle. But it was a constant trickle, and it was easy to spot them after a while, these mostly middle-aged men, almost always dressed in business suits, who, when they passed you on the stairs, acrobatically avoided eye contact. None of them looked to be from the neighborhood, but once I recognized a man I'd seen on posters advertising a series of lectures on architecture at Cooper Union, and the imp in me would not be suppressed. "Have fun, professor," I called over my shoulder, though I dared not turn to see his response.

A few years earlier I might have been scandalized. But in college I'd known women who worked in topless bars or strip clubs, and at least one who acted in porn films. I always thought the claim that large numbers of women in other professions—nurses, schoolteachers, even policewomen—moonlighted as prostitutes was an exaggeration. But it was a sign of the times that you heard this claim often, along with the opinion that the selling of sex, like the selling of marijuana, should be legal. I'd also recently seen the movie *Klute*, in which Jane Fonda played a new breed of hooker: educated and stylish, articulating for her high-class analyst how she thrives on the feeling of control she gets from trick-ing. (And of course tricking doesn't stop her from winning the detective-hero, either.)

Those were the days when my model for how not to behave was my parents, who had alienated me as far back as high school by being proud Goldwater Republicans, and who would have had the police on Inna's case in a heartbeat. On the other hand, the friends with whom I shared my discovery about my neighbor took it in stride. Who were we to judge her, man? It was her body, and it wasn't like she was hurting anyone. But I did wonder about her, this ordinary-seeming young woman with her pretty, high-cheekboned face and Alice-in-Wonderland hair, who I was certain was not an addict like, say, the streetwalkers in Times Square, those ghastly, battered-looking wrecks who could never be mistaken for anything but the smack whores they were. Who knew how or why Inna had gotten into the Life? Maybe she was trying to earn money to put herself through clerical school or open her own nail salon. Maybe this was the only way she could pay off some crushing debt she'd been unfor-tunate enough to incur. Or maybe she was sacrificing herself to help someone else, a loved one who needed a life-saving operation.

Speaking of money, I couldn't help being curious about how much she charged—and did she have a pimp? Could one of those men who visited her be her pimp? If so, she never had any trouble with him that I could tell. I never heard any violence—I never heard any noise at all—coming from her apartment. (Or maybe instead of a pimp she had a madam; maybe that's who Viktoriya was.) I wondered also what her apartment was like, whether it was decorated in some special style. What sprang to mind was silly and improbable but remarkably persistent: red-plush furniture, Oriental rugs, a brass bed, satin sheets, ginger-jar lamps with fringed crimson shades. . . .

I wondered about the cat. What if a customer was allergic to cats, or hated or was spooked by them, as many people are?

But all this makes it sound as if I gave far more thought to the situa-tion than I really did. In fact, I saw it as just one more adjustment to be made in a crazy city that demanded many such adjustments. It was part of the darkness of that neighborhood, the seamy strangeness of that building. Downstairs, the madly cooking and squabbling Ukrainians; next door, the Polish couple who, now that their child had been born, went at each other worse than ever; across the hall, Raskolnikov, and, next door to him, Inna the hooker. Though I'd never lived with people like this before, it didn't take long for me to get used to them all enough to be able to ignore them.

I continued to say hello to Inna when we met, and though I never got the sense she would welcome conversation, at times her smile struck me as a bit brighter or more relaxed, as if she might be warming up to me. But I didn't see her in Phebe's again, and, as I say, except for when I ran into her I didn't think much about her. I was busy with my own life and my growing number of new friends, which now included a special one: an NYU philosophy grad student named Josh.

Early one morning, right after I got up, I heard an urgent tapping at my door and a small voice calling "FEE-be, FEE-be," just like the bird. I could tell that it was Inna, and that she was crying, and when I opened the door I could tell from her red and swollen face that she had been crying a good long time—maybe all night. She was breathing asthmatically through her mouth, and I saw for the first time that one of her front teeth was chipped and discolored, like old tile. She looked so distraught, my throat tightened in alarm and pity for her.

It was her mother. "She is in hospital. She is having infarct."

Her mother lived in Chicago, and Inna could not wait to go to her. She had managed to get on a flight departing in a few hours. She didn't know what to expect when she reached her mother's bedside, but would I look after the cat while she was gone? I said yes, of course.

Just before taking a cab to the airport, she dropped off a set of keys and told me she had left enough food to last the cat at least until the following night. But I let myself in moments after she'd gone.

Her apartment was like mine: the same three little rooms, the tub in the kitchen, the toilet in the closet, but her windows looked out on the back of another building. There wouldn't have been much light in any case, but the windows were covered by thick army-green curtains so that the apartment was almost pitch-dark even in daytime. Nothing like the Victorian boudoir of my imagination, it reminded me of a modest motel or dorm room. No frills, just a few pieces of plain furniture and some cheap scatter rugs. There was one small bookcase that held no books but a pile of magazines, American and Russian. A fat Russian-English dictionary sat on top of an antique-looking portable TV set, which interested me because I had no TV of my own. But when I turned it on I got a picture like a pointillist painting. She had a radio but no stereo. The bed was a double mattress on a box spring and took up all the space in that room. There were no pictures or photographs of any kind, no decorative accessories except for some throw pillows and a large number of scented candles that made the air smell like fruit on the cusp of rot. No whips or bonds or costumes or masks, nothing of that sort—not in view, at least. (It remained to be seen whether I'd be able to resist snooping through closets and drawers.) But there was what I took to be one telling sign: on the kitchen counter sat half a dozen bottles of liquor and a couple of glasses of the kind my parents used to drink their nightly old-fashioneds.

She was very tidy. The cat's litter box was hidden in a corner of the living room, behind a bamboo screen. The cat itself, even more regal up close, looked out of place in that humble dwelling, as if it were slumming. Inna had told me its name, but it was a foreign name and I hadn't quite caught it: something something *ka*.

After a few minutes, I wanted to leave. It seemed so meager and bleak—like the house of a suicide, I couldn't help thinking. No books. So what did she do when she wasn't—working? Sit here by herself watching that crummy TV? It occurred to me that she might have another place somewhere—her real home—and used this one only for business. But all the evidence was against that. And then another unlikely idea came to me: Inna had run away. She'd given her pimp the slip, she was escaping the Life, she was never coming back to Sin City.

I was almost at the door when someone knocked, and I jumped like a burglar caught red-handed. I had no intention of answering, and when the door opened I was badly startled. Without checking I had assumed that Inna's door, like my own, would have automatically locked behind me.

He was startled, too—enough to blurt the obvious: "You're not Vicki."

At that moment we heard footsteps on the landing above, heading for the stairs. The man stepped over the threshold, stealthily letting the door click shut.

Either, in her hurry and distress, Inna (but he'd called her Vicki, hadn't he) had forgotten to cancel this customer's appointment or she had tried but had been unable to reach him in time or, maybe, under the circumstances, she'd decided just to stand him up.

He was peering past me, as if he expected her to emerge from somewhere in the apartment. He was in his forties, I guessed, with a thick head of black hair evenly seamed with silver. He wore a brown suit and a blue shirt but no tie; his collar was open enough for me to see the top of his undershirt. His throat was hairy. I spied a thin, nearly invisible gold chain. He was heavy, but in a manly, well-proportioned way. He wasn't particularly scary, but I was scared anyway. I was panicky.

Calm down, idiot, I told myself. *All you have to do is explain.* And he was eyeing me now, clearly waiting for an explanation. Meanwhile, the cat, on tip-toe, was tracing mincing figure-eights around his calves. At last I found my tongue.

He listened, nodding, looking vaguely concerned and sympathetic. He said, "That's sad," and "That's very bad," and went from nodding his head to shaking it slowly. It was sad and bad, he repeated. He was a poet.

"It happens," he murmured reasonably. "Act of God. It's okay." But though he was looking at me, and not unkindly, it was as if he was talking to himself. And I was still scared. Maybe because I knew what he was there for, he seemed to fill up the space with his maleness; there might have been ten men pressing in on me, in all their maleness, and I was afraid to breathe normally, afraid to inhale that reek: the reek of a men's locker room.

I could not wait for him to leave. Instead, he strode through the apartment as if he owned it and threw himself onto the bed.

It was so unexpected, I had to sit down. I sank onto one of the kitchen chairs, and instantly the cat jumped in my lap. The air had changed, becoming charged and palpable like the air in the woods right before a storm. The cat started purring. I felt the vibration and heat of its small sleek body in my lap. It got louder and louder. I had never heard a cat purr that loud before, like a white-noise machine.

"Here, kitty kitty."

The cat and I looked at each other, but we both knew who he meant.

In one bound the cat sailed onto the counter amid the glasses and liquor bottles. There was a light tinkling, a dim but merry sound, like wee bells chiming: a fairy wedding. The cat looked back at me over its shoulder, narrowing its splendid eyes.

A bewitched voice said, "Would you like something to drink?"

Thump, came the response. And then another thump. His shoes hitting the floor.

Thump thump thump thump thump. My heart.

"Come to Daddy," he called. So I went.

The day after Inna returned (her mother's condition turned out to be less serious than at first feared; she was sent home from the hospital at the end of a week), she came again to my door. As I held out her keys, she snatched them roughly out of my hand. Her eyes were gleaming slits, like the cat's, and her voice was deep as a man's.

"You owe me money."

She must have misread my frozen response. She planted her fists on her hips, stamped her foot without moving it, and hissed, "*Half.*"

From then on she was cold toward me, responding to my greetings with such a sullen moue I stopped offering them. Customers came and went as before, but I never ran into that particular man again—though I might well have if I hadn't moved shortly after. My one-year lease was up and, rather than renew it, I decided to move in with two other women I'd met working at Phebe's and who were looking for someone to share a large apartment they'd found in the West Village. I left the old place without ever resolving the question of my neighbor's real name or the more confounding mystery of why she wasn't afraid of getting busted.

Perhaps misled by *Klute*, or by the free-love spirit of the times, I told my new boyfriend the whole story.

What was it like? he asked.

Incredibly sexy, I told him.

He wanted to hear every detail, and then he wanted everything to be just the way it had been with me and the john, and that was incredibly sexy, too. But after that night—because of what he now knew about me? Because of what he knew I now knew about him?—I never saw Josh again.

Men.

For years, even though I no longer lived in New York, and never practiced law there, I worried that, somehow, somewhere, that john was going to reappear—perhaps in the form of one of our firm's major clients—and blow the whistle on me, ruining my career, putting my mother and father in their graves, driving away my friends, destroying my marriage, and turning my own children against me.

If you do something wicked, although you can never undo it, you should at least try to make up for it by doing something good. So I was raised. I remember how shocked I was when I saw the hundred dollar bill he took from his wallet. I could have paid the next month's rent with it and had enough left over to take myself out to dinner. I remember deciding to give every penny to charity. Instead, with the half I got to keep, I bought the vintage motorcycle jacket I'd been coveting since the first moment I saw it.

From South Haven

John O'Connor

John O'Connor is from Kalamazoo, Michigan. His writing has appeared in
Quarterly West, The Believer, Gastronomica, *and* Best Creative Nonfiction.
His essay "The Boil" appeared in Open City *25, and was reprinted in the*
Utne Reader. *He lives in New York.*

IT WAS THE SUMMERTIME AND WE WERE WITH OUR
families out at Sleepy Hollow, an old resort just north of
South Haven, Michigan, right on the big lake. I was
twelve. She was a year or two older and came from a
town called Anderson, near Indianapolis. Her family
had once been farm people but she seemed cast from far
more exotic stock. Her name was Angelique, for
instance, an uncommon name in central Indiana and
not, in her case, a family name but an affectation of her parents, who
were artists and lapsed hippies. She wore leather cowboy boots in the
heat of summer and let her hair spill onto her face and across her shoulders to her chest, where it clotted among a few beaded necklaces. She'd
go down to the water with it untied and snapping in the wind, and in
one staggeringly erotic flourish her fingers would dart up to brush it
from her neckline and tuck it into her T-shirt collar. She was even
known to drink coffee.

Although I'd never been to Anderson, I imagined it a squalid hick
town full of BMX hooligans and budding rapists, a place where most
girls have been pregnant before high school and boys in acid-wash hide
brass knuckles in their boots. There was a bruised quality to Angelique
that suggested this, something unwieldy and breakable, as if she'd been
pushed into life too early and didn't know what to make of it. I knew
Anderson was tornado country, so I imagined Angelique to be more vulnerable than she was, having presumably spent a lot of time huddled in
storm cellars and roadside ditches and so on. Of course Anderson was
likely no different from my hometown of Kalamazoo, which was an hour
east of South Haven on dry flatland surrounded by celery farms; not

exactly a high-orbit of refinement. But back then it seemed remarkable that Angelique lived in Anderson and managed to escape unscathed.

To me, she belonged to that breed of beachvolk I grew up around during the summers on Lake Michigan: athletic, prodigiously tanned people who wore nothing but sandals and swimwear and considered lake water their salvation. She was a starlet of this set, flawless in a nylon one-piece Speedo, exploding with a soft, meticulous beauty that was vaguely pornographic. After a swim she'd slip into a pair of cotton gym shorts and the wetness would draw a relief of her backside that tripped a subterranean chord in me. You cannot imagine how good she looked lying next to me in the sand. The roundness of her bottom, the white of her inner thighs, smacked me with loony desire I'd never felt before. That she was a farm girl, more or less, with dirty fingernails and a passion for aerial fireworks, only made it worse.

I don't recall much of what we said to each other. With few exceptions, all seemed to pass silently between us, though that's probably just my memory switching off. Other details have blurred away, such as why she agreed to the thing in the first place. Although she didn't need to, she offered us a defense of sorts, I suppose so she wouldn't appear too sluttish. But this was twenty-five years ago and I've forgotten her reasoning. I remember vividly, however, what it was like to lose my fear of sex and enter a world of panting, zoo-animal lust. I recall the early feelings of dread, my tangled nerves, and the sense of bewilderment at what we were doing and the worry that it was somehow illegal or dangerous or both.

My family vacationed at Sleepy Hollow every summer until I was fourteen. It was a big wide-open place with lots of grass and sand and a rim of white cottages around a giant pool. A restaurant called Ichabod's was the lone expansion on the Washington Irving theme. The roads were unpaved. Sand swept down from high rolling dunes and spilled into the black water. On a clear day you looked for Chicago.

It was the kind of place people returned to year after year, though there were interlopers like Angelique's family who came just once or twice. She told me it was either there or a beach near Gary, where her father had a fishing place neither she nor her mother liked much, on account of their relatives, who from the sound of it had a spiritual acquaintance with booze. South Haven was her father's big concession, though once he saw it he didn't complain. They rented one of the pricier units by the beach, surrounded by great elms and maples. Ours was a breezy two-bedroom deal thrown back in the pines, lacking telephone and coffeemaker but deliciously cool at night.

My own parents were struggling. When I was older I saw that my dad had been withdrawing from us back then, had begun to separate himself in little ways, something I'm sure he loathed but considered necessary. I never felt that he didn't love us, only that there was a detachment. Although the downfall was a ways off, and there remained some affection between my parents, I sensed our days at Sleepy Hollow were coming to an end.

My best friend there was Hayes. We were the same age but he seemed older, with the quiet, affable poise of a British golfer. His parents were divorced and pawned him off on his grandparents every summer, and as a result he had a bit of a wild streak. He suckered me into rock fights on the beach that ended terribly, with blood gushing from our heads. But grown-ups loved Hayes because of his abandonment, so he was permitted an occasional outburst.

It was Hayes who approached Angelique at the pool one day. She was lying on a patio chair, wrapped in a towel at the waist and dripping with Coppertone, black Wayfarer sunglasses hoisting a pile of hair from her forehead. We'd seen her around, found out she was from Anderson, and plotted our approach. Hayes, who came from a remote Chicago suburb, said that small-town Indiana girls were notoriously loose and that Angelique, with her long neck and pouting lips, looked like love.

That day Hayes was a resident-pro in seduction, a man of raw courage and resolve, his voice a steady lustrous thing that made you *believe.* Which was fortunate, because the mere mention of her name — elegant and foreign-sounding—struck me mute with fear. It was like I'd never even imagined a girl before Angelique, and I could never have approached her alone. Hayes's cunning was extraordinary. Words came out of him fixed and shining, burnished by his strange adolescent confidence. Somehow he arranged for the three of us to meet on the beach stairs the following night.

Hayes and I had amassed a caché of porno magazines, which we stored in a small covered hole at the edge of a ravine that ran behind some cottages. We'd gather there secretly, huddled over the pale, soiled flesh, our sweat dripping onto the pages, ferns brushing our calves. My penis would rise in my shorts like a tiny bone and suddenly it would seem like I was standing on uneven ground. My sexuality was tentative then. I played with myself in private but rarely ejaculated, leery of the slick, incriminating mess of semen. It was foreboding, this whole darkened thing with women and insertion. I had hoped the porn would clarify things, provide a segue to real flesh-and-blood girlhood of the sort embodied by Angelique. But it only left me more puzzled and angst-ridden, unable to fathom how to go from half-jerking-off under the covers to wholesale vaginal berserking.

We'd stolen the magazines from a wayward lifeguard who drove a black T-top Firebird Trans Am, recently rebuilt. His name was Wyatt (I was apparently the only one in southwest Michigan with a boring name). He had a stingray haircut with the part down the middle. His smoky room near the tennis courts was a library of pornography: *Hustler, Penthouse, Playboy,* even *Juggs.* Hayes and I would browse the periodicals while Wyatt sat drinking Apple Schnapps and smoking Winstons and talking of loose women. He let us drive his Firebird once, with him riding shotgun and Hayes and I taking turns down a dirt road hemmed on one side by a cliff overlooking the beach. We came down hard on the curves, spitting out the window and listening for the sound of gravel zinging off the guardrail. Wyatt never allowed us drink or cigarettes, but he encouraged us with women, and with Angelique in particular. He'd noticed her himself, he said. When Hayes told him about our impending rendezvous on the beach stairs, Wyatt didn't miss a beat.

"She seems like a modern lady," he announced. "Maybe she'll have you both."

Hayes's eyes locked onto mine. Across the ten feet of floor between us, he whispered, "We can share."

This hadn't occurred to me, but it made sense. I would've been lost without Hayes. Worse. I'd become epileptically unhinged, the sun-dappled neckline and deviant sexual appetites of Angelique from Anderson leaving me convulsed on the beach stairs' splintering, shadowy top landing. That kind of humiliation would follow me through life. I needed Hayes's counsel, his steadying hand. In a way it wouldn't be so different from the magazines, I told myself. Keep my head down, mouth ajar, and try to remain upright.

This was the summer my parents first appeared to me as sex people. It didn't happen overnight—I didn't walk in on them or anything—but I started to sense that they existed in a realm apart from me, a solemn place that adults never talked about or did so obliquely with a kind of smirk, as if only they knew how the world operated. For the first time I saw something more in my parents' affection for each other. When they touched, I looked away.

I didn't realize the connection to Angelique, to the peculiar roil of terror and anticipation she let loose in me that for so long afterward hung on the edge of my desire, never completely vanishing. It also had to do with the summertime in South Haven, I think, with the endless parade of flesh that spoke of all kinds of weird possibilities. We were beach-savants. Our world was of the half-naked and sun-prone. My mom resided in one of those low-slung canvas beach chairs, her rear-end brushing the sand, a hardcover novel in her lap. I remember thinking for the first time she was beautiful and that men would die broken-hearted from never having had her, though I couldn't have explained exactly what that meant.

Bring on the Dancing Horses

Ed Park

Ed Park is the author of the novel Personal Days *and a founding editor of* The Believer. *He was born in Buffalo and lives in New York with his family.*

WHEN I CALL MY PARENTS, MY MOM TELLS ME MY dad is busy teaching a class on the Internet. That is, the class is in a classroom but the topic is the Internet. More specifically, he's teaching seniors—that is, old people—how to blog, write anonymous comments on news articles without panicking, poke their children on Facebook, and get away with not writing h, t, t, p, colon, backslash, backslash, w, w, w, dot before every web address.

I had no idea my dad liked the Internet so much. "Who said anything about like?" my mom says. I can hear her clicking away at her keyboard in the background.

My dad is retired—or was. Is it that they need the money? I fantasize about a heretofore unknown gambling problem, hush funds, love children. My mom sells my old comic books and De La Soul cassingles on eBay. She doesn't know I know. Every so often I'll think about stuff I loved in my youth, and a search inevitably brings up her dealer name. I amp the bidding when it seems safe. You could say I'm looking out for her. But how is it that her four grown kids have neglected their parents' financial needs?

I go to bed with a nagging sense of guilt, though this is how I usually go to bed.

My girlfriend, Tabby, reviews science fiction for a living, which just goes to show you that America is still the greatest, most useless country in the world.

She went to Penumbra College in Vermont and is ABD in comparative literature at Rue University. She's been ABD ever since we met, back when I didn't know what it stood for. Her dissertation is about one or possibly all of these things: manservant literature, robot literature, and the literature of deception.

Tabby is considerably older than me, and by considerably I mean over ten years. I told my parents five, but I don't think they were fooled. Tabby not only remembers life before the Internet, but life before the affordable and relatively silent electric typewriter.

She reads fast, writes faster. She does monthly columns for the *California Science Fiction Review*, *Planets* magazine, *Satellites* magazine, and the web site for the Northwest Airlines Frequent Flyer Book Club, which is getting a soft launch.

I didn't think it was possible for someone to read as fast as Tabby does, and for a long time assumed she must be skimming. But whenever I'd quiz her on a novel that we'd both read, she knew every detail. I'd sit there with the book open and ask things like: "Who answers the door in the middle of chapter seven?"

I tried to keep up with Tabby's reviewing, but it's hard when someone's so prolific. I am not friends with many writers, mostly because that means having to read all their articles, stories, essays, books, and even poetry. They expect you to have read it all. With Tabby, I tried. I really did.

But she's what she calls a stylist. I gave up on her *Planets* magazine column after the third one. I got stuck on the opening line: "All time travel is essentially Oedipal."

Tabby is a brilliant genius in her own way, but sometimes I worry that she is turning into an alien. Lately we don't go out much, and she has taken to wearing what she calls a housecoat about the house. Whenever I'd come across the word "housecoat" in a brittle British novel of misaddressed correspondence and quiet adultery, I would try to picture what was meant. I was never sure, but surely it isn't this thing that Tabby more or less lives in, a sort of down-filled poncho with stirrups.

At the same time I'm attracted to this girl at work. I don't even want to know how old she is. My guess is that she's younger than me by a margin nearly as great as that separating me from Tabby. But what do I know about age? I thought Tabby was my age when I met her. I'm not a good judge of these things, possibly of anything.

The girl at work. I think English is her second language or possibly her third. She has a lisp and does crazy things with her hair. Her name is Deletia. I think it's the most beautiful name in the world.

Here's a secret. I wrote that down on a Post-It once—*You have the most beautiful name in the world*—and carried it stuck to the inside of a folder. All day I was hideously excited as I sat at my desk, roamed the corridors. Then I forgot about the note for a week. When I saw it again the words filled me with disgust. Before throwing it away, I used the sticky edge to clean out the crevices of my computer.

I have two older brothers, whom I despise, and a younger sister, whom I adore. My brothers have always been exceedingly nice to me, including me in all manner of conversation and sport, yet I can't stand the sight of them. At least individually. When the three of us sons are together, my ill will dissipates somewhat, into a sort of tan-colored cloud of indifference. My sister, Grace, on the other hand, speaks sharply to me and expects me to do things like pick up her dry cleaning and find her cheap tickets to Cancun on the Internet. I mean the real Cancun, not some virtual *playa*. But she's the baby of the family and I'm happy to oblige.

We children all live in the city, and gatherings are complicated for me. If it's me, my eldest brother, and my sister, I get argumentative the second I walk in, under the impression that he is picking on her, being the bully that he undoubtedly is. If it's me, my other brother, and my sister, I'll tell jokes nonstop, poorly thought-out jokes that hinge on antiquated wordplay. I'm trying to defuse the tension caused by the fact that this brother is a withholding control freak.

In fact my brothers are exceedingly nice to my sister as well, and she does not speak sharply to them or expect them to run her errands. Sometimes I think she respects them because they make money and I don't, really. Or because their wives are elegant, capable women, and Tabby is something of an eccentric and a bit of a slob.

Once I was on the crosstown bus and saw Grace and my brothers walking out of a restaurant, laughing. They looked gloriously happy. They posted a picture of their lunch on Facebook. I don't know what they were thinking.

After Internet class, my dad e-mails me. His spelling, in longhand, has always been impeccable, but something about e-mail makes him spell like Prince. Sometimes I have to read his messages aloud, pronouncing the letters and numbers until I figure out the meaning.

He tells me that 2day in class he did a 2torial on how 2 delete spam without opening it. Next week he's going 2 teach them how 2 upload videos 2 Utube. His students R loving the Internet!

I e-mail him back and ask if he wants to chat online. No response, though I know he's still awake. He keeps updating his Facebook posts. Doesn't he know I can see them? Doesn't he know I'm his friend? I stay up till two watching his wording get terse.

Every day, sometimes more than once, science fiction books arrive at the door by mail or messenger. Tabby tears into them. Slabs of space opera line the hall, mortared with alternate history.

There's this one FedEx guy who drops by a couple times a week, bearing such goodies. He's practically family at this point. He buzzes from the lobby three times, impatiently, like he's doing an "O" in Morse code. Tabby hits the door button without asking who it is.

The FedEx guy looks, she once said, like an underwear model with clothes on. Of course Tabby's not attracted to FedEx, as she's easily twice his age. But you can never be sure. They always make a suspicious amount of small talk, so much that it probably qualifies as regular talk. Today she tells me that he's an aspiring writer and wants her advice on where to send stories.

"Are they even science fiction?" I ask.

"They're *speculative* fiction," she says. FedEx has given her some of his work, and apparently it's pretty good, a self-conscious throwback to the age of the pulps, with a tawdry modern veneer. She's thinking of writing a column about him.

"But he hasn't published anything yet," I say.

"Oh he will, and he has," she says, like someone well acquainted with time travel.

I never told my siblings that I saw them from the bus, though I put up a cryptic post on my secret blog. "Sometimes the people you think you can depend on turn out to be *not* so dependable," I wrote. No one knows I have the blog. I've had it for years. It averages three readers a week, who stay on anywhere from zero and four seconds. I keep meaning to delete the thing but the required authentications have changed so much that I can't even figure out how to do it.

Maybe my dad could help me. Lately I've been wondering if he can do my sister's Internet chores for her, like get those plane tickets or update her Facebook status. Grace hasn't logged onto Facebook in a long time. I know this because I keep getting little messages in the corner: Reconnect With Grace. Write on her Wall.

Something tells me Tabby will never finish her dissertation. Part of her wants to finish just to finish. She wants PhD after her name. But realistically, she's never going to teach. There are no jobs in robot literature or manservant literature. I don't know what the literature of deception is.

The latest twist is that Rue University no longer exists in the material sense. It became a low-residency institution two years ago, then an online-only entity, with all teaching, discussion, and advisement done via e-mail. Now it's just a diploma mill. "It's not even worth the paper it's printed on," Tabby says cheerfully. The joke is that they don't even send you a diploma, but rather a PDF that you can download and print if you like.

Tabby gives me a book for my birthday. It's a review copy of something called *The Truculata: A Tale of the Weemim*. I thank her and we have sex. She keeps on the poncho, stirrups and all. Later I escape to the study with my gift. The prologue begins:

> Ten thousand years have passed since the S'rwrwa conquered the outer colonies of the Confederation, enslaving its peoples by means of superior firepower and the Naxx, a form of mass hypnosis perfected by the rogue wizards known as the Qmzic.

"Oh, good God," I say. I glance at the cover art: a bowtie-shaped spaceship whirling into the void. I notice that *The Truculata* is book two in the third of four projected trilogies. I force myself to read on.

> Only the mysterious Weemim, a clan of psychic Hffr'z descended from the Grand Vizier Fungwafer VIII and his half-horse concubine, continues to offer resistance. But overwhelmed by the S'rwrwavian robot army, and the rise of the vicious Green Lord Exanthatrill, the Weemim are dying out.

I am clawing the side of my head, in agony.

> Their only hope is to bribe the Qmzic with the hallucinogenic seaweed they harvest, and use their powers to unlock the secrets of a small "cube" of impossible geometries called . . . the Truculata.

I'm forever reading about people who get so incensed at a book that they fling it across the room. This always seemed to me journalistic boilerplate, like those ten-minute standing ovations you read about, or audiences booing something at the Cannes Film Festival. Nevertheless, for the first time in my life, I fling a book across the room. The six hundred-page bulk of *The Truculata* leaves a dent in the wall, which I attempt to conceal by moving the lamp.

Later Tabby and her poncho glide into the study. She picks up *The Truculata*, moves the lamp back into position, and begins underlining passages of note.

That evening Deletia sends me text messages that are either extremely suggestive or simply misspelled. I don't think Tabby would ever go through my phone, but anything's possible.

I delete the texts. I delete Deletia. She texts me again an hour later. I don't write back. What could she be thinking?

At work the next day she explains to a bunch of us that someone hacked her phone and e-mail. I can't tell if she's saying that the hacker is an ex-boyfriend or a criminal from her home country, or if these two shadowy figures are one in the same.

My one-liner falls flat, more obscene than I intended. Our secretary looks scandalized, but Deletia smiles. English, I've learned, is her *fourth* language. Later I write her name on a Post-It, over and over again, a downpour of Deletia, and put it in my shirt pocket, right over my heart.

For the past year, and without my knowledge, Tabby has been running a heroic fantasy Web site called Swords of Amber Mist.

"I didn't think you'd be interested," she explains, after I stumble on the bookmark.

She's right: I'm not interested. I am, however, inscrutably, deeply upset. I peek as she updates the site. It's largely fanfic, with characters from different books and movies interbreeding. Aliens, animals, homo sapiens. This is what happens, in post after post. The copulation, as it's often called, takes place in caverns, on ancient battlefields, or in "antechambers." The background is a starlit black, undulating with digital smoke that rises from skull-shaped braziers.

You need to be over eighteen and a member to read or contribute to Swords of Amber Mist. There are banner ads for online role-playing games, medieval-sounding deodorant.

"Does FedEx write for this?" I ask.

"You mean Bob? He's on SoAM all the time," she says. "Oh, he stopped by while you were at the cleaners. There's a package for you in the hall."

On the bench in the hall is one of those silky impermeable FedEx envelopes. The texture's like that of Tabby's futuristic poncho. It's from my mom, or rather her eBay avatar, and it's addressed to my user name, which she has put in quotation marks. Somehow this kills me.

There's no note inside, no indication that she knows who I am. This is Tabby's address, not mine.

I pull out something sky blue, the cloth as thin as tissue in places. Then I get it: I've unwittingly won the auction for my old Echo and the Bunnymen T-shirt, from that show I didn't even go to. It was sort of after their heyday. I put in the bid two months ago and promptly forgot about it. On the back of the shirt it says: Bring on the Dancing Horses.

Cathedral Parkway

Vince Passaro

Vince Passaro's fiction and essays have appeared in The New York Times
Magazine, Harper's, Esquire, *and other publications. He is the author of the
novel* Violence, Nudity, Adult Content.

EVEN WITH THE WINDOW CLOSED I RECOGNIZE
the voice of Mrs. Klein. I am sitting at my desk, still in
a robe although it is late afternoon, waiting for my wife
to come home. I open my window and see below me in
the building's entranceway two women facing each
other, one white and the other black. The black woman,
a Jamaican, is Mrs. Klein's caretaker; Mrs. Klein stands
before her, shrieking at her in German. Mrs. Klein's
Alzheimer's Disease has grown steadily worse since the death of her husband a few months ago; she now requires care around the clock. I know
the details because my next-door neighbor on the fifth floor, Marya
Klein, is the sister of Dr. Klein, the man who died. She tells me about the
deteriorating condition of her sister-in-law.

Marya, like her brother and sister-in-law, is a Jew who escaped Hitler.
She is a painter, at eighty, one still very active, but not up to the recent
strain of her brother's chaotic estate and her sister-in-law's increasing
madness. She confides in my wife, who is seven months pregnant, and of
whom Marya is very fond; she calls my wife "an angel." She tells us Mrs.
Klein is becoming increasingly violent, irrational and incontinent; that
Mrs. Klein's daughter (Marya's niece), who was troubled before her
father's death, has after it become quite dangerous, and has repeatedly
abused her mother; that the daughter is now forbidden by court order
from seeing her mother and even from entering the building (if we see
her we are to call the police); that, among other disgraces, the family dog
bit Mrs. Klein several times, so severely it had to be put to sleep, which
caused more rage from the daughter, who favored the dog (she claimed
it was not the family dog but hers alone); and worst of all, that Mrs.
Klein often escapes from her caretakers and gets lost, Marya fears that
one day she will disappear completely. We are aware of this last problem

on our own, because on several recent occasions Mrs. Klein has gotten loose in the building, has come to the fifth floor and pounded on our door, thinking she is on her own floor, the seventh. She cries and pleads in German to be let in. The first time it happened she pounded for a while and then went away; that is, my wife and I, sitting at dinner, listened to her pounding and did not answer the door. This was a long and leaden moment. Sin, which is often tedious, demands a particular kind of endurance when one has a partner. We sat in silence and looked at each other and then avoided looking at each other until the racket in the hall had passed, the knowledge too explicit between us that we didn't want to deal with the troubled Mrs. Klein. But when it happened a second time my wife went out and spoke kindly to her and took her upstairs. I remember listening with a tremendous relief to my wife in the hall, as she spoke softly to Mrs. Klein; I heard mingled with my wife's words Mrs. Klein's half-sobbed, undecipherable German (the sound carrying down to me through the apartment's long corridor), and hearing this, the woman's desperate need and my wife's kindness to her, I took the kindness as kindness to myself and was soothed by it. Later, when Mrs. Klein returned, crying and pounding again, and I was home alone, this feeling came back to me, a very palpable thing, of having been loved by my wife, a mysterious genesis of erosion surrounding this woman who had always been a stranger to us. And so this time I escorted her home myself. I guided her by her elbow; she did not resist but only mumbled to herself in German and cried while we waited for the elevator. I tried to say things that would soothe her, fearing some outbreak, but she was quiet. Inside the elevator we both stood looking straight ahead, the way people do in elevators, with a rigid sanity, our only connection my hand on her arm. Her skin, even at the elbow, was soft, not at all the scaly, dry skin I had expected when I'd reached for her.

Today she is standing in the entranceway below my window shouting at the Jamaican woman, angered apparently because she does not want to go inside the building, where it seems they had been headed, but back out to the street. As she shouts she gestures to the left, down 110th Street toward Broadway. I lean out and watch, my hands balled up on the rough concrete of the window ledge. A French woman who lives below me also leans out; the back of her head seems to jut out from among the bricks. I am aware of myself as the disturbed neighbor (a look on my face as I lean out the window), but I am not disturbed, merely tense. It is 4:30 on a humid day in spring, I've been trying in a half-hearted way to work, outside the daylight is failing, and soon my pregnant wife will be home. Tomorrow, I have to go and do a job in an office, which I dread. I want no commitments. Even this distant observation of the troubles of the woman in the passageway threatens to entangle me. I want to believe that the caretaker, without my involvement, can do just what the name of her position implies: take care of things, and of me, absorb the shock of this woman and bring her safely home. It occurs to me that I would like the same guarantee made for my wife, that her "outburst" will be properly handled, and that she will be returned in good order, sound, safe, intact.

Right now, for Mrs. Klein at least, the issue is in question. Even if she is quieted, it seems to be a matter of time before some catastrophe befalls her. Not long ago I saw her wandering alone on Broadway near a produce market where I was shopping, and a group of boys for no reason except their flawless instinct for cruelty picked up a bunch of grapes and began throwing them at her. It was a barrage of grapes, probably four or five of them struck her at once. She turned, and seeing nothing at first that explained what had happened to her, merely looked confused. Then the boys ran off, and Mrs. Klein let out a piercing scream; she stood and shook her arms at them and cursed them. *Gott-damn* were the only words I understood. And then she darted off, up Broadway and away from the market, leaving me wondering whether I should go after her and take her home, or, really, knowing that I should do this and would not, afraid that if I were to interfere with her I would not only be inconvenienced, but she would scream and shout at me. So I stood there, and she disappeared. She hadn't seen me.

The two women stand below, framed in the entranceway by the descending walls of the building: Mrs. Klein, mad and visibly spiteful, jumps and shouts and gestures with her arms; the caretaker is firm, resolved to contain her although perhaps not fully equipped to do it. Out by the curb, our part-time doorman sits on a kitchen chair and watches; he will not interfere. He is an older, timid man who speaks Spanish and not very much English; he has before him a fight between a woman who shouts in German and her caretaker who responds in a kind of lilting and rounded Jamaican English, and for him there is probably not on all of 110th Street a language sufficient to address the problem. He sits quietly. He is small and spry, perhaps fifty-five or sixty years old, with a neat mustache and thick glasses that make him look a bit like a bird. He glances quickly from side to side as a bird does. People pass and he pretends, as they do, that nothing is happening, although before them a woman with Alzheimer's Disease shouts and waves her fists at her caretaker. She moves frantically to the left and to the right, trying to get past, but the caretaker continually blocks her way. Finally they struggle. Mrs. Klein shouts again and then, at last, strikes her caretaker, one punch on the left arm, followed by a kind of pause and evaluation for both of them (the caretaker doesn't react), then another punch (again no reaction, very little time has passed) and finally a very strong blow to the caretaker's chest, which has both the sound of a smack (skin on skin) and a real thud, like a barrel being struck, something giving way, the displacement of air, a pop.

Above, although I don't realize it at first, I am shocked by what I have just seen: an old woman punching a younger one, punching her with a fist, hard, I clearly saw it and very clearly heard it, even five stories above; in the moments after it I realize that a kind of law has been broken in plain daylight, or a number of laws, that a woman should make a fist and punch, rather than use an open hand, that it should be a thin old woman besides, striking a far younger, more robust one, and most of all that an absurd violence has erupted in the passageway, a place as familiar to me as my own living room. And then another law, one that makes 110th Street livable, also is broken: although I don't know German I can tell that what Mrs. Klein says next has to do with the caretaker's race . . . *schwartzer.*

After this she tries again to go around the caretaker and out to the sidewalk, but now with less energy; she has for the moment lost the edge of rage she had before she struck. Yet she will not give up. She tries two more times. The caretaker stops her. Mrs. Klein gestures repeatedly toward Broadway. There is something she wants. The caretaker's patience is at its limit: time to go home, she says in a strained singsong, as if to a difficult child. *Nein, nein,* Mrs. Klein answers, angry again. The caretaker stretches her arms to keep Mrs. Klein from getting past and so leaves herself vulnerable to a sharp slap in the face. It makes a terrible sound and reminds me of seeing a child struck. The caretaker reaches for her face to rub the spot where she's been hit, while Mrs. Klein yet again tries to dash around her; the caretaker blocks her way, there is more shouting and threatening, they grapple, all in a few moments.

At last, a large Puerto Rican woman who lives on the sixth floor and who cares for children comes out of the building, wheeling a stroller. She knows the two women and she tries to calm Mrs. Klein, who briefly weeps and then shouts again. The Puerto Rican woman takes Mrs.

Klein's arms and pats them and rubs them; she is saying something kind in her rough voice. She too doesn't speak English very well and so her speech is more noises than words really, distinct vocal units conveying pure emotion. This is how she speaks to everyone, warmly, voluminously, even if they speak no Spanish. Her name is Mrs. Rivera, and she is a very large woman, an inch or perhaps two under six feet, with wiry gray hair and a rasping voice; seeing her I always think of the mountains, because she looks like a woman of the mountains, large and natural. She rubs Mrs. Klein's arms and embraces her. From above it looks like a visitation scene, the greeting of two women on the verge of confinement; there are two pairs of female arms, of different shape and shade, entwining, making motions that replace language . . . The stroller sits unobtrusively among the three women, the baby quiet. The women reassure, assert, and move around each other, using the simplest syllables. The caretaker, in the presence of a third party, has relaxed and moved off to the side a bit. Above, I too am relieved by Mrs. Rivera and the sense that someone has arrived who will calm Mrs. Klein. So I am taken by surprise, as is the caretaker, when Mrs. Klein dashes out to the sidewalk and to the left, toward Broadway, out of sight. The caretaker goes after her. Mrs. Rivera walks slowly with her stroller out to the curb, cheerful looking, after all, she had done what she could, and talks there to the doorman. Suddenly the street has shifted back to normality. The two combatants are out of sight. Mrs. Rivera speaks to the doorman, as on any other day. They are probably talking about the weather: it is the first warm day and the doorman has put his chair out by the curb to get the breeze. He is not a doorman, really, just a man who lives on the block and who works part time sitting in the lobby of this building in the afternoons. The tenants pay him four dollars an hour; some call him Joe, and others, who speak Spanish, use what must be his real name, Jose . . .

After a few minutes the caretaker brings Mrs. Klein back. She looks defeated and exhausted, the way a very active child might look at the end of a long day. Mrs. Rivera speaks again to her, again touching her arms and reaching for her hands. And in this way the scene manages to come to an end: the caretaker brings Mrs. Klein inside, tearful, shocked, and impenetrably alone. Mrs. Rivera wheels off the stroller, containing the silent child, and the French woman withdraws her head from the fourth-floor window. But from the fifth floor I watch long after it is quiet, gazing down at the street, taking in the smell of the spring's first hot day and the unusually thick feeling of the air. I am glad of the air, although I am not tempted actually to dress and go out and do the things dressed people do. I look at the people going by and at Joe out by the curb, sitting, his head swiveling back and forth as he also observes the people passing. My wife is due home soon. She may call before coming, she may not. She is pregnant. I feel as if everything is volatile, ready to break apart. For my wife's sense of well-being, I know I should be dressed when she arrives, and so I get dressed, without showering. I stick my head in the sink and run water through my hair and use the washcloth a bit and pull on a pair of pants and a shirt. Then I go back to my desk and wait. What I can't get out of my mind is the slap, the savageness of it, the awful sound, and the Jamaican woman's remarkable sacrifice of dignity for the sake of this lost old woman; I am also realizing that there were certain flawed but enduring human principles which guided Mrs. Klein, even madly: the caretaker is black, and her employee, and will not strike her in return. Mrs. Klein is mad but her madness is cunning, even criminal. As the slap replays in my mind, I think, Nazi.

The only other person who looked out, the French woman on the fourth floor, has two very tall mulatto daughters. She makes her living refinishing furniture. I have seen her through her kitchen window, which is across the air shaft from my kitchen window and below it, cleaning and repairing things around the house. I've also watched her teenage daughters, who use the kitchen a great deal at night. They are very tall and full in the body, almost plump; often they wear nothing but open robes and underpants. They've seen me, standing at my stove, which is by the window, cooking something or pretending to. We never acknowledge each other; sometimes one of them will walk over and close the curtain, sometimes not. We see each other on the elevator and greet each other politely; I do not say, I saw you the other night, fixing tea, brown-bellied, in blue panties. . . They look about nineteen and sixteen; they dress stylishly, with severe haircuts and much leather, I run into them once in a while when they are going out on dates with vain and awkward-looking boys. Alone, the girls seem very haughty; with boys, less so. My involvement is confined to their lives in the kitchen, mostly at night, the French mother has decorated it warmly, with baskets of fruit on the windowsill, wood block counters, etc. Everything is clean; whenever I see the French woman at work, repairing or cleaning, I compare her apartment unfavorably to my own, and her habits unfavorably to my own, because what I'm usually thinking of as I watch her work is my own work and how much difficulty I have doing it. The disparities I feel translate over to the objects in view, and these become the tangible expressions of a successful style, a way of living that seems much more at ease and productive than mine, I notice that her kitchen floor is nicer than ours, for instance, that the tiles are better, attractive black-and-white squares, old-fashioned looking in a reassuring way, pleasant and clean, as a home should be.

I open the window again and lean out, looking down the sidewalk toward Broadway, watching for my wife. I see our superintendent talking to the super of the next building; I don't see anyone else I know until Mrs. Rivera returns with the stroller. Mrs. Rivera's husband is a waiter in the Italian restaurant around the corner, a fact which led Joe once to tell me that the Riveras were "rich." The husband made four hundred dollars a week in the restaurant, Joe said, and the wife took in children; they were rich. Joe's voice rose comically every time he said the word "rich." People say he is slow. He is not slow, but he does have a speech impediment, a stutter and a kind of stiffness around his mouth that makes it difficult to understand him in English and in Spanish also. He is from a family of twelve children: first his parents had nine boys (Joe is the last of them), and then finally a girl, and they decided that one girl with nine boys was "too hard" so they decided to have another baby, hoping for a girl; it was a girl. After that they had a last baby, also a girl. Twelve children. I try to picture my wife and I having twelve children. The only thing I can think of about having twelve children is that after the first few, the births must go quickly. If this were our twelfth child, I wouldn't be nearly so afraid; after all, what's one more? Joe, with eight older brothers, has thirty nieces and nephews, many of them older than he. He likes music, and often while he sits he plays guitar or listens to the radio. Otherwise he talks about cars with all the men who live on this street and seem to be around all day. Everyone owns a car: mid-sized American cars from the 1970s, Darts and Dusters and a few rumbling LTDs. They stand in groups over open hoods, conferring. To own a car on this block is to be part of an organization; all repairs, parts, parking problems, etc., can be addressed without ever actually driving the car away. For a while I had a sky blue 1963 Buick that I'd paid a hundred dollars for, an enormous automobile, an ocean liner. It attracted a lot of attention on 110th Street. Joe and my super each had wanted to buy it; the super owned a Volkswagen Beetle, a turquoise vintage model from the 1950s with a flat windshield, a car which he pointed out (going for the sympathy angle) wasn't big enough for his wife and his four children. Joe wanted it because he knew it was a bargain; he offered five hundred dollars. Neither of them bought the car, after all, as it was wrecked in an accident in Pennsylvania, being driven by a retarded boy (or a near-retarded boy, accounts differ), who is a friend of my wife's mother, the kind of woman who befriends people in need, brings them home and gives them things, like cars.

Still no wife. Around the corner from here stands a cathedral, the largest Gothic cathedral in the world. This street officially is named Cathedral Parkway, although not many people use that name anymore, they use its number: one hundred and tenth street. The building where we live rises around a narrow entranceway to form a shaft up which sounds from the street seem to travel with full clarity and volume. Right now, it is quiet. I rise and lean out again to look down the street, watching for my wife; at this late stage in her pregnancy she walks very slowly. She never waddles. She tells me she has to think about this as she's walking, and often she asks me, Am I waddling? No, I always say . . .

Across the street from here is an older, Gothic-looking building with a series of ornamental gargoyles hanging from the first-story facade. From my desk I get to see many of the people who come to look at the gargoyles, people with tripods and cameras to photograph them, couples who pause and point them out, one to the other, as if they are saying: You see these are the gargoyles I told you about . . .

What I am doing, watching all these people, these strangers, seems like an attempt to understand something outside myself, but it's not just that. I am trying to discover something about myself as well. I think people are like bats, sending out sounds and placing themselves by the echo, except that for us the sound is our imagination, not the glorious imagination of the genius, but the everyday imagination all of us have: the imagination we need to be able to love one another. I watch, I see the couples across the street, pointing at the gargoyles, and I see the two superintendents, leaning against the brick; I see the doorman Joe, a small, shy man who loves music; I see a young woman in an open robe making tea in the late evening for her sister, who sits at the table behind her; they are talking. I see Mrs. Klein screaming with rage. And I see a black Jamaican nurse, Mrs. Klein's savior, who was brought into this world like a savior, by a woman in agony, and finds herself now like a savior, reviled, spit at and slapped.

Who By Fire

Victor Pelevin

Victor Pelevin is the author of the novels Oman Ra, The Yellow Arrow, *and* The Life of Insects, *as well as several other novels and collections. He lives in Moscow.*

 THE MAGAZINE FEATURED A PHOTOGRAPH OF A beefy man in a sweat suit who stood beside a yellow Ferrari. The Ferrari was parked in front of a large villa built in the style of the old *Empire du mal.* Steam rose from the red coffee cup trimmed with a gold stripe that rested on the roof of the Ferrari. The rectilinear shape and color scheme of the steaming mug made a visual rhyme with the grinning owner of the car. The man wore a heavy gold chain over the hairless chest that peaked out from his unzipped red jacket, and in his color scheme he resembled the coffee cup quite closely. The words under the photograph read: *Nescafé Gold. Real coffee for real people.*

"Idiots, "exhaled Boris Marlenovich as he tossed the magazine under his seat. The two men sitting across the aisle threw a suspicious glance in his direction (though in his dark glasses and toupee Boris Marlenovich was totally unrecognizable). Having concluded that his exclamation was not directed toward them, the two men went on with their conversation. They were, however, mistaken—Boris Marlenovich was referring precisely to them. Their conversation had been getting on his nerves since before take-off.

"The Russians," said one of the pair, a bald and bearded man who resembled Lenin after successfully opening a German line of credit and investing in a new wardrobe, "are still waiting for their first taste of liberty. The typical state of affairs in Russia is a complete freeze. During its entire history the country leaps from one thaw to the next, always aiming for liberty and missing every time. But at least when the thaw comes you can feel it. It's not about politics or economics. That's just fluff, written to order by the political analysts. But something appears in the air and for a while it gets easier to breathe. We were lucky: We had the

Gorbachev thaw. We were breathing easy until this latest 'Denim Revolution.' Now we'll have to wait thirty years for another thaw, maybe a hundred."

"Well, that's not quite the case, really . . ." the second answered quietly. He looked like a cross between former Prime Minister Chernomyrdin and a big mama bear. He kept silent most of the time and, instead of paying much attention to his neighbor, he incessantly fingered his impressive ring of keys and Tamagotchi virtual pets, which hung from his hand like a rosary. Boris Marlenovich could tell by the size of the key chain that he was watching a former janitor from the old Soviet school. But things weren't as obvious with his garrulous sidekick.

"No sir, Pavel Sergeevich, we'll live to see another Soviet regime, but with the addition of whorehouses and gambling establishments. It'll stink, in short, like it did under Brezhnev. It already stinks a bit anyway, what with all the stolen cash. The smell of all that dirty money already exceeds the codes set by Moscow's Department of Sanitation . . . Why should we be surprised when people who can't live a lie finally take up arms against their oppressors?"

That was too much for Boris Marlenovich.

"Listen," he said, turning to the Nouveau Lenin, "if your nose is too sensitive for Delta, and first-class to boot, then perhaps you should be flying Aeroflot. In luggage."

Lenin shuddered. He splashed a bit of vodka from his plastic cup. Looking at Boris Marlenovich he floundered for a retort.

"Right," he said finally," I see we have here your typical right-wing extremist. You area right-wing extremist, aren't you? Go on, confess."

Boris Marlenovich was already sorry he had broken into the conversation.

"I've got your right-wing extremists sitting outside my office in the waiting room," Boris said. "The ones that haven't thrown in the towel. I've got your left-wingers there, too. The right-wingers sit on the right and the left-wingers sit on the left. Got it? Now shut up baldy. I need some shut-eye."

"So you're a real strong man, huh?" the janitor chimed in, aiming a pair of heavy eyes at Boris Marlenovich. "I've seen your kind before. And where do they all end up?"

"That's right," said the bald one. "If you're so goddamn high and mighty, why aren't you flying your own Boeing?"

Boris Marlenovich shook his head. He could have mentioned that he owned an Airbus A-320, currently in the shop getting a new engine, and not a Boeing like some tasteless Arab, but his new acquaintances weren't worth the trouble.

Moreover, some of his men were approaching through the corridor, two from the pilot's cabin and three from the tail end. Boris Marlenovich saw one of the men take the Tamagotchi chain off the janitor's hand while another quickly and carefully uncurled Lenin's fingers from the folder of papers which he nervously clasped to his chest. The two passengers did not resist out of sheer surprise. It was hard to watch, and Boris Marlenovich turned to the window. Bits of muffled conversation reached his ear. Then a stewardess babbled something excitedly in English.

"But they want to change seats," one of the men explained to her in careful English. "Of course it is of their own free will. They want to be closer to the back of the plane. They're superstitious. They think it is safer there. I'm their translator."

"Just keep it quiet, bitch," another one of his assistants hissed at the flustered stewardess.

Boris Marlenovich wrinkled up his face and put on his headphones. He listened to Vivaldi. The white clouds in the azure below were unbelievably beautiful and Boris Marlenovich imagined that the music in his headphones emanated from the plane's shadow sliding over the frozen white hills and chasms like a phonograph needle. After a few minutes he was touched politely on the elbow. Boris Marlenovich turned his head and saw that his nervous neighbors were gone.

"We've identified them," said the aide. 'The bald one is Valentine Gowestovich, lawyer for Buranchik, a don from Brighton Beach. I suppose he was rehearsing his closing remarks. His defense strategy is that Buranchik got tragically lost in his search for identity, a victim of cultural paradigms and climactic conditions."

"A-a-ah," said Boris Marlenovich, stretching. "So that's it. I was wondering who was taking up arms without orders. Now I get it. And you know they'll find Buranchik innocent, simple as pie. The son-of-a-bitch is convincing."

"The second one is Pavel Lobkov. He's in nickel trading. He also controls one-third of the cocaine market in Northern Siberia. But he keeps his private stock in ideology."

"I thought he seemed familiar. Are they messed up in the same case?" The aide nodded.

"Look at what he was holding," he said, lifting the chain of flat electronic amulets. "At first I thought they were your usual Tamagotchi. And then I noticed each has a last name on the bottom. And instead of a virtual infant on the screen each one shows a little parliament member standing at a podium. Fifteen of them speak from the podium while three of them hold their hands out. These three just fell over. I can't tell if I should feed them, or . . ."

"Well, what else?"

"Here, that's the battery. See this wire coming out of it? And this here is like a cellular phone, only the buttons are weird. And its all in GSM XPro. Get it? He carries his whole regional Duma faction around with him on his keychain."

"Interesting," said Boris Marlenovich, examining the electronic rosary. "I've heard about these things but I've never seen one. The miracles of technology . . .. Well, I'm not envious. We've only got one of those cyber thing-a-ma-gigs, but it's the primary one."

"Look, one of the parliamentarians just keeled over. And there goes another! Unbelievable. And another, mother of God!" "Hey, you been pushing any buttons?" asked Boris Marlenovich suspiciously.

"Just this red one. It started ringing so I pushed it . . ."

"Why don't you give it back to its rightful owner. Keep it out of harm's way, or we'll regret it later. How much longer to New York?"

"Six hours."

"Wake me when we get there."

As usual, finding a spot where you wouldn't hear any frantic Russian speech in JFK was a depressing impossibility. Dispensing quickly with the formalities at Customs and passport control, Boris Marlenovich hurried toward his welcoming party. The scene reminded his chief aide of a monumental canvas the aide had once seen in Paris, which portrayed the arrival of Napoleon in Africa.

"Well?" asked Boris Marlenovich, walking up to his henchmen. "Everything's in place," answered a young man with a barely noticeable earphone resembling a tiny snake crawling halfway into his ear. "We've got the whole situation under surveillance and in our control. Since morning the subject has been located in the vicinity of South Street Seaport, as usual."

"Good," said Boris Marlenovich. "Where's the stylist? I'd like to get ready . . .No, right here. We don't have much time."

His retinue held up a canvas tarp to shield him from the rest of the airport. The stylist, wearing immense horn-rimed glasses, jumped behind the tarp after Boris Marlenovich. His chief aide thought that it was behind such fabric canopies that Japanese princes once equipped themselves before battle.

"Let's begin with the basics," the stylist warbled behind the stretched fabric. "Bold and playful: husky-fur underwear by Gitrois . . . The silk shirt is strict yet stylish, by Valentino . . . Here is a tie to match that watch, by Pierre Balman. The suit is light, of course, Claude Montana . . . Do you like it?"

"Montana?" replied the invisible Boris Marlenovich cheerfully.

"Your socks can stay. They match. And now your little shoes, Cesare Paciotti, spats. You'll be a real Cinderella in these, hee-hee . . ."

"What do you mean?"

"A guaranteed magical evening. Unfortunately, by morning time they'll fall apart completely. If you walk a lot."

"I won't be walking much," said Boris Marlenovich as he exited the improvised changing booth. "I'm not planning on it."

Forty minutes later his white limousine with tinted windows stopped on Fulton Street, the first in a long caravan of cars.

"You said you wanted to stop just short of your target, so we will let you out here," said the aide. "She's within three-hundred feet."

"Excellent," said Boris Marlenovich. "Hand over the gear."

"Here," said the aide, opening the small briefcase on his lap. "This thing goes in your ear . . .No, the other way. This ear-piece goes behind, and this wire with the headphone goes under your ear lobe. You stick it right inside.. .It's skin color, so it's practically invisible. The microphone is sewn into the lapel."

"And if I take off the jacket?"

"No problem. It has a radius of a hundred feet. You're connected to a prompter and several consultants. The earphone connection is multi-channel. See that long blue van over there? They will monitor you from inside. It's like having a quiz show team plus the Library of Congress on computer, all at your disposal."

"Is the prompter good? My English isn't always up to snuff . . ."

"It's all been taken care of. If you forget a word, or you need some local cultural reference, cough once. If you want to make a joke, cough twice. If you want to say something subtle or lay on some heavy intellectual argument, three times. Security is standing by."

"Just make sure they're not close enough to trip me up."

"Boris Marlenovich," the aide said, gently taking his boss by the arm. "Think it over, just once more. I mean, the boys and I could round up a whole chorus line for you instead. Completely risk-free."

"See, that's what none of you young people understand," said Boris Marlenovich, removing the aide's wrist from his arm. 'These days you can even order a lion from your office without going on safari. They'll knock the animal off from a helicopter and deliver him right to your door. But in the end a man has to go out and hunt for himself."

"At least take the screwdriver."

"What screwdriver?"

"With the universal head," the aide replied excitedly and in his hand appeared a small black hand gun. "It'll screw anybody, even in a bullet-proof vest. And by the time trouble starts, our boys will be all over the place."

Boris Marlenovich glanced at the weapon disdainfully and reached out as if to take it but at the last minute his hand changed its trajectory and he plucked a violet carnation from a vase attached to the wall. He broke the stem and threaded the flower through his buttonhole.

"Why don't you just put a gold chain around my neck," he said, "and fill my mouth with the taste of a new day. I'm not serving up any screw-drivers, or any White Russians for that matter. I don't have the stomach for it."

"I know. You're a kind man," sighed the aide. "A romantic. How funny it is that in Russia everyone thinks you're a shark, cold and unmerciful."

"That's the way it should be," said Boris Marlenovich, "It's not like that's an accident. It's just that it's of symbolic importance to me. How do you say that in English?"

"Symbolic meaning," said a voice in his right ear.

"Seembolik Minin," Boris Marlenovich repeated, opening the limou-sine door, "and seembolik Pozharsky. Why does it stink like fish out here? Do you read me? Over."

"Loud and clear," said the voice in his ear. "That's the Fulton Street Fish Market. The subject is still located at South Street Seaport. Straight ahead . . ."

The crowd on the wooden boardwalk swarmed in circles around the various street performers. Boris Marlenovich stood for a minute or two at the edge of a ring of people watching people watch a black guy who limbo'd beneath a low plank to the beat of drums, twisting miraculous-ly to stay on his feet. But from his perspective Boris Marlenovich could-n't even catch a glimpse of the performer.

The woman looked exactly the same as she did a month ago when he first spotted her from a car window, on his last visit to New York. She was a woman of thirty, maybe thirty-five. She was wearing a light-green tunic, a briar wreath with long green thorns and green sandals. Her plain, sweet face was covered in green make-up to match her clothes. Green gloves adorned her hands. In her right hand she held a green torch and in her left hand a green prop book. A bored photographer stood nearby. When it was clear that Boris Marlenovich was approaching no one but her, she lifted her head and smiled.

"Do you want to take a photograph with me?" she asked. "You'd better hurry before it gets dark."

"Maybe you won't believe it," said Boris Marlenovich putting some effort into the English words, "but I'd just like to . . . eh . . . eh . . . eh . . . make your acquaintance."

"You have a strange accent," she said. "Where are you from? Let me guess . . . Greece?"

"Yes and no," said Boris Marlenovich. "I'm a bit from Russia and a bit from Cyprus. And my name is Boris Marlenovich Pickle. The last name's an odd one, but very Chekhovian. Haven't you heard it on television? That's funny."

"My name is . . ."

"Hold it," said Boris Marlenovich. "For today I'd like for you to be just Liberty. Would you mind my calling you that? Its important to me."

"Okay," said Liberty and smiled. "Okay, how's life, Boris?"

"Not bad, Liberty. Maybe we could take a walk?"

"Actually, I'm working," said Liberty and glanced over at the photographer.

A thick white envelope appeared in Boris Marlenovich's hands.

"And I'm offering you a job," he said.

"What kind of a job?" Liberty furrowed her brow.

Boris Marlenovich coughed and cleared his throat.

"Your field of expertise," he said with a smile and extended the envelope to Liberty. "Free me from my loneliness for just a few minutes. That's all I'll ask of you, I promise."

Liberty took the envelope cautiously, looked inside and blinked her green eyelids.

"What are you, an Arabian prince from Siberia?" she asked.

"I've got Arabian princes sitting in my waiting room," said Boris Marlenovich, "between the right-wingers and the left wingers. So what do you say?"

"A rich guy," said Liberty, "I get it." They rested their elbows on a wooden railing beyond which dark water splashed to and fro.

"Just don't get it in your head that the photographer's my pimp," said Liberty, gazing into the multi-colored lights of Brooklyn glimmering across the East River. "It's just not the season. Is this your first time in New York? If you want I'll give you a tour. See those white and yellow lights? That's the River Café. And that bridge is . . ."

"I know," Boris Marlenovich interrupted. "Mister Brooklyn Bridge. I can tell you stuff about that bridge even you've never heard.

"For example?" Boris Marlenovich cleared his throat quite thoroughly.

"Well, for example, eh . . . There was this Russian poet, maybe you've heard of him, Mayakovsky. He wrote a poem about that bridge. That's what it was called: 'Brooklyn Bridge.' So, in this poem, these Negroes, I mean Afro-Americans, jumped off the Brooklyn Bridge into the Hudson. Because of the unbearable lightness of being, I suppose. Into the Hudson, take note, though this is the East River. That means they flew three miles, across Manhattan. By the way . . . eh . . . your man Castaneda's Don Jenaro could jump seven miles further, but our guy did it fifty-two years earlier."

"Very interesting," Liberty smiled. "Are you just as knowledgeable in music as you are in poetry?"

"Of course. That song, for instance. The one they're spinning on that sailboat . . ."

Boris Marlenovich coughed again. "That's Leonard Cohen."

"Amazing," said Liberty, gazing at Boris Marlenovich with sincere curiosity now. "It really is Cohen. Do you know what the song's about?"

"Of course . . . eh . . . Chelsea. I mean it wasn't Chelsea he wanted. He wanted Janis Joplin. At the Chelsea Hotel . . . Yeah. Any how, there was this singer, Janis Joplin, who had an affair with Cohen. And they made love at that hotel. Do you like Cohen?"

"Do I like him?" Liberty sighed. "There was a time when I dreamed of renting the room at the Chelsea where they met. But I realized that the room would always be taken."

"You know what," said Boris Marlenovich, "I've got this hunch that if we go to that hotel right this minute that room will be free. I repeat, a hunch that the room will be free in . . . How long does it take to get there? About twenty minutes? In twenty minutes then."

The room truly was unoccupied, but for some reason it had been left in disarray. It seemed that its occupants had left in a hurry; the bed was completely unclean, a man's sock and a few crisp hundred-dollar bills were strewn on the floor and the electric teapot by the door was still warm. The room seemed unusual to Boris Marlenovich, who was used to a more pristine decor. The wall of mirrors above the headboard was reflected in another mirror on the opposite wall making it seem that the bed was in a tunnel that ran to a progressively fading infinity on both ends.

"They could have at least made the bed," Boris Marlenovich grumbled.

Liberty examined the room with obvious interest. A coffee table and two armchairs stood by the window. A large stuffed monkey sat in one of the armchairs resembling a poor Brooklyn cousin of Mickey Mouse. The other held a virgin violin made of glued plywood which had never even known a toy bow. A pair of dice, somehow suspicious, lay in-between them on the table.

Boris Marlenovich quietly cleared his throat.

"You got a cold or something?" asked Liberty. 'You're always coughing."

"No," said Boris Marlenovich, "Just thinking, eh . . . the unmade bed—it's symbolic. Remember, like in the song. Giving me head on the unmade bed while the limousine waits in the street."

Liberty looked at Boris Marlenovich with empty green eyes.

"That's a lovely coincidence, about the limousine I mean," she said putting her fingers gently on his shoulder. "But that stuff about giving you head . . .I don't know about that. Generally speaking, that's not part of my game. But since we're having an evening of karaoke . . .We'll have it your way, but only if you can remember the next line . . ."

"You told me again that you prefer handsome men," Boris Marlenovich said quickly and licked his dry lips, "but for me you would make an exception."

"Okay," said Liberty and smiled. "For you I'll make an exception."

The corridor, locked off by security guards, was empty save for the aide and a young man standing by the door in a white waiter's coat too tight for his Special Forces build. Next to him stood a tray on wheels adorned with a box of candy, a champagne bucket and something covered with a white napkin.

"Do you read me, Number Five?" whispered the man into a small walkie-talkie as he read off the list scrawled on a crumpled shred of paper. "It's ready. Let's do a run down. A rose and chocolates for 'Everybody Knows' (track number seven on the CD.) Check. KY Jelly and a vial of crack for 'The Future' (track number eight.) Check. Champagne (no track number . . .) No, we didn't light the violin . . .Because, moron, its

not the burning violin from 'Dance Me To The End Of Love', which is
track number twenty-three, but the plywood violin from 'First We Take
Manhattan,' (number nine.) That's a wrap. Got it. We wait for the cue
and bring it in . . . Listen Vanya, I don't get it, who's this Cohen guy, anyway? And what do you mean—who by fire?"

"Back to work," the aide hissed fiercely and tore the walkie away from
the waiter. "You can gab later."

He wanted to add something else but just then the door opened and
Boris Marlenovich appeared in the corridor. Taking two steps he
stretched his arms, slowly extending them sideways. The look on his face
expressed something indefinite and indefinable. The chief aide reflected
that whatever Leonardo DiCaprio and James Cameron might shout out
as they played golden soldiers under the clear skies of Los Angeles, the
prince of the world (although not yet the king) was to be found in a
completely different realm. And the aide didn't have to look too far to
see him, either.

"Boss! You've got a green stain on your pants!" said the aide getting
a grip on himself. "Huh? Oh, I get it. We'll have them cleaned later.
What's the plan now?"

"Now?" Boris Marlenovich shook his head to put himself back
together. "What now? . . .We go back to the ranch."

The aide stepped off to the side and sputtered into the walkie-talkie:
"Attention all cars and security. Roll out to the airport. Repeat: the airport."

Liberty peeked into the corridor from the twilight of the hotel room
with a frightened look on her face.

"What happened?" she asked quietly.

"Nothing," said Boris Marlenovich. "I've gotta run. As Cohen would
say, ahem . . .oppressed by the figures of duty. You know how it is."

He took the toupee off and gave it to his aide. Seeing his balding pate
with tufts of rough hair spread far and wide as though burned by the
fires of hell, Liberty stumbled backward. Boris Marlenovich shrugged
his shoulders and walked down the corridor. After a few steps he looked
back at her and ran his palm over his scalp.

"Never mind," he said with a charming and somewhat guilty smile.
"We are ugly, but we have the music."

Translated from the Russian by Matvei Yankelevich.

Happy Pills

Mark Jude Poirier

Mark Jude Poirier grew up in Tucson, Arizona, the fifth child in a family of eleven children. He is the author of the novels Goats *and* Modern Ranch Living, *as well as the short story collections* Naked Pueblo *and* Unsung Heroes of American Industry. *He has written the screenplays for* Smart People, *as well as an adaptation of Alice Munro's short story "Hateship, Friendship, Courtship, Loveship, Marriage."*

YOU AND ROBBY SIT IN ROBBY'S MESSY DORM ROOM and wash down the last of your wisdom-teeth codeine with Rolling Rock, while you watch a video from the sixties made for retarded girls about to hit puberty. You should be studying because it's the week before finals, but Robby's brother, who's up at Johns Hopkins, discovered a cache of old sex-ed films in a closet somewhere in the public health library, and called Robby last night. Robby took a train to Baltimore this morning to get the film, missed his organic chemistry study session, and you transferred the film to video this afternoon. You and Robby spent hours in the audio-visual lab, trying to figure out the equipment, pissing off a group of overdriven MBA students who were videotaping a presentation about conflict resolution.

The sex ed for retards film is better than you hoped. It's about menstruation, and the star is a Down's Syndrome girl named Jill who asks everyone about periods. "Does Aunt Mary get a period? Does Daddy get a period?" The climax of the film is when Jill follows her older sister into the bathroom for a maxi-pad change. Jill's sister pulls a bloody one out of her panties and straps on a fresh one with the little elastic belts they used back then. Her bush is clearly visible. You're incredulous. It's unruly. You and Robby rewind it twice and you're sure you can see pink, what Robby calls her "roast beef curtain." You can't understand why they felt the need to show this. Jill helps her sister by wrapping the bloody maxi-pad in toilet paper and carefully placing it in the trash. There's the menstrual blood. It's bright, like cherry pie filling.

You imitate Jill's voice, even though you know it's cruel and that you shouldn't. The codeine and beer make it easier. For the next few months, you use "Jill" as an adjective. Robby loses his keys and he's Jill. Your phone gets cut off because you forget to pay your bill for two months, and you are totally Jill. You keep track, though, and each time you use "Jill" as an adjective, you have to walk the five flights of stairs in your dorm. It's like a bank. You can walk the stairs before you use "Jill" as an adjective or after, but you can't owe any stairs before something important, like your econ final or your father's medical tests. If you do, you will bomb the test and your father will have cancer.

Robby is rarely Jill because he's a genius. He will go on to place second in the 1990 College Jeopardy Tournament, losing to a horse-toothed chick from Rutgers because he won't know some trivial bullshit about the Beatles' manager. He'll win a washer and dryer and five thousand. He'll tell you that Alex Trebek wears thick makeup.

Two months after that, his sister will find him on the floor of the laundry room of their parents' sprawling Nantucket house. He will be clutching a tin of shoe polish. His headphones will still be blaring De La Soul, he'll be wearing your old lacrosse shorts, and he will have a bluish pallor. He will be dead.

The grief will take residence in your stomach and make it difficult for you to return to D.C. for your senior year. Your parents will say it's okay if you want to take a semester off, think about things, see a few professionals. But you'll return that fall, and when you realize no one on campus has even a vague sense of humor, no one is good at wasting time like Robby was, you'll actually study and do well and graduate on time and stop using "Jill" as an adjective.

You take Paxil. Twenty milligrams per day. One pink oval pill before you go to bed. On the television commercials for Paxil, a woman can't cope at work. A man is afraid to meet people at a party. They touch their foreheads to show inner turmoil. All the actors in the commercials are attractive, with smooth skin and nicely combed hair. Even though you feel the commercials are comically unrealistic, you know these pills have helped. You no longer have an anxious pang in your gut, you no longer suffer bouts of super can't-get-out-of-bed depression, and you no longer count your steps or have to enter a room with your right foot and leave with your left. The nocturnal teeth grinding has ceased, and your jaw has stopped clicking. You can eat bagels again.

You could be a spokesperson for Paxil except that you're a district-marketing manager for Lilly, the company that produces Prozac. You tried to like Prozac, you tried really hard, but you couldn't sleep, and after about a month, you started to look like your alcoholic grandfather, full purple bags under your bloodshot eyes. It was better than Desiprimine, though, the drug they put you on after college, which made you a constipated zombie and left you a legacy of hemorrhoids that flare up when you eat Mexican food or have mustard on a sandwich.

You keep your pills in your suit pocket because the airlines have lost your bags twice this year. Lost for good. A mad scramble for receipts, and several arguments with airline employees trained to detect when someone is lying. Your Paxil was in there, and you spent that first out-of-town meeting dizzy and nauseated from withdrawal until you had time to find a twenty-four-hour pharmacy. When you finally took the pill, about a day and a half late, you felt as if you could feel the happiness chemicals burrowing into the crinkles of your brain.

You sit in coach, and the woman seated next you, a big potato with dull brown hair, is chattering on about where you should eat in Indianapolis. You already told her that you've been to Indianapolis before, you are familiar with its restaurants, but she won't shut up about a sports bar that she thinks you would love. "They have one room for football, one for basketball, and . . ."

But you are thinking about Amy. She's your wife. Married four years, and you're pretty sure that you hate her. The elaborate scene unfolds: Amy in an elevator, heading up to an abortion clinic in the sky, the one hundred and thirty-seventh floor, the cables snap, and she begins to fall, the bell chiming for each floor she passes, she rises like an astronaut, she is pinned against the ceiling, the bell chimes, faster and faster—*ding ding ding ding ding*—but Amy has plenty of time to know that she's about to die. She has time to regret. She has time to think that she's selfish and cruel. One of her shoes has come off. It floats below her. She wants it. She wants her shoe, a pointy Gucci sling-back, something a witch might wear to a barbecue, and she fights the G-force to reach for it, barely touching the stick heel with the tip of her fingernail before the crash. You take comfort in knowing that this animosity toward your wife and these vivid scenes can be controlled, perhaps with a simple increase in your Paxil dosage. From 20 mg to 40 mg.

You pull the *Sky Mall* catalog from the seat pocket. You flip to a page called 'Successories'. Your ironic favorite item is a poster of a husky dog with the quotation: THE ATTITUDE OF THE LEADER DETERMINES THE SPEED OF THE PACK. You wonder how your sales team would respond if you spouted something like that at your next meeting. You turn to the monotonous hag next to you who is still speaking and you say, "Quiet time."

"Excuse me?" she mumbles. You notice her neck skin is loose—like she lost a significant amount of weight. Hundreds of pounds. Good for her.

"It's quiet time," you say. "Please abide by the rules."

You can't play kickball because they have already chosen teams and they're in the fourth inning. Chris Zizza says you can, but Doug says no way. You wish you had done your math last night like you were supposed to and that Mrs. Campobello didn't make you stay in at lunch until it was done, until now. You want to play second base and hang out with your teammates. There is safety in numbers. Thelma never comes over to the kickball game. You saw her this morning, so you know she's here, somewhere, maybe over near the swings with her friends, or outside the science room playing Chinese jump rope and grunting like she does.

You have every reason to be afraid of Thelma. She is retarded and smells like your grandmother, like cigarette smoke and cleaning fluid. Her eyes are crazy; there is nothing behind them. She is a Metco kid, bussed in from Boston. She has freckles even though she is black. If she decides to get you, she will, and everyone will help her. Everyone will chase you. When they catch you, they will hold you down while she kisses you and licks you and squeezes your balls. Teachers never stop her.

Thelma caught you once in the beginning of the year. Patches of melted early-fall snow dotted the playground. Your back and hair were muddy when they finally let you up. You were crying and you couldn't breathe. Thelma's tongue felt bigger than it looked. She wasn't seeing you. She was only seeing your mouth.

The Thelma attack returns with an unwelcome carnal immediacy that scares you into action. You jog off into the woods, back behind the janitor's building, where you and your friends once found a dead cat— back when you had friends, before everyone didn't think you were weird, before Margaret Hickey told everyone on the bus you had a boner when you really didn't, which was a miracle because you often did get boners on the bouncy bus, especially in the morning. You wait for the bell to ring. You pee against a tree and are amazed to see steam rising from your piss. It doesn't seem that cold out. You turn over a log and look for salamanders, but this log has been turned over many times before by many science classes, and nothing alive is under it.

Later in the year, four older boys will bring Thelma to this very spot in the woods. Rumors will fly. Thelma sucked all of their dicks. They poked her pussy with a stick. They fucked her. Rumors will escalate to such an extent that the principal will call an assembly where he tells the whole fourth, fifth, and sixth grade what really happened: Thelma brought some marijuana from Boston for the boys to try. Nothing sexual happened. Because you live in a community of rich, concerned parents, a few moms will take time off from shopping and planning meals to come to school and talk to each of the classes individually about drugs and sex. They will be trained by an educational psychologist for one afternoon before doing so. Doug's mom is pretty, you will think—like the lady on the shampoo bottle: fluffy blonde hair and big eyes. She will field questions, along with your teacher, Mrs. Campobello, about marijuana and rumors you will have heard about Thelma. Kim Pond will ask what marijuana is. The word "marijuana" scares you and it will scare you then. You will be surprised that kids at your school smoke it or would want to. You will wonder if they are likely to go crazy and stab you with knives. As if Leonard Nimoy and killer bees and UFOs weren't enough to worry about. You have heard a few things about Charles Manson and Helter Skelter. You are not allowed to watch the movie on TV. Your cousin Stephen has a *Helter Skelter* book, a thick floppy paperback, and in the middle there is a section of photographs. You looked at them once, saw Manson's crazy eyes, the hippie girls who followed him, the victims, the messy crime scenes. You will never look at those photographs again, and when Stephen wants to play Helter Skelter, you will say you have a stomach ache. But you will fear—you'll be sure—that if you don't play Helter Skelter with Stephen, some day you will be murdered by drug-crazed psychos. After going inside, presumably to lie down, the fear consumes you, and you will change your mind and run outside and find Stephen and tell him yes, yes you will play Helter Skelter, of course. The game won't be that scary. Stephen will yell, "There they are!" and you will both run the other way until he yells it again, and you turn around and run again. Over and over. For an hour or so. You will think he should call the game "There They Are" instead of "Helter Skelter."

Your hotel in Indianapolis is a square. It looks like it should be part of an office park on a road with a name like "Service Lane West" or "Passway 102." It edges a sad public university, a branch of Indiana State, or Purdue, or Indiana University. All the buildings on campus look like shipping and receiving centers. Peering out your window tonight, you see no students. The grass is brown and patchy under yellow lights. You are thankful that you went to a nice university with attractive buildings that weren't built in this century. It's March 30, and when you landed in Indianapolis three hours late at 5:03 p.m., the pilot told you it was eighteen degrees outside. The woman next to you broke the Quiet Time rule and hesitantly said, "A little colder than Los Angeles, huh?" Now you place your suitcase on the bed and question your decision to come to Indianapolis a few days early. It's better than being at home with Amy, though, you promise yourself that.

Amy won't look you in the eye when she tells you. You wonder if she would have even told you if you hadn't asked. You would have eventually asked, noticed that she wasn't getting bigger, noticed when September rolled around that you didn't have a baby son or daughter. "There was either something wrong with the fetus, or something wrong with me," she tells the table. She doesn't use the word "baby" and you ask her why. "Fourteen weeks does not a baby make." She seems more annoyed than sad. You want to puke. You want to smack Amy. You want to leave. In minutes, you will decide to go to Indianapolis a few days early. You wonder if it's the Paxil that scrambled the genetic code in your sperm, made your baby a retard with its heart on the outside of its body. You know Amy is lying, that she aborted your baby. It's a bit too convenient to have a miscarriage a week after the tests, which, she said, went well, and showed the baby to be in good health. Wrong. It showed something else, the worst, and she couldn't handle it. "I would appreciate it," she says as she walks out of the kitchen, "if you tell the truth and say I miscarried to anyone who cares, and keep your creepy paranoia to yourself." You want to pick up the butter dish in front of you and hurl it at Amy. It would be nice to nail her in the back of the head, to get butter in her hair. You don't even bother yelling at her. You long for the Midwest. Polite, wholesome people. Tough people. Hard workers. People who aren't tan. You decide now that a few extra days in Indianapolis might do you some good. "I'm fine!" Amy yells from upstairs. "I'm fucking fine! Thanks for asking! Thanks for your fucking concern!"

You don't remember downtown Indianapolis being all part of a giant mall. Skywalks stretch and snake from office buildings, to hotels, to restaurants, to department stores. A giant Habitrail. There's a food court around every corner of every skywalk. It's freezing outside, so you don't mind that downtown is now a giant tangled mess of careless architecture, though you are aware that this sort of over-the-top retail has stripped Indianapolis of any individuality it may have once possessed. You recall it having individuality, but you can't be sure.

You walk into Sam Goody Music and you're greeted by a robotic voice: *Welcome to Sam Goody.* The source of the welcome is a deformed woman awkwardly perched in a wheelchair. When a customer walks in, she presses a button on a panel that sits in her lap: *Welcome to Sam Goody.* You don't look closely at her. You can't. Is it nice that Sam Goody has given her this job, the job of greeter? They could be using her. People will assume that Sam Goody is a charitable company for employing the handicapped and the same people won't think twice about spending $18.99 on a CD that they could get at Target for $11.99. You begin to flip through the common overpriced CDs, and, like every time you're in a CD store, your bowels tell you to find a toilet fast.

You push through throngs of tanned kids just back from spring break. They wear faux retro T-shirts that advertise gas stations, pizza parlors, and sport teams that never existed. Where are their winter coats? As you walk through a food court on the way to the rest room, you notice that people in Indianapolis eat poorly—fried chicken, Cinnabons, barbecued ribs—and are generally overweight. You decide that you too will eat poorly this week, beginning with a cheeseburger after you finish in the bathroom.

The stall you have chosen is the cleanest you have ever been in. Leave it to good midwesterners to make their public rest rooms pleasant. The person who cleaned it most likely did so with a genuine smile and a firm sense of pride. There is no graffiti. The tile work is actually interesting, sort of southwestern influenced, navy and terra cotta. It doesn't stink. You know you won't catch anything from this toilet, so you sit right down and think you could stay here forever.

As you enjoy your cheeseburger and fries and onion rings and deep-fried mozzarella sticks in one of the food courts, you realize that you can find a deformed or mentally retarded person no matter where you look. You will always be able to do so. You look around until you spot a man with only one leg wheeling into Abercrombie & Fitch.

Amy is out. You don't know where and you don't care. It is only seven months into your marriage, you're sitting on a leather couch that cost more than your last car, trying to relax in your new house in Rancho Palos Verdes that set you back seven hundred thousand because of its ocean view and good school district, and you don't care where your wife is. It would be very easy for you to get in your car and drive three miles to the video store and pick out a porno, but the Paxil makes masturbation an arduous and often exasperating experience, so you opt to flip through the channels and eat an avocado sandwich.

You stop on a documentary about Down's Syndrome kids whose parents want them to have plastic surgery to make them look as if they aren't retarded. The idea repulses you. You decide the parents are doing it for themselves, not for their kids. You then wonder if Down's Syndrome kids have a camaraderie. They do all look alike. You saw some in South America who looked like twins of ones you've seen in the U.S., only with darker skin. Jill with darker skin. If one sees another in the supermarket is there some sort of atavistic recognition and sympathetic attachment between them? You think, yes, and that these vile parents are robbing their kids of one the few special feelings they might have during their short lives. You are disgusted by the doctors who perform these surgeries, grossed out that someone even thought of doing it in the first place. You finish your sandwich and head to the video store.

When you return, you see Amy's car in the driveway, so you turn around and take back the porno unwatched.

You slept really well last night. Ten solid hours. While the ugly patterned bedspread was made of an abrasive synthetic material, the mattress was perfect: soft with a hard center. The sleep makes coming early to Indianapolis worth it.

Other people from Lilly have begun to inhabit the hotel. You see them in the lobby and in the halls, men and women from all over the world, shades of skin ranging from deep black to nearly translucent. Some wear turbans. Others are in ill-fitted suits from the Third World. Bad eyewear from Eastern Europe. Good eyewear from Western Europe. Dots on foreheads. Accents. Almost everyone carries a black leather Lilly folder. Most smile. You smile. You don't even want coffee this morning. You look forward to spending the day in the mall, perhaps catching a movie, eating poorly again.

You share a cab with Oswaldo, an Ecuadorian with *90210* sideburns. He wears a well-tailored suit. He's in charge of launching the Prozac Weekly campaign in three South American countries.

"Ah, eh, Indy is pleasing to you, no?" he asks as you drive out of the hotel's parking lot. His breath is visible.

The cold vinyl seat has drained all warmth from your ass. "I like it well enough," you say. "Too cold."

"I like it very much," he says, grinning, looking through the cab's window at the brown, freezing gloom.

You have been to Ecuador. You and Robby were there for three weeks between sophomore and junior years. You smoked a lot of pot. You got food poisoning and puked for two days in a hostel called the Magic Bean. A nice girl from Australia helped you, made you sip bottled water and take showers. You lost almost ten pounds in forty-eight hours. When you finally stopped puking, Robby brought you Gatorade and convinced you to get on a bus with him to a jungle town called Mindo. As hard as you try, you cannot remember much of the few days you spent in Mindo because you ate some psychedelic mushrooms. You visited a reptile zoo, you know that. You have a snapshot of you and Robby holding a giant boa—although, that may have been back in Quito. You remember crawling under a building in Mindo, finding a shoe in the mud, and hundreds of tiny black and orange frogs, the size of crickets, jumping all over you. Nothing else.

"Where are you from?" the cab driver suddenly asks.

You can't tell if he's asking you or Oswaldo, so you answer for the both of you. "I'm from Los Angeles and Oswaldo is from Quito, Ecuador."

"You a Jew?" he asks you.

"What?"

"A Jew from California?"

"I am a Jew," you lie, wondering what he's getting at.

"You look like a Jew," he mumbles. "A Jew and a Mexican in my cab at the same time." He breathes audibly through his nose.

"Oswaldo is from Ecuador, not Mexico," you say. "You have a problem with us?" The cab driver is scaring you. His hair is thin and greasy. His face is pink. The back of his neck is cratered with acne scars.

"I have lots of problems!" he yells. You notice the letters DARE tattooed across his red knuckles. The letters have faded into a dirty green color.

"What is happen?" Oswaldo asks you.

"El es un racista," you tell Oswaldo, wondering if "racista" is even a Spanish word.

Oswaldo nods.

"Let us off at the gas station up there," you tell the driver through a nervous lump in your throat.

But he doesn't stop. Instead, he takes a right on a road, which you're pretty sure isn't leading to downtown. "Come on!" you yell. "Let us out!" You would just jump out of the cab at the next light if it weren't for

Oswaldo. You can't leave him alone. You can't tell him to jump out. You can't remember the word for "jump" in Spanish.

"Where are we going to?" Oswaldo asks.

"I don't know," you say. "He is loco."

Oswaldo laughs nervously.

The driver mumbles something about all Mexicans being sodomite faggots.

Your cell phone is charging at the hotel, sitting on the bathroom counter. You're Jill for not taking it with you.

Is this it? Is this Nazi redneck it?

"Stop this cab!" you yell. You try to open the window, but it's locked. You pound on it. "This is ridiculous!" Warehouses and run-down, winter-beaten homes. Dirt lots. A spray-painted, gutted-out bus. A few crows pecking at a shredded mattress in someone's front yard. The buildings thin out. Not even a neighborhood. The sky is brown. The cab speeds ahead. Oswaldo prays aloud.

Think of strangling the driver from behind, or at least pulling his greasy hair. Imagine the cab crashing into one of the formidable trees that line the road. There are no seatbelts.

You could be honest with the driver, tell him you're thirty-three, you're not Jewish, you're married but don't like your wife who you think recently aborted your unborn child without consulting you because she found out it was defective, you take Paxil but work for Lilly, the company that keeps Indianapolis alive, although you wonder why they don't move their world headquarters to a decent city. You could go on. You could tell him about the time you saw your grandmother in the hall in the middle of the night, a rubber tube hanging from her asshole like a tail. Tell him about the long-haired kid outside a T station in Boston, blasting Whitesnake on a boom box, playing air-guitar with a fucked-up arm. And speaking of fucked-up arms: that beggar kid in the bus station in Quito. His arm was more like a foot, his fingers all like baby toes. Ask the driver if he thinks the kid's mom worked in some horrible chemical factory when she was pregnant. That same day, a guy carried a woman onto the bus, sat her down across the aisle from you and Robby. Her feet were on backwards, no shit. If she had looked down, she would have seen her heels, not her toes. Even Robby couldn't come up with anything funny to say. You were both depressed until you reached your destination a few hours later. Can this driver think of anything to say about that? Did you hear the one about the lady with the backwards feet?

The driver stops the cab. "Get out," he says. "Get out of my cab." He unlocks the doors and you step onto the frozen dirt. He drives away, leaving you and Oswaldo among naked trees.

"I am confuse," Oswaldo says. "It is cold."

Oswaldo is handsome. A wonderful mixture of European and native Ecuadorian features, so perfect you want to cry. You know it's all just a rush of chemicals in your brain that's making you feel this way, a wave of relief that washes the right receptors and lights them up like Christmas trees with a perfect cocktail of neurotransmitters, but it's real nonetheless, and you're part of it and it's part of you. Oswaldo smiles and looks around. You hug him; you have to. You bury your nose in his sideburn, breathe in his cologne and the cold air, hug him tighter. He hugs you back, and you feel like everything bad falls away.

From On the Cliff

Gregor von Rezzori

Gregor von Rezzori was born in Bukovina in 1914, which at the time was an outpost of the Austro-Hungarian Empire and is now a region divided between Ukraine and Romania. In 1969 The New Yorker *published his story, "Memoirs of an Anti-Semite," which subsequently appeared as a section of a novel of the same name in 1979. His other books include* The Death of My Brother Abel *and* The Snows of Yesteryear. *He died in 1998 in Italy. What follows is an excerpt of a novel left unfinished at the time of his death.*

AMONG THE DREAMS THAT HAUNT ME, THERE IS one, more persistent and tormenting than others, which conceals that which represents—if I am to express it in literary terms—"the unfathomable mystery of my being." The dream proceeds in an unquiet flow, interrupted by blank periods of unconsciousness and by raggedy specters, yet draws on with an inexorability which fills me with terror. The logic of its images is deceiving. It holds true only for as long as I let myself drift in its flow. When I watch this dream from within itself, as, so to speak, from a diving bell, the images drift by me like so much flotsam carried by an inundation. There is no apparent significance to be found in them, even though, in their original context, they are sure to make sense, just as in the waters of a flood, the drifting bird cage with the dead bird, the face of the grandfather clock without hands, and the floating dresser drawer, in which a cat has sought refuge, gain a connective meaning when these diverse items are understood as parts of the house in which all of them originated. There exists a similarly unifying concept for the images of my dream. It may be called "I" and in its totality it represents an aggregate of individual character traits. But this "I" is not the tenant of the flooded house, even though I know with the certitude of the dreamer that whatever I experience relates to something I cannot name, but which constitutes the core of that concept of "I" and, thus, the core of myself. This, incidentally, is a thoroughly malevolent core: it is the origin of the flood which destroyed the house. Although this is to be understood merely in all the ambiguity which epitomizes the state of dreaming. In it, images are experienced and experiences are imagined. Metaphors flow into one another in a semantics of meanings all their own. But what they signify to me is unambiguous: my "I," in reality, does not exist. It is an abstract concept. Alike, in the realm of geometry, a point through which an infinity of lines are running and which by itself, nevertheless, is without dimension. It is the vanishing point of a cyclopic vision, a one-eyed perspective, in which all that is happening is gathered up in an existential experience of beingness. It is exclusively my own and yet I cannot define it by the declaration: "This is I!"

I was about to prepare my dinner: roasted calf's heart. I was hungry after an overcast day spent in a brown mood. I'm alone in my house. My servant—attendant, gardener, companion in solitude, call him what you wish (he, too, is now alone since the woman with whom he entered my service has left him), after having finished with his chores (whatever these may be; they are not of my concern), probably sits in dull apathy in front of the TV screen in the improved barn where he lives. We hardly exchange more than three words in a week. This morning he brought me from the village butcher some calf's heart for the dogs, still warm, for Monday is slaughtering day. I fed the dogs the cartilaginous, fatty ventricles and reserved some of the tender pieces for myself. I love to eat heart. Quickly broiled with a little butter, flavored with a bit of pepper and nutmeg, it is more succulent, heftier, and "heartier" than any other kind of meat.

The dogs, too, are wild for it. The greed with which they wolf down the pieces is frightening. They are heavy-set Neapolitan mastiffs, mouse-gray with broad white chests and enormous dark-gray heads, reputed to be highly dangerous. I have been warned repeatedly not to feed them by hand. I did it all the same today, even though my fear of them makes the hair at the nape of my neck tingle. On the butcher block where I always cut my meat, the points of the heart lay in front of me, plump and rosy, with delicate purple veining beneath the silkily shiny skin, that already had begun to dry out: sharply dissected, malignantly inflamed and swollen glands.

I understand why the women with whom I lived in the end all abhorred me. I used to suffer from an all-consuming paranoia. Time and again I was caught up in the manic concern that I had caught one of those venereal diseases, of which, during my childhood and adolescence,

I had been given graphic descriptions to rival medieval presentations of hell. Their coloring was the same as that of altar panels of the Sienese school: the fiery red of festerings, the livid green of pus, the yellowish liquefaction of decomposition. When these came to haunt me, I lost all reason. The slightest reddening of my penis would send me into ludicrous frenzies. I could not keep myself from checking several times daily whether the pure cyclamen-shaded silkiness had not been marred by a small, hard, raspberry-colored primary symptom, which soon would proliferate into fearsome sores; or whether from the slit of my urethra that, with its slightly protruding opening formed a kind of thin-lipped mouth which showed an embarrassing resemblance to the mouth of my mother, was not issuing the mealy drip of an ever more corrosive flow which would dissolve my testicles. Obsessed by such fantasies, I inspected the part of my body in which my sense of selfness was concentrated even more intimately than in any other, such as, for instance, my hand, that obedient and devoted servant, indeed my most humble one, without which I would be nothing and even would be unable to make a living. (For I am by profession a woodcarver of sacral figures and not a bad one: my sculptures of the Madonna are displayed in some of the most prestigious art galleries.) In this, my hand, myself is much more concentrated than in whatever is inside my skull, where allegedly all originates that elevates life above the dumbness of sheer animal existence. (While, in fact, nothing grander takes place there than a succession of surrealist images, not unlike those in my nocturnal dreams.)

At first, women usually were amused by my eccentric obsession. A sprightly creature, whom I had picked up out of a tour bus when I was still living at the seashore above a cliff and who then stayed with me for some weeks, always participated with diligence in my self-inspections. She was a puckish thing, graceful and lively, full of droll fancies and always cheerful. I would have every reason to be grateful to her. She helped me to get over a difficult time, when I lost all my hair. This happened so unexpectedly and with such thoroughness that, at first, I was as if spellbound by the process itself and hardly considered to what an extent if transformed my whole appearance. One morning, as I was combing, I suddenly held whole tufts of hair in my hand. As I wiped my face with a washcloth, I rubbed away my eyebrows. I no longer had to shave. My pubic hair disappeared; my chest and my armpits, my arms and my legs became as smooth as those of a child. Soon, my head, too, was totally bald and of a silky sheen, flushing to roseate pink under the weakest rays of the sun. It was fascinating. But then, when several physicians told me that there was no known remedy against this loss of hair, that one knew nothing of its causes and could only surmise that those were psychosomatic in their origin, so that I had to conclude that I would remain a freak for the rest of my life, a bleak albino, a livid worm, only then did I really get panicky. The girl, her name was Lisa—incidentally, the same name as that of the girl to whom, as common parlance has it, I had lost my innocence—this the second Lisa in my sexual career; this girl, then, in the most disingenuous and natural way prevented my ending up in an insane asylum. She not only took the liveliest interest in my sporadic inspections of my penis, but also in the rapid progression of my baldness. She said I now looked altogether like a penis in full erection, since my glabrous head in its taut plumpness resembled nothing so much than a hardened glans.

She was witty and without prejudices. Once I told her the story of the maid, her namesake Lisa. She was the daughter of Furlan peasants, with whom I, a naïve and readily aroused adolescent, used to wrestle as with my schoolmates, until one warm Sunday afternoon, when my mother happened to be out of the house and our scuffling in her room got out of hand, ended up in another activity, which left us both, still panting and not fully realizing yet what had happened, with a dull feeling of guilt and a vague repugnance and disgust for each other. The change in our reciprocal behavior, so totally different from that day onward, when previously we had dealt with each other almost like siblings, aroused the suspicion of my mother. She dismissed the girl and then, to test the reaction this would provoke in me, told me that she had to let Lisa go because this supposedly innocent country child had contracted a venereal disease.

I managed to appear unconcerned. But in reality, my fear was horrifying. Even though I knew it to be a calumny, merely a trick of my mother's to find out how far I had gone with this girl; the latter herself might not even have known that she had been infected. Although she kept herself very clean, she hadn't been a virgin. And who is to know the type of men with whom a maid knocks about on her days off. I hated my mother. I hated her anyway, but now I hated her all the more for the low cunning of her ruse, with which she had tried to entrap me. I went about with murderous thoughts; I was a mere sixteen. I would have been capable of an act of violence, if I had found only the slightest sign of an infection on me and, without rhyme or reason, would have held my mother responsible for it. The aversion that filled me when I thought of what had happened in the maid's room, the bestial, obsessive, despicable coupling of the sweating bodies in the messed up, crumpled clothing, exposing only the genitals, the sliminess of the secretions, the disheveled bed linen, which had not been freshly changed for God knows how long and from which emanated an obtrusively female odor, the sticky, loose hair of the maid, her hot, bloated face, distorted by lust—all flowed together in the loathing I felt for my mother.

My mother was reputed to be very beautiful, in spite of her thin lips; someone once remarked that she drove men crazy with her hangman's smile. Even today it is only with distaste that I recall the overblown rifeness of her femininity, her glorying in the role of the arch-female, in which she saw herself and as which she found herself confirmed by everybody around her; it is only with intense repugnance that I remember the strong smell of her hair, which was her constant preoccupation and which Lisa had to brush and pin up mornings and nights, so that hairpins would be lying all over the house and I would find them between the pages of books and on the breakfast table; even the entrance hall was pervaded with the smell of that blonde mane, which my mother wore towering on her head. It drove me to insanity to see the men who came to visit us—those suitors with the comportment of lounge lizards, whom my mother called "admirers"—dilate their nostrils in the effort of catching a whiff of her "female effluvium." I knew that my mother was—as the saying has it—as cold as a fish, incapable of any affection, let alone of any tenderness. It was said that she had driven my father to an early death; I had never known him. Her suitors she kept on a string, and, in my own belief, none of them actually were her lovers. I would have been aware of it, for such things cannot remain concealed in a middle-class apartment one shares together.

What I clearly remember is that an aura of sexuality always surrounded the female whom I'm obliged to call my mother. She led an indolent life, but raised me with Spartan harshness. The only proof of affection I ever got from her was the permission, later the command, to join her in bed during her after-lunch siesta. As long as I was a child, I derived a certain pleasure from this, although even then I avoided touching her overly smooth, heavily scented skin or even her underwear. But the bed was large, warm, and soft, it was the matrimonial bed of my parents and the only place of voluptuous safeness I knew at the time. Yet, all too soon it also became a source of disturbing emotions. She lay there almost naked, merely covered by a thin silk robe under which I imagined her heavy breasts held by a bra. Soon other parts of her body crowded my imagination. I felt sick when thinking of those other carnalities: the slick belly with the indented navel and its swelling out to the edge of the brief panties, which she presumably wore and which I fancied to be so tight as to define clearly the mound of her pubic hair underneath. She made little effort to hide her corporeality and, at home and during most of the day, went around in nothing but her thin dressing gown, unless she—as she termed it—"dressed to kill." In our small provincial town, she was thought of as always being in the height of fashion. In the secret of my own heart, I called her a slut.

During puberty and even more so in its aftermath, this sultry siesta hour, next to a woman I loathed, caused me intense anguish. With that lust for domination peculiar to her, my mother had known how to shape this ritual togetherness into a duty I owed her. I sweated next to her. Needless to say, I couldn't sleep. The thought of what my schoolmates— I had no real friends—would say, if they knew that each day, during the best leisure time, I was ordered into the bed of my mother, made me blush all over. What bothered me most was that I was unable to prevent certain effects on my awakening virility. Hard as I tried, I could not constrain the surge of my blood. It got so that the thought alone of that siesta produced an erection with me. I was strongly developed and my pubic hair was precociously full. The idea that my mother could consider or, even worse, might actually become aware of my condition, brought me to the verge of despair. Had it happened—or rather, had she betrayed in any way that such had occurred—I would have killed one of us, her or myself. Meanwhile, however, I had to continue fulfilling my daily postprandial duty of our shared siesta. Nor was I exempted from it after the affair with the maid.

Lisa—not the maid, but that person with whom I lived years later and not so long ago in that house on the cliff above the sea—happened to be the only human being with whom I ever spoke of that episode. Not so much because I might have set any special trust in her; rather I believe it was the shock over the loss of my hair that made me confide in her. She had the gift of making light of everything, without taking anything lightly. At times, she reminded me of a tightrope walker I had seen at the circus in my childhood: I saw her balancing a delicate Japanese umbrella above her silver wig, while her feet groped and glided forward on the rope, then tripping swiftly and lightly over its entire length. Nor did Lisa ever lose her equilibrium and poise while hearing my confessions. She listened to me, alert and with concerned attentiveness, and then said: "I thought of a good metaphor for expressionism: instead of speaking of primary symptoms having the color of raspberries, you should rather speak of rasberries having the color of primary symptoms." It had no connection whatever with what I had been telling her (I had not mentioned any primary symptoms, least of all any raspberry-colored ones; a disgusting idea!), and yet I felt relieved in a strange sort of cheerful way. Women are odd creatures indeed.

But let me get back to what I had started to recount: today, as the points of heart lay before me to be cut up, I suddenly was overcome by the feeling that once more I was back there, hovering above the cliff. I shall try to describe this more accurately: it is a kind of hatred, intensified to a celestial degree. It renders the world transparent to my eyes. I somehow feel that this hatred is part of God's essence, in which I share. At the same time, it crushes me down to the very depths of the humanly experienceable. If, at the beginning, I spoke of those images as being the flotsam of my life's story as it appears in my dreams, such seizures of divine hatred are the eddies in that flood. They pull me down to the bottom. Above them swirls the froth of my existence.

I was about to cut the meat. I take pleasure in cutting meat with very sharp knives, particularly heart, which is firmer and more elastic than other kinds of meat and which, under the blade, bursts open more satisfyingly, displaying so to speak more carnal cuts, from which only a few sparse drops of blood seep out. Before I start cutting, I sharpen the knives on the whetstone. I do this, sensuously taking my time, with a quick crossing of the blades in front of me, as I have learned to do it from butchers. I appreciate fine tools; my carving knives, my chisels and scaupers I also keep shiny and sharp. Wood is a responsive material, which I carve with a pleasure proportionate in its voluptuous intensity to the wood's degree of hardness. The case with meat is different and very special. The sinking in of the blade is an experience of erotic immediacy, albeit only if the knife is exceedingly sharp, for then one feels as if the meat actually were to open itself to the blade. Ordinary knives do not cut well. That's why I acquired a set of real butcher knives, from cleaver-like heavy ones, with which to hack apart bones, all the way to tiny ones, viciously curved, with which to peel, with short, hissing, strokes, the tendons from their enveloping sheaths.

But the local butcher here is an average man of no particular interest, who knows little of all that. Only his appearance is out of the ordinary. He is one of those blaze-faced redheads, who are frequent among Ashkenazi Jews, and whose skin is not merely freckled, but spotted and flaming like that of salamanders. They pinch their faces into a permanent grimace, as if they were squinting all the time into the heart of flames. Someone told me once that they are the descendants of the tribe of Juda, to which the mother of Christ belonged. For Jews, the ritual kosher slaughterer, the so-called *shochet*, is respected as someone holding almost priestly rank.

The slaughterer who advised me when buying my set of knives was not the local butcher, but the one in the village at the seashore, above which I lived on top of a cliff in a tiny white-washed house built of rocks and pieces of marble and made up of three rooms around a patio overgrown with bougainvilleas. The way I see it now, I was very free then, master of my own destiny, of greater zest, and experiencing my life much more intensely than now. This ended when my hair began to fall out. The butcher down in the village took as lively an interest in this phenomenon as the blithe creature who was living with me at the time. I was probably the butcher's best customer and I treated him like a friend. In return, he favored me with his choice pieces of meat. He was a handsome man, not overly tall, but imposing in stature. His hair in front was getting sparse. I recall a pair of rather disturbing gray eyes, radially striped with lines of yellow, as the eyes of cats or goats. If one looked into them, the iris, nailed down by the black pin-point of the pupil, seemed to start whirling around it, as a wheel of fortune turns around its hub. The eyeballs were of that bluish white, peculiar to freshly peeled hardboiled eggs. In my memory of him, I see those eyes above a bloodsmeared, white linen apron. Those eyes rivet my own, while his hands, in a kind of autonomous and almost unconscious dexterity, continue to manipulate his knives. I admire any kind of craftsmanship and I am proud of my own skills. His hands were well-formed, strongly veined, with sensitive fingers and spatulate nails which, despite all the wallowing in blood, he kept spotlessly clean. The hands of an artist. What was most impressive were his arms: massive and muscular, powerful, as if fed by the constant handling of raw meat. The skin of the forearms was ivory matte and covered by a black, silken fleece; on the inner side, however, they were hairless and above the elbow of such smooth and swelling whiteness, as elsewhere one only finds in the breasts of comely women. All the movements of the arms and the handling and strokes of the knives were skillful and precise in their execution, irrespective of whether these served to heave a whole side of beef down to the cutting block from the murderously pointed, S-fashioned hooks, affixed to the ceiling of the store; or, with incredibly well-aimed hatchet strokes, to split open a joint; or separate ribs with broad, heavy blades; or peel crunchingly the red fleshy parts from their surrounding cushions of fat with short, dagger-like knives. I bought from him only the very best meat of young steers which, in addition to a few lambs, he slaughtered regularly each week. The village was tiny and, apart from myself, he didn't have many regular customers. He treated me as a privileged client. A kind of trusting relationship developed between us. Once, when he got into trouble, I was able to help him out. But of this, more later.

The place where this occurred was renowned for its beauty. Whether this is so still today, remains to be seen. Even then, swarms of tourists invaded it in summer, but kept to the beach, where heretofore only the huts of fishermen had stood, so that all too soon a rank proliferation of villas, hotels, dance halls, boutiques, espresso bars, and self-service stores began to form a new subdivision, climbing the slope of the hill to join the old *borgo*, whose houses were glued to the precipice like a colony of swallow nests. The hill itself rises sharp and abruptly from the flat shore to form a cape protruding into and towering over the sea. Since days of old, this striking formation was seen as a petrified giant reclining, his chin supported by his hand and gazing out at sea. Along his back and during my time, the olive groves still climbed unchallenged and unspoiled within rubble-walled retaining terraces all the way to the cork oak woods, which extended their stunted growth along the ridge of the hill. Nights, the thrushes sent their sweet strains, a succession of three simple notes, up to the heights of the star-blazing heavens. A road, hewn from the rock, winds its way in serpentines up to the ridge, and then turns into a stony path ending where the rocks, bare and vertiginous, drop down to the sea's foamy surf below. Barely a dozen steps from the abyss, on the highest point—the bald crown of the giant, if you so wish—there stood my house.

Translated from the German by H. F. Brock de Rothermann.

Eidetic

Rick Rofihe

Rick Rofihe was born in Bridgewater, Nova Scotia and lives in New York City. His book of short stories, Father Must, *was published by Farrar, Straus and Giroux. His e-book* BOYS who DO the BOP: 9 New Yorker Stories *can be freely downloaded via the online literary journal Anderbo.com, of which he is publisher and editor-in-chief. He is a Whiting Writers' Award winner, and the judge of the RRofihe Trophy short story prize.*

DEAR HANK,

I know this is unceremonious, writing on my daughter's "Care Bear" stationery but, nonetheless, you haven't written to me and I feel like our dialogue has ended abruptly. Writing to you without getting a reply is like jerking off.

Not much is happening here in Wainscott. Adrian is penis-obsessed. Fortunately next week his father is joining me so I'll let *him* deal with it. (Another reason I'm glad I'm not a single mother.)

And if you want to know what penis-obsession *means* in a four-year-old, it means him clipping little Spider-Man weapons around his penis and shooting them. And threatening his sister by holding his penis like a hose and chasing her around pretending to pee on her. (On the other hand, I did catch Emma just as she was about to tie a little doll apron and bonnet around Adrian's penis to make "a penis woman," she told me.)

All this is too much for me. But I can relate all the way around. I mean, if *I* had a penis, I would find all *kinds* of fun things to do with it too.

Now, Hank, what is this note about that I just received from my mother? What is she talking about when she says "us"? YOU AND ME? And she says she *approves*—OF WHAT?? *RÉPONDEZ S'IL VOUS PLAÎT!*

In any case, her sensationalism knows no shame. Yesterday she called and told me in a quavering, tear-filled voice that my grandmother had fallen down the stairs. I thought it had just happened. She filled me in, blow by blow, slo-o-owly, in that teary voice with lots of sighs: how grandma landed on the concrete basement floor, that she may have been lying there for "who knows how long," that the doctors wouldn't tell the family for sure if she was ever going to walk again. Finally I asked if my grandmother was going *to die* and she responded in a perfectly normal voice that this all happened *days* ago and that grandma is now sitting up in her hospital bed, eating, speaking, and drinking. (My mother is truly a product of the tabloid age.)

Of course, the whole thing is horrible, because even though I don't really care about most of them, I do have a vague fondness for my grandmother. Furthermore, I know a huge confrontation will happen when I don't attend either or both my grandmother's logically imminent funeral or my sister's remotely possible wedding. But what can they do? Put a familial curse on me? Cut me out of a will that I'm not in anyway?

Hank, have you ever read any interesting fiction or drama about mailmen? Not postal workers, only the people who schlep it to your door. I recently imagined a scene in which a mailman throws bunches of letters into the ocean. Can you imagine how appalled and upset certain people would be if they found out a mailman might have *done something* to their mail? There could be a public lynching. (What I'm trying to say, Hank, is, *Please* write.)

I'm going to bed now. It's very late for me (a quarter to midnight) and I've obviously missed the last letter pickup.

OK, now it is 5 a.m. and although I'm sipping a cup of coffee while the kids are still sleeping, I'm not *really* awake because I jumped out of bed when the alarm went off, thinking I was late or maybe reacting to a dream or something. (Ignore me if I'm babbling.)

I think that all night I dreamt about people I knew when I was in high school. I woke at 2 a.m. composing in my head the meaningful letter I would write to Shirley, my high school drug pal and sex partner who, twelve years ago, when I ran into her out in Missoula, was a telephone-repair person and looked like a cowboy with breasts. Then I slept and woke again, sure that I would call and visit Ellis, my flamboyant and brilliant boyfriend but *not* sex partner (he was always gay) and show him the photo of us running naked through the campus of the college I would soon attend. I rediscovered Ellis when I taught a term in Santa Cruz and then re-rediscovered him a couple of years later on a trip (before I met you) to New York. He writes essays that often wind up in good places under different names. The last one was about his having AIDS. I'm frightened to contact him again because I think he's quite sick and even though I've never really been around one, I have a feeling I would be a lousy bedside companion for a terminally ill person.

Did I ever tell you that I have an eidetic brain? I never really thought of it as a virtue because nobody else cares if a person has this ability or not since it doesn't really translate outside one's head, but anyway I can see the wildest things clearly. I'm really at my best when I can visualize the pine floor of your house up there, and the newspaper beneath the maple table with benches at either side and something on your stove that was pretty, probably an enamel teapot. And a beige shirt that you wore. And how I got you hard with my hair.

Now it's 8:30 and the kids here have had breakfast. I'm watching them through the patio door but, let's face it, you can't raise your children through glass, so this will be short.

What I wanted to tell you was my favorite passage in that insert you sent me from *Sassy* (an appallingly racy post-toddler magazine that I often did look at—and I know you did too) is the one where the foxy guy buys a "hardbound, coffee-table-size book" (and I thought Madonna's *Sex* was oversized) and then tells the cashier that she has "a good bod but no brain cells" because she short-changed him.

Who do you think are the true intellectuals? I'm a fan of both Gore Vidal and Harold Bloom although most people can't stand either of them. George Plimpton is interesting. (I wish you were here with me so you could say Yes-No-Yes or something.)

I'm seeing Adrian getting his penis out. Gotta go.

The mailman's not here yet, but now I have a little girl with a toothache in my lap. Poor Emmikins. I'll have her write her greetings to you—she's a very smart little girl.

Now it is 1 p.m. I am most definitely awake. Got your two hilarious post-cards just now, along with an envelope full of annotated clippings. The cards killed me. You are so funny Hank Hillon.

But I'm trying to respond to your real letter. The older letter about love and sex and relationships. You're right about the getting close and pulling back thing and how I did that and you too. But why when I was pregnant with Adrian? Just timing? I don't know why I did that with you. I can only make things up because I can't remember why, and my eidetic mind can't seem to see anything either. Maybe it had to do with the sex. You're right, sex can really screw things up. (You said "make you sad" but I don't feel that way although I see how you can because you are a romantic person and I'm not, although I wish I was. I'm too pragmatic.)

Sex used to define me in a sense. Especially when I was a teenager and it was one of the only ways I knew how to communicate, since I was raised in a family where sexual abuse and innuendo trumped academia and sincerity. Seduction and sex was a hard habit to break. Some time after I started college I found out that I had another way to relate to people, and after all isn't that what life is about—always looking for other people to relate to? So I changed my appearance— short hair, no make-up, and found that sexual energy toward me changed and I wasn't flirting with every dick-head on the street. Though I do tend to flirt with men and women after I know them and trust there is something about me they like that doesn't include sex. Because sexual energy between friends is inevitable especially when it's one of the biggest things you really don't know about each other. So what if I can't help but wonder about other people's sexual responses—does that make me a kind of voyeur? Anyway, I'm a *would-be* fly on the wall.

I'm glad (I hate that word) . . . I'm happy . . . I'm pleased? . . . It's nice (awful). . . It is *simpatico* that you now have in your life a woman who something's going on with . . . (no, no, no) whom you're interested in (worse). HEY DUDE, GOOD LUCK W1TH THE BABE! Now for your question: How would *I* feel if *you* were married? . . . hmm . . . I guess it would be just another thing. I had a very close friend in Santa Fe who worked at a place called the Borrowed Money Café. His name was Eugene. We tried the sex thing about ten years ago and it wasn't right, but we were (and still are in a remote sort of way) close friends. For a while, way back when neither of us had a partner. Then he met a wild Texas chanteuse, but my never-ending presence led to their demise. Years later, after I was married, he met a woman who he'd eventually marry and he said to me, "Dee," (that's what he always called me—Dee DiLorenzo), "BACK OFF!" I've always backed off but she's never been entirely comfortable with me.

And so it goes . . .

I'm going to stop writing this letter now.

Popcorn

Strawberry Saroyan

Strawberry Saroyan is the author of the memoir Girl Walks into a Bar. *Her poetry, journalism, and essays have appeared in* The New York Times Magazine, The Believer, Zyzzyva, *and* Salon.

SHE CLOSES HER EYES AND SEES BLACK AND THEN stripes of color like on television when they do broadcast testing and say this is a test, this is only a test, if this were real . . . and then the screen disintegrates into a rainbow of microdots swirling around like in a cartoon when someone vanishes into thin air, only this is the opposite of that because the dots make her appear, swirling into an image of her walking down Madison Avenue, and it's her but it isn't really her, she's a movie star circa 1945 and the camera loves her and her style is real instead of just retro, and she's carrying a black cell phone and talking to someone nonstop but the sound is turned down so she can't hear what she's saying, and she worries about it but then she realizes it isn't a cell phone at all, it has a big black cord, shit, she's forgotten to leave her phone at home, but it doesn't matter because the cord keeps stretching as she keeps walking and talking, and the conversation she's having is really important to her movie-star self, but her real self is curious about her apartment so she follows the cord back to her place, and when she arrives it's just like she always thought it might be, it has a chocolate and cream color scheme, it's like walking into a big cup of coffee, it's comfortable, you can sit down, have a drink and there's a rainstorm on the stereo and big abstract paintings everywhere, and she breaks the fourth wall and climbs into a picture of a skyscraper on fire, and once she's inside she wants to get to the top of the building where the flames are so she doesn't even think about it, she just starts flying, she flies standing, it's more like levitation, and when she gets to where she needs to be to save everybody, it isn't actually a building at all, it's a red hot Rothko suspended in the sky, and she wants out, so she rides a wet droplet of paint she finds at the bottom of the canvas down until she hits a lit streetlamp, which burns a little but not that bad,

500

and then she lands on the ground, dusts herself off, and starts walking to a dinner party she has to be at on the Upper East Side and on the way she sees a copy of the new *New Yorker* in the window of Hudson News, and she walks in and buys it and her coins clink on the counter, and as they do she hears a faint ringing and she realizes it's the phone but she decides not to get it, and she doesn't but she starts to think she might be awake, and then she starts thinking about her life and what she's doing with it, and the idea of anonymity frightens her like nothing has ever frightened her before, and she is in a slow panic, and she thinks she might as well just commit suicide, the only thing happening is that she'll be twenty-six and then twenty-seven and then thirty, and then her ex-boyfriend appears out of the blue, like changing the channel, looking better than he ever does in real life, looking like a fucking Kennedy, and they're standing on the lawn, and he gives her a copy of his novel and there's an angel on the cover, and she thinks it's weird that he hasn't mentioned her wings but then she thinks he's probably just trying to be polite and she walks upstairs then and flings herself out a window, and she realizes she's falling, but luckily she lands on a bed, and Courtney Love has been sleeping there, but now she's awake and big black cameras with flashbulbs popping but no photographers are pointing at them, and Courtney says let's go into the living room there's a party in there, so they put on matching nightgowns and tiptoe out to surprise every-body but nobody notices, and the Beach Boys are playing but it's all instrumentals, no lyrics, and she starts dancing to the keyboards that sound like they're coming from the future, and then she speeds through a tunnel to a drum solo until she comes out the other side, and then she's at a desk, in an office, and there's a big sign suspended above her that says MEDIA SLUT, and another one that says MORE, and she starts phoning people she doesn't know and asking them if they still love her and some of them say yes, and the hand she's dialing with has black nails that look like someone stepped on them but they also look chic, and she's smok-ing a Parliament Light, and she worries about smoking indoors but then she remembers that no one cares, it's okay to light up in the office because she's in London, and the thought that she's so far away makes her happy, and she tells the person on the line in L.A., listen we can't talk long because I'm halfway across the world, but then she realizes it does-n't matter because the company's paying and screw the company, and then she walks out to get some lunch somewhere and she sees a white limo, and it looks like Larry Flynt's but someone else rolls down the win-dow and says hi, and she doesn't know who it is at first but then she recognizes Burt Reynolds, looking like he looked in the seventies, and he opens the door and motions for her to come sit on his lap, and she says wait, let's take a walk first, I don't really know you, I mean, I know you from the movies but I don't know you as a person and then he convinces her that that's silly she's just scared, and she doesn't want to look scared so she gets in the car, she figures the driver will protect her if nothing else, and then Burt looks into her eyes and tells her to stop thinking, and she does, and by the time they hit the freeway they're making out to the *Mission: Impossible* theme and moving so fast it feels like they're flying, and then she looks up and realizes the car is driving itself, and it's okay as long as they're going in a perfectly straight line but if they come to a turn they're in deep, and Burt thinks the whole thing is funny at first but then he gets pissed because her fear is killing the mood, but she doesn't care, she's going to save herself, so she climbs up front, and the whole time she's praying there are no cops around because she's practically naked and speeding, but then she forgets about it, this is about life and death not traffic tickets, and then she gets off on Sunset, and Burt's asleep in the back, and the *Mission: Impossible* disc skips and then dies, but she keeps her eyes on the road and her hands on the wheel, and then the car swerves, and then it swerves again, and she sees the faces of other drivers coming at her head-on but she keeps driving, and then she realizes she's killing people but the brakes aren't working and crashing actually feels kind of cool, but she has to look upset for insurance purposes so she starts faking it, and suddenly she's screaming and crying like a girl in a horror picture, and then she realizes everything is just special effects, the people are crash-test dummies and the fire isn't really hot and everyone is still alive, and then Burt opens his movie-star eyes and says don't worry honey, it's all popcorn, and she knows it's a line but she falls for it anyway, what the hell.

My Mother and the Stranger

Saïd Sayrafiezadeh

Saïd Sayrafiezadeh is the recipient of a 2010 Whiting Writers' Award, and the author of the critically acclaimed memoir, When Skateboards Will Be Free, *of which "My Mother and the Stranger" is a chapter. His short stories and nonfiction have appeared in* The New Yorker, The Paris Review, Granta, *and* The New York Times, *among other publications. Born in Brooklyn to a Jewish American mother and an Iranian father, he was raised in Pittsburgh.*

MY MOTHER'S NAME IS MARTHA HARRIS, WHILE MY name, on the other hand, as you already know from the byline, is Saïd Sayrafiezadeh. If we lived in a matriarchal society, my last name would also be Harris. I would be a Harris right now sitting down to write this story this evening about the evening a stranger forced his way into my mother's home, if men did not—do not—view women as property. This going back thousands of years, a history I am unfamiliar with, have not researched with any authority, yet know it to be somehow true as I sit down to write, decidedly not a Harris.

It is twenty-nine years ago when this tale takes place. It is 1973. It is Fort Greene, Brooklyn. It is nighttime. I am five years old. My mother is forty. She gave birth to me when she was thirty-five, and by thirty-six she was separated from my father.

Shortly after the abrupt and unceremonious departure of my father, who also happened to be her husband of ten years, my mother abandoned the name Sayrafiezadeh and returned to her maiden name of Harris. "He gave me twenty-four hours notice," my mother has told me dramatically more than once. And I imagine the scene unfolding in the perfunctory way it does when one is laid off, effective immediately, and escorted from the building. My mother's return to Harris was a way to be away from Sayrafiezadeh, it was a way to divorce herself from my father who would not legally divorce himself from my mother for twenty more years, that is until he was ready to remarry again, and his legal status in the United States was no longer in jeopardy. But my mother's return to Harris not only succeeded in divorcing herself from her ex-husband but also of divorcing herself from her present son. Written on the mailbox in the lobby of our apartment building was "Harris/Sayrafiezadeh," as if roommates resided there, or an unmarried couple, or a progressive married couple, a progressive married interracial couple at that.

"Supper is almost ready," my mother calls to me twenty-nine years ago when this story begins. Together we are alone in our apartment. I am playing on the floor in the living room, while my mother is busying herself in the kitchen. I place this colored wooden block on top of that colored wooden block. Silence surrounds me, interrupted only by the faint *clink-clank* of my mother's dishes in the sink. It is that time of night in New York City when everything seems to fall silent and still. And on the sixteenth floor of the apartment building we live in, everything is even more silent and more still, the sounds from the street falling short of us. And it is also at this time of night, for reasons unbeknownst to the scientists, that strangers choose to enter people's homes unannounced and do evil things. It is during this pre-supper séance then that the stranger, who has decided against being detected in the elevator and has climbed sixteen flights, enters our apartment and silently, stealthily, creeps, quietly, whisperly behind my mother and waits. His presence my mother and I are unaware of.

I have lied to you, reader. My mother's name is not Martha Harris. I have lied and I apologize for it. My mother's name is, in fact, Martha Finklestein. I am sketchy on the details, because my mother is sketchy on the details, but sometime during World War II when my mother was about ten years old and living in Mount Vernon, New York, her father decided that his eldest son would have an easier go at finding a job if he was not so obviously Jewish. Thus in one swift pen stroke the family did away with Finklestein forever, replacing it with the generic and rather boring Harris that I first introduced my mother to you as. If we lived in a matriarchal society and if we lived in a society that did not have its own history of anti-Semitism, I would be writing this story tonight not as a Harris, but as a Finklestein. But since none of this is the case, I use the byline Sayrafiezadeh. The Jew in me has been completely supplanted by the Iranian.

My mother is in the kitchen. She has called out to me that supper is almost ready. And now she turns from the dishes, innocently, turns with whatever collection of inconsequential thoughts are running through her mind at that moment, and turns to see not the empty space she had imagined and wholeheartedly expected, but to see the space filled with the large form of the dastardly stranger, who has been waiting patiently, because he has known that she will see him eventually, turn toward him eventually, the way a spider knows that the fly will eventually have no choice but to fly into its web. And my mother screams. It breaks irreparably the silence of the evening as well as the world of my colored wooden blocks. And the dish my mother is holding in her hand drops and shatters on the floor, giving a nice exclamation to the drama at hand.

My mother is a Jewish woman, I've already said. You can tell this by the name she does not go by. You can also tell, I have always thought, by her physical features. Her prominent nose, for instance. Her tiny, five-foot-one frame, the hunched way she has about her, the old beyond-her-years attitude. She was a senior citizen by the time this story takes place, at age forty. Of course, none of these features may have anything to do with Jewishness, but rather with my own anti-Semitic associations, which I admit I am in great possession of. In ways that I am not quite clear about, but will defend as if they can be proven mathematically, I have always asserted that my mother's Jewishness is why I have found her so ugly my entire life, and why as her offspring I have often found myself to be so ugly. It is certainly not helped by the fact that my mother does not have her hair done, does not wear makeup, does not paint her nails, does not wear perfume, does not dress in colorful, fitted outfits, does not date men ever, does not have sex with men ever, does not exhibit any sexuality, homosexual, asexual, or otherwise. The last man she had sex with was my father, which was when she was thirty-six years old. My mother, in effect, took a vow of celibacy after my father's departure, and became a nun, a secular nun, a secular Jewish nun. When my mother walks down the street in what amounts to her habit, men are not compelled to look at her tits or ass. And the one time she wore a skirt I was confused and made vaguely uncomfortable by the sight of her calves and thighs in stockings, uncomfortable in the way one is when one watches a handicapped person attempting to dance, for instance. It is a painful attempt. All of these details I have somehow come to associate with the fact that she is Jewish, and I am happy to have that part of myself disguised, suppressed, repressed, hiding the mother in me away, happy to not be a Finklestein, happy to have been born into a patriarchal society.

And my mother turns, sees, screams, and the plate breaks, and my child's play on the floor with colored blocks promptly comes to an end. I rise fearfully, and pad toward the kitchen, peeking cautiously around the corner, imagining the worst, imagining myself saving my mother and in turn being saved by her.

In the kitchen my mother stands erect, paralyzed, her back presses against the refrigerator, the stranger faces her menacingly from across the counter where he leans. His size is overwhelming, and made doubly so by the fact that there have been no adult men in our apartment since my father's exit. The stranger is bulbous, and he casts a shadow that falls across the kitchen, across my mother and myself. We are infected by his shadow. My mother is motionless like a cadaver, rigid with fear. The stranger is motionless, too, but his posture is loose, relaxed, an athlete about to take off. Better to be relaxed when you are the assailant. My mother and the stranger watch each other, they wait, they plot, each wondering what the other's first move will be.

A brief word about the missing patriarch. My father has gone off to work diligently attempting to overthrow this society of ours. He is a subversive. He is a communist. He is a Trostkyite. He has lived in exile. He has also spent time in jail. He writes long articles with phrases lifted directly from Marx and the Russian Revolution. Articles that the coal mining layman would have difficulty deciphering. He refers to his fellow party members as "comrades." In my mother's home there is a reverence for my father, he is a divinity and I am taught by my mother to be happy and proud and respectful of the work he is doing to better the world. This is all I am going to say about my father. He is a figure in the world, but a non-figure in our lives. Nor is he what I have sat down to write about tonight.

Tonight I am writing about how a stranger has managed to ingeniously infiltrate a double-locked door. And my mother speaks to me in a low, breathy whisper, as if knowing she will be granted one wish and one wish only. "Get me," she says, "go get me a shoe." And I do as I am told. I scamper into the closet for her weapon of choice, and return to her at once, where she clutches the shoe in her hand.

The stranger sees this weapon and does not like it. The balance of power has shifted, he knows this. There has been an unexpected sea change. He was attracted by the smells of dinner and he thought that his jaunt through the kitchen would be an easy one, that he would collect his three or four crumbs into his basket and be gone before anyone so much as noticed. He has done this many times before, this is how he has survived and made his living.

"You son of a bitch," my mother is saying and the tone of her voice frightens me and frightens the stranger, and his antennae begin to move this way and that, trying to map out the best possible escape route. And he moves away from my mother abruptly, quickly, his six footsteps patting out a rhythm across the counter, over a plate, and up the side of the Maxwell House Coffee can where he stops to survey the lay of the land, catch his breath, and gather his bearings.

And where we can observe him more closely. He is, to put it mildly, a behemoth. The subject of legends, of folklore. He stands nearly six inches, with antennae that adds another six inches. We notice a scar running along one of his legs, from the knee down. When he looks, we can see where he is looking. We can make out the consternation on his face. A single bead of sweat breaks on his forehead and falls, plunking into the Maxwell House Coffee can.

"Where did I enter from?" he says to himself, angry at himself for having lost the way. "Where did I enter from? I was sure it was from over here!"

From where she stands, my mother raises the shoe like a gunman taking aim. The insect has no choice but to move, caught in the crosshairs. My mother raises the shoe higher. The insect moves more quickly, scurrying further along the counter, and then down into the sink, and then up the sink where he hangs upside down from the faucet.

"If I don't move, perhaps she won't see me here." The thought of a delusional man. A man whose options are slowly running out.

And now my mother, having summoned her courage, begins to move toward him.

Once very late at night, well past midnight, my mother carried me in her arms home from the Clinton-Washington subway station in Fort Greene, Brooklyn. It's the G line. She walked along a completely empty Dekalb Avenue and from nowhere a man suddenly appeared and stood in our way. I remember his face clearly. I was in my mother's arms so I was at eye level with him, an odd perspective for a child so used to looking up toward adults, and I made eye contact with him. We looked at each other briefly. My mother stepped to her left and the man stepped to his right, blocking her. My mother stepped to her right and the man stepped to his left, blocking her again.

Now my mother and I are running across the wall, knowing that if we can make it to the cabinet we will find safety. Safety among the plates and cups and bowls. He'll never find us in there, my mother whispers to me. We will be safe in there. We will hide ourselves in the maze of the dishes and we will wait and wait until he has exhausted himself from hunting for us and gives up. If it takes hours, we will wait for hours. If it takes days, we will wait for days. And when he has finally exhausted himself, bored himself and turned the light off and left the kitchen we will emerge and return home and pick up where we left off.

Reader, I have lied to you twice. I promised I would not bring my father into this description. But how could I avoid the obvious? Couldn't we, my mother and I, have used him now? A strong, large man to set the world in order. He, no doubt, would have reasoned with my mother and the cockroach. He would have shown them that their oppression is the same oppression. He would have shown how the ruling class exploits my mother in the same way it exploits the insect. "They tell you that there is only supply enough for one of you," he would explain in his emphatic accented English. "And in this way they pit the two of you against one another in order to drive down your wages and increase their profit. This is a historical fact. Marx has written extensively about it." Perhaps he would even have some literature to give out. And in this clear reasoning of my father, the bug would see this, and understand. And my mother would see this, and understand. A sweet reconciliation between them would ensue. And then my father would be off, to save and educate the other workers.

But as I have said, my father is not present. This bloody task is up to my mother and my mother alone. And the bug passes by the bowl of beans, pausing ever so briefly. "My, that would have made for a nice snack," it thinks wistfully, using that far off calm inner voice that one uses for thinking thoughts during the most inappropriate moments. And in this pause within a pause my mother finally, swiftly, brings the shoe down, catching the insect on its shell, knocking it off the counter and onto the floor where it lands on its back.

The pain ricochets through its body. It has felt pain before, but never pain like this. It knows the situation is dire. "I'm OK," it thinks in the way you think when you have dislocated your shoulder or broken your leg, and you are trying to convince and comfort yourself that you have not dislocated your shoulder or broken your leg and that all you really need is a good night's sleep and you'll be as good as new in the morning. The psychologists have discovered that in times of duress we will often lie to ourselves and evade the lie simultaneously. "Here I go, you see," the bug says to himself, "right back on my feet, you see, and right around the corner of the counter, to the oven, as I planned from the start." But as it races toward the oven, it is unaware that now it is moving at half the speed it was before. And my mother, mercilessly, strikes the bug again. The pain again. Ricocheting again. Commingling with the former pain. Suddenly feeling numb, drowsy, wouldn't it be nice to just sleep right here in the corner, curl up in the corner. Just a short pre-supper nap. But no! Now is not the time for sleep! I must continue or all is lost! But wouldn't it be nice?

And my mother again, like a matador. And again. The sport suddenly cheapened for the pleasure of the lower classes.

The cockroach is still now, quiet. Resting on its back. It's antennae involuntarily waving this way and that, still trying to pick up the good news, though there is no good news it can pick up that will do it any good. So this is how it will end, it thinks. Here on this cold linoleum floor in these fools' apartment. There's still so much I wanted to do with my life. I would have wished for a better parting. In the arms of my lover. With my children gathered around. Will they know of my death? Who will inform them? They will wait up tonight, hoping for me to return with the goodies that I promised. They will wait the next day and the next. And they will always wonder after me.

And my mother is sobbing now, great sobs shaking her body, tears and snot running down her face, the exhaustion that comes after the execution, the exhaustion of the hangman who weeps after the trapdoor has been pulled, the prolonged involvement leading to the condemned's death has left him susceptible to his most vulnerable emotions. And my mother suddenly scoops me into her arms and sits down in the kitchen chair clutching me tightly. Her fingers digging into my back. Her body heaves, waves of grief, and I go up and down in those waves. The ocean's moan in my ear. Tears for a lost family, poverty, uncertainty, tears for a distant, nonexistent husband. We sit there together, the three of us, she in the kitchen chair, I in her lap, the cockroach on the floor, fading away, it's life slowly ebbing from its pores. The moments. My mother's moments, my moments, the insect's moments, all together in one moment. The deathwatch filling the room. The bug feeling no pain now. The contradiction: in great pain, no pain. My mother rocking back and forth, clutching me, I her teddy bear. The three of us all witnessing the cascading moment that is coming, coming, comes. And then passes. The antennae still. And the cockroach gone. My mother and I alone again. We will be the only living witnesses to what transpired in that night.

La Vie En Rose

Hubert Selby, Jr.

Hubert Selby, Jr. (1928–2004) is best known for his novels Last Exit to
Brooklyn *and* Requiem for a Dream, *both of which were adapted for film.*

YOUR SONG EDITH. BUT WHAT MELODY OF THE BRO-
ken heart wasn't your song? Chevalier named you the
Little Sparrow, and so you were . . . small, petite, easily
unnoticed in the world of glamour . . . fragile yet so
indomitable. What demons haunted your life? What
angels sang in your heart? Were you constantly forced
to choose between the angels and the demons? Did you
know the difference? Did you believe you were putting
angeles in your arms? And, perhaps you were, for surely it quieted the
demons for a while . . . for a while and though the demons always
returned, it was worth living with the angels for a moment, looking at
life through rose-colored glasses.

But even when those glasses were shattered, and the demons ripped
at your tattered heart, the angels sang from your throat and stirred our
hearts, helping us see a glimmer of light where none was thought to be.
How did you do that, my Piaf? How did you turn the pain and agony of
constant tragedy into the songs that gladden our hearts?

And did you mend your own broken wings over and over so you
could fly to yet another nest . . . only to once again fall so hard against
the pavement that gave you birth?

Yes, you were a Little Sparrow, yet when you sang the Nightingale
blushed, and marveled at your distinct ability to transform your pain
with a lightness the nightingale doesn't know . . . because it does not
know the heaviness in your heart.

I never saw you, but feel such a kinship. I never saw you, yet we are
sisters . . . brothers . . . one in the heart. I never saw you, but I know you
were so slight, so pale . . .

Yet so like Lady Day who was black. And, like you, when Billie sang
she transformed hundreds of years of tragic history into a towering victory of spirit. She too carried on a tradition, one in her blood, and one

510

she learned from Bessie, and so many others. As I love your pale fragility, so I love Lady's black strength. But who could think of color when she sang, or you, because the music went right to the heart and resonated with the love from the soul.

The Little Sparrow, Lady Day, and me. Different arms, different tracks, same path. We took the journey together and I know what manner of tortured heart beat under our blue-dotted flesh.

There were times when Lester Young would play behind Billie. She'd stand at the edge of the stage, swaying, getting ready for the next tune . . . and the Prez would swish up behind her and put the bell of his ax against her bottom and play, LOVER MAN, and Billie would wiggle her cute little thing, smiling, and sort of croon kind of deep and throaty, OOOOOOO PREZ. It was always like the phoenix rising from its ashes as the indomitable spirit rose from the tragedy of its existence.

Billie's gone, Little Sparrow. And to the end it seemed like the TREES THAT BORE A STRANGE FRUIT were determined to strip her of every vestige of dignity before she could go quietly into the much needed night. Friends would bring her a little dope, something to sniff so she could thumb her nose at the generic pneumonia that was killing her. A nurse saw the white smudge on Billie's nose, easy enough to see, and blew the whistle, and so the visits were cut off, those allowed in searched, and a police officer guarded the dangerous prisoner as she slipped into the comfort of the sleep where those concerns no longer exist, and she could sing her song in the light. Lady had her day, but it seems like her nights were so despairingly endless, and now both have joined to shroud her with sleep.

How many days did you have, Little Sparrow? A few, here and there, but always swallowed by the darkness. It seems the sunshine came only on a man's shoulders . . . and it seems it was always inappropriate . . . and ill fated. Then Marcel Cedan entered your life. He too fought his way up from the streets. Yours were Parisian, his Algerian. His streets became a ring, and then cheering thousands of fans, as with you, and his hunger clobbered men into submission. As with you, he fought his way to the very top, and into your Sparrow's heart. Another inappropriate liaison, but this time it seemed to be blessed. But you had your nurse and guard too and a routine flight to Paris, and you ended in strewn wreckage and black headlines. And once again the Little Sparrow is alone, seemingly abandoned and rejected by the very angels that gave her the song she sang. And in time the angels defeated the demons and you too were free of the struggle. And another part of me is gone.

Yet I somehow continue, not knowing, from time to time, if it's the mercy of the *angeles* that keeps me going, or my defiance of the demons. There have been so many songs cut off in mid verse, so many seemingly lost bridges.

I was locked up with Bud Powell shortly before he died. A man I used to see, and hear, almost weekly at one time, along with so many others like Prez, Bird, and countless others who walked our path. But was one of the greatest musical geniuses of the twentieth century, and when I think of him the image that comes to mind is not of him at the old Roost or Birdland, but leaning against the wall in the psyche ward at King County, eating a candy bar and grinning the grin of a man separated from himself. So many times I have seen him hunched over the keyboard, a quart container of beer on the piano, with imagination and brilliance, creating music second by second. But that's not the image of Bud that comes to mind, but rather Bud hanging over the piano they rolled into the ward, that same grin on his face, hunting, hunting, hunting across the keyboard, unable to find what he had many years before found and had already given to us.

So many are gone. I loved them . . . and still do. And so many of them are gone. Have been for many years. And yet I remain. Here. Now.

And from time to time, I think.

Not why I'm here and they're not. Not a case of: they were so much more talented than I. I am far beyond wondering and/or comparing. I think about finishing their song by singing mine. I believe not only that I can, but that I must, or what is heaven for? I believe there is only one song in the universe, and we are the song. . . . You, me, Billie, Piaf, Bud all singing the same song in our own way. Only one song . . . so we must keep singing.

O God, help me . . . help me to sing my song so theirs can go on and their nonexistent flesh cast off its scars, those blue-dotted cries of pain. O my dear, sweet God, I love my friends as I do You and would sing their songs for them so their spirits can rejoice and cast off the habitual shackles that kept them chained in their cells. I pray that no pain goes unsoothed, no fear unloved, and that I will continue to hear Your song sun by Your kids, and we will all rejoice in the spirit that continues to see not beauty in ugliness, nor joy in pain, but infinite possibilities in each other.

The Sparrow showed us it can be done. As did Billie, Bud, and millions of others who everyday sing. Your song through endless heartbeats of pain. I thank all of you . . . all of you . . .

And every time I managed to get one more breath into this body I will sing a song of thanks to you my brothers . . . my sisters . . . my friends . . .

May your sleep be peaceful and angels sing sweetly in your ears.

Winners

Jessica Shattuck

Jessica Shattuck is the author of the novels Perfect Life *and The* Hazards of Good Breeding. *Her writing has also appeared in* The New Yorker, Wired, Mother Jones, *and* Glamour.

I HAD HEARD ABOUT SCOTT McMILLAN FROM HIS mother. He was switching his major from English to film studies. He was spending the summer in Scotland. His college dorm room was a pigsty, but even so he had girlfriends. His friends were just the best boys, the sweetest, funniest, wildest boys—what a time they had in college! Things like that. It gave me a picture of him; I had gone to the same college he went to so I could put all this in context, at least generally, and it brought all these old, probably-best-forgotten memories of my own undergraduate days back.

The summer I met Scott I was alone for June and July. My husband, Ellery, who is a physicist, was at a conference in Aspen to which we had both decided he should go without me. And my son Charlie was away from me for the first time at Camp Kenneboro, a summer program for gifted children, to which I had sent him off with both of us in tears.

Charlie is a delicate boy. He was born early and that fragile, blue-veined vulnerability he had lying in his incubator has never really left him. He is fiercely intelligent and, *I* think, very funny. But he has never been happy in a classroom setting and has never had friends to invite home; he would rather build elaborate multi-tiered housing complexes for his matchbox cars than play with other children outside, no matter how beautiful the day. I worry about him horribly, although, as Ellery points out, he has all the makings of a brilliant person, which, to his way of thinking, is much more important than being able to make friends at a playground sandbox.

It was shortly after Charlie left that Knutsa invited me to Scott's twenty-first birthday party—a tent-and-band-and-champagne mini-wedding she was throwing for him and referring to as a "dance." Knutsa was the closest thing I had to a friend in the Connecticut suburb we had moved to on account of Ellery's career. She was twelve years older than me and something of an eccentric—at least for the country club scene she was a part of. She did things like fix her own garage door when it was broken, and speak frankly, and eat raw garlic when she had a sore throat. Other than that she wore lots of pink and green and played golf and bridge, just like all the other New Meriden mothers. But she was Swedish, which set her apart and gave her a kind of down to earth cosmopolitanism that New Meriden in general seemed to lack.

"You must give Scott advice on his studies," she said when she called to invite me. This was, I think, in reference to my work as a printmaker, which she had somehow found out about despite the fact that since we had moved to New Meriden, I had not made a single print. "And you can help me sing the Swedish birthday song," she added by way of further enticement. Both prospects sounded unsettling, but I was bored and lonely so I put on a pretty red-and-white wrap dress that I hadn't worn in forever (what occasion did I have in my life for a sexy party dress?) and went.

It was a gorgeous day out—seventy-four degrees and vibrantly blue-skyed. The sloping lawns of the neighborhood glowed green gold and the shadows of the old oak and maple trees looked round and substantial, like friendly elephants. The McMillan house practically shone with all-American prosperity—the white clapboard and black shutters, the fabulous, Victorian wrap-around porch, and the generally grand way it faced the street, chin high and chest out. It was one of those rare days that I saw beauty in New Meriden, which I usually saw as dull and confining—tinged with the creepiness inherent in great privacy and sparse population, central air and no sidewalks.

As it turned out, I wasn't the only friend Knutsa had invited to help set up early—the cast of characters ooing and ahhing over the flowers when I walked in was a who's who of the Benton Beach Club, tanned and blow-dried, and buttoned and belted into tasteful summer suits. I felt immediately like a floozy snugged into my clingy, outdated sundress. And I had worn my hair down, which too seemed suddenly suspect.

"Do you all know Jane?" Knutsa said solemnly, putting one hand on my shoulder. Being from Northern Europe, she doesn't smile gratuitously, which lends an awkwardness to social interactions. So despite the condescension, I was grateful to the Nancys and Bitsys and Katherines when they piped up with chirpy greetings and compliments on my "darling" sundress. Mr. McMillan was away, as usual, on business—a fact of Knutsa's life that I was in no place to comment on. We had that in common I suppose.

For the next hour, I did my best to make conversation with the other ladies—*ladies* was how I thought of them, as if I was the only *woman*, or possibly, *girl*. We distributed bowls of grand, fluffy peonies and attached ribbons to little silver napkin rings that Knutsa was giving out as favors, and I tried to joke about dining hall standards rising. But no one seemed to find this very funny, so eventually I just put my head down and tied bows. When I got up to bring my first batch of favors out to the tent, one of them tucked the tag of my dress in and gave me a little pat on the shoulder. "Happens to the best of us," she said, in a way that meant precisely that it didn't.

The guests began arriving before Scott did—cute girls in strappy sundresses and awkward makeup, tall boys in khakis and blue blazers. All handsome and healthy and well-adjusted—the kind of kids who understood how to maintain eye contact and write a good thank you note. There was a clique of pretty girls in black dresses, and a group of boys with shaggy hair and ironically donned vintage madras shorts. There were jocks and theater kids and stoners, and it was not un-diverse either: there were Asians and black students and a pair of compact looking Sri Lanken twins who were introduced to me as "great divers." They were not all preppy exactly: what they had in common was the fact that they seemed to be winners—all of them, I could see this. They were capable, confident young people, starting life off on the right foot. Which, God knows, didn't mean they'd end up on top, but that they seemed to have the kind of grace and social know-how that put the odds in their favor, and made the possibilities great.

"Scott," I heard Knutsa cry in a burst of uncharacteristic excitement. "He's here, everyone! The birthday boy at last!"

It would have been enough to make even the heartiest twenty-one-year-old collapse in embarrassment, but the tall, shaggy-haired young man who had just walked in the front door didn't miss a beat. "What did you think, I wasn't coming?" he said giving her a hug and swinging her a little off her feet. Knutsa gave him a playful slap on the arm and positively glowed in his presence: her darling, handsome son the joker, the irrepressible fun lover, here at last.

He was a handsome boy all right: tall enough to make Knutsa look small despite the fact that she was nearly six feet, and bold featured, with strong but not overwhelming eyebrows, and the easy stance of someone at home in his body, aware of his grace. He was not a pretty boy, but a real looker—the kind of man who will be handsome still when he's sixty. His hair was as snowy blond as hers. Under his blazer he had on a red Chairman Mao T-shirt. So *cool*, so frivolously rebellious, when in fact the T-shirt made a mockery of rebellion, turned a potent political symbol into a fashion statement. I could hear Ellery's voice in my head as I thought this.

"Jane," Knutsa cried as I started out through the kitchen. She had Scott by the hand and was pulling him away from a pretty, ponytailed girl who was laughing and throwing her head back like some sort of mating goose.

"Hey," Scott said, when they reached me, extending his hand. "So you're the fellow graduate I've been hearing about." He had a little smirk as he said it, which made fun of his mother rather than me.

"A long time ago," I laughed.

"Not *that* long ago," he said inscrutably—was it chummy or flirtatious, this reference to my age? "Wait a minute—you need a refill." He took my elbow lightly, and began leading me toward the bar, but before we reached it Knutsa had swept him off into a new round of introductions. Which was just as well, I told myself, but I have to admit there was a telltale hot patch on my skin where his fingers had rested—a slight but unexpected ruffling of my nerves.

Knutsa had instructed me to be the "point person" on the band—she had a fondness for business speak terms ("bottom line" and "net, net" were two of her favorites) that always sounded jarring in her accent— like the odd metaphors they actually were. The band was comprised of two of Scott's roommates, a skinny, delicate looking girl in a silver tracksuit, and an older black trombonist who introduced himself as "Scott's Godfather," which seemed to be some sort of joke. They were a demanding bunch as it turned out; they had not brought enough extension cords, and needed lots of beer and glasses of water. But I liked them, and anyway, I felt more comfortable in their presence than I did with the other New Meriden matrons—which, it occurred to me, unpleasantly, was what we were.

The tent was filling up and Scott's friends were getting good and liquored from the kamikaze shots caterers were passing, along with trays of mini hamburgers and quesadillas, and, at Knutsa's insistence, caviar toasts. Meanwhile, I rooted around in the McMillan's immaculate basement looking for electrical cords with Marissa, the silver suited bassist, who told me all about her endometriosis and the fact that Max, Scott's roommate and the impromptu band's drummer, had dumped her last Sunday. Poor Marissa, I wanted to say, boys like Max are always going to dump worried, unstable, sensitive girls like you. She was the first person I had encountered here who did not seem to be a winner, with the possible exception of Scott's "Godfather," who seemed, actually, to be homeless.

Before they went on I did a shot with them and felt immediately guilty.

Here I was, a grown woman, the mother of a troubled ten-year-old, at a twenty-first birthday party, doing shots. I pictured Charlie on some narrow camp cot, sucking his thumb (which he still does,) and weeping. Tears come so easily to him, as if his whole body is a great unstable glass of salt water you have to be careful not to tip. "Only —— more days," was how he began every one of his brave, worried, little letters, and only Ellery's threats, via cell phone, kept me from racing up to New Hampshire to retrieve him. "He has to learn, Jane," Ellery would say. "Jesus Christ, do you want to have a son who never copes?"

I must have been looking stern or gloomy or something thinking of this, because as I stood there pretending to watch the band Scott approached me with a kind of cautious, respectful expression. "Sorry about earlier," he said. "We got cut off."

"Oh that's all right." I meant it. "It's your party—you don't have to entertain your mother's guests."

"But I *wanted* to talk to you," he said, earnestly. "You don't look like the rest of them," he shrugged and kind of rolled his eyes in the direction of the ladies. "You're nice to be friends with her—she's cooler than most of those people she hangs around with. She gets bored here. I always tell her she should get out more, meet new people. " He had a tiny smear of mustard on his chin.

"You do?" I said, trying to picture this conversation. So this, perhaps, explained Knutsa's program of outreach toward me.

"Sure," he shrugged. "Someone has to."

It was a novel idea—this hunky young man as mama's confidant.

"So you're an artist?" he asked and took a sip of his drink—something dark and strong looking.

"Sort of, I haven't worked in forever—" I began. "Or at least since I moved here."

"Ahhh." He nodded, as if this were logical. "And what brought you here?"

"Family," I found myself saying.

Scott gave me the kind of serious, searching look that calm, confident people can employ, even with strangers, without seeming rude or insincere. We stood there for a moment and I was aware of how tall he was next to me, and that my face was flushed from all the wine I'd been drinking. Out of the corner of my eye, I could see a centimeter of black bra peeking from the V of my dress.

The conversation moved on. Scott was a good talker. He knew how to ask questions: what art school had I gone to, and what did I think of that artist who made the girls stand around naked in high heels? How did I like New Meriden? Which I turned around and got him talking about what it was like to grow up here, and all the pranks and capers he had pulled off as a kid to break up the tedium: sneaking into the club swimming pool at midnight, throwing water balloons at cars from the golf course, driving his mother's car into Putnam County before he got his license.

None of which I could imagine Charlie doing, now or ever. *Why aren't I out there?* he had asked me one day when we could hear kids in our neighbor's yard playing. *Why am I up here in my room reading?* For such a young person, his voice was full of great existential angst. *I don't know, sweetie,* I had said. *Why don't you go out and join them?* He had just looked at me with those big, sorrowful eyes. *I don't know how to,* he answered. It was not sulky, or reproachful really, just sad.

I pushed the thought away and nodded at whatever Scott was saying. He had a calming way about him, this big, handsome, rich kid who could have been such an asshole or a spoiled brat, but seemed instead to be funny and thoughtful, even kind. He had an ironic distance from the stories he recounted that made the telling of them appealing, as if he was aware of the events he was describing as part of a whole genre of coming-of-age stories, a clichéd legacy of growing up in the suburbs.

Now and then someone would come over and add something to our conversation, or clap him on the shoulder, or catcall his name, and standing with him, I felt this warm glow of Americaness, the tug of this strong, unspoken bond he shared with so many kids under the tent who had shimmied down trees outside their own bedroom windows, barfed in neighbors bushes, and canonballed, after hours, into forbidden swimming pools. It seemed beautiful and stupid, and at the same time marvelous—such a lucky way to grow up. Here were the fetes and challenges of adolescence in a society spoiled enough to spend billions on orthodontia and produce teenage girls who made themselves throw up perfectly good food.

I was overcome by a hot flush of longing standing there as he spoke. Had there ever been a time when my life had been as light as his, as care-free? Would there ever be such a time for Charlie?

"Hang on," Scott said, interrupting himself. I have no idea how long we'd been talking—ten minutes? Twenty? "Hang on a minute," he put his drink down and took mine from my hand, put it down too. The band was just warming into a cover of a Culture Club song, which must have come out before the party guests could walk. "Come," he said, "enough zany New Meriden stories."

"Oh—I don't—" I protested, but he was pulling me, by the elbow so as to be more gentlemanly than romantic, to the dance floor, and I felt genuinely flummoxed by how to resist. Not that I didn't want to dance, but it didn't seem right, really; even in my growing white wine haze I could see this. It occurred to me also, for the first time, that he was possibly stoned—that he had that chatty intensity of a stoned person—it explained why we'd been talking for so long. But then we were dancing, and he was a good dancer. He knew how to lead and spin and twirl me around without being confusing or clumsy. It was hardly surprising—he was good at everything according to Knutsa— but I had forgotten how much fun dancing could be. How free and unhinging. From the raised dais the band was on, Marissa was singing with Max and seemed over her attack of endometriosis, and I forgot for a minute that I was almost forty, that I hated New Meriden, that I had a son who had never made a friend in his life, and how the last time I had been under a tent dancing, it was with Ellery, and he had stormed off in a sulk when I complained about his stepping on my toes.

When the song came to an end, I was breathless, and for a moment I actually harbored the illusion that the clapping was for me and Scott. It was, of course, actually for the band, which was a good thing, and I excused myself to get a glass of water. Scott was descended on by two pretty, dark-haired girls in glittery eye shadow who wanted to have their picture taken with him.

At the bar, I sipped my water, and tried to smooth my hair. The light was beginning to change—turning to that lovely soft gold of New England evenings, and from what I could tell the crowd was pretty sauced. To my left five boys did shots in a cheerful huddle, and on the dance floor someone was putting on an ironic break dance exhibition. The cheese and fruit table looked like it had been mauled by a hungry animal and there were paper napkins fluttering out on the lawn, like some sort of enthusiastic native species that had sprung up in the last few hours.

I pictured my quiet condo at the end of the road: kitchen counters littered with a week's worth of dishes, Charlie's little desk empty of projects, the rest of the rooms dusty and solemn. I had been living slobbily on my own, leaving ashtrays overflowing on the porch and shoes everywhere, letting the mail pile up on the kitchen table and newspapers collect around my bed. The condo would be in the deep shadow of the scraggly fir trees that hovered over the front porch. It would have none of this rich gold light that gave everything the veneer of contentment— of joy and love and promise.

I was waiting in line for the downstairs bathroom when I next saw Scott. His T-shirt had come untucked and his hair looked less clean and shiny than it had earlier, but he looked more handsome if possible, and even taller. He was wearing a tattered, ancient looking straw hat. "Jane," he said, stopping and turning as he passed on his way down the hall. "What are you doing?"

"Waiting for the bathroom," I said saucily. "What did you think?"

"The bathroom," he said as if this were akin to a visit from Jesus. Then he seemed to gather his wits about him. "Hillary, Laura," he nodded to the girls in front of me, "Excuse us a moment." He took my elbow. "I'll show you one upstairs."

It wasn't really fair, I protested, I was last in line, but he was already guiding me around to the stairs.

I followed him, feeling the thick carpeting squish under the heels of my sandals, and my chest prickle with a sense of giddiness and unease. I had never been upstairs in Knutsa's house before. It was no more personal than being downstairs: freshly vacuumed carpeting and a series of braggy-framed family vacation pictures, a lot of closed doors. "Right through there," Scott gestured when we arrived at what appeared to be his bedroom, which gave me a more acute twinge of unease. But I walked across the threshold as though nothing unusual had crossed my mind. "Thanks," I said crisply, making my way around a weight-lifting bench and past a series of gangster movie posters, and shutting the door behind me. In the bathroom, I checked the mirror. The face that stared back was a little unfamiliar: flushed and slightly drunken, but pretty. Youthful, actually, and surprisingly calm. I concentrated on applying a new coat of lipstick and retying my dress.

When I came out, Scott was still there, lying flat across the bed with his feet on the ground. His eyes were closed and the hat he had been wearing lay under his hand beside him, like a small animal that might otherwise escape.

"You're still here," I said involuntarily, at which his eyes flew open.

"Waiting for you." He sat up on his elbows.

I felt my face color at this. What had been pretend was now real. The pleasant patter of my heart turned into an anxious, brittle chatter and my knees felt watery, my cheeks hot.

"So has this always been your room? From childhood?" I said. My voice came out too high, too artificially cheery.

"Mm hm." It was low throaty sound that managed to dismiss the question as irrelevant. I could feel his eyes on me, even with my back turned. The whole room smelled of warm boy—Speed Stick and summer dust, a touch of alcohol and sweat. I should go downstairs right now, I told myself. What did I think I was doing? But the thought crossed my mind with little urgency, as if it were about someone I was watching on TV. I noticed the red in the stubble of hair in his sideburns and the slight flush of razor burn along his jaw.

And to buy myself time I looked over at his bookshelf. There was a small silver crown on the edge of it, not much bigger than a monopoly piece. "What's this?" I asked, picking it up and turning it over.

"Oh that," Scott groaned and sat up fully. "That's just this thing they gave me in high school." He tapped his knuckle against the photo framed on the shelf behind it: a stylized shot of two people on the back of a convertible bedecked with streamers and the word *Homecoming* spelled out over the hood. The boy was Scott with shorter hair, and a slightly rounder face.

"Homecoming king," I said aloud.

"It was totally stupid." He took the crown from my palm. And then with one deft move he was leaning in, his nose comically large on approach, and his mouth startlingly alive and real. My whole body electrified in an almost more violent than pleasant way. And then he was kissing me: his lips surprisingly soft and his teeth hard beneath them—an invitation of sorts. I won't say it wasn't perfect: everything an old married woman would want from such a kiss.

I don't know how long it lasted: twenty seconds? Seven minutes? I was lost in the thrill of it—the rush of being wanted, the steady urgency of Scott's hands making their way down my back, my neck, the delicate ridge of my collar bone. But then there was a sound outside in the hallway—a sort of scraping bump, like someone stumbling against the wall. I don't think Scott heard it, and I don't know what it was. A drunken party guest? The McMillan's cat? A figment of my own imagination? But it shook me out of this dream world I was floating in. With the threat of discovery I became foolish to myself. Here I was, a grown woman—a mother no less—making out with a twenty-one-year-old: a boy who had just barely, legally become a man.

And it gave me a sudden flash of anger at Scott for being confident enough to make a pass at his mother's friend, a woman eighteen years his senior, for having been elected homecoming king and not even caring, for having all those lovely, happy friends outside, and for being so infinitely likeable and attractive and blessed with that serendipitous combination of luck and grace and good fortune that makes life as light and flexible as a good shoe—something comfortable enough to dance in. And for having no idea that this was at all unusual—a beautiful stroke of luck.

It made me do something peculiar, if that is not too generous a word. "Oh," I said, ducking and stooping to fix an imaginary crisis with my sandal. It was not mature, or fair, or dignified at all. But it was effective—Scott drew back and looked at me with an expression of astonishment and concern. And as he stood there in confusion, I put my hand out to the shelf and covered the tiny silver homecoming crown. Instead of moving aside, I closed my fingers around its spiny head and straightened.

Was I okay? Had he overstepped—he was sorry if—Scott was saying, recovering the situation with his usual poise and good manners. With even a sort of genuine contrition.

No, no it was just my sandal, the buckle—but I should get downstairs, really, I should get going—I responded with less finesse. I avoided making eye contact by chattering about the time—where had it gone? How had it gotten to be so late? I could feel the points of the little crown digging into my hand like a fistful of thorns.

Together we soldiered our way back downstairs and at the bottom were enveloped by an influx of his roommates clamoring for mini-hamburgers and more caviar toast.

"Sorry," Scott mouthed over his shoulder as he was pulled out on the crest of them, and I managed a kind of tight smile. Standing there at the foot of the stairs, face to face with the Taj Mahal of Knutsa's vacation photos—a twelve-by-fourteen gold-framed print of all six McMillans at the top of some gorgeous alpine peak—I still liked him! That was exactly it:

he was irreproachable, this bright, blond, happy son of Knutsa's. I almost had to laugh, but I didn't.

It wasn't until out on the street that I allowed myself to peel my fingers open and look down at the object I had stolen. It glinted a little in the last light of evening, and its points had bored five tiny dots into the sweaty surface of my palm. It was ridiculous really—a cartoonish Monopoly toy of a thing, with its little molded silver cushion and florid inscription, the whole silly royal conceit.

But I had it now and all the way home, down quiet Sherman street with its old oaks and gleaming lawns, its bright swimming pools and million dollar houses, I clutched it in my palm, slick and uneven, sharp and at the same time smooth. I told myself I was taking it for Charlie, my own homecoming king, a boy who had none of the good grace and auspicious beginnings that Scott McMillan was born with, and who would never be a winner in the democratic, Darwinian sense Scott was. He would appreciate the way the crown glinted in the sunlight and glimmered in the darkness; he would catch the whiff of power that clung to its humble points. But I know I took it for myself too: a souvenir of youth and lust and possibility, a reminder of luck. It would be a little secret Charlie and I could chuckle over together—ballast to right the scales.

Peg

Sam Shaw

Sam Shaw graduated from Harvard and attended the Iowa's Writer's Workshop; he currently lives in Los Angeles. "Peg" was anthologized in Best American Nonrequired Reading *following its appearance in* Open City.

Reception

 FIRST THAW, AND THINGS WERE GOING TO BE ALL right. George sat on the cinderblock prow of his chimney with a compass and a level and a short length of twine. Here was the sun, streaming on wet conifers. And beneath the teeming sounds of early spring—tinny FM rock, the cannonade of pickup basketball, a lone honest hammer beating time—beneath it all, there was the steady cheerful murmuring of snowmelt in gutters and drains.

The view had put him in an expansive mood. From this vantage, Prospect seemed a gentle and orderly place, all right angles and perfect arcs. Cars rolled slowly down the streets. Somewhere a rifle cracked, and George felt a fleeting kinship with the town's forefathers, small rational men who had almost certainly commanded the respect of their wives.

George restored the satellite to its proper azimuth and elevation. The work was slow, but agreeable too, and as he tightened the last bolt he had the sense that he had also brought his life into a kind of alignment. It was March, and the colors of the world shone bright and true.

He found Rita in the threshold to the den, regarding the TV screen with her arms folded. The picture was crystalline, brilliant even.

"How about that," he said, in the tone of a surgeon who has just completed a radical new procedure.

"Don't start," she said, "It was the cord, not the dish. Practically detached. I fixed it myself an hour ago."

He stood there with his compass in his hand.

"What are you smiling for? Anne Pomerantz phoned in a panic. She thought you were going to jump."

George sprawled across the sofa. On the television, a couple of tigers were screwing in a vast green dale. Before long, the sights and sounds of this Technicolor world had displaced the paler appurtenances of the house—the rattan chairs arranged just so, the animal hum of the furnace. George closed his eyes. It was a perfect day on the veldt. But Rita kept intruding, talking dimly to herself, pacing, shutting kitchen drawers. Undoubtedly, she was filling out contest forms. It was Rita's talent in life to win prizes through the mail. Their closets were full of crockery, birdseed, baby clothes. The hallways, too. Blenders and radios, water picks, snorkels, leather-bound books. All manner of athletic and gardening equipment. What were George's talents? There was billiards. In high school, he'd played snare drum in the marching band.

A while later, the mailman arrived with today's bounty of junk mail and glinting sweepstakes appliances. Then it was dark, then dawn, then dark again.

Sleeves

George and Rita had been married only three years—they were newly-weds practically—but already an anxious silence had fallen on the house, and they greeted each other with the same weary enmity that had passed as tender between George's parents after five arid decades. It was troubling. George had been a recluse all his life, an exile of sorts, and he'd looked to Rita for relief. But his solitude was all the more complete for her presence. She was constantly shutting off lights or worrying the thermostat gauge. It unnerved him, the way she never fully came to rest, the way she skimmed from room to room, in darkness, like a shark.

At first, Rita had seemed to George the most fragile and lovely creature in the state. She'd had a skittish greyhound named Silver, who followed her on errands. One afternoon, they were ambushed by another dog: it overtook them, a wiry murderous thing, and when Rita came to Silver's aid, he bit her wrist, which promptly snapped. It was the ruined arm that won George's heart. He loved to carry things for her, to open doors and cut her steaks at Vern's. He loved to brush her red bangs from her eyes. After the wrist had healed, he would sometimes drape his coat over her shoulders on chilly night walks. It brought him a great deal of pleasure to look at the limp sleeves hanging at her sides.

Now her every gesture spoke of disappointment: around the house, she wore the loose sweats and haggard eyes of a patient on a death ward;

neglected jars of powder and containers of eye shadow and lipstick lined the bathroom counter like a monument to her vanished beauty.

Failures

It was raining, and as he fumbled for the house key in the low light from the kitchen window, George slipped and split the seat of his pants.

"God bless," he sputtered.

He balanced his cigarette on the iron rail and probed the tear with both hands.

Probably Rita could sew it up, but the thought of asking vexed him. Not that she'd refuse. Rita relished the few household chores she performed, as if through suffering her life might acquire an aspect of the heroic; she'd become a kind of domestic martyr, a saint of Cascade Pure-Rinse Flakes and Lemon Cheer.

He knocked his cigarette into the hedge, opened the door and draped his coat on his wife's listless hydrangea.

Among the bills and gaily-colored circulars fanned across the floor, there was a postcard from his brother:

Beware the Ides, etc., etc.!
Fondly, Chuck

George turned it over in his hands. In the picture three coffee-colored ladies washed a sports car. One of them was drinking from a hose. George held the card to his face. It had a sweet, gluey odor.

After his divorce, Chuck had fled to Pompano Beach, where he lived in a condo with a whirlpool tub and a marble bar. It was a bachelor's paradise: sixty-five in winter, and his job as trainer at the airport Marriott gym guaranteed him a steady diet of svelte, undemanding sex partners, many of them actual flight attendants. George had always hated his brother, who was unequivocally his better—older, stronger, quicker and more handsome. Even in the final throes of his marriage, Chuck maintained a brute, vigorous health. He and Susan fought like wolves; more than once the police appeared at their door, called by sleepless neighbors. There were shattered glasses and plates, a ten-gallon tank full of startled fish upended on the bedroom floor. Occasionally he had shown up at George's late at night with a wide humorless grin and a six-pack of Pabst, once with a frozen steak-tip sandwich held to his purpled eye. George would give him a blanket and Chuck would lay on the couch in the dark, the TV roaring.

With George and Rita it was steady and silent, a sort of intravenous drip. There was no violence, no betrayal, no tearful recrimination. In this too it seemed that he had failed.

Penny's

George worked the night shift at Penny's video. Some of his most loyal customers were young women, about whom he indulged lavish filmic daydreams. Typically his fantasies involved acts of sacrifice or heroism: there were blazing fires, bar fights, donations of blood that left him pale and depleted. Occasionally, he'd spy one of his lady patrons in town talking with another man, and he would want briefly to die.

Tonight, two girls from the high school had spent nearly an hour in the store, and he had scrutinized them head to toe while they roved through the interminable shelves of movies. They were all of seventeen, he guessed. The more conventionally attractive of the two wore a man's hockey jersey, altered to expose a few inches of tender stomach. The other was more to his liking: squat and round, with powdered eyes that lent her a haunted racoonish aspect. Or Asian, somehow, and geisha-like. She was precisely Chuck's type.

George's temples throbbed. This was the weight of yearning, green love expressed as barometric pressure in his head. He felt that he knew this one, really and truly knew her, better than her friends and family even, perhaps better than she knew herself. Light flared in her reddish hair with a special brilliance that suggested she was different from the others, touched. Her future was elsewhere, far from Prospect; no bagging waxy fruit or filing memos in a windowless box—though probably she would make a fine secretary, the sort of quiet dutiful employee who is consistently passed over for promotion, and George felt a wave of hatred for her grey-flanneled tyrant of a supervisor, who wouldn't know raw talent if it was sharing his thirty-dollar entree in a restaurant in Tokyo, or thirty yen he guessed, and he pictured her dressed in a sheer kimono, and choking on a square of unchewed eel, clawing the air, and in his mind he shoved aside the useless gaping manager and swept to Raccoon girl's aid, applying first a Heimlich, then slow CPR, below the tables now on the soft carpeted restaurant floor, tasting dusky soy sauce on her lips.

"My card?" she asked, and George found that he'd stowed it in the pocket of his shirt.

After they'd left, he retrieved her record on the office computer and penned her home number on his wrist.

Telephone

Seated now in his kitchen and looking into a glass of milk, George tried to picture Raccoon girl's face. Black eyes and full disappointed lips. Through the tear in his pants the chair was cold, though not disagreeably so. What a pleasant shock it would be to hold her round face, to breathe life into her parted mouth.

George considered the number written on his arm. He picked up the Nortel Execu-talk—one in a long and distinguished line of sweepstakes phones—and pondered the electric void of the dial tone. Then he restored the handset to its cradle. Down the hall, the bedroom door was ajar. The thought of sinking into bed with Rita stung his eyes. He stood up and poured his milk into the sink where it pooled over carelessly stacked dishes and cups. He put on his coat, opened the door, and stepped into the night.

Vern's

At the corner, George turned south toward town. All in all, Prospect wasn't much on the eyes. The houses were more or less identical: prefabricated single-story numbers, painted white or yellow or sometimes powder blue. Desiccated hedges flanked the yards, and every forty feet or so a street lamp threw circles of sallow light on the blacktop. Where was he going? The options were few and too familiar. There were three bars in town, only one that would be open. Vern's: a falling-down house at the foot of the highway, a structure that had formerly served as a Methodist church.

During the months of their courtship, Rita had been sick with mistrust, sure that half of Prospect wanted George, and though he knew that she was wrong, the notion had pleased him. Whenever he shot pool at Vern's, whenever he broke a date or failed to call, she requited him with reddened tearful eyes. Since the wedding, though, she was a new woman, coolly disinterested. It was as if George were one more object gained in a contest—as if all pleasure lay in acquisition, none in ownership.

A Friend

In hope of reviving Rita's passions George had contrived a phony mistress. Late at night he would whisper loving phrases to the dial tone on the pink Princess phone in the den. He would sleep in a chair at Penny's, return home at dawn with rumpled clothes and dampened tousled hair. On an airless summer evening, he had given her a name. Rita sat in the bed, clipping proofs of purchase from spent packages of cereal and long grain rice. George paced the yard, talking on the black Precision cordless.

"No, no," he said to the shrill note in his ear. "I'm the lucky one. A woman like you is a once-in-a-lifetime special gift."

In his enthusiasm, he almost believed there was someone on the line.

Periodically, he veered past the bedroom window. On each such occasion, he furtively angled his head, hoping to catch Rita watching him. After a while he gave it up and joined her in the bedroom.

"Don't worry," he said. "She's a friend, and nothing but."

Rita paused, scissor raised at a martial slant. "Who?" she asked.

"Peg," he said. Where had it come from? George had never known a Peg.

"Peg," George said again, testing the sound of it. "From Vern's. I'm sure I've mentioned her. My billiards partner, Peg."

She resumed cutting.

"I'm thinking of inviting Peg to dinner. She's recently divorced."

"So invite her," said Rita.

"I'm thinking that I will," said George.

120 V AC

Had the game progressed too far? That fall, George had cried "Peg" in the heat of sex. The next week, he'd found Rita in the darkened bedroom, making love with a small plastic cylinder.

"What are you looking at?" she'd panted, and the thing had seemed to mock him with its nasal insect hum.

Waltz

In truth, Rita seemed only vaguely aware of his comings and goings, and if his talk of Peg concerned her, she betrayed no sign. Despite all his maneuvers, she seemed implicitly to trust him. And perhaps she was right: that winter, at Vern's, he'd met a true Peg—or was it Paige?—and in his beery condition he'd felt it was fate, that she'd been sent to free him from his cell. They danced a slow waltz, and she let him rest his hands on the firm plane of her back, and at closing time, in the rain-glossed parking lot, she kissed him roughly on the mouth. But George withdrew. Because in spite of everything, he wasn't a man who broke a vow. In spite of everything, he was true to Rita, true as north.

Lack

"Peg," he said to the empty street. "Peg."

For the first time, he heard the name for what it was. Empty. Mournful. A word expressing everything he lacked.

He was halfway to Vern's when he heard the sound—a rupture in the night stillness, a howling of metal and glass. He held his breath for a minute. An uneasy quiet fell. He jogged to the corner and turned down the street.

The car stood a hundred yards away, a little white sedan. The hood had split around a tree. Steam rose from the engine, and the ruined windshield grinned. George approached it, tasting queer metallic smoke on the air. The car was bleeding. He dipped his toe in the fluid—oil or fuel, he didn't know—and traced a line on the ground.

Through the fogged glass of the side window, he discerned a figure bent across the steering wheel, inert. It took him a moment to understand what he was looking at. Like some exotic zoo animal: legs, a torso with crooked arms, and finally a neck that flared into nothing. George's eyes rested on the incomplete body awhile. At last, he stood upright, and surveyed the area. There were no houses in sight, no one to call for help. And frankly, he thought, the time for help had passed.

"Oh, man," George said to the thing in the car. "I wish I could do something. I wish there was something I could do."

He crossed to the front of the car and laid his hand on the wrinkled hood. It burned his palm. Reflexively, he touched his fingers to his mouth. And at that moment, he saw it. At first, he thought it was a possum nestled in the tall grass, and then he knew better. It was several feet away, lost in shadow: dark hair, and a glimpse of skin.

George crouched beside the head and reached to touch its ragged neck, tentative and deliberate like someone attempting a difficult shot in billiards. An older man, sixty at least, with a sharp nose, thin lips, and wide pearly eyes. Something in the face brought his brother to mind.

The stare had an eerie limpid quality: it was as if the head had something to impart to him.

In school, George had read accounts of guillotined kings and queens who blinked and hissed in death.

"Hello?" he said, just to be safe.

The blood matting the hair and coating the cheeks and teeth was altogether too red, the color of grenadine. George cleaned the face with the cuff of his shirt. In spite of what must have been a terrible flight, its features were poised. This put him in mind of a circus act he'd witnessed as a boy: child trapezists describing slow arcs in the summer air.

George cradled the head as one might hold a child. With his free hand, he lit a fresh cigarette. Then he opened and shut the jaw as if to make it speak. The teeth made a quiet clicking noise. Shamed by this act, George pressed the face to his chest.

Overhead, the cruciform lights of an aircraft winked.

He zipped his jacket over the head, turned his back on the ruined car and walked briskly home.

Homecoming

George closed the door gently so as not to rouse his wife. He stood there in the darkness of the hallway, listening to the wash of heated air through vents. Having judged Rita asleep, he laid some newspapers on the kitchen table, and set the head on top.

He walked around the room, running his hands over counters, opening and shutting cabinets and drawers. Inside the freezer he found two plastic ice-trays, some TV dinners, a few packages of ground beef, a stick of butter and a tub of yogurt missing its lid. He stacked these objects on a chair. Then he placed the head at the back of the freezer and walled it behind the frozen foods.

Next there was the business of cleaning. He wiped the counter and the floor, and deposited the slick newspapers along with his pants, his jacket and his shirt in a paper bag beneath the sink. The water from the tap was pleasant on his hands, and he gave them a vigorous washing, and his arms, and even his armpits, and then he wet his hair. Afterward, he crept to the bedroom. For a long minute, he stood overlooking the prostrate shape of Rita, who was fast asleep. He could hear the steady tidal noise of her breath, but her chest was still. In sleep, she remained his wife.

Flight

They had taken the house in autumn, just weeks before the wedding. It was empty of furniture then, and the walls shone startling white. Silver had yet to be killed, and the high *tick tick* of his pacing filled the air, a sound as of fingers typing an interminable memo. On the first night they'd found a sparrow, stone dead on the kitchen floor; Silver offered it to Rita, who offered it to George. How had it come to be there? Through the chimney? George imagined its last days in the house: the dizzy indoor flight, its hundred frenzied dives against the glass panels of the sliding kitchen door. He would have fed it to the dog, but Rita demanded a proper burial in the yard, in a Dixie cup coffin. Afterward, they lay together on the bedroom floor, she facing outward. He touched her cheek and found that it was wet, and he held her as tightly as he could. He had felt then that she was the kindest and most loving person he would ever know, moved to tears by the death of a bird.

Nocturne

George climbed into bed. Gingerly, he tucked a hand under the bottom of Rita's cotton shirt. Her stomach was an oven. He slipped a finger into the hollow of her navel and closed his eyes and lapsed into sleep.

Provisions

The next morning, George feigned sleep while Rita dressed for work. Before she left the bedroom, she paused in the doorway.

"I know perfectly well you're awake," she said.

He waited with his eyes shut until he heard the front door close.

While he ate breakfast, George stared fixedly at the freezer. What would've happened if she'd taken something out to thaw? He opened the freezer door, dug through the barricade of frozen foods and retrieved the head. The skin had lost its color; the brows were thick with frost. George set the head down on its side in the center of the table and finished eating.

The head notwithstanding, it was a weekday like any other. He showered and brushed his teeth, made up the bed, and cleaned the dishes, watched *Knight Rider* and *Baretta* at lunchtime. Throughout the day, the head sat on the table sizing him up.

At four o'clock, he dressed for work, then leaned against the counter and contemplated the head.

"How about a drive?" he asked it.

George rummaged through the front hall closet until he found a red-and-white Igloo cooler, which he filled with ice. To his great satisfaction, the head fit perfectly. Atop its chilly bed, it looked like something from the seafood counter at the Freshmart. George swiveled the top of the cooler, and it locked in place with an authoritative click.

He was very glad not to encounter any neighbors on his way to the car. At the corner of Treasure Hill Road, he slowed to a crawl. Police tape lashed in the wind. There were cruisers, and a couple of deputies trailing shrewd-looking dogs through the high grass. George sped toward town, his right hand tapping syncopations on the cooler.

Devices

At the video store, he felt a nagging urge to take out the head and put it on the counter. It didn't seem right to keep him locked up all night. He compromised by opening the lid a crack, exposing a sliver of red ice.

Later, a bored-looking redhead appeared, and George felt his heart turn over like the engine of a car. She laid her tape on the counter, and asked, "Where's the picnic at?"

George followed her eyes to the cooler.

"It's a heart," he said. "For transplant. Still beating if you listen."

She turned her head and closed her eyes. Outside, a car horn cried. George had been watching a trick-shot billiards tape; there was the sound of balls colliding, then damp applause. She gave him a high forced laugh and shook her head and left.

At closing time, George took the head and propped it against a stack of tapes.

"This is where I work," he said. "It's called Penny's Video. But there is no Penny. Penny is what you'd call a marketing device."

The head watched him as he dusted the shelves and extinguished the lights.

Foil

In the car, George posed the question that had troubled him throughout the day: "How does it feel?"

"You'd be surprised," the head answered. The voice was high and hoarse. It made a sound like wrinkling tinfoil. "It feels like nothing. Nothing at all."

"That's good," George said. He tuned in a ballad on the radio and lit a cigarette.

"What about taking me out of the box?" the head asked. "It's cold as a polar bear's tit."

George lifted the head out of the cooler and set it on the seat beside him.

"Actually, it's all right," the head said after a time. "I'm grateful not to be wherever it is they've taken my body, for example."

"Probably the hospital," George offered, exhaling smoke that billowed against the windshield. "Or for all I know, they've buried it."

"A savage custom if I've ever heard one," said the head. "It's easy enough on the living. I don't guess they can stand the idea of death."

The sound of steel guitar washed over them. At a red light, George offered his cigarette to the head, and for a few moments they both considered the problem of inhaling without lungs.

"Now there's something I'm going to miss," it said.

George parked a little ways from the house. He sat a while, looking through the filmy windshield and biting his lip. As if sensing his ambivalence, the head made a faint clucking sound. The cigarette in George's hand had burned down nearly to the filter, and a long column of ash buckled and dropped onto his lap.

"I'm going to have to put you back in the box," he said to the head.

Homecoming II

Mercifully, Rita had made herself scarce. George took a browned banana from the fruit basket on the counter and peeled and ate it.

"How about you wrangle us a date," said the thing in the cooler. It was an interesting proposition.

"I don't know," he said. "Really?"

The number on his wrist was only faintly legible. He dialed, feeling a strange warm calm. There was ringing—once, twice. Then all at once her breath was in his ear.

"What happened to ten o'clock?" she asked.

George faltered. It was not a question he'd anticipated.

"Louis?" she asked, and George set the phone on its cradle. He collected the cooler and walked to the bathroom. He shut the door behind him and laid the head on its side in the sink.

"We ought to give you a proper cleaning," George said to the head. And truly, it looked unwell, the features wilted, the skin raw and white.

George turned on the faucet, so that a weak stream of water doused the hair and trickled onto the face.

"Too hot," said the head. George adjusted the temperature.

A Wedding

"If you'll permit," said the head, "let me tell you a story. When I was young like you, I had a lady, and what she wanted more than anything was to marry. She was sweet, like to rot your teeth. But I tell you that there's nothing that'll take the life out of a man as surely as a band on his finger."

George nodded, because he knew this to be the truth.

"Finally I gave in to her, and we drove to Las Vegas and had ourselves a safari wedding with a black priest and a choir of lady singers in tiger suits. When we got back to our hotel room, I took out an empty suitcase and put it out on the bed for her to see. I told her, 'Every time you fuck this thing up, every time you do me wrong, I'm going to take a piece of clothing, a shirt or pants or whatever, and I'm going to put it into the suitcase, and once the suitcase is full, I'm gone.' We weren't married a year before I'd packed my bag, and I stuck it in the back of my car and I left."

"You know," George said to the head, "in another time and place, I might have been a very good professional billiards player."

"Billiards," said the head, "is the sport of kings."

Improvements

George looked closely at the nicked cheeks. They were covered with stubble. When he squinted, he could almost see tiny hairs snaking out of the follicles. He spread shaving cream on his hands and lathered the face. In slow careful strokes, he shaved it clean. He dried it with one of Rita's hand towels, and set it in front of the mirror to contemplate its reflection.

"I've looked worse," it said.

George rifled through Rita's makeup drawer and took out a compact of rouge. "Let's see what we can do about giving you some color," he said. He applied the makeup in generous streaks, massaged it into the loose jowls until the head had a pleasant ruddy complexion.

George was poised with a tube of lipstick in one hand and a hairbrush in the other when the door swung open. Rita stood in the hallway, pale and bedraggled.

Rita

"Who's in there?" she demanded. Her eyes were fire. "I know it's not a woman, in our house. In my bathroom."

And then she saw the head. She stopped in the threshold, a shaky hand covering her mouth. George went cold.

"It's not how it looks," he stammered, gesturing at the head with the hairbrush. He saw himself through Rita's eyes, and he felt ashamed. "I thought I'd clean him up. I couldn't leave him, could I? There are dogs and whatnot."

Rita made a low watery sound. She took a clumsy backward step and pointed an unsteady finger at George.

"You get out of here right now," she cried. "You go to your Peg. You get out of this house."

She retreated toward the bedroom, past chess sets and Walkmen and free weights and cordless phones, and George watched her shrink away and disappear behind the door, which shut without a sound.

Fauna

George sat down on the tiled floor of the bathroom. He leaned his head against the toilet.

"What am I supposed to do now?" he asked.

The head made a fine suggestion. "Let's drop in on your brother Chuck," it said. "And listen: pick out a golf club from the closet in the hall."

"What for?" George asked.

"If this thing's going to work out," it said, "you'll have to learn to trust me."

George held the edge of the counter and staggered to his feet. He collected the head and lurched through the kitchen to the closet and out the front door. The air smelled fresh, like Christmas. It was a fine night for driving, mist suspended over vacant yards, curtains drawn on the few lit windows of the town. Through the windshield, the mailboxes suggested human forms, and George had the impression of his neighbors gathered at the ends of their driveways to see him off. Some time later, the car passed a bull elk idling in a stand of pines, still and noble and grave. The whole world seemed to pause to take in its breath. A premonition of light etched the mountains in fine relief, and the highway uncoiled, a kind of gentle offering. George was speechless, and on the seat beside him, so was the head.

From Say Please

C. I. Shelton

C. I. Shelton is a graduate of Wabash College. This is an excerpt of his first published story.

 JEMMIE MCKINLEY RATIONED HERSELF ONE CIGArette per day, that she smoked with great delight and often left out on her coffee table to remind herself that something soothing awaited her.

Jemmie McKinley once told her mother to go fuck herself and meant every word of it.

Jemmie McKinley was an anthropology student of the lowest order and spent the majority of her school time dodging lectures, avoiding professors, asking for extensions on papers, or citing some new sort of learning disorder that necessitated more time for test-taking and disallowed pop quizzes. She fudged doctor's evaluations and was prescribed cutting-edge, corrective pills (supply) that she sold to her attention-deficient peers at a moderate markup (demand).

Jemmie McKinley wore vintage T-shirts emblazoned with the faces of conservative pundits in an ironic way. She kept a dog-eared copy of *The Chrysanthemum and the Sword* in her purse at all times but had yet to read past the preface.

Jemmie McKinley had a small, pursed mouth full of straight, white teeth that hadn't required braces. When people caught sight of them they immediately went about gaping open their mouths, pointing out this incisor or that bicuspid, describing in graphic detail their own orthodontic horror stories, romantic entanglements, professional befuddlement and subsequent defeats in life.

For this reason, Jemmie McKinley avoided smiling.

She spent most of her spare time and all of her weekends with her boyfriend, Maxwell, in the seclusion of his apartment: drinking pots of coffee, listening to public radio, randomly engaging in protected sex and arguing in great detail about how this whole country was going straight to hell in a handbasket.

They'd been dating for three months, still engaging in the latter stages of feeling one another out, slowly muddling through the awkwardness inherent in new things with new people. Max was gangly and tall, wiry and despite the immense amounts of food that he ate, never seemed to gain weight. He resembled a basketball player from some European country that she didn't know or couldn't pronounce the name of—an Eastern one, whose indigenous people had dark, curly hair, large noses, and often neglected showers.

She liked Max because of the look on his face when a particularly engrossing piece of information flashed across the newswire at the bottom of the television screen. She liked how little he knew about foreign policy and how distressed he became when profiles of endangered species were shown on the nightly news. She liked him because he seemed like even more of an underachiever than she was, yet somehow managed to wear it more graciously. When people asked him what he did for a living he replied that he was "in between things" or "weighing his options" rather than simply saying "unemployed" or, more accurately, "uninterested."

They over-ordered takeout on Friday nights which typically lasted through Saturday evening. On Sundays, they scraped by on untouched cartons of white rice smothered in soy sauce, fortune cookies, and bags of fried wanton strips. There were times when Jemmie would look across the kitchen at Max as he hunkered down to the microwave, entranced as the food on his Styrofoam plate hissed and popped, and decided that she would be more than content if this cycle of things could last forever.

Max raked the uneaten portion of her food onto his plate. "You must know everything," he said, his mouth still open with surprise.

She raised her hands in a sort of shared disbelief. "I don't know that I'd go that far," Jemmie said. "They just skipped me ahead a few grades."

"Just like that?" he asked.

She snapped her fingers.

"And then what?"

"All I know is that they made me take these silly tests and then somebody, some person, who I suppose was anointed the authority came about and showed us all of these pie graphs and flowcharts and explained that I was 'gifted.'"

"The 'genius czar.' And how old were you?"

"Six. Give or take," she said, peering over her newspaper.

"The only things I cared about when I was six were recess and pizza."

"I think those were the only things that I cared about too. If it were up to me, I would have just stayed the course. But there's something about talent that makes other people grab ahold and claim their share, somehow. It really boils down to the fact that my parents were bound and determined that one of their children was a wunderkind of some sort. And I was the one that panned out," she peered into her mug. "I suppose if I wouldn't have pulled it off then they would have kept trying. Like manifest destiny or something."

"That must have been something for your brothers and sisters," Max squeezed an enormous glop of honey into his coffee, then returned the plastic bear to the center of the table.

"Oh, it had to have been. It had to have been eviscerating. My parents used to take me with them to their friend's houses for grown-up parties. You know? Real fondue, Pictionary-type crowds. I'd do math problems and things like that on a small chalkboard and the people would clap and then I'd curtsy. I was like a walking parlor trick. My parents always left my brother and sister with a sitter," she gave herself applause. "I'm actually pretty sure that's why the other two are so close—mutual dislike of their kid sister. I was like some sort of retroactive measuring stick for the both of them. If you'd ask my parents to this day about their children they'll make excuses for Margot and George Jr.. It isn't like they didn't have the exact same upbringing and meals that I did, same schools, same aunties and uncles. And *Mrs.* McKinley's the worst of the two of them about it. It's practically how she introduces me to people. Little Jemmie: our genius."

"I don't know what I'd do if they said that I was that smart when I was that young," he shook his head, still mired in disbelief and then raised his hands to the stucco-ceilinged God overhead. "The powers that be."

"That's the thing about it," she clapped her hands onto her thighs. "What do you do with that besides rub it in other people's faces? It's like the ultimate trump card. But, I think that it was the worst thing that could have happened to me. I mean they tell you that and where do you go from there?"

"Hey," Max closed his eyes and plugged his fingers in his ears. "Read my mind."

Keeping Time

Rachel Sherman

Rachel Sherman holds an MFA in fiction from Columbia University. She is the author of a novel, Living Room, *and a story collection,* The First Hurt, *which was shortlisted for the Story Prize and the Frank O'Connor International Short Story Award, and was named one of the 25 Books to Remember in 2006 by the New York Public Library. Both books were published by Open City. She teaches writing at Rutgers and Columbia Universities and lives in Brooklyn.*

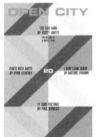

BUNK K IS MADE OF LOGS AND SCREENS AND FILLED with eleven-year-old girls. These girls still wake up easily and early; they do not wear deodorant yet. They are still lithe, still children, and pretty, still, in an undeveloped way. I am their counselor, and sometimes they watch me in the shower.

My co-counselor, Wendy, is chubby and silly and the girls like her too. But I am the one they sit up for in their pj's way after lights out. I am the one that brings the chilly, beer-filled air in from outside to listen to my girls.

"What were you doing?" they whisper. "Where have you been?"

On the first Friday of camp we sit Indian-style on the wood floor of our bunk. Walking inside the circle of girls, I pour M&M's into each set of small, cupped hands.

"Oh, I know this game," Janet says. She is a camp veteran, here the year before.

"Well, let's try it again," I say. "Don't eat them yet."

The "get-to-know-you" game is simple: Eat one M&M for each thing you tell about yourself.

Red is for love. The girls love chocolate and swimming and pets. Love is easy.

Green is for hate.

"I hate Easter Bunnies," April, a girl whose hair has never been cut, says and swallows.

Colleen hates snakes and Jenny M. hates butter and Alex and Jenny B. both hate having to go to the bathroom in the woods on campouts.

There are two girls with braces who hate them. I hate circuses.

"I hate liars," Trisha, the skinny girl with the whitest skin in the bunk, says. She tells us she also hates the sun. I decide, after this first full week of camp, that she is my favorite. My favorite because of her glasses that make her eyes look bigger than they are, and her skinny legs and one-piece bathing suits; my favorite because she will tread water by the diving board the entire swim time just to talk to me; my favorite because in a few days she will tell me I should take my underwear off to sleep so that my vagina can "breathe."

"Let's do red again!" someone says. We go back to loving.

When it is my turn I say I love pearls.

"What about Chris?" Trisha asks, looking at a brown M&M that she has balanced on her pointer finger.

"Yeah, what about Chris?" the other girls echo.

I look over at fat Wendy who smiles.

I have the urge to make them wait until nighttime and then put a flashlight under my face. Part of me wants to tell them about Chris, the cute counselor I won during counselor training week by teaming up with him in volleyball. That during the day, when Chris is a counselor for the boy's bunk B, he is thinking about what he does at night. During the school year Chris goes to a good college because he played lacrosse. In the dawn Chris is a dreamer who forgets his dreams in the morning.

I wanted to tell the girls, while they sat Indian-style on the floor in their pajama tops and bottoms, that Chris, the boy everyone loved, unbuttoned his shorts and pulled himself out while I lay on my back and watched in the back of his van. I watched him watch me while he touched himself; I watched his blond hair begin to stick to his forehead from sweat.

I listened to the sound of his palm against himself, against his shorts. When he came I watched his face, watched him close his eyes and giggle, watched him as he lay back down on top of me, getting my stomach wet. He kissed me, smiling and embarrassed, lighting a joint and passing it over.

During the day I keep time. It is my job all day long. I watch the girls with one eye while I sit on the edge of the diving board, swinging my legs back and forth.

When their time is finally up, I blow my whistle and put my hands above my head. I motion for the girls with water-logged ears and the girls who are still underwater: those lucky girls who see me blurry from underneath, lost in the only good sound.

My second night off, I put the girls to bed and make sure that Wendy is okay. I finish my job and meet Chris at the pool.

It is dark and he is naked, already swimming without me. I watch him look up at the sky.

I go up to the rim of the pool and splash water on his stomach with my foot.

"Come in," he says, smiling, swimming to the edge of the pool where I am standing. He holds onto my ankles with his wet hands.

"Come in," he says, looking up at me.

Even though it is chilly, his wet hands feel good.

"Come on," he says, stroking my shins.

I feel like a man the way I want him. It is sad the way I want him. But I look past him, over him. I feel myself in the air above him when I dive in.

Afterward, I would answer the girls' questions. One at a time I would point to their small, raised hands, their fingernails polished with my only bottle of nail polish left. Each girl in my bunk has red lacquered nails, slowly chipping away with each day in the lake or the pool. I would even let fat Wendy ask me questions: fat Wendy who I found one night with her pillow between her legs and her head pushed against the thin mattress, shaking the springs.

Colleen would raise her hand first.

"Was it big?" she would ask when I called on her. No one would laugh because Colleen is popular.

"Yes," I would say, holding out my hands to show the length of a hammer, then closing the space slowly, trying to remember if it was really that large.

"Was it sticky?" Trisha would ask, and all the girls would giggle.

"Yes," I would say, "it got on his pants. He was trying to be gentle and trying to concentrate."

"Someday," I would say, "you'll get to look in a boy's eyes when he surprises himself."

I would tell my girls, "It is something to see."

During free time we sit on the bunks writing letters, making string bracelets, playing games.

Trisha sits on my bottom bunk and braids my hair. Her small fingers touch me behind my ears and on my neck.

"I saw you and Chris," she whispers.

The bunk—the girls—seems to get even smaller. I close my eyes and feel my face get hot then cold. I do not move, but my neck sweats beneath her breath.

"Where?" I ask, still looking forward so she cannot see my face. "When?"

"In the sand, by the lake," she says. "Wendy took me to the infirmary on your night off and I saw you."

"Do you know Chris?" I ask.

"Of course! He's my volleyball instructor," she says.

"Did Wendy see too?" I whisper.

"No," Trisha says, finishing the braid and wrapping the elastic around the bottom. She snaps the last band against my hair and pats my head.

"Just me," she says.

Trisha sits next to me on the diving board. She has white sunblock striped down her nose, and freckles on either side of it. She tells me about her new canopy bed at home and her mom who is a social worker and has an office attached to the side of her house. She tells me how she was going to have a little brother or sister but then her mom had a miscarriage.

"Look! It's Chris!" she says, pointing toward the gate of the pool.

We both watch as Chris walks toward us, waving to the girls like a rock star.

"Hi, Chris," Trisha says. She runs to him and he picks her up and hangs her upside down while he walks over to me.

"I got a live one here," he says, flipping her over and poking her in the belly button of her one-piece. Then, picking her up by the armpits, he throws her in the pool.

"No!" she yells, just before the water hits. He laughs and watches her splash, then he sits next to me on the diving board. I watch as Trisha swims to the other end of the pool and holds on to the far edge to watch us.

"How's it going?" I ask.

"Oh, just resting with the boys down by the flagpole," he says, touching my fingers with his pinkie so no one can see.

I want to listen to the sound of the girls with my eyes closed.

He puts his finger in the crease of my palm and whispers, "I wish I could fuck you right now."

I close my eyes for just one second, and hope no one is drowning.

I look down and Trisha is treading water beneath us. I take my hand back from Chris.

"I think swim time is over," she says, her teeth chattering.

I put my whistle in my mouth and look at my watch.

"It's time," I say, standing up and putting my arms over my head, then exhaling hard into my whistle. I watch the girls until they are all out of the water and safe. Then I blow the whistle again for lineup and watch as Chris walks out of the gate. The girls stand inside their towels with blue lips and puddles beneath them. They wait for me to lead them to where they are supposed to go.

Chris and I sit in the woods on a stiff, green camp blanket.

"You know," I say, "Trisha saw us."

"When?" he asks.

"The other night. When we were on the sand."

He laughs, "Maybe she learned something!"

"Shut up," I say, pushing him over. I take a swig of the cheap wine he brought.

"She's my favorite," I tell him.

"I thought I was," he says.

We drink more wine and touch hands and make love. I want to feel the way I do when I watch the girls fight or talk or sleep. I want to feel the way I do when I think of them growing. I want to feel that way when Chris kisses me with his eyes closed while I watch him. He has done nothing wrong.

Afterward I lie on his chest and he lies on his back. He looks at the sky and I look at his chest. We breathe together and I wish I could look at the sky too.

"I forgot to tell you," he says.

He strokes my head. I remember how I used to think when boys did things like that it meant love.

"What?" I ask.

"Well, I didn't forget. But I wanted to tell you. I've decided to be the groundskeeper here during the year."

I pick my head up to look at him.

"Really?" I ask. "What about school?"

He is looking at me with a serious face.

"Well, they need someone up here year round, and I quit school. I quit in the spring. Plus, up here I can go skiing . . ."

After camp I am going back to my life. I am going back upstate to my college where I have a dorm room with a futon and a guy down the hall I sometimes sleep with. I am signed up for two lit classes, a math requirement, and a gender-studies class called "Gender, Patronage, and the Decorative Arts in the Renaissance." I am already talking with friends about a trip to Aruba during winter break.

"Aren't you going to be bored?" I ask.

"Well, I don't know. I don't really have a choice. I mean, the truth is, I got kicked out. Grades and stuff. Bullshit. But I think it's going to be awesome up here, you know? All alone in the wilderness. I think it will be awesome to be the only one here."

I imagine him a skinny wolf-boy, growing hair all winter and running naked through the girls' bunks, tearing the mattresses with his teeth.

"I don't know what to say," I tell him.

"Say you'll visit me," he says, squeezing my hand.

I put my head back on the blanket and look at the sky. I imagine the snow on top of the mud and the sand. Snow that will help start the dirt to get ready for next year's girls to grow on. There was no point to camp when there was no one to keep track of.

"What?" he says. "It's no big deal."

I can see that Chris is trying to smile. I put my finger to his bony nose.

"I know," I say, and we go back to kissing.

In the water, the girls pull at my legs and shoulders, dunking me under. The girls are rowdy today: the summer dance was announced in the mess hall last night.

Now it is time for dates. It is time for notes thrown from boy to girl: notes flung in the shape of planes across the mess hall. It is time for counselors to relay messages from one camper to another. Campers mouth to each other at bonfire "yes" with a smile. Or they make their best friends mouth "no" while they look the other way.

Trisha sits in the sand. She has her usual traces of white sunscreen on her nose and neck. I wave to her from the water, smiling while I am dunked by the other girls. This mess of girls pushes me beneath dirty lake water where there are green weeds and other things I do not want to see.

I swim away from them as fast as I can toward the shore. I wonder what these girls will be like one day. I have gotten them at the beginning of their stories, when all they have are buds for nipples, little crushes, and waists so small that their towels wrap around them three times. I want to know how they will end up. I want to know who in the group will turn ugly. Who will end up a worrier, and who will end up a slut? I want to know who will turn out like one of the other counselors. Who will turn out like me?

I get out of the lake and lie down next to Trisha on my towel.

"I don't have a date!" Trisha says. She looks at me, her green eyes behind her glasses. Then she lies on her stomach and puts her face in her palms. I reach out to pat her back but she flinches away. Some nights I've watched her sleep.

"Not everyone has a date, Trisha," I say, and wish I hadn't said her name. We both know I am lying.

Trisha is right. Everyone has a date except for her.

Suddenly I feel wetness and weight on my back: one slick body after another—a pile of wet girls—fall upon me. Beneath them I am trapped on my towel, pressed against the sand.

They giggle and crush me, then tickle me until I scream "Mercy!" Finally, they slowly dismount. I can feel the shift of weight as each girl leaves. When the last one stands I feel a new, cold breeze.

Chris has suddenly appeared and I watch as Trisha wiggles in his lap. Chris is tickling her, trapping her. Her eyes are closed; her mouth is open. Her face has the feeling I wish I had when Chris touches me.

The girls get ready for the dance. They have washed their hair the night before and braided it so that today it is wavy. Colleen has an aqua-blue eye pencil and the girls line up so she can draw around their eyes.

"How do I look?" they all ask, trying and retrying different outfits that they trade each other and then give each other back.

Trisha sits on my bed. She is wearing white shorts and sandals and my white tank top with small pink flowers on it. I wore it with Chris last night—it is dirty and smells like me—but Trisha insists on it.

Outside the mess hall, the girls start whispering and giggling. The boys punch each other and laugh too.

Colleen goes right up to her date—a boy who has those rosy cheeks that can make boys look beautiful. She kisses him, straight on the mouth.

Chris stands next to his boys. He looks especially attractive in the nice light. It makes everything whiter, just before it gets dark. His teeth glow when he smiles at me.

When all the bunks have arrived we start lining up to get in. Trisha holds one of my hands and Chris, secretly, rubs his pinkie in my palm.

"What a beautiful shirt," Chris says to Trisha. He leans over and pokes her in the belly of my tank top where his hand touched my stomach last night.

Trisha giggles. She is not a giggler.

"You gonna dance with me?" Chris asks her.

Trisha smiles and blushes.

"Yes," she answers, quietly. It is almost a whisper.

Inside the mess hall it is dark with balloons and music and punch. Some of the older girls are already in the middle of the dance floor, all doing the same dance.

Some kids hit balloons back and forth. Some of the younger boys run around the room, touching the walls, making bases. Slow songs start and couples pair off.

I grab some M&M's from the snack table and Trisha and I play on one side of me, while Chris and I poke each other in the ribs on the other.

I pick up a red M&M and say to Trisha, "I love camp."

"See the kid with the high-tops?" Chris says. "That's the one I caught masturbating."

He points out one boy's hand on another girl's ass and laughs.

Chris will be cleaning this floor in a month, and there will be nothing to laugh at.

I look back to Trisha as she picks a green.

"I hate camp," she says.

I pick red again. "Bunk K," I say.

Trisha pops a green one and chews while she says, "Breakfast." She kicks the legs of her chair.

"You better ask her," I whisper to Chris. "You promised."

"Yeah," he says, smiling and leaning over me, putting out his hand to my girl and asking, "Ready?"

Again Trisha blushes. She steals a red one from my palm.

"Yes," she says, and takes Chris's hand.

I watch as they dance to a fast song. Trisha's skinny legs try to keep a beat. Chris dances like boys do and holds her hands and twirls her around and around.

He looks over at me and makes silly faces while Trisha concentrates on her turns.

A slow song comes on. I want to butt in on either of them. I want to dance.

Chris picks Trisha up by her armpits and she puts her legs around his waist. He spins around with her straddling him while she leans her head back, laughing.

I see some of the other girls, looking over their boyfriend's shoulder to watch as Trisha holds on. She puts both arms around his neck, her head on his shoulder, and Chris takes his arms away, looks at me, laughs, and shrugs.

On the sidelines, I am laughing too.

I alternate my M&M's, then eat them.

Green: mowing my father's lawn.

Red: the pool.

Green: chapped elbows.

Red: my white tank top with its tiny pink flowers.

The song begins to fade, mixing into the next song, which is fast. I get up from my seat so Chris can twirl us both around.

Chris takes Trisha under her arms to put her down but she holds on and puts one hand on his face. They look at each other, and then she leans in. She kisses him on the lips, softly, a second too long.

I watch him forget everything and then remember as he drops her down and pushes her onto the hardwood floor. He wipes his mouth with his hand, then runs to the screen doors of the mess hall, pushing them open and running out.

Everyone looks. The mess hall doors slam. The music stays beating: oblivious.

Trisha is on the floor, looking up at the ceiling. Her tears drip down the sides of her face but she does not wipe them away. I watch as Wendy and the other counselors run to her while I stay frozen. They huddle around her, making a counselor tent. I watch and stand. Then I run out the screen doors.

Camp might be the meanest thing you can do to a child. Especially if your counselor runs after her boyfriend instead of holding you. Especially if you are the smallest, palest girl in the bunk and you have seen something you should not have seen.

Especially if, after leaving your parents, all you want is a kiss.

"Chris!" I yell and run outside, "Chris!"

I run toward the lake to him because no one else is, I tell myself. It is better to be at camp with someone than to be alone.

I find him in the water, splashing his face with his hands, still wearing all his clothes.

I dive in and when I am deep enough I swim to him.

Chris and I get deep enough so that only our heads are above water. I can tell that he is crying.

"It's okay," I say, trying to reach out and touch him.

"I don't know why I'm fucking crying," he says. He rubs his eyes and tries to smile.

Chris kisses me while underwater there are things I do not want to see.

He says my name, and I straddle his legs while he holds me up. I lean back to float and look up at the dark sky.

We can hear the dance still going on. The sting of what has happened is still there, but the counselors whisper and smile, hoping the kids will be distracted by the music and the punch.

I let Chris carry me out of the water and put me on the sand. I sit up and look back at the mess hall, the colored balloons tied to the railing: oblivious.

The balloons are pink and yellow and white. They are girl's colors that stand for nothing. They are the colors in between.

Yellow is the feeling of hitting the blond wood that is forever worn from summers of sneakers and sandals and Parents' Day heels. There is dirt no one can get out of the cracks despite the mopping after each meal. All along her back a girl would be yellow if the years before her could disappear then make her new.

Pink is for the feeling of a puffy-eyed girl, in the infirmary with ice for her elbow and knee. She quietly opens the plastic bag and hits the ice on her face, making it spotty. It turns dark pink, then darker still. When she hits her arms, the skin on them turns blotchy like a rash she once had. She tries and tries, but the skin will not turn red.

White is the inside of the pool, underwater, where the girls open their eyes to play clapping games. Girls go under for just a second. Girls hold their breath, turn upside down, blow bubbles until they can't take it.

White is the color of leaving and coming up for air. It is the moment before the water breaks.

It is the color of the water in the night with the lights on.

It is the color of staying a girl, trapped in the only good sound.

Sports

David Shields

David Shields is the author of twelve books, including Reality Hunger: A
Manifesto *(named one of the best books of 2010 by more than thirty publica-
tions) and* The Thing About Life Is That One Day You'll Be Dead *(a* New
York Times *bestseller). His work has been translated into fifteen languages*

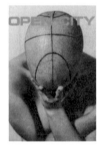

IN HIGH SCHOOL I WAS ATHLETIC AND THUS, TO A
certain extent, popular. However, I worked unduly hard
at it, at sports, with very little sprezzatura, which made
me extremely unpopular among the dozen or so really
popular, athletic people. Why?

Because I made popularity or grace look like something less than a pure gift. Only the dozen or so really
popular, athletic people knew I was unpopular, so I
could, for instance, be elected, if I remember correctly (I don't: I'm making this up), vice president of the junior class and yet be, in a sense,
underappreciated. It was a frustrating place to reign, really, consigned to
the highest ring of the Ringstrasse, unable to escape or improve. Every
Halloween I cowered in my basement bedroom with the doors locked,
lights out, shades down, and listened to the sound of lobbed eggs. In the
fall of 1973 I broke my leg, badly, playing football on the beach (so
Kennedyesque!), and the first day I was home from the hospital I lay
immobile in a body cast in the living room, an aluminum pin in my
thigh. Two medics carrying a stretcher stormed the front door, looking
for someone who had supposedly fallen on the front steps. Later that
afternoon, a middle-aged man, slightly retarded, tried to deliver a pep-
peroni pizza. A dump truck started pouring a ton of gravel into our
miniscule backyard. A cop came to investigate a purported robbery.
Another ambulance. A florist. An undertaker from central casting. A
paint salesman. My popular, athletic friends, who had gathered together
to watch the proceedings with binoculars in one of their houses at the
top of the hill, orchestrated this traffic all night and deep into the
morning. They meant it as a terrorizing, thoroughly evil prank, and
my mother certainly saw it that way, but I never took it as anything other

than the most moving, collective confession of the pain which consists of the inability to identify with pain other than by intensifying it. Vehicles from most areas of the service sector were, at one point, parked virtually around the block.

The Truce

Said Shirazi

Said Shirazi lives in Princeton, New Jersey. His stories have appeared in The Paris Review, New England Review, Ninth Letter *and other journals. He teaches creative writing at a maximum-security prison in Trenton.*

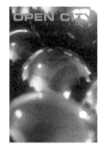 LEIGH CHENG IS A GUY I WENT TO HIGH SCHOOL with. His poetry was better than mine, it was quiet and had symbols, but he wasn't very serious about it. He was a joker, like his hero David Letterman. Leigh and his friends used to take a video camera out and do interviews on the street, imitating that half-mocking style which draws on people's natural friendliness to make them look foolish.

He didn't make his schools and went to U. of M. for a year, then transferred to an Ivy. After college he moved to New York, was a production assistant on music videos for a while, switched to being a paralegal because the pay was better, and then quit that with plans to travel. Leigh was between jobs in the last weeks before Brad and I were starting grad school, and the three of us used to play Hearts all night on the roof and then go for breakfast before crashing.

Leigh could talk to people. You would come down to meet him and find him commiserating with the doorman; they had started with the weather and soon Leigh knew the man's salary and union dues and family background, things we didn't know about one another. It would turn out the man had an advanced degree in his own country but hadn't been able to find work in his field here.

After crashing on people's floors for a few weeks, Leigh finally took off on his trip. No one saw him for a long time and supposedly not even his parents knew where he was. Someone else from high school reported running into him on a train in Pennsylvania but without really finding out where he was coming from or where he was going.

Brad would sometimes hear rumors, which never failed to be exaggerated in his custody. The legend was that Leigh was driving around the country, sleeping in his car, and eating cold corn from the can. He would pull into a town, take a seat at the bar, and watch the game on TV, striking up a conversation with the locals on either side of him. When he ran out of food money, he took a crappy job for a few weeks wherever he was. For a while he had even been scooping ice cream at a Häagen-Dazs in Boulder. Most importantly, he wasn't doing all this to write about it; he'd quit writing a long time ago.

I was really envious. Leigh had become the fabled man of means by no means, the King of the Road. He was a bigger bum than I was, and without betraying any effort. I felt like an athlete beaten in his best event, doomed to be second-rate even as a failure. I was a garden variety ne'er-do-well; Leigh was an unrepentant hobo.

Years pass. I went back up to New York the last weekend in June for a fight party and to see some old friends. Monday night I took the train back down. On my way back from the dining car I ran into Leigh coming up the aisle. He was wearing shorts with a polar fleece pullover and a pair of Ray-Bans and had on boating shoes with no socks. Despite the sunglasses, I recognized him first. I blocked the aisle, waiting for him to figure out why.

We got seats together and started catching up. Pretty soon Leigh was saying that the two of us should start a company. Every idiot our age was making a bundle off the Internet and we had to get in on it. I was too stunned to do more than humor him but he didn't seem to notice that I was teasing. "So, what would our company *do*?" I asked.

He didn't know the first thing about it, not even the buzzwords. He had thrown off his proposal before he even remembered that I once actually did know something about computers, back in the days of the three-hundred-baud modem and the five-and-a-quarter-inch disk. I got out before C had two plusses pinned to its chest for bravery in the field of object orientation, before it was cashiered to make way for HTML and Java. To get back in now would be starting over and starting late.

"So when did you decide you wanted a piece of the action?" I asked.

"Last winter," he said. Who could blame him? Seven years is a long time to hold out, especially when no one's watching and there's nothing to hold out for and even if you held out forever nothing would happen—plus winter. He mentioned he was coming back from a college friend's wedding in Boston. What he didn't have to say is that he must have been totally freaked out to see everyone else in clover. The legacy of an Ivy League education is a life haunted by other people's successes. Because you were once on familiar terms with them, it seems preposterous that you should be impressed now, and all success comes to seem like a backroom scam, a corrupt deal struck between mediocrity and connections.

As little as I knew about computers now, I told him, I knew even less about business. Since my father had retired, I had been trying to learn enough to help him figure out how to invest his savings. I had found the stock market a far less sane and regulated activity than, say, the making of verse. The pit was a daily riot, madness in a necktie.

Our conversation surged and lapsed, murmured itself out and blew up in laughter. We were being funny and pretty loud and I couldn't help wondering if the people around us were listening and enjoying the show. He mentioned an actress who'd gone to the same school as me, asking if I had known her. We broke her down into constituent parts like a chop shop stripping a stolen car, but there was no weight behind his trash on women, no bitterness to make it solid and give it force. It sounded, to my ear, false. What he said had the same lightness a fan's talk has when he pictures himself on the court, faking out a defender and then smashing the backboard glass with his mighty, wholly imaginary dunk.

Without my asking, Leigh began to talk about how he was planning to go to Taiwan soon. By this time I had gotten the real story from Brad. Leigh hadn't been traveling across the country; he didn't even have a car. Most of the time he had been living at home in Potomac, in his old bedroom. At some point, he had gotten a drive-away to Boulder and hung out there awhile, scooping ice cream the whole time, but that was a long time ago. Since then he kept saying he was about to go to Taiwan. He'd been saying that for years. Now he was telling me how he was getting into golf. He had been borrowing his younger sister's clubs but she'd taken them with her to law school. "We should hit some balls sometime," he said.

I caught myself trying to read my fate in him. Everything he said or did went sideways. His every comment was dismissive of itself, and half-hearted to boot. He didn't look at you when speaking. Leigh Cheng had passed through native irony to a second-order sincerity, where you realize that if intelligent culture has turned out for you to be only so much crap, then regular people just trying to get by shouldn't be looked down on, and then through more irony to a third-order sincerity, where you decide that you yourself must be a regular person at the core and must have certain basic psychological needs—home, family, self-esteem, affection, meaningful work, purpose—even though you still can't locate any of those feelings inside yourself.

By this time I had the real story on me as well. I had dropped out of grad school after one semester, worked in an office awhile, moved twice and was now living at home again with my dad. I had a question for Sinatra about New York: If you *can't* make it there, does that mean you *won't* make it anywhere? I had only been back a few weeks. Everyone I knew was gone. In the suburbs, everyone leaves, and if anyone comes back they keep to themselves like Leigh was, like I would have to in the months to come. Either he was numb or he had to be absolutely miserable. I wanted to say to him: Hey, it's me, man, you can be honest, you can say that your life is horrible and you have found yourself living completely outside of civilization, that you live in the suburbs the way a bear might live in the woods. But there was no way to say that. Unhappiness is a secret society with no handshake of recognition, a vast club no one's proud to be a member of.

All of my old high school friends were turning into Salinger characters, delicate misfits hiding out in the corners of the world. The class of '86 was a good year for bananafish. What I did know was that I didn't want to wind up that way, spitting out the letters to get them on the page. What I did know was that being sensitive is about the stupidest thing you can do.

At Union Station we transferred to the Metro. The Washington Metro isn't much like the New York subway. There are no musicians and no graffiti, and before the start of their journey the passengers have urinated elsewhere, in urinals. The stations are giant concrete tubes built to double as bomb shelters, with high, waffled ceilings that are cushioned to absorb sound. Majestic escalators carry people at a dizzyingly steep angle up to and down from the street.

The train pulls in with a delicate whoosh, announced by a row of flashing lights along the track. The cars are clean, quiet, and well-maintained, like the elevators at a prestigious law firm. Half the seats face one way and half the other so the trains won't have to turn around. It looks as if partisan rivalry has split the car down the middle, leaving the passengers with their backs aimed at each other. Around the door the seats are arranged in such a way that the standing room has an air of the stage. Leigh and I sat down in the first open seats, which would put us in the front row. It was well past rush hour and the train was not very crowded.

A couple of young executive-types came on at the Metro Center stop, carrying their jackets. It had been a long happy hour and now they were stepping out of it into the bright car. They were drunk and uncertain about how to carry it, vaguely embarrassed and a little defiant. Their faces had the look of newborns when they first stop crying, that fear and patience, that suspense.

Their white dress shirts were shiny and creased. The cloth didn't hang naturally but puffed out, as if it had been inflated to transport a breathable atmosphere. The shirts were like balloons tethered down by tie and belt. Both men wore conspicuously expensive frames in the hopes of exuding professional ascendance. Underneath everything they were probably our age.

I'm going to call them the Cow and the Bull. They continued their previous conversation. I was only half-listening to what they were saying. After a few minutes the Cow seemed to have a solution. "You've got to make a sperm deposit," he said. "You've got to drop it in the crack."

The Bull suddenly turned toward Leigh. "What do you think?" he asked.

Leigh sat up like he had been called on in class. "I'm sorry," he said, "but I have to disagree." The guys waited, puzzled, for him to elaborate.

"Didn't you say you had to drop the wood?" Leigh asked. Either he thought they were talking about golf, or in the course of his travels he had picked up some new sexual slang unknown to me.

"This guy's got big trouble," the Cow confided to us, indicating his friend. He was clearly in love with him though he would have killed anyone who said so.

"So what's the problem?" Leigh asked. "Are you guys coming from an engagement party?" The Bull didn't want to talk. He had turned to Leigh out of embarrassment about his friend's being so explicit in public. He'd had to say something fast to cut him off. "What then, a divorce?" Leigh persisted.

"That sounds like a good idea," the Bull said, almost to himself.

The metro opened its doors to an empty platform. "Who do you work for?" the Cow suddenly asked Leigh, lurching off the subject. In Europe the question is considered rude.

"Is this a woman problem?" Leigh asked, trying to establish a category. But the Bull held quiet. He was weighed down by troubles he could not bear to think about and could not forget, he had to stay on top of his public drunkenness, and he had to ward off his co-worker's doggish admiration. He was struggling for self-possession.

"Who do you work for?" the Cow repeated, roughly. I wondered what I would say if he asked me. He was talking the way people talk in a bar, either because they had just come from one or because they were still drunk. Everything he said he said a couple times, as if he were still shouting over a jukebox.

The Bull hung overhand from the grip, his biceps flexed, looking away. These were guys who were made out of steak. At the neck and waist and wrists they were thick with muscle. Guys like these never turned their attention to something without directing their whole frame toward it and putting their whole body behind their challenge to it. They were turned out toward the world and challenged it first of all physically. They did not flit around like marionettes when trying to make a point; they had no palette of gestures to accompany their words except dropping their shoulders or leaning forward. These were the guys out there yelling at the quarterbacks and cheering on the strippers. Civilization was invented to hide their nature. They were coarse men dressed finely.

People getting off were using the other end. It began to sound like the interrogation of a spy. "Who do you work for?" the Cow asked Leigh.

If we had wanted to be executives, we would have started as these guys' bosses on the first day. We'd had the grades and the scores and diplomas you could redeem for gold in any city in the world. "Who do you work for?"

Who *do* I work for? Nobody? Myself?

"Hey, there," Leigh said to the Cow, "I thought this was a friendly conversation." He hadn't been avoiding the question so much as gently ignoring it as indiscreet.

"Answer the question, Leigh," I teased, half on their side. "Who do you work for?"

"I temp," he said.

"Temp," the Bull repeated, dully.

"Yeah, I'm a temp. I do office work. What do you guys do?"

"We're stockbrokers," the Bull said. He sounded embarrassed.

The Cow, at last satisfied on this point, wasted no time moving on to the next item on his agenda: "You wear sunglasses on the subway."

"I have a retina problem," Leigh explained. He was on the line between putting them on and just joking around. They went back and forth a little on it.

"A retina problem is only with sunlight," the Cow said, finally. "This is fluorescent light."

"Okay, you got me," Leigh said, giving in. "I'm bullshitting."

After the fancy schools and the downtown book parties, I had forgotten that back on our home turf we were freaks. It is not at all unusual in Washington to see an elderly man in a blue seersucker suit and a bowtie; no, that's normal. The city has the air of a Southern plantation, right down to the segregated living quarters. Its famous monuments are so passionless and misplaced that one might imagine their pictures on money came first, that a group of architects got together and decided to build a city on the model of the one, the five, the ten and the twenty, pulling the bills out of their pockets and throwing them on the table for blueprints. The Egyptian needle and the Roman temples are overgrown lawn ornaments no less tacky than jockeys and flamingos. With its broad steps built at twice the human scale, as if in anticipation of being conquered by a race of giants, and the long flat blocks that seem to pass in slow motion, the city sits there like a filibuster in stone, duller arguably even than Boston. Once you outgrow the Air and Space Museum you've had all the fun to be had here. The most interesting thing in Washington is the Metro, actually, where the Cow, now turning to me, said, "Your glasses are really small. You can see through those?"

"They're not real," I told him, taking my cue for a solo. "I only wear them to look intelligent." He frowned as I pushed on. "I have 20/20 vision, but it was either this or carry a book with me all the time. You know, for the ladies." I knew from Leigh's crash that the odds were strongly against it going over; I felt a little like a pilot taking off in a storm. I wanted to say something funny enough to make one of the passengers behind us crack up, but because I was seated the opposite way I couldn't see their faces.

I'm not usually wrong about who you can play with, but we both misplayed these guys. We were fucking with them because they were stupid, but because they were drunk they were on their guard against being fucked with, and so they caught us. When someone's drunk, you can't really put them on. They're too off-balance to be taken in. You might be able to confuse them a little but that's no victory, since they're already confused. You have to clinch it, and you can't because their minds aren't clinching, their mental fingers will not close to grip.

"Bullshit," he announced firmly, to my surprise. They weren't stupid.

"Turn your head," he demanded. If I turned my head, I was doing what he told me to, but if I didn't, I either had to glare at him directly or cleverly change the subject, and I couldn't think of anything. I tilted my head a little and he took a step to the side to see better.

"You shave your legs?" the Bull asked Leigh.

I laughed. "Answer the question, Leigh. Do you shave your legs?"

"And you don't shave at all," the Cow said, referring to my beard, as if to remind me that I couldn't change sides on a whim.

Now I started to become aware of something inescapably effeminate about us, although I couldn't put my finger on it. Was it Leigh's shorts?

The fact that we had been talking with animation? Our loose posture? Leigh and I are not particularly effeminate. By real world standards, however, we and everyone we know and the roughest guy we have ever hung out with is a fairy—slight, slouching, sprawled, relaxed.

The Cow went back to basics, to his bread-and-butter move. "This guy's wearing sunglasses on the subway. Isn't that the stupidest thing you ever heard of?" he asked me. He'd run out of inspiration himself now and slipped down from teasing into mere threat.

By saying the word "stupid" he'd crossed the line. Seeing my reaction, he drew back: "And this guy's ready to say fuck you." He had caught me angry before I did. The Cow had his horns too; he'd shown his, and without meaning to I'd shown mine, such as they were, and that's how things stood then, us sitting, them standing, the earth rolling round and the car whizzing its load of wage-earners beneath the streets and through the dark toward dinner.

If we were in a bar they would have been picking a fight but on the Metro it just made no sense. They were belligerent and genuinely curious at once. They either didn't know how they were supposed to act or they kept changing their minds on it. They were almost trying to pick a fight and almost trying to pick us up. Manhood is a giant fag-hunt, but nobody knows what you're supposed to do when you catch one: punch them, kiss them, or ask a few questions and let them pass.

"As long as I'm being an asshole," the Bull announced, fumbling in a pocket, "I might as well be a complete asshole." He was cutting things short again. He slipped two business cards out of a leather case and gave one to Leigh. "We need a lot of temps."

I think the fact that we tried to trick them was understood to be playful and friendly. They had been trying to play with us by being threatening, and we had been trying to play with them by putting them on, but we all knew we'd gotten too old to rumble. Pound for pound they could kick our asses, but sadly for all concerned it didn't even matter anymore; it was just sniffing and growling.

The train was slowing as it came to our station. Leigh and I got up. Now that it was almost over, I wished I had played a little more, pushed it further. "Any stock tips?" I asked over my shoulder.

"Seagate," the Bull said.

"Seagate? Get outta here." Seagate was a hard-drive manufacturer that had just taken a bath. I admired the guy for having the wit to get in one last subtle jab, on time-release so to speak, by giving us a bum tip. Perhaps he was being honest though.

After all, the best time to buy a stock is just after it bottoms out.

Chicken Pox and Other Stories

Hal Sirowitz

Hal Sirowitz is the author of several collections of poetry, including Mother Said, My Therapist Said, *and* Father Said. *His books are huge commercial successes in numerous countries, chief among them, for reasons that are not entirely clear, Norway. He lives in Pennsylvania.*

WHEN I WAS SIX MY MOTHER WANTED ME TO CATCH the chicken pox. She said if I got it when I was an adult it could be more severe and make me sterile. No woman would want to marry me, because I couldn't have children. But if I got it when I was young I'd only have a mild reaction and would never get it again.

She found a girl on the block who had chicken pox. She arranged for her to come over and play with me. She was a year older, and wasn't very nice. She pushed me around. She wouldn't even let me play with my own toys. She kept hogging them.

My mother kept coming into the room and saying, "did you touch her yet? Make sure you touch her a lot so you'll get the chicken pox. Otherwise, I'll have to invite her to play with you again."

I didn't want to play with her again. I'd rather play with boys. So I touched her in an infected area on her cheek. She smashed me on the head with one of my toys, and said she didn't like to be touched.

My mother came back into the room, and wanted to know how many times I touched the girl. I said only once. She said that was not enough. I had to touch her more.

So I touched her again. She beat me up. But while beating me up she had to touch me. I was sure I caught it.

The next day I started to itch. I caught it. My mother said I should thank the girl the next time I saw her. But I didn't feel very grateful. It was very itchy.

OPEN CITY

Porno Film Star

Ki asked me if i wanted to star in a porn film. she said she was planning on making a feminist movie in which a good looking guy makes love to ugly women. I felt complimented that she found me good looking, because looks are very subjective. But I wondered how she could convince women she thought were ugly to be in her film. Maybe she was a trickster, and told them she was making a feminist movie about pretty women sleeping with an ugly guy. But the whole idea was anathema to my concept of romanticism. So I told her I couldn't be in her movie.

Hide and Seek

My Aunt Doris and Uncle Jack would take my older sister to the country with them. They kept promising to take me next. But whenever it was my turn my mother would ask me to do her a favor and not go. She'd prefer it if I let Iris take my place, because she wanted her out of the house. She needed a vacation from her, because Iris didn't do what she was told. She didn't mind me, because I was always respectful. She said she'd make it up to me by buying me a present.

Iris took my place. I realized it didn't always pay to be good. Iris was bad, and got to go away more.

Finally my aunt and uncle took me to the country. I met some other kids. We played hide and seek. When it was my turn I found a spot in the barn behind a bale of hay. I knew it was the perfect spot. They could never find me. I stayed there for an hour. Then I got bored. I realized the whole point of hide and seek was to be found. If you hid too well then you defeated the purpose of the game.

I went to look for the other kids, and found them playing another game. I told them I won, because they weren't able to find me. They said I didn't win, because they never looked for me.

My Gettysburg

When I was thirteen I went to Gettysburg with my parents. They said they couldn't afford two motel rooms, so they got an extra cot for their room.

My father always drove fast. His theory was that the faster you drove the safer you were, because if you exceeded the speed limit then you weren't around other cars. It was always other drivers who got you into accidents. Someone could make a sudden stop, and no matter how fast your reflexes were you might not be able to avoid hitting him. I felt he used that same philosophy with me. He was never around much. He was always busy working, playing his mandolin, or watching TV.

At Gettysburg he was annoyed at me for something I said. He was speeding. Then he took a turn too fast, veered off the road, and crashed into a farmer's fence. The cows came over to see what he had done. So did the farmer. Then the police came. He got a ticket for reckless driving.

We went back to the motel, and went to sleep. The cot wasn't comfortable, so I just kept my eyes closed, didn't move, and pretended I was asleep. My mother called my name. I didn't answer her, because I knew she'd have been annoyed if I wasn't sleeping. Then she started whispering to my father. The room was small, so I was able to hear. She told him he shouldn't be too annoyed at me, because I was always a little strange. Then I heard him snoring. Soon she was asleep, too.

I stayed up the whole night memorizing what she had said. It didn't take long to memorize, because it was only one sentence, but I had to be sure I'd remember it in the morning. It felt like the whole world had turned against me. My classmates used to tease me for the way I spoke. But I always felt my home was a safe haven. Suddenly my parents were no longer on my side.

Without a Door

My father removed the door to my sister's room from its hinges. Iris lived downstairs. My mother would call us when dinner was ready. Iris always came late. That got my parents mad. Iris claimed she didn't hear her calling.

One day my father took his screwdriver and removed the door. They said now she has no excuse not to hear them.

Another time Iris put some peroxide in her hair to make it lighter. My parents told her that if she wanted to make herself the center of attention they'd be happy to oblige her. They removed the curtains and shades from her windows. They said now everybody can see you. We're giving you what you wanted.

She could no longer yell at me for entering her room without knocking, because her door wasn't operable. Her room looked like they were in the process of remodeling it.

Once in a while someone will tell me my poetry is too much about my mother yelling at me. Why don't I write a poem about talking back? This is why.

Better Lucky Than Good

Peter Nolan Smith

Peter Nolan Smith left New England for New York in stolen car in 1976. He spent many years as a nightclub owner and doorman in New York, Paris, London, and Hamburg. After a career in the international diamond trade, he traveled extensively throughout the Far East before residing most of the twenty-first century in Pattaya, Thailand. Success at failure forced his return to the states in 2008, when he resumed his life as a diamond salesman. He is currently plotting another early retirement to devote his life to the study of leisure.

THE COLUMBUS DAY WEEKEND BEGAN WITH A grizzly rain splattering on the Hudson. I shut the windows for the first time in months and dressed in heavy clothes for breakfast. The shoes and jacket were unnaturally heavy after a season of shorts and sandals. Luckily global warming guaranteed that the city would heat up before the leaves fell from the trees.

I ran from my apartment building, dodging the raindrops on East Tenth Street. Halfway onto Ninth Street a young man and woman walked my way underneath an umbrella. The long black raincoat acted as a *chador* and a scarf covered pale blonde hair. The hyena laugh betrayed the woman's identity. I almost said hello, but Gabrielle appeared happy and I lowered my head.

She must have recognized my walk, for she called my name with a touch of disbelief.

I feigned surprise. "Gabrielle, I'm surprised to see you in New York."

"I'm shooting a film here, so it's nice to be out of Paris." She tugged the scarf and unleashed her casually coiffed hair. Her beauty remained as intoxicating as our goodbye kiss in Paris. "You haven't aged a day."

"Most men say that." The timeworn compliment was lead to her ears.

"It's the truth." I had seen her in a film by Claude Lelouch the other night. She had been naked. Her breasts lay flat against her chest. Her blonde hair hung down her back. It was too familiar to view the film's entirety.

"Thanks." She introduced the handsome young man as the lead actor in the movie. "He'll hit it big."

"Only if the camera lets me." His agent must have promised him a golden career.

"Congratulations," I offered, and the actor started a discourse on acting. I cut him short with a question to Gabrielle. "How long are you in town?"

"Just another week. Maybe we can meet for lunch." She stepped closer to the young man to either reheat his interest or for shelter under the umbrella.

I stuck my hands in my pockets. "I'm at the same number."

"The same apartment?"

When we had been contemplating a life together, she had visited the three narrow rooms of 3E. A loft or a hotel room on the park was more a movie starlet's style. "I've been living there since 1977."

"Except for when you stayed with me?" She lilted her head to the side and a golden curtain slipped across her face.

"And a couple of other places." Gabrielle and I might have spent part of a lifetime with each other instead of less than a half-year. It took me a long time to discover that she gave me months more than her other lovers. Wanting more had been asking too much.

"Your friend, Jeffrey, he introduced us."

"Jeffrey's dead almost seven years and his girls are almost grown." Paris and Manhattan were populated by ghosts of both the living and dead. She touched my hand as a silent apology for our failed romance. "And your friends in Paris bet you would go to an early grave. In fact, I heard you died in a motorcycle accident."

"A truck hit me head-on in Burma and killed me instantly." I lifted my bent left wrist. Gabrielle shook her head. "You're joking?"

"I hit the windshield and flipped to land on a pile of rice and an old woman. She looked in the air for the airplane from which I had fallen."

"You were always lucky."

Her words aged me a hundred years, because they weren't true in love. A slide show of our meeting flickered from my memory. She had been the lead in a movie. I had been cast as a thug. The director asked me to rough her up. They should have used a stunt man. I didn't know what to say other than to ask about her one true love. "How's your pig?"

"He passed away a couple of years ago."

I derived no pleasure from her pig's death. "Sorry, you really loved that pig."

"You had a pig?" The young actor expressed his emotive range like he was auditioning for the role of her lover.

"A little pig." I had bought flowers and she had cooked meals fit for a deposed king. Even the end at the airport had been romantic. The hurt came once I got back to New York. "She considered cats and dogs dirty."

"And pigs are clean?" he chuckled and Gabrielle narrowed her Atlantic green eyes.

I decided to further damage his prospects by quickly adding, "Cleaner than humans. They only wallow in the mud to stay cool. Her pig was toilet-trained."

"So you're a pig-lover." The actor was struggling with his composure. I had him right in my sights. "Why not? They saved my life."

"How?"

"It's a long story and we have to rehearse our lines," Gabrielle said. She had heard the tale a long time ago. She leaned forward to kiss me. I knew better than to let my lips touch hers. I turned my head. The twin pecks on the cheeks were a far cry from making love in the shadows of the Tuilleries. "Still wearing Chanel."

"Some things stay the same." The tolling from the St. Mark's steeple broke the spell of the past and she tucked her arm under his. "Good seeing you. Take care."

"Don't worry about me, I'm indestructible." I walked away, soaked by the rain.

I confused her lust for love. My error had hurt and she was right. None of my friends, enemies, or family had expected me to live into my forties. I had been drowned by a double-overhead wave in Bali, beaten to a pulp with baseball bats on the Lower East Side, and survived an Olds 88 T-boning my VW in front of the Surf Nantasket. The other near-death scrapes were countless. A second sooner or later crossing a street and a car might have crushed me on its fender. A slip in the bath and I drown. Fitness had no influence on survival, especially since I had entrusted my life to luck, which offers little protection against the deadliest assassin of all.

Yourself.

In *The Comedians*, Graham Greene writes, "However great a man's fear of life, suicide remains a courageous act, for he has judged by the laws of averages that to live will be more miserable than death. His sense of mathematics has to be greater than his sense of survival."

I had majored in math during college and gambled in Reno on my twenty-first birthday, yet nothing had prepared me for a sudden lurch toward the brink of self-destruction in 1988.

That summer, my faux-cousin, Olivier Brial, had thrown me the keys to his family's beach home. Carnet-sur-Mer wasn't the Riviera. Only the Riviera was the Riviera, but the Mediterranean was just as blue.

I wrote during the day and ate the evening meal with Oliver's family. The town had no nightlife outside the cafés and by the end of August I had completed a collection of short stories. I thanked the Brials for their hospitality and bid Perpignan farewell, fully confident that my book would conquer Manhattan's literary world. I hitchhiked to Avignon and headed into the Luberon Valley, where my friend, Jeffrey Kime, was renovating an ancient villa on the outskirts of Menerbes.

Summer ends slowly in Provence. Jeffrey's dog barked at my arrival. His wife and kids shouted their warm greetings from the terrace. Lunch was set for ten guests. Another place was set at the long table and Jeffrey introduced me as an "author."

After a long repast of fresh vegetables, succulent fish, and melons accompanied by countless bottles of red wine, I read them a story of swimming naked in the Quincy Quarries. Jeffrey's wife claimed I was the "next big writer." Their friends toasted my upcoming success and I retired to the attic bedroom for a dreamless sleep.

Late-August blessed the ruined towns stretching through the Luberon with delightful weather. The company was smart. We read books. Conversations covered the cares of the world punctuated by wit-whipped laughter. The night sky swirled with the cosmos. I should have been happy, only every morning awoke an increasingly profound despair.

This depression was not the result of a mere hangover. I was inflicted with a disease and I diagnosed its source, peeking out the attic's tiny window. Jeffrey's youngest daughter was holding on to the tail of their golden retriever and relieving herself au naturel. Her mother joyously declared, "Matilda's getting toilet-trained by a dog."

My friends were happily married and their lives were moving toward reachable goals. I hadn't had a girlfriend in years and no one really published stories of arson and stealing cars. My future was a life sentence of solitary confinement and I secluded myself in the attic, asking, "What next?" Lifting my eyes to the sky gave me the answer.

Jeffrey's house rested under an escarpment separating the Luberon from the coast. A dirt trail through the vineyards climbed past a quarry. Centuries of labor had created a three-hundred foot cliff. The sheer white face murmured a single syllable. I soon deciphered their whisper into one word.

"Jump."

Not like David Lee Roth sang on Van Halen's second album.

Simply, "Jump."

Jeffrey sensed my dismay. We had all had friends go crazy, some fatally. He didn't leave me on my own, although his surveillance wavered with the preparations for a Sunday lunch. His wife commanded his company for a shopping trip to Avignon. His kids begged me to come along. I had different plans. "You go without me."

"Will you be here when we return?" Jeffrey opened the door to his Volvo. His wife corralled their two daughters into the rear and said, "Where else can he go?"

"Just for a walk in the beautiful French countryside?" I waved goodbye and as soon as the car disappeared around the curve, I set out for the path skirting the cliff face. I rested atop the hill. To the west the River Rhône shimmered as a silvery snake under the noon sun and the northern horizon wore the broken toothed smile of the snowy Alps. Not a cloud spoiled the sky and fragrant wildflowers scented the wind. It was too beautiful for any more words and I walked toward the edge, determined to excise the word "jump" from my vocabulary.

Only twenty feet from eternity I heard an inhuman snort to my right and a nasal grunt to my left. The underbrush rustled apart for two little pigs. They were unusually hairy, primeval, and cute. I took a single step toward them and they shivered out a squeal. A louder snort trumpeted from behind a rock. I froze in place, as a massive boar with yellow curling tusks and coarse black hair coating her sinewy spine trotted protectively before the piglets. The black pearl eyes glared maternal hatred and the beast methodically scraped the earth with a cloven hoof. Its horrible head lowered to charge in a slather. "Jump" was replaced by "run" and I climbed a wizened tree. The boar rammed the trunk several times. Its babies scooted into the bushes and the ugly brute vanished from the plateau. Not sure it wasn't playing a trick, I swayed in the tree for another minute, exhilarated that my will to survive had overpowered my will to die.

Some priests might have deemed the incident a miracle and I might have offered a prayer in thanks, only I wasn't sure which saint was the patron of pigs. I dropped from the tree and headed to Jeffrey's house.

The kids were chasing each other in a squall of shouts, the guests were drinking rosé and conversing about a nearby neighbor's book about life in Provence. Jeffrey's wife was slicing a slab of meat for the barbecue and my friend was peeling potatoes. Obviously relieved by my reappearance, he asked, "Where have you been?"

"Out for a walk." Explaining my mad dash from suicide was a topic for another day and I helped chop the potatoes with a knife. It was sharp and I was careful. "What are we having for dinner?"

"A nice roasted pork." Jeffrey beamed with a lean hunger.

"Pork?" I protested and Jeffrey scowled, "You convert to Islam?"

"No visions, a change of heart." Grateful to the boar's intercession, if only momentarily, I said, "I'll stick to the potatoes for today."

"Suit yourself," Jeffrey shrugged and I basked idiotically in my triumph over a desperate desire to leave this life before my time. In Paris Jeffrey introduced me to Gabrielle. I was happy for a while. Not forever, but that romance is a story for a day without the sizzle of bacon waffling on the drizzle.

I entered Veselka and the counterman took my order. At fifty, asking for anything more from life than breakfast becomes risky, but I can deal with surprises, because I've had practice, for while pigs can't fly, they sometimes can save your life.

From The Egg Man

Scott Smith

Scott Smith's screen adaptation of his novel , A Simple Plan, *was nominated for an Academy Award. He also wrote the adaptation of his novel,* The Ruins, *which was released in 2008. The following is an excerpt from a novella that originally appeared in its entirety in* Open City.

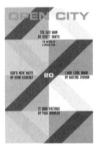

THOMAS GORDON WAS A HEALTHY MAN; HE RARELY had difficulty with his digestion. So it was immediately apparent that something was wrong on the morning when he shat the egg.

First of all, there was the pain. It started high in his gut, right beneath his diaphragm, and eased slowly downward with a sharp ripping sensation. Thomas groaned—he couldn't help himself—and gripped the toilet seat, a sheen of sweat emerging across his entire body. He could feel the egg, his anus stretching to accommodate it, then stopping, then stretching some more, his sphincter contracting and relaxing, contracting and relaxing, the process completely out of his control, the onset of each spasm making him double over in anguish. He tried to rise, as if he hoped to flee the situation, abandon his body there to its misery, but his legs refused to obey him. They were shaking—his hands were, too—and the egg seemed to be growing larger inside him, his sphincter pushing, pushing, pushing. Later, he'd wonder why its shell hadn't cracked from the pressure, but at the time he was much more concerned for his own body; he felt certain that his anus was on the verge of tearing.

And then, with a loud, splashing PLOP, Thomas was free of it, more sweat seeping out across his body, his ears ringing, tears blurring his vision. He didn't stand for nearly a minute, didn't even glance into the bowl to discover what had caused him such distress. He remained seated, breathing deeply, returning to himself, his hands massaging his knees. Thomas assumed that it must've been some aberrantly-shaped piece of shit, or—at the most exotic—a large, inexplicably undigested hunk of food, and he began, briefly, to review the previous day's meals, searching for a likely candidate. He certainly didn't expect it to be an egg;

the possibility never would've occurred to him. But—when he finally, gingerly, wiped himself, struggled to his feet, and turned to examine the morning's results—there it was, bobbing up and down in the center of the bowl: a large, white-shelled egg, three times the size of a chicken's, smeared with excrement and a thick, yellow, mucous-like slime.

Thomas's first impulse was to wash it down the pipes. This wasn't something he needed in his life. But of course you can't shit an egg and then immediately flush it away. Shitting an egg is a noteworthy event: it demands to be investigated. Thomas bent and retrieved the egg from the bowl. He took it to the sink, washed the shit and mucous off its shell, then patted it dry with a towel. It was far heavier than he would've anticipated; it felt droppable, and when he left the bathroom, he used both hands to carry it.

Thomas lived on the Upper West Side of Manhattan. His apartment was nothing more than a box, really: twenty feet long, fifteen feet wide, with a tiny bathroom on one side, and a barely larger kitchen on the other. He had two windows, both of which looked out onto 111th St., but they were small and didn't offer much light. He had a futon bed that he could convert into a couch, an armchair in which he liked to read at night, a trunk that doubled as a coffee table, a five-drawer bureau and matching nightstand. In the kitchen there was a card table with two plastic chairs. And that was all. So when Thomas stepped out of the bathroom with the egg, there were only so many places he could take it.

He shuffled past the armchair, past the trunk, the bureau and the bed, and stepped into the kitchen, moving reflexively toward the refrigerator. That was the wrong idea, however—Thomas knew it as soon as he paused to think—the egg was so warm to the touch, far too warm to set on one of those cold shelves. The only possibility left then was the card table, which was where he sat, the egg cradled in his hands. He needed to find a NEXT STEP, but what might it be? Should he call someone? His parents, perhaps? Thomas's mother and father had retired the year before and moved to California, where, three hours earlier, it was nearing five o'clock in the morning. He tried to imagine telephoning them at this hour, waking them up, telling them he'd just shat an egg, but his mind flinched from the prospect: clearly nothing good would come of it. What about a doctor? Should he make an appointment, take the egg in with him? Thomas envisioned himself sitting on an examining table, offering the egg to a stranger in a white coat, and this scenario seemed equally unpromising, equally ludicrous.

Thomas heard his watch beep on his bureau in the other room. It was eight o'clock. He was running late: he still had to shower, fix his breakfast, drink his coffee, throw on his clothes. He set the egg on the table, surrounding it with the sugar bowl, the napkin holder, the salt and pepper shakers, to keep it from rolling off and smashing on the floor. This was a simple step, yet it had a profound effect upon Thomas, giving him an unexpected sense of freedom. He'd shat an egg that morning: so what? He didn't have to do anything with it; he could just place it on the kitchen table and move forward into his morning.

Which was what he did. He took a shower, and then—having ventured back this far into his normal routine—realized that it would be silly not to proceed even further. So Thomas stood at the counter with a towel around his waist and ate a quick bowl of granola, two slices of toast, a banana. Normally he would've sat at the card table to eat, but he felt a little rush of panic each time he glanced in the egg's direction. It seemed far easier to remain on the opposite side of the kitchen, facing the cabinets, while he spooned the cereal into his mouth, chewing and swallowing, chewing and swallowing, humming loudly to himself in an effort to keep from having to think.

Next came his coffee, then his clothes, and Thomas was out the door by 8:30, ten minutes late, which wasn't too bad, considering the extraordinary nature of his morning.

Thomas worked as a data processor for a large insurance company in Midtown Manhattan. Eight hours a day, five days a week, he sat at a desk typing names and numbers into a computer. Thomas had originally accepted the position as a stepping stone, a way to help fund his passage through law school. But it had quickly become apparent that he had no future as an attorney (his first semester's grades had been the only hint he needed). And then the job was all he had. It was a mind-numbing manner in which to spend one's days—there was no way to disguise this—but the salary was more than adequate, and, as the years had passed, Thomas had grown almost content with the position. He was one among more than thirty data processors on the same floor, and the sense of anonymity this provided suited Thomas's personality almost as much as the job's reassuring predictability, the repetitive, trance-inducing nature of his duties.

Today it was even more of a solace than usual. With the right attitude, transferring names and numbers from a printed page to a computer screen can become a Zen-like occupation. The passing data takes up all the available space in one's brain, keeping anything even remotely resembling a thought safely at bay. Thomas didn't have to contemplate the fact that he'd shat an egg that morning, didn't have to debate what this event might now demand of him. He typed in birth dates and addresses and social-security numbers, names of spouses and children, occupations and previous illnesses, his mind filling and emptying with these details, filling and emptying, like a bucket bailing out a leaky boat.

At 10:15 Thomas had a coffee break, lunch followed at 12:30, and it was in those moments that the egg's presence reasserted itself. His coffee break was the most difficult. Thomas spent the fifteen allotted minutes in a state of pure anxiety. By lunchtime things were better, however. The entire affair had already begun to seem a bit unreal, so much so that Thomas started to wonder if he might not have dreamed the egg, one of those tricky, early morning, half-awake reveries: perhaps he'd drifted off while he was sitting on the toilet. God, it would be awfully funny to arrive home that night and find the kitchen table empty—ha-ha-ha—wouldn't that be comical? Thomas smirked down at his tuna ish sandwich, envisioning the moment, the egg gone: no, the egg never there. He was overtired—that was the only way to explain it—he needed to get himself to bed a little earlier each night.

Thomas knew better in his heart, though—for one thing, he was still in a fair amount of pain from the egg's passage—and the proof came when he arrived home that evening, when he stepped into the kitchen and flicked on the light. Because he felt no surprise to see the egg waiting for him, exactly as he'd left it, propped into place between the sugar bowl and napkin holder, the salt and pepper shakers—a degree of disappointment perhaps, but no surprise at all.

Thomas loosened his tie, sat down at the table, contemplated the egg. The simplest thing would be to get rid of it right now, without another moment's hesitation, crack it open and pour it down the drain, never pause to think of it again, and Thomas might've attempted this, too, had there not been, once more, that disconcerting warmth when he reached forward to pick up the egg, making it seem almost alive.

He quickly returned it to its spot on the table.

And came to a decision.

When the egg cooled, he'd throw it out. He'd take it down the hall to the incinerator chute and drop it through the little door. But in the meantime, while its shell maintained its uncanny heat, he'd simply continue to pretend that it wasn't there.

Thomas draped a napkin across the egg.

"Okay," he said, speaking out loud to himself, as he sometimes did in moments of heightened anxiety. "That should do." He rose from his seat. "Now what about dinner?"

Thomas had plenty of food in his cabinets, but as he started to scan the shelves, he felt the weight of the egg's presence behind him, as if there were a cat in the room, sitting on the kitchen table, peering at his back. The sensation was too much for him; it pushed him into an uncharacteristic spontaneity. He decided it might be a good idea to eat out that night, and, still in his work clothes, he hurried from the apartment.

Unfortunately, Thomas chose his restaurant poorly: a Chinese place which appeared to pride itself on its efficiency. Thomas had hoped to linger over his meal, but the waitresses and busboys conspired to hasten him along. His order arrived with startling alacrity; his plate vanished before he'd had a chance to clean it properly, and was instantly replaced with his bill. Thomas didn't have the strength of character to resist this pressure, to order another cup of tea, pull out a newspaper, lounge backward in his chair. He sensed the entire establishment's desire to have him vanish, liberating his table for the next customer, and, ever-accommodating, Thomas struggled to comply. He paid without his customary check of the bill's arithmetic, swiped his mouth with his napkin, jumped to his feet, and was gone.

Out on the street, Thomas realized that it was still much too early to return home. He couldn't possibly fall asleep yet, and to spend the next two hours reading in his armchair was unthinkable. He'd never be able to concentrate with the egg lurking in the kitchen, would have to keep getting up to touch its shell, that eerie, implacable warmth gradually pushing his anxiety to a higher plane, until soon it would begin to feel more like fear than simple nervousness, his heart thumping in his throat.

A movie was the obvious solution, and Thomas chose more wisely here, a romantic comedy that was so innocuous he began to forget the story even as he watched it, the perfect panacea for his present situation. Thomas sat with a bag of popcorn in his lap, chuckling off and on throughout the film, not because he thought it funny, but because others in the crowd were laughing, and he found their merriment infectious.

It was late when the movie finally finished—on most nights Thomas would already have been asleep by now—and he hurried home, striding straight into his bedtime preparations, the brushing of his teeth and washing of his face, the donning of his pajamas, the setting of his alarm. He couldn't resist the egg's pull entirely, however; he gave it one quick check before he turned out the light. It was still there, unchanged. Thomas touched the napkin, felt the shell's heat radiating toward him, and immediately fled to the safety of his bed.

Did he sleep?

Later, Thomas wouldn't be able to say for certain. It was possible that he'd begun to drop off, his thoughts starting to slide away from him, his body growing heavy beneath the sheets, sluggish and inert, because he had the sense that the cracking noise had been going on for some time before he finally became aware of it—*crack, craaaaack, crack-crack*—the oddity of the sound gradually dragging him back up into consciousness. He knew immediately what it meant, though he yearned for it not to be true, and spent a few moments straining for a different solution, the tap dripping, a branch scraping against the window, a mouse nibbling at a box of crackers in the cabinet. But no, now that it had happened, Thomas recognized its inevitability. The only surprise was that he hadn't anticipated it. This was what eggs did, after all: they hatched.

Thomas lay in the dark, listening to the slow dismantling of the shell. The louder cracking sounds slowly gave way to softer ones, the softer ones to a damp sort of rustling, and then something fell over with a thump. The salt shaker, Thomas guessed. He pictured it on its side, a cascade of white crystals spilling from its perforated mouth. And behind it? Thomas didn't think of reptiles, though that might've added a whole new dimension to his rising sense of terror; no, he pictured a bird, sharp-beaked, cocking its head to examine the kitchen with its yellow eyes—yes, a hungry, freshly hatched bird, searching for sustenance. Thomas imagined this creature tottering to the edge of the table, hesitating there, flexing its wings, while it listened for sounds of prey, the hush of Thomas's breathing in the neighboring room, the rapid beating of his heart. It would take flight then—maybe it already had—two or three powerful wing beats, and a long, silent glide toward the bed, a clot of darkness swooping down upon Thomas, talons extended for his throat . . . .

There was another muted thump, as something else fell over on the table. Perhaps it was the pepper shaker this time, or the napkin holder, or even the creature itself. Because the silent raptor winging toward him was nothing but a foolish fantasy; no matter what else the thing might be which had just emerged from that egg in Thomas's kitchen, it was first and foremost a newborn, and therefore weak, vulnerable, easily disposed of. All Thomas had to do was stride in and twist its neck, slam it dead with a heavy book, or crack a window and fling it out onto the street.

Come to think of it, why hadn't he had the foresight to leave a window open? That would've been the simplest solution, allow the creature to escape of its own accord, stagger to the sill, spread its wings, tip forward into the night. Thomas could've discovered the fragments of shell in the morning, could've swept them off the table onto the palm of his hand and dropped them into the trash. The creature would be gone, its egg disposed of; there'd be nothing to trouble him except his memory of the event, which—feeling so anomalous, so absurd—would fade more quickly than most. He would've been able to move on into his life, to thrust the incident from his mind.

But no, it was November: the nights had turned chilly. Thomas had left the windows closed.

The rustling had stopped; the apartment was silent. Thomas knew that the moment had come for him to climb out of bed and go welcome this new arrival, yet he resisted it. He didn't want to venture into the kitchen, didn't want to turn on the light and see what had pecked its way into being through that thick white shell. It was bad enough to have his body produce an egg, but then, to have that egg produce a bird . . . well, this seemed like far too much to ask of him. And yet something had to be done, didn't it? Some action taken? Gathering his resolve, Thomas decided to count to ten, then pull himself out of bed. A weak man's strategy, with its predictable pitfall: when he reached eight he changed his goal to one hundred, and then, while he was only in the low forties, it suddenly became two hundred. Theoretically, this process could've continued indefinitely. Dawn might've come and found Thomas still counting, slogging his way toward fifty thousand—yes, had it not been for the voice, Thomas might not have gotten up to check at all.

But there was the voice.

"Tho . . . mas!" it called. "Help . . . me!"

Even then Thomas assumed it was a bird, a talking chicken. Why not? It was no more preposterous than any other possibility, certainly no stranger than the prospect of a six-inch tall man, naked, half-blind, covered in slime, which was what he found waiting for him in the kitchen when he finally mustered the courage to go and answer the creature's pitiful pleas for assistance.

The immediate need for action saved Thomas, gave him a brief buffer zone of non-time during which he didn't have to think too closely about what he was doing. The little man was lying face-down on the table in an obvious state of distress, calling Thomas's name, begging for help, his legs hidden beneath a thick, yellow, glue-like goo. Thomas acted on instinct, straight from the spinal cord, without any intervention from his higher faculties—and this was fortunate, too, since they'd collapsed into an impotent state of shock at the sight of the tiny man. He scooped the creature up, carried him to the sink, began to rinse him off beneath the tap.

"Warmer," the man groaned, and Thomas adjusted the flow accordingly. The water seemed to give the naked man strength. He squirmed down out of Thomas's grip and stood on the floor of the sink, hunched over beneath the faucet, as if it were a miniature shower. Thomas would've assumed that anything coming out of an egg would possess noticeably infantile qualities, but there was nothing particularly juvenile about the little man. He looked like an adult, with thick blond hair covering his chest, the beginning of a bald spot on his scalp, a pair of love handles hanging from his hips.

The man stepped away from the faucet's flow. He stood dripping in the sink's basin—-naked, the yellow slime rinsed from his body—and turned to peer up at Thomas. Almost instantly, he started to shiver. Thomas grabbed a dish towel, wrapped it around the creature's tiny shoulders.

"The table," the man said, his voice still sounding weak, the threat of a cough lurking behind it. "Take . . . me . . . back."

Thomas quickly obliged, lifting his guest from the sink, returning him to the table. With the dish towel clenched around his shoulders like a cape, the man made his way unsteadily toward the remains of his egg, the fragments of shell, the smears and globs of thick yellow slime. It was the mucous he was after: he dropped to his knees and began to eat it, scooping the goo up with both hands, ladling it into his mouth. Thomas's stomach lurched upward. He turned away, but couldn't escape the ravenous slurping-munching-gulping sound of the creature's feasting. The burning taste of bile seeped into Thomas's mouth. "I have to use the bathroom," he said, his voice emerging slightly slurred, thick with saliva. "I'll be right back."

The little man was lost in his gorging. He didn't respond.

Thomas rushed from the room, his hand pressed to his lips.

He spent a few minutes crouched over the toilet—coughing, gagging, spitting—but he didn't vomit: his spring rolls and wonton soup and Hunan chicken remained safely ensconced within his stomach. Afterward, he splashed some cold water on his face, then sat on the edge of the tub and tried to gain some perspective on his situation. He'd shat an egg. The egg had hatched. And now he had a six-inch-tall man roaming about his kitchen. Thomas felt an urge to laugh, and he surrendered to it, thinking it might make him feel better, only to realize as soon as he heard himself—the high-pitched, anxious-sounding giggles bouncing back at him off the bathroom's tiled walls—that it was a bad idea. He'd hoped for a quiet, world-weary sort of chuckling, something which might convey a self-confidence, a jaded amusement with the willful absurdity of the world, but what had emerged was much more revealing of his inner state, and therefore far less reassuring.

Thomas felt a need to take some decisive step; the circumstances seemed to demand it of him. But he couldn't think what that step might be. He'd already gone through this process when he shat the egg—the desire to reach for the telephone, followed almost immediately by the realization that there was no one whom he could call. The fact that the egg had now metamorphosed into a little man changed this not one bit. Thomas had chosen to live his life in a solitary manner, and now, in this time of crisis, he was paying the price. He had no one to lean upon but himself.

It was becoming increasingly clear to Thomas that he didn't want to think after all, and—as a means of avoiding having to do so—he started to recite the alphabet in his head. He went from A to Z, then backward from Z to A, then stood up and opened the bathroom door, hoping that enough time might've elapsed for the little man to have finished his meal.

More than enough, as it turned out: when Thomas made his way back to the kitchen, he found that his guest had fallen asleep. He was lying on his side in the center of the table, the dish towel wrapped around him like a blanket. Thomas frowned down at him. He couldn't let him sleep there, could he? What if he rolled off the table in the middle of the night? Thomas considered for a moment, then stepped back into his bedroom, opened his bureau's bottom drawer, made a little nest among his socks and underpants. The tiny man didn't wake when Thomas lifted him off the kitchen table, carried him across the apartment, and set him in the drawer; he simply curled a little more deeply into himself, tucking his right fist under his cheek, like a pillow.

Thomas returned to the kitchen, swept the shell fragments off the card table, dropped them in the trash. He used a sponge to wipe away the few remaining traces of yellow slime, and then—except for the little man sleeping in the next room—it might've seemed as if the egg had never existed. Thomas stood for a moment with the sponge in his hand, scanning the table, the refrigerator, the counters and cabinets, feeling a vague sense of disappointment at the ease with which he'd managed to clean the kitchen. He yearned for some further task to keep him occupied, dreaded the idea of sitting up all night, his thoughts churning pointlessly from the egg to the little man and back again, like a rush of static in his head. Naturally enough, he assumed that he'd never be able to sleep after the events of the evening, yet when he stepped back into the next room to check on his guest, he was surprised by an inexplicable wave of fatigue. It was as if the little man's slumber—so deep, so hungry—were contagious. Thomas stood over the drawer, watching the creature, and the steady rise and fall of the little man's chest seemed to have an hypnotic effect upon him. A gauze-like sensation crept into his skull—a feeling of fuzziness, of padding, began to surround his thoughts—and, hardly realizing what he was doing, he shuffled back across the room to his bed.

Lying down, he thought, *This might not be so bad. It's like having a pet.* Many times over the years Thomas had considered bringing a cat into his life, or even, in his more ambitious moments, a dog. With a cat one had to be constantly changing its litter box, though, while a dog needed to be walked several times a day. Neither of these difficulties would apply to the egg man. Which meant that, at least from one perspective, the little man might be *better* than a dog or a cat, simpler, less of a weight upon Thomas's life. Of course, there was the disturbing detail that he could talk, not to mention the fact that he was a miniature human. But parrots talked, didn't they? And monkeys weren't that far from being miniature humans, and people kept both of these for pets . . . .

The bridges between Thomas's thoughts were starting to collapse, his mind skipping and stuttering into sleep. Without really intending to, he found himself ranking pets by order of difficulty—parrot, cat, dog, monkey—and trying to decide where the little man might fit in. Then, abruptly, he was thinking about babies, how infants wake in the middle of the night, screaming, demanding to be nursed, was imagining the egg man climbing out of the drawer, making his way into Thomas's bed, searching for his nipple, and it was here, with one last gasp of thought— *how did he know my name?*—that Thomas finally slipped into sleep.

Thomas's alarm went off at 7:30 the next morning, yanking him out of a dream in which he'd been running to catch a plane. He was late—the plane was scheduled to take off at any moment—and he was lugging a large, heavy suitcase, which he knew was too big to carry on board, but which for some reason he'd neglected to check at the ticket counter. Neglected, he slowly began to realize, because he hadn't yet been to the ticket counter—dear God!—he was nearly at the gate but now he had to turn around and deal with his luggage. The airport was so crowded, too, everyone moving in the opposite direction, pushing against him, and when he rounded a corner he suddenly saw that he wasn't at the airport, after all. He was at the Port Authority bus terminal on Forty-second Street; he'd come to the wrong place. Now he'd have to find a cab, but which way was the exit, and what was that insistent beeping, a truck backing up, he had to get out of the way, why wasn't anyone else trying to move? They needed to get out of the way, damn it, the truck was nearly upon them, only it wasn't—no, the beeping was his alarm clock, and Thomas's eyes were open, staring at the ceiling of his apartment. Then he was sitting up, lowering his feet to the floor, reaching to turn off the alarm before he stood and started toward the bathroom, his body still only half-awake, his mind even less so, carrying his dream's urgency into the day, the sense of being late, of having to rush to catch up.

He was nearly to the bathroom before he remembered his guest. He saw a blur of movement in the corner of his eye, and when he turned he found the little man rising into a sitting position in the drawer, yawning, stretching his arms over his head. The creature had grown dramatically during the night, doubling in size: he was over a foot tall now. Thomas felt a wave of vertigo at the sight of him, as if he'd stepped forward and his foot had sunk through the floor. He turned and stumbled back to his bed, sat down on the edge of the futon.

"Morning," the little man said. His voice was deeper now, stronger.

Thomas realized with a shock that they looked like each other, that the man in the drawer was a miniature version of himself. It was such an astonishing development that he found himself speaking the thought out loud: "We look the same."

The little man nodded. "We *are* the same."

Thomas blinked at him. He still hadn't gotten used to the fact that the creature could speak.

"I'm you," the man said. "And you're me. There are two of us now."

"But you're only—"

"Inside, Thomas." The man tapped at his head. "Inside we're the same. We have the same mind. The same memories. I know everything you do. Your dream? With the suitcase, the crowds, the truck backing toward you? That was my dream, too."

Thomas couldn't think of any way to respond to this. In the past few days his life had grown far more complex than he'd ever imagined possible. Each time he'd convinced himself that he was regaining some sense of equilibrium, a new development had arrived to bump him back off his feet, and Thomas was beginning to wonder how much more he could take. Thinking this, part of his mind started to slink away from the encounter, as if in retreat, shifting toward the clock beside his bed, the minutes slipping by one after another. He still had to shave and shower and eat and dress. If he didn't hurry, he'd be late.

The man in the drawer seemed to read his thoughts: "You better get going," he said. "No point in staying home. Eating and sleeping—that's about all I'll do today."

Thomas didn't move. It wasn't that he found the idea of rushing off to work unattractive—right now it seemed by far the most appealing of the morning's options, simply to run away. But he know that he couldn't escape this situation that easily. There was so much that needed to be sorted out between him and his guest; he could see no point in postponing the moment of reckoning from now until this evening.

Once again, the tiny man appeared to sense the drift of Thomas's thoughts. "Go on," he said. "We can talk later. Just bring me a slice of bread and a saucer of milk before you leave."

Thomas stood up without a word, went into the kitchen, got the food. He felt relieved to have someone telling him what to do, even if it was a foot-tall version of himself, sitting naked in his bureau's bottom drawer. Left to his own devices, Thomas knew the course he'd have taken: he would've sunk irretrievably into a stunned state of inertia. It was only the little man's air of decisiveness which allowed him to creep forward, with a false air of resolution, into his day.

When Thomas returned with the food, his guest climbed out of the drawer. He was big enough now that he didn't need assistance. Thomas set the saucer on the floor, and the little man dropped to his hands and knees beside it. Watching the creature lap at the milk, Thomas couldn't help but remember his faltering attempt at self-reassurance the previous evening, how, as he'd drifted off to sleep, he'd struggled to equate the little man's presence with that of a pet. Now, fully awake, the idea seemed absurd. If Thomas could've traded the little man for a cat, he would've done so in an instant. He would've exchanged him for an entire pet-shop's worth of animals, in fact, dogs and hamsters and ferrets, would've lined the walls of his apartment with fish tanks, filled his drawers with snakes, lizards, turtles, hung a dozen parrot perches from his ceiling. A cat lapping at a saucer of milk, a small, purring presence—by God, the lovely simplicity of such a creature! Thomas imagined picking the little man up, setting him in his lap, scratching him behind his ears.

The man lifted his head, turned to smile at Thomas, milk dripping from his chin. Again, there was that eerie sense of his intuiting what Thomas was thinking—*I know everything you do*, he'd said. It was a disturbing moment, and, as was his tendency, Thomas fled from it, hurrying to the bathroom, immersing himself in the tenuous comfort of his morning routine.

Tenuous because Thomas couldn't quite manage to enter it with the necessary gusto. A fairly large percentage of his mind seemed to remain behind in the bedroom, watching the little man eat, struggling unsuccessfully to find a mundane explanation for this creature's presence in his life. He dropped the toothpaste cap down the drain, gave himself a nasty cut on the chin while he was shaving, then stood in a daze beneath the shower, forgetting to wash his hair.

By the time he returned to the bedroom, the little man was already back inside his drawer. He'd drained the saucer, finished the slice of bread, and now, wrapped in a pair of Thomas's boxers, was drifting into sleep again. When he heard Thomas enter, he lifted his head, and—in a raspy, slightly slurred voice—said, "Put . . . out . . . more . . . food."

"What kind?" Thomas asked, but the little man didn't answer. He rolled onto his side and began, very softly, to snore.

Thomas got a box of saltines from the kitchen, an orange, the remaining loaf of bread, set them on the floor before the bureau. Then he started to fix his own breakfast. As he was taking his first bite of granola, though, he realized that the little man wouldn't be able to open the box of saltines on his own. Nor, probably, would he be able to peel the orange. Thomas set down his cereal, grabbed a plate, returned to the bedroom. Crouching beside the bureau, he peeled the orange, then arranged it and several handfuls of crackers on the plate. But would this be enough to see the little man through the day? It seemed like a paltry amount of food, laid out like that on the floor, so Thomas added a bowl of pretzels, an open jar of peanuts, two slices of American cheese. And the creature would need something to drink, too, wouldn't he? Thomas poured another saucer full of milk, and then, when this didn't seem sufficient, filled a second one with apple juice, a third with water. By the time he was finished, the bureau had the cluttered look of a pagan altar, the floor before it crowded with offerings to his tiny god.

Suddenly it was 8:20. Thomas still had to finish his cereal, his toast and orange juice, then throw on his clothes, drink his coffee and hurry out the door. He did so at a run, hardly conscious of the little man's presence, his mind focused on the ticking clock beside his bed. Fifteen minutes passed, and—though he was a little breathless, a little frazzled—all was accomplished: he was late, but not disastrously so. On his way to the door, he gave a quick parting glance into his bureau's bottom drawer. He should've resisted the urge, as it turned out, because he couldn't help but notice that there was a cut on the sleeping creature's chin, a shiny slash of bright red blood, in the exact spot where Thomas himself had nicked his own face while shaving that morning. Thomas wished he hadn't seen this. He tried to reassure himself that it might be nothing more than a coincidence, that the little man could've fallen and banged his chin as he was climbing back into the drawer, but of course he knew better. Why else would his heart have begun to race with such violence at the sight of the creature's wound? And why, having just downed a cup of coffee, should his mouth taste so oddly, so insistently, of bread and milk?

Fortunately, Thomas had no time to lose himself in the maze of these imponderables: he was late. He turned from the little man, hurried out the door. This isn't to say that he departed with anything like equanimity, though. His guest was only a foot tall, but a stranger nonetheless, and it felt odd to Thomas, leaving him alone in his apartment like that. Twisting shut the lock behind him, he experienced a strange flutter of foreboding, as if the creature might steal something in his absence.

The Pride of Life

Christopher Sorrentino

Christopher Sorrentino is the author of four books, including Trance, *a National Book Award finalist. He is currenlty working on a novel about identity.*

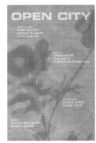

TOLLER'S MOTHER WITHDREW FROM THE WORLD AT the age of forty-five, when Toller's parents moved to California after Toller's father accepted a job with a computer company in Santa Clara. Toller's mother instantly found the region to be uncongenial, and retired to her bedroom, where she would stay, more or less, for the next twenty years. Toller himself was young then, in the pride of life, and to the extent that he was aware at all of his mother's reclusiveness he assumed that since she was now old, she had every reason to stop being an active participant in life. Toller's father was absorbed in his work and either paid little attention to his wife's increasingly eccentric behavior or did not confide in his son about his concerns.

After Toller graduated from college, he and the girlfriend he'd had since his sophomore year broke up and Toller decided to follow his parents to California, having heard, as everyone used to hear, about how inexpensive and easygoing it was in the Bay Area.

"Great," his father said. "Can't wait to be able to see you all the time, sport."

"Oh, Toller," his mother said, "why would you want to come to this miserable place?"

Toller came anyway, bouncing around for his first few months before settling in the East Bay, in Rockridge, where he took a room in a big house on Bryant Avenue he shared with four other people. Once a month or so he borrowed a car from a friend and drove to Palo Alto to visit his parents at their small house in College Terrace. His mother would come out of the bedroom, and the two of them would usually spend some time sitting alone on the patio in the backyard, a quiet little space that caught the breeze and was shaded by a mature cotoneaster and a lemon tree. Richly colored bougainvillea climbed over the fence and up the rear of the house. His mother had hung a hummingbird feeder from the kitchen window overlooking the patio and often one of the creatures would buzz past them to feed. Toller would watch the blur of the bird's wings as it hovered, dipping its beak into the feeder's fuchsia-shaped port.

"There he is," Toller's mother would say, "my best friend."

"Wow, he's really great," Toller would say, admiring the bird's ruby throat and precise, almost mechanical, movements.

"My best friend out here," his mother would repeat.

Toller would find this sort of exchange disconcerting: he'd bargained on admiring a bird (or a pretty house nearby, or the smell of eucalyptus, or whatever seemingly innocuous subject had briefly shuffled into position before them), and now he felt obliged to console his inconsolable mother in her loneliness. She would explain to him, again, that it was impossible here: no one interesting to talk to, nothing interesting to do, and nowhere interesting to go; and although Toller found none of these things to be true, at twenty-three he wasn't yet prepared to reject sweeping, categorical generalizations, least of all when they came from his mother. In any case there was little to do other than to agree with her, since she seemed to grow irritated with him if he did otherwise.

Things happened to Toller over the next few years—he grew close to some people and drifted away from others; he took jobs that interested him, that bored him, that paid well or poorly; he traveled, he enrolled in courses, he moved to San Francisco with a friend, he played in a band. He took advantage of some opportunities and missed out on others. He was an ordinary person whose life began to take on a reliable shape, and when he took stock of his small share of failures he did not, as a rule, have regrets, or anyway he didn't dwell on them.

Throughout, he returned again and again to the patio. The plastic hummingbird feeder grew cloudy and opaque and his mother replaced it. If it was rainy or cold, he and his mother would sit in the wing chairs adjacent to the fireplace in the living room. They'd talk while waiting for Toller's father to arrive. His mother hated the weather and felt that it was making her sick. His mother, who refused to learn to drive, hated having to wait to be driven everyplace. His mother hated the shape in which sticks of butter were manufactured on the west coast, and she hated the taste of the milk. Since it had been some time since Toller's father had tried to persuade her to accompany him to the various parties, dinners, barbecues, banquets, and other functions that he liked or felt obliged to attend, she no longer talked too much about how she hated the people who were being presented to her as potential friends. She did, however, forge intense, empty attachments to supermarket clerks, pharmacists, medical technicians, hair cutters, and tradesmen who came to the house to make repairs, and though she knew nothing more about them than the things she learned making small talk, she would relate the information to Toller in minute detail. His mother would tell him the elaborate plots of the television shows she watched. If Toller told her about the things that were happening to him, she would grow silent, as if he'd rudely brought up an awkward subject.

When Toller was thirty, various circumstances coalesced so that he found himself, all at once, without friends, single, unemployed, and quite unhappy. Now, abruptly, he was receptive to his mother's particular view of things. For six months he sat on the patio or in the wing chair once and sometimes even twice a week, immersing himself in his mother's opinions. He felt, rightly, that they were closer than they'd ever been before. It was her invigorating sense of futility that helped him get past the difficulties of the period, that and the cash subsidies that his parents pressed on him. Eventually, he found a place to live that he could afford, he found a new job, he made new friends, he met a girl. Things eased; life began to regain its reliable shape, and for the first time Toller began to resist his mother's judgments, as though his fleeting keen appetite for them was overly reminiscent of the circumstances that had stimulated it. Besides, now that things had turned out well, so well, they seemed slightly ridiculous.

His new girlfriend, Margaret, was a lively and sensible young woman to whom a life like the one Toller's mother was living was incomprehensible, and she bluntly pointed out to him that it was more than merely *odd*, the apologetic word Toller had taken to using to describe his mother, but: pathetic, limiting, pathological, antisocial, paranoid, and crazy. She'd majored in East Asian studies at Stanford and Toller—who was both offended by this evaluation and strongly enough infatuated with Margaret to lend credence to her every utterance—pedantically questioned her qualification to make such a diagnosis.

"It's not a diagnosis, Toller. These are colloquial expressions in everyday use. When someone tells someone else that a third person they both know is paranoid or antisocial everyone's clear on the meaning."

They'd left the house in College Terrace and were stopped at a light on Page Mill Road. Glass office buildings sat facing the road from the south behind acres of parking and a wide strip of landscaping that ran parallel to the sidewalk; on the north side, hidden behind thick growths of trees, were the winding, circular residential streets nestled at the base of the Stanford foothills. Though it was a cool night, they had the windows partly open and the good smell of wood smoke came into the car.

"I'm not clear on it, Margaret."

"Wind chimes."

His parents' new neighbors were a couple around Toller's age who had moved into the house next door earlier that year; they had installed in their backyard a set of wind chimes whose presence, Toller had noted, was gradually unhinging his mother, who now seemed to view wind chimes as a prominent element in an imagined version of the loathsome state's coat of arms. For several months, no conversation with her had been without its obligatory reference to the ubiquitous device, whose percussive tones—when he'd even noticed them—Toller had always found pleasant. Tonight, Toller's mother had subjected them to an extended harangue about the neighbors' chimes: how the slightest stirring of the air caused them to jangle, how their particular pitch was especially annoying and atonal, how the breeze itself—once so welcome and refreshing—seemed to be conspiring against her, invariably starting up at exactly the moment when she sought out a quiet moment on the patio . . .

Margaret had interrupted: "Have you talked to the neighbors? Maybe they'd be willing to move the chimes, or even take them down."

Toller's mother waved the idea away irritably, her lips pursed. "I've never spoken to those people," she'd said.

Now the light turned green and Margaret put the car into gear. "That was really something," she said, softly.

"Yeah," Toller said. "She's odd. I agree. But it's been hard on her out here. Totally new place, no friends."

"Toller, she's made it hard on herself. She's made it impossible. How long has she been out here? Twelve years?"

"About."

"Does she even go to the movies?"

"She can't. She doesn't drive."

"Toller. My grandmother drives. She's eighty-two. Born and raised in Taishan. She learned when my dad finally persuaded her to move down to Campbell from the city."

Toller didn't know how to respond to the news of this awesome accomplishment.

"And friends, Toller? Doesn't she have any old friends she stays in touch with?"

Toller explained that his mother had perfectly naturally lost touch with some friends, had fallen out with a few others, and so forth. He did not mention the occasion, a year or so earlier, when an old family friend had called to say that she was traveling in the Bay Area and that she'd love to drop by for drinks one evening. Toller had been there on the evening in question, and was disturbed that his mother pulled the curtains and left the lights off when it began to grow dark. When the doorbell finally rang, at about six o'clock, his mother had raised a hand for silence, and the three of them had sat there in the dark, his mother with her index finger laid across her lips, until the intruder had departed.

"Let's assume for the sake of argument that she's right," Margaret continued. "That it's horrible here: horrible, vapid, unwelcoming. Which isn't true, Toller. You know it isn't. I'm from here. It's very hard for me to sit across that table from her and politely listen while she tells me that everything I identify with is stupid and phony. And also when you agree with her, which, really. But let's assume just for the sake of argument that she's right. How often does she leave?"

"Leave?"

"You know. Get on a plane and go back to whatever home means to her. Take off for a week in Rome or Paris. Hawaii. She doesn't work. Your dad makes money. How often does she get away from this horrible place?"

Toller remained silent, half-expecting to hear about the heroic grandmother's annual pilgrimages back to Taishan.

"You're the one who told me that your mother never leaves the bedroom. What is she, a character from a nineteenth-century novel? Some Victorian lady with the vapors? What is that if not antisocial, and pathetic?"

"I wouldn't have told you if I knew you were going to use it against her."

"First of all, reminding you of something that you yourself told me is not using it against her. Second of all, you wouldn't have had to tell me a thing."

Margaret was right, but for now Toller only amended his thoughts of his *odd* mother to characterize her as someone who'd *lost her way*. That her actual life, a life that held her interest, had always seemed to exist at some point in time prior to the present, that the possibility of fulfillment had always seemed irretrievably lost to her, were conclusions that eluded him, as if the long crisis and profound isolation of the current setting threw these essential truths into such sharp relief that they were unrecognizable. Margaret was right, and for love of her Toller did find the limit to which he was willing to subjugate himself in order to align his behavior with his mother's expectations, as always defined by her cloistered outlook. Margaret was right, and she alone seemed to have established a rapport with Toller's mother, a rapport she felt she'd achieved through the respectful exercise of candor. She thought the older woman needed to be stood up to; needed—to use another colloquial expression in everyday use—a reality check. But Toller's mother's refusal to accept her adult son's assertion of his adult prerogatives was beyond Margaret's understanding, and she couldn't imagine how reckless nearly everything that he undertook seemed from the vantage of the bedroom. So when Margaret was seven months pregnant with Toller's baby and the couple decided to take advantage of their underemployment to spend two weeks alone at her parents' cabin on the north shore of Lake Tahoe, Margaret urged Toller to assert himself while he nervously prepared to inform his parents over the phone of their plans. She didn't understand his nervousness. He was thirty-two.

"Why would you want to go there?"

"It's beautiful, Mom."

"Toller, nothing in California is beautiful. It's all ugly. And you sound like a jackass, a true California jackass. One of those jackasses who's always talking about *getting away*, about *taking the weekend*. One of those sun fetishists who worships the weather and the fresh air. One of those self-righteous jackasses who belongs to hiking clubs, who wears a baseball cap, who—"

"Mom, we're going. Margaret really wants to take this time before the baby comes."

"And what about the baby? Don't you think you ought to be more careful about money, now that you're expecting a child?"

"I don't . . . I'm not . . . I—"

"How are you going to take care of it, hm? It's a big responsibility, a baby. Have you given it any thought? Any thought at all? Or is it all you and Margaret can do to think about your fun, your vacation at this lake? This is a life, a human life, that you are responsible for—forever! Neither of you has a real job. If I were in your shoes I'd just take those two weeks to hunker down with the classifieds each morning and try to find work. It's time to be an adult, Toller, not one of these jackasses here in

California, grown men and women driving pickup trucks, who think life is all about fun and bicycling in silly shorts and a helmet and wind chimes. Wind chimes! For God's sake!"

Toller drew his attention from the abyss that had opened in the telephone receiver he held in his hand; looked around the apartment, that his mother had never seen, the apartment in which he and Margaret lived; at the books and pictures, the newspapers and mail stacked on the table, the stasis and the flux, at Margaret herself and her wondrously swollen belly, all the evidence of his life that his mother refused, at the risk of derangement, even to acknowledge. The fullness of it all, the friends she would never meet, the adventures she refused to take interest in, the enthusiasms she could not comprehend—even his own child, this grandchild, she would never really know; her stunted awareness would derive only from the monthly appearances it would make on the patio. Toller's mother should have understood him as well as anybody, but she understood only that he was the suddenly recalcitrant instantiation of the child who had once unquestioningly accepted her authority over every sphere of his life.

"Toller!" she brayed. "I don't want to hear about it if you find yourself in financial trouble! When you were coming down here a couple of years ago so upset and unhappy, I thought you were coming to your senses! But it appears that you're forgetting every lesson you should have learned!"

For the very first time Toller understood that his mother was truly the enemy of everything he was, all the things he'd sedulously worked to become, and that their connection had always been entirely, deceitfully, dependent on his successfully masking those things from her. Even her embrace of Margaret seemed doubtful: with the spat pronunciation of the hard consonants in words like *California* and *jackass*, words struck against the palate as if to generate sparks, he knew that she was identifying for him what she saw as the exact source of the contamination.

"Mom," he said, "I know what I'm doing. It's a vacation. People take them."

"*People*. Only in California would *people* take a vacation when they're not working! Vacation from *what*?"

"I don't have to ask your permission, Mom."

"How dare you!" she said. "How dare you! You little so-and-so!" There was a strangled noise, as if the heart of her indignation was beyond expression, and she slammed the phone down, leaving Toller, and Margaret, shaken.

Toller's father, vivid to him in nearly all other contexts, seemed to him (it must be said) to be a cipher in connection with his mother; Toller had no idea whether his father was concerned about his mother or not, whether he truly agreed with her condemnation of their lives or simply humored her, whether that placid agreeability masked a secret life of his own. Toller knew that his father got up and dressed and left the house every morning, that he came home every evening with stories of the greater world, that he sometimes met other people for lunch or golf, that he kept in touch with old friends. When he would join them on the patio, or by the fireplace, or around the dining table, he listened to Toller's mother attentively, although she could not possibly have been drawing anything new to complain about from within the enclosure of her life. His father's uncanny equilibrium was such that Toller had sometimes felt, before he met Margaret, that his mother's *oddness* was entirely a product of his own imagination. Perfect loyalty is what it was; Toller's father was loyal to a fault—but Toller wouldn't have understood this if he hadn't grasped, three weeks after their return from Tahoe and nearly six weeks since he'd spoken to either of his parents, the furtiveness of the call he received from his father one morning.

"Toller, you have to call your mother and apologize."

"Why do I have to apologize to her?"

"She feels very strongly that you spoke out of turn."

"And that's how you feel about it? Out of turn. She's the one who spoke out of turn. It was her. I can run my own life. I'm having a kid. I'm thirty-two years old."

"I know you are, Toller."

With each declaration of maturity, Toller felt more flustered and infantile. It went on like that for a few minutes. Toller wanted badly for his father to acknowledge that his mother had been wrong—wanted his father to acknowledge more than that, actually, although he was sensible enough not to share his developing opinions on his mother's mental condition—but the subject was taboo.

"How about her apologizing to me? Have you asked her that?" Toller asked again.

"I can't, Toller." His father was calling from his office, but he lowered his voice. And here Toller recognized the fragilely balanced forces holding together the marriage, and what must have seemed to his father to be his own life; his having reached, at sixty, the limits of its adaptability. Toller's father wasn't calling as his mother's envoy, or as Toller's ally, but as a man maneuvering to avoid a choice that would result either way in an unbearable loss. Toller understood; he hoped for the best with his mother, but he couldn't stand the idea of losing his father. He called and apologized.

Toller's mother continued scrupulously for a while to all but ignore Toller. It was so awkward, the way that she would talk around him if possible, as if he weren't there, or brusquely tell him that she would call his father to the phone if she happened to answer when Toller called, that Toller half-expected her to stop the discomfiting game; to ask him if she had demonstrated to his complete satisfaction that—as with her other feats of self-estrangement—she was fully capable of sustaining this act of will: would he now conform to her requirements? For all that she required of him, she may as well have asked such a question of the entire despised state of California. Unexpectedly, she took to Margaret again wholeheartedly, which bothered Toller, who suspected that it was her coded way of denigrating the relationship; of subtly informing him that she saw a clear and definite separation between the two of them that she could emphasize by placing the wedge of herself in it, which seemed to be confirmed by Margaret's curious reciprocation of her evident affection.

"When a nasty old cat decides it loves only you, you always love it back," Margaret explained.

Margaret had attained the condition of hallowed and empty bonhomie embodied by the Safeway cashier, the phlebotomist, the man who sawed off the dead branches of the live oak in the front yard, all those *dear people* his mother thought so highly of. It didn't matter how or why. To remain in Toller's mother's good graces meant to have sustained the glow of some positive impression, no matter how arbitrarily it had been registered. The impression didn't need to have any depth. Toller's mother certainly didn't want to know any more about Margaret than she did about those cherished strangers of hers: she became visibly uncomfortable if Margaret spoke to her of her childhood in the South Bay; or of her father, a radiologist in San Jose, and her mother, the owner of a Hallmark store in Los Gatos. She did clap her hands with glee when Margaret told the story of her refusal to bend to her parents' will and follow a pre-med course at Stanford, but became perplexed and sullen when it was made clear that the resulting rift had been temporary and superficial, as if the deepest and most mysterious disappointment of the human psyche was the willingness to forgive other people. And when things finally eased between Toller and his mother, when she began again to speak to him as if he were more than an unwelcome stranger, it was plain to him that she had neither forgiven him nor stopped being disenchanted with him.

Toller might have wondered why he'd bothered apologizing at all; it was obvious that his mother suffered his presence only in order to see Margaret and the baby, a girl, who was—as Toller had predicted—delivered to the patio each month in the back of the late-model Toyota sedan that the new parents, having somehow avoided the financial ruin their vacation was sure to bring on, had bought used. He might have wondered if not for the fact that, as intended, his apology enabled him to continue to see and speak to his father—more so than before, even, since the job of sitting with his mother in the shade of the cotoneaster and the lemon tree now was delegated largely to Margaret and the baby, allowing Toller and his father to spend time together. His father was now partially retired, providing consulting services to his former employer for several well-compensated hours each week. Though Toller never pointedly inquired about his mother's habits, his father made it clear to him that the things he was doing in his now-abundant spare time he was doing by himself.

"And Mom?" Toller would ask, casually.

"Oh, you know your mother," his father would say. "She has her books and her cards and things. I just try to stay out of her hair."

Toller followed this obliquely delivered advice to the letter; he persisted in hoping for the best with his mother, but he had little idea what the best might be, and the degree of deformation inherent in the family mechanism became painfully evident on occasion, most notably when his mother refused outright to attend his wedding to Margaret and insisted that his father remain behind to chauffeur her to a scheduled doctor's appointment. Even the illusion he maintained of unfettered access to his father became strained to the breaking point in such instances, and in the case of their wedding Toller had to beg Margaret not to call his mother and give her a piece of her mind, fearing that if Margaret made it onto what they called his mother's "shit list"—this ordinary phrase evoked in Toller's imagination an actual lengthy document, with names inscribed indelibly upon it—he would never be able to see his father again.

Toller and Margaret continued to make their monthly pilgrimages to Palo Alto, eventually from the suburban town of Brisbane, where they moved into a house built on one of the lower slopes of a mountain. They raised their daughter, had another. Sometimes, in the evening, when he stepped out of the kitchen door and stood on the little redwood deck overlooking his backyard with a bottle of beer in his hand, watching his older daughter play in the soft light remaining with the sun now behind the mountain, listening to a mourning dove calling, that desolately beautiful sound he associated with the pale orange of twilight here, he'd think of the precipitating offense, of the misconception at its heart— wasn't this his house, his deck, his daughter, his beer? What had he done so badly? He was able to shrug it off, though: aside from the hunkering mystery of his mother, life was good to Toller, reliable and satisfying, and it was typical of a simplicity of mind that he would have been the last to suspect that he believed it would continue this way forever.

When Toller was forty-two, his father was diagnosed with a brain tumor, and he died six months later. Toller learned that his father was dead when his mother called while he was on his way to the hospital.

"Don't let them take him away," Toller said automatically. It was the most reflexive thing he had ever said, completely unprompted and unscripted, and he pondered it, this primal desire, as he drove along 280, exiting at Sand Hill Road and coasting down the long incline toward the Stanford campus and the medical center at its edge, Hoover Tower rising in the distance. A malfunctioning sprinkler operating on one of the emerald swaths of grass on either side of the road sprayed the windshield and passenger side windows of Toller's car as he passed, startling him from his reverie, and he fumbled for the wiper switch.

At first, after the diagnosis, Toller had been tremendously hopeful— hopeful that his father would survive, and hopeful that the crisis would repair the rift between his mother and him. Who else, he'd wondered, could she turn to? And who else, he might have wondered, did he have? Even a hated son resists the idea of his own orphaning. But although he'd carefully dressed and groomed himself for his appearances in his role as concerned adult son, hoping to gull his mother from behind the disguise of his ongoing success, she'd been unrelenting, and when Toller had checked the time on his wristwatch, a wristwatch he was proud of, as the two of them waited for his father to emerge from surgery, she had casually ridiculed it, gesturing at it as if to the very unseen audience to whom Toller was playing. "What kind of a watch is that? That's an absurd watch for a grown man." And, after the surgeon had finally appeared to deliver the unhopeful news, when Toller had leaned toward his mother and begun to say vaguely reassuring words, she had twisted the section of newspaper that she held in her hands—a section he had offered her in the courtly manner that he imagined was befitting a considerate and beloved son—into a club, as if she intended to strike Toller with it. His own newspaper!

"For God's sake, Toller. I don't need comforting. I don't need you to comfort me."

When he arrived at the hospital on the day his father died, he found his mother standing at the nurse's station, a paper grocery bag on the counter before her. He started for his father's room, but his mother's voice stopped him: "He's gone, Toller." He pushed through the voice; she couldn't possibly mean what she seemed to be saying, but when he reached the room it was empty, the bed already efficiently stripped.

"I wanted to see him," Toller said.

"You didn't want to see him like that."

"I *did*," Toller insisted. "I *did* want to see him."

"Well, I didn't want to wait in there with him while you took your time getting here," she said. "All right? Please, don't make a scene. If you want to see him, you can go down to the morgue. The morgue, right?"

A nurse looked up brightly from the computer terminal and open files before her and nodded. Toller's mother had one hand on her hip and rested an elbow on the counter. She looked as if she was at the front desk of a hotel, checking out. It dawned on him that in the grocery bag were his father's things. Toller sat down in a chair to wait while his mother squared things away. The chemo nurse came upstairs to hug her, the CT scan technician, the floor nurse, wearing a preposterous tunic depicting Sylvester and Tweety—stalking, chasing, pouncing, fluttering away, laughing. More of his mother's *great friends*.

Toller returned home to Brisbane that night—his mother having refused his perfunctory offer to stay with her at the house—and ate voraciously. He had his father's address book with him, and he wore his father's signet ring on his finger. The girls were in bed and Margaret sat across the kitchen table watching him. He ate what was before him and then returned to the stove to get more from the pot. He drank an entire bottle of wine. Margaret said nothing when he started on the whiskey. He felt elated. A feeling of well-being spread throughout his body, easing a knotty tautness that seemed to have entered deep into each of his muscles months and years beforehand. He wondered if this was what his father had felt as his own depleted body began its final shutting down, an easeful surrender of all the worst things life had thrust upon him.

What, with that gone, would have been left to worry about? Surely he couldn't have been worried about that boulder of refusal, of imprudent harsh resolve, that turned up at the hospital each day disguised as a wife, disguised as a *person*, to stand at his bedside, imparting her spurious good cheer to the personnel who jabbed, who poked, who choked, who abraded, who tormented his father throughout those final weeks. That fantastic act, honed over the course of decades while the malignancy of her genuine feelings burned glowing within her, lavished upon those who professionally and without the least emotion presided over his father's destruction. After all that she could not forgive, all that fell short against that scale of rigid values she'd erected over the years, he found, with joy, that he could not forgive those smiles and tears she expended on them even after allowing their collaborators to haul his father away like meat. The two of them, mother and son, were free of one another at last. Thinking of his father dead—the imagined corpse that would always have to stand for the real one he hadn't seen—he began finally to cry for the first time that day, and Margaret reached out to take his hands in hers with the incomplete but heartfelt understanding that is the best, really, that we can hope for.

A King in Mirrors

Matthew Specktor

Matthew Specktor is the author of two books, including the novel That Summertime Sound. *His writing has appeared or is forthcoming in* Harper's, Black Clock, *and* Canteen, *among other places. He is senior editor at the* Los Angeles Review of Books, *and is currently at work on a screenplay with the actor James Franco.*

The New Soft Shoe

 MY FATHER TOSSES ME INTO THE AIR. I HAVE NO IDEA when, or if, I will come down. My face splays out like a race car driver's, pinned back against my skull. I feel my bones, my stomach, my heart, my kidneys—all things I have seen pictured in a book—sliding around inside their loose cage of skin. When he's finished, and all of my worst fears have been shown but not proven, he hands me to my uncle.

"Here." He is doughy, soft and huge like a walrus. He walks away, laughing.

Such is my introduction to my body. Inside my room, I practice with it. What does it do? I put on side three of *The White Album* and spasm uncontrollably to "Helter Skelter," to "Everybody's Got Something to Hide." Every day is my birthday, until my uncle—a joyless hardass, who lives alone in Mar Vista—asks me what I'm doing.

"Dancing."

"That's not dancing," he snaps. He shows me instead what might be, moving around the room in a sequence of elaborate steps that seem chalked across the floor, diagrammed in white. He hums under his breath, "Moon River," and for a moment we are in the South Pacific, on one of the nameless atolls that decorate the globe over in the corner. Palms sway outside my window. My uncle is lost too, I think, in whatever world of Waves and Wacs, scarlet fever and diphtheria—I am aware my parents grow backwards, into a world that predates the polio vaccine and the Beatles—he came from. Eventually, he loses interest, drops my hands and brushes me off his feet. My poor uncle, who never married and has no kids of his own. Sadness ticks off him, there in the corner, as he stands with his hands on his knees. The needle hisses in the run-out groove. Behind the house they are digging a hole in the yard. I listen to the men shouting, the bulldozer's solemn rumble. My uncle straightens and walks from the room. He has a finely fuzzed head, soft like a peach, and he smells like hot skin, cleaning fluid: some sweet, decaying smell I can't name. I try to imagine what he was like when he was funny. When, for instance, he very elaborately switched out the family's Cream of Wheat with wood shavings, so his father sat down—this would've been in March of 1939, when my mother was seven and he fourteen—to a hot bowl of sawdust. I picture this perfectly: the stern savage who is supposed to look like me, pouring himself some orange juice, and then whipsawing suddenly, keeling forward to hit the table face first. For a long moment, no one speaks. My mother's family are all absurdists, deadpan practitioners of jokes that aren't funny. Orange juice dribbles over the side of the table and Spencer, the dog, laps it up. Nails scrabbling atop linoleum. Finally someone laughs and my mother reaches over and pokes her dad's clammy, inert skin.

All this has been explained to me, with talk of a *congenital defect*, a *closed valve*, but I think it's the most terrifying thing I've heard in my life. It finds its mirror in the racket the Beatles are now making, a clatter of found sounds and restaurant scrapings—*number 9, number 9*—I'll never listen to again. Outside, the men keep shouting, the bulldozer digs its hole. Eventually this will be a swimming pool. For now it's a grave, a pit I climb in and out of at will, rehearsing my own retirement. The record, the shouting, the nightmare grind. These things blur, they run together: my grandfather, born with a bad heart, and the hours, the world, the ordinary clamor of the day.

Flaming

My parents take me to see a psychiatrist. A boy I know has just died hang-gliding.

"Why are you afraid?"

I don't have an answer. His office looks like an abstract painting, grid-like and disorderly. He is a set of glasses concealing, somewhere far behind him, a man. Bald like my uncle, my grandfather, like me someday. *A maternal gene.*

"Are you afraid of other things? Besides dying?"

I am afraid of light fixtures, uncooked hot dogs, chicken livers; I am afraid of the bright blue gizzard I've seen in a disemboweled rattlesnake, a scream that is emitted on the second side of the *Hair* soundtrack. I am afraid of my own heart. My mother stands in the kitchen on one foot, talking on the phone while she burns sandwiches.

"Oh that's awful," she says, tapping her cigarette against the edge of the counter. Her frail, pale face like the lady on the Yuban can, framed by platinum strands. "How did it happen?"

Flakes drift down toward the floor, gray snow. My sandwich when she hands it to me is black, carbonized, the cheese almost liquid. I like it like that, eat it cheerfully while I listen to the gardener attack the grass outside. I can't help but notice, however, that people are dying, that men are marching on the moon. I eat and feel weightless, uncertain. I walk up to the television while Marlon Perkins is talking. "I know him," I proclaim, hands against the glass, as if I might tumble through it to Africa.

"No you don't," my mother says. "Sorry honey, but you don't."

Sunday evening, I'll be asleep by 7:30, the living room rug the same color as the Serengeti. While I sleep, perhaps, a friend of my mother's is killed in a shootout with the police. Another, a colleague of my father's, commits suicide in his garage. *Monoxide, closet, Black Panther.* The words are suggestive, but don't make sense.

"Did Sheila know?" my mother asks. While I sit on the floor and strike blue-tipped kitchen matches against ribbed glass; sniff the inside of a cedar-lined box, like a silver coffin. "How could she not know, he was flaming?"

I could ask, but I don't. It's more interesting not to know, to say nothing of safer. *What's gunrunning, who are pigs, why is Roman Polanski crying?* My parents barricade their doors against things that haven't happened yet. In their room, and through the door, my mother speaks the word "leukemia." I hear my father say, "That's too bad, Ren, that's too bad."

At Roxbury Park, a little girl I've been playing with—her name is Mariana Dopp—stops coming. My mother sits with the profile of a statue, while I tumble alone below the trees. *Dopp, rhymes with stop.* These things make a crooked, associative pattern, spinning out around death. I look up at the moon, pale and vaporous in the afternoon sky. A eucalyptus rains sticky pods on my palms. *Why is she bald, mom, why is she bald?* Later in the evening my parents throw a dinner party. I listen to them, from bed, the voices drifting up the stairs. I'm not in the least sleepy. I take three curtain calls, steal slices of prosciutto—tattered, disintegrating like dried skin—off slices of greening melon. When I am out of excuses, I go back upstairs. Their voices are garbled, faraway, like passengers' on a ship. They are singing, singing "Auld Lang Syne." I am wide awake. Over the hedge the neighbors are awake too, every light in their house blazing. I lie perfectly still. A chandelier hangs above me like a bomb. The singing collapses at last into laughter, my mother's voice riding drunkenly above the rest. *Goodnight, goodnight.* My eyes stay locked upon the window next door, counting the seconds, the minutes, the hours, just waiting for the light to go out.

The Good Doctor

"Let's go to Martindales," my father says. "Let's go to Beverly Hills."

It's Saturday morning, the day spreads endlessly before us. His friend, The Good Doctor, picks us up in a Grand Am. He's not a doctor he's an actor, an Englishman: I've seen him on TV, scrutinizing viruses through a microscope, playing a scientist striving to save the world. He smells sweet and vaguely urinous. He is handsome, in just the way his nickname implies: leathery, box-jawed, hair flecked with early silver. I am older, I can read a menu, my mother has given me a copy of *Tom Sawyer* that will obsess me for the next year-and-a-half. In the darkness of the Hamlet on Century Park East—a room like a casket, velveteen and windowless—we eat our Rex Harrisons, the Number 9 with Russian dressing, the waitresses fail to recognize The Good Doctor. What could be wrong with them? *I'm fine, thank you and you,* my father says to everyone who greets him and I wonder who the ghost is, the invisible second to whom my father is also speaking?

Outside, there are pyramidal steps, a shape like a ziggurat that I wind my way around, trying to keep my balance while my dad and The Good Doctor discuss business.

"They're squeezing our balls," my father says, "but I'm going to get you what you deserve. We'll take you to another network if we have to."

"Those bastards." For a moment, they forget I am here. "I can't afford not to get picked up, you know that don't you?"

The Good Doctor holds my hand so I don't fall. What would I do without him? A Ferris wheel lifts into the air, in the distance. The Good Doctor looks that way too. His wife, Peggy, is having tests run at Cedars of Lebanon. Something is not right, a problem with her ovaries. Neither of these men, wise grown-ups, is yet forty years old. The air is the color of ash, there where the Ferris wheel touches it, beyond the tops of the conifers that mark the edge of a golf course. He lets go of my hand a moment, reaches up to adjust his glasses. My father sits, his chinless face—he looks like a Hell's Angel gone tender, gone soft—trained upon the ground. Maybe he's counting the bricks, which I do too: the pinkish rectangular tiles that line the restaurant's courtyard. His own father is in the same hospital, coughing up his lungs. Later, we go visit him, just the two of us now. We stand in the hospital elevator, on our way to see a person neither of us understands, his accent thickening under so much phlegm I can barely decipher a word of it. I rub the Braille plate, next to the regular buttons, as we lurch skywards. I look at my copy of *Tom Sawyer*, so full of things I don't understand either—what is "ambuscade," what are Arabs, what are bulrushes?—yet I don't care. I vanish inside the sounds.

Shadow Dancing

My father throws away his cigarettes, takes up running.

"Come on," he says. It's six o'clock in the morning. "Come on."

We're living in Santa Monica now, home of the newlywed and the nearly dead, my mother calls it. It's 1977. The pier, the mall, the promenade are all derelict, and crumbling towers crouch at the base of Ocean Avenue, their balconies pendular with dead ferns. There's no one awake at this hour. The sky is gray, a plain dull mother of pearl. We run to the ocean and back. I wake up, warm into hating my father the way I do. Every step hurts, feels concussive and unnatural even in my soft shoes. I wear headphones, a transistor radio tuned to an AM station plays Andy Gibb. The day cracks open like an egg as we jog along Ocean, and yet there's nobody here. The wide streets, the brass balustrades of the Shangri-La Hotel and the Bellevue, places where the retirees cluster to eat Crab Louis at twilight. We go home and I dress for school, while my father lines up his vitamins and chokes them down, two by two. He's shaved his face in an effort to look younger. I still recognize him, but it's possible my mother doesn't. The Zegna ties, the manicures, the spritzers. Up in my room, Suzie—the dog I've had since I was two—lies perfectly still beneath the windowsill. Her side rises and falls, rises and falls, her gray fur mottles with the carpet. She is blind in one eye, limping, she smells like wet feathers, like slow rot. Soon she will fall into the swimming pool and drown. "Hello?"

The voice on the other end of the phone is garbled, gross with its own weight and importance when I pick up on Saturday afternoon. I call my dad and pretend to hang up, though of course, of course, I listen.

"Freddy, Freddy, I've got to get off this picture—"

"I can't get you off of it. It's a contract. It'll be a horse's head in *your* bed, next time—"

I crouch in the den, barely daring to breathe. I've seen the movie, blood streaking the producer's silk sheets. There might be marbles in the man's mouth, coins on his eyes. How can he talk this way?

"Freddy, Freddy, what can you do?"

Over my bed, in my room, there is a poster that summarizes female beauty. A woman with ringlets, raccoon eyes, a maroon tube top. This image is everywhere—in three years, it'll be antique—but now it's in everyone's room, all around the world. I come home to find her standing inside the vestibule, talking to my mom about shoes. She looks like her own quotation, like an echo of something that didn't exist before she invented it. I yawn, plod upstairs. When your fantasies belong to everybody they cease to be interesting, cease to be yours. Maybe, instead, they cease to be credible. Yet—the signs are everywhere. Why can't I read them? Every morning the boulevards are crowded now with men like lemmings, stampeding to the sea and back. My father and I are no longer alone. Their greasy torsos and hollow eyes, their stallion bodies as they run, breathing violently, pivoting upon the Pacific's coolness and back, back to their ranch-style bungalows and unhappy children, their jilted wives softening beneath the kiwi trees. Or else to their condominiums in Brentwood, the empty two bedrooms let furnished, rooms and refrigerators bare except for crushed boxes of Monopoly and Scrabble, half-bottles of Soave Bolla and rancid hacks of salmon. At one of these, belonging to a friend's father, I find a dildo underneath a couch. When A___'s dad is murdered, it seems almost a relief to the rest of us. We waste our time acting it out, garroting one another or stabbing, leaving fist-sized bruises on one another's skinny chests. That this life, with its dream of infinite extension—I've heard my father, too, use the word *cunt*—should end just like any other.

Bone, or Cream

"'Till death!' You said, 'Till death!'"

My parents are fighting downstairs, my mom's voice hysterical. I lie in bed and listen, try to find some other explanation beyond the obvious. I hold my breath, my tongue tastes of hashish. "Moonage

Daydream" blares through headphones, but I can hear everything: the ice rattling in my mother's glass, her voice more animal than human.

"Who is she?" she shouts. "What's her name?"

I am beginning to feel doomed to unoriginality, beginning to suspect an adult life is more wearisome than a child's. Like it or not, I am a conscript in true love's army. At this hour, certain songs mean everything to me. "City of the Dead." "Watching the Detectives." When my father leaves, I shake his hand and watch him walk off, tramping across the shabby grass. That's his car, parked at the curb, a Mercedes I've never seen before. It's white, and sinister in the moonlight. Its ragtop is rolled back in the rain.

"What's her name?"

My mother asks me now, plaintively this time, and I shrug. I know, but I can't tell her. She knows, but pretends not to. Their marriage lasted seventeen years and suddenly—she confides in me—he changed everything it is possible to change, everything outside his own skeleton. I realize— as my mother uncorks a second bottle of wine for the two of us—that this has been bothering me—my father's new car is not white, but "bone," or "cream." Or both. Can it be both? It doesn't matter, he has a new one—newer still—when he shows up to visit, when he spends the night in a moment of deep contrition and then bails again, leaving behind a tan Members Only jacket, several sizes too small. My mother weeps and weeps and weeps. Her cheek is flush with the butcher's block table in the kitchen, where she is asleep or unconscious, I can't tell. Her nightgown hangs open. I pass by, ignoring her, ignoring the sight of my mother's tits. Up in my room, I play David Bowie, the one about the Thin White Duke, "throwing darts in lovers' eyes." What I, after all, would like to do. It's late, I'm awake, and somewhere outside my father's Porsche roars throatily along the avenues, the ghostly sound of the automotive suburbs. I pour myself another shot, draw one more line. My face is numb, my teeth like a beaver's, hard enough to chip wood. My father is out there, leading his obscure and elegant life. Mine might last longer, but only—I lift my face from the mirror and close my eyes—only if I'd like.

Rehearsal

My father collapses at The Palm. He takes a bite of his dessert and then turns blue, swooning across the table, leaving skidmarks of chocolate mousse on white cloth.

"Oh my God!" my stepmother yells, more convincingly than she ever has on screen. "Oh my God!"

For a moment, no one notices. Her voice sounds off the walls and marbles with the gossip, the murmur of all the other diners, the pictures of Lew Wasserman and Tony Perkins, Don Rickles and Harry Cohn.

"Oh my God!" she screams again. And people look up from their piles of shoestring potatoes finally, those towers that look like tiny kindling. A waiter runs and wraps his arm around my father's waist, squeezes. Maybe she is less convincing than I thought for I don't, even while this is happening, believe her. Around the room faces are raised from plates of scallops, skin tones red and gold, to look at my father writhing and choking, before he coughs up whatever was blocking his windpipe. A bit of cake, so they can go back to eating their own.

No story here. Nothing has happened. My stepmother touches her hair, that rat's nest of brittle darkness, and forks ring out against china. My father drinks a glass of water. When John Belushi died, Leigh Brillstein showed me her true face, which was everyone's true face, streaked with tears. She sat beneath the halogen tubes, the hum of electric typewriters and telex machines around her, while she hung up the phone quietly. When the news was announced, three hours later, Leigh was already in crisis mode, regal as a queen while she fielded condolence calls, leaving it to the media to weep and moan. Had my father died, this would've been my job. No one here would do it sooner. I am twenty-two, a paperback *Hamlet* jammed deep within my pocket, a college diploma—still bleeding ink—rolled up in the backseat of my car. People resume eating, their faces placid as cows. *No one we know, anyway.* Around them, around us all, the caricatures on the walls bound up like superheroes, gigantic heads attached to cricket bodies. Don Rickles to the rescue! Please tell me how to live, what to do.

Allergies

D___ goes to London. Theater is his life. He sends me a Dadaist postcard decorated with stick figures, a long, long letter detailing everything—the conversion rates, the coldwater flat in Hampstead, the view from the buses along Charing Cross Road, the man whose nose is half his face— until I am jealous. I yearn to be him. The pages of the letter are dusted with hair, he writes: *I am allergic to everything, I can't stop sneezing, this flat smells funky.* It belongs to a poet, an older man who has gone abroad. *These fucking cats!* What does it matter? He is living a dream. In high school we wore long coats and ate peyote, staggering around the campus after dark. We broke into the science building, chased each other down the long, dark halls, banging fiercely against the empty lockers. *Are you scared yet*, we'd yell. *Are you scared yet??* Not yet, not ever. If they couldn't catch us now, how were they supposed to do so in the future? Flashlights under our faces, skin dripping off our bones. In London he lives on porridge and orange juice, a healthy lifestyle. We've moved on. *But why does this place reek so,* he asks in a letter that reaches me at a temp desk in San Francisco, where I am adjudicating a suit between Mastercard and Visa, typing and retyping nearly identical forms. *Fruitless, fruitless.* I really ought to be in London, instead of temping for the man, dying (I suspect, and it feels like) by inches. I write back, in Liquid Paper. *S.O.S! Some Pig! Help Me Please!* Soft, calligraphic brushstrokes, on blue stationary. I wait and I wait. I get no response. On the phone with my mother, one day she says, "Honey, I'm sorry to tell you but that boy in your class? The one who won a Fulbright? He died."

"Died?"

Yes, died. The explanation tumbles out in a rush, something about a gas leak, a few beers, a headache, a nap. He never woke up. I sit at my desk staring out at the Transamerica Pyramid, Coit Tower at twilight, ruins of a civilization that hasn't collapsed yet as my mother—suddenly sober, shuttling herself from meeting to meeting—apologizes. For what, I wonder? Because I am young, I think too, never sorry enough.

I quit my job. But not before I get one last letter, which comes as I'm cleaning out my desk. I open the airmail envelope and find—a ziplock baggie full of mold? Are they spores, toxic, a new drug? They look like an old man's pubes, gray-green, something scraped off a peach: only when I find the note do I understand.

I shaved the cat, he has written. The solution! *I shaved the cat!*

The Stupidest Movie in the World

This is how it goes, for a while. We have entered the new territory. We have found our feet, it appears. For example G___, last seen scavenging in a Dumpster behind the Santa Monica Promenade, reinvents himself as a successful stockbroker. He shows up gleaming, in a new suit, his red hair and freckles still screaming Trust Me!, the needle marks invisible along his arms. Wonderful, we want to applaud! Bravo! I knew you'd make it, I almost tell him, but don't. So-and-so directs the Stupidest

Movie of All Time, then laughs his way to the bank. We attend the premiere, applaud with enthusiasm. The movie is so bad we can enjoy it without feeling envious of his model girlfriend, the pimpwear he sports—irony, irony—as he glides across the lobby of the DGA. There he goes! Waiting to embrace him, why—it's The Good Doctor! He's in the movie too, but who isn't? His turn as an animal rights activist who gets mixed up with the mob is an homage or a parody, whereas our own— my own, performance as myself—is what, precisely? I go over to say hello to him. He squints at me like an assailant. *Oh,* he says. *Yes, I remember. How's your father?* I tell him, and think: maybe I am the second self, the one my father was always talking to. He pats my shoulder and then walks away to join a woman I don't recognize. Peggy is dead, their own children both grown, both suicides.

We keep on, though. We just keep getting away with it. Until P___'s sister dies of an aneurysm, collapsing on the floor of her terrace in Westwood, peach-colored nightgown bunched around her ankles, textbooks scattered around her head. Until X___'s mother gets bone cancer, and some kid we barely remember succumbs to kidney failure, then has a building named after him. Memorial services are held on the Paramount lot. Respectfully, we attend. I preen agelessly in a restroom outside the theater, a white chrysanthemum in the buttonhole of my blue jacket. Unless—wait! That's at my wedding. I am there, to my own amazement as well as anybody's. *Remember that night you crashed behind the ice machine, wearing argyle socks?* I do not. I hardly remember anything, although the words, spoken below the clustering thunderheads, are as present as can be. *I will,* I say, looking over my wife's shoulder at the cemetery, where the stones are all eroded beyond legibility, all covered with a radiant green moss. Should I attribute to any of this a special significance? To the clouds rolling in over the bay? Of course I shouldn't, of course I don't. I take a drink from a passing waiter and watch these—soft pink, edged with lemon peel—drifting across the lawn, shimmering in the dark like fireflies. There go my parents, on speaking terms! And here comes my bride, inexplicable in her dress, like a column of melting foam or like everything I have neglected to ask for in my entire life.

God's Eye

I wake up screaming. It happens naturally. There's a crick in my neck, my knees don't work the way they used to. My wife leaves, almost before she was ever here. I wake up, lifting my face off the pillow that is wet, and has muffled my animal groan. *Are you a camel*, my daughter says? *Daddy, are you a giraffe?*

"Something like it," I said, turning my face away. She shouldn't see me like this, I shouldn't see me like this. "I'm a primate."

"What's a primate?" she says.

"A primate's a monkey. Just like—you!"

I leap from bed and attack her, giggling. She hiccups with laughter. I won't let her stop. Sunlight lops off the bottoms of the palms, plantains dangled past my window. Does anything ever change, besides everything? Besides the need for colonoscopies and the meaning of the shopping list—not my writing—still taped to the fridge? I have no idea, and yet the same sad Santas go drooping across Wilshire Boulevard, the same gay tinsel marks the gateway to Beverly Hills. My daughter oohs and aahs at the same fountain—the one my father once peed in after a function at the Hilton—on the corner of Sawtelle and Sepulveda. Only there is no such corner, the streets don't cross.

I lie on my back, under the linden trees. I sit on the bench, where my mother's friend—the one who was arrested for gunrunning and who died in prison—used to do God's Eyes. I drive by the Hamlet and see it is gone, the whole edifice replaced by a Jamba Juice, which is something my daughter loves anyway. Should I have been informed about all this? Down in Tarzana, the last Orange Julius in southern California finally shuts its doors.

"Tell me again," my daughter says. "Daddy, tell me again about the seasons."

"Go to sleep," I say. We are lying in a hammock stretched across the backyard.

"No, tell me."

She needs a nap, I merely want one. Okay, okay.

"Listen—" the hammock sways—"Spring, summer, winter, fall."

"Hmm," she mumbles around her thumb. "Again."

"Spring, summer, fall, winter."

I almost repeat myself. The hammock sways. As if in the scramblings and half-continuities of experience, there is order after all. The sun pours through the trees and Vivi rotates on her side, curling over her fist. Somewhere across town, my father sticks his belly with needles, injecting himself with Human Growth Hormone. As if he is going to live forever and death were just a superstition to be avoided, the man his own voodoo doll. My mother's body floods with radiation, her tumor shrinks from six centimeters to two. And I am consumed by ghosts, of people I have known and others I have merely guessed at, yet been lucky enough to live with for a while. Shadow spatters like a can of black paint across the patio's far white wall: the last thing I ever look at will probably mean as much to me, though it's impossible it ever could more. The wind picks up and rocks the hammock back and forth. My daughter shivers like a hummingbird. Before she is lost in the provinces of sleep and I beside her, wide awake and also, strictly speaking, dreaming.

Gordito

Jerry Stahl

Jerry Stahl is the author of the memoir, Permanent Midnight, *which was made into a move starring Ben Stiller and Owen Wilson. His novels include* Perv, Plainclothes Naked, I Fatty, *and, most recently,* Pain Killers. *"Gordito" appeared in his story collection,* Love Without *(Open City Books).*

ALL PURAY EVER TALKED ABOUT WAS ZELDA Fitzgerald. It was kind of creepy, but I've listened to sadder insanity.

"Zelda used to do this thing with carrots, I swear. She'd braise them, get them just a little hot and tender, then slide them in."

I didn't have to ask where. But I did anyway.

"Do you have olive oil?" she asked. "I can show you. Sometimes I sprinkle cayenne."

I suppose I should tell you now, Puray was a little person. Pre-PC, a midget. A stacked half-pint. Knee-high. But where do you put *that* in the story? March it out in the first sentence, then that's what it's about. It's one of those hot sexy midget stories. Then you make the associations. Stereotypes. Male midgets are massively hung. They all look like thumbs. Ignorance. Or not.

But march the news out in the middle—*"And, by the way, the love of my life was genetically predisposed to never make forty inches"*—and what is that—O. Henry?

The least important detail was her stature. It was her Zelda thing. How much she wanted alcohol, more or less constantly. I once asked her why she drank. She said, "My father was in the circus."

"And—?"

"There is no *and!* Slide the carrot in real slow. Put the right music on. *Like there is any right music.*"

When she was being dramatic, her eyes would bug out. Frida Kahlo–adjacent. The unibrow made her more beautiful. She was half Guatemalan, half Armenian.

"A sultry mix, Daddy used to say, but unduly hirsute."

After the circus, her father wrestled. She showed me a poster that first day, while she braised.

"*GORDITO!*" The name in flaming letters across the bottom.

His expression was weirdly subdued. He had a professorial look, despite the leopard-skin toga, and a creased forehead like his daughter.

"He could have been a doctor of literature in Guatemala City. But, of course, his size. No one wanted to hear about Henry James from a tiny hombre who looked like Mickey Rooney, but smaller, darker. Mickey Rooney with machismo. Do you know why I was his favorite?"

There were probably a dozen answers to that I didn't want to hear.

"Because I was dangerous," she said, letting that hang in the air for a while. "To myself."

This was the kind of thing she said. The kind of thing that stirred feelings inside me I'd never had before. Like I wanted to kill her and take care of her at the same time. Like love was something foul you had to wipe off or extract with tweezers. Sometimes I saw the space over her head as tainted. What she gave off was so powerful it stained the air. But it wasn't a smell, exactly. It was absence. All the space she didn't take up: the grease-stained wall behind her, where a normal woman's breasts would be. How can I explain this? When her friends came over, I felt hulking. I didn't see them as small. I saw myself as an embarrassment of size.

"Some men think Puray is a little doll," she whispers, her voice raspy as an old black man's. "They want to play with Puray and dress her up. Bounce Puray on their knees."

"That's because they've never *had* you on their knee."

Our little joke. Puray's flesh had some density that makes her heavy as a standard human. I don't know the physiological explanation, but despite her stunted height, I could barely lift her. It's as if she was condensed. Hypersolid. After sex she liked to slap her ass and holler, "pig iron." Or when she'd been fucked *and* fucked up, "pig irony." For her the joke was fresh every time. She'd giggle her throaty giggle and hop in my lap, her leaden shanks nearly driving me through the floor.

Once, at a bus stop on Figueroa, she finished off a short dog of schnapps some rummy had left in a paper bag, then leaped up, balanced herself on the back of the bench, lifted her pink skirt high enough to show baby-blue thong, and stage dived into my lap. The impact was like a sandbag, dropped from a great height onto my femurs. But the pain was made small by the image preceding it: the robin's-egg ribbon buried in her black thatch, pubic hair thick as Castro's beard. Only slightly matted. She had good hygiene, she just sometimes forgot to finish what she started. I've seen nastier things. I just can't remember because of the hole this one burned through my medulla longata.

In the grips of some passion spaz, I grabbed her by the hair and yanked her face up to mine. I just wanted to stare at her, then kiss her. Mistaking my advance for attack, Puray slid a blade out of her bra and slashed. She missed my face but caught the hand I'd swung in front, what we know is called a defensive wound from TV cop shows. I saw my fingertip fly somewhere under the bus bench and, without thinking, I smacked her. Or tried to. She'd done some novelty boxing, and ducked me easily, so my fist crashed into Plexiglas. Apparently, my scream softened her up. She slipped the blade back in her bra and just slapped me.

I still wanted to punch her, but saw the eyes of the taquería patrons across the street. It was lunch hour. You don't know shame until you've fought with a female little person in public. Punch a pretty midget in the face, see the stares you get. When she kissed me, shame coursed through my system like bad speed, making me excited and nauseous all at once.

"Do you love me?"

Her eyes glazed when she got this hot. Violence got her like that. But it had to be accidental. She could tell the difference. If she ever thought I was faking—playing mad 'cause mad got her hot—she came right at me. "You only like me because I make you feel big."

She knew just where to slide the knife.

On an old-fashioned mercury thermometer, Puray Magic Marked a slash at her normal temperature: 99.9. Half conscious on booze and party pills, she'd tell me stories about being a child in freak shows. Her skull, more or less normal size now, had reached adult diameter by her fifth birthday. Which made her resemble, in her own words, a hydrocephalic toddler with a swagger. Gordito dressed her in a matching leopard-skin mini-toga, safety pinned, like his, at the left shoulder. When she was nine a lady from the Department of Health offered her mother twenty-five dollars not to breed any more. That was the going rate for handicap tube-tying.

"My mother was nearly six feet, and stacked. Daddy called her Mt. Olympus. He'd climb her with a knife in his teeth." (The same one, it turned out, that she'd tried to filet my face with at the bus stop. It was a family heirloom, originally stolen from the Times Square Howard Johnson's.)

Jerry Stahl

"Daddy overheard the D.O.H. lady talking to my mother and went into Gordito mode. He told her I wasn't handicapped. Even at nine, I felt redeemed. I thought he was sticking up for us. For the family. And then I heard him say, '*I know the rules. Non-handicap gets fifty.*' Hah! I learned everything I needed to learn about life, right there."

I loved the brazenness of her nightmare history. There was no gray area. My mother made me cuddle naked till I was eleven. But she didn't put me in a sideshow with Lobster Boy. I had certain advantages. Puray believed, more than anything, that her past connected her to Zelda's. When the future Mrs. Fitzgerald was ten, she telephoned the Montgomery police department to tell them a child was in danger of falling from the roof of a building. Then she climbed out her third-story window and onto the roof, waiting naked for their arrival. Her father was on the Alabama Supreme Court, so the house was big.

"Even then, Zel understood," Puray muttered, in her fetching slur.

"Understood what?"

"What do you think? You don't need to get drunk to indulge in irrational behavior. You need to get drunk so you can explain it."

Puray braised her carrots every morning. It was what she did, instead of vitamins. We lived in a studio apartment near the corner of Normandie and Sunset. Little Armenia. The tiny kitchen area was full of potted plants. None of the plants seemed to die, but none of them looked healthy. Unless they were supposed to be yellow. The first time we met, she told me she had hepatitis, on and off. "*Liver stuff, so we should be careful—if you want to be careful.*" It occurred to me that she might have given the houseplants hepatitis, if such a thing were botanically possible. I didn't want to find out. I'd seen what she could do with a root vegetable.

Our days passed simply. "I'm sleepy because of the hep," Puray would yawn, no more than two or three hours after rising. Up at ten, back in bed by noon. The good hours she spent in a high chair at the three-legged kitchen table, writing in legal pads. When she wrote she made sucking noises with her lips and ate compulsively. Her prose resembled Zelda's only at a distance. Mostly it involved drinking and losing control, in no particular order. Our first month together, she showed me her memoir, *What Are You Looking At?* It had an arresting beginning. "*Sometimes little Cinderella dropped a load in a blackout. . . .*"

Puray could not decide whether to refer to herself as Little Cinderella or Teeny Zelda. But names weren't the issue. I thought "load" was little crude, but it wasn't just that.

"Blackout loads?" I said with as much tact as I could muster. "I think that's something I'd have noticed."

Puray didn't see anything strange. "When a girl's survived as long as I have, she learns a few tricks."

But I wasn't buying it. "Some things even a trained professional can't hide."

"Wanna bet?" She barely bothered to sneer. "Ever wonder why I menstruate five times a month? Why I sleep with a pad in my panties? Maybe it's not a pad!"

Since she didn't like to be touched while sleeping, she might not have been lying. We never had sex in bed. Besides which, I wasn't sure I wanted to know.

We shared a Murphy bed, which unfolded to the lip of the bathtub separating the tiny living area from the kitchen proper. Puray daynapped in the tub. Around 10 a.m. her lids would start closing. She'd climb the stepladder to the raised tub, equipped with a dog bed. It was a perfect fit.

"Brain fog," she'd sigh when I tucked her in. "This Mami needs sleepy-sleepy." We kept the shades down, so it was only daytime in a technical sense.

If what Puray said is true, Zelda undid her husband with her carrot routine. In front of the maid. In front of the mailman. In front of Hemingway, who called her Flapper Sadista.

"The miracle was that it never appeared in a story. Though of course it does, in subtext. . . . Zelda liked it, right up in *here*. Mmmmff . . . and sometimes *here* . . . You want to hold this? *Mmmm.* Easy, like you're cleaning a pencil sharpener. Daddy liked vegetables, too."

When it got good she kind of sang, in a whisper. *Gordito!*

I know about mutants. The women they end up with. Women you want in private.

When what you get is a Puray.

You get a mutant, beautiful or not. And you love them. Because they're just like you.

"The secret," she said, "is you never peel them. You leave them dirty."

Toby Dead

Laurie Stone

Laurie Stone is author of three books of fiction and nonfiction and has published memoir pieces in Creative Nonfiction, TriQuarterly, *and* Threepenny Review, *among other publications. She has recently completed* My Life as an Animal, *a memoir, and is at work on* The Pain of Language, *an essay collection.*

AT EIGHTY-NINE, MY MOTHER LEARNS HER ARTERIES are clogged with plaque like tubes with toothpaste, but she brushes off the news and goes into cardiac arrest. A squat little machine that looks like R2-D2 is attached to her by a vacuum cleaner hose, and my sister is holding a clipboard. Ellen is tapping it with a long, hard fingernail saying, "You have two choices, Ma, sign the form or dead. Which is it, Ma, the form or dead?" I am glancing from the machine to my mother, who looks like a chimp caught in a lab experiment. She trains her beady eyes on Ellen, as if she's being conned, but she takes the pen in her monkey paw and signs on for three more years of life—as well as a stroke and the twenty-four-hour care of home aides. My mother and I don't like each other, don't see eye to eye, don't get along, but love is somewhere in the room. I feel responsible for her no matter what. It's like watching your own death.

The last time I see her, she's a pile of sticks in the hospital. "Get away," she screams when I enter her room, in a voice so loud the woman in the next bed pleads with me to stop her. "How?" I ask, "I'm open to suggestions."

We don't pick who we love. We don't pick who we don't love. People say: I'm sorry for your loss, and I wonder, *What is my loss?* When I am thirty-five and my father is dying of liver cancer, Toby sends me to the hospital then blames me for his death. At nineteen, as I am walking to the rabbi to marry Bruce, she tells me to get killed because Bruce's parents want their friends at the ceremony, and I don't have a problem with that. In your life, do the passages play out operatic, or are they civilized, like in *Our Town*? Everyone has stories. Some people let go of them like stones from their pockets. Some people keep them because it's what they have.

When I am little and crossing streets, my mother and I squeeze hands in pulse beats. We live in Washington Heights, near St. Nicholas Avenue, and it is a river of shops and strangers. Foreign words, sausages wrapped in greasy paper and eaten on the fly. We are moving, and we are together. My sister is at school, my father at work, and Toby and I are on the streets. People talk to us. Strangers talk to my mother. She is beautiful with deep-set eyes and high cheekbones, clip-clopping in high heels and pencil skirts, and there is something about her. She says more than she needs to at the butcher's, a man with a bloody apron stretched tight across his paunch, and they consult about brisket, Jew to Jew in the sawdust, and you can sense the despair of the carcasses hanging in the back, and it makes the occasion tender, all of us feeling closer to the chopping block. Toby prefers strangers to most people—strangers on buses, at the automat, in the park. She can say anything she wants. What can it hurt? In the morning, I watch from her bed as she drifts around naked, splashing on My Sin and attaching nylons to dangling garters. She will take me to the park to shovel sand, but it's the streets she's after, clip-clopping, and she's waiting for Ellen. My mother can't juggle two friends, and Ellen is first. You can tell by the looks they exchange in the school yard and the way they laugh at things I will still not understand by the time Toby dies and I am sixty-one.

In Long Beach, we have dinners out. The rest of us share, but my mother eats her own portion of roast pork with Chinese vegetables. It's bok choy, but we don't know the name. Long Beach is not a city. You drive from here to there. When my father and sister are away, I will go anywhere with my mother, even though I can't tell if she is happy or sad. It looks like a spell you fall under when you learn to play mahjong. My mother says she doesn't like games, but there she sits with other women, shifting tiles that make a clicking sound like cubes of hard candy. We drift to shopping malls where there are stores and strangers but no streets. She's dying to get lost. I adore her. She embarrasses me. She will say someone is ugly so they can hear. I want to look like her. I spend as much time as I can sleeping at my friend Linda's house. When I am five, I go to sleep-away camp for two months for the first time. I miss her. I thrive. When she visits, she reaches for Ellen first. "Because she's older."

The Toby of Long Beach is backing up a finned, yellow Plymouth, looking over her shoulder with a cigarette twisted in her lips. We're headed to the Malibu Beach Club, and I am fat. In a home movie, she sits outside her cabana wearing a turquoise halter top pulled up to her bronzed shoulders. In the late afternoon, she pads to the ocean where waves lap her copper legs and foam surrounds her trim waist. Each splash is a shock because she doesn't know how to swim. She tells strangers about the time my father rigged a float behind a rowboat and Ellen, then a toddler, slipped out and almost drowned. "She turned blue," my mother says to anyone on the sand.

Near the end of her life, she would ask what's it all about? And I would wonder how, if you hated games, you could master the intricacies of something like mah jong, and if you could do that, what else might you have learned?

She sits across from me at Starbucks, her hair fluffy and white—a color close to her platinum bleach jobs. She's out of her wheelchair, on a wooden seat, spooning up a Frappacino and licking her lips. "I never eat between meals. I'm only doing it to please you." I broach the subject of money. Usually I don't ask her for things, but she's given Ellen her diamond ring worth $40,000, while I have received nothing. I'm commuting to Arizona because I've fallen in love with a Brit named Richard. We met at an artist colony, and he teaches museum studies in Phoenix. I am sixty, and I want my mother to be nice. We want what we want. I propose she give me $5000 a year for four years, half the value of the ring. She narrows her eyes, and her head snaps back. "I won't give you anything."

I have expected this reaction but have given it a shot. What can it hurt? Money is what my mother has, the way she used to have beauty— a little leverage, a little bait. She can reward my sister, because Ellen's love isn't in doubt, plus Ellen can't be tantalized—she has plenty of loot of her own. Toby can see my yearning—or maybe it's love—and I can't wipe it off my face. Generally, she likes talking about money—how much you earn, when it could run out. I like talking about money. Money is desire before it's transformed into something that can disappoint you. I want her jewelry and the little bowls she sets around. I want her things the way I want her.

She tries to stand but can't, and I feel her entrapment. She's bellowing, and we're getting looks. I suggest we talk about something else— Ellen's grandchildren or the biography of Harry Truman she's reading. Why does she admire Truman? I'm not going to get into it. She doesn't think it matters he dropped the bomb. It wasn't on her people.

She squints, pushing aside her drink and reaching for her walking stick, her good arm shaking, her back twisting into a C shape. I help her up, and she leans into me, making a face. Because we're touching? Because I can still walk? She instructs me on how to position my feet, move the chair, and lock the wheels, as if I haven't performed these tasks before. The chair takes on an alien aspect, and I forget to swing aside the foot rests to allow her a clear path. As she shuffles forward, she nearly falls, and we sway like drunken lovers at the end of a tango—a broken double act, Dean and Jerry embracing and looking daggers. I laugh. When Toby is tickled, her nostrils quiver and her eyes tear. She once accidentally attached her sable scarf to my winter coat, and when I arrived at school and saw the furry snake poking out of a sleeve, I called her and she fell on the floor. She plops her backside onto the seat and squirms. I slip my hands under her armpits, feeling the dough of her, and I hoist her up until she's settled. All the way back to her apartment, she shouts, wishing for me to be shot or run over by a car, chin up, her voice raining down. Passersby stare. What does she care? I get a helicopter view of Fifty-seventh Street and see a shrunken old woman in a worn brown hat and her sixty-year old daughter in need of Botox.

I once emailed a man on a dating site and when I signed my name, he wrote: "I always thought your writing at the *Village Voice* was overrated." I didn't respond. What can you say to that? But the thing is, the remark went into me. I'm a few months short of my sixtieth birthday, riding in a taxi to an artists' residency in Nebraska City. The driver is detailing his gastric bypass surgery and pointing out the hospital where it was performed. I'm in a taxi from Omaha, because there is no public transportation to Nebraska City, and when we pull into town, I see why. The main street looks like a mouth with missing teeth, stores framing in their windows clues to their tragic abandonments: books scattered on the floor with their spines broken, apples rotting on a table under an inch of dust, chairs overturned like beetles on their backs. It looks like me, I think, this place.

Gertrude Stein, when she didn't know if she had anything to say, before she concocted the pellucid but indecipherable style that gave away nothing as it gazed with seeming serenity at everything, before she invented herself as a fat Buddha, devised a system to divide people into two categories. You could divide anything into halves, like loaves of the brain. Stein's idea was derived from her study of psychology with William James, before she dropped out of medical school saying, "You don't know what boredom is." She thought there were people whose natural way of fighting is the attack and people whose natural way of fighting is resistance. When I read this, I thought: Toby and I, attack; Ellen and my father, resistance. My sister says she was subsumed by Toby while I escaped. She says, "You got the better deal."

"Yeah," I say, "but you got the diamond."

During my mother's last months, she sits with her eyes closed, her hand propping her chin. "It's as if she's going to sleep, but she's thinking," Ellen says, "waiting for death."

In December, Toby asks Ellen, "When is Laurie coming?"

Ellen says in a week.

"Then I'll have both my daughters with me."

I think, whatever she wants, I think, what can it hurt? Oye.

When Toby is eighty-seven, we visit the Guggenheim and walk down Madison Avenue. The streets are thronged with kids arriving home from school, and I remember running into our house in Long Beach and calling, "Mom, I'm home." I want her to be there. I want to think she is waiting for me, even though I will grab my bike and be gone. On Madison Avenue, women with headbands are walking dogs. Toby places her hand gingerly on the the head of a cocker spaniel. "I'm afraid of dogs," she says to the owner. "That's how I was raised."

"You don't seem afraid," the woman says.

"I'm afraid of everything. You have no idea. I could tell you."

We pass a bakery. Toby stands at the window, imagining how the pastries taste.

"You could buy one."

"Are you out of your mind?"

At a flower shop, I buy her a bunch of hyacinths. "Put them beside your bed. They'll make your room smell like perfume." The stalks are long, the buds unopened.

"They look like vegetables. Should I cook them and eat them?" She laughs.

After she dies, I see her inside a chicken instead of a gizzard, a heart, and a liver. She used to chop chicken in a wooden bowl, along with green pepper, god knows why, and lace it with mayonnaise from the health food store, and she said to me on more than one occasion but not often that I should have it, and I have to tell you it was tasty. I slip slivers of garlic into chicken I stab, opening little mouths and the memory of the knife when her chest was slit and it wouldn't heal and she pointed to the stitched red gash with a cockeyed grin and said, "Like a chicken." "Like a chicken," I said. She once typed a paper for me in high school, and as she unscrolled the first page we noticed bits of chicken were stuck to it. "They must have fallen into the roller," she said.

In the days following her bypass operation, there are bruises on her arms from the IV, a large bandaged wound in the middle of her chest, and incisions on her legs where arteries have been removed for her heart. Her limbs are slack, and her skin looks like a paper bag. One of her nostrils is larger than the other, and it quivers around the canula that feeds her oxygen. Several of her toes are bent in different directions, as if they cannot decide which way to go. A corn on one toe is hard and deep, as if it has logged all the miles she has walked.

One day when I enter, she is sitting up, and a banana, cut into pieces, is in a bowl before her. She can hold a spoon with her good hand, but she can't understand why her other hand won't steady the bowl. She looks at one hand, then the other, her brow furrowed. She could pick up pieces of banana and place them in her mouth, one at a time. Instead, she picks up the bowl and tosses the contents at her face, catching whatever she can on her tongue, chewing fast and scowling at anyone who tries to remove the fallen pieces from her pillow and chest.

Slowly, she improves. Even so, a lung specialist counsels against sending her to a rehab facility, predicting she will die in a matter of months or weeks. Still, Ellen and I work to place her at Helen Hayes. Before the transfer is assured, she keeps asking, "Will they think I'm worth saving?" Yes, we say, but you know, really, she was right to wonder.

While she is still in the hospital, a social worker enters with a clip board. Toby needs to decide if she wants to be resuscitated in the event of another heart attack. "I don't want to be alive now," she says. The social worker pats her shoulder and suggests she give it more thought. My mother asks me what I would do, and I say I would want to live.

"What's so great about living?"

"The story."

She waves me away. "I don't care about the story. I was never interested in the story. What is the story?"

"Your future."

"I don't understand. I never have."

"All right, the story is history."

"Ah, that is a subject I happen to like. That is a subject I have studied. I have seen things. I've seen enough. People tell you, you are supposed to live for others, but who believes that? Don't misunderstand me. I'm happy to see my children, my grandchildren. I'm happy they're all right. But that is not a reason to live." She tries to hitch herself higher on her pillows. She is collapsing into her weak side, twisting around. I help her adjust herself. I get another pillow from the closet and arrange her weak arm so it is comfortable.

When the social worker returns, my mother says, "I don't think I want to sign."

After Toby completes her three weeks at Helen Hayes, she's admitted to the Hebrew Home in Westchester for additional rehab, and one morning before I visit I dream I have a beard. At first only a few black hairs sprout under my chin and on my neck, but as I study my face the hairs formed a carpet from my sideburns to my collar bone. This makes me unhappy, but it's funny.

When I arrive, she's in the hall, resting between laps with her physical therapist. She waves, sitting up taller. She's wearing a workout suit and sneakers, and she looks like a walker at a mall, inching along in Alexa's embrace. She is pushing a half-walker with her good hand, while Alexa supports her on the other side. Alexa says, "Head up, walker forward, right foot forward, weight on right foot, that's right, you're doing it, bottom in, head up, that's right, now the left foot. Lift. I've got you, you won't fall, you can do it." She can.

When she's finished, I wheel her to the patio and we sit under a tree and watch boats. The Hudson is wide and majestic up here. Towering oaks shade the lawn, and geese venture up from the river, hunting for food.

"Remember in *The Night of the Iguana* when Deborah Kerr wheels her grandfather out and he recites a poem he's been working on for a year?" I ask.

"I'm the grandfather."

"He's like an ancient sea turtle, depositing his last egg."

"How can a male turtle lay an egg?"

"How can you be here with leaves falling into your hair when you were this close to dead a few weeks ago?"

"I need a dye job." I say she can get one in the beauty shop. She says, "Deborah Kerr played spinster types who were hot under the hood. That's the way they show the English, refined." She looks at her stick arm. "I was never hot under the hood." She points to a woman in a wheelchair. "Did you ever see anyone so fat?" The woman fills the seat, and her legs are sausages. "How can a person live like that?"

"Maybe she's loved for her imperfections," I say. She is surrounded by her family. Near her, two little girls chase geese.

"Every misshapen person who comes along, you defend."

"I woke up this morning with a beard."

"I never wanted children," she says to the air. "Move my arm, it hurts." I shift her weak hand on the pillow. Her fingers are gnarled. A goose waltzes past, and she tries to pet it with her good hand. She can't reach it. "What did the poet say in the play?"

"He gave a summation. He was nearly a hundred."

The goose sashays up again and looks at my mother. "It wants something. They all want something." Her spine is twisting, and I straighten her. A vein pulses on her neck. Another goose seems on a collision course with her chair. It flaps its wings, and she looks happy until it veers toward the fat woman. "I won't be laying any turtle eggs, if that's what you're hoping for," my mother says. "If that's what you're waiting for, you might as well load up the wagons and hitch up the horses."

In the 1970s, Ellen's husband buys a health food store on Fifty-Second Street, and my parents work there, my mother in the front, the Czarina of vitamins, my father, the ex-coat manufacturer, in the back, whipping up smoothies and lunch specials. "Where is Toby?" people ask, first thing. My mother is never happier. The streets are inside the shop. She kibitzes with Greta Garbo, pretending not to recognize her. "You, Toby," Greta asks, "you know what it is, a man?" My mother shoots a look at Murray, who is slicing an avocado. "That's what I know, end of story." The store booms for ten years, but the landlord jacks up the rent and Mark is forced to sell. After my father dies, my mother cooks for God's Love We Deliver, the organization that feeds homebound people with AIDS. She stands on her feet during three-hour shifts, dicing onions, potatoes, and carrots. She's part of a crowd again, and they drag her out for coffee and Chinese food. God's Love is what she talks about: Karen's dating debacles, Ben's heart murmur. I volunteer there, too, and one day the head chef calls me, complaining that Toby is making racist remarks. They've put up with it for more than a year. "Talk to her," he says, and so I go to her apartment and we sit at the cherry wood table with walnut inlays.

"May I be struck by lightning if I ever said such a thing." She doesn't look me in the eye. "They're lying."

"Frankie says you talk about 'them,' use the word 'swartzers'. Everyone knows what that means."

"You're siding with strangers?" She shakes her head and presses her lips together. "I should have known you'd sell me down the river."

"I'm on your side," I say, but how can this be true? She wants my allegiance no matter what. I want hers. What else is new?

She eyes a plaque on the wall. A lion is crouching at the feet of galloping horses, mighty in himself with eyes ablaze but cornered. "Who the hell are they to tell me what I can and cannot say? What, I'm going to be fired from a volunteer job?"

"How would you feel if people slammed Jews?"

"They hate Jews! That's why they're ganging up on me."

"Ma, you're doing the same thing."

"People are jealous of Jews. Blacks deserve what they get."

"*All* black people?"

"No. Some, I like."

"Well. You have to think about other people's feelings."

She sets down her cup, and the saucer rattles. "I thought about other people my whole life. I don't want to be gagged."

"Just stop being nasty. How hard is that?" What am I talking about? Mornings, I wake up with lists of friends I've offended and lost. The rats that survive the longest are the ones that adapt. The rats with the longest lives cart around the fewest unhappy memories.

Toby is silent, searching for a way to be herself and yet remain at the party. In the end, she's asked to leave. Reporting this, she looks sad and ashamed, and I feel for her, but then blood flows into her cheeks. "I don't need them. I don't need to work there anymore."

During her last months, she goes in and out of dementia. When her aides go shopping, she flings herself from her wheelchair onto the floor and tumbles to the door, bringing down tables and chairs. She can't walk, but there is strength in her right hand and leg. She strips off her pants and underwear, crawls into the hall naked, and bangs on neighbors' doors. She wheels herself to the elevator, rides to the lobby, and tells the doormen she's being beaten by her caretakers. She wants contact. Every time she falls, she has to be picked up and held. Before she's disabled, she's uncomfortable with touch. Afterward, she kisses people's hands and slides them across her cheeks. She is scared that Primrose, who has been with her since she returned from rehab, will leave. I say she won't.

My sister tells a story. My mother is having coffee after attending a class at Hunter College when a voice burns through the cafeteria din. "So you're still alive." It's my mother's sister, Bell, who disappears again, or maybe Toby lowers her head. Next a card arrives in the mail with a picture of a snake on it, signed Bell. "You believe this happened?" I ask Ellen. My mother's address and phone number aren't listed.

One time when Ellen calls Toby, Primrose asks my mother if she knows who Ellen is. Toby says, "My sister." I think she may have confused Ellen's name with Bell's, or mixed up the words *daughter* and *sister*. When Ellen visits, Toby remembers a quarrel with Bell, and Ellen says, "She's probably dead." Toby bursts into tears, saying she has seen her sister on TV, waving to her.

On the phone, my mother tells me, "Primrose says you come to New York every week and don't visit." It's not true, I say.

"That's what Primrose says."

My mother reminds me of my grandmother when she was old and confused. She once called to report she'd read Toby's obituary in a newspaper and wanted to know where her daughter was buried. Did she want Toby dead, given that my mother had refused to speak to her for more than ten years?

On the phone, Toby asks if I have children.

"No."

"Why not?"

"They're not that easy to produce."

"I thought you would have six by now."

I look at my hands that are hers, small boned and veiny.

I am pushing Toby's wheelchair up the hill on Fifty-seventh Street. She is nearing ninety-two. Primrose walks beside her.

"Toothpaste, cotton swabs, witch hazel," my mother says, fists waving. She is bundled in a wool coat and a fake fur hat that frames her pretty, hollowed face.

"You told me twenty times." Prim's jaw is clenched, her eyebrows to the roof. Prim is what separates my mother from a nursing home. She's wearing a navy parka and a wool hat pulled low over red dreadlock extensions. My mother absently holds a glove, and Prim pockets it.

I ask my mother if she's happy to be out.

"How can I be happy?" she says in a reedy voice, a question she might have posed at any time in her life. I see more strain than usual beneath the dimples that etch her cheeks—a smeared, blitzed look, like one of those murdered or murderous faces painted by Francis Bacon.

"Don't give up your apartment," she says, as we wait for a light on Columbus Circle. "Don't be stupid."

Cars whiz close to the curb. The glass of the Time Warner Center—New York City's first enclosed shopping mall with posh restaurants and boutiques—rises impassively over the empty fountain surrounding a statue of the Italian mariner. It's as if he's come all this way to be in the center of the world, the New York everyone noses to and feels ship-wrecked from if they have to leave. When Richard lived here, he thrived among people who were charmed by rather than snooty about his nonOxbridge vowels—*toof* for *tough* and *soofer* for *suffer*. Two mounted police patrol the gate of the park. Vendors sell souvenirs and framed photographs, including the famous shot of John Lennon with his round specs and shoulder-length mane, perched on a ledge on the Upper West Side. Richard and I have talked about coming back. My place could be a base, although it's too small to stay in for long and he needs the right job. It is a law of the universe—as firm as the principle that mass and ener-gy are interchangeable—you don't give up a rent stabilized apartment in New York. You maintain your resident status, holding a chair against landlords who want to slash your throat so they can triple the rent.

I seem not to care. I am floating, blimplike, over my past, all of which—my early years in Washington Heights, my student days at Barnard and Columbia, my long tenure at the *Village Voice*, my love rela-tionships and passionate friendships—have been tangled in the spaghetti streets of the city. It's so much my medium, I can't feel it. I mean, does a fish know it's swimming in water?

At Columbus Circle, it doesn't cross my mind that when my mother speaks about my apartment she is thinking about *hers*—fearing her aides will leave, worn out by her demands, and that she'll be exiled from the only existence that breathes life into her and that she contributes to with her huffing theatrics, my mother the character, my mother with a role in the only show she wants to attend. Even in her wheelchair, she buses to Fairway, searching for a nectarine that won't break her heart. I say her aides won't leave, but it makes no impression. I don't consider she's worried about me. I can't hear her, can't hear my friends who say, "Don't lose your bearings. Don't lose yourself." I think they're saying,

"You can't have love. You can't have happiness." They say: Look before you leap, but the horizon looks like Richard.

"Laurie's not going to give up her apartment," Primrose says. She turns to me. "I tell her the same thing every day."

The sky is gray and pillowy, and a light rain falls that Toby doesn't notice. A police horse walks close, its wet hair scenting the air. It snorts, and my mother jumps. "I'm afraid of horses. Laurie, don't let the horse get so close. It will step on me. It will bite me."

"More likely you'll bite the horse," Prim says, eyeing Toby with the affection of their early days, her mouth swerving to the side. She's played reggae for Toby and danced, my mother exclaiming how talented she is, how sexy. They talk about sex, Prim lying beside Toby on her bed. Toby says she was afraid of sex, too. For a moment Prim is Island Girl again, her hips swaying and her laugh full-throated, the beauty from St. Ann's and later Kingston who walked through fields of ginger and annatto, a gorgeous woman pursued by men, who married one, only to cut him loose when he proved more an anchor than a float. She has made me swear not to tell Toby about the new man she's seeing, fearing my mother will tear him down.

"Me bite a horse? I don't even like horses," my mother says.

"You don't like anything. You don't need anything, do you, Toby?" Prim says.

"That's right. I wish I could live by myself."

The light changes, and we cross. A pack of teenagers with a rainbow of skin colors lopes by, behind them an elderly couple navigate by themselves. My mother regards them enviously. Two Wall Street types in long coats and leather boots bound up from the subway, jog to make the light, then disappear into the Time Warner Center. A bus wheezes to a halt and coughs out sundry denizens, some heading for the shops, others for 8th Avenue. On the other side, I press down on my mother's wheelchair, and she swings back like a patient in a dentist's chair.

"Why are you going to Arizona?"

"To be with Richard." I hoist her up to the curb.

"Do you pay for the plane tickets?"

"Yes."

"Why?"

"I want to be with him."

"I wish I had your money." She chuckles and twists her head. "Why are you giving up your apartment?"

"I'm not."

"You said you were giving up your apartment."

"I didn't."

"You don't know how things will turn out. Where will you go? Don't be a fool. No one gives up an apartment in New York. Why doesn't he come to you?"

"He has a job in Phoenix."

She turns her face to the side as we make our way through the glass doors, and I wheel her across the marble rotunda. Her profile is still beautiful. Her cheekbones jut glamorously. "He's a poor slob," she says in a dreamy, mad hatter voice, addressing the air more than me.

Eight weeks before my mother dies, she's admitted to the hospital with mysterious bleeding. Bladder cancer is suspected, but I don't believe she has it. I think she'll return to her apartment and I will see her again. I think she'll meet Richard, even if she has no idea who we are. It turns out she doesn't have cancer. She dies in her bed, approaching ninety-three.

"She's gone," Ellen says on the phone, driving to Toby's apartment. After my mother's stroke, she learned she had fibrosis of the lung, which is incurable and untreatable. It was supposed to have killed her a long time ago. Finally, it did. According to the coroner, she suffocated in her own fluids.

Richard speaks about two types of museums. The kind like Noah's Ark that aim to exhibit samples of everything that exists, such as The Museum of Natural History in New York. And memory palaces: idiosyncratic collections, commemorating local history you find in any small town.

I sleep in Toby's bed, organizing her things. When Ellen and I learn that her furniture has value—a lamp, for instance, is the work of the Italian designer Gino Sarfatti—I vote to auction it, including a small table I've thought of keeping. Toby wore a deco diamond ring on her left pinky I would follow as her hand swept this way and that. "You'll have it when I'm dead," she would say, smiling, unable to imagine her extinction, same as everybody. I didn't understand why she was wearing it in the hospital. I thought it might be giving her comfort, and so I didn't remove it for safe keeping. When it was stolen, I felt the ground tilt, just as I do as I write, still falling for the same old con.

I make my way through Toby's freezer, cooking chicken pieces bent like her arthritic fingers. I pack up a set of plates, black and silver-rimmed, service for twelve, never used. Outside, my mother still skitters along 58th Street, still stands in front of the Plaza Hotel on the red carpet secured with brass rivets, still chats with the doorman while scanning the distance for the dot that is me. Maybe I've been abducted by aliens. I should be so lucky.

My mother wouldn't have cared about the garbage bags stuffed with her clothes, still in plastic from the cleaners though some with stains, and her chipped, everyday plates with the autumn leaf design worn faint. I throw away a dozen pairs of Easy Spirit shoes, character style, with a strap across the instep. I see her at the dining table with the harlequin inlays, above her a modernist chandelier, a burst of twelve tulip fixtures selected by Julie Stein, the interior decorator she trotted behind in the late 1950s when our bungalow was converted into an all-year-round house. Toby is hunched over a book that rests on a stand. A conservative talk show is blasting on the radio.

Eight months before she dies, she's admitted to St. Luke's Hospital after a psychiatrist deems her in crisis. The aim is to start her on a new mood stabilizer—the previous ones having failed. My sister is fed up with Toby, who is screaming pretty much all the time. Ellen is disowning her mother with the freedom of the loved child. But Toby touches me and reminds me of Al Swearingen, the sympathetic monster at the center of the HBO series *Deadwood*, who also reminds me of myself. Played by British actor Ian McShane, his dark eyes ringed with pain, he is always stealing himself for the next brutality he is going to unleash on the world, as if his savagery is against his will, as if his cruelty is a tyrant driving the obliging but reluctant servant that is also him to carry out his deeds.

I call my mother on her ninety-second birthday, and she sounds groggy but present. "I disappointed you by not giving you money and calling Richard 'a poor slob.'"

"Why did you say that?"

"I didn't mean anything. I say the same things about Mark."

"You've known Mark for forty years. You've never even met Richard."

"You're right."

She is seeing herself more clearly as she slips away. She's sorry about the money but doesn't give me any.

In Arizona, from our patio, Richard and I watch lightning fracture the black sky. Pollack flings of furious beauty skip across the night, and the darkness shudders like a body waking from the dead. I squeal with each illumination, night becoming day in a confusion of the natural order. "Everything gets rubbed," Richard says, looking up at the crackling night.

I propose we write about the concept of the muse, a marble of a thought that's been tumbling in my head. A professor friend has been teaching my work and has referred to Toby as my muse. At first I shoved the idea away, but I have come to see that every piece I write about long-ing—and isn't everything we write about love or something hurting what we love?—starts with an ache for my mother. It has the shape of shadow moving over desert mountains, across giant saguaro cacti with their arms outstretched, across higgeldy-piggeldy rocks, some red col-ored, some blackened and inscribed. It is a blank sky—like a brain before it's marked with impressions.

At the start of a hike, I stand on the road while Richard studies trail maps. He explains where we are going, but I don't care. I know the walk will be arduous and hot and that I will not exactly enjoy it, rather will want to go along, hoping to see lizards and birds. Hikers share trails with mountain bikers. What they do—bobbling up crazily steep paths and hurtling down the other side—looks torturous. It's the ordeal you choose rather than passively suffer, the dare that feels like a right to exist.

Shade is beautiful in the desert, cutting a knife edge against glaring light, bleeding across wide, vacant space. One day, we arrive at the top of a hill, and Richard sees a still higher point crowned by black, jutting rocks. As we scurry up, we realize we've come to the old wall of a forti-fied area. A small sign indicates an archaeological site, but It isn't marked to attract visitors. Around us are hundreds of petroglyphs: designs scraped out on desert varnish by people who lived in the region 900 years before. All traces of them have vanished except for these markings, variously thought to be astrological and astrological symbols, direction-al pointers, territorial markers, and personal and artistic expressions— forms of ancient tagging. I copy a design into my notebook that looks like a Giacometti figure, a pared down, twig thing—a remnant of our-selves we carry inside.

When I think about New York, I see my mother's feet stretching down to the Lower East Side, her fingers up to Carnegie Hall. She dreams of her legs running for a bus. "I'm not young anymore," she says to the mustached man who guides her up the steps. "I wish I had your youth, darling, I wish you good health, you are so kind." I see her on her bed, pulled behind a boat. She is flying across waves and she is afraid, but that is the element she remembers as her music. Even as a young girl, her eyebrows knit as if seeking each other in consolation. We don't know who we are. It isn't a human capacity, so you might as well wish for a golden beak to sprout from the parrot colored feathers on your face. I'm sorry for your loss, people say, but what is my loss? I'm glad I won't see her again. I wish she were alive.

High Wire

Robert Stone

Robert Stone's most recent work is short story collection, Fun With Problems.
He is the author of seven novels, including A Hall of Mirrors *(winner of the
National Book Award),* A Flag for Sunrise, Children of Light, Outerbridge
Reach, Damascus Gate, *and* Bay of Souls, *as well as the nonfiction work*
Prime Green: Remembering the Sixties. *His short story collection,* Bear and
His Daughter, *was a finalist for the Pulitzer Prize. The recipient of a
Guggenheim Fellowship, Stone lives in New York City.*

I FIRST MET LUCY AT A MOVIE PREMIERE AT
Grauman's about midway between the death of Elvis
Presley and the rise of Bill Clinton. Attending was a gesture of support for the director, who happened to be a
friend of mine. The film's distributors had made a half-
hearted lurch toward an old-style Grauman's opening,
breaking out a hastily dyed red carpet. A couple of
searchlights swept the murky night sky over downtown
Hollywood. By then these occasions were exhausted flickers of the past,
so there were none of the much-parodied rituals some of us watched in
black-and-white newsreels at the corner Bijou. No more flashbulbs or nar-
rators with society lockjaw telling us what the talent was wearing. Neither
simpering interviewers nor doomed starlets walking the walk. The camera
flashes and the demented fans crowding the velvet rope were all memories. Hollywood Boulevard was even rattier then than it is now. The only
people around the marquee that night were frightened-looking Japanese
tourists and bright-eyed street freaks with slack smiles.

The picture was no good. It was the forced sequel to a 1960s hit with a
plot cribbed from a John Ford movie of the fifties. It featured two very old
actors, revered figures from the time of legend, and the point of it was the
old dears' opportunity to recycle their best beloved shtick. The withered
couple and its more agile doubles shuffled through outdoor adventures
and a heartwarming geriatric romance stapled to some bits of fossil
Western. Attempts had been made to make it all contemporary with winks
and nods and brain-dead ironizing.

The audience consisted mainly of people who were there on assignment, out of politeness, or from fear. There were also members of the moviegoing public, admitted by coupons available through the homes-of-celebrities tours and at the cashier counters of cheap restaurants. Raven-haired Lucy, with her throaty voice and dark-eyed Armenian fire, was actually in the picture briefly, as an Apache maid. I later learned she was not in the theater to take pleasure in the picture or even in her own performance. She had come in the service of romance, her own, involving an alcoholic, Heathcliffish British actor, the movie's villain.

Heathcliff had made Lucy crazy that night by escorting his handsome and chic wife, suddenly reunited with her husband and relocated from London. It seemed that the sight of them had stricken her physically; when I saw her sitting alone a few seats down from me she was cringing tearfully in the darks and lights from the screen.

My first impulse was to leave her alone in her distress. I was certainly not impelled to a hypocritical display of concern. But it was one of those bells; I was unattached, still single, due to leave town in a week. Maybe I'd had a drink or smoked a joint before the appalling show. Anyway I moved one seat toward her.

"Nice scenery," I said.

She looked at me in a flash of the big sky country's exterior daylight, removing her stylish glasses to dab at her tears and sitting upright in her seat.

"Oh, thanks."

Her tone was predictably one of annoyed sarcasm but I chose not to interpret it as the blowing off she intended. Sometimes you can parse a hasty word in the semi-dark and I decided not to be discouraged, at least not so quickly. I realized then that she had some connection with the picture on the screen. An actress, a production girl?

In those days I was confident to the point of arrogance. I assumed I was growing more confident with time. How could I know that the more you knew the more troubled and cautious you became, that introspection cut your speed and endurance? We watched for a while and she shifted in her seat and touched her hair. I interpreted these as favorable portents and moved over to a place one seat away from her. At that distance I recognized her among the film's cast. Scarcely a minute later on screen, Brion Pritchard, her real-life deceiver, callously gunned down her character, the Apache soubrette. I watched her witness the tearjerky frames of her own death scene. She appeared unmoved, stoical, and grim.

"Good job," I said.

Lucy fidgeted, turned to me, and spoke in a stage whisper that must have been audible three rows away.

"She sucked!" Lucy declared, distancing herself from the performance and turning such scorn on the hapless young indigen that I winced.

"So let's go," I suggested.

Lucy was reluctant to go, afraid of being spotted by our mutual friend the director who had also produced the film. She expected to look to him for employment before long. However, she seemed to find being hit on as a consolation. It was the first glimpse I had of her exhausting impulsiveness.

We sneaked out in a crouch like two stealthy movie Indians, under cover of a darkness dimly lighted by a day for night sequence. The two stars on screen told each other their sad backstories by a campfire. Their characters had the leisure to chat because Apaches never attacked at night.

Across the street, appropriately, a country and western hat band from Kyoto was crooning rural melodies. The two of us jaywalked across Hollywood and into the lobby of the fading hotel where the band was performing. A man in a stained tuxedo—an unwelcoming figure—directed us to a table against one wall. I ordered a Pacifico; Lucy had Pellegrino and a Valium.

"It's Canada," Lucy told me.

"What is?"

"The scenery. In the thing over there."

"The thing? You don't remember what the picture's called?"

"I like repressed it," she said and gritted her teeth. "Sure I know what it's called. It had different titles post-production."

"Such as?"

"*Unbound. Unleashed. Uncooked.*"

We introduced ourselves and claimed we had heard of each other. For a while we watched the hat act sing and swing. The lads looked formidable under their tilted sombreros. Their lead singer sang lyrics phonetically, rendering interpretations of "I Can't Stop Loving You," "I'm Walking the Floor," and other favorites. Their audience was scant and boozy. There were a few other bold escapees from the premier across the street.

"You were a great Apache."

She only shook her head. Plainly even qualified professional regard would take us nowhere. For some reason I persisted.

"Come on, I was moved. You dying. Featured role."

"Dying is easy," she said. "Ever hear that one?"

I had. It was an old actor's joke about the supposed last words of Boris Thomashevsky, an immortal of the Yiddish stage. Surrounded by weeping admirers seeking to comfort him, he gave them a farewell message. "Dying is easy," said the old man. "Comedy is hard."

"They shot different endings," Lucy explained. "One sad, one happy."

"Really?" It was hard to believe they would perpetrate a sad ending with the two beloveds, which would only have made a fatuous movie even worse. When riding a turkey, I believe, cleave to the saddle horn of tradition. But sad endings were a new thing in those years—the era of the worst movies ever made. Industry supremos who hadn't been on the street unaccompanied for forty years were still trying to locate the next generation of dimwits. So they tried sad endings and dirty words and nude body doubles. There was no more production code, movies were supposed to get serious and adult. Sad endings were as close as most of them could reach.

"So I hear. I wasn't there. I didn't read the endings. Like I had other things on my mind. I didn't see it, did I? We're over here."

"O.K."

"I bet they went with the happy though." She sneaked a quick look around and bit a half of her second ten-gram Valium. I told her the happy seemed likely.

"Oh," she said, and she smiled for the first time in our acquaintance, "Tom Loving. You're a writer." She either guessed or actually had somehow heard of me. Her smile was appropriately sympathetic.

She told me they had reshot a lot during the filming, different versions of different scenes.

"I die in all of them," she said.

Eventually we drove our separate cars to an anchored trailer she was renting on the beach in Malibu. As I remember, she was tooling around in a big Jaguar XJ6. We sat under her wind-tattered awning on the trailer's oceanfront deck and a west wind peeled wisps of cold, briny fog off the ocean. It was refreshing after the sickly perfume of the theater and the haze of booze and smoke in the lounge.

"I'm not happy." Lucy told me. "I'm sure you could tell, right?"

"I saw you were crying. I thought it was over the movie."

"If we'd stayed," she said, "you would have cried too."

"Was it that bad?"

"Yes," she said. "Yes! It was deeply bad. And on top of it that bastard Pritchard whom I've always loved." She looked at me thoughtfully for a moment. "You know?"

"I do," I said. "We've all been there."

She looked away and laughed bitterly, as though her lofty grief must be beyond the limits of my imagination. I was annoyed since I had hoped to divert her from pining. On the other hand, it was entertaining to watch her doing unrequited love with restraint and a touch of self-scorning irony.

"This man is deliberately trying to make me crazy," she said. "And to kill himself."

"It's a type," I explained.

"Oh yeah?" She gave me another pitying glance. "You think so?"

She had crushed my helpful routine. I put it aside. "Was that the wife?" I asked. "The blonde?"

"Yes," Lucy said. "Think she's attractive?"

"Well," I said, "on a scale of yes or no . . ."

"All right, all right," she said. "All right."

"Met her?"

"I have met her," said Lucy. "When I did I thought hey, she's not a bad kid. But she's a fucking bitch it turns out."

I kept my advice to myself and little by little Lucy detached herself from her regrets. Later I came to know how suddenly her moods could change. It was of course an affliction, in her case untreatable. She kept her ghosts close at hand and always on call. They were present as a glimmer of surprise that never disappeared behind her eyes.

After a while I got her to walk with me; we shed our shoes and went across the moonlit beach. Brion seemed to be off her mind.

The sand at the water's edge had a steep drop-off to the surf. We clambered down to the wet sand where the waves broke. The sea's withdrawing force was nearly enough to pull us off our feet. Lucy lost her balance and I had to put an arm around her waist to preserve her.

"It could take you away," Lucy said.

We had a hard time climbing the four feet or so to the looser sand, hard enough to leave us out of breath. As we walked back, Lucy told a story from her earliest days in town. She had fallen in with some fast-lane hipsters. Many of them came from industry families. One night she and a friend found themselves on the beach with the daughter of a world-famous entertainment figure. The daughter passed out on the sand, so when Lucy and her friend saw somebody coming they ran off into the nearby shadows. Two men arrived, equally world famous. They encountered the daughter sprawled on the sand and tried to rouse her. The adolescent had responded with dazed, rude mutterings. One man told the other whose daughter she was. Lucy always remembered his Viennese accent.

"Ja," the man said to his friend. "Kid's a valking disaster."

Lucy and her friend giggled in the dark. Who could walk?

"I don't drink anymore," Lucy told me.

In spite of her solemn reflections, when we got back to the trailer she produced some quaaludes and cocaine for me. I did a sopor and a couple of lines on her beautiful goatskin table. We drank champagne with it, which I feared would be a mistake. We were ready to get it on, both of us, but I wondered briefly if she might not suffer a morning after the fact change of heart. She was a woman on the rebound, I was a stranger and I was afraid there might be recriminations. That was not Lucy but I didn't know it then. She seemed so mercurial. I think we watched a little of Carson that night and found it uproariously funny in the wrong places. It was true that she smoked incessantly and smelled of tobacco. Otherwise she was a Levantine angel, one of the celestial damsels awarded to the devout and to me. In the sack she told me about her early life in Fresno.

"Know what people called Armenians?" she asked.

"What, baby?" We had gone to bed to Otis Redding, "Dock of the Bay," and there beside me Lucy addressed her après cigarette with such intensity and style that, after three years clean, I wanted one too. "Tell me what they called the poor Armenians?"

"They called us the Fresno Indians. Not so much people in Fresno. But in other towns. Modesto."

"How appropriate in your case."

She daintily set her smoke down, turned around and poked me in the ribs hard, forcing me back into focus. She was wild-eyed. "Don't fucking say 'poor Armenians!' You're disrespecting my parents."

She was not really angry although she had me fooled for a moment. She ran her fingers down my bones like a harpist and we slept the sleep of the whacked until drizzly dawn. Getting up, it struck me that I was due in New York in less than a week and what fun Lucy was. She would be on location in Mendocino until I left. This saddened our morning. We swore to keep in touch, the contemporary West Coast vow of enduring passion.

The gig in New York was the rewrite of a script that had been worked by two different writers unaware of each other's efforts. The dawning era of serious adult movies (a term which did not then altogether carry the meaning it has today) had inspired them both to attempts at revolutionizing the film idiom. They both seemed to think that some ideal director would be guided by their novel scene settings and subtle dialogue. The thing had to be done in New York because the indispensable star lived in Bucks County and hated the coast. Naturally the synthesis was a turgid rat's nest and the job shameful and distressing. It was a project only God could have saved; I failed. I didn't like failing but I got paid and thanks to Him the thing never got made. If it had you can be sure I would have eaten the rap for it all by myself.

Then a doctoring job on a picture in production in England came my way. The project was an Englishing of a French movie for which the producers had actually paid money, and the translation of it by a British writer in command of good French was not at all bad. But the setting had been transferred to Queens, and the producers thought his draft both too faithful to the original and too un-American. This was one to grab though, a worthwhile credit. I went over, got hired, and started looking for a pad. Meanwhile the producers put me up in a crummy room at Brown's. The weather was sleety so I read my way through Olivia Manning's trilogies, Balkan and Levant. At this time Britain had no daytime television lest weak-minded people play hooky from their dark satanic mills. For the same reason nighttime television went off around eleven, to the national anthem.

One night I turned on the tube to see that ITV was running a soap Lucy had done two years before. The moment I recognized her I felt a rush, a fond longing. I wasn't inclined to explore the feeling. Without prejudice—I think without prejudice—I was struck with how good she was in it. She looked altogether youthful and lovely and she had a substance in the role that was worlds away from the poor Pocahontas routine my pal John had thrust on her. Days later I watched another episode. She played a villainous character—slim sexy brunettes were usually villainesses then—who did a lot of lying. She managed to render deceit without sideward glances or eyerolling. Her character had heart and mystery. Also intelligence. Vanished were the trace elements of Valley Girl adolescence that I had become rather fond of. But I preferred Lucy the pro because in those days I loved watching real artists deliver.

Now I wonder if it wasn't about then—that early in the game—that I started doubting myself, distrusting the quality of the silence in which

I worked. Anyway, in Lucy's performance on that soap I thought I recognized the effort of one who lived for doing the voices, the way good writers did. Equipped with a sheath of fictional identity, she turned incandescent.

In the morning I phoned her across eight time zones and tried to tell her what I had seen her do. She tried to tell me how she'd done it. Neither of us in that sudden conversation quite succeeded.

So I asked her: "How's life?"

She said: "Oh man, don't ask me. I don't know, you know? Sometimes bearable. At others fucked."

"The pains of love or what?"

"I miss you," she said all at once and I told her, from the heart, that I missed her too. I hadn't been asking her about us but I can tell you she put me in the moment.

The next day I got a call from John, the perpetrator of *Unbound Unleashed Uncooked*. During our conversation I had mentioned to Lucy that I was house hunting. John told me that none other than Heathcliff, Brion Pritchard, had an apartment in St. John's Wood I could borrow for a moderate fee. I was so enthused, and tired of hearing landlords either hang up or purr with greed at the sound of an American voice, that I went for it at once. The studio that had green-lighted us paid. Distracted, I failed to focus on the distastefulness of this arrangement. Anyway, prowling and prying about the place when I should have been writing I discovered many amusing and scandalous things about Mr. and Mrs. Heathcliff that sort of endeared them to me.

Then a strange and wonderful thing happened. One evening at the interval of a play at the Royal Court I saw a girl—and she was so lovely and gamine that I could not think of that creature as anything but a girl—who was speaking American English to a female friend she had come with. I noticed that she was wearing Capezios. Catching her alone for a moment I made my move. My predations back in the day often had a theatrical background.

"You're a dancer," I told her.

She was in fact a dancer. I asked her if she cared for dinner or coffee or a drink after the play, but she didn't want to leave her friend alone. Today I would have given her my phone number, but not then, so I asked for hers and she gave it to me. On our first date we went to an Italian place in Hampstead. Jennifer had spent two years with the Frankfurt Ballet and when we met she was in England pondering options. European cities were losing their state art subsidies and there was no shortage of young dancers from Britain and the States. I took her home, not pressing it. Our second meeting was on Highgate Hill and as we walked to Ken Wood we told each other the story of our lives. This was the wonder-of-me stage of our courtship and it was genuinely sweet.

It turned out that Jennifer, notwithstanding her adorable long-toothed smile and freckled nose, had been around the block, a runaway child and an exotic dancer—a teenage stripper—in New Orleans. Her nice parents in River Oaks had reclaimed her and sent her back to ballet school, first in Dallas, finally in New York. As a student she had gotten into cocaine and danced a *Nutcracker* in Princeton where the falling snow effects, she said, made her sneeze. We were so easy with each other, at the same time so intoxicated. It was lovely.

In London, although there was plenty of blow about, she abstained and in that hard-drinking city she stayed sober. She put up with my boozing, but sweetly let me know she did not want to see the other. I thought often about moving her into the place on Abbey Road. Since the Pritchards showed no sign of returning I had stayed in it after the script was done and kept it on my own for months afterward, working on originals. For some reason we never quite got to the point of moving in together that year. Then I got a call—like all your Hollywood Calling calls it came in the middle of the night—asking me if I would come out and talk about another deathless number. I decided to go and when I told Jennifer she cried.

"I thought we were long-term."

It just about broke my heart. "We are long-term," I hastened to say. I wondered if she would ask to come with me. I probably would have taken her. At the same time I wanted to see Lucy.

Back in L.A. it was dry, sunny winter inland with a mellow marine layer at the beach each morning. The place I liked that I could have was a condo in Laguna. Laguna was pretty nice then but for some reason I had not known about the traffic and had not quite realized what was happening to Orange County. The apartment overlooked the sea and had sunsets.

I had batted out three original scripts in London. Mysteriously, the first two drew from my then agent—Mike? Marty?—more apparent sympathy than admiration. Out in the movie world two of them were promptly skunked. I was still used to being the boy wonder and a midlife bout of rejection was unappealing. I didn't much like rejection. Maybe I had tried too hard, attempting to scale the new peaks of serious and adult, naïvely imagining for myself an autonomy that neither I nor anyone in the industry possessed. The third one anyway was optioned, went into turnaround and years later actually got made. But my deathless number expired.

Frustrated and depressed I postponed calling Lucy. During my third week back I finally invited her down for another walk on the beach.

Climbing out of her dusty Jag she looked nothing but fine. She wore turquoise and a deerskin jacket, my Fresno Indian. With her smooth tan, her skin was the color of coffee ice cream and her eyes were bright. Ever since watching her perform in the soap I had begun to think of her as beautiful.

As we set out down the beach, beside the Pacific again, she put on a baseball cap that said Hussong's Cantina, promoting the joint in Ensenada. It was a sunny day even at the shore and you might have called the sea sparkling. A pod of dolphins patrolled outside the point break, gliding on air, making everything in life look easy. Lucy told me she had tested for a part in our friend John's next movie, a horror picture. She was still worried about whether he had somehow spotted the two of us walking out of Grauman's. The horror flick sounded like another bomb at best. This time Lucy had read the shooting script and knew what there was to know of the plot.

"She's a best friend. Supposed to be cute and funny. She dies."

I said that in my opinion she, Lucy, was ready for comedy.

"Tom, everyone pretty much dies horribly except the leads. It's a horror flick."

We had a nice day and night.

A week later I went up to Silver Lake where Lucy had moved after selling her nice trailer in Malibu. Her bungalow had some plants out front with an orangey spotlight playing on them, and in its beam I saw that the glass panels on her front door were smashed and the shards scattered across her doorway. Among them were pieces of what looked like a dun-colored Mexican pot. This was all alarming since her door would now admit all that lived, crawled, and trawled in greater L.A. Moreover, there was blood. When she let me in I asked her about it but got no answer. She brought us drinks and I lit a joint I had brought and she began to cry. Suddenly she gave me a sly smile that in the half-darkness of the patio reminded me of the weeping Indian maid I had rescued on the next seat at Grauman's.

"I'm in difficulty," she said.

I said I could see that. It turned out to be all about bloody Heathcliff, Brion Pritchard, still on the scene and newly cast in the horror movie.

Third-rate art was staggering toward real life again; Brion was the man who got to stab her repeatedly in the forthcoming vehicle.

"How can they do that?" I asked her. "Another of John's movies and Pritchard gets to kill you again. Isn't that like stupid?"

"He's relentless," she said. "Tommy, don't ask! What do I know?"

I suppose it was I who should have known. Brion was in serious decline, succumbing to occupational ailments in a tradition that went back to the time of nickelodeons. He drank. A man of robust appetites, he also smoked and snorted and stuffed and swallowed. On top it all he had started lifting weights and pioneering steroids. He boozed all day and through the night, drove drunk, punched some of the wrong people. Along the Rialto, all this was being noted and remarked upon. He was a violent working-class guy, one of A. E. Housman's beautiful doomed ploughboys, who but for talent and fortune would have drunk himself into Penrhyndeudraeth churchyard long before. Predictably, he had identified Lucy as the font of his troubles.

Shortly after dawn on the morning before my visit Brion had come banging on Lucy's door, haranguing her in elegant English and low Welsh. Impatient to enter and mess with her, he had taken her ornamental pot and shoved in the door, cutting himself in the process, badly enough to sober him slightly and slow him down. This bought time for Lucy to call 911. She told me that when the cops came Brion gave them the old Royal Shakespeare, which by then in Hollywoodland impressed no one. They all but begged her to press charges although he had only succeeded in hitting her once, hard. Naturally she denied it heroically— I could well picture her playing that one—and sent them away. At least she hadn't raced to his side at the hospital.

That evening it was plain we were not going to have much of a party. I asked Lucy to come down to Laguna with me. She dawdled and I hung around until she tuned me out. I was angry; moreover I was feeling too much like what you might call a confidante. In the end I made her swear to get the door fixed, even replaced, and I said I'd do it if she wouldn't. I told her to call the cops and me if the loutish Welshman accosted her again. I have to admit that if it came to action I wanted the cops on my side.

Driving back that night was depressing. I had expected to stay with her. I should mention that in this period there occurred the last brief gas panic—odd and even numbered days and so on. In my opinion the fuel shortages of those years played their part in the vagaries of romance. People often went to bed with each other because their tanks were low.

I picked up work at that point with HBO, which had then started showing its own productions. The project involved some interviews around the country in the subjects' hometowns. It was a Vietnam War story, echoing the anger of the recent past. This took me out of town for the next three weeks. In a hotel in Minneapolis I picked up a *USA Today* with a back-page story announcing that Brion Pritchard was dead. It was shocking, though in fact with the advent of AIDS a sense of mortality increasingly pervaded. We could not know it but death was coming big time. In that innocent age no one had imagined that anything more serious would happen to Brion than his dropping a barbell on his foot. I felt nothing at first, no relief, no regret. He was no friend of mine. On the way back to L.A. though, I became drunk and depressed, as if a fellow circus performer had fallen from a high wire. All of us worked without a net.

I had some doubts about calling Lucy too soon, mainly because I no longer fancied the role of consoler. Eventually I realized that if I wanted to see her again I would have to endure it. When I called she sounded more confused than stricken. At first I couldn't be sure I had the right person on the line. My thought was: she doesn't know how she feels. This is a role thrust on her and her feelings are down in some dark inaccessible region much overlaid. With what? Childish hungers, history, drama school? Capped by unacknowledged work and guilty ambition. A little undeserved notoriety of the tabloid sort. By then I thought I knew a few things about actors. I had even been one years before.

When I saw Lucy next she gave a display of what I now recognized as false cheer. In this dangerous state she could appear downright joyous. When I expressed sympathy over Brion she gave me an utterly blank look. Being the pro she was, Lucy was almost always aware of how she looked but the expression she showed me was unpremeditated, unintentionally conveying to me that Pritchard's death was literally none of my business, that neither I nor anyone else shared enough common ground with her and the late Heathcliff, *ensemble*, for even polite condolences. But, somehow, a couple of weeks later we found ourselves on the road to Enseneda. Enseneda and Tijuana could still be raggedy fun in those days. We managed to borrow a warped convertible from an actor pal and took off down the coast road. I hope we told him we were crossing the border.

The drive was an idyll, precisely defined, I was unsurprised to learn, as a happy episode, typically an idealized or unsustainable one. Down south that April afternoon there were still a few blossoming orange groves to mix memory and desire on the ocean breeze. Over the emerald cliffs people were hang gliding, boys and alpha girls swooping like buzzards on the updrafts. In the sea below surfers were bobbing, pawing ahead of the rollers to catch the curl. And on the right, a gorgeous gilt—no golden—dome displayed a sign that read, as I recall: SELF-REALIZATION GOLDEN WORLD FELLOWSHIP. It was the place the surfer kids called Yogi Beach and there we overcame Lucy's peculiar grief and spent the happiest half-day of our lives.

In Tijuana, which was as far as we got, we put the convertible in Caesar's protected parking and ate the good steak and the famous salad. We did not talk about Brion. For a while we traded recollections of Brooklyn College drama school where, strangely, both of us had put in time.

It seemed, as the day lengthened, that the elations of our trip stirred a mutual yearning. Not about the night because of course the night would be ours. I thought we might find our way through the dazzle of our confusions to something beyond. In my memory of that day—or in my fond dream of a memory—I was about to guide us there. In this waking dream I'm suspended at the edge of a gesture or the right words. All at once a glimmer of caution flickers, goes out, flashes again. Who was she after all? An actor, above all. I was wary of how she brought out the performer in me. I mean the performer at the core, ready to follow her out on the wire where she lived her life. At that age I thought I might walk it too.

I could have been a moment short of giving her the sign she wanted, whatever it was. These days I sometimes imagine that with the right words, a touch, a look, I might have snatched her out of disaster's path, away from the oncoming life that was gathering ahead of her. I held back. Surely that was wise. The moment passed and then Lucy simply got distracted.

I let us drift down the collonnades of the farmacia tour at the busy end of Revolución, chasing green crosses and phosphorescence. I wanted a party too. Joy's hand, they say, is always at his lips bidding adieu. That melancholy truth drove us.

We crossed back to Yanquilandia without incident. On the drive up the freeways we talked about ourselves.

"You and me," Lucy asked. "What is *that?*"

I didn't know. I said it was a good thing.

"Where would it go?"

Not into the sunset, I thought. I said exactly that. Lucy was ripped. She chattered.

"Everything goes there," she told me.

I ought not to have been driving. I was stoned myself.

As Lucy talked on I kept changing the subject or at least tweaking it.

"I have a kind of plan for my life," she said. "Part of it is career shit." She had picked up the contemporary habit of referring to people's film and stage work that way, including her own. As in "I want to get my shit up there." Or "I saw you in whatever it was and I loved your shit." It was thought to be unpretentious and hip, one social deviant to another. I particularly hated it, perhaps for pertinent but at the time unconscious reasons. "Actually," she went on with an embarrassed laugh, "artistic ambitions."

"Why not?"

Her fancies involved going east to Off-Broadway. Or working in Europe. Or doing something in one of the independent productions that were beginning to find distribution. Beside the artistic ambitions she entertained some secular schemes for earning lots of money in pictures. In retrospect, these were unrealistic. We found ourselves back on the subject of us.

"Don't you love me?" she asked.

"You know I do."

"I hope so. You're the only one who ever knew I was real."

I politely denied that but I thought about it frequently thereafter.

"What about Brion?"

"Poor Brion was a phantom himself," she said.

"Really? He threw a pretty solid punch for a phantom."

"I wasn't there that time either," she said. "I hardly felt it."

Passing the refinery lights of Long Beach she shook her head as though she were trying to clear it of whispers.

"You know," she said, "as far as shadows and ghosts go, I fear my own."

"I understand," I said. Hearing her say it chilled me but for some reason I *did* understand, thoroughly. I was coming to know her as well as was possible.

"Why do you always treat me with tea-party manners, Tom?"

"I don't. I don't even know what you mean."

"You're always trying to be funny."

I said that didn't mean I didn't love her. "It's all I know," I said.

We were driving along the margins of a tank farm that stood beside the freeway. Its barbed chain-link fence was lined with harsh prison yard arc lights that lit our car interior as we passed and framed us in successive bursts of white glare. In my delusion, the light put me in mind of overbright motel corridors with stained walls tunneling through some gnomish darkness. My head hurt. In the spattered white flashes I caught her watching me. I thought I could see the reflected arc lights in her eyes and the enlarged pupils almost covering their irises, black on black.

"Everybody loves you, Tom," she said. "Don't they?"

How sad and lonely that made me feel. Out of selfishness and need I actually grieved for myself. It passed.

"Yes, I'm sure everyone does. It's great."

"Do I count?" she asked.

Yes and no. But of course I didn't say that. In the twisted light I saw her out there sauntering toward a brass horizon and I wanted to follow after. But I was not so foolish nor had I the generosity of spirit. I was running out of heart.

"You more than anyone, Lucy," I said. "Only you really."

That's how I remember it. As we drove on Lucy began to complain about a letter she said I'd written.

"You used these exquisite phrases. Avoiding the nitty-gritty. All fancy dancing."

"I don't do that. I don't know what letter you mean. Come on— 'exquisite phrases'?" I laughed at her.

A couple of miles later she informed me she had written the letter to herself. "In my style," she said.

"So," I asked her, "what were the phrases you liked?"

"I don't remember. I wanted to get it down. The way you are."

"Lucy, please don't write letters from me to yourself. I can do it."

"You never wrote me," she said, which I guess was partly the point. "Anyone can jump out of a phone."

Suddenly though, without apparent spite she declared: "John's going to expand my part." She was talking about the now-revived horror movie in which John had hired a live British actor to strangle her. However, on consideration she thought he might now transform her into a surviving heroine. I said it was great but that it probably wouldn't be as much fun.

"You know," she said, "you don't get credit for being scared and dying. It doesn't count as acting. Anyway I can live without fun."

"If you say so."

"John," she said, "wants to marry me." For some reason at that point she put her hand on my knee and turned her face to me. "Seriously."

I wondered about that for a while in the weeks following. Once she showed me a postcard of the Empire State Building he had sent her from New York. He had adorned it with embarrassing jokey scribbles about his erection. One day I took John to Musso's for lunch but he said not a word to me about her. Over our pasta I asked him if it was true that he was sparing Lucy's character in the thing forthcoming.

"Oh," he said, as though it was something that had slipped his mind. "Absolutely. Lucy's time has come."

I suspected that the lead would be the kind of supposed-to-be-feisty female lately appearing as part of the serious and adult wave. I knew Lucy could deliver that one all the way from Avenida Revolución.

"She can give a character some inner aspects," I told him.

"You're so right."

"Good actress," I suggested. "Great kid."

John went radiant but he didn't look like a bridegroom to me. "You know it, Tom. Tops."

He didn't marry Lucy. Instead, when the funeral-baked meats had cooled he married Brion Pritchard's widow, Maerwyn. He didn't even promote Lucy to insipid ingénue. Halfway through the horror movie her character died like a trooper. In spite of my infatuation I had to admit there were many great things one could do with Lucy but marrying her was probably not one of them.

We went out a few times. She began to seem to me—for lack of a better word—unreal. I kept trying to get close to her again. At the time I was selling neither scripts nor story ideas. There were no calls. I might have tried for an acting gig; I was owed a few favors. I had no illusions about my talent but I was cheap and willing, well-spoken enough for walk-ons as a mad monk or war-mongering general. I offered a Brooklyn Heights accent, which sounds not at all the way you think. But I had grown self-conscious and all the yoga in the world wasn't going to bring back my chops or my youthful arrogance. That was what I'd need in front of a camera. My main drawback as an actor had always been a tendency to perform from the neck up. I might have thrived in the great days of radio.

Somehow I got a job with a newspaper chain working as their West Coast editor. It took up a lot of my time and part of my work was resisting being transformed into a gossip columnist. I almost got fired for doing a piece for the *New York Times* Arts and Leisure section. The news chain paid a lot less than writing for the movies but it paid regularly. I had plans to engineer a spread for Lucy but nothing came along to hang it on.

Out of what seemed like nowhere she took up with a friend of mine named Asa Maclure, pronounced *Mac*-lure, whom people called Ace. Ace was an actor and occasional writer (mostly of blaxploitation flix during the seventies) with whom I had liked to go out drinking and drugging and what we insensitively called wenching. Ace was a wild man. What inclined me to forgive him at all was a telegram he had once sent to a director in Washington for whom he was going to act Othello.

CANT WAIT TO GET MY HANDS AROUND THAT WHITE WOMAN'S THROAT.

Ace had just arrived back in L.A. from Africa where he had portrayed a loyal askari who saved a blonde white child from swart Moorish bandits in the Sahara. The white child, supposed to be French, was from Eastern Europe somewhere. Ace was unclear as to which country. She had gone on location with her mother along as chaperone. The mom was, as Ace put it, a babe. Ace was suave and beautiful, the kind of guy they would cast as Othello. In no time at all his romance, as they say, with Mrs. Vraniuk was the talk of every location poker game. Restless under the desert sky Ace decided to shift his attention to young Miss Vraniuk. Consummation followed, producing some uneasiness since the kid was not yet twenty-one. Nor was she eighteen. Nor, it seemed, perhaps, was she fifteen. But it was in another country, another century, a different world. At the time, in the circumstances, it represented no more than a merry tale.

"This child was ageless, man," Ace told us. "She had the wiles of Eve."

If any images or other evidence of desert passion existed, no one worried much about it. Talk was cheap. And most American tabloids then did not even buy pictures.

Ace and Lucy became a prominent item, appearing in the very magazine that now employed me. The stories were fueled by Ace's sudden trajectory toward stardom. Though she was blooming, as she aged more beautiful then ever, she was noticed only as Ace's companion.

It happened that one week the papers dispatched me with a photographer to do a story on kids in South Central who rode high stakes bike races. The races ran on barrio streets, inviting the wagers of high rolling meth barons and senior gangbangers. Lucy decided to come with me and when I went down a second time she came along again. Both times she seemed a little hammered and could not be discouraged from flirting with a few speed-addled pistoleros. A local actually approached me with a warning that she was behaving unwisely. Driving back to Silver Lake she said: "You and I are sleepwalking."

"How do you mean?" I asked her.

"We're unconscious. Living parallel lives. We never see each other."

I said I thought she was involved with Ace.

"I mean really see each other, Tommy. The way people can see each other."

"You're the one who's sleepwalking, Lucy."

"Oh," she said, "don't say that about me." She sounded as though she had been caught out, trapped in something like a lie. "That's frightening."

"That's what you said about both of us. I thought you were on to something."

Maybe she was confounded at her own inconsistency. More likely she never got there. She sat silent for a while. Then she said: "Don't you understand. Tommy. It's always you with me. Ever since Grauman's."

It was not a joke. I don't think she meant to hurt or deceive me with the things she said. For some reason, though, she could leave me feeling abandoned and without hope. Not only about us but about everything. She was concerned with being there. And with whom to be. It occurred to me that perhaps she was going through life without, in a sense, knowing what she was doing. Or that she was not doing anything but forever being done. Waiting for a cue, a line, a vehicle, marks, blocking. Somewhere to stand and be whoever she might decide she was, even for a moment.

"That can't be true, Lucy."

"Oh yes," she said, urgently, deeply disturbed, "Oh yes baby, it is true."

There was no point in arguing. A couple of miles along, she put her hand on my driving arm, holding it hard and I suspected she might force the wheel.

"I have such strength," she said. "I don't know how to use it. Or when. I accommodate. That's the trouble."

One strange afternoon, Asa Maclure, Lucy, and myself decided to go bungee jumping. Seriously. It might have represented the zenith of our tattered glory days. The place we chose to bungee jump from was a mountainside high above the Mojave flats, reachable by cable car from Palm Springs. There, over a rock face that rose a sheer few hundred feet from the desert floor, two actual Australians, a boy and a girl, had the jump concession.

I might say that I can't imagine how we came to plan this but in fact I know how. Ace was well aware of the fraught status between Lucy and myself. I'm sure she talked about me to him, maybe a lot. He would tease me, or both of us, when we were together.

"You all are actually pathetic," he declared once. "A gruesome twosome. Tommy, she sighs and pines over you. I believe you do the same. I don't mind."

I was provoked. He was saying that our strange affair notwithstanding, he—Mister Mens Sana in Corpore Sano—was who she turned to for good loving. It was a taunt. So I decided I'd play some soul poker with him for Lucy and win and take her away. Thereafter he tried to see that she avoided me. When we were all together Ace and I would watch each other for cracks in which to place a wedge. Though I liked to believe I was smarter than Ace, he was verbally quite agile.

The bungee incident began as a bad joke and started overheating, the way one kid's playful punch of another will gradually lead to an angry fistfight. In fact it was completely childish, nothing less than a dare. It was I who made the mistake of talking bungee jump; I'd seen the Australians referred to in the *Times*'s weekend supplement and it occurred to me I might get my employers to pay for us. Ace was famous, Lucy semi-famous, beginning to get noticed, frequently called in to test, and cast at times to help lesser actors look good. There were also reruns of her several soaps.

I felt I had to do this. I had made a jocular reference to this scheme in the presence of Ace, and Lucy and Ace called me on it. While I was trying to prod the higher powers to spring and assign a photographer the two of them went and did it. Would Lucy descend into the ponderosa-scented void after her paramour? A thing never in question. It was an eminence she'd sought lifelong, a Fuji disposable Lover's Leap. They survived.

All my life I have regretted not being there. For one thing, regarding *Maclure*, I held my manhood cheap. He had foxed me and bonded with her in a way that I, who had made something of a career out of witnessing Lucy's beau gestes, would never experience. She hurt me bad.

Suffering is illuminating, as they say, and in my pain I almost learned something about myself. I repressed the insight. I was not ready, then, to yield to it.

"I wanted it to be you," Lucy said, like a deflowered prom queen apologizing to the high school athlete whose lettered jersey she had worn and dishonored.

"I wanted it to be me too," I said. "Why did you go and do it?"

"I was afraid I wouldn't do it if we waited."

I shouted at her, something I very rarely did.

"You'd have done it with me! You goddamn well would have!"

Of course this exchange was as juvenile as the rest of the incident but it stirred the unconsidered home truth I had been resisting. This kind of juvenalia goes deep and you can also approach self-awareness after acting childishly.

Still, I wasn't up to facing it. For days and days I went to sleep, stoned, half-drunk, whispering: What was it like, Lucy? I meant the leap. I very nearly went bungee jumping by myself but it seemed a sterile exercise.

I was bitter. I had excuses to avoid her and I used them all. She called me at the office and in Laguna but I was tired of it. The next thing I knew I had quit my job and gone over to England to find Jennifer.

Jen had got a Green Book and was teaching dance with some friends in Chester. When we saw each other I knew it was on again. I had to peel her loose from some painter from over the border. Another fucking Welsh boyfriend!

I took her home to Dallas and met the high-toned folks and married her in the high-toned Episcopal equivalent of a nuptial mass, dressed up like a character out of Oscar Wilde. She conscientiously wore red, though I pointed out that neither of us had been married before. We moved to Laguna and, lovely and smart as she was, Jen got herself a tenure-track job in dance at UC San Diego. I watched her work and she was peppy and the good cop bad cop kind of teacher, and you never saw a prettier backside in a leotard. We moved to Encinitas.

My bride all but supported me while I worked on a few scripts. She had loans from her parents and the UC salary. I don't know exactly what had changed in the movie business; I hadn't noticed anything good. However, I optioned two scripts right away.

One day I was coming out of the HBO offices on Olympic when I ran into Asa Maclure. The sight of him froze my heart. In those years you knew what the way he looked meant. He was altogether too thin for his big frame, his cool drape sagged around him. The worst of it was his voice, always rich, Shakespearean, his preacher father's voice. It had become a rasp. He sounded old and he looked sad and wise, a demeanor that he had used to assume in jest. I hoped he wouldn't mention the bungee jump but he did. Plainly it meant a lot to him. From a different perspective, it did to me too. We traded a few marginally insincere laughs about how absurd the whole thing had been. He looked so doomed I couldn't begrudge him the high they must have had. I didn't ask him how he was.

A couple of weeks later I got a call from Lucy and she wanted to see me. She was still in Silver Lake. I lied to Jennifer when I drove up to visit her. Jen had not asked where I was going but I volunteered false information. I felt profoundly unfaithful though I realized that there was not much likelihood of my sleeping with Lucy. No possibility at all, from my point of view. So I felt unfaithful to her too.

Lucy, in Silver Lake, seemed at once agitated and exhausted.

"Ace said he saw you," she told me, when we were seated in the patio dead Heathcliff had demolished.

Passing through her living room I noticed that the house was in a squalid state. The floors were littered with a scatter of plastic flowers and charred metal cylinders. There were roaches on the floor and in the ashtrays, along with beer cans and other post-party knickknacks. Lucy had been running with a new set of friends. I imagined these people as a kind of simian troop, although I never got it clear who exactly they were and how Lucy had been impressed into being their hostess. I did know that it had somehow to do with supply and demand.

I had been out of town and I was not familiar with free-basing. I can't be sure that Asa turned her on to it. Basing was the rage then in extremist circles like his. She talked about it with a rapturous smile. I had been around long enough to remember when street drugs hit the industry big time, and I remembered that smile from the days when each new advance in narcosis had been acclaimed as somebody's personal Fourth of July. A life-changing event. To cool the rock's edges Lucy had taken to easing down behind a few upscale pharmaceuticals: 'ludes, opiate pills. Unfortunately for all of us, genuine quaaludes were disappearing even south of the border. This left the opiates, which were still dispensed with relative liberality. While I watched, Lucy cooked up the brew in her kitchen as she had been instructed. She told me she had always liked to cook though this was a side of her I'd never seen.

Cooking base, we ancients of art will recall, involved a number of tools. 7-Elevens then sold single artificial flowers in test tube–like containers so that crack scenes were sometimes adorned with sad false blossoms. Lucy mixed quite a few gram baggies with baking soda and heated them in a cunning little Oriental pot. The devil of details was in the mix, which Lucy approached with brisk confidence. Alarmingly, the coke turned into viscous liquid. People who have put in time in really crappy motels may recall finding burned pieces of coat hanger on the floor of the closets or wardrobes. Lucy had one and she used it to fish the brew out so it could cool and congeal. It was then that the stem came into play and a plastic baby bottle and a burned wad of Chore Boy, which was a kind of scouring pad we used as a filter. On the business end of the stem, appropriately enough, was the bottle's nipple, which the adept lipped like a grouper on brain coral.

We did it and at first it reminded me of how, when I was a child, my mother would have me inhale pine needle oil to cure a chest cold. The effect however was different, although if someone had told me it cured colds I wouldn't have argued. It was quite blissful for a time and we were impelled toward animated chatter. I commenced to instruct Lucy on the joys of marriage, for which I was then an enthusiast. She soared with me; her eyes flashed. In this state she was always something to see.

"I'm so happy for you. No I'm really not. Yes I am."

We smoked for an hour or more. As she plied the hanger end to scrape residue from the filter and stem, she told me about her career prospects, which seemed stellar. She had been cast for what seemed a good part in a film by a notoriously eccentric but gifted director who had assembled a kind of repertory company for his pictures. Some of these made money, some tanked, but all of them got some respect. For Lucy, this job was a good thing. And not only was there the film part. As schedules permitted, she was going to do Irina in *Uncle Vanya* at a prestigious neighborhood playhouse. I rejoiced for her. As I was leaving, supremely confident and looking forward to the drive, I kissed her. Her response seemed less sensual than emotional. I was hurt, although I had no intention of suggesting anything beyond our embrace. Sometimes you just don't know what you want.

Around Westminster, I began to feel the dive. Its sensation was accompanied by a sudden suspicion that Lucy's reversal of fortune might be a little too good to be true. When I got home I took two of the pain pills and believed her again.

Not long after this we read that Asa Maclure was dead too. He had AIDS all right but it wasn't the disease that killed him. The proximate cause of his death was an accident occasioned by his unsteady attempt to cook some base. He set himself on fire, ran as fast as he could manage out of his San Vicente apartment and took off down the unpeopled sidewalks of the boulevard. He ran toward the ocean. Hundreds of cars passed him as he ran burning. According to some alleged witnesses even a fire truck went by, although that may have been someone's stroke of cruel wit.

Asa Maclure was a wonderful man. He was, as they say, a damn good actor. He was also enormous fun. In the end, he was a good friend too, although obviously a difficult one. Suffice it to say I mourned him.

Jennifer and I went to his funeral. It was held at a freshly painted but rickety-looking black church in what had once been a small southern town not thirty miles from where her parents lived in River Oaks. Asa's father presided, his master in declamation. Asa had resembled his father and the man was strong and prevailed over his grief. There were few people from the industry, mostly African-American, all male. Praise God, Lucy did not appear.

Back in Dallas at my in-laws' stately home we had a few bourbons.

"Your friend has the kiss of death," Jennifer said. She delivered this observation without inflection but it remained to hover on the magnolia-scented air of that cool, exquisitely tasteful room.

Both of my optioned scripts were being green-lighted.

From what I read in the papers it seemed Lucy had been replaced in the mad genius' picture. The neighborhood production of *Vanya* opened with no mention of her. I presumed she had read for it. Maybe she had assumed the part was hers. Once I met her for a sandwich in a Beverly Hills deli and we talked about Ace's death. Lucy spoke slowly, with great precision and was obviously high. I was worried about her and also concerned to discover where Ace's death had left her.

"I've compartmentalized my life," she declared. She had brought with her a huge paperback book with dog-eared pages and she showed it to me. It was a collection of drawings by Giovanni Piranesi that featured his series called "Imaginary Prisons," in which tiers of prison cells are ranked along Gothic stone staircases and upon the battlements of vast dungeons that ascend and descend over spaces that appear infinite. For reasons which many art lovers will immediately comprehend on seeing some of his drawings, Piranesi is a great favorite among cultivated junkies. His prisons are like their world.

On the blank pages in the book Lucy had written what she called plans. These were listed in columns placed across from one another, each laid out in variously colored inks and displaying Lucy's runic but attractive handwriting. When she handed the book to me for comment I could only utter a few appreciative sounds. Every word in every paragraph of every column was unreadable. I still have no idea what she had written there. Finally I could not, for my life, keep myself from saying something meant to be friendly and comforting about Asa. I got the same cold suffering look I had seen when Brion Pritchard died.

In the weeks after that, in a craven fashion, I kept my distance from her because I was afraid of what I might see and hear. She didn't call. Also the trip to Texas had left Jen and me closer somehow—at least for a while.

After a few months Lucy left a message on our machine absurdly pretending to be someone else. Suddenly I thought I wanted to see her again. The desire, the impulse, came over me all at once in the middle of a working afternoon. On re-examination, I think the urge was partly romantic, partly Pavlovian. I was concerned. I wanted to help her. I wanted to get seriously high with her because Jen didn't use. So my trip back to Silver Lake was speeded by a blend of high-mindedness and base self-indulgence. It's a fallen world, is it not? We carry love in earthen vessels.

Lucy's house was not as dirty and disorderly as it had been on my last visit but everything still looked dingy. She did not garden or wash windows and no longer employed her help. She no longer cooked either since crack, the industrialized version of base, had obviated that necessity. It was safer too and far less messy than basing. The rocks went straight from the baggie into the stem. For me the hit was even better. She had Percocet and Xanax for coming down, a lot of it. She was still very attractive and I later learned she had a thing going with a druggy doc in Beverly Hills who must have been something of an adventurer.

"I'm going to Jerusalem!" she said. She said it so joyously that for a second I thought she had got herself saved by some goof.

"Yes?" I approved wholeheartedly. Seconds after the pipe I approved of nearly everything that way. "How great!"

"Listen to this!" she said. "I'm going there to live in the Armenian quarter. In a monastery. Or, like, a convent."

"Terrific! As a nun?"

She laughed and I did too. We laughed loud and long. When we were finished laughing she slapped me on the shoulder.

"No, ridiculous one! As research. Because I'm going to do a script about the massacres. I'm going to sneak into Anatolia and see the Euphrates."

She had an uncle who was a high-ranking priest at the see of the Jerusalem patriarch. He would arrange for her stay and she could interview survivors of the slaughter.

"I want to do this for my parents. For my background. I won't say 'heritage' because that's so pretentious."

"I think it's a great idea."

I was about, in my boisterous good humor, to call her project a pipedream. Fortunately I thought better of it.

She saw the thing as eminently possible. The Russians had unraveled and she might film in Armenia. There were prominent Armenian-Americans in the movie business, in town and in the former USSR. She had me about a quarter convinced though I wondered about the writing. She had the answer to that.

"This is yours, Tommy! Will you do it? Will you go with me? Will you think about it? Please? Because if you wrote it I'm sure I could direct. Because you know how it is. You and me."

Naturally the urgency was intense. "It's a sweet idea," I said.

"You could bring your wife, you know. I forget her name."

I told her. She had somehow deduced that Jennifer was younger than she.

"They're all named Jennifer," she said.

As if to bind me to the plan she pressed huge handfuls of Percocet on me. Starting to drive home I realized that I was too rattled to make it all the way to Encinitas. I checked into a motel that was an island of downscale on the Westwood-Santa Monica border and called Jen, home from her classes. I explained how I had come up to inquire into something or other, and suddenly felt too ill to make it back that evening.

"Don't drive then," Jen said. I could see trouble shimmering on the blacktop ahead.

Next Lucy disappeared. Her phone was suddenly out of service. The next time I was up in town I went to her house and found it unoccupied. The front garden was ochre rubble and the house itself enclosed in scaffolding. It was lunchtime and a work crew of Meso-Americans in faded flannel shirts were eating In-and-Out burgers on the roof.

Once I got a message in which she claimed to be in New York. It was rambling and unsound. She said some indiscreetly affectionate things but neglected to leave a number or address. I did my best to tape over the message to stay out of trouble. I had only partial success.

A little serendipity followed. I heard from a friend back in New York, a documentary filmmaker whom I hadn't seen in many years. He had gone into some boutique on Madison and met the gorgeous salesperson. She seemed glamorous and mysterious and dressed enticingly from the store so he asked her out. He thought she might go for a Stoppard play so he took her to the play and to Da Torcella and then to Nell's. People recognized her. It turned out she was an actor, a smart actor, and could talk Stoppard with insight. She was a wild but inspired dancer and had very nearly nailed a part in an actual Broadway play. She knew me, was in fact a friend of mine.

"Oh," I said. "Lucy."

He was disappointed she hadn't asked him home that night. Casual couplings were not completely out of fashion by then, though white balloons were beginning to ascend over West Eleventh Street. My friend thought he liked her very much but when he'd called one evening she sounded strange. It sounded, too, as though she lived in a hotel.

I thought I knew the story and I was right. She could hardly have asked him home because home then was an SRO on 123rd and Broadway and he would not have enjoyed the milieu. All her salary and commissions, as I later learned, were going for crack and for scag to mellow it out. Pain pills were not doing it any longer. I quoted him the maxim made famous by Nelson Algren: "Never go to bed with someone who has more problems than you do." He understood. I didn't think I had deprived anyone of their bliss.

There was something more to my friendly cautioning. It wasn't exactly jealousy. It was that somehow I thought I was the only one who could handle Lucy. That she was my parish.

When she showed up in California again it was in San Francisco. I got a call from her up there and this time I didn't bother to erase it. Jennifer and I were in trouble. I had a bit of a drug problem. I was drinking a lot. I suspected her of having an affair with some washed-up Bosnian ballet dancer she had hired down at UCSD. The fellow was supposed to be gay but I was suspicious. Jennifer was a well-bred, well-spoken East Texas hardass a couple of generations past sharecropping. Amazingly, the more I drank and used, the more she lost respect for me. At the same time I was selling scripts like crazy, rewriting them, sometimes going out on locations to work them through. Jennifer was largely unimpressed. Everything was stressful.

I was full of anger and junkie righteousness and I went up to see Lucy, hardly bothering to cover my tracks. She had rented an apartment there that belonged to her stockbroker sister, not a bad one at all though it was in the dreary Haight. I guess I had wanted a look at who Lucy's latest friends were.

Her live-in friend was Scott and she introduced us. I had expected a repellent creep. Scott surpassed my grisliest expectations. He had watery eyes, of a blue so pale that his irises seemed at the point of turning white. He had very thin trembly red lips that crawled up his teeth at one corner to form a kind of tentative sneer. He had what my mother would have called a weak chin, which she believed was characteristic of non-Anglo Saxons. There were no other features I recall.

Scott was under the impression he played the guitar. He plinked on one for us as we watched and waited. Lucy avoided eye contact with me. As Scott played his face assumed a kind of fanatical spirituality and he rolled his strange eyes. Watching him do it induced in the beholder something like motion sickness. In his transport he suggested the kind of Jehovah's Witness who would kill you with a hammer for rejecting his *Watchtower*.

When he had finished Lucy exclaimed: "Oh wow." By force of will I prevented us from applauding.

Scott's poison was methamphetamine. I was not yet familiar with the drug's attraction and this youth served as an exemplar. Having shot some, his expression shifted from visionary to scornful, paranoid and back. I had seen many druggy people over the years—I knew I was one myself—but Scott was a caution to cats. To compare his state with a mad Witness missionary was demeaning to believers. His transcendent expression, his transport, ecstasy, whatever, was centered on neurological sensation like a laboratory rat's. The mandala at the core of his universe was his own asshole. It was outrageous. However there we were, beautiful Lucy, cultivated me, livers of the examined life, in more or less the same maze. What did it make us?

When Scott had exhausted conversation by confusing himself beyond explication, he took a pair of sunglasses off the floor beside him, put them on and moved them up on his forehead.

"I invented this," he told us, "this pushing shades up on your head thing."

Weeks later Scott was removed from her apartment with the aid of many police officers, screaming about insects and imitating one. It was history repeating itself as farce, a particularly unfunny one. Lucy lost the place and the stockbroker sister was forced out. The upside was losing Scott as well.

Back home it was cold and Jennifer grew suspicious and discontent. When she was very angry her mild educated Anglo-Southern tones could tighten and faintly echo the speech of her remote sharecropping ancestors in the Dust Bowl. Sometimes her vowels would twist themselves into the sorrowful whine of pious stump farmers abandoned by Jesus in the bottomland. You had to listen very closely to hear it. I had never heard the word "honey" sound so leaden until Jennifer smacked me in the mouth with it. She could do the same thing with "dear." Dust Bowl, I thought was by then a useful summary of our married state.

I started going to bars. I listened to production assistants' stories about the new-style dating services. I did not pursue these routes because I was no longer so young and beautiful and because I was bitter and depressed. I did have a few one- or two-nighters on location. The best, carnally speaking, was with a stunt woman with a body like a Mexican comic book heroine who, it was said, had once beat an Arizona policeman half to death. Of course bodies like hers were not rare in movieland. Straight stunt girls were more fun, at least for me, than actresses. What they might lack in psychological dimension they made up for in contoured heft and feel and originality. They were sometimes otherwise limited unless you counted insanity as psychological dimension. Once I had a weeklong liaison with an unhappily married Las Vegas mounted policewoman who wanted to break into movies. As for the young women once characterized as starlets—they all knew the joke about the Polish ingénue, the one who slept with the writer.

I was not so obtuse that I failed to observe certain patterns in my own behavior—not simply the greedy self-indulgence but all the actions that were coming to define me. This seemed at the time a misfortune because I didn't reflect on them with any satisfaction. There they were however, beginning to seem like a summary, coming up like old bar bills. As for root causes, I couldn't have cared less. There were limits even to my self-absorption. Also I worried about getting ever deeper into drugs.

I saw Lucy every few months. Jennifer and I finally had it out around that one. She accused me of infidelity and I told her plainly that yes I was sleeping around. Safe sex of course, I said, though I don't know how much that would have mattered since we had not made love for months. However, I told her truthfully that I had not been to bed with Lucy for years and not at all since we had married. I also challenged her own virtue.

"What about your supposed-to-be-faggot colleague down there at school. Fucking Boris." The high-bouncing lover was called Ivan Ivanic and I had hated him since the day Jennifer corrected my pronunciation of his name, which was I-van-ich. "He's not getting in your pants?"

She was furious, naturally. You can't use that kind of malicious language about gays to most dancers. But I saw something else in her reaction. She was shocked. She cried. I resisted the impulse to believe her.

I visited Lucy more frequently. One thing I went up for was dope. She had moved into a fairly respectable hotel just uphill from the Tenderloin and by then she was scoring regularly in the Mission. After numerous misadventures, ripoffs, and a near rape she had learned how to comport herself around the market. She had the added protection of being a reliable customer. Lucy was not yet penniless. Her television work was still in syndication and her residuals from SAG continued. But she was spending her money fast.

By the time I arrived from the airport—this was still in the days of fifty-dollar flights—Lucy would have done her marketing on Dolores and picked up her exchange spike at the Haight Free Clinic. My contribution to the picnic was the coke I had bought down south. Lucy kept her small room very neat. We would embrace. Sometimes we would hold each other, as chaste as Hansel and Gretel, to show we cared. We hoped we cared. Both of us were beginning to stop caring about much.

I would snort coke and Lucy's smack. I never shot it.

Sometimes it made me sick. Often it provoked brief hilarity. I would watch her fix—the spoon, the lighter, the works as they say—with something like reverence. Listen, I had grown up to Chet Baker, to Coltrane, to Lady Day. To me, junkies, no matter how forlorn, were holy. Of course at a certain point if you've see one you've seen them all and this was as true of us as of anyone. Much of the time we looked into each other's eyes without sentiment. This was better than staring at your toe. In each other's dilating pupils we could reflect calmly on the uneasy past. The lambent moments expanded infinitely, all was resolved for a while. Once she even began to dream aloud about going to Jerusalem to do research for the script that I would write, and about kicking the jones in the Holy Places.

We chose silence sometimes. It wasn't that we never spoke. In a certain way you might say we were weary of each other. Not bored, or fed up, or anything of that sort. Worn out after the lives we'd tried to make intersect, and conducting a joint meditation on the subject. There were times I'll admit I cried. She never did but then she was always higher.

Every little once in a while Lucy would try to persuade me to fix the way she did. We never went through with it and I felt guilty. I was after all the guy who had not gone bungee jumping. Lucy never pressed it.

"If you died I would feel like I killed Shakespeare," she said.

I was never sure whether we thought this would be good or bad.

Mortality intruded itself regularly into our afternoons because it seemed that half the people we knew were dead. I supposed that down in sunny Encinitas my Jennifer was expecting to hear that I had succumbed to the kiss. During one of my later visits—one of the last—Lucy told me about a conversation she'd had at the UC hospital emergency room. A doctor there had said to her: "You're rather old to be an addict." She laughed about it and did a self-important, falsely mellow doctorish voice repeating it.

To me Lucy was still beautiful. I don't know how she looked to other people. She was my heroine. I noticed though that lately she always wore long sleeves and that it was to hide the abscesses that marked the tracks where her veins had been. Her eyes didn't die. Once she looked out the small clear window that looked up Nob Hill and made a declaration.

"The rest of my life is going to last about eleven minutes."

The line was hardly lyrical but her delivery was smashing. She looked great saying it and I saw that at long last she had located the role of her lifetime. Everything before had been provisional but she had made this woman her own. It was as though this was finally whom she had become and she could do almost anything with it. Found her moment, to be inhabited completely, but of course briefly.

I went home then, the way I always had, and saved almost everything. I saw that Lucy and I, together, had finally found the true path and that this time we were walking hand and hand, the whole distance. Again I refused the jump. She was more than half a ghost by then and it would be pretty to think her interceding spirit saved me.

One of us had to walk away and it was not going to be Lucy. She was the actor, I thought, not me.

I May Look Dumb

Maxine Swann

*Maxine Swann's first published story, "Flower Children" won the Cohen
Award, the O. Henry Award, and the Pushcart Prize, and was included in* Best
American Short Stories. *Swann received degrees in literature from Columbia
University and the University of Paris. She is the author of two novels,* Serious
Girls *and* Flower Children. *She lives in Buenos Aires, Argentina.*

ON THE WEEKENDS, OUR FATHER PICKS US UP IN HIS
funny-smelling car and takes us out into the world.
"C'mon, c'mon, c'mon," he says, though we've been
waiting for hours. He wears loose collarless shirts with
embroidered fronts, bright red pants. He lives in the
city now. We almost never go to his house. It isn't much
of a place, on a little street in a not so good neighborhood, and there's nothing to do there. Rather, he always
takes us on an adventure. Windows all down, hair flying, we peel out of
the driveway. The dust rises behind us on the dirt roads. The fields fall
away. We're never sure what we're doing, where we're going, only that
we're rapidly, recklessly, farmhouse by farmhouse, leaving all we know
behind.

At the golf course, we turn. "Golf," our father says, "now who in his
right mind would be so stupid to play golf?" We pass the neighbor, Ed
Trout's house, with the perfect garden. Every leaf and flower is in place
and gleams. "You know what's going to happen to Ed Trout?" our father
asks.

"What?!" Clyde, the littlest, screams.

"Jesus, Clyde, shut up." Lila, who's oldest, covers her ear. He's
screamed right into it.

"He's going to die and go up to Heaven and at the gates where God
is, God's going to ask him, 'What have you done?' And he's going to say,
'God, I've kept this perfect garden. It was perfect every day.' And God's
going to shake his head, 'Sorry Ed, that's not enough.' 'But I watered it
every day.' 'Sorry, Ed.'"

By now we're looping up and down hills, soon to enter the little town. The funeral parlor is its stateliest building. There's the Vets Club, the post office, the elementary school. We stop at the gas station. We love the smell of gas. As soon as we pull in, we all start sniffing. Already some of us have to pee. We scramble out. There's a thin man with gray hair pumping the gas.

"Who wants an ice cream sandwich?" our father asks.

"Me!" we yell.

He goes into the office and gets ice cream sandwiches, one for each of us and two for himself. When we're back from the bathroom and our father's back from the office, we sit in the car unpeeling our ice cream sandwiches and waiting for the gas tank to be full.

"You know, it's the damnedest thing," our father tells us, gobbling his first sandwich in two bites, "old guys just love it when you call them Pops."

"Really?" Lila says. She licks her sandwich delicately, wrinkling her nose.

"Yes, they do. They do!"

The attendant comes over to our father's window and our father hands him some cash.

"You mean like that guy?" Clyde asks.

"Well, I don't know about him. He's not that old—"

Clyde leans his whole upper body out the window, his ice cream sandwich streaming down his hand, and screams, "Howdy Pops!"

The guy, walking away, turns and shakes his fist at us.

Our father has already started the car and now pulls out fast. "Jesus, Clyde, not like that!" But he's hunched over, laughing. We're all laughing, and hunched over now too like him, peering back at the guy as we make our getaway.

Our father hits on an enthusiasm and runs with it. Every weekend for months we go cave exploring. Then he switches. We go to tractor pulls or skiing or to meditate in ashrams. Sometimes he brings us places it takes hours to get to, like the top of a mountain, and then almost immediately, he wants to leave. "C'mon, c'mon, c'mon," he says a thousand times over, herding us forward with his arms.

Occasionally he makes a scene. Once when we're walking down a street in Washington D.C., he points out a group of punk rocker kids loitering near the park. They have high mohawks, black and green, and wear spiked collars around their necks.

"You know what really drives these kids nuts?" our father says. "It really drives them nuts if you tell them they look nice. I'm going to go over there and tell them they look nice."

"No, Dad!" Lila says, stamping her foot.

But he's already on his way, head low, sidling slightly sideways. He looks back at us and wiggles his eyebrows up and down a few times.

We're standing on the sidewalk. Lila, desperate, turns away. I want to turn too but I can't make myself. I'm too curious. What are they going to do?

Our father edges up to the kids. The girl with the green hair deepens her sneer. The guy with the highest mohawk leans back, looking our father up and down. Suddenly it occurs to me that they might attack him. Could they kill him? He's obviously provoking them. Might they not have knives?

Our father stands in front of them, wagging his finger, neck out like a turtle, telling them they look nice.

But instead of attacking him, they seem at a loss. They don't get it. Why's he doing this?

Having said his piece, our father turns away. But even then, it takes the kids a moment to recover. "Loser!" the one with the tallest mohawk calls when he's already yards away. "Wanker!" the girl yells.

Our father looks back over his shoulder, nods and smiles at them, as if they've all just shared a little secret, and sidles his way back to us.

All of us are watching except for Clyde, who's kicking a tire on a nearby car. He kicks so hard his foot bounces back. This is what makes it fun. Jack, who's six, is looking at our father, mystified. I feel like squirming. Lila's mad.

"Dad, why did you do that?!" she asks.

Both she and I want to get away fast.

Sometimes, because of his stutter, our father makes a scene without even meaning to. He gets stuck on a word and can't get it out. He stands there in front of whomever he's trying to talk to, mouth open, eyes closed, for the longest time. If we know what he's saying, we can help him out. The worst though is when he's on the phone. The people on the other end can't see his face, so have no idea what's going on. Sometimes they hang up or say something rude. We can't help either in that situation, so instead we start giggling crazily out of nerves.

"My kids are all laughing at me," our father tells the person on the line. For some reason, at this part he doesn't stutter at all.

Whole blocks of our lives take place in the car. Our father talks a mile a minute, explaining things, telling us things, saying how "his mind was blown" by this or that. As he talks, we're supposed to tell him when he's hunching his shoulders—it's when he hunches that he stutters. "Dad, you're pulling down," or when he's wrinkling his forehead, "You're wrinkling, Dad." He's concerned about the wrinkles on his forehead and about going bald. His hair is receding a bit in the front. He's all fired up about all kinds of things, a recent bill in Congress on education, a design for a new brick stove, the lunatics and assholes all around us on the road. He loves it when we tease him. We tease him. We play games. We laugh so hard we pee. When someone farts, everyone yells and we roll all the windows down. Our father tells us that if you ever fart when there's a dog around, always act like it was the dog.

We scoot through a city, stopping at stoplights. The houses are all stacked on top of one another, the buildings full of little windows. Who lives here? The cracked sidewalks have grass sprouting up. We see two kids talking on the street down below. If a flood came, would all this be washed away? Then the light changes. We're out again, driving. We pass coal mines and dumping grounds with bulldozers lifting up and repositing loads of trash.

"Keep your eyes out for cops," our father tells us. The cop cars wait stealthily in the center strip of grass. They usually pick a dip so they're out of sight. Sometimes our father gets stopped for speeding. One time he gets in a fight with the cop. He swears and bangs the top of the car with his hand.

"I'll see you in court," the cop says.

"Are you going to court?" I ask, once our father's back inside, thinking that means you go to jail.

He rants and raves about what an asshole the cop was and forgets about my question. It takes him a while to simmer down.

We get carsick, cranky. We beat on each other—no one wants to sit on the hump in the middle, someone in the back seat is taking all the room, whoever's in the front seat has been there too long. One of us cries or screams. Our father lets us go until it gets too bad. "All right, cut it out, you guys, Jesus Christ!" We fall silent, exhausted, and stare out the windows for hours and hours at the blue fog of New Jersey, the roadside developments, the thousands upon thousands of fleeting trees.

"Where are we going?"

"Are we almost there?"

Pit stops, pee stops. We love stopping and getting out of the car. If we're going north, our favorite place to eat is the Skyliner Diner. It's a silver metal building by the side of the road. We always order manicotti. One time, when we walk into the Skyliner, our father gets confused.

"Jesus Christ," he says, looking around, "what the hell's going on here? You've changed this whole place around!"

He's saying it to no one in particular. Clyde, standing beside him, does the same, imitating him, arms up, baffled, looking around. The cashier, a teenage girl with thin bangs and braces, is the only person working there in sight. She stares at our father blankly.

Our father tries again, edging nearer her. "Didn't you change this whole goddamned place around?"

She shakes her head slightly, then glances toward the back as if she might need help. It's not clear to her if he's crazy or not. Except for Clyde, who's stepped up to the cash register with our father, we're all lingering back.

"I swear to God," our father says, "they changed this whole place around." He turns and looks at us, one hand out, gesturing emphatically. "Didn't they? Didn't they?!"

The girl at the cash register still looks edgy. There's a little bell by her hand she can ring if she's in trouble.

Lila suddenly breaks away, walking past the cash register and down the aisle between the booths, her bright slab of hair swinging back and forth. A moment later, she turns and runs quickly back to us.

"It's because we came in the other door!" she says. "Usually we come in that door!"

"What?" our father says, full of disbelief. Or is he just playing? It's never quite clear if he's playing or not. He follows her back the way she went, with Clyde at his heels.

The cashier watches them go.

"Well, I'll be damned!" We hear our father laugh. Jack and I follow the others across the diner. It *does* look more familiar on the other side.

"Damn," our father says, laughing, slapping his thigh. "She's right!" Clyde slaps his thigh too and laughs loudly like our father, only his laugh is fake, an imitation. "Good for you, Lila!" our father says. He loves it when he's shown up to be a fool.

By the time we finish eating, it's dark. At night the road looks different, the red lights going away from us, the white lights coming toward us. Someone has to stay awake to keep our father awake. Lila and I pinch ourselves hard on the neck or inside of the thigh. Sometimes our father pulls over to sleep. He tilts the seat back. If you're wide awake, you have to just sit there quietly. Or else he turns the radio on. This always helps because the love songs drive him crazy. "Mandy" by Barry Manilow came on the radio.

"Jesus Christ, listen to this horseshit! Now this is the kind of crock of shit only grown-ups would come up with."

"Grown-ups?" we say, "What's wrong with grown-ups?"

"What's *wrong* with grown-ups? What *isn't* wrong with grown-ups?" We're speeding through the night. We all lean up to listen, except Clyde who's asleep. We love it when our father rants and raves about grown-ups. "The real problem," he explains, "the overall problem, is that grown-ups think they're smarter than kids. When the fact of the matter is, the older you grow, the dumber you get. What happens is that you start hoarding up opinions. Pretty soon you've got an opinion stuck to everything and, before you know it, your poor little brain is so crowded with opinions the damned thing forgets how to think! Now if grown-ups would only listen to their kids, if they'd listen to their kids, they might learn a thing or two." I laugh. Jack grips his hands in his lap, excited. I can see Lila smiling to herself in the dark.

When our father brings a girlfriend along, things are different. She takes the front seat. The four of us in the back are crushed and quieter, waiting to see what she'll say. No matter what, we know we're in for a surprise.

Each of our father's girlfriends is weirder than the one before. There's Ginny, with a bowl haircut, who gets very nervous in the car. She keeps clutching the dashboard and the emergency brake. Whenever we stop, she gets out and walks off to the edge of the parking lot to try to calm herself down. Marcia puts a tape of people chanting mantras in the tape deck. Once when we go to a modern dance performance with her, instead of clapping along with everyone else, she lifts her arms up high in the air and twists her hands silently back and forth. Suzanne is a miniature person, so tiny you feel that she could fit into a box.

Although our father's girlfriends are very different from one another, not one of them, in any case, is at all like our mother, which turns them into a group. The unspoken line when we meet them is that our mother is the woman our father still loves, even though she told him to leave, and they, the girlfriends, are nothing more than stand-ins. We prefer it, of course, when our father comes on his own, but if a girlfriend's there, we're always curious. It's like an experiment in our science class. You put something in a petri jar, then nudge it, add water, waiting to see what it'll do.

For instance, our enthusiasm is sparked again by Ginny when we discover that she can't spell. We realize this one night in a hotel room when we sit down to play Boggle. Even the littlest, Clyde, can spell a few things. But when she comes up with a list of the most childishly misspelled words, we can't believe our eyes. At first we just stare at her, stunned. We hadn't realized that such a thing could happen to a grown-up. Then, without laughing, we're merciless. We very politely correct each word. Whenever possible, we take a special delight in letting Clyde do it. From then on, we insist on playing Boggle at every opportunity, over lunch, in the car. Even if she refuses, it's enough of a pleasure simply to be playing in front of her.

One day our father brings a woman named Abigail. She's the weirdest of all. She has her jaw wired shut due to an operation to get a bigger chin. This means she can only speak through a clenched jaw and take in liquids.

What's our father thinking? With these girlfriends, it's as if he's trying to convince himself of the uselessness of pursuing any woman but our mother and, with such peculiar choices, he proves himself right over and over again. Not that he isn't pretty weird himself. He is—he even tries to be. In this way, his girlfriends are like expressions of his own weirdness, in which he delights, but they never seem to step beyond that role. Until Lonnie.

It's our spring break and our father's coming to take us to our grandmother's in New England. This is where we go to ski in the winter and, when it's warmer, we sail or swim. We'd thought our father was coming on his own, but when he drives in, we see, to our annoyance, that there's a woman in the car. From our perches, on the porch railing, at the edge of the driveway, up above on the swing, we're all ready to attack her, however silently, but then stop. She's the kind of woman we've only seen in magazines or on the rare occasions when we've watched TV—we don't have a TV at our house—but never in real life. Stepping out of the car and shaking out her perfumed hair, she looks like an exotic bird that's just landed on our lawn. She wears a see-through lime green blouse that clings to her breasts, a yellow skirt that stops above her knees. Her hair is long and curly and dyed orange-red, her eyelashes long and thick, her lips glossed and shiny. This is a kind of glamour that has nothing to do with the hippie style of our mother and her friends. Suddenly, we feel ashamed of the way we look, our straggly hair and corduroys. We feel ashamed of our yard, which is muddy from the rain. How is she supposed to get from the car to the porch in those high block heels?

She wobbles her way over, leans down and kisses us. She's brought presents, perfumes for my sister and me, shaving brushes for the boys. "For when you're old enough," she says in a playful voice. Jack, his eyes on her, mesmerized, brushes the shaving brush back and forth across his chin. "And until then, you can use them to tickle girls." She laughs, winks at our father.

Only Clyde, it seems, is exempt—he's beating on the back of our father's leg with a stick, too much his own ball of energy to pay attention to anything else for long. But the rest of us are spellbound. No, she's definitely not "one of us." But is she maybe better instead of worse?

Once in the car, she promptly starts talking, in her light, flat, playful voice, like a girl's. Jack, sitting on the hump in the middle, leans up close between the two seats and stares at her. She turns to kiss him. "This is my little man," she says. His cheeks are already bright red as always; now the edges of his ears flame too.

She looks back at Lila and me. "I've been dying to meet you," she says. "You know your father talks about you all the time. Ever since the first time we met. Did you tell them how we met?" she asks him. "Your father wooed me at a party with his dancing. You know, he's a wonderful dancer. Do you girls like to dance? No one these days knows how to dance like that. Only aristocrats." She giggles. "So I knew right away he must be an aristocrat. An aristocrat in hiding, is what I thought. Because no aristocrat who wasn't hiding would wear such goofy clothes." She giggles again. "And I was right! Of course I was right! I'm always right about a man. So anyway, we danced. Everyone else was doing, you know, whatever funky dance, jiggling around, and then they put on a waltz and everyone got afraid except your father. I could see he wanted to dance. I was standing right there, looking at him. I don't know how to waltz either, but I figured I could learn." She hits our father lightly on the arm. "I figured there were a lot of things I could learn from an aristocrat."

"What's an aristocrat?" Jack whispers to Lila.

Lila shrugs, putting up her hands. "Like kings and queens." She stares back at Lonnie, squinting, listening, trying to understand what she means.

I forget to peer out at the roadside houses, the rocks rising. I can't take my eyes off Lonnie. It's as if we've caught by accident a butterfly in the petri dish and rather than scrutinizing it, have become hypnotized.

Most astonishing of all is that our father is mute. This is the first time we've seen this happen in our lives.

"When I went to Europe, I thought I was going to see aristocrats left and right," Lonnie goes on. "And, of course, I didn't see a single one! I told you about my trip to Europe, didn't I?" she says to our father, then turns back to us. "A man took me. He was very in love with me. But I said I'd only go if he didn't lay a finger on me." She giggles and puts out one dainty finger. "And he didn't. He didn't the whole time. I knew he wouldn't."

Then it occurs. Right in the middle of Lonnie's chatter, someone farts. We can't believe it. Mortified, we don't say anything at first. Lila very subtly rolls her window down. Only Clyde has no clue and acts the same as if it were any old day.

"Dad!" he yells.

"What?" our father asks.

I quickly hit Clyde on the leg, but it's too late.

"You farted!" Clyde yells, grabbing his leg.

"What?" our father asks, in his mock innocent voice. "Have I ever farted?"

Lonnie laughs her girlish laugh. "That's another thing I've learned. Only aristocrats fart like that."

"Damn!" our father says, leaning his head back. It's the look he gets when one of us has done or said something he finds wonderful. He couldn't be more pleased.

Last year, before it got too cold, we had been going with our father to leap off quarry cliffs. Now he's found out about a quarry that's right off the route to our grandmother's and wants to take us there.

"You got your suits, right?" he asks us, as he veers off the main road. Yes, we've brought our bathing suits. He nudges Lonnie, "You? You got your suit?"

"Oh, I couldn't," Lonnie says, "Jump off a cliff? I'd be much too scared. But I'll watch all of you."

Now we don't want to go either. It means walking through the woods. How will she ever manage in her sandals? Her legs will get scratched. Burrs and leaves will stick in her hair. Suddenly, this seems a dirty and boring pursuit.

But our father insists. We're going down side roads, our father ducking and peering to see if he's found the spot. Finally, we stop in front of something that looks like a path. Our father parks the car and gets out. "C'mon, c'mon, c'mon," he says, since we seem to be lingering.

We trudge back along the bramble-lined path. I see Lonnie up ahead, picking aside the brambles gingerly with her fingers so she can pass.

"Why do we have to do this?" I ask.

Our father, right in front of me, turns and looks back, truly surprised. I'm the one who's usually up for anything. "What d'you mean, why do we have to do this? Jesus Christ, I thought this was *all* you wanted to do!"

In some of the quarries, the water is crystal clear, but this time it's muddy. We're going to plunge into muddy water right before Lonnie's eyes. We climb the cliff grudgingly. She waits below, a lime green and yellow figure by the side of the water. I'm the first to leap. When I'm in the air, I hear Lonnie scream. Then when I come up again, my head bobbing on the surface of the water, she jumps up and down and claps her hands. "Whoo-ee!" she calls. She leans down to greet me as I swim over. "That was fantastic!" she says. Okay, I think, so maybe this isn't so bad. I pull myself out of the water. It's freezing, March, my skin is all blue. But this is definitely worth it all the same. Lonnie will clap and scream and jump up and down. The others leap behind me. Lonnie does the same for them. They beam too as they climb out of the water and then we all swagger as best we can midst our shivering up the cliff to do it again.

Afterward, we stop at a gas station. We're wet and bedraggled, but Lonnie looks splendid. When she steps out of the car, all the men look at her. Lila brings a comb with her into the bathroom to try to fix her hair. She usually wouldn't bother, but it's because Lonnie's there.

"Here," Lonnie says, "can I help you do that? You have the prettiest hair, you two. So thick." She begins combing out Lila's hair and fixes the part. "Your father's just wonderful to me," she says as she works. "I only tell him these stories about other men to make him jealous." She turns on the hand dryer and makes Lila stand in front of it to dry her hair. Next she turns to me. Her perfume, when she's this near, is rising off her skin. Whereas I always tear at my hair, she's very gentle. Once it's all combed out straight, she turns on another dryer and has me stand there.

Then she looks at herself in the mirror, her face and hair. She opens her purse and takes out a makeup bag. Lila and I watch as she touches herself up, putting a layer or two more of mascara, pats of powder and lip gloss. "Hey!" she says, turning, "Do you two want me to make you up?" Usually it's a race between us and the boys to see who's done first in the bathroom. Now we're taking so long, but we don't care. Lila and I nod. Lila steps up first because her hair is already dry. Lonnie makes her close her eyes. She puts eye shadow on Lila's lids and curls her lashes.

"You don't want mascara," she says. "Mascara's messy." She dabs lip gloss on Lila's lips and a touch of blush on her cheeks. "There!" she says, stepping back and looking. She steps near again, wetting a finger in her mouth and shaping Lila's eyebrows. My hair is dry now. Lonnie runs her hands through it. She shivers. "Oh, it's like silk," she says. She puts makeup on me too. I love the feeling, eyes closed, of her cool, smooth hands running over my face.

Our father knocks on the bathroom door. "What's the hold up?"

"It's a surprise, you'll see," Lonnie says.

"Jesus!" we hear him say, turning away. We giggle. We know how he hates just hanging around.

When we come out, our father's back in the car with the boys. Both Lila and I have eye shadow on and very pink cheeks.

"Look at them," Lonnie says, "Did you ever see such pretty girls?"

Lila, with her makeup on, has an uncertain smile.

"What do you have on?" Clyde asks. He swipes at Lila's face.

Jack looks at us for a minute then goes back to staring at Lonnie. "This one doesn't need makeup," Lonnie says, rubbing Jack's chubby cheeks and kissing him.

Our father snorts a little. Besides having been made to wait around, this, makeup and so on, is not at all his line.

Usually with our father we stay in a cheap hotel. Or we just drive straight the whole way through, him stopping to lie back for naps now and then. But this time, he's made arrangements to spend the night with a friend of his in Boston. We twist and turn our way through Boston until we find the street; quiet, clean, lined with large trees. The house is a brownstone, the door painted a shiny dark blue. Our father holds Clyde up so he can bang the knocker. He bangs it loud.

The man who appears, our father's friend George, looks much older than our father though they're the same age. Amazingly tall, with a protruding belly, he already looks like an old man.

"Good Lord," he says to our father, "what a wondrous shirt." As he says hello to Lonnie, a slight smile plays at the corners of his lips. He gives the four of us perfunctory nods, then leads us all into the house.

The house is dark inside and, though it's the height of spring, it feels like winter here, the windows small and lots of dark furniture all around. A woman, who must be a maid—though we've never seen a maid, but she wears a black and white costume—peers out of a door.

"Do you need anything?" she asks.

"No, no, that's fine, we'll eat when Maeve returns," George says. "Maeve's out teaching a class," he says over his shoulder, leading us down a dark hallway.

"She's teaching, is she?" our father asks. "A professor, you said? Damn! Good for her."

"Well yes, I suppose so." George sounds surprised.

We follow him down the hall to a room where there's a TV on. Two kids are there. They look up.

"Say hello, boys," George says.

The boys, his sons, look just tiny, given their father's massive size, and seem to be sitting on miniature doll chairs. Or at least one of them does. The other is handicapped and in a wheelchair. He's very frail. His arms and legs wobble. The first one, short, pale and chubby, sits very near to take care of his brother.

At first we feel offended by being brought in here. When he's ranting about grown-ups, our father goes on and on about how stupid people are not to want kids around.

"And," we ask, egging him on, "what about parties where there are no kids allowed?"

"No kids allowed?! Who would want to go to a party where there were no kids allowed?"

These children, it seems, are always shut up in here.

But we stop thinking about it a moment later because we're watching TV. Since we never watch TV, we don't know how to do it. I look at Jack. He hasn't even sat down but his eyes are already spinning. Clyde sits open-mouthed, very close to the screen, his legs tucked underneath him. Lila and I are soon doing the same. We forget about everything, the boys, the house, even our father and Lonnie. We don't know how much time has passed when the maid comes to get us. The maid pushes the boy in the wheelchair into the dining room and the rest of us follow behind.

The dining room is dark, with a dark wood oiled table and a sideboard. George's wife, Maeve, is there. She has dark hair, slim legs, and an ironic expression that never seems to go away. She, like the rest of the family, wears somber clothes, burgundy and dark blue. We all look completely out of place, our father in his hippie clothes, Lonnie in her transparent lime green blouse, Lila and I in our velour V-necks from JCPenney, and Jack, with the Indian belt he wove himself, holding up his corduroys. The boy in the wheelchair is placed at one end and the rest of us kids around him.

The maid brings out the food, a meat and potato stew in a deep dish. Lonnie, as usual, immediately starts talking. "Are you really a professor?" she asks Maeve.

"I am," the woman says, smiling her ironic smile.

"I think that's wonderful," Lonnie says. "So romantic."

Maeve's laugh sounds like a bark. "Well, I don't know about that. What do you do?" Maeve asks. She has a throaty voice. She doesn't look at Lonnie as she's asking because she's serving herself food.

Lonnie clasps her hands and props her chin on them. "Oh, nothing," she says, "loll around."

Maeve looks at her, raising one dark eyebrow.

"That's not true," our father says, pointing at Lonnie. "She's a n- n- nurse. And not just any kind of nurse. She works in a mental institution."

This is news to us. We all look at Lonnie. I try to picture her in nurse's uniform, with those white shoes. She must look very pretty, I decide. I picture the part around her boobs very tight.

"Did you have to tell them that?" Lonnie says, playfully, looking down at her hands. "Well, anyway, that's just my day job." She flutters her eyelids and laughs. Suddenly, as opposed to Maeve, she seems to have the most charming giggly laugh.

Our father persists, still pointing at Lonnie. He must be nervous because he's stuttering. "She p- p- put herself through college and nursing school all on her own—"

"Oh, come on, let's not talk about that," Lonnie says. "I want to talk about other things, romantic things, art and literature. That's what we came here for. Isn't that what you all usually talk about?"

There's a beat of awkward silence. Lonnie looks around, dazzled, then down at her plate. "These plates are so pretty!" she says, "Are they new?"

"No, no, dear," George says, that same amused expression on his face he had when he first saw her, "those plates are very old."

Lonnie blushes. "Oh well, of course, listen to how gauche I am. They're very pretty anyway. I guess the oldest things are the prettiest, like those paintings. I guess those paintings are very old too."

"Why, yes dear, they are."

Lonnie puts her flirty eyes. "Do you call all women 'dear' or only the ones who ask silly questions?"

"No, not at all, your questions are most perspicacious," George says. He leans back, folding his long-fingered hands on his chest, and smiles. He seems to be enjoying this.

"See now, there's a word I don't know," Lonnie says. "I knew I'd learn things if I met some of Sam's friends. I asked him, I said, on this trip I want to meet some of your friends, not your new friends—he's got the weirdest friends now—but your old friends from the past. But he keeps you all in hiding, I don't know why. If I had such nice friends, I'm sure I'd introduce them to everyone. I'd bring whole troops of people in here."

George, listening for a moment, then turns to our father and addresses him, interrupting. "You sure ducked out of sight," he says. "What have you been up to?"

Lonnie looks very surprised. Although the rest of us are still listening to her, she lets her story peter out.

"Aww, all kinds of things," our father says. He's acting different, not like himself. "Writin' a bit, got some other projects, started up a little business."

"Oh, really? What kind of business?"

"Roofing. We do roofs."

"Roofs?! Good Lord, you're just as bullocks as ever! Have you kept up with any of our partners in crime at the AD?"

"Naww, not so much."

"C'mon, fella, where's your allegiance? A group of us get together once a month."

"Oh, yeah, who do you see?"

Lonnie leans across the table toward us and asks in a loud whisper, "What's the AD?"

Lila shrugs, lifts her hands. "Dad, what's the AD?" she interrupts.

George looks confused by such impertinence from a child. Maeve is watching all of us, amused, as if we were a circus act.

"Aww, it's a club at Harvard," our father says.

"What's Harvard?" I ask. Lonnie laughs delightedly.

"It's a school where George and I went."

George has a kind of harrumphing laugh. "Well, you've certainly been keeping them in the dark," he says.

"Oh yes," Lonnie says, "he's been keeping us all in the dark. About everything. Believe me, he's got things up his sleeve. And I don't mean just you two. I mean all sorts of projects, not to mention women. And here I am an open book. I guess all aristocrats are secretive, aren't they?" She turns to Maeve, pointing at George, "Is he secretive too? I tell everything. He knows about all the men I've dated and slept with. I've told him all the stories. I try to make him jealous, but he doesn't get jealous.

Isn't that the weirdest thing?" Again turning to Maeve and pointing at George, "Does he get jealous? Maybe that's another trait—"

"Charming, you're charming, dear," George interjects, as if trying to put some order into the proceedings. "Yes, we're all very secretive, aren't we? I, for example, hardly ever enumerate to my wife the women I slept with before I met her. Or perhaps I did once. Did I once, darling?"

"Yes, dear, once," Maeve says, "in Cairo, right before the war."

"Cairo? Before the war?" Lonnie looks confused. There's a tremor on her lips, though she keeps her smile. "You're making fun of me, aren't you?"

"No, dear, not at all," George says.

"Why do you seem to have a British accent?" Lonnie asks. "Are you British? Or is it just a little play-acting? We all do a little play-acting, don't we, even aristocrats, to get by?"

George, annoyed, scrapes back his chair. "I think we've finished here, haven't we?" He calls the maid. "We'll have coffee in the living room."

Everyone stands. Lonnie's comment was a barb, but now she looks sorry. George is already lighting up a cigar. He doesn't look at her. There's a move toward the living room, George first. The chubby son pushes the one in the wheelchair out past the living room and down the hall again to where the TV room is. Clyde follows them. But Lila, Jack, and I linger in the hall, not sure where we're supposed to go. Our father, George, and Maeve are already sitting down in the living room. Lonnie has gone to the bathroom. When she reappears coming down the hall, she says to us in a whisper, "Let's go watch TV, okay?"

She pauses in the door of the living room. "I'm going to go watch TV with them," she says. "I'll let you aristocrats talk amongst yourselves."

George looks relieved, but our father seems disappointed. He holds out a hand to Lonnie. "Honey," he says, to our surprise. We've never heard him call a woman "honey" before. But Lonnie's decision has been made.

We bring her into the TV room with us. We sit down on the couch with her, Lila and me on one side, Jack on the other. We hand her the flicker so she can choose a good channel. We find her a blanket for her bare knees. "Oh, whew," she says, still blushing, recovering, "This is so much more fun in here with you."

The next day begins as the previous one, only something seems to have shifted in the night. Who decides it? Me? Lila? We have to get rid of Lonnie, or depose her at least. She requires too much attention. She's disrupted everything. Our father has been silenced, he calls her "honey"; we're all decorous now. Gone are the games, the farts, the hair-flying fun. The night before at dinner we saw her weak spot. This gives us a grip. We're no longer helpless, blindly enthralled.

Once again, in the car, Lonnie begins chattering right away. "Spanish men are just wonderful. Have you ever dated a Spanish man? Well, I guess, of course, you haven't. Though your father might have, knowing him." She giggles. "Your father's a complete schizophrenic, you know that, right? But that's what I seem to like, crazy people. I spend my life surrounded by them. At least they're always full of surprises. Your father is definitely always full of surprises. And that's what a woman wants, isn't it, to be surprised? It's the biggest aphrodisiac."

"What's an aphrodisiac?" Lila asks, but differently now, warily.

"Oh, they don't need to know this yet, do they?" Lonnie says. "It's what your father has. It's what brings the girls around. Everyone's in love with your father. Wherever we go, all the girls are wild for him."

I give a little snort, picking up on our father's snort yesterday over the makeup.

Jack sits slowly back. Lila sighs, looking out the window. Lonnie must have felt us all pulling away, but chatters valiantly on.

"I think the Italians are way overrated. That's just a movie myth. The ones I've met all look like worms."

She takes out some lip gloss and puts it on, then hands it back to Lila and me.

"No thanks," Lila says, her hand flopping down casually, staring back out the window again. I'm torn. I remember how the lip gloss felt on my lips the day before and how it had the nicest strawberry taste. "No thanks," I say, my voice a bit weak.

"Are you sure?" Lonnie asks.

I nod, somewhat pained.

"It stinks in here," Clyde says after a moment.

We all look at him. We don't smell anything.

"Did someone fart?" Jack asks. We're not even worried now about talking about farts in front of Lonnie, whereas yesterday we were so concerned.

"No, it's not a fart," Clyde says, laughing, slapping his knee. "It smells like something else. Even stinkier."

"Perfume," Lila and I murmur softly in unison.

Lonnie turns around in her seat and gives us a quick stung look, then addresses Clyde. "You don't like my perfume?" There's a tremor on her lips, that same tremor that was there the night before, only she kept trying to smile. Everyone sees it except for Clyde. He's not even looking.

"No, I don't!" he says, laughing.

"All right, Clyde," our father says. "That's enough."

We drive on for a little while. Lonnie actually isn't talking. When she starts again, her voice sounds different. Not so much like a little girl's. "You know, I didn't have a childhood like you all do. You're very lucky. You have two parents who love you. You don't have to work all the time. You're free to play. We lived in a trailer. My father abandoned us. I worked nonstop. I almost never had any fun."

Our father looks over at her, uneasily.

She tries to rally one last time, in her girlie voice again, giving our father eyes. "That's why I've made up for it as an adult."

Our father laughs with relief, but we, by this point, are all looking away.

A little while later, in the gas station bathroom, in what seems like a last ditch effort, Lonnie tells Lila and me that she's so in love. Our father, she says, is the love of her life. Lila, without looking at her, shakes the water off her hands. I eye Lonnie warily. I go into one of the stalls after her.

"Did you write that on the wall?" I ask.

She giggles. On the wall in the bathroom were the words "Lonnie will marry Sam this year" in lipstick. Lila goes into the stall to look too and comes back out and stares at Lonnie. Lonnie blushes.

"Yes, I did."

"Why?" I ask, on my lip a slight sneer.

"Why? Because I wanted to. Didn't you ever like a boy and write his name on a wall?"

"No," both Lila and I answer.

"Well, you should."

"Why?" I ask.

"We don't want to," Lila says.

We can tell from the look on Lonnie's face that she sees that everything has changed. She turns to the mirror and fixes her makeup silently. Lila and I head for the door.

Later, it occurs to me that Lonnie illustrated perfectly one of our father's favorite lines: "I may look dumb." He loved the idea of someone "looking dumb." Her Barbie doll act was just that, an act, the way she'd come up with of getting by.

Back in the car again, we drive on. Lonnie is quiet. Sensing something wrong, our father jokes around a bit. But he seems to be waiting for Lonnie to talk and can't get his usual monologue off the ground. After a little while, Lonnie asks if we can stop again, saying she has to use the bathroom. Once our father pulls over, she steps out, taking her purse and then, leaning down at the window, asks for the keys. Our father hands her the keys. She goes around and opens the trunk, takes out her bag, baby pink, and comes back around.

"Thanks," she says, leaning down, dropping the keys on the passenger seat, "I'm going. Your kids, you know, are mean."

We're all struck silent, as she walks off. Only then does our father make a move. "Jesus Christ," he says, getting out of the car and following her into the office. We can see the two of them through the glass window. Lonnie has asked the guys behind the counter to use the phone and is making a call when our father comes in. He waits for her to finish. When she puts the receiver down, he begins gesturing, pointing back to the car. She shakes her head, her long red curls flopping around. He moves toward her. She steps back. He throws his arms up in the air, in a helpless gesture. The guys behind the counter are watching with the animated faces of spectators fully engrossed in the show. Lonnie starts talking forcefully, pointing a finger at our father. Then she's yelling. He puts his hands up in front of his face, as if he's being hit by hail. A blue cab pulls up in front of the office. Lonnie picks up her bag and steps out. Our father dodges gingerly after her. Outside, she gets in the cab and slams the door. He taps on the window. She doesn't look. A few seconds later, the cab drives off. She doesn't look back at any of us.

Our father stands outside the office, looking after the cab. Then he looks over at us and raises his hands again, helpless, in the air. He slinks back to the car. "Damn!" he says, getting in. We kids are all a bit excited. This is surely exciting. Of course it would have been more so had Lonnie screamed more. And if it had gone on. If she hadn't driven off like that without looking back. We giggle nervously. But much too soon, the blue cab is out of sight.

Our father leans back for a moment, hands in his lap, staring out the windshield. We almost never see him like this, not talking or moving. Then he starts the car. Lila climbs through the space between the seats into the front. We drive out of the gas station, drive on. Silence. No one talks. Isn't this what we'd wanted? The situation was impossible. There was no question. She had to go. I glance around, but no one is looking at one another. Are we ecstatic, triumphant? Do we feel that we've done a terrible thing? Have we even *done* anything at all? I lean up to look at our father's face. He's staring out impassively at the road. I settle back and stare out too. We're on the highway. The landscape looks lonely, the cliffs and road signs, the wayside houses.

As we drive on, I keep noticing for some reason the deposits of roadside trash, tumbling down the hills beyond the guardrails. You can see the way the stuffed armchairs, the bedsprings, and toilet bowls have dropped and, by their own weight, bumped down the hill. I know that Lonnie went off of her own accord, yet I can't help feeling at the same time that we dumped her. That we rolled her out of the front seat and dumped her by the roadside. Sitting there, I can almost feel it, the strain in my arms, from heaving a body out of the car.

From Gone

Toby Talbot

Toby Talbot's books include A Book About My Mother, Early Disorder, The World of the Child, *several children's books, and, most recently,* The New Yorker Theater and My Life at the Movies. *For many years she was the cultural editor of* El Diario de New York. *She runs the Lincoln Plaza Cinema with her husband, and teaches Spanish literature and translation at New York University, as well as documentary film at The New School. The following piece is an excerpt from* Gone, *a novel.*

Anna: December

BARCELONA WAS A GHOST TOWN. EMPTY STREETS, shops closed, shutters lowered for the midday break. It was 1:35 p.m. when Anna checked into El Duque Hotel on the Passeig de Gràcia. She remembered the hour, for the receptionist, glancing at the clock through steel-rimmed glasses, said she was early and that her room wasn't quite ready, but it wouldn't be long. She was startled at being addressed by her maiden name, having forgotten it was the one under which she'd made the reservation. When asked for her passport, she said it was in her luggage. The clerk, noting her reluctance to be served a refreshment in the lobby, suggested the bar.

Settled grudgingly on a stool, she sipped juice from fresh Valencian blood oranges. The barman was alone. He set a dish of almonds before her, and remarked on this unseasonably hot November weather: a loyal native, apologetic to tourists for unseemly spells of heat, cold, or rain. To show appreciation for his civic concern she nodded, whereupon another small dish, green olives stuffed with anchovies, appeared.

In Madrid it was twenty-nine degrees, he told her, and so dry that people had been hospitalized for dehydration. "*Tiempo feo*"; he screwed his brow at foul weather. As Anna set to calculating the Fahrenheit equivalent of twenty-nine degrees centigrade—in the eighties probably—she heard his voice in the background: "But that's Madrid for you."

OPEN CITY

The eternal rivalry of two cities: Barcelona berating Madrid's provincialism, snobbism, and indolence; Madrid spurning the other's materialism.

Here she was, in the same mirrored lounge as on that first visit—nine, ten years ago? The same blue carpet, the same tufted maroon leather chairs. Arturo, invited by his Spanish publisher, had insisted that she come. It was shortly after their marriage; she was his mooring, he insisted, and not just the translator of *We the Disappeared*, his book about being kidnapped and tortured in Argentina. Hard to believe that Arturo, given up for drowned last July, was in Barcelona now.

Mentally, she replayed the scene of the dance in Selores, the village where she'd been visiting Wendy and Gregorio: *"What the hell are you talking about!"* she shouted when Wendy drunkenly blurted out the news that Arturo was alive. Grabbing Wendy by the shoulders, she shook her and kept shaking her: tt was like shaking a rag doll. Suddenly the music, with a discordant scraping of the fiddle, stopped. Dancers came to a halt, glued to their spots, holding each other like figures trapped in Pompei. Firecrackers exploded in Anna's head; Wendy remained mute. Anna dug her fingers into the doll's arms and imagined clawing her till all the sawdust fell out. "Talk! Say something!" she commanded. Wendy, sweating, eyes bulging, jaw limp, put up no struggle.

Their neighbor Cuca came over and separated them. *"No, hija, no!"*

For days, immobilized by shock, Anna sat in front of her translation of Arturo's book, scheduled to be published posthumously. How could it be? How could the person she trusted most engage in such deception ...after all she'd done for him. These last months of loss, hope, and then mourning were sheer delusion—the double bereavement. At one point she came close to tearing up the manuscript: *Get the hell out of my life!*

When Wendy was asked for details, she only shook her head. Her husband, Gregorio, loyal to Arturo, had bound her to secrecy. Did Wendy know more than she revealed, but was loathe to be a messenger of bad tidings?

Why was Arturo in hiding? Had he committed a crime—though knowing him so well (or did she?), criminal behavior seemed unlikely. Had he received threats from the Argentine secret police and vanished in order to protect her? The words of *We the Disappeared* rang in her ears: *I live in fear of being alive. I'm the memory of a life, and memory fills me with fear.*

680

Yet, fury aside, what a relief knowing he was alive. An incredible, god-damn relief. And by the end of the week, she set out to find him. To confront him, accuse him, abandon him.

Gregorio had insisted on driving her to the airport in Santiago de Compostela, almost an hour away, though she wanted to take the train. She glared at his banalities: "It's a process . . . It's in God's hands . . . Time will tell." More than once, he assured her that Arturo was well: "I spoke to him just last week." But he could not, or would not, predict the precise date of his return. What to believe? Somehow, she believed Gregorio when he gave her Arturo's most recent phone number, and believed when he vowed that Angel had left no forwarding address.

At the gate, he waved goodbye, Wendy did not, her face a chalky mask. "Be sure and phone us," were her last words.

"*La señora Pereda, por favor.*" A bellhop entered the lounge: Room 317 was ready.

Anna paced up and down before the phone, preparing what to say if Arturo answered—a voice from the grave. Spinning zero for an outgoing line, she dialed the number in her notebook. The phone rang four times before a machine with a woman's voice answered in Catalan. All Anna could decipher was *vacaciones.*

Güell Park had been one of Arturo's favorite spots in Barcelona. Set on a mountain overlooking the city, it was close to the cemetery where his parents were buried. Antonio Gaudí, its visionary creator, and a virtual recluse, had been run over by a tram in 1926 on his way to church. A pale, bearded man, God knows how old or young, gospel book in hand, rusty black jacket fastened by safety pins, empty pockets. No ID.

The four spires of his renowned church, the Sagrada Capilla, dominated the city. "It's the best place to worship," Arturo had remarked, standing in its hollow center exposed to the sky, towers soaring above like candles of molten wax. "No sermon, open air, not one straight line." Unfinished, like Gaudí's life.

Now, wending her way through the spiraled arcade of the park, asymmetrical pillars leaning in, it felt like treading beneath waves of curling rock. Each bend yielded echoes of children playing hide-and-seek, and glints of Arturo's image. She headed for the Crocodile Plaza with its serpentine ceramic bench. A riot of greens, reds, yellows, and purples, embedded with shards of crockery—tiles, plates, bottles collected by Gaudí's workers. Leaning back against the shimmering mosaic, arms outstretched, she felt herself becoming part of that constellation of curlicues, icons, and cryptographs.

Children, deaf to maternal admonition, clambered gleefully on the ceramic paws and flanks of the Crocodile, poking their fingers into its harmless maw—little Pinocchios flirting with the whale. A wedding party was gathering for photographs around a newlywed couple, bride in ivory satin, groom in dove-gray morning coat. Young couples strolled by, arms linked, dutiful daughters guided elderly mothers, pensioners with canes and berets conversed in Catalan. Anna felt her solitude keenly.

Wife shadowing husband. How original! A Dashiell Hammett yarn: shadow-shade-spirit-ghost. *I have a little shadow that goes in and out with me, and what can be the use . . .* The verities of children's chants; shadows indeed left no footsteps. Anna Santos Pereda, a dangling marionette, movements decreed by a phantom puppeteer. Damn this tired script, damn Arturo! What in the world had prompted this vanishing act? Something *she* had done? Or had he simply flipped? Guess again. Another woman? Supposing she found them, in some nice little roost? In Spain, under Franco, a crime of passion bore small penalty. Her thoughts rambled on, disjointed as the bits and pieces of Gaudí's bench. She shut her eyes to blot them out. But a child's laughter and a mother's outcry penetrated: *"Juanito, ven aca!"*

"Se puede?" She looked up. Silhouetted against the sun, with camera and tripod, was the wedding photographer. Yes, she *did* mind. With hundreds of yards of bench, why must he plant himself here? But she merely shrugged, since he was already seated and arranging his gear. Locking a pouch, closing straps, folding the tripod into his black canvas bag.

Busywork done, he turned to survey the panorama. Treetop foliage, terra-cotta roofs, church spires, and yonder the sea. Linking thumb and index finger, he encircled his eye as to frame a shot, then swung around to observe the children perched on the crocodile. Finally, with background and foreground exhausted, he turned to her.

Dubrovnik

Cannon Thomas

*Cannon Thomas was born in Youngstown, Ohio and now lives in Manhattan.
He's written for* The Philadelphia Inquirer, The Dallas Morning News, *and
many other newspapers. "Dubrovnik" is an excerpt from a novel in progress
and was his debut publication.*

DUBROVNIK WALKED DOWN THE HALL FROM HIS
bedroom and entered the living room, shuffling softly
over the construction-orange carpet in a pair of
moose-hide slippers that he more or less lived in since
he'd moved back in with his parents. Dubrovnik's
mother forbid the wearing of shoes as a preservative
measure for the new carpet. She policed the situation
fairly fanatically. If she saw footprints on her orange
carpet she'd squeal, "Who's wearing shoes?"

Dubrovnik had moved back home to save money after the steel mill
closed. He'd lost his job as an inspector in a tin-plate mill. This reprise
of his childhood was one of the unforeseen consequences of the mill
closing. One of the least analyzed but nevertheless most deeply felt
effects of the ascent of Japan's economy was that Mitchell Dubrovnik no
longer got to wear shoes in his own house.

He noticed his father beached in a blue velour La-Z-Boy on the far
side of the living room. Mr. Dubrovnik was swaddled in a white terry
cloth bathrobe—his chapped and bleeding, toenail-less feet with yellow
patches of dead skin flapping off them, hanging over the edge of the
footrest. He had terrible feet—the ugliest feet most anyone had ever
seen, but he wasn't ashamed of them. He'd gotten something called jungle rot while in the Pacific during the war. The Dubrovniks were proud
of Mr. Dubrovnik's feet. If anybody ever asked about them, it gave them
an opportunity to talk about where Mr. Dubrovnik had been and what
he had done in the war. "He was in the Pacific," someone would say and
everybody knew exactly what that meant. He'd fought the *Japs.*

At the moment Mr. Dubrovnik wasn't doing much of anything. He
was sleeping, on and off. A copy of a book—*The Devil and the Deep Blue*

Sea: My Life as a Navy Seal—was laying facedown and open, bellowing up and down upon his chest.

Dubrovnik was relieved to see that his father was unconscious. It was 11 a.m. and he felt guilty. During these morning appearances he always felt like a prisoner being pulled out of a drunk tank to face the local magistrate. He felt obligated to explain his belated presence to his father, usually greeting him with some detail of a program he'd been watching: *Have you ever seen that penguin documentary? The Charlton Heston one? That thing's incredible. It was on late. Have you seen that? Sixty degrees below and they're outside walkin' around! Charlton Heston says they're the most courageous things on Earth. Sixty degrees below.*

He'd go on like that and Mr. Dubrovnik would grunt and groan, but he'd never get the absolution he was seeking and he usually regretted talking. Mr. Dubrovnik would obliquely change the subject, bringing up, in this case, *Ben-Hur*, his favorite picture. The most Dubrovnik knew of his father's feelings about his nocturnal hours came whenever he'd hear the soft knock on his bedroom door, and his father's voice saying: "Last call for the human race, Mitchell. Last call. Rise and shine."

Today Dubrovnik crept into the kitchen, treating his father like a sentry. He saw the note his mother had left on the refrigerator. In large letters in red Magic Marker it said: MITCHELL! PLEASE EAT THE KIELBASA. He stood still for a minute and listened for the sound of the washer and dryer coming from the basement. Nothing. His mother was apparently out somewhere. "Good for her," he muttered.

Dubrovnik cautiously opened the door to look for the kielbasa. His appetite was subordinate to his mother's need to not throw anything out. Since moving home he sometimes felt she was using his digestive tract as a garbage disposal. He alternated between resentment and, in more elevated and mature moments that never lasted long, the realization that feeding him was the way she showed her love. While her doting may have kept his stomach full it often turned against his other urges. Without saying a word she'd confiscated fireworks out of his closet that he'd brought back from a visit to South Carolina. And his copy of *The Happy Hooker* had disappeared without a word from its hiding place in the lining of his mattress. But he kept quiet about it.

Opening the refrigerator door he saw Tuesday's pork roast sitting in a snowy bed of congealed fat. Sunday's ham was down to the fatty ends near the bottom of the bone, resting on a blue china platter and on its way to becoming ham salad and, finally, navy bean and ham soup. This soup had something of a reputation in the Dubrovnik household based on its historical significance. It was the only dish his father had enjoyed while serving in the Pacific. Whenever it was on the menu the dinner conversation inevitably teed off with this anecdote. It was part of the family gestalt that none of them could look at a ham without thinking about his father's time in the service. And then, finally, in a blue Tupperware crypt hiding behind a large-mouthed bottle of ketchup, Dubrovnik found the kielbasa, enough for two large sandwiches. He went over to the counter and sliced it up, put it between two slices of Lady Lee white bread, and smothered it so thoroughly with ketchup that his sandwich looked like a bandage that needed to be changed.

He sat down to eat at the kitchen table. A copy of the want ads from that morning's *Ironton Vindicator* was waiting for him there. His mother always left them out just to be sure that her son and the want ads would cross paths sometime during the day. Dubrovnik had stopped reading the classifieds six months ago, after a year of unemployment. *What was the use?* he'd thought, somewhat reasonably, with four thousand unemployed steelworkers chasing after a handful of low-paying jobs. Nobody was looking for a sheet inspector in a tin-plate mill, or a hot-mill tapper, or a switchman for dumper cars that fed iron ore into a skyscraper-sized Bessemer converter—or any of the other jobs Dubrovnik had held as a steelworker during the twelve years since he'd graduated high school. Those occupations had been modernized out of existence by a new generation of steelmaking technology that never arrived in his rusty, polluted corner of Ohio.

Most of the unemployed, men with families of their own, had run off to the Sun Belt to become convenience store managers and bank tellers and security guards in non-union towns like Tampa and Houston and Phoenix. But Dubrovnik, thanks to his bachelor status and the graciousness of his parents, got to stay behind in Ironton and wait for better days while eating his mother's cooking.

Sometimes he went out after jobs for the sake of household diplomacy. Once, after his mother pestered him into answering an ad for a swimming pool chemicals salesman, he took revenge on her by responding to an ad for subjects for a medical experiment.

His friend Eddie Richetti, who'd also worked at Sheet and Tube and had hung out with Dubrovnik since high school, had pointed out the ad to him. Doctors at the University of Akron were looking for male subjects between the age of 18–40 to participate in a study of fat cells. For ninety days they would have to consume nothing but protein supplements and raw or steamed vegetables. You couldn't even put anything on the vegetables. Dubrovnik knew this because he asked the nurse who made he and Richetti's appointment for an interview. He'd ask her, "What about oleo?"

The idea of her son selling himself into vegetarianism irritated his mother and Dubrovnik knew it. He couldn't have tweaked her much worse if he'd shaved his head, put on a sarong, and started begging for money at airports. He and Richetti drove up to Akron and tried to sign up. A doctor in a lab coat interviewed them in an office wrapped in frosted glass. The doctor told them that they couldn't drink alcohol during the study, something the ad hadn't mentioned and neither of them had considered. Their idea of the experiment consisted mainly of a fantasy of them living among all those lovely suburban girls who shielded their breasts with their books. They'd both missed out on college. But what sense was their being around all those beautiful girls if they couldn't get drunk? How would they communicate? That news damaged their enthusiasm, but the idea officially died when Dubrovnik's mother had called the Ohio Department of Labor Bureau of Unemployment Compensation and found out that any compensation he took in would cause his benefits to be reduced. Dubrovnik wasn't risking that. Not for $50 per day.

Dubrovnik was still hungry. He went back to the refrigerator, opened it absentmindedly and looked in. His plans for the day were beginning to solidify. He'd spotted a story in the *Vindicator* saying that today the demolition experts were going to blow up the blast furnaces at Ironton Sheet and Tube. A brief campaign to preserve them as a museum had failed due to a lack of government interest. A steel museum was already being planned in Birmingham, Alabama. Ironton would get nothing.

Dubrovnik thought he would watch the demolition. He wasn't sentimental about it. Whatever sentimentality he had about the mills was attached to the men who'd worked in them. Behind the bar in the Dubrovnik basement was a black-and-white photograph taken during his grandfather's days at the mill. It showed a couple of sooty-faced hard-hats smiling beneath a sign at the entrance to the mill that said: DAYS SINCE LAST DISABLING INJURY. A blurry 9 was written below in chalk. No, Dubrovnik wasn't sad about today's events. He simply loved explosions.

He then spotted a single can of Iron City hiding behind a two-pound tub of I Can't Believe It's Not Butter. It was noon. A beer was tempting, as long as he opened it quietly enough not to awaken his father. He pulled the top and the beer let out a loud snake-like hiss.

A couple of minutes into dinner that night Mr. Dubrovnik spoke up on behalf of his favorite vegetable. "I love carrots this way," he said. His mother took it from there. "That's because they're cooked right down in the grease, beside the meatloaf. They really soak up the flavor that way."

Sometime between Dubrovnik's first stint with his parents and his second, food had replaced sex as the medium of exchange in their relationship. That was fine with Dubrovnik. He sat there silently forking his way through his meatloaf, mashed potatoes, and carrots, hoping not to be drafted into the conversation.

Near the end of the first helping his mother poked him. "What's wrong with your milk, Mitchell?" she said.

It took Dubrovnik a second to realize what she was referring to. Then he realized that Mrs. Dubrovnik was speaking rhetorically. She knew exactly what was wrong with his milk: it was getting warm. To her the kilowatts that went into cooling a glass of milk were part of its quantitative value. Her son was throwing money out the window.

"Well, if you're so doggone worried about it then why don't you drink it?" Dubrovnik said, raising the glass to her. "Here! Go for it."

"Put that down," she said. "Stop wasting it."

"Wasting *what?*" he asked.

Dubrovnik's father cleared his throat, his way of warning people he wanted to change the subject. "Mitchell, did everything get blown up OK?" he asked.

"Yeah, yeah," said Dubrovnik.

"Were there a lot of people?" he asked.

"Couple hundred, maybe," Dubrovnik said, without looking up from his plate.

Actually, the demolition disappointed Dubrovnik. The old open hearth went down in a puff of smoke that rose up and swallowed the best parts of the performance. All he saw was a strategic series of blue flashes followed by a rumbling that sounded like a bunch of trash cans being blown down an alley. Then came a blinding cloud of dust that drove everybody back to their cars.

Mr. Dubrovnik rested his palms on the edge of table and pushed his chair back a foot or so. By this gesture he meant that he was about to broaden the scope of the conversation. "They'll all be back," he said, patting his stomach. "As long as we have water, we'll have industry. They're not going to be doing much without our water. That's why they all came here to begin with."

The water theory was Mr. Dubrovnik's sole contribution to economics. It had a biblical ring. It went like this: you couldn't have industry without lots of water. Ironton's industrial success was ordained by nature. They were lucky to live so close to Lake Erie. Companies were disappearing to the Sun Belt for non-union labor and tax breaks. Eventually, the laws of reality would catch up with them. They'd run out of water. They'd come running back.

Mr. Dubrovnik looked at his son. "What are they going to do when they run out of water? What then?"

"I dunno," said Dubrovnik. "Write it off on their taxes."

Dubrovnik had himself lately started thinking of defecting. A friend of his, Anthony, had moved to Atlantic City and he'd been pestering Dubrovnik to take advantage of his couch.

Mrs. Dubrovnik stood at the counter holding an electric knife over a cutting board, staring down an enormous lump of meatloaf.

"Is anybody thinking about more meatloaf?" she asked. In the middle of dinner she usually sought some kind of meat forecast. Mr. Dubrovnik said he'd have more. Dubrovnik turned her down.

"Why don't you do something with your hands, Mitchell?" she asked. "You're good with your hands. I wish you'd use them."

The "good with your hands" thing started in Dubrovnik's high school days. During his junior year he had been caught building pipe bombs in shop class. During a disciplinary conference, Dubrovnik's shop teacher, Mr. Roncone, tried to console Mrs. Dubrovnik by saying repeatedly that he'd never seen a kid quite so good with his hands. In doing so he'd given her her favorite idea of her son—a boy with subtle physical creativity. After graduation she urged Dubrovnik to do something with his hands, but instead he'd gone straight into the mill.

After dinner Dubrovnik marched off to his bedroom. The first thing he saw when he opened the door was a pink envelope sitting on his pillow. Mrs. Dubrovnik always left his mail there. There was only one source of pink envelopes in his life: the Ohio Department of Labor's Bureau of Unemployment Compensation, which used them to deliver urgent bad news. The last one he'd received was a summons to visit the local unemployment office. He'd had to go down and enter the brightly lit linoleum world of the unemployment office, stand in line for a couple of nervous, rubber-legged hours, and meet with a counselor.

His employment counselor was George O'Connell, a big beefy balding red-haired guy whom Dubrovnik suspected was the same George O'Connell who bowled with his parents. Dubrovnik had heard his parents say that this O'Connell had a plate in his head from Korea.

Dubrovnik spent the first part of the interview scouting O'Connell's scalp for signs of staples, stitches, rivets and his bookshelves for anything that might link him to either the Korean conflict or the St. Anthony's bowling league, but all could see were family photos and a couple of unframed certificates conferred by the Northeastern Ohio Development Corporation.

O'Connell asked Dubrovnik what he was doing about a job. Dubrovnik, sensing he wanted something anecdotal, told him how he'd made it to the final interview for a swimming pool supply salesman job. He told O'Connell how, during the second interview, the owner asked him to take a personality test. "I never heard back," Dubrovnik said.

"Did you ever call to find out what had happened?" O'Connell asked.

"No," said Dubrovnik.

"Ahhh, you should always call, always," said O'Connell. "What if the guy had lost your phone number? Geezus, Mitchell, you have to be more persistent. He might have kept you in mind if something came up. A lot of getting a job is luck. The right place at the right time. Always follow up. You never know. Have you ever heard the expression that ninety percent of life is showing up?"

"I missed that," Dubrovnik said.

O'Connell asked Dubrovnik what he'd like to do if he could do anything and Dubrovnik had said he'd like to do something with his hands. He told O'Connell how he'd applied to the Electricians, the Plumbers, and the Carpenters but hadn't heard anything back.

"That's because you don't know anybody," O'Connell said. "You need to know people to get those kinds of jobs."

"What kind of people?" Dubrovnik asked.

O'Connell took his hands out from behind his head and slid on his elbows across his desk toward Dubrovnik until they were nearly nose to nose. "Well, let's put it this way," he said. "It doesn't hurt to be Italian. Not in this town anyways."

O'Connell signed Dubrovnik up for another personality test. "You need to take more advantage of the Department's resources," he said. He ordered him down to the Skills Assessment Center, where he said a woman named Kathy would be waiting with a personality test. Dubrovnik stood up and made a final inspection of O'Connell's skull. It was shiny and spider-veined but without a single trace of shrapnel. O'Connell took Dubrovnik's lingering attention as a sign he was reluctant to go searching for Kathy. "Don't worry, you'll find her," he said. "You can't miss her. Big black hair and bright red dress." Dubrovnik marched down the hall but all he found was a scattering a folding chairs and some blackboard notes. An arrow connecting the words *lazy* and *answering machines*. After a couple of minutes, he bolted.

Now, seeing the pink envelope on his pillow, he wondered if the missed personality test had finally caught up to him. He opened it and read:

MITCHELL AUGUSTUS DUBROVNIK:

THIS IS YOUR FINAL PAYMENT. YOUR CURRENT PERIOD OF ELIGIBILITY HAS EXPIRED. IF YOU WOULD LIKE TO APPLY FOR AN EXTENSION OF BENEFITS OR, IF YOU BELIEVE YOU HAVE RECEIVED THIS NOTICE IN ERROR, THEN CONTACT YOUR LOCAL OFFICE OR CALL 1-800-JOBSNOW, EXT. 17.

Dubrovnik didn't know what to make of it. He lay back on his bed with the notice on his chest. He stared at the swirls of paint on the ceiling. A series of huge explosions were going off on the television on the other side of the wall behind his head. Mr. Dubrovnik was out in the living room digesting and watching *The World at War*. He knew this episode by heart. The Germans were nearly surrounded and escaping back to Paris. The Americans held them in a noose, but Ike, that bureaucrat, was holding back General Patton.

Dubrovnik heard an asthmatic wheeze at his door accompanied by a faint knock. "Mitchell, you alive in there?" It was his father. "What," Dubrovnik said, louder than he meant to.

"Your mother wants to know if you need shoes," he said. "There's a sale here in the paper." He rustled the paper.

"I'll think about it," said Dubrovnik.

His father went away. He went back to thinking. He told himself the state was doing him a favor. He remembered Al Martinelli, a retired electrician who had enormous tufts of hair growing out his ears, saying he had no regrets about things he'd done in his life; it was the things he didn't do that he regretted. "My motto: Do something—even if it's wrong," he'd said. Dubrovnik liked it so much he asked the bartender for a pen and wrote it down on a cocktail napkin beside a drawing of a naked woman lying in a martini glass.

Dubrovnik noticed something fluttering softly outside the window. He sat up and looked out. It was snowing. Snow everywhere. The neighborhood was turning a magical white. He opened the window and inhaled—he liked that cold mentholated taste snow put in the air. He watched a couple of cars make tracks back and forth down the street He pledged that tomorrow, no matter what, he'd call his friend in Atlantic City just to see what was happening.

Anthony told him that Atlantic City was going great guns. He'd made $250 last Saturday night—driving a cab. "Sinatra was in town," he said. Dubrovnik told him he was finally coming out to take a look around.

Dubrovnik spent the rest of the day feeling expansive. For the first time in years his brain was too stimulated to watch TV. He saw himself living on a higher plane—with cameos by Old Blue Eyes and the Atlantic as a backdrop. That night he walked into the living room to to tell his parents. His father was rereading a book about Patton's campaign in Sicily. His mother was knitting, getting a jump on Christmas. Dubrovnik was nervous. After he told them they just sat there looking around the room uncertainly. Then he mentioned Sinatra being there last Saturday. The words popped out of his mouth, almost involuntarily, in a desperate attempt to add some positive weight to his decision. It worked. His parents perked up. "He was here about forty years ago," his mother said. "I have his autograph floating around here somewhere," she said, aiming a knitting needle at the bankers desk in the corner, where the family archives sat amid postage stamps and pile of coupons for antifreeze and antacid. "He was just a skinny kid."

On the morning of Dubrovnik's last day in Ohio his mother accosted him through the bathroom door. "What would you like on your sandwiches?" she asked. She was mad at him for making such a late appearance on a day he needed to drive eight hours to Atlantic City. Talking to him through the bathroom door was her earliest opportunity to show it. She knew he hated talking when he was in the bathroom. And he knew she knew. Nothing was better for making Dubrovnik feel infantile than the sound of his mother's voice just inches away while he was sitting bare-assed on the toilet.

"Mustard," he barked, rooting for her to jump back.

But Mrs. Dubrovnik, a fighter by nature, gladly took one to give one. She stepped back up to the door. "You *want* mustard on turkey. That it?" she said, making mustard on white meat sound incredibly unkosher.

"Yes," he said, "Mustard!"

When Dubrovnik reached the living room his father was waiting. Mr. Dubrovnik had devoted his morning to thinking about his son and the Pennsylvania Turnpike. He worried his son didn't understand the risks.

"Only a guardrail separates you from oncoming traffic," he said. "If it rains you'll be blinded every time you try to pass a truck. And I mean totally blinded."

"Sounds terrible," Dubrovnik said, unconvincingly.

"It used to be much worse," his father said. "Much worse. Your grandfather drove that way before there was a turnpike. Imagine going through those mountains before tunnels."

The legend of the Pennsylvania Turnpike always began with Dubrovnik's grandfather, who blazed the trail from Ohio to Florida, returning with grapefruit, conch shells, and Joe DiMaggio's autograph on the menu of an Italian joint in St. Petersburg. Any time anybody in the household was about to take a long journey by car, the spirit of Augustus Dubrovnik was invoked—the wise grandfather who wrapped his car seats in plastic, belonged to Triple A from the very beginning, and brought road flares, undercoating, and steering wheel clubs into the family.

Dubrovnik couldn't be bothered about the turnpike. He was more worried about the bag of pot he'd lost a couple of months ago. It kept reappearing in the form of miniature nervous breakdowns whenever he was about to leave the house for a spell. He could just see his mother reclaiming his bedroom on behalf of her sewing machine, stumbling into a dime bag and wondering where she'd failed as a parent. Dubrovnik walked to his bedroom, swept his hand behind the dresser and under the mattress, gave his old athletic socks a final squeeze for contraband, stuck his hands up the bung hole of the ceramic kangaroo atop his dresser to see if there was a shred of plastic hiding anywhere up there, and then said a final goodbye to his room.

When it was time to go his mother and father were standing by the front door, waiting. His mother handed him the traditional Dubrovnik traveler's kit—a plastic bread bag stuffed with pounds of sandwiches, cookies, and potato chips. She pointed to a large metal canister sitting on a bench beside the door—a five pound can of Cheetos. Dubrovnik had spotted the Cheetos a couple days ago and mistook it for a sign she was hosting club. "That's yours," she said, giddily.

"Really, mine?" he said. "All that."

"You don't have to eat it all today," she said, smiling.

Dubrovnik studied the canister—a solid metal cylinder with an orange, blue, red, white paint job. He was touched. He realized these Cheetos were his mother's way of remaining in his life a while longer—first as snack food, then, possibly, as a wastebasket. He hugged her.

The Cheetos gave Mr. Dubrovnik an idea. "Wait a minute," he said. "I have something." He ran off through the dining room toward the garage, setting off a glassy tinkle in the china cabinet that caused Mrs. Dubrovnik to place a hand over her stomach. Mr. Dubrovnik returned with a couple of jugs of sky-blue liquid—windshield washer fluid. "You'll want this if you run into anything on the turnpike," he said. "Any kind of weather at all." He handed it over and started in about the time Grandpa ran out of windshield washer fluid on the turnpike and everybody was sold out so that he could barely see to drive. "He had to think about getting a motel," he said.

"For Christ's sake, that's enough," Mrs. Dubrovnik interrupted, then turned to her son. "You better get going if you want to get in before dark. You don't want to be caught on the turnpike at night. Not in those mountains. It's pitch black."

The first part of Dubrovnik's trip was dedicated to finding a place to snort the pink perfumed amphetamine powder—crystal meth—that his friend Bob Reid gave him as a going away present. Dubrovnik popped in on Bob the night before to say a quick goodbye. Bob dealt to Dubrovnik for the last couple years. He used to be everybody's drug dealer but then, after a stint in prison, he only sold to friends.

Bob and his girlfriend, Else, were hanging out as always, sitting around in their underwear watching some nonsense on TV, and arguing whose turn it was to go to the store. When Dubrovnik told Bob he was moving away, Bob got sad. "Hold on," he said, "I've got something for your trip." He came back from his bedroom with a tiny Ziploc packet stuffed with pinkish powder.

"Ever done crank?" he asked.

"I don't think so," Dubrovnik said. "I've eaten a ton of yellow jackets and Christmas trees and shit like that, and some of my mom's Ritalins, but I don't ever remember snorting anything. No."

"Crank is relatively new around here," Bob said. "It's a big deal in Philadelphia."

"I'm going through there on my way to Atlantic City."

"Well, buddy, you'll be crossing home plate then. Just ask for the Pagans. They've got tons of this shit."

Dubrovnik held up the envelope for examination, then sniffed its perfumey contents.

"Don't think too seriously on that stuff," Bob said. "It'll make you crazy." Bob rolled his eyes as a way of alluding to the proof, his apartment. Four months earlier meth inspired Bob to try and understand his motorcycle better, so he took it apart. Now his apartment looked like a parts schematic for a Harley Goldwing. The frame was leaning against the back of the couch. Some cables, possibly brakes, were slung across the top of the refrigerator, and the household smelled like motor oil.

Until he got into his car Dubrovnik wasn't sure he'd take the meth. But soon he decided it was better to do meth than to be caught with it, so he pulled into the first rest stop on the turnpike. He drove to the far edge of the parking lot, away from the facilities, and lined his Dart up with a historical marker in front of a picnic area. He figured the historical marker would explain to law enforcement types what he was doing parked way over there by himself. He read the marker. It told how some Indians from New York came down to Pennsylvania to kill some German settlers on behalf of the French in their war with the British for control of the Monongahela Valley. The actual site of the massacre, it said, was out there under the eastbound lanes. Dubrovnik looked off in that direction, where the J.B. Hunts and the Roadways blasted along, and tried to imagine Indians in buckskin scalping the Pennsylvania Dutch.

When he looked back he noticed a bunch of Moravian seniors were straying from their tour bus toward the picnic area, many of them armed with ice cream. They swerved around his car like a school of fish. None of them looked at him, but he smiled anyways so they could see how harmless he was. After the Moravians passed, he dug a fresh dollar bill out of his pocket and rolled it tightly. He spread out some lines of meth on the vinyl bench seat of his Dodge Dart, took a final look around, submerged himself below the dash and blasted off.

His turnpike ended up being different than his father's or grandfather's turnpike. The need to urinate was a bigger force than trucks or guardrails. It kept forcing Dubrovnik to confront the fat Germanic female joviality and bright linoleum fluorescence of HoJos. He bought breath mints at New Stanton and a hefty lady in a full-length apron said, "Would you like some ice cream?" He bought a comb in Tuscarora and, again, the lady brought up ice cream. "It's free," she said, "with a fill-up."

"That's all right," he said. One of the ladies was about his mother's age. She was enormous. He recalled his mother saying Germans are fat because they eat nothing but dessert. And his father saying they blow up like balloons once they're married.

At Valley Forge, he asked one of the ice cream ladies if she sold alcohol. She leaned forward on her fat palms and looked dead at him, like some kind of crab that lived underneath a hair net. "No," she said, "Alcohol is forbidden on the Pennsylvania Turnpike. If you want alcohol you'll have to get off the turnpike altogether."

Dubrovnik wasn't interested in leaving the turnpike. He just wanted something to take the edge off the speed. His high needed maintenance. He'd been chewing the same stick of Juicy Fruit for seven hours. The lovely energy that flowered in his brain earlier in the day was now branching out into his body with less uplifting effects. A dull ache was beginning in his stomach. He needed to put something down there, so he broke down and bought some ice cream.

From Killed on the Beat

Helen Thorpe

*Helen Thorpe lives in Denver, Colorado and works as a freelance journalist.
Her first book,* Just Like Us, *tells the true story of four Latina friends who are
split down the middle in terms of their legal status; it was named one of the
best books of 2009 by the* Washington Post. *Her magazine stories have
appeared in* The New York Times Magazine, The New Yorker, *and* Texas
Monthly. *Thorpe is married to John Hickenlooper, the governor of Colorado,
and they have one son. This is an excerpt of a longer piece that originally
appeared in* Open City.

EARLY IN HER CAREER AS A REPORTER FOR THE SUN-
day *Independent*, the largest selling newspaper in
Ireland, Veronica Guerin met with a low-level hustler
who was friendly with some of Dublin's criminal bosses.
She was new on the crime beat, struggling to sort out
what was taking place in the murky Dublin underworld, and the hustler was exactly the type of person
she needed to get to know: while he had never been
convicted of any crime, he knew all the pub talk and some of the truth
about what was happening in Dublin's criminal circles. And he was a
born gossip. Guerin would never be able to print anything he said without checking it, but he could point her in all kinds of directions.
Following an introduction provided by a mutual acquaintance in the
insurance business, Guerin badgered the man with phone calls until he
finally agreed to meet her for coffee just to get her off his back. "After
months of driving me mad, I met her in a café in Baggot Street," recalled
this person recently. "I fucked her over. I called her all the names you
wouldn't use for a woman. I called her more names than you can imagine."

Guerin was attractive, and she always dressed well; frequently the first
word that an acquaintance will use to describe her is elegant. That day
she was probably wearing some sort of business suit. She was a small
woman, with short blonde hair, and a square, open face. To the man who

had agreed to meet with her, she did not look like the sort to be able to weather verbal abuse. But Guerin had grown up in Artane, a lower-class neighborhood on the north side of Dublin—the Liffey River divides Dublin culturally, as well as geographically, and the northside has always been known as the wrong side of town—and she calmly sat and listened to the man's tirade without saying a word. As he got up to leave, the man looked back to see how Guerin had taken his lecture. He was stunned to see that she was grinning.

"Now sit down and talk like a man," Guerin told the hood.

In the months that followed, Guerin collected an odd assortment of ex-cons, bad guys and shady characters that she would see on a regular basis. At a certain point, when she secured an interview with a man known in Dublin as the Monk, she invited him to her home and interviewed him at her kitchen table, even though he has been unofficially credited with several murders and the largest armed robbery in Irish history. The Monk probably found the invitation disarming. "Even if I am not working on a crime-related story, I will call or meet for coffee with a couple of criminals, because you are going to hear something and it is important that you keep up," Guerin later told Catherine Donnelly, an advertising copywriter, in an interview that was recorded before her death. "You are keeping in touch, keeping in contact, and ensuring that there is some element of trust there."

Most of these people had never talked to a reporter before—Dublin has a cohesive, insular criminal community, with its own slang and its own rules—but they talked to Guerin, whose greatest strength as a reporter was her ability to get people to open up to her. Her northside background gave her the ability to relate to anybody at all, regardless of station. "She never had any notions about herself, even though she was probably one of the best people in her profession," said Mary Hallissey, one of Guerin's friends at *The Sunday Independent*. She was irrepressible and she was cocky, and there was something about her manner that allowed her to establish immediately the kind of rapport that most people achieve only over time. Gerry Quigley, an officer who had been assigned to protect her after several initial assaults on her person, wrote in a police magazine about the time they first met: "Being slightly officious, I told her who I was and showed her my I.D. card. She looked at it and said, 'Yeah, yeah, come in; I'm just making tea.' I said something about taking a patrol around the house first. She looked at me, grinned, and said, 'Would ye ever go and shite.'"

The crime beat is considered tough to break into, but Guerin didn't have any trouble developing sources. While growing up in Artane, Guerin was active in Fianna Fail, one of Ireland's leading political parties, and asa result, she had a vast network of contacts throughout Irish society, which she used to her advantage. Although Guerin was devoted to her family, went to Mass every Sunday, and rarely drank alcohol, she could curse like a truck driver, an ability she used to great effect with both detectives and criminals. As a schoolgirl, she represented Ireland internationally in basketball and soccer, and even as an adult, she remained fanatically devoted to Manchester United, the English soccer team that traditionally has the most Irish players. Sports probably made her competitive at any rate, Guerin had a passion for beating other reporters to a story that was unusual even in the newspaper business. And she used her sports vocabulary, like her profanity, to break the ice. She spent more time in her sports car chasing down stories, than she did in the office. She was a famously avid talker, carrying two mobile telephones with her everywhere. Detectives at garda stations around the city recall getting swept into conversation with her despite their best intentions not to be, and apparently somebody high up in police headquarters was happy to feed her documents, as on several occasions she managed to acquire internal police files that even most detective sergeants would have had a hard time obtaining.

Because she did not restrict herself to police contacts, Guerin soon attained a reputation and a national following for her offbeat, spicy, detailed profiles of Dublin's major criminal characters. Other crime reporters did not rely on criminal sources because they felt doing so would put them in danger, and they also felt it was pointless, since they thought criminals were inherently unreliable. "It's become popular in the last few years to interview criminals and print what they say as if it's gospel," said Tom Brady, a reporter who covers crime for *The Irish Independent*, the sister publication to the weekly paper that Guerin wrote for. "It's an unfortunate trend, and it leads to falling standards in journalism. It's about circulation wars, that's all."

Guerin disagreed. She thought that the closer she got to criminals, the less likely they were to come after her, in the way that crooks sometimes look after people in their own neighborhoods, once they decide they are alright. She also thought that criminals were the only sources who could reveal certain things to her. "What makes them want to go out and murder somebody?" Guerin asked in the interview with Donnelly. "Is it avarice? Is that why they are dealing in drugs? Is it avarice that makes them go out and hold up a bank? What is it that motivates them? I want to know that, and I think people need to know."

This relentless curiosity would lead Guerin into areas of Dublin society where few other people of her milieu ever strayed. Finally it led her into confrontations with members of Dublin's criminal underworld that brought about her doom. If Guerin had not comprehended the risk she was taking, she would have been a foolhardy woman, but she knew full well what was at stake. That was why, when she was shot at point-blank range on the Naas Road, the Irish responded by canonizing her in their long, much-peopled hall of fallen heroes. Beyond what it said about Guerin, the assassination set off months of noisy debate because of what it said about Ireland as a whole. In the history of the country no journalist had ever been killed because of his work—not even in the north. Now the best-known woman in the Irish press had been murdered in the middle of the day on one of the busiest roads in the country's capital. Guerin's murder clearly stated that, despite her own efforts as a crime reporter, nobody in Ireland had correctly imagined how dangerous its criminals had been allowed to become.

During the time that Guerin wrote about Dublin's underworld, a sea-change took place in it. In the years leading up to her death, there were many intimations of the new order, and her assassination was a clear sign that Ireland's shadow economy had undergone a revolution, but if any further confirmation was needed, it appeared on August 14 of last year in the guise of a coal ship called the *Front Guider*. That vessel had set out from Colombia, crossed the Atlantic, and berthed in Co. Clare, where police and customs officials discovered fifty kilograms of cocaine hidden behind false ceiling panels in the ship's gymnasium. Police later found the cocaine was 75 percent pure, and estimated it would fetch about £16 million on the streets, making the find of cocaine the largest in Irish history.

Ireland has always tolerated a certain level of black market activity—I know of respected businessmen who have furnished their entire houses with stolen goods—and that toleration has allowed an indigenous criminal community to thrive in Dublin's public housing. In the last five years, however, as large quantities of narcotics have begun to move through the country a situation that was once viewed as acceptable has bloomed into a catastrophe with regional implications. In part, the change was brought about by the formation of the European Economic Community. Membership in the E.E.C. has invigorated Ireland's legitimate business world, but it has caused the country's illegitimate enterprises to catch fire as well, largely because the E.E.C. suspended border restrictions on traffic within its member countries in 1992, permitting goods of all kinds to circulate more freely. The first unintended consequences of this action was to bequeath Ireland with a burgeoning local drug scene. Younger heroin users have started turning up at clinics around Dublin in significant numbers—in 1994, 2,978 individuals sought treatment, an increase of 50 percent in four years—and both ecstasy and marijuana are now available throughout the country. Along with the problems of addiction has come an epidemic of petty crime such as break-ins, car thefts, and muggings. In the past, the residents of Dublin's poorest neighborhoods have been willfully blind to the crimes that occur in their midst, but by last summer, they had begun building anti-drug protest shanties and organizing marches in their streets. When they marched in Ronanstown, they were chanting "Pushers, pushers, pushers, out, out, out!"

Proust and the Rat

Nick Tosches

Nick Tosches was born in Newark and lives in New York City. He is the author of over a dozen books including the novels Cut Numbers, Trinities, *and* In the Hand of Dante, *as well as the biographies* Dino, Hellfire, *and* The Devil and Sonny Liston. The Nick Tosches Reader *is an anthology spanning the first thirty years of his career. He is currently working on a novel.*

A QUIET, DESOLATE-FEELING WINTER AFTERNOON: Johnny, Jean-Jacques, and I are sitting together. The talk has turned to Proust. This may be because Johnny and I have acquired some bottles of the Calon-Ségur wine that Proust is said to have favored, or because Jean-Jacques has acquired the newly published *Carnets* of Proust. Or it may be because of the convergence of these acquisitions.

And so it comes to pass, in the wintry quiet of this afternoon, that Jean-Jacques tells us of Proust and the rat.

In his nocturnal roamings, Proust was a furtive frequenter of the old brothels and hammams. One evening, he posed a strange question:

"Do you have rats here?"

The mistress, or master, of the establishment was taken aback and became defensive for a moment, as if Proust were questioning the cleanliness of the place. But the look in Proust's eyes seemed to be one of innocent hopefulness, and his question received a natural and nonchalant answer.

"Of course we have rats."

"Can you please bring one to me?"

Then, in a chamber upstairs, it unfolded. There was the big black rat in a cramped makeshift cage. There was the maid of Eros, holding between thumb and forefinger the pearl head of a gleaming, needle-sharp hat pin of perhaps twenty-five centimeters in length. There was Proust, with his cock in his hand, giving precise instructions: the hat pin must be directed slowly but steadily through the snared rat, so that this piercing would bring to it a death that likewise came slowly but steadily. Proust tried to synchronize the process, so that when the point of the hat pin exited the underbelly of the rat, the drops of his semen fell simultaneously with the drops of blood that fell from the point of the hat pin, and his orgasm and the death-throe of the rat were as one. In the secret course of the years to come, Proust perfected this act.

Johnny and I are transported by this tale. Here, we feel, is sex supreme. Here, we feel, is Proust—beyond the starched collar and cork-lined room—revealed to be, yes, spiritually free. As we sit wordless, savoring the beauty of it all, Jean-Jacques delivers the coup de grâce:

"I think there was also a picture of his mother. A small photograph of his mother. Yes. In a frame. He placed it by the rat, so that he could look at both the rat and the picture."

This is it. Johnny and I decide to search out antique hat pins immediately. I feel that there can be no greater love.

But what, we ask, is the source of this tale? Georges Bataille, says Jean-Jacques.

Soon we are joined by Michel, a gentleman of great erudition who even knows the location of Proust's favorite hammam. Yes, he confirms, the source of the tale is Bataille. He seems to mention a title: *L'érotisme et le mort.*

I later discover that there is no *L'érotisme et le mort.* There is *L'Érotisme* and there is *Le mort*, and there is *La littérature et le mal*, which has much to say of Proust but nothing of the rat. In fact, probing through the dozen tomes of the *Oeuvres complètes* of Bataille, I find no glimpse of the rat.

Seasons pass, and in the *Times Literary Supplement* of July 26, in an essay by Malcolm Bowie on two new biographies of Proust, I read Bowie's observation that the death of Proust's mother, Jeanne, on September 26, 1905, was for Proust "far too troubling to be transposed directly into his fiction. It not only left him incurably wounded but gave him a new freedom, shadowed by guilt, in his pursuit of sexual pleasure."

The summer passes. It is good rat weather. I sit with a strange and obscure book about Proust by Maria Paganini-Ambord. It is called *A la pêche au poisson-loup*, and it is a study of the three letters of the alphabet— *a*, *r*, and *t*—whose verbal permutations are seen to form a pattern in Proust's writing through passages in which his prose is wrought through the repetition of words such as *art*, *rat*, *tare*, and *rater*. But, while noting that one scarcely needs to be reminded of the fascination that rats exerted on Proust, there is not a hint about Proust and the rat; and the author is far more concerned with the word *rat* than with the creature itself. A note appended to the study refers to Jeanne Bem's article "Le Juif et l'homosexuel dans *À la recherche du temps perdu*: fonctionnements textuels," in the

February 1980 issue of *Littérature*. This article calls our attention to the passage in *À la recherche du temps perdu* (I:576) where the madam, in praising the charms of a whore named Rachel, cannot articulate the name of Rachel beyond its first syllable, which is the sound of the word *rat*.

In my search for the perfect hat pin, I have learned that these pins likely began, in the early-nineteenth century, as decorative hairpins, which grew into the longer hat pins to accommodate the bigger and bigger hats that dominated women's fashion from the last decade of that century through the second decade of the twentieth century. As the size of hats increased, so did the length of hat pins, from an early average of twelve and a half centimeters to known specimens of up to thirty-five centimeters, with heads that were often ornately jeweled. All of them made for lethal weapons. Injuries were inflicted frequently throughout Europe and America, and legal measures were taken against their use in Germany and in New Orleans. In Germany, the police threatened that safety finials must be affixed to the points of all hat pins worn in public.

A thirty-five-centimeter hat pin could do even the fattest and biggest river rat quite nicely indeed.

But the tale itself: is it true? Johnny and I wonder about it. In the end, we resolve the matter. If it were not true, it is true now.

I have lately also located a copy of Bataille's rarest volume, *Histoire de Rats*. This small volume, with three original etchings by Alberto Giacometti, was published by Les Editions de Minuit in 1947 in a limited edition of two hundred and ten copies, of which forty were numbered copies with a suite of three additional etchings, and ten were *hors commerce* copies with the additional suite on Rives paper. In "Georges Bataille ou l'impossible" (1984), Daniel Leuwers, maître-assistante à la Faculté des lettres de Tours, stated: "Les expériences relatées dans *Histoire de Rats*, mettant en jeu l'érotisme et la mort"—there: that phrase, that chimerical title—"se justifient par [la croyance] que 'l'outrance du désir et de la mort permet seule d'atteindre la vérité.'"[1]

When the holy days of Christmas giving come, I will give this rare volume to my beloved.

---

1. "The experiences related in *Histoire de Rats*, bringing into play eroticism and death, are justified by [the belief] that 'excess of desire and death alone makes it possible to reach the truth.'"

Mistress

Lara Vapnyar

Lara Vapnyar is the author of the story collections There Are Jews in My House *and* Broccoli and Other Tales of Food and Love, *and the novel* Memoirs of a Muse. *Her novel* The Smell of Pine *is forthcoming from Open City Books. "Mistress" was her debut publication.*

THE DERMATOLOGIST HAD A MISTRESS. FOR THE PAST few weeks, it had been the main topic of conversation in his white waiting room, decorated with a lonely, lop-sided palm in the corner and bright dermatology posters. There were about eight patients seated on red patent-leather chairs, most of them Russians, because of the office location on Kings Highway, a Russian area of Brooklyn. The doctor even had a few Russian newspapers lying along with dated issues of *Time* and *Sports Illustrated* in a plastic magazine rack. Nobody was interested in them though.

"He took her to Aroba in November. The mistress," Misha's grandmother was confiding in Russian to a gray-haired woman in a sports jacket, sneakers, and long skirt. "Aruba," Misha corrected her mentally. He tried to read a book, but the grandmother's excited whisper filled with fat, rich words like "Aruba" or "mistress" wouldn't let him concentrate. Sometimes she attempted to talk to a woman in a gray beret, seated next to Misha. To do that she leaned over Misha, putting her heavy elbow on his knee for balance. He had to press his opened book to his chest and wait until she was through, trying to keep his face away from her mixed aroma of sweat, valerian root drops, and dill. "First he went on vacation with his wife, but the mistress made a scene, and he had to take her too. They are all like that, you know." The gray-haired woman nodded. At some point, other Russian patients came closer and stayed there to chat. "You mean doctor Levy has a mistress?" "Yes," the gray-haired woman said eagerly. "He even took her to Aroba." And Misha's grandmother looked at her with reproach, because she wanted to be the one to tell about Aruba.

Every second Thursday, after school, Misha had to take his grand-mother to the dermatologist. He served as an interpreter, because the grandmother didn't speak English. He didn't mind these visits—there wasn't much to translate. Doctor Levy, a small, skinny man with dark circles under his eyes, just glanced at the sores on her ankles, scribbled something in the chart, and asked: "How's it going?" Grandmother said "Better" in Russian and Misha translated it into English. Misha didn't mind the eye doctor and the dentist either. Misha was saved by his grandfather from visits to a gynecologist. "A nine-year-old boy has no business in a gynecologist's office," he said firmly, surprising everybody, because since they had come to America it was a rarity to hear him argue, to hear him speak at all. Misha was happy—for some reason he was afraid of pregnant women with their inflated bellies, fat ankles, and wobbly domineering way of walking. His mother had to take several hours off work to take the grandmother there. She complained about it and looked at Misha and the grandfather with reproach.

Nobody saved Misha from monthly visits to an internist. This doctor let Misha and his grandmother into his sparkling cabinet with cream-colored walls covered with diplomas, and walked confidently to his large mahogany desk. He sat there tall and lean, with a thick mane of bluish-white hair, red face, and very clean white hands, listening patiently to the grandmother's complaints. Unlike other doctors, he never interrupted her. Misha would have preferred if he did. "My problem is . . ." she would begin with a sigh of anticipation. She prided herself on being able to describe her symptoms with vividness and precision. "You should've been a writer, Mother," Misha's father once said, when she described per-spiration as a "heavy shower pouring from under my skin." Misha's mother looked lost. She didn't know if she should smile at the joke or scold her husband for being ironic about her mother. She chose to smile then. "No, a doctor," Misha's grandmother corrected, oblivious to his irony. "I would've become a doctor if I hadn't devoted my life to my hus-band."

While she talked to the doctor, Misha usually stared down, following the pattern on the checkered beige-and-brown linoleum floor with his eyes, the pattern broken at places with furniture legs and his grand-mother's feet in wide black sneakers. Her words were loud and clear, emphasized by occasional groans and changes of tone. "I can't have a bowel movement for days, but I have to go to the bathroom every few hours. It usually happens like this. I feel the urge and go to the bathroom immediately. I push very hard, but nothing happens. I come out, but I feel as if a heavy rock is in there inside me, weighing down my bowels. I go in and try again." The grandmother pressed one of her feet hard onto the floor when she was describing the "heavy rock." Misha looked at her thick dark stockings. She brought a big supply of them from Russia, along with a supply of wide, striped garters. Misha felt how the edge of his patent-leather chair became moist and slippery under his clutched fingers. He also felt that he was blushing all over, especially in his ears. He wondered if the doctor noticed how red they were. But he didn't look at Misha, he looked at the grandmother with a patient, polite smile.

"Come on," Misha thought, "stop her. There must be other patients waiting." But the doctor didn't move. Maybe he used these minutes to sleep with his eyes open. "When at last it happens, I feel exhausted, I feel as if I had won a battle. My head aches and I have a heartbeat so severe that I have to take forty drops of valerian root, lie down, and stay like that for at least an hour." When the grandmother was through, she turned to Misha. The doctor turned to him too, keeping the same polite and patient expression on his face. Misha thought about darting out the door, past the receptionist, past the waiting room, onto the street. He thought about rushing out the window, a large clean window with a plastic model of a split human head on a windowsill. He could see himself falling onto the grass, then rising to his feet and running away from the office. But he didn't jump. He sat there, thinking how to avoid mentioning "heavy rock" or the grandmother's sitting in the bathroom. "Um . . . she . . . my grandmother . . . her problem is . . . she has a . . . she often gets a headache and her heart beats very fast." The doctor smiled at Misha approvingly and wrote a prescription with his beautiful, very clean hands. "Tylenol!" his grandmother later complained loudly in the dermatologist's waiting room. "Look at the American doctors! I tell him that I have constipation and he gives me Tylenol! Can you believe that?" The Russian patients eagerly sympathized. Misha hid his burning ears behind *The Great Pictorial Guide to the Prehistoric World*. He wished they would switch to the safer subject of the dermatologist's mistress.

Once, they saw her. She flung the door open and walked straight to Dr. Levy's office, not smiling, staring ahead. She was a short stout woman in her late thirties, with short reddish-brown hair, in tight white jeans and a shiny leather jacket. She was clomping with her high-heeled boots and tinkling her gold bracelets as she walked. She was swinging car keys in her hand. Everybody in the room went silent and followed her with their eyes, even Misha. She had a beautiful mouth, painted bright red. "Shameless!" somebody hissed in Russian. Maybe it was Misha's grandmother.

At home, Misha did his homework in their long white kitchen, because in his mother's opinion it was the only place that had proper light and wasn't too drafty. For about a year, four of them—he, his mother, his grandfather, and his grandmother—had been living in this one-bedroom apartment with unevenly painted walls, faded brown carpet, and secondhand furniture. Everything in the apartment seemed to belong to somone else. Misha and his mother slept in the bedroom, Misha on a folding bed. The grandmother and grandfather slept on the sofa bed in the living room. Or rather it was his grandmother who slept, snoring softly. The grandfather seemed to be awake all night. Whenever Misha woke up, he heard the grandfather tossing and groaning or pacing heavily on the creaky kitchen floor.

In Russia, they had separate apartments. They even lived in different cities. His grandparents lived in the south of Russia, in a small town overgrown with apple and peach trees. Misha and his mother and father lived in Moscow, befor his father left to live with another woman. In Moscow, Misha had his own room, a very small one, not bigger than six square meters, where the wallpaper was patterned with tiny sailboats. Misha had his own bed and his own desk with a lamp shaped as a crocodile. His books were shelved neatly above the desk, his toys were kept in two plywood boxes beside his bed. When his parents were arguing, they said: "Misha, go to your room!" But during the last months before his father left, they didn't have time to send him to his room. They argued almost constantly: started suddenly, without any warning, in the middle of a matter-of-fact conversation, during dinner, while playing chess, while watching TV, and ended after Misha had gone to bed, or maybe they didn't end at all. Misha went to his room himself. He sat on a little woven rug between his bed and his desk, playing with his building blocks and listening to the muffled sounds of his parents yelling. He played very quietly.

Misha liked doing homework, although he would have never admitted that. He laid out his books, papers, pencils, so that they took almost all the surface of the table. He loved coloring maps, drawing diagrams, doing math problems, he even loved spelling exercises—he was pleased with the sight of his handwriting, the sight of the firm, clear, rounded letters. Most of all he loved that during homework time nobody bothered him. "Shh! Michael's studying," everybody said. Even his grandmother, who usually cooked dinner while Misha was studying, was silent, almost silent—she quietly hummed a theme from a Mexican soap opera that she watched every day on the Spanish channel. Her Spanish was not much better than her English, but she said that in Mexican shows you didn't need words to understand what's going on.

The other thing she loved to watch on TV were weather reports, where you didn't need words either: a picture of sun was for a good day, raindrops for drizzle, rows of raindrops for heavy rain. Misha's mother was against subscribing to a Russian TV channel, because she thought it would prevent them from adjusting to American life. For the same reason, she insisted that everybody called Misha "Michael." Misha's mother was well-adjusted. She watched news on TV, rented American movies, and read American newspapers. She worked in Manhattan and wore to work the same clothes that Misha had seen in the waiting room's magazines, but her skirts were longer and the heels of her shoes shorter and heavier.

The problem with the homework was that it only took Misha about forty minutes. He tried to prolong it as much as he could. He did all the extra math problems from the section "You Might Try It." He brought his own book and read it, pretending that it was an English assignment. He stopped from time to time as if he had a problem and had to think it over, but he just sat there, watching his grandmother cook. She took all these funny packages, string bags, plastic bags, paper bags, bowls, and wrapped plates out of the refrigerator and put them on the counter, never forgetting to sniff at each of them first. Then she opened the oven with a loud screech, gasping, saying, "Sorry, Michael," and took out saucepans and skillets, put them on the stove, filled some of them with water and greased others with chicken fat (she always kept some chicken fat handy, not trusting oil or cooking spread). While the saucepans and skillets gurgled and hissed on the stove, the grandmother washed and chopped the contents of packages and bowls, using two wooden boards—one for meat, the other for everything else. Misha always marveled at how fast her short and swollen fingers were. In a matter of seconds heaps of colorful cubes disappeared in the saucepans and skillets under chipped enameled lids. "I was wise," the grandmother often said to her waiting-room friends. "I brought all the lids here. In America it's impossible to find a lid that fits." The women agreed; something was definitely wrong with American lids. To make ground meat, the grandmother used a hand-operated, metallic meat grinder, also brought from Russia. She had to summon the grandfather into the kitchen, because the grinder was too heavy—she couldn't turn the handle herself, she couldn't even lift it. The grandfather put his newspaper down and came in obediently, shuffling with his slippers as he walked, with the same tired, resigned expression that he had when he followed the grandmother home from the Russian food store, carrying bulging bags printed with a stretched, red "Thank You." He took his dark checkered shirt off and put it on the chair. (The grandmother insisted that he do that. "You don't want pieces of raw meat all over your shirt!") He put an enameled bowl of meat cubes in front of him and secured the grinder on the windowsill. He stood leaning over it, dressed in a white undershirt and dark woolen trousers. He brought five good suits that he used to wear to work in Russia to America. Now he wore the trousers at home and the jackets hung in a closet with mothballs in their pockets. The grandfather took hold of a rusty meat-grinder handle and turned it slowly, with effort at first, then faster and faster. His flabby pale shoulders were shaking and tiny beads of sweat came out on his puffy cheeks, long rounded nose, and shiny head. The grandmother sometimes tore herself from her cooking and made comments: "What have you got, crooked fingers?" or "Here, you dropped a piece again" or "I hope I will have this meat ground by next year." She never talked to him like that in Russia. In Russia, when he came home from work, she rushed to serve him dinner and put two spoonfuls of sour cream into his *shchi* herself. The grandfather sucked the soup in loudly and talked a lot during dinner. Now he didn't even answer the grandmother. He just stood there, clutching the meat-grinder handle with yellowed knuckles, turning it even faster, which made his face redden and blue twisted veins on his neck bulge. His stare was focused on something far away out the window. Misha thought that maybe his grandfather wanted to jump, like he wanted to in the doctor's office. Only their apartment was on the sixth floor.

While the food was cooking, the grandmother went to get her special ingredient, dill. She kept darkened, slightly wilted bunches spread out on an old newspaper on the windowsill. She took one and crushed it into a little bowl with her fingers, to put it in every dish that she cooked. At dinner, everything had the taste of dill: soup, potatoes, meat stew, salad. In fact, dinner hardly tasted like anything else but dill—the grandmother didn't trust spices, put very little salt in the food, and no pepper at all. Misha watched how she moved from one saucepan to another, dressed in a square-shaped dark cotton dress, drying her moist red face and her closely cropped gray hair with a piece of cloth, sweeping potato peels off the counter, groaning when one fell to the floor and she had to pick it up. He couldn't understand why she put so much work into the preparation of this food, which was consumed at dinner in twenty minutes, in silence, and didn't even taste good.

Misha couldn't pretend to be busy with his homework forever. Eventually the grandmother knew that he was done. She watched a weather report on TV, and if nothing indicated a natural disaster sent Misha to a playground with his grandfather. "Go, go," she would yell at the grandfather, who sat on the sofa in his unbuttoned checkered shirt buried in a Russian newspaper. "Go, walk with the boy, make yourself useful for a change!" And the grandfather would stand up, groaning, go to the bathroom mirror to check if he should shave, usually decide against it. Then he would button his shirt, tuck it into his trousers, and say gloomily: "Let's go, Michael." Misha knew that after they left, the grandmother would take over the Russian newspaper. She would put her glasses on (she had two pairs, both made from cheap plastic, one light blue, the other pink), and slump on the sofa, making the springs creak. She would sit there with her feet planted far apart and read the classifieds section, the singles ads. She would circle some with a red marker she borrowed from Misha, to show them later to Misha's mother, who would laugh in the beginning, then get irritated, then get upset and yell at the grandmother.

All the way to a playground, while they passed redbrick apartment buildings and rows of private houses with little boys in yarmulkes and little girls in long flowery dresses playing on sidewalks, Misha's grandfather walked a few steps ahead, with his hands folded on his back, staring down at his feet, never saying a word.

Back in Russia, it was different, maybe because Misha was younger then. When he spent summers at his grandparents' place, the grandfather took him to a park willingly, without being asked. He talked a lot while they strolled along the paths of a dark, dense forest: about trees, animals, about how fascinating even the most ordinary things that surround us could be. Little Misha didn't try to grasp the meaning of the words. They just reached him along with other noises: a rustle of a tree, a bird's squawk, a nasty screech of gravel as he ran his sandal-clad toes through it. It was the sound of the grandfather's voice that was important to him. They walked slowly, Misha's little hand lying securely in the grandfather's big sweaty one. From time to time Misha had to release his hand and wipe it against his pants, but then he hurried to take the grandfather's hand back.

Now, once they reached the playground and stepped on its black spongy floor, the grandfather said: "Okay, go play, Michael." Then he passed round the place, searching for Russian newspapers left on benches. He usually found two or three and walked to a big flat tree stump, in the farthest corner from the domino tables, where a heated crowd of old Russian men gathered, and from the benches where old Russian women sat discussing their own ailments and other people's mistresses. There, for the full hour that they were on the playground, he sat unmoving, except to turn the newspaper pages. Misha didn't know how he was supposed to play. Three-year-olds on their tricycles rode all over the soft black surface of the playground. The slide was occupied by shrieking six-year-olds, the swings by little babies, rocked by their mothers or by fat teenage girls, who had to squeeze their bottoms hard to fit between the chains. Misha usually walked to the tallest slide, stepping over dabs of chewing gum and pools of melted ice cream. He climbed up to the very top and crawled into a plastic hut. There he sat huddled on a low plastic bench. Sometimes he brought a book with him. He liked thick serious books about ancient civilizations, archaeological expeditions, and animals who became extinct millions of years ago. But most of the time it was too noisy there to read. Then Misha simply stared down at the playground that seemed to move and stir like a big restless animal, and at his immobile grandfather.

The notice about the English class was printed in bold black letters on pink neon paper. The color was so bright that it arrested your look wherever the notice was lying. Since the beginning of March it could be seen lying anywhere in the apartment: on the kitchen table, in the bedroom on a crumpled pillow, on the toilet floor between a broom and a Macy's catalog, stuffed under the sofa (the grandmother pulled it out from there, blew the pellets of dust off it, smoothed it with her hands, and scolded the grandfather angrily). Everybody studied it, read it, or at least looked at it. It was being discussed if the grandfather should go. He fit the description perfectly. Any legal immigrant who lived in the country less than two years and possessed basic knowledge of English was invited to attend a three-month long class of American conversation. "Rich in idioms," was stated in letters bigger than the rest. "Free of charge," in even bigger letters. "It's an excellent program, Father!" Misha's mother raved at dinner, pulling bones out of catfish stew on her plate. "Taught by American teachers, real teachers, native speakers! Not by Russian old ladies, who confuse all the tenses and claim that it's classic British grammar." At first, the grandfather tried to ignore her. But Misha's mother was persistent. "You're rotting alive, Father! Think how wonderful it would be if you had something to do, something to look forward to." Misha's grandmother made dishes clatter, moved chairs with a screech, and often interrupted this conversation with questions like "Where are the matches? I just put them right here" or "Do you think this fish is overcooked?" She was offended that nobody thought of her going to the class, even though she knew that the words "basic knowledge of English" hardly applied to her. The best she could do was spell her first name. The last name required Misha's help. But Misha's mother couldn't be distracted by the grandmother's questions or clattering of dishes. "You'll begin to speak in no time, Father. You know grammar, you have vocabulary, you just need a push." The grandfather only bent his neck lower and sipped his tea, muttering that it was all nonsense and that in their area of Brooklyn you hardly ever needed English. "What about yours and mother's appointments?! Michael and I are tired of taking you there all the time. Right, Michael?" Misha's mother said, and moved their large porcelain teapot, preventing her from seeing Misha's face across the table. Misha nodded. It was decided that the grandfather would go.

On the first day of class, the grandfather took one of his jackets from a hanger and put it on, on top of his usual checkered shirt. He asked Misha if he had a spare notebook. Misha gave him a notebook with a marble cover, a sharp pencil, and a ballpoint pen. The grandfather put it all in a plastic "Thank You" bag. In the hall, he took from the top shelf of a closet the box with his Russian leather shoes, and asked Misha if they needed shining. Misha did not know, and the grandfather shoved the box back and put his sneakers on. He shuffled out to the elevator, holding the bag under his arm.

From then on, for two nights a week—the class was held on Mondays and Wednesdays—they had dinner without the grandfather. His absence didn't make much difference, except maybe that Misha's mother and the grandmother bickered a little more. It usually started with a clipping from a Russian newspaper, a big colorful ad—"Come to our party and meet your destiny! Price: fifty dollars (food and drink included)"—and ended with Misha's mother yelling: "Why do you want to marry me off? So you can drive the next one away?" and the grandmother reaching for a valerian root drops bottle. "I never said a bad word to your husband," the grandmother said plaintively. "You said plenty of your words to me. Didn't spare money in long-distance calls!" "I only wanted to open your eyes!" Then Misha's mother rushed out of the kitchen and the grandmother was yelling at her back, carefully counting the drops into her tea cup: "How can you be so ungrateful! I came to America to help you. I left everything and came here for your sake!"

Misha's mother came to America for Misha's sake. She said it to him once, after she came back from a parent-teacher conference. She came home and said: "Come with me to the bedroom, Michael." He went, feeling his hands getting sweaty and his ears red, although he knew that he didn't do anything bad at school. His mother sat on the edge of the bed and removed her high-heeled shoes, then pulled off her pantyhose. "The teacher says you don't talk, Michael. You don't talk at all. Not in class, not during the recess." She was rubbing her pale feet with small crooked toes. "Your English is fine, you have excellent marks on your tests. You have excellent marks in every subject. Yet, you're not going to make it to the top class!" She left her feet alone and began to cry, spreading black paint around her eyes. She said to him, sniffing, that he, his future, was the only reason why she came to America. Then she walked to the bathroom to wash her face, leaving her rolled-down pantyhose on the floor—two soft dark circles joined together. From the bathroom she yelled to him: "Why don't you talk, Michael?"

It wasn't true that he didn't talk at all. When asked a question, he gave an accurate answer, but he tried to make it as brief as possible. He never volunteered to talk. He registered everything that was said in class, he made comments and counter-arguments in his head, he even made jokes. But something prevented these already formed words from coming out of his mouth. He felt the same way when his father called on Saturdays. Misha spent a whole week preparing for his call, he had thousands of things to tell him. In his head, he told him everything that had happened in school, he described his classmates, his teachers. He wanted to talk about things he read in books, about lost cities, volcanoes, and weird animals. In his head, Misha even laughed, imagining how he would tell his father all the funny stories he read about dinosaurs, and how his father would laugh with him. But when his father called, Misha went numb. He answered questions but never volunteered to speak and never asked anything himself. He sat with the phone on his bed, facing the wall and hooking old layers of paint with his fingernail. He could hear his father's impatient, disappointed breathing on the other end of the line. Misha thought that his reluctance to talk could be the reason for his father's not calling some weeks.

Now the grandfather had to do his homework too. Misha came home from school and found him at the kitchen table in Misha's usual place with his notebooks and dictionaries spread across the table. The grandfather even cut himself little colorful cards out of construction paper and wrote down difficult words from the dictionary on them: an English word on one side, a Russian meaning on the other. He studied seriously and couldn't be bothered during that time. The grandmother had to go to the Russian food store alone, and she usually brought back smaller, lighter bags because she couldn't carry heavy things. Nobody used the meat grinder now. It was stored in a cupboard along with other useless things brought from Russia: baking sheets, funny shaped molds, a small dented samovar, a gadget for removing sour cherry stones. The grandmother wasn't happy about it. She muttered that she had the whole household on her shoulders and threw looks of reproach at her husband. Misha's mother said: "Please leave him alone; Father has to learn something, it's only for three months anyway." Misha wondered if the grandfather enjoyed his homework as much as he did. He also wondered if the grandfather cheated like he did, pretending that his homework took much more time than it really did.

About three weeks after the class started, the grandfather took the box with his leather shoes down from the shelf. He went to a shoe store and bought a small bottle of dark-brown shoe polish. To do that he had to look up the English word for "shoe polish" in a dictionary. Before each class, he polished his shoes zealously with a piece of cloth. "I don't want the teacher to think that Russians are pigs," he mumbled, answering the grandmother's stare. He sat squatted, with his head down, and his face and neck were very red, as red as they were when he said that he wasn't making enough progress and had to go for extra lessons on Saturdays. The grandmother was putting things into a cupboard when he said that. She shut the white cupboard door with a satisfied boom. "All that studying and you are not making progress!" One evening the grandfather got up from the sofa, put on his jacket, put some money in the pocket, walked to Kings Highway, and came back with a new shirt, a light-blue one with dark-blue stripes. "It was on sale," was all he said to the grandmother.

"'It was on sale!' was all he said to me," Misha's grandmother announced in the dermatologist's waiting room. "If I didn't know him, I would have thought he had a mistress." Her listeners, two Russian women, one wearing a thick knitted beret of a lustrous purple color and the other a plain black one, nodded to her sympathetically. "But I do

know him." The grandmother grinned and raised one brow to emphasize her words. She looked meaningfully at the women, leaned closer to
them, and whispered something. "That—for several years now," she
added. The woman in a purple beret said: "But this is good, this is better." The grandmother considered her words and said: "Yes, yes, this is
better, of course."

Misha imagined his grandfather with a mistress, with the dermatologist's mistress, because she was the only mistress he'd seen. He imagined his grandfather strolling with her along a Sheepshead Bay embankment among other couples, one of her hands sticking out of the shiny
leather sleeve holding his grandfather's hand, her other hand swinging
car keys. Then he imagined her kissing the grandfather on a cheek and
leaving a mark with her bright red lipstick. The grandfather would wrin-
kle his nose and rush to wipe it off, the way Misha always did when his
mother kissed him after work. The image of his serious grandfather vigorously rubbing his cheek made Misha smile.

Sheepshead Bay was the place where the grandfather took Misha for
his evening walks now. For a few weeks after the class began they continued to go to the playground, but the Russian newspapers were abandoned. The grandfather took his colorful word cards with him. He spread
them on his stump securing each with a small stone to prevent the wind
from picking them up. Sometimes he read them slowly, in whispers or
with his lips moving or with his eyes. But more often he just looked
around with an incredulous expression as if he saw all this for the first
time. Then one day, the grandfather said that he was going to take
Michael to Sheepshead Bay to look at the ships and breathe the fresh
ocean air. The grandmother protested at first, saying that it's a long walk,
and it's windy there, and the boy might catch cold. But the grandfather
was firm, almost as firm as he used to be back in Russia. He said that the
boy needs exercise and that's that.

On Sheepshead Bay, they didn't stop to look at the ships. They
crossed the creaky wooden bridge and proceeded along the embankment, passing fishermen, tall trees, and chipped green benches occupied
by lonely looking women. At the end of the path they turned back and
repeated their route three or four times. The grandfather walked ahead,
maybe a little faster than usual, limping slightly in his stiff leather shoes.
He stared ahead, sometimes turning to look in the direction of the trees
and benches. A few times Misha had an impression that the grandfather
nodded to somebody on one bench. Once he slipped on a fish head on
the pavement and almost fell while looking in that direction. Misha

made frequent stops to look at the fishermen's shiny tackles, fish heads, and tails they used for bait, and the inside of their white plastic buckets, which were usually empty. When the wind was so strong that it chilled Misha's ears and tried to tear his little Yankees cap off his head, there were sharp dark waves in the water, and Misha could see fish jumping with a big splash. While somebody was pulling his fishing rod out, Misha followed it with his eyes, holding his breath and licking his lips. He hoped at least once to see a fish being caught. When the grandfather's class was over, Misha was sure that they wouldn't come here anymore. He would have to go back to the plastic hut on the playground, which would get hot in summer and smell of burnt rubber.

The grandmother had all her appointments written down on a big wall calendar. It hung next to refrigerator, a bright spot on a pale kitchen wall. It was called "Russian Famous Monasteries," printed in Germany and bought in Brighton Beach. Below the beautiful, glossy picture of the Zagorsk Monastery, with golden cupolas floating in the brilliantly blue sky, was the schedule for June. The fifteenth, the date when the grandfather's class was to be over, was circled with Misha's red marker. "See, you didn't want to go, but when it's over you will miss it, Father," Misha's mother said when she passed the calendar on her way to dump her plate into the sink. The grandfather only shrugged. He didn't look moved in any way by her words. It was the grandmother who looked moved, even animated, every time June 15 was mentioned. The great things were to be done then. The grandmother spoke about the ten pounds of cucumbers she wanted the grandfather to bring for her from Brighton Beach. "They are twenty-nine cents per pound there! I will make pickles." She also spoke about the plums and apricots she needed for jam, about sour cherries to make sour cherry dumplings, about little hard pears for marinating, about apples for apple pies. She threw longing looks in the direction of the locked-up meat grinder, telling about a wonderful recipe she heard in the dentist's office. "I'll make *zrazy*. Anna Stepanovna says that they come out much better with scallions instead of onions. I'll need a lot of ground beef for them." Then she found a Russian travel agency, which offered discounted tours to elderly people. "We'll go to Boston, to Washington, to Philadelphia. Women in waiting rooms talk about their trips nonstop, and I just sit there too shy to open my mouth. And you will have to go with me," she said to the grandfather. "I won't go alone, as if I weren't married. They put unmarried women on bad seats in the back, next to a toilet." Misha thought that maybe for his grandmother it wasn't such a bad idea to sit next to a toilet, but he didn't say anything. The grandfather didn't say anything either. He only buried himself deeper in his textbook.

On June 2, a weather report on TV showed a neat gray cloud and dense oblique rows of raindrops. "Heavy shower," the grandmother announced, turning the TV off and walking into the kitchen where Misha and the grandfather were doing their homework, or rather sat with their textbooks open. "You're staying home tonight." The sky in the window was mostly gray, but with a few patches of blue. Misha looked farther down. People weren't carrying umbrellas and the gray asphalt of the road was dry and dusty. He looked at his grandfather. The grandfather examined the sky carefully, then lifted the window a few inches up to stick his arm out. The howling gushes of icy wind dashed in, but the arm, although covered with goose bumps, was dry. "We'll come back before the rain starts," he said. The grandmother shrugged.

The first raindrops started falling as soon as they left the building. They made dark marks on the pavement but missed Misha and his grandfather. Then a raindrop fell right on the tip of Misha's nose. He wiped it off. Close to Sheepshead Bay, the grandfather stopped and stuck his open palm out. Some drops fell on it. "It's not rain, is it, Michael?" the grandfather said, turning to Misha and wiping his damp face with his damp palm. Misha shrugged. They both looked in the direction of the bay. It was very close, they could see the ships, and the dirty-gray high waves, and the tops of the trees bending low under the pressure of the wind. Newspaper pages, probably left on the benches, were flying up. "It's not a heavy rain. Let's make one round. Okay?" Misha nodded, holding tight to his cap. They crossed the street, the only ones to walk in the direction of the park. The majority of people hurried out. Big round raindrops were now falling fast, hitting the pavement one after another with a smacking sound, and turning small wet spots into intricate ornaments, then into puddles. The grandfather stopped hesitantly and looked in the direction of the benches. There was nobody there. "I think we better head home, Michael," the grandfather said. "It's starting to rain."

The heavy downpour reached them while they were waiting for the street light to turn green. With all the wind's howling and sounds of rain, they didn't immediately hear somebody calling for them. Or rather, Misha heard, but he didn't grasp at once that it was his grandfather's name being called. "Grigory Mikhailovich! Grigory Mikhailovich!"

Nobody had used his surname since they left Russia. A small old woman in a brown raincoat, holding a plastic bag above her head, was running to them, stumbling in black water-resistant boots too wide for her. Misha pulled the grandfather on the sleeve, making him stop and turn. "Grigory Mikhailovich! Come to my place, come quickly, the boy will catch cold," she said breathlessly, trying to position her plastic bag above Misha's head.

street from the park. They walked up a dark staircase, which smelled of something unpleasant. "Cats?" thought Misha, who had never smelled a cat. The woman led the way. She was still out of breath and spoke in short, abrupt sentences. "Poor boy. Grigory Mikhailovich. How could you. In a weather like this. I was there on a bench. But I left. As soon as the rain started. I saw you from across the street. I'm worried about the boy." The grandfather was also out of breath, and silent.

Inside Misha could only notice that the apartment was very small and dimly lit before a big rough towel, smelling of unfamiliar soap, covered his face and shoulders and back. He felt the woman's swift little hands rubbing him. He became ticklish and wanted to sneeze.

"My name is Elena Pavlovna. We go to school together, your grandfather and I," the woman said, after Misha and the grandfather had refused dry sweatpants but accepted dry socks and their shoes had been stuffed with newspapers and put to dry in the bathroom. They were drinking hot chocolate at the one-legged round table in the tiny kitchen. Misha's grandfather and Elena Pavlovna made hot chocolate together. The grandfather was pouring boiling water from the kettle, holding it by the wooden handle with both hands, Elena Pavlovna put the mix into three yellow mugs and moved them closer to the kettle. They said "thank you," "please," and "would you" to each other, and smiled frequently. They spoke like characters in Chekhov's adaptations that Misha's mother loved to watch in Russia, yet Misha could feel that with his grandfather and Elena Pavlovna it wasn't an act. "What's your name?" Elena Pavlovna asked. "Michael," said Misha. "Michael?! You don't look like Michael. Misha would suit you better. Can I call you Misha?" Misha nodded, blowing with pleasure on his too-hot drink (at home the grandmother usually added cold milk to his cup) and biting on a cookie with delicious raspberry jam inside. "Store-bought," Elena Pavlovna had said. "I don't bake. Why bother when there are so many delicious things sold in bakeries? Right? But that's not the real reason. I am simply a very bad cook." Misha could see that she wasn't ashamed to admit that.

Her apartment was smaller than theirs. One room and a kitchen. It was furnished just like theirs: a hard brown sofa from a cheap Russian furniture store, a scratched coffee table and chest of drawers brought from the garbage, heavy lamps bought at a garage sale. A delicate Russian tea set and books in a dark cabinet with glass doors. Misha read the titles—the same books as they had—Chekhov, Pushkin, historical novels with dark, gloomy covers, Maupassant and Flaubert translated into Russian, thick dictionaries, Russian–English and English–Russian. Some titles were covered with two big photographs. Two serious, curly-headed girls, both older than Misha, on one. "My granddaughters," Elena Pavlovna said with a sigh. "They live in California with my son." On the other picture, black and white, was a smiling young man in a uniform. *Her son*, Misha thought, but Elena Pavlovna said that it was her husband.

Elena Pavlovna had a braid, a thin gray braid coiled on the back of her head. Misha had never seen an old woman with a braid before. The hair coming out of the braid framed her face with a crown of fluffy gray-ish-white curls. Her skin was dry and thin with neat little wrinkles that looked drawn on her face with a pencil. Her eyes were small and dark. They misted over when she was reading them her sister's letter from Leningrad. "Everything is the same, the Neva, the embankment, the Winter Palace, only you, Lenochka, are gone." The grandfather patted her hand, showing from a faded blue sleeve, when she said that. She wore a blue woolen dress with the high collar covering her neck and a large amber brooch. "Want to look at my brooch, Misha?" she asked, unpinning it. "My mother said that there was a fly inside." Misha held the large, unpolished piece of amber in his hands. It was cool and smooth on top, rough on the edges. There was a strange black mass inside with thin sprouts looking a little like an insect's legs. "I am not sure, myself, maybe it's just a crack," Elena Pavlovna said. "Do you know, Misha, what amber is?" "Yes," he answered eagerly, turning the piece of amber in his hands. "It's hardened tree tar, flies could get stuck in it while it was still soft and gluey. Yes, I think it is a fly, only a deformed one." Misha raised his eyes off the brooch and blushed, seeing that both Elena Pavlovna and his grandfather looked pleased with what he said.

Outside everything was wet and brightened by the rain. The trees sent showers of raindrops on their heads when they passed under them. They walked very fast, close to each other, their wet shoes squishing on the black wet asphalt. They left Elena Pavlovna's apartment as soon as the rain ended. Their shoes were still damp, but they took the sodden newspapers out and put the shoes on. Elena Pavlovna didn't protest, she didn't say that they must wait, that Misha might catch cold from wearing damp shoes. On the staircase she took his hand in her dry, little one and said: "Come again, Misha." But Misha doubted that he would ever see her again. He also knew that she wasn't to be mentioned at home. They would probably have to say that they waited until the rain was over in a hallway of some building or inside a deli. Elena Pavlovna, a woman with a gray braid and an amber brooch, would be his and the grandfather's secret. For some reason, Misha felt an urge to take his grandfather's hand, but then he thought that nine-year-old boys don't walk holding their grandfathers' hands. Instead, he began talking about the formation of amber, about volcanoes, about chameleons, about dinosaurs that swallowed big rocks to help them grind the food, about crocodiles that did it too. He talked nonstop, breathlessly, sputtering, chuckling in excitement, interrupting one story to tell the next. He looked at his grandfather, whose eyes were focused on Misha, who nodded in amazement and muttered from time to time: "Imagine!" or "Imagine what living things have to come up with to survive!" And Misha wanted to tell him more to hear the "Imagine!" again and again. Close to their building, the grandfather suddenly stopped, interrupting a story about Komodo dragons. "Misha," he said, sounding a little out of breath. "You know what, my class won't be over on June 15th. I mean it will, but I'll find another class, then another. Misha, there are a lot of free English programs in Brooklyn. You have no idea how many!" A big raindrop fell on the grandfather's head from the tree. It ran down his forehead, lingered on his large nose, and hung on the tip. The grandfather shivered and shook his head like a horse. Misha laughed.

Nothing Happened

David Foster Wallace

David Foster Wallace (1962–2008) is the author of several works of fiction and nonfiction, including Infinite Jest, Girl with Curious Hair, A Supposedly Fun Thing I'll Never Do Again, *and* Pale Fire, *a posthumously published novel. This story, originally published in* Open City, *later appeared as "Signifying Nothing" in his collection* Brief Interviews with Hideous Men.

HERE IS A WEIRD ONE FOR YOU. IT WAS A COUPLE OF years ago, and I was nineteen, and getting ready to move out of my folks' house, and get out on my own, and one day as I was getting ready, I suddenly get this memory of my father waggling his dick in my face one time when I was a little kid. The memory comes up out of nowhere, but it is so detailed and solid-seeming, I know it is totally true. I suddenly know it really happened and was not a dream, even though it had the same kind of bizarre weirdness to it that dreams have. Here is the sudden memory. I was around eight or nine, and I was down in the rec room by myself, after school, watching TV. My father came down and came into the rec room, and was standing in front of me, like between me and the TV, not saying anything, and I didn't say anything. And, without saying anything, he took his dick out and started kind of waggling it in my face. I remember nobody else was home. I think it was winter, because I remember that it was cold down in the rec room, and I had Mom's TV afghan wrapped around me. Part of the total weirdness of the incident of my father waggling his dick at me down there was that, the whole time, he did not say anything, (I would have remembered it if he said anything), and there was nothing in the memory about what his face was doing, like what his facial expression looked like. I do not remember if he even looked at me. All I remember was the dick. The dick like claimed all of my attention. He was just sort of waggling it in my face, without saying anything or making any type of comment, shaking it kind of like you do in the can, when you are shaking off, but, also, there was something threatening and a little bully-like about the way he did it, I remember, too, like the dick was a fist he was putting in my face and daring me to say anything, and I remember I was wrapped up tight in the afghan, and could not get up or move out of the way of the dick, and all I can remember doing was sort of like moving my head all over the place, trying to get it out of my face, (the dick). It was one of those totally bizarre incidents that is so weird it seems like it is not happening even while it is happening to you. The only time I had even glimpsed my father's dick before was in locker rooms. I remember my head kind of moving around, all over the place, on my neck, and the dick kind of following me all over the place, and having totally weird thoughts going through my head while he did it, like, "I am moving my head just like a snake," etc. He did not have a boner. I remember the dick was a little bit darker than the rest of him, and big, with a big ugly vein down one side of it. The little hole-thing at the end looked slitty and pissed off, and it opened and closed a little as my father waggled the dick, keeping the dick threateningly in my face no matter where I moved my head around to. That is the memory. After I had it, (the memory), I went around my folks' house in a haze, in like a cloud, totally freaked out, not telling anybody about it, and not asking anybody anything. That was the only time my father ever did anything like that. This was when I was packing, and going around to stores getting boxes to move with. Sometimes, I walked around my folks' house in shock, and feeling totally weird. I kept thinking about the sudden memory. I went into my folks' room, and down to the rec room. The rec room had a new entertainment system instead of the old TV, but my mom's TV afghan was still there, spread over the back of the couch when not in use. It was still the same afghan as in the memory. I kept trying to think about why my father would do something like that, and what he could have been thinking of, like what it could have meant, and trying to remember if there had been any kind of look or expression, during it, on his face.

Now it gets even weirder, because I finally, the day my father took a half day off and we went down and rented a van for me to pack and move out with, I, finally, in the van, on the way home from the rental place, brought it up, and asked him about the memory. I asked him about it straight out. It is not like there is a graceful way to gradually lead up to something like that. My father had put the rental of the van on his card, and he was the one driving the van home. I remember that the radio in the van did not work. In the van, out of (from his perspective) nowhere, I suddenly tell my father that I recently remembered the day that he came down and waggled his dick in my face when I was a little kid, and I sort of briefly described what I remembered, and asked him, "What the fuck was up with that." When he simply kept driving the van, and did not say or do anything to respond, I persisted, and brought the incident up again, and asked him the same question all over again—I pretended as if maybe he did not hear what I said the first time. And then what my father does—we are in the van, on a brief straightaway on the route home to my folks' house, so I can get ready to move out on my own—he, without moving his hands on the wheel or moving one muscle except his neck, turns his head to look at me, and gives me this look. It is not a pissed off look, nor a confused one like he believes he did not quite hear. And it is not like he says, 'What the hell is the matter with you,' or, 'Get the fuck outta here,' or any of the usual things he says when you can tell that he is pissed off. He does not say anything, however, this look he gives me says it all, like he cannot believe he just heard this shit come out of my mouth, like he is in total disbelief and total disgust, like not only did he never in his life waggle his dick at me for no reason when I was a little kid but just the fact that I could even fucking imagine that he ever waggled his dick at me, and then like believe it, and then come into his presence in the rented van and like accuse him. Etc., etc. The look he reacted and gave me in the van while he drove, after I brought up the memory and asked him about it straight out—this is what sent me totally over the edge where my father was concerned. The look he turned and slowly gave me said he was embarrassed for me and embarrassed for himself for being related to me. Imagine if you were at a large, fancy, coat-and-tie dinner or track banquet with your father, and if you all of a sudden got up on the banquet table and bent down and took a shit on the table, in front of everybody at the dinner—this would be the kind of look that your father would be giving you as you did it. Roughly, it was then, in the van, that I felt like I could have killed him. It is weird—the memory in itself did not, at the time, get me pissed off, but only freaked out, like in a shocked daze. But, in the van that day, the way my father did not even say anything, but merely drove home to their house in silence, with both hands on the wheel, and that look on his face about me asking about it—now I was totally pissed off. I always thought that that thing you hear about seeing "red" if you get mad enough was just a figure of speech, but it is real. After I packed all my shit in the van, I moved away, and did not get in contact with my folks for over a year. Not a word. My apartment, in the same town, was two miles at most away, but I did not even tell them my phone number. I pretended they did not exist. I was so disgusted and pissed off. My mom had no clue why I was not in contact, but I sure was not going to mention a word to her about any of it, and I knew for fucking-A sure that my father was not going to say anything to her about it. Everything I saw stayed slightly red for months, after I moved out and broke off contact, or at least a pink tinge. I did not think of the memory of my father waggling his dick at me as a little kid very often, but hardly a day went by that I did not remember that look in the van he gave me when I brought it up again. I wanted to kill him. For months, I thought about going home when nobody was there and kicking his ass. My sisters had no clue why I was not in contact with my folks, and said I must have gone crazy, and was breaking my mom's heart, and when I called them they gave me shit about breaking off contact without explanation constantly, but I was so pissed off, I knew I was going to my grave never saying another fucking word about it. It was not that I was chicken to say anything about it, but I was so fucking over the edge about it, it felt like, if I ever mentioned it again, and got any sort of look from somebody, something terrible would happen. Almost every day, I imagined that, as I went home and was kicking his ass, my father would keep asking me why I was doing it and what it meant, but I would not say anything, nor would my face have any look on it as I beat the shit out of him.

Then, as time passed, I, little by little, got over the whole thing. I still knew that the memory of my father coming down into the rec room and waggling his dick at me was totally real, but, little by little, I realized that, just because I remembered the incident, that did not mean that my father necessarily did. I started to see that, maybe, he had forgotten the whole incident. It was possible that the whole incident was so weird and unexplained that my father psychologically blocked it out of his memory, and that when I, out of (from his point of view) nowhere, brought it up to him in the van, he did not remember ever doing something as bizarre and unexplained as coming down and threateningly waggling his dick at a little kid, and thought I had lost my fucking mind, and gave me a look that said he was totally disgusted and embarrassed. It is not like I totally believed that my father had no memory of it—it was more like I, little by little, was admitting that it was possible that he blocked it out. To me, it seemed, little by little, like the moral of the memory of any incident that totally weird is, "anything is possible." After the year, I got to this position in my attitude where I figured that, if my father was willing to forget about the whole thing of me bringing up the memory of the incident in the van, and to never bring it up, then I was willing to forget the whole thing. I knew that I, for fucking-A damn sure, would never bring any of it up again. When I arrived at this attitude about the whole thing, it was around early July, right before the Fourth of July, which is also my littlest sister's birthday, and so, out of (to them) nowhere, I call my folks' house and ask if I can come along for my sister's birthday and meet them at this one special restaurant that they traditionally take my sister to on her birthday, because she loves it so much. This restaurant, which is in our town's downtown, is Italian, expensive, and has mostly dark decor, and has menus in Italian. It was ironic that it was at this restaurant, on a birthday, that I would be getting back in contact with my folks, because, when I was a little kid, our family's tradition was that this was my special restaurant, where I always got taken for my birthday—I somewhere, as a kid, got the idea that it was run by the Mob, in which, as a kid, I had a total fascination, and always badgered my folks until they took me on my birthday—until, little by little, as I aged, I outgrew it, and then somehow it passed into being my littlest sister's special restaurant, like she had inherited it. It has black and red checkered tablecloths, and all the waiters look like Mob enforcers, and on the restaurant's tables are always wine bottles with candles stuck in the hole, which have melted, and various colors of wax run and harden up all over the sides of the bottle in lines and varied patterns. As a little kid, I remember having a weird fascination with the wine bottles with all the dried wax running all over them, and of having to be asked, by my father, over and over not to keep picking off the wax. When I arrived at the restaurant in a coat and tie, they were all already there, at a table. My mom looked totally enthusiastic and pleased just to see me, and I could tell that she was willing to forget the whole year of me not contacting them, she was just so pleased to feel like a real family again.

My father said, "You're late." His face had zero expression either way.

My mom said, "I'm afraid we already ordered, is that okay."

My father said that they had ordered for me already, being as I was a little late getting there.

I sat down, and smilingly asked what they had ordered me.

My father said, 'A chicken pesto dish thing your mother ordered for you."

I said, "But I hate chicken. I always hated it. How could you guys forget I hate chicken?"

We all looked at each other for a second, even my little sister, and her boyfriend with the hair. There was one long split second of all looking at one another. This was when the waiter was bringing everybody's chicken. Then my father smiled, and drew one of his hands back jokingly, and said,

"Get the fuck outta here!" Then my mom leaned her head back and put her hand up against her upper chest, like she does when she is afraid she is going to laugh too hard, and laughed. The waiter put my plate in front of me, and I pretended to look down and make a face, and we all laughed. It was good.

Westchester Burning

Amine Wefali

Amine Wefali made her debut in Open City. *She is the author of* Westchester Burning: Portrait of a Marriage, *and is working on a collection of linked stories about Nyack entitled* The River, *as well as a children's book. She owns three restaurants in Manhattan.*

1. You Can Be Sure

IN 1984 PHILLIP AND I BOUGHT A HOUSE IN BEDFORD as an investment. We planned to rent the house out. The money we received in rent would almost pay for the mortgage, and the appreciation on the house would, through the years, pay for our children's college education.

We bought the house from Mrs. Keenan. Her husband had owned a chain of taverns in the Bronx, Erin Forever. He died of a heart attack the day they moved in, leaving her alone to raise their six sons. Her youngest was going to Michigan University on an athletic scholarship and she didn't need a large house anymore.

We had the eleven rooms painted Navajo White, the downstairs floors refinished, and the upstairs recarpeted in a medium pile, light green. We rented the house to a divorced orthopedic surgeon and his two grown sons. After six months they stopped paying rent. The doctor quit his practice and became a bodybuilder. His sons held part time jobs as landscapers.

"It's not easy evicting tenants," a litigation partner told Phillip.

Four months later they were gone.

They took their forty sets of bodybuilding equipment and opened "Bodies by George" in Hartsdale. The business was registered in the doctor's mother's name. They left five dogs, two of them dead, eight cats, and two ferrets.

Phillip took a day off from work, got the animals in cages, and brought them to the local ASPCA. The Department of Public Works removed the dogs that had died.

The house was fumigated and the real-estate agent advised us to reno-vate the house before putting it on the market.

"You have a great investment here. Money you spend on it, you'll dou-ble. It's in a great location, great family neighborhood, and the house is on five acres. Yes, the land in the back slopes down suddenly, but that's not a problem. Five acres is still five acres. Bedford zoning law allows one horse per acre. You can have five horses here."

Phillip told me the house was now my baby, but he would still have to approve all expenditures.

There were three estimates for the work; Phillip went with the middle bid.

"Mrs. Calt," said the contractor, "you can't get these urine stains out. No amount of sanding will do it. The whole downstairs. Upstairs? It went right through the carpeting. All the floors. In every room. You'll have to retile the bathrooms, it went right through the grout. It's a good thing that the floor in the basement is cement. Cement is pretty indestructible. All we need to do with that is wash it down with a strong chemical solution and then paint it. A nice battleship gray.

"Mrs. Calt, since your husband okayed replacing the floor, why don't you suggest knocking out the wall between the kitchen and family room to him? There's a big hole in it anyway. This way you'll get to see a nice fire burning in the fireplace as you're making dinner."

The contractor hired a subcontractor for the kitchen counters and cab-inets. The contractor was paid, but instead of paying the subcontractor, he became ill and moved to Florida, where bankruptcy laws are lenient.

Phillip hired the contractor who had come in with the highest bid.

"Mrs. Calt, did you know that they laid the new flooring over rotted subflooring? There's no way you can save what was put down. Everything will have to be ripped up. If you like, we'll cut it up for you and you can use it for kindling. We'll give you a new subflooring and we'll use wood that's been kiln dried. This way it won't buckle up at you. We'll lay down brand-new oak floors and you can be sure the job will be done right this time."

The house didn't sell. It was a problem that most of the five acres were unusable. It was advised to landfill the gully, remove the weeping willows, and create an expansive lawn. I saw the two sons of the doctor on the land-scaping crew. One was operating the bulldozer and the other one was dri-ving the truck with the rocks.

It took about a year after the Wall Street crash of l987 for the bottom to fall out of the real-estate market. It was then that Phillip told me I had ruined his life.

Why do I believe, at age fifty-two, that by spraying Yves Saint Laurent's Rive Gauche near the open window of my attic bedroom, it will replace the smell of my first cigarette of the morning? That the strong, sweet, scent will be enough to mask what I have done? What can he say? Can he hurt me more?

He came home last night after I finally fell asleep. He did come home, because when I came downstairs his door was closed, shut tight by the black sock he uses as a doorjamb.

During the renovation of the house, the doorknobs from all the doors were removed. The doors were stripped of old paint, planed, sanded, primed, and repainted. The doorknobs were placed in two large plastic buckets.

"Mrs. Calt, we can't find the doorknobs. Someone must have taken them or else they were thrown out by mistake. They're gone. I don't even know where to tell you to get them. They're an odd size. They'd have to be specially made up. It'll be expensive, since they were solid brass and old."

Phillip now uses one of his black socks to hold his door shut. The door that opens to the room that was once ours and is now his. He sleeps alone.

He'll have someone. He takes care of himself. Cycling on weekends, using lite mayonnaise, having one brimming glass of red wine to help clear his arteries and to be safe, a small piece of Belgian chocolate. He uses firming neck cream. He takes vitamins E, A, C (l000 mg.), and B complex, zinc, calcium, folic acid, and selenium. He reads *Paramahansa Yogananda*. Lying in bed, after taking a cold shower, a large white towel wrapped around his waist, he exercises his gums with a rubber-tipped metal instrument.

It won't take long for him to have someone. He won't have to take someone somewhere. That someone can come here and lie next to him on the queen-size bed. Lie. Together. When I leave, I'll take the dust ruffle. It was specially ordered from England. It cascades, in folds, to the plum-colored carpet. I'll take it. It'll remove the softness from the bed.

2. Friends

Her hand moves through her thinning hair. Her eyes focus on mine and then she looks away. "I'm going to stop dyeing my hair as soon as it turns all gray," she says.

In the fading light of a humid August evening she and I sit on her terrace, waiting for the rain. The roses I brought lie between us on the table. The geraniums in clay pots haven't been watered and the terrace needs to be swept. Her neighbors tore down the wooden shed that separated their two backyards, replacing it with a chain-link fence. An attempt was made to spray paint it dark green. "I should have planted ivy there," she says. "They could have at least told us. Bobby could have built something with the old wood."

In her right hand she holds a cigarette, in her left, an empty wine glass; her dexterity serves her well. Three bottles of red wine lie in an open cooler several yards behind us. I move to bring the whole thing closer and she says, "Don't. I need the exercise." And she gets up and peels away the wrapper from the neck of an unopened bottle and, calling on years of practice, pushes the cork down with her thumb.

She was a dancer with Martha Graham. Now her waist has thickened, her legs are thin, and the cornflower blue of her dress can't take away the weariness from her face.

Her mother called me last night. "Katya. It's terminal. Don't let her know I told you. Maybe she'll tell you herself."

With her glass refilled she moves her chair closer to mine, leans into the cushion, and says, "Why is Brooklyn suddenly on the way for you? Last time you said you were coming I cleaned the house and waited and you never showed up. This time you just drop in. I haven't seen you in, what? Three years? Next time I won't be home."

"I miss you," I say.

"Bobby made a Greek salad. Let me give you some," she says.

"How is it that you get husbands who cook for you?" I ask.

"I guess I'm just lucky." She laughs. "Are you and Phillip still together?"

"Yes." I recross my legs.

"When are you going to wake up and leave him?" she asks.

"How's Paul?" I ask.

"My brother is fine. You know he married her. Candy. Now she wants a baby and she makes him take vitamins to help her do it. He told her he had a vasectomy and she told him to reverse it. What? She wants to make a father out of him again at fifty-five? He has two with Ada. You have four with

Phillip. And I have none with Bobby. What should that average out to? Two apiece?"

"Let me put the roses in water," I say.

"No. Don't. It'll rain soon and we'll go in. He's moved his company to Seattle. Bobby and I spent a few days out there. He's built this twenty-thousand-square-foot home that suspends over the Pacific. The master bathroom is as big as this house and it has a glass ceiling that if you touch one of the buttons it disappears and you see the stars at night. I asked him if he ever touched the button when there was a storm outside and he said that could never happen. Fourteen people can float around in the Jacuzzi that's surrounded by calla lilies and he takes the vitamins Candy gives him and throws them into the heads and says to me, 'Maybe they'll make them grow.' They're coming to New York at the end of the month, but he's not staying in Brooklyn with me, no, he can't do that. It's the penthouse at the Four Seasons."

"I wish I could see him again."

"You can't. She doesn't leave his side. He's lucky if he floats in the Jacuzzi by himself. I talk to him about you in front of her just to see her squirm. No. He's gone. Packaged. Done and gone." The strap of her dress falls off her shoulder and she doesn't bother bringing it back. "Did you notice my nose? I finally got it fixed."

"I never thought anything was wrong with your nose. What do you say to him about me?"

"I make things up." she says.

We hear the siren of a fire truck.

"I wonder how they maneuver these narrow streets?"

"Just like we all do."

The rain starts to fall and I reach for the cushions to bring them in.

"Leave everything."

We walk down the steps to the basement. She pulls out damp sheets from the dryer and I follow her into a room that is now a bedroom. Bobby lies on the unmade bed, their dog, Mookie, beside him.

"Let me help you make the bed," I tell her.

"No. Let Bobby sleep. Mookie threw up last night and when she did, I did. It was a mess. It took me hours to clean." And she drops the sheets in a pile on a chair.

We climb the stairs to the room that takes up the entire second floor. The windows are open at both ends and the breeze breaks through the smell of dust and cinnamon. She lights candles that stand on the side-board, softening the light cast by the chandelier hanging from the sixteen-foot ceiling. She reaches into a cabinet and brings out an opened bottle of white wine; she pours it into a thin crystal glass, not caring that it's warm. We walk to the far end of the room. I sit on one of the couches that surround the glass table I had given her when Michael started to walk. She stands by the fireplace and from the mantel takes down an icon. She walks over and hands it to me. "I bought it in a village outside of Moscow. An old woman wanted five dollars for it, I gave her five hundred and still got a bargain."

It's old and it's covered by the tarnished silver *oklad*, allowing only the thin, dark faces of the mother and child to stare through.

"You should hang it," I say.

"Where should I hang it?" she answers.

"Above your bed," I say.

"It's not blessed," she says.

"I'll go with you to the synod and we can get it blessed," I say.

"Should I wait for you to come so we can go together? When did you become religious? Put it back for now."

On the mantel I see a framed photograph resting against the wall. It was taken the summer the three of us were counselors at a camp in the Catskills. Paul stands between his sister and me with his arm around my waist. We hiked twenty-five miles that day on roads that wove through neck-high corn. A cardinal flew low and I knew how happy I was.

"I didn't know this picture existed," I say.

"Paul gave it to me when I saw him," she says.

"He had it all this time?" I ask.

"Why are you surprised? Remember the dress you let me wear?"

White chiffon with small apricot polka dots. The slightest movement would set it in motion. She asked me if she could wear it to a party. I noticed my dress one Saturday, folded, in a laundry basket beneath a leaking bottle of bleach. Impulsively she cut her hair; she kept the long, thick braid in a box on the top shelf of her closet. I took her braid and wore it until it stopped being anything. She told me it wasn't an even trade.

"Do you know what I miss most? My hair."

"I know," I say.

"You do? How do you know? Your hair didn't go down to your waist and you didn't have a mother who spent an hour every day brushing it. All you had was a mother who told you my brother wasn't good enough for you. Who could amount to something. You threw my brother away like he was nothing. Like he was nothing. And you got Phillip. What a prize! Are you happy? You can't be. He can't make anyone happy. Happiness? And you knew Phillip and I were getting it on and you did nothing."

When did her eyes become lifeless?

"Say something."

"Let me have some of that Greek salad Bobby made."

3. Smile

Madison Avenue was wet and cold. The first snow of the winter disappeared as it hit the pavement.

Martin's wife said this wasn't a retrospective, just some photographs Martin put together for a show representing his work through four decades.

As I walk in I see Dooley. He and Leslie still live in the town Phillip and I left two years ago. Dooley tells me that it's always so wonderful to see me, that Martin and he went to Yale, that they and their wives try to get together at least twice a year, that it's always so much fun. I smile and say, "That's wonderful."

"You've lost weight, haven't you?" Dooley asks. I smile.

"I hear that you and Phillip are moving back to our little town."

I smile and know if he's heard this, he's probably heard the rest. "I guess you and Leslie are still together?"

His eyes quickly leave mine and we move our separate ways.

I stand before a large black-and-white photograph. A dark- haired girl sits, holding onto her cigarette. A boy, his head raised, lies beside her. The Coney Island boardwalk stretches out behind them into a summer haze.

"Isn't it amazing how close they let him come in?" a stranger beside me says.

"He was probably their age when he took this," I reply.

"Of course." The stranger laughs. "May I ask where you were then?"

"I was riding my bicycle to the library to sneak in to read *Nancy Drew and the Secret of the Girl Who Couldn't Remember*. And you?"

"Stationed in Germany."

It's then that I see him.

He walks by, his hand holding hers; guiding their way through the crowd.

She's taller than he is, her thick, curly hair held together by pins.

A friend who knows her tells me he's cleared up her face. The same way he cleared up my weight.

I wonder if he tells her he is in awe of her? Does he serve her tea sweetened with rose-petal jam in his darkened office? And does he tell her, softly, to bend lower as he enters her from behind?

I move to the bar and a young man gives me my vodka with no ice in a wineglass and I make my way back to where I know they might be.

My hand reaches out and touches him on his deep blue cashmered back. "Hello," I say.

He turns and looks at me with no surprise. "Hi."

"Martin lives in our building."

"Who's Martin?" he asks.

"He's the photographer. We're at his show."

"You're still in the city?"

I turn and walk away and as I pass the stranger leaning against a pillar of that low-ceilinged room, I smile.

4. Birdseed

There was no birdseed left for the parrots, Lorritta, who we've had for eighteen years, and Vanya, who remained with us after my mother died, and I drove the ten miles to the feed store.

I haven't been to this store in two years, ever since we moved out of our house in Westchester and into an apartment on West Eighty-sixth Street. Phillip said he could no longer afford paying for the house and the apartment and he was tired of paying New York City taxes and he's finished with trying to make me happy. It hasn't worked. So a month ago we moved back to the house that's surrounded by the pines and the quiet.

It was Phillip who had usually done this errand on Saturday mornings, either before or after the garden center, the dry cleaners, and the liquor store, the one that stands at the top of the hill. How many pounds of rabbit food did we buy through the years? Annie loved her bunnies.

As I walked in, the owner, leaning back in his swivel chair, his feet up on a stack of canned dog food, said, "Are you back? It's not what you thought it'd be. Right?"

I smiled and made my way to the bin where the birdseed was kept. The bin was empty; on the floor beside it stood an open sack of seed. He came over and we each filled a plastic bag.

"You've lost weight," I said.

"Actually I gained a little. I really lost it when my wife left two years ago. She ran off with an old guy she worked with at the electric company. This guy of hers put his wife in a nursing home and had my wife move in with him. Something happens to them, they sort of go nuts."

"Was your wife going through menopause?"

"Yeah, how did you know? Right. I guess you would." He laughed. "He died, this guy of hers. A half a year after she moved in. She's paying for it now though. Big time. She's taking care of her sick mother. Do you still have dogs?"

He and I walked over to the cash register and I took a wrapped piece of candy from a glass jar that stood by the hamster cages.

"She tried divorcing me, but it was lame and the judge threw it out."

"You don't want to give your wife a divorce?"

"No. She's not getting half of anything. She's really gotten old looking; she never took anything for it. And she's gotten to be afraid of things. Now it's the air bag in her car."

He followed me out carrying a twenty-five-pound bag of dog food. He put it on the front seat while China barked at him from the back.

"Give your parrots broccoli; it's full of calcium. That way they'll live longer. Nice seeing you again. Take care of yourself."

5. The King Alfreds

Carole called this afternoon. She asked if I'd go to the ballet. She finally has a subscription and no one in her family will go with her. She'll pick me up, but I will have to drive in. She can't stand the maniacs on the road.

I know Carole won't come into the house and I know Phillip will watch her drive up. She avoids Phillip ever since George, her husband, came over and asked Phillip not to move the stone wall that stands between our properties. George and Carole buried both their Irish setters by it. Phillip pulled out the new survey that showed his property going beyond the wall into "land George shouldn't think is his anymore." George couldn't claim it, said Phillip, by using their two dogs as an excuse. And my husband had the stone wall moved. Now, fifteen feet of grass and two dead dogs are on our side of the stone wall.

I walk out of the house into a cold May evening. Spring is late this year, the dogwoods are just coming out. It will probably be a brilliant fall.

I wait for Carole to finish beating her car mat against the corner of the garage.

Carole hasn't lost her looks or the blonde in her hair. We both worry about our calcium. I eat cottage cheese and sardines. She takes Tums, three rolls a day. She doesn't smoke or drink coffee or eat any processed meat.

She likes her champagne with a splash of raspberry vodka and she's wearing the black cashmere coat we flipped a quarter for at last month's St. Anthony's rummage sale.

She straightens up after putting back the mat and says, "I still miss the King Alfreds."

Carole is remembering the daffodils. It took us a week of afternoons to plant them. We laid the bulbs in five tight rows along the path leading to the playhouse. They came up stronger every May for fifteen years. When the new well needed to be dug, an underground spring was disturbed and it flooded the whole area where the daffodils grew.

I back Carole's Suburban to the front. I can't stop myself from looking toward the house and seeing Phillip sitting in his chair by the windows.

Last night, Phillip told me I was irrelevant to him. We stood a few feet apart by the stairs to the attic and he said, "Katherine. Don't you understand? You are irrelevant to me."

It takes only a few minutes to leave our country lane and be on the parkway going south. Carole unfastens her seat belt and says, "I don't want to get wrinkled."

I glance over to her as she begins to play with her hair. She'll take a strand and begin twirling it around her finger, using the twisted end, like a paintbrush, to dot her lips. She looks out the side window. "My mother had rosebushes. I wanted to dig them up from her yard and plant them where our tennis court used to be, but that cheap, miserable bastard sold them. She had a bush of blue ones. Roses don't smell anymore. They've strained the smell right out."

"Roses take so much time. I've tried covering them, not covering them. It doesn't seem to matter," I reply.

"Her roses grew from May to . . . November? There were roses on the table at Thanksgiving. Funny, I just remembered that."

"We always had a bowl of fruit on the table for Thanksgiving."

"She made the best apple pies. She'd have the kids pick the apples off the ground. She'd make six, seven pies. They'd be gone in two days. I asked her to give me the recipe. She'd say, 'Watch me.' I never was in the kitchen long enough to watch."

I thought of my own mother and all of the questions left unanswered.

"I'd have her out to the house in Shelter Island. She wouldn't be there two days when she'd say, 'Take me to the fruit stand. I want to get those peaches to make your father a pie.' A pie! When I saw the bastard take the bedpost and beat her with it. He kept it unscrewed and ready."

"Did she ever fight him back?" I ask.

Carole laughs. "Are you still hoping I'll say yes? I walked in on them once. He had her right on the kitchen table. He was mean. Mean. I'd ask him for a nickel to buy a Good Humor. You know what he'd say? 'Go earn it.' I was five years old. The only thing he ever gave me was a radio for my graduation and he bought it at the Salvation Army thrift store. And she had to die before him. He left everything, the house, the apartment buildings, everything to the archdiocese. He really thought it would get him to heaven. May his soul rot in hell."

"Rita Simmons died."

"I know. Finally," Carole says.

"They say she went down to sixty pounds. You could see her heart."

"That's not possible," Carole says.

"Yes. They say you could see it beating."

"Promise me, Katie. If I ever get that way, leave me off somewhere in the desert. Give me a sun reflector and tell me to just keep walking, that you'll pick me up real soon. Rita held on too long. There's a point where you've got to say, okay, that's enough. Thank you. Goodbye."

When is enough enough? Rita was president of the Garden Club. There were eleven of us. We'd pile into two station wagons and go planting around statues. Carole and I are the only ones left. Everyone else has moved away. Rita's husband was transferred to Keene, New Hampshire.

"I have to tell you the latest," Carole says. "I get a call from a dealer this morning. There's a show at the County Center. He tells me he's got what my husband wants. George has been looking for a BB gun like the one he had when he was twelve. His mother made him sell it. He got four dollars for it. Now, this dealer, how many years later? Has one just like it. In its original box, tissue paper, the whole thing. But now, of course, it's five hundred dollars. Today is George's birthday. Funny, he gets his wish on his birthday. He buys the gun, brings it home. By now he's had a few. I'm in the library, polishing the porridge bowl where I keep the gummi bears and I see him standing in the doorway, pointing the gun at me. He says, 'Let me just blow away that beaver. It's not doing me any good.' I tell him, 'Go ahead,'" and she laughs. "If only he knew where the beaver was last night, how wet and wild it was. I really cannot stand him. We did nothing for his birthday. I wanted to go to the Kittle House for brunch but he was out buying a gun. None of the kids showed up. Their father's sixty-fifth birthday. Can you imagine? I'll blow it away. It's not doing me any good." And she laughs.

"One of these days he might just do it."

"George? You know what he said to me? 'If I'd killed you when we still lived in Scarsdale I'd be out by now.' He's funny." She laughs. "Katie, what do I have? Maybe another five good years? As soon as we sell the house, I'm out. I'll get a house in Westport, on the water, close to town, where I can walk to everything. I can take the train to the city. I've had it with the driving."

"I thought you were going to Florida?"

"No. The whole state is one big air conditioner. I told you Frank is buying a house in Captiva. I'll make him open all the windows when I visit. It was so convenient having him so close by. Now? I'm really going to miss him. He says I'm like a river."

I wonder why they call it the Saw Mill River Parkway? There had to have been a river here. Once. Large enough to have a saw mill on it. Where did it go?

"Frank is the same age as George. Incredible. George can't get it up anymore. It's the drinking. It's sad. George was so good. Once. Still, not like Frank. It's also the genes. George's father left before George was born, so God knows what he was like. Frank's father is ninety and they have to restrain him in the nursing home."

I think how lucky Carole is that her parents died quickly. It wasn't very quick for my mother. But then she was with me and I held her when she died.

"The only problem with Frank is he repeats himself. He forgets and I don't want to tell him, 'Frank, I've heard this.' Listen, as long as he fucks me the way he does, I don't care. I put a smile on my face and say, 'Oh, Frank, what an interesting story.' He's a great cook, too. George remembers everything, when he's sober, which is not a lot of the time, and he can't get it up. Frank remembers close to nothing and can go on for days. Wouldn't it be great if I could splice them together and throw away what's not working?"

"With Phillip it's a mystery."

"Well, Katie, while you're trying to figure that one out, climb down those attic stairs of yours and join the world. Find yourself a man. All I have to do is put it out to one of Frank's brothers and you're in."

"I don't want that."

"I know. You want love. I was in Barnes & Noble the other day. I was looking through some books and I read something. It said, 'Love is something you don't have and you give to someone who doesn't want it.'

"That's not true."

"Why are you holding on? Are you waiting for him to say, 'Katie, you're the best thing that's ever happened to me?' He's never going to say it. Get over it. He's incapable of it. Leave him."

"I am."

"Right. You'll be up in that attic of yours for a while yet. You've made it too cozy. And you won't let go. You keep your mother's ashes by your bed, for God's sake. And where would you go?"

"I'm going to U.C. Berkeley."

"To do what?"

"I am going to get a degree in archaeology."

"Being with one dead man is not enough for you? You haven't said anything to me about this. When did you decide this?"

"Last night."

"Last night? You're not serious. You're not going to do this. Anyway you're too old."

"I'm not. I'm doing it."

"It's too late to apply."

"I'm applying to the summer session. I'll be enrolled by fall."

"When are you leaving?"

"At the end of May."

"No you're not."

"I am."

Carole and I sit still watching the New York City Ballet perform *Sleeping Beauty*. A bar of dark chocolate rests in my lap. I try not to let the rustle of the thin foil be heard as I give Carole and myself a piece.

Carole leans over and whispers, "Isn't it magical?"

6. By the Railroad Tracks

Thanksgiving Day. Phillip made an omelette for five, for himself and the children. I take China for a walk. She won't leave my side as we walk the old golf course overlooking the Hudson.

Phillip made reservations at the Kittle House for six at four. I'll sit between my two daughters, and for the first time in thirty years I'll eat turkey that I haven't put in the oven. Maybe I won't have turkey. Maybe I'll order goose.

I had planned Thanksgiving at home, inviting friends to relieve the tension.

Phillip told me that's not what the children want.

"Why?" I asked.

"Ask them," he answered.

I did, and they said he told them there weren't going to be anymore Thanksgivings at home.

I planned to go to the Grand Union to buy eggs and toilet paper and instead I sit on a bench in a small park by the railroad tracks. I give China half my bagel with cream cheese. The car radio mentioned two Macy's balloons were damaged by high winds, one shredded completely, the other causing a lamppost to fall on a woman.

A black girl walks by in a camel-hair coat with a leopard print bag slung over her shoulder. Is it a mince pie or a plum tart in the plastic bag she's holding? Below me the New York City–bound train pulls in. The girl starts to run and I hope she makes it.

It's a blue, cloudless morning. The hardware on the empty flagpole beats against the metal.

A policeman walks over to where I sit.

"What are you writing?" he asks.

"My life story," I answer.

"Well, that's probably better than mine. Are you from around here?"

"The next town over," and I motion to where I think north is while telling China to sit.

"Where the snotty people live?"

"Yes, the self-important and boring ones."

"Brooding?"

"Boring."

"I'm from the Bronx."

"You know, there's not a person from the Bronx that I haven't liked."

"Yeah, it used to be a great place. They have a bunch of guys that take care of your town. We're all New York City cops come over."

"The pay is better here?"

"Nah, it's less aggravation. It's the aggravation that gets you. If you finish off your day without anyone getting killed or robbed, you've done your job. Anything else is an aggravation. Your first year, you want to help everyone. After twenty, you don't care if they live or die. It messes up your life. You bring your work home and your relationships suffer."

"You were married?"

"Yeah. She took off eight years ago."

"Did she run away with another man?"

"Maybe she did. Who knows? But she ran away with my daughter." He shoves his hands into the pockets of his sateen jacket. "That's enough to spoil your day."

"Have you seen your daughter since?"

"Nope. She took her to Italy." His eyes vanish as he looks into the sun. "What are you gonna do?"

"Have you remarried?"

From his jacket pocket he pulls out a blue photograph book and hands it to me.

The first picture is of an infant placed in a pumpkin wearing a hat shaped into leaves and the second picture is of the little boy being held in his father's arms.

"Your wife takes very good care of your son."

"She does shit. I'm the one who cooks and cleans and she calls me a fanatic. Relationships? Relationships are an aggravation. The holidays are the worst. It's supposed to be a happy time and all it is is more depressing. You'd think it'd be your family that supports you, but it doesn't work out that way. It's the barber or the dry cleaning man or an old lady. They listen to you and give you support. Your father, mother, brother? Nothing. It's the people you don't know that give you what you want."

"Isn't it wonderful you have the kind of job that lets you be in touch with a lot of different people."

"Well, it was nice talking to you. I need to check up on the train station, see if they didn't trash it during the night. Are you married?"

"Yes."

"Happily?"

"We're separating." And it's the cold wind that's just made me shiver.

"Well, be good."

7. Rats

Phillip is squeezing juice from an orange when I walk into the kitchen and without looking up he says, "Are you aware of the twenty-one-thousand-dollar bill your lawyer sent me? Why don't you get a job and pay for it?"

"I have a job."

"Why don't you get a job that earns money?"

"My job eventually will."

"Fuck you."

Using both hands, he brings the glass of juice to his lips. I decide to make a poached egg for myself. Waiting for the water to boil I again tell him to get an exterminator. We have rats in the basement.

"Michael and I put poison down."

"They're too smart for poison. Why can't you just call an exterminator?"

"What do you think an exterminator is going to do?"

The bell rings. The big, bronze ship's bell that was hung to the right of the front door by the admiral who had the house built in 1907. He named his home "The Anchorage."

"Are you expecting someone?"

"Kormandy."

Phillip must have called Mr. Kormandy to get an estimate on the damage done to the ceiling and the garden-side wall of the kitchen when the pan he was frying french fries in caught fire.

"Mr. Kormandy, you don't have to take your shoes off. Nobody else does."

He smiles and extends his hand and wishes me a happy and healthy new year and continues to untie his laces. He's not as thin anymore and his dyed hair makes his face look older. The last time he was here seems so long ago.

"It is holding up," he says, looking at the rooms as he stands by the staircase.

He doesn't know we had someone else after him. Someone recommended by the contractor. If Mr. Kormandy had done the painting maybe we would still have our doorknobs.

"Mr. Calt. How are you, sir? I was saying to your wife that my job still looks good. How long has it been?"

"Awhile," replies Phillip, remaining seated. "I take it you've been well?"

"Actually, not so good. I married again. A twenty-year-old girl that I got from Hungary."

This must be his fourth wife.

"She bought fifty-nine pairs of shoes and filled two closets with clothes. In two years she spent twenty-five thousand dollars. I knew she would be a girl with problems; her father was an alcoholic. He told his children he would throw them out of the window so she is a nervous girl. I thought when I brought her to America it would be okay. She bought a six-hundred-dollar dog and she does not pay rent. I have to divorce her. I met a girl in Hungary. She is different, but who knows? Maybe they are all the same. I want to marry her."

The pot I was boiling water in is burning and I remove it from the stove. I look at Phillip. He sits and eats raw cashews from the bowl I keep filled.

"Does your wife work?

"Oh yes. She has a very good job cleaning houses, and I got her a green card so she is okay."

"Did you buy Amazon.com?" asks Phillip.

"No. Did you?" and they laugh. "But do you know what I have been buying? Museum-quality paintings in Budapest for two thousand dollars. I have thirty-two paintings. I think it is going to be very, very good."

"Mr. Kormandy, while you're here, would you look in the sitting room?"

He interrupts me. "It's that outside stone wall. I will see how bad it is." And he leaves Phillip and me alone.

In a lowered voice Phillip says, "I'm on a limited budget. I'm not having any extra work done. You got that?" And his eyes become like two ink spots.

"Get an exterminator. I saw a rat coming out of your room."

8. By The Clock

I'm to meet my lawyer in Grand Central by the clock. He and I will walk to Phillip's lawyer's office. It's been ten months since the four of us have had a meeting. Nothing's changed. Phillip and I still live in the same house. It's now a question of who moves out.

I'm taking the train into the city. I won't have to deal with the traffic or the expense of midtown parking. I've given myself fifteen minutes to walk down the hill to the station.

A light rain has started to fall. On my way to the coat closet to get an umbrella I see part of the ceiling lying on the piano, the Steinway grand Phillip bought Anne when she was eight and asked her father if she could learn how to play. I told Phillip there was a leak in the master bath shower and he said all we had to do was reposition the shower head so that the water would fall right into the drain and wouldn't collect along the sides where the leak probably was. I guess the ceiling couldn't take it anymore. The plaster is wet and I've got to get it off the piano before it stains it and I've got to cover the piano with something that's waterproof in case the rest of the ceiling falls. Do I have anything large enough? Maybe I should roll the piano out of the way? No. Then the plaster will fall on the wood floor and stain that. What should I do? I'll move the piano. I'll lay a couple of blankets that I still keep in the closet from the time the children used them and the cushions from the couches to make teepees.

I barely make the train.

The conductor asks for my ticket.

"I didn't have time to get a ticket."

"How much time did you have?

"Five minutes."

"That was enough time. I won't charge you the two-dollar penalty. Next time get your ticket at the station."

I notice a young man sitting diagonally across from me. I had seen him on the platform while I was catching my breath. He's so clean. He has a new suit on. Everything he's wearing is new. Does he shave? He must. I'm not near enough to know if he uses cologne. Probably. He's still talking on his cellular phone.

"I'll figure it out." "You know what?" "The truth is." "Profit." "You know." "I'd buy it." "Sure." "Exactly." "No rush." "As long as it's in our possession." "I'll call you when I get to the office."

A thick gold band encircles his left ring finger. They probably bought one of those prefab modular homes starting at $790,000 on Hardscrabble Road. Did they choose to have it assembled on level ground or on a knoll? They have two acres to landscape. In the fall they planted fast growing pines to obliterate the view of the neighboring power lines.

I think of Lillian Hellman. Her farm was on Hardscrabble Road and this new development is part of her farm. Her farm, where she grew bleached asparagus and raised poodles. I was in her farmhouse once, now owned by friends of friends. I sat in the library where she wrote and I was shown the linen closet where the shelves have been left labeled MISS HELLMAN and MR. HAMMETT. She sold the farm to pay for Dashiell Hammett's defense. She didn't have a choice.

The young man sneezed. A balding man in a pin-striped, white-collared shirt says, "Bless you."

"Thanks."

He's coming down with a cold. He's overworked and he goes outside with wet hair.

He stands up and goes to the doors as we pull into 125th Street. The doors open and he gets off.

Of course. He's one of the ones who is going to make Harlem presentable.

I pretend not to see Phillip in the building's lobby. We take separate elevators up. We're all right on time.

"The tuition for the Columbia University course Katherine is taking is completely unaffordable. To the extent that she wishes to pursue adult education, the budget should indicate the cost of classes at Westchester Community College, within reason of course, not Columbia University or a comparable college," says Phillip's lawyer. She looks smart wearing a size two beige Calvin Klein suit, ticking off at $350 an hour, Elsa Peretti's gold misshapen heart dangling from her throat.

I wonder who paid for law school.

"We'll get to that. First, I'd like to discuss Katherine and Phillip's living situation. Phillip should move to an apartment in the city. Katherine and Stephen should live in the house while Stephen is still in school, which is for another five years, and then, if Phillip wants the house, he can buy Katherine out."

"That's unacceptable. Katherine hates the house. Has always hated the community. She's stated this time and again. Phillip loves his house. Let Katherine be the one to rent an apartment in the city. She should live where she has always wanted to live. Phillip works in the city and he loves coming home to the fresh air."

"Stephen is in school here and Katherine stays with her son until he graduates."

"Let her rent a house."

"Katherine is not renting a house. If Katherine moves it will be into a house of her own. This is non-negotiable."

"Katherine is well aware there is no money for her own house."

"The Nantucket house can be sold."

"The Nantucket house is for Phillip's retirement."

"You know very well, Nancy, if this goes to court there will be a division of property, and aren't we here trying to avoid court at all costs?"

I wonder if the rest of the ceiling has fallen down.

Eurotrash

Irvine Welsh

Irvine Welsh is the author of seven novels and four short story collections. His novel, Trainspotting *was adapted into a film whose global success presented Welsh with a cult following. A prequel to* Trainspotting, *entitled* Skagboys, *will be released in 2012. "Eurotrash" was his first publication in the United States. He lives in Edinburgh.*

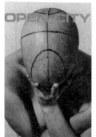 I WAS ANTI-EVERYTHING AND EVERYONE. I DIDN'T want people around me. This aversion was not some big crippling anxiety, merely a mature recognition of my own psychological vulnerability and my lack of suitability as a companion. Thoughts jostled for space in my crowded brain as I struggled to give them some order that might serve to motivate my listless life.

For others Amsterdam was a place of magic. A bright summer; young people enjoying the attractions of a city that epitomized personal freedom. For me it was a dull, blurred series of shadows. I was repelled by the harsh sunlight, seldom venturing out until it got dark. During the day I watched English and Dutch language programs on the television and smoked a lot of marijuana. Rab was a less than enthusiastic host. Without any sense of his own ridiculousness he informed me that here in Amsterdam he was known as "Robbie."

Rab/Robbie's revulsion for me seemed to blaze behind his face, sucking the oxygen from the air in the small front room on which I had made up a couch-bed. I'd note his cheek muscles twitch in repressed anger as he'd come in, dirty, grimy and tired from a hard, physical job, to find me mellow in front of the box, the ubiquitous spliff in my hand.

I was a burden. I had been here for only a fortnight and clean for three weeks. My physical symptoms had abated. If you can stay clean for a month you've got a chance. However, I felt it was time I looked for a place of my own. friendship with Rab (now, of course, reinvented as Robbie) could not survive the one-sided exploitative basis I had remodelled it on. The worse thing was: I didn't really care.

One evening, about a fortnight into my stay, it seemed he'd had enough.

—When ye gaunny start lookin for a job, man? he asked, with obviously forced nonchalance.

—I am, mate. I hud a wee shuftie aroond yesterday, trying tae check a few things out, y'know? The lie of the land, I said with contrived sincerity. We went on like this; forced civility, with a subtext of mutual antagonism.

I took tram number 17 from Rab/Robbie's depressing little scheme in the western sector into the city center. Nothing happens in places like the one we stayed in, Slotter Vaart they call it; breeze-block and concrete everywhere; one bar, one supermarket, one Chinese restaurant. It could've been anywhere. You need a city center to give you a sense of place. I could've been back in Wester Hailes, or on Kingsmead, back in one of those places I came here to get away from. Only I hadn't got away. One dustbin for the poor outside of action strasser is much the same as any other, regardless of the city it serves.

In my frame of mind, I hated being approached by people. Amsterdam is the wrong place to be in such circumstances. No sooner had I alighted in the Damrak than I was hassled. I'd made the mistake of looking around to get my bearings.

—French? American? English? an Arabic-looking guy asked.

—Fuck off, I hissed.

Even as I walked away from him into the English bookshop I could hear his voice reeling of a list of drugs. —

Hashish, heroin, cocaine, ecstasy . . .

During what was meant to be a relaxing browse, I found myself staging an internal debate as to whether or not I would shoplift a book; deciding against it, I left before the urge became unbearable. Feeling pleased with myself, I crossed over Dam Square into the red-light district. A cool twilight had descended on the city. I strolled, enjoying the fall of darkness. On a sidestreet off a canal, near where the whores sit in the windows, a man approached me at a threatening pace. I decided quickly that I would put my hands around his neck and choke him to death if he attempted to make any contact with me at all. I focused on his Adam's apple with murderous intent, my face twisting into a sneer as his cold, insect eyes slowly filled with apprehension.

—Time. Do you have the time? he asked fearfully.

I curtly nodded negative, striding satisfyingly past him as he arched his body to avoid being brushed onto the pavement. In Warmoesstraat it was not so easy. A group of youths were fighting a series of running baffles; Ajax and Salzburg fans. The UEFA Cup. Yes. I could not handle the movement and the screaming. It was the noise and motion I was averse to more than the threat of violence. I took the line of least resistance, and slipped down a side-street into a brown bar.

It was a quiet, tranquil haven. Apart from a dark-skinned man with yellow teeth (I had never seen teeth so yellow), who was wired up to the pinball machine, the only other occupants of the place were the barman and a woman who sat on a stool at the bar. They were sharing a bottle of tequila and their laughter and intimate behavior indicated that their relationship went beyond that of publican-customer.

The barman was setting the woman up with tequila shots. They were a little drunk, displaying a saccharine flirtatiousness. It took the man a while to register my presence at the bar. Indeed, the woman had to draw his attention to me. His response was to give her an embarrassed shrug, though it was obvious that he couldn't care less about me. Indeed, I sensed that I was an inconvenience.

In certain states of mind I would have been offended by this negligence and would definitely have spoken up. In other states of mind I would have done a lot more. At this point in time, however, I was happy to be ignored; it confirmed that I was as effectively invisible as I intended to be. I didn't care.

I ordered a Heineken. The woman seemed intent on drawing me into their conversation. I was just as intent on avoiding contact. I had nothing to say to these people.

—So where do you come from with an accent like that? she laughed, her X-ray gaze sweeping over me. When her eyes met mine I saw a type of person who, despite their apparent camaraderie, has an instinctive drive toward manipulative schemes. Perhaps I was looking at my reflection.

I smiled.

—Scotland.

—Yeah? Where about? Glasgow? Edinburgh?

—All over really, I replied, bland and blasé. Did it really matter which indistinct shite-arsed towns and schemes I was dragged through, growing up in that dull and dire little country?

She laughed, however, and looked thoughtful as if I'd said something really profound.

—All over, she mused.

Just like me. All over. She introduced herself as Chrissie. Her boyfriend, or he who, given his indulgence of her, intended to be her boyfriend, was called Richard.

From behind the bar, Richard stole injured glances at me, before I turned to face him, having clocked this in a bar mirror. He responded with a ducking motion of his head, followed by a 'Hi' in a dislocated hiss, and a furtive grope of a ratty beard that grew out of a pock-marked face but merely seemed to accentuate rather than conceal the lunar landscape it sprang from.

Chrissie talked in a rambling, expansive way, making observations about the world and citing mundane examples from her own experience to back them up.

It's a habit of mine to look at people's bare arms. Chrissie's were covered in healed track marks; the kind where ugly scar tissue is always left. Even more evident were the slash marks; judging by depth and position, the self-hating, response-to-frustration type rather than the serious suicide-bid variety. Her face was open and animated but her eyes had that watery, diminished aspect common to the traumatized. I read her as a grubby map of all the places didn't want to go to: addiction, mental breakdown, drug psychosis, sexual exploitation. In Chrissie I saw someone who'd felt bad about herself and the world and had tried to shoot and fuck herself into better times without realizing that she was only compounding the problem. I was no stranger to at least some of the places Chrissie had been. She looked as if she was very ill-equipped for these visits, however, and that she tended to stick around a bit too long.

At the moment her problems seemed to be drink and Richard. My first thought was that she was welcome to both. I found Chrissie pretty repulsive. Her body was layered with hard fat around her gut, thighs and hips. I saw a beaten woman whose only resistance to the attentions of middle-age was to wear clothes too youthful, tight and revealing for her meaty figure.

Her doughy face twisted flirtatiously at me. I was vaguely nauseated at this woman; gone to seed, yet unselfconsciously attempting to display a sexual magnetism she no longer possessed, and seemingly unaware of the grotesque vaudevillian caricature that had supplanted it.

It was then, paradoxically, that a horrible impulse struck me, which appeared to have its origins in an unspecific area behind my genitals: this person who repulsed me, this woman, would become my lover.

Why should this be? Perhaps it was my natural perversity; perhaps Chrissie was that strange arena where repulsion and attraction meet.

Maybe I admired her stubborn refusal to acknowledge the remorseless shrinking of her possibilities.

She acted as if new, exciting, enriching experiences were just around the corner, in spite of all the evidence to the contrary. I felt a gratuitous urge, as I often do with such people, to shake her and scream the truth in her face: You're a useless, ugly piece of meat. Your life has been desperate and abominable so far, and it's only going to get worse. Stop fucking kidding yourself.

A conflicting mass of emotions, I was actively despising someone while simultaneously planning their seduction. It was only later that I acknowledged, with some horror and shame, that these feelings didn't really conflict at all. At that stage, though, I was unsure as to whether Chrissie was flirting with me or merely trying to tease the seedy Richard. Perhaps she wasn't sure herself.

—We're going to the beach tomorrow. You must come, she said.

—That would be great, I smiled lavishly, as the color drained from Richard's face.

—I may have to work . . . he stammered nervously.

—Well, if you won't drive us, we'll just go alone! she simpered in a little-girl manner, a tactic commonly used by whores, which she almost certainly once was, when she still had the looks to make it pay.

I was definitely pushing at an open door.

We drank and talked until the increasingly nervous Richard shut the bar and then we went to a café for some blow. The date was formalized: tomorrow I was forsaking my nocturnal life for a day of seaside frolics with Chrissie and Richard.

Richard was very uptight the following day when he drove us down to the beach. I derived pleasure from watching his knuckles go white on the steering wheel as Chrissie, arched around from the front passenger seat, indulged in some frivolous and mildly flirtatious banter with me. Every bad joke or dull anecdote that spilled lazily from my lips was greeted with frenetic peals of laughter from Chrissie, as Richard suffered in tense silence. I could feel his hatred for me growing in increments, constricting him, impairing his breathing, muddying his thought processes. I felt like a nasty child jacking up the volume on the handset of the television control for the purpose of annoying an adult.

He inadvertently gained some measure of revenge, sticking on a Carpenters tape. I writhed in discomfort as he and Chrissie sung along.

—Such a terrible loss, Karen Carpenter, she said solemnly. Richard nodded in sombre agreement.

—Sad, isn't it, Euan? Chrissie asked, wanting to include me in their strange little festival of grief for this dead pop star.

I smiled in a good-natured, carefree way.

—I couldn't give a toss. There's people all over the world who haven't got enough to eat. Why should I give a fuck about some over-privileged fucked-up Yank who's too screwed up to lift a forkful of scran into her gub?

There was a stunned silence.

—You've a very nasty, cynical mind, Euan! Chrissie wailed. Richard wholeheartedly agreed, unable to conceal his glee that I'd upset her. He even started singing along to "Top of the World." After this, he and Chrissie began conversing in Dutch and laughing.

I was unperturbed at this temporary exclusion. In fact I was enjoying their reaction. Richard simply did not understand the type of person Chrissie was. I sensed that she was attracted to ugliness and cynicism because she saw herself as an agent of change. I was a challenge to her. Richard's servile indulgence would amuse her from time to time; it was, however, just a holiday retreat, not a permanent home, ultimately bland and boring. In trying to be what he thought she wanted, he had given her nothing to change, denied her the satisfaction of making a real impact in their relationship. In the meantime, she would string this fool along, as he indulged her boundless vanity.

We lay on the beach. We threw a ball at each other. It was like a caricature of what people should do at the seaside. I grew uncomfortable with the scene and the heat and lay down in the shade. Richard ran around in his cut-offs; tanned and athletic, despite a slightly distended stomach. Chrissie looked embarrassingly flabby.

When she went to get ice cream, leaving Richard and I alone for the first time, I felt a little bit nervous.

—She's great, isn't she, he enthused.

I reluctantly smiled.

—Chrissie has come through a lot.

—Yes, I acknowledged. That I had already deduced.

—I feel differently about her than I've done about anyone else. I've known her a long time. Sometimes I think she needs to be protected from herself.

—That's a wee bit too conceptual for me, Richard.

—You know what I mean. You keep your arms covered up.

I felt my bottom lip curl in kneejerk petulance. It was the childlike, dishonest response of someone who isn't really hurt but is pretending to be so in order to justify future aggression toward, or elicit retraction from, the other party. It was second nature to me. I was pleased that he felt he had my measure; with a delusion of power over me he'd get cocky and therefore careless. I'd pick my moment and tear out his heart. It was hardly a difficult target, lying right there on the sleeve of his blouse. This whole thing was as much about me and Richard as it was about me and Chrissie; in a sense she was only the battleground on which our duel was being fought. Our natural antipathy on first meeting had incubated in the hothouse of our continuing contact. In an astonishingly short time it had blossomed into fully fledged hatred.

Richard was unrepentant about his indiscreet comment. Far from it, he followed up his attack, attempting to construct in me an appropriate figure for his hatred.

—We Dutch, we went to South Africa. You British oppressed us. You put us into concentration camps. It was you people who invented the concentration camp, not the Nazis. You taught them that, like you taught them genocide. You were far more effective at that with the Maoris in New Zealand than Hitler was with the Jews. I'm not condoning what the Boers are doing in South Africa. No way. Never. But you British put the hatred in their hearts, made them harsh. Oppression breeds oppression, not resolution.

I felt a surge of anger rise in me. I was almost tempted to go into a spiel about how I was Scottish, not British, and that the Scots were the last oppressed colony of the British Empire. I don't really believe it, though; the Scots oppress themselves by their obsession with the English, which breeds the negatives of hatred, fear, servility, contempt, and dependency. Besides, I would not be drawn into an argument with this moronic queen.

—I don't profess to know a great deal about politics, Richard. I do find your analysis a tad subjective, however. I stood up, smiling at Chrissie who had returned with cartons of Häagen-Dazs topped with slagroom.

—You know what you are, Euan? Do you? she teased. Chrissie had obviously been exploring some theme while she was getting the ices. Now she'd inflict her observations on us. I shrugged. —Look at him, Mister Cool. Been there, done it all. You're just like Richard and me. Bumming around. Where was it you said you wanted to head for later on?

—Ibiza, I told her, or Rirnini.

—For the rave scene, the ecstasy, she prompted.

—It's a good scene to get into, I nodded. —Safer than junk.

—Well that's as maybe, she said petulantly. —You're just Eurotrash, Euan. We all are. This is where all the scum gets washed up. The Port of Amsterdam. A dustbin for the Eurotrash.

I smiled and opened another Heineken from Richard's cold basket. —I'll drink to that. To Eurotrash! I toasted.

Chrissie enthusiastically bashed my bottle with hers. Richard reluctantly joined in. While Richard was obviously Dutch, I found Chrissie's accent hard to place. She occasionally had a Liverpool affectation to what generally seemed to be a hybrid of middle-class English and French, although I was sure it was all a pose. But there was no way I was going to ask her where she was from just so that she could say: all over.

When we got back to the 'Dam that night, I could see that Richard feared the worst. At the bar he tried to ply us with drink in what was obviously a desperate attempt to render what was about to happen null and void. His face was set into a beaten expression. I was going home with Chrissie; it couldn't have been more obvious had she taken out an advertisement in the newspaper.

—I'm shattered, she yawned.

—The sea air. Will you see me home, Euan?

—Why don't you wait until I finish my shift? Richard desperately pleaded.

—Oh Richard, I'm completely exhausted. Don't worry about me. Euan doesn't mind taking me to the station, do you?

—Where do you stay? Richard interjected, addressing me, trying to gain some control over events. I flipped up my palm in a halting gesture, and turned back to Chrissie. — The very least I could do after yourself and Richard giving me such a good time today. Besides, I really need to get my head down too, I continued, in a low, oily voice, allowing a dripping, languid smile to mold my face.

Chrissie pecked Richard on the cheek. —Phone you tomorrow baby, she said, scrutinizing him in the manner of an indulgent mother with a sulking toddler.

—Goodnight, Richard, I smiled as we made to leave. I held the door open for Chrissie and as she exited I looked back at the tortured fool behind the bar, winked and raised my eyebrows: —Sweet dreams.

We walked through the red-light district, by the Voorburg and Achterburg canals, enjoying the air and the bustle.

—Richard is incredibly possessive. It's such a drag, Chrissie mused.

—No doubt his heart's in the right place, I said.

We walked in silence toward Centraal Station where Chrissie would pick up the tram to where she stayed, just past the Ajax Stadium. I decided that the time was ripe to declare my intentions. I turned to her and said. —Chrissie, I'd like to spend the night with you.

She turned to me with her eyes half shut and her jaw jutting out.—I thought you might, she smugly replied. There was an incredible arrogance about her.

A dealer, positioned on a bridge over the Achterburg canal, caught us in his gaze. Displaying a keen sense of timing and market awareness he hissed —Ecstasy for the sex. Chrissie raised an eyebrow and made to stall, but I steered her on. People say that E's are good for shagging, but I find that I only want to dance and hug on them. Besides, it had been so long that my gonads felt like space hoppers. The last thing I needed was an aphrodisiac. I didn't fancy Chrissie. I needed a fuck; it was as simple as that. Junk tends to impose a sexual moratorium and the post-smack sexual awakening nags at you uncompromisingly; an itch that just has to be scratched. I was sick of sitting wanking in Rab/Robbie's front room, the stale musty smell of my spunk mixing with the hashish fumes.

Chrissie shared an apartment with a tense, pretty girl called Margriet who bit her nails, chewed her lower lip and spoke in fast Dutch and slow English. We all talked for a bit, then Chrissie and I went through to the bed in her pastel-colored room.

I began kissing and touching her, with Richard never far from my thoughts. I didn't want foreplay, I didn't want to make love, not to this woman. I wanted to fuck her. Now. The only reason I was feeling her up was for Richard; thinking that if I took my time and made a good job of this, it would give me a greater hold over her and therefore the opportunity to cause him much more discomfort.

—Fuck me . . . she murmured. I pulled up the duvet and winced involuntarily as I caught a glimpse of her vagina. It looked ugly; red and scarred. She was slightly embarrassed and sheepishly explained:—A girlfriend and I were playing some games . . . with beer bottles. It was just one of those things that got a bit out of hand. I'm so sore down there . . . she rubbed her crotch,—do it in my bottom, Euan, I like it that way. I've got the jelly here. She stretched over to the bedside locker, and fumbled in a drawer, pulling a jar of KY out. She began greasing my erect cock.—You don't mind putting it in my bum, do you? Let's love like animals, Euan . . . that's what we are, the Eurotrash, remember? She spun round and started to apply the jelly to her arse, beginning with the cleft between her buttocks, then working it right into her arsehole. When she'd finished I put my finger in to check for shite. Anal I don't mind, but I can't handle shite. It was clean though, and certainly prettier than her cunt. It would be a better fuck than that floppy, scarred mess. Dyke games. Fuck that. With Margriet? Surely not! Putting aesthetics aside, I had castration anxiety, visualising her fanny still being full of broken glass. I'd settle for her arse.

She'd obviously done this before, many times, there was so much give as I entered her arsehole. I grabbed her heavy buttocks in both hands as her repulsive body arched out in front of me. Thinking of Richard, I whispered at her, —I think you need to be protected from yourself. I thrust urgently and got a shock as I caught a glimpse of my face in a wall mirror, twisted, sneering, ugly. Rubbing her injured cunt ferociously, Chrissie came, her fat folds wobbling from side to side as I shunted my load into her rectum.

After the sex, I felt really revolted by her. It was an effort just to lie beside her. Nausea almost overwhelmed me. I tried to turn away from her at one point, but she wrapped her large flabby arms around me and pulled me to her breast. I lay there sweating coldly, full of tense self-loathing, crushed against her tits, which were surprisingly small for her build.

Over the weeks Chrissie and I continued to fuck, always in the same way. Richard's bitterness toward me increased in direct correlation to these sexual activities, for although I had agreed with Chrissie not to disclose our relationship to him, it was more or less an open secret. In any other circumstances I would have demanded clarification of the role of this sweetie wife in our scene. However, I was already planning to extract myself from my relationship with Chrissie. To do this, I reasoned, it would be better if I kept Chrissie and Richard close. The strange thing about them was that they seemed to have no wider network of close friends; only casual acquaintances like Cyrus, the guy who played pinball in Richard's bar. With this in mind, the last thing I wanted to do was to alienate them from each other. If that happened, I'd never be shot of Chrissie without causing the unstable bitch a great deal of pain. Whatever her faults, she didn't need any more of that.

I didn't deceive Chrissie; this isn't merely a retrospective attempt at self justification for what was to happen. I can say this with confidence as I clearly recall a conversation that we had in a coffee shop in Utrechtesstraat. Chrissie was being very presumptuous and starting to make plans about me moving in with her. This was glaringly inappropriate. I said overtly what I had been telling her covertly with my behaviour toward her, had she cared to take note of it.

—Don't expect anything from me, Chrissie. I can't give. It's nothing to do with you. It's me. I can't get involved. I can never be what you want me to be. I can be your friend. We can fuck. But don't ask me to give. I can't.

—Somebody must have hurt you really badly, she said shaking her head as she blew hashish smoke across the table. She was trying to convert her obvious hurt into feelings of pity for me, and she was failing miserably.

I remember that conversation in the coffee shop because it had the opposite effect to the one I'd wanted. She became even more intense toward me; I was now more of a challenge.

So that was the truth, but perhaps not the whole truth. I couldn't give with Chrissie. You can never put feelings where they're not. But things were changing for me. I was feeling physically and mentally stronger, more prepared to open myself up, ready to cast aside this impregnable cloak of bitterness. I just needed the right person to do it with.

I landed a job as a reception-clerk-cum-porter-cum-dogs body in a small hotel in the Damrak. The hours were long and unsocial and I would sit watching television or reading at the reception, gently ssshhing the young drunk and stoned guests who flopped in at all hours. During the day I started to attend Dutch language classes.

To the relief of Rab/Robbie, I moved out of his place to a room in a beautiful apartment in a particularly narrow canal house in the Jordaan. The house was new; it had been totally rebuilt due to subsidence of the previous building into the weak, sandy Amsterdam soil, but it was built in the same traditional style of its neighbors. It was surprisingly affordable.

After I moved out, Rab/Robbie seemed more like his old self. He was more friendly and sociable toward me, he wanted me to go out drinking and smoking with him; to meet all the friends he'd vigilantly kept away from me, lest they might be corrupted by this junkie. They were typical sixties time-warp Amsterdam types, who smoked a lot of hash and were shitscared of what they called "hard drugs."

Although I didn't have much time for them, it was good to get back onto an even footing with Rab/Robbie. One Saturday afternoon we were stoned in the Floyd café and we felt comfortable enough to put our cards on the table.

—It's good to see you settled, man, he said. —You were in a bad way when you came here.

—It was really good of you to put us up, Rab . . . Robbie, but you weren't the friendliest of hosts, it has to be said. You had some coupon on ye when you walked in at night.

He smiled. —I take your point, man. I suppose I made ye even more uptight than ye were. It just freaked me a bit, y'know? Workin like fuck aw day and ye come in and there's this wasted cunt whae's trying tae git oaf smack . . . ah mean I was thinkin, likes, what have I taken oan here, man?

—Aye, I suppose I did impose myself, and I was a bit of a leech.

—Naw, you wirnae really that bad, man, he conceded, all mellow. —Ah was far too uptight, likes. It's just, you know, man, I'm the sort of punter who needs my own personal space, y'know?

I can understand that, man. I said, then, swallowing a lump of space-cake, smirked. I dig the cosmic vibes you're sending out here, man.

Rab/Robbie smiled and toked hard on a spliff. The pollem was very mellow. —You know, man, ye really caught me out acting the arsehole. All that Robbie shit. Call me what you always called me, back in Scotland. Back up Tollcross. Rab. That's who ah am. That's who ah'll always be. Rab Doran. Tollcross Rebels. T.C.R. Some fuckin times back there, eh man?

They were pretty desperate times really, but home always looks better when you're away from it, and even more so through a haze of hash. I colluded in his fantasies and we reminisced over more joints before hitting some bars and getting ratarsed on alcohol.

Despite the rediscovery of our friendship, I spent very little time with Rab, due mainly to the shifts I was working. During the day, if I wasn't taking my language classes, I'd be swotting up, or getting my head down before my shift at the hotel. One of the people who lived in the flat was a woman named Valerie. She helped me with my Dutch, which was coming along in leaps and bounds. My phrasebook French, Spanish and German were also improving rapidly due to the number of tourists I was coming into contact with in the hotel. Valerie became a good friend to me; more importantly, she had a friend called Anna, with whom I fell in love.

It was a beautiful time for me. My cynicism evaporated and life started to seem like an adventure of limitless possibilities. Needless to say, I stopped seeing Chrissie and Richard and seldom went near the red-light district. They seemed a remnant of a seedier, more sordid time I felt I had left behind. I didn't want or need to smear that gel on my cock and bury it in Chrissie's flabby arse anymore. I had a beautiful young girlfriend to make love to and that was what I did most of the day before staggering onto my late shift, strung out on sex.

Life was nothing short of idyllic for the rest of that summer. This state of affairs changed one day; a warm, clear day when Anna and I found ourselves on Dam Square. I tensed as I saw Chrissie coming toward us. She was wearing dark glasses and looked even more bloated than ever. She was cloyingly pleasant and insisted we went to Richard's bar in Warmoesstraat for a drink. Though edgy, I felt that a greater scene would have been caused by cold-shouldering her.

Richard was delighted I had a girlfriend that wasn't Chrissie. I had never seen him so open toward me. I felt a vague shame about torturing him. He talked of his home town of Utrecht.

—Who famous comes from Utrecht? I gently chided him.

—Oh, lots of people.

—Aye? Name one?

—Let me see, eh, Gerald Vanenberg.

—The PSV guy?

—Yes.

Chrissie looked at us in a hostile manner. —Who the fuck is Gerald Vanenburg? she snapped, then turned to Anna and looked at her with raised eyebrows as if Richard and I had said something ridiculous.

—A famous international footballer, Richard bleated. Trying to reduce the tension he added —He used to go out with my sister.

—I bet you wish he used to go out with you, Chrissie said bitterly. There was an embarrassed silence before Richard set us up with more tequila slammers.

Chrissie had been making a fuss of Anna. She was stroking her bare arms, telling her that she was so slim and beautiful. Anna was probably embarrassed but was handling it well. I resented that fat dyke touching up my girlfriend. She became more hostile toward me as the drinks flowed, asking me how I was getting on, what I was up to. A challenging tone had entered her voice.

Only we don't see him so much these days, do we, Richard?

—Leave it, Chrissie, Richard said uneasily. Chrissie stroked Anna's peach cheek. Anna smiled back awkwardly.

—Does he fuck you like he fucks me? In your pretty little bottom? she asked.

I felt as if the flesh had been stripped from my bones. Anna's face contorted in discomfort, as she turned toward me.

—I think we'd better go, I said.

Chrissie threw a glass of beer over me and began verbally abusing me. Richard held her from behind the bar, otherwise she'd have struck me. —Take your fucking little slut AND GO! A REAL WOMAN'S TOO MUCH FOR YOU, YOU FUCKING JUNKIE VERMIN! HAVE YOU SHOWN HER YOUR ARMS YET?

—Chrissie . . . I said weakly.

—FUCK OFF! JUST FUCK OFF! BANG YOUR SILLY LITTLE GIRL YOU FUCKING PEDOPHILE! I'M A REAL WOMAN, A REAL FUCK-ING WOMAN . . .

I ushered Anna out of the bar. Cyrus flashed his yellow teeth at me and shrugged his broad shoulders. I looked back to see Richard comforting Chrissie. —I'm a real woman, not a silly little girl.

—You're a beautiful woman, Chrissie. The most beautiful, I heard Richard say soothingly.

In a sense, it was a blessing. Anna and I went for a drink and I told her the whole story of Chrissie and Richard, leaving nothing out.I told her how fucked up and bitter I was, and how, while I'd promised her nothing, I'd treated Chrissie fairly shabbily. Anna understood, and we put the episode behind us. As a result of that conversation I felt even better and more uninhibited, my last little problem in Amsterdam seemingly resolved.

It was strange, but as Chrissie was such a fuck-up, I half thought of her a few days later when they said that the body of a woman had been fished out of Oosterdok by Centraal Station. I quickly forgot about it, however. I was enjoying life, or trying to, although circumstances were working against us. Anna had just started college, studying fashion design, and with my shifts at the hotel we were like ships in the night, so I was thinking of chucking it and getting another job. I'd saved up quite a healthy wad of guilders.

I was pondering this one afternoon, when I heard someone banging at the door. It was Richard, and as I opened up he spat in my face. I was too shocked to be angry.

—Fucking murderer! he sneered.

—What . . . I knew, but couldn't comprehend. A thousand impulses flowed through my body, fusing me into immobility.

—Chrissie's dead.

—Oosterdok . . . it was Chrissie . . .

—Yes, it was Chrissie. I suppose you'll be happy now.

—NAW MAN . . . NAW! I protested.

—Liar! Fucking hypocrite! You treated her like shit. You and others like you. You were no good for her. Used her like an old rag then discarded her. Took advantage of her weakness, of her need to give. People like you always do.

—Naw! It wasn't like that, I pleaded, knowing full well it was exactly like that.

He stood and looked at me for a while. It was like he was looking beyond me, seeing something that wasn't apparent from my vantage point. I broke a silence which probably lasted only seconds, but seemed like minutes.—I want to go to the funeral, Richard.

—He smiled cruelly at me. —In Jersey? You won't go there.

—The Channel Islands . . . I said, hesitantly. I didn't know Chrissie was from there .

—I will go, I told him. I was determined to go. I felt culpable enough. I had to go.

Richard examined me contemptuously, then started talking in a low, terse voice. —St Helier, Jersey. The home of Robert Le Marchand, Chrissie's father. It's next Tuesday. Her sister was here, making arrangements to take the body back.

—I want to go. Are you?

He scoffed at me. —No. She's dead. I wanted to help her when she was alive. He turned and walked away. I watched his back recede into nothingness, then went into the flat, shaking uncontrollably.

I had to get to St. Helier by Tuesday. I'd find details of the Le Marchands' whereabouts when I got there. Anna wanted to come. I said I'd be a poor traveling companion, but she insisted. Accompanied by her, and a sense of guilt that seemed to seep into the body of the rented car, I drove along the highways of Europe, through Holland, Belgium and France to the small port of St. Malo. I started thinking, about Chrissie, yes, but about other things, which I would generally never concern myself with. I started to think about the politics of European integration, whether it was a good or bad thing. I tried to marry up the politicians' vision with the paradox I saw in the miles of these ugly highways of Europe; absurd incompatibilities with an inexorable shared destiny. The politicians' vision seemed just another moneymaking scam or another crass power-trip. We ate up these dull roads before reaching St Malo. After checking into a cheap hotel, Anna and I got roaring drunk. The next morning we boarded the ferry to Jersey.

We arrived Monday afternoon and found another hotel. There were no funeral notices in the *Jersey Evening Post*. I got a phonebook and looked up Le Marchand. There were six, but only one R. A man's voice came down the receiver.

—Hello.

—Hello. Could I speak to Mister Robert Le Marchand?

—Speaking.

—I'm really sorry to bother you at this time. We're friends of Chrissie's, over from Holland for the funeral. We understand that it's tomorrow. Would it be alright if we attended?

—From Holland? he repeated wearily.

—Yes. We're at Gardener's Hotel.

—Well, you have come a long way, he stated. His posh, bland, English accent grated. —The funeral's at ten. St Thomas's chapel, just around the corner from your hotel as a matter of fact.

—Thanks, I said, as the line clicked dead. As a matter of fact . . . It seemed as if everything was simply a matter of fact to Mr. Le Marchand.

I felt totally drained. No doubt the man's coldness and hostility were due to assumptions made about Chrissie's friends in Amsterdam and the nature of her death; her body was full of barbituates when it was fished out of the dock, bloated further by the water.

At the funeral, I introduced myself to her mother and father. Her mother was a small, wizened woman, diminished even further by this tragedy into a brittle near-nothingness. Her father looked like a man who had a great deal of guilt to shed. I could detect his sense of failure and horror and it made me feel less guilty about my small, but decisive role in Chrissie's demise.

—I won't be a hypocrite, he said. —We didn't always like each other, but Christopher was my son, and I loved him.

I felt a lump in my chest. There was a buzzing in my ears and the air seemed to grow thin. I could not pick out any sound. I managed to nod, and excused myself, moving away from the cluster of mourners gathered around the graveside.

I stood shaking in confusion, past events cascading through my mind. Anna put her arm tightly around me, and the congregation must have thought I was grief stricken. A woman approached us. She was a younger, slimmer, prettier version of Chrissie . . . Chris . . .

—You know, don't you?

I stood gaping into space.

—Please don't say anything to Mum and Dad. Didn't Richard tell you?

I nodded blankly.

—It would kill Mum and Dad. They don't know about his change . . . I took the body home. I had them cut his hair and dress him in a suit. I bribed them to say nothing . . . it would only cause hurt. He wasn't a woman. He was my brother, you see? He was a man. That's how he was born, that's how he was buried. Anything else would only cause hurt to the people who are left to pick up the pieces. Don't

you see that? she pleaded. —Chris was confused. A mess. A mess in here, she pointed to her head. —God I tried, we all tried. Mum and Dad could handle the drugs, even the homosexuality. It was all experiments with Christopher. Trying to find himself . . . you know how they are. She looked at me with an embarrassed contempt. —I mean that sort of person. She started to sob.

She was consumed with grief and anger. In such circumstances she needed the benefit of the doubt, though what were they covering up? What was the problem? What was wrong with reality? As an ex-junkie I knew the answer to that. Often plenty was wrong with reality. Whose reality was it, anyway?

—It's okay, I said. She nodded appreciatively before joining the rest of her family. We didn't stick around. There was a ferry to catch.

When we got back to Amsterdam, I sought out Richard. He was apologetic at having dropped me in it.

—I misjudged you. Chris was confused. It was little to do with you. It was nasty to let you go without knowing the truth.

—Naw, I deserved it. Shite of the year, that was me, I said sadly.

Over some beers he told me Chrissie's story. The breakdowns, the decision to radically re-order her life and gender; spending a substantial inheritance on the treatment. She started off on a treatment of female hormones, both estrogen and progesterone. These developed her breasts, softened her skin, and reduced her body hair. Her muscular strength was diminished and the distribution of her subcutaneous fat was altered in a female direction. She had electrolysis to remove facial hair. This was followed by throat surgery on her voice box, which resulted in the removal of the Adam's apple and a softening of the voice, when complemented by a course of speech therapy.

She went around like this for three years, before the most radical surgery, which was undertaken in four stages. These were penectomy, castration, plastic reconstruction and vaginoplasty, the formation of an artificial vagina, constructed by creating a cavity between the prostrate and the rectum. The vagina was formed from skin grafts from the thigh and lined with penile, and/or scrotal skin, which,

Richard explained, made orgasmic sensation possible. The shape of the vagina was maintained by her wearing a mould for several weeks after the operation.

In Chrissie's case, the operations caused her great distress, and she therefore relied heavily on painkilling drugs which, given her history, was probably not the best thing. That, Richard reckoned, was the real key to her demise. He saw her walking out of his bar toward Dam Square. She bought some barbs, took them, was seen out of her box in a couple of bars before she wandered along by the canal. It could have been suicide or an accident, or perhaps that grey area in between.

Christopher and Richard had been lovers. He spoke affectionately of Christopher, glad now to be able to refer to him as Chris. He talked of all his obsessions, ambitions, and dreams; all their obsessions, ambitions, and dreams. They often got close to finding their niche; in Paris, Laguna Beach, Ibiza, and Hamburg; they got close, but never quite close enough. Not Eurotrash, just people trying to get by.

Harold Brodkey: The Great Pretender

Edmund White

Edmund White is a novelist, memoirist, and biographer. He is the author of many books including A Boy's Own Story, The Married Man, The Flaneur, *and biographies of Marcel Proust and Jean Genet (winner of the National Book Critics Circle Award). This piece is excerpted from his memoir* City Boy: My Life in New York During the 1960s and 70s. *He is also a professor of creative writing at Princeton.*

A TALL, BLOND BIOLOGIST NAMED DOUG GRUENAU, four years younger than I but like me a graduate from the University of Michigan, was living with the novelist Harold Brodkey on West Eighty-eighth Street.

Harold had an immense underground reputation—which sounds like a contradiction in terms. Everyone in New York was curious about him, but few people outside the city had ever heard of him. Long ago, in 1958, he'd published *First Love and Other Sorrows*, a book of stories that had been well reviewed, but they weren't what all the buzz was about. Now he'd bring out a story occasionally in *The New Yorker* or *New American Review* or even *Esquire*. The one in *New American Review* (a quarterly, edited by Ted Solotaroff, which had once brought out a dirty chapter from Philip Roth's *Portnoy's Complaint*) was highly sexual but not dirty—a fifty-page chapter, published in 1973, about a Radcliffe girl's first orgasm. The prose in "Innocence" could be strained if striking: "To see her in sunlight was to see Marxism die." It seemed the longest sex scene in history, rivaled only by the gay sex scene in David Plante's *The Catholic*—and reminiscent of the sex scene, "The Time of Her Time," included in Norman Mailer's *Advertisements for Myself* (except that one had been anal!). Then there had been troubled, labyrinthine stories about Brodkey's mother in *The New Yorker* of a length and complexity no one else would have gotten away with. This was obviously a writer, we thought, who must be, above all, extremely convincing. The mother stories nagged and tore at their subject matter with a Lawrentian exasperation, a relentless drive to get it right, repeatedly correcting the small assertions just made in previous lines. Everyone was used to confessional writing of some sort (though the heyday for that would come later) and everyone knew all about the family drama, but no one had ever gone this far with sex, with mother and with childhood. We were stunned by this new kind of realism that made slides of every millimeter of the past and put them under the writer's microscope. In *Esquire* in 1975, Brodkey published a short, extremely lyrical story, "His Son, in His Arms, in Light, Aloft," about a baby boy being carried in his father's arms. Mother might get the niggling, Freudian treatment, but Daddy deserved only light-drenched, William Blake-like mysticism.

All these "stories," apparently, were only furtive glimpses of the massive novel that Brodkey had been working on for years and that would be the American answer to Marcel Proust. Brodkey's fans (and there were many of them) Xeroxed and stapled into little booklets every story he'd published so far in recent years and circulated them among their friends, a sort of New York samizdat press. His supporters made wide fervent claims for him. Harold was our Thomas Mann, our James Joyce. That no one outside New York knew who he was only vouchsafed his seriousness, his cult stature, too serious for the unwashed (or rather the washed, a more appropriate synecdoche for Midwesterners like me).

He and Doug lived in a big, rambling West Side apartment with a third man, named Charlie Yordy, whom I met just once but who reeked of a hoofed and hairy-shanked sexuality. He was a friendly, smiling man but seemed burdened, as all people possessed by a powerful sexuality are.

Harold was as bearded and hooded-eyed as Nebuchadnezzar but tall and slim and athletic as well. He must have been in his forties. His constant swimming and exercising at the Sixty-third Street Y (the one I'd lived in when I first came to New York) kept him as fit as a much younger man. His moods and thoughts were restless, rolling about like ship passengers in a storm. Sometimes he looked as if a migraine had just drawn its gray, heavy wing across his eyes. The next moment he'd be calculating something silently, feverishly to himself—then he'd say out loud, "Forget it." Cryptic smiles flitted across his face. He seldom paid attention to what the people around him were saying because he was concocting his next outrage—for most of his remarks were outrageous, and he could not be cajoled out of them.

Harold had lived with Doug for some eight or nine years. Doug was so polite and respectful that even whenever Harold would say something absurdly farfetched, Doug would cock his head to one side and up a bit, as if he were a bird trying to make sense of a new, higher, quicker call. Doug was a big man with a bass laugh but around Harold he didn't take up much space. I think he'd decided that Harold was both cracked and a genius and that even his insults were, ultimately, harmless, but Doug taught biology in a private school and had endless hours of grading and preparation and counseling and teaching to do, whereas Harold appeared to have enough money to be idle—and to meddle. When I told David Kalstone about Harold, David sang, "Time on my hands . . ."

I wasn't quite sure what Charlie did, though I must have been told (Americans are never reluctant to ask strangers what they do). I think he was a math teacher and then he manufactured clothes in the Adirondacks. He wasn't around often, and in any event he seemed to be more Harold's boyfriend than Doug's, though I'm sure Harold told me they were all three lovers. The apartment was big enough to accommodate them all and even give each one of them privacy. Harold was on the prowl. Not all the considerable amount of time he spent at the Y was devoted to swimming. People who knew who he was said he was a tireless, overt cruiser.

Harold seldom talked about his own work but he loved to deliver pronouncements about literature and how to make it. He particularly enjoyed giving other writers—even older, more successful writers—advice. As the years went by I kept hearing strange and then stranger stories about him. One of his great defenders was Gordon Lish, a top editor at Knopf and the man who had virtually invented minimalism. Gordon apparently walked into the office of his boss, Bob Gottlieb (who'd started his own career as the editor of *Catch-22*, and had even been the one to persuade Joseph Heller to change the title from *Catch-18*), and said something like, "You've published a few good books, Bob, but nothing that will make people remember you after you're gone. Now you have the chance to publish Proust—but you must write a check for a million dollars and not ask to see even a single page."

At that point Harold had been signed up with Farrar, Straus for years, but they'd paid him a considerably smaller sum—and they weren't willing to give him the full attention he demanded. Harold needed not one editor but several to go over with him the thousands of pages he'd already written. As far as anyone could tell, he was years away from delivering. But their reluctance to put the full resources of their staff at his disposal roiled in Harold. Responding to the challenge, Gottlieb wrote the check.

The Elegant Rube

Malerie Willens

"The Elegant Rube" was Malerie Willens's first published story. It was anthologized in Best American Nonrequired Reading *after its appearance in* Open City. *She grew up in Los Angeles and lives in Brooklyn, where she's at work on a novel and more stories.*

WALLETS, LADIES. NOW!

That's what the mugger said to Michael and Wade when he ambushed them. They had just come out of a late movie, and were rounding the corner onto a residential block when he emerged from some shrubs. The teenaged assailant with lippy peach fuzz and a confusing accent called the brothers *ladies*. He held the grip of some weapon, stuck into his pants at the waistband. Michael dropped his popcorn, which flew up and then scattered onto the pavement. He tossed his wallet to the skittish kid, and then his brother did the same.

Turn around or I'll shoot off your face!

Michael and Wade turned and stood with their arms at their sides until the boy's staccato footsteps grew faint. Because it was late at night in Los Angeles, nobody was there to see them. They looked like life-sized wooden soldiers who'd been positioned on the sidewalk and then abandoned. Michael, whose scarecrow body and tentative manner made some women think of poets, stood with his back straight and long. He maximized each distinct vertebra but he still felt delicate in the presence of his brother's much larger body, just inches away. He glanced over at the spiny orange birds-of-paradise that separated one duplex from the next. The flowers looked like plastic from the ninety-nine cent store—odorless probably, and coated in a fine layer of dust. He conjured up the kid's voice. *I'll shoot off your face* is what he'd said, as though he and Wade shared one face—the meshing, hapless visage of a single victim.

The night on which a crime occurs is always the wrong night—always incongruous, inappropriate, charged with meaning. This night was no exception. It was the brothers' first encounter in nearly a year. In the early days of their estrangement, Michael had been optimistic. Because he couldn't trace it back to a decisive insult, it seemed like an adult's rift—a barely perceptible accumulation of subtle wrongs—rather than a brawl, beef, or blow-up. He visualized it as an artery, occluded with the plaque of misunderstanding, until, after too many awkward phone calls and canceled breakfasts, the blood barely pumped.

He could still see the two of them as boys, falling back onto the couch with the loose-limbed ease of brothers. He saw Yoo-Hoo spewing out of each other's noses, he saw Wade spinning Nina Marsak's tiny, mysteriously obtained underpants around his forefinger, and he heard the echo of handballs against the garage. Their parents had believed in the sanctity of the fraternal bond. "When we're gone," they would say, "it'll only be you two." And the boys would answer, "yeah-yeah" as they chased the dog past the TV, slammed bedroom doors papered with raunchy bumper stickers, and slouched sullenly around on Sundays in mismatched socks.

And then their parents were gone—run off the road three years earlier, on their way to San Francisco. It happened north of San Simeon but below Big Sur, the point at which the viscous coastal fog wraps itself around the road like a big gray cat. On childhood car trips, Michael likened this misty stretch of Highway One to the Middle Earth in his books, where white cliffs arched and preened, like women getting dressed. It was their parents' favorite strip of the coast, which made Michael feel simultaneously better and worse that they had died there.

Attempts to stay in touch had been sporadic since then. After the accident, the brothers collaborated in the work of death, meeting in corner booths over french fries, cloaking their grief in logistics. Finally, after what felt like months but were in fact only weeks, the affairs of their short, round, easygoing parents had been streamlined into paper statements and reduced to receipts.

The brothers would make casual plans and then break them each time. It had been gnawing at Michael for a year. At home in his bed, after mixing sound for cartoons all day, he wondered about his brother. He'd allow himself one beer for two that were non-alcoholic, and then two reals for one fake and so on. He felt bloated and muzzy-headed, but he rarely got drunk. He spent his days wedged tightly between headphones and in front of screens—rising and falling to the manic, high-speed rhythms of big color and voice. This did sinister things to his nights, when the silence sounded loud and the stillness dizzied him—like sitting in front of a television that had just been turned off, the click and the blackness piercing the center of his forehead: a bindi of sudden quiet.

Michael doubted that Wade was as preoccupied with their estrangement as he was, not because Wade was a bad or callous person, but because his superpower was the ability to make himself slippery, so that nothing ever touched him. Michael assumed he was busy with his own life, which had always been somewhat mysterious. Wade had dropped out of law school and gone into "investments." Michael assumed he earned money making rich people richer. He was defensive and noncommittal when Michael asked.

Had one brother bullied the other or stolen a girlfriend, the situation would have been clearer. But Michael began to understand, during his bedtime alchemy of drinking, and not-drinking, and then drinking, that his problems with Wade were not fixable, and that Wade was a person he wouldn't have known had they not been related. They'd always been comfortable at home with their parents and on holidays in restaurants. They were good at being brothers. Boys. But the family made sense only as a foursome, and now the surviving two were thrust back into the world, maladroit on the skinny legs they'd inherited from their father. There were memories to unearth and stories to tell and retell, but without the parental glue, the brothers had come apart.

Michael called Wade on a Monday night. He made himself sound casual because Wade responded well to lightness. The ease of the call surprised him; they decided on Vincenzi's remastered 1948 triumph of Leftist desolation, *The Elegant Rube*. A movie date might have been a strange choice for a potentially tense reunion, but for Michael and Wade it made sense.

Fifteen minutes before the show, Michael arrived to find Wade in his usual seat: middle section, five rows from the front, on the left aisle. It was just the two of them, save for a woman in the front row, with long, wild gray hair and a complicated scarf. The deco sconces that lined the walls were the same ones that stood watch over Michael and Wade's childhood matinees and teenage late shows. Their parents had never understood the boys' interest in revival house fare—often the same movies they'd watched when they were kids—but they were relieved that their very different sons had this in common. Michael's magic lessons and Wade's soccer practice began dwindling in exchange for Westerns and war films at age ten. And during teenage weekends, when Michael painted naked women (although he'd never seen one) and Wade played Atari, they'd line up together late at night for the culty, bloody, and bawdy. They'd sit together in that blue-lit space—that timeless, placeless fish tank of shadow and sound. At sixteen, Michael wrote an essay entitled "Breathing Underwater: Ode to the Cinema," in which the viewer watches a movie while pleasantly submerged in the indeterminate space of the theater: a warm, undulating zone of contrast, a fusion of land and sea.

Michael didn't want to creep up on Wade and scare him, so he weighted his gait enough to make it audible as he walked down the aisle.

Wade turned and smiled. He'd gotten fatter.

There was a simian brushing of hands and bumping of limbs against shoulder and knee. Michael sat down.

Wade handed him a half-eaten bar of expensive-looking chocolate. "So?"

"So?" said Michael, who broke off three squares, already wondering where they'd go when the movie ended.

They finished the chocolate too fast. Michael wanted to slow everything down. He wanted them to take their time but he didn't know how to pause and linger in a way that wouldn't alarm Wade.

"You got fat," Michael said.

"I know. All I eat is meat and candy. Mirabelle's putting me on a diet."

Wade had always dated rich girls, who'd been carefully named: Mirabelle, Tatiana, Tallulah. Whenever Wade mentioned a girlfriend, Michael sensed he'd never be allowed to meet her. He knew little about Mirabelle, even though she and Wade had been dating for some time. She was a rock critic whose not unimpressive trust fund allowed her to work on an extremely part-time basis. There was always a story about Mirabelle's disappointment when some rock legend turned out to be shockingly dull in person.

Michael tried to formulate a question about Mirabelle that would shepherd them past the small talk but Wade maneuvered the discussion back to familiar territory.

"Remember when we tried to freeze our nose hairs, like dad?" he asked. He was referring to a story their father had told repeatedly: an army story. He was stationed at Fort Devins in the middle of a bad Massachusetts winter. While marching back and forth on the parade ground one frigid, windy morning, he felt his nose dripping. He reached up with a gloved hand and squeezed it, wincing at the sharp pain inside his nostrils: his nose hairs had frozen into glasslike shards. He began to bleed as he marched. It was a morning of bleeding and marching, bleeding and marching: a wretched moment in a relatively comfortable life. He thought the story might ensure that his boys chose college over the service, although there was never any real danger that they wouldn't. What the story did do was encourage the boys to freeze their own nose hairs by shoving crushed ice from the refrigerator up their nostrils.

"Popcorn?" Michael asked, and with Wade's mildly irritating double thumbs-up, he left for the concession stand.

In line in the lobby, Michael studied the posters for the Vincenzi retrospective. They were all pop art and primary colors, as if to dupe today's moviegoers into thinking that the bleak neo-realist world of Vincenzi might be kitschy and mod. And the films' English titles had all been changed. *Crime Tale* was now *Riotous Corpse*, and *God Is Here* became *The Boss of Us*. The strangest of all was the movie they were about to see; the gently wrenching *The Elegant Rube* had been renamed *Uncle Paolo Is No Criminal.* Michael paid for the popcorn, pumped it full of liquid butter, and told himself to tell Wade about the title.

There was no one new in the theater, still just the wild-haired woman. Her ragged attractiveness, coupled with the fact that she sat alone and in front, made her seem self-possessed, European, and a little morose. She had begun to read a book.

"But Uncle Paolo's a minor character," said Wade with a mouth full of popcorn.

"What I don't understand," said Michael "is why *Uncle Paolo Is No Criminal* is a better title than *The Elegant Rube.*"

"It's his best film," said Wade.

"I like the later ones, after the stroke."

"But he was paralyzed. Dude couldn't even talk!"

"He said those were the movies he'd always wanted to make, that he wasn't a genius until he had the stroke."

The European woman whipped her head around as though startled by a loud noise, and surveyed the brothers before returning to her book. Michael had mentally named the woman "Veronique," but then he changed it to "Simone."

The lights faded, which meant that in two minutes it would be dark. Michael stuffed a fistful of popcorn into his mouth and then rubbed his palms together so that the butter and salt stung the chapped grooves. He felt a fluid surge of trust in the next two and a half hours, as though he'd just taken a Valium on an empty stomach. He and Wade would sit there like they always had, snug in each other's idiosyncratic breathing and the periodic shifting of weight. They'd swell and break in tandem, like wrestling on the kitchen floor or kneeling over Tinkertoys, the stove popping with the first sounds of dinner. And after the movie they'd sit in silence for as long as they could stand it. They'd wait for the theater to empty and then they'd look at each other and smile—exhaling—slightly embarrassed at having just seen something great. They'd walk their identical hunched-over walk up the aisle, through the ancient lobby with its flocked wall-paper and whorehouse candelabras, and they'd rejoin the night. And before they began their postmortem, they'd look at each other again and just say, "Wow."

Wallets, ladies. Now!
   Turn around or I'll shoot off your face.
   They stood there until they believed the kid was really gone. Then they turned around and walked ten feet to the tub of popcorn and its splayed contents. The pieces of popcorn looked violated, as if they'd been alive before and now they were not.
   "Great," said Michael, hands in his pockets.
   Wade reached up and fingered the cartilage of his upper ear, a habit he'd had since he was a kid. "I think he was Latvian," he said. They weren't far from the Baltic section of town. "Lucky I only had a few bucks. Did you have cash?"
   "None in my wallet. Five bucks in my pocket, which I kept," said Michael, kicking the tub of popcorn toward the gutter.
   "He called us 'ladies.'"
   "Ladies with no money," said Michael. "Little douche bag chose the wrong ladies."
   They circled slowly around the pieces of popcorn, as though it might provide some insight into the situation.
   "Now we have to cancel everything," said Wade. "I hate that."
   "Like credit cards?"
   "Credit cards, gas card, driver's license . . . my whole life was in there."
   "If that's your whole life, Wade, I don't know. Not a good sign."
   "Very funny."
   "It takes five minutes to replace everything. You do it on the computer now. You'll have all your cards by next week."
   "Okay. Relax."
   "I am relaxed. You're the one who's worrying. Why do you care so much about your cards?"
   "Jesus, Mike, calm down. If I irritate you so much, why'd you arrange this? Why'd you invite me out?"
   "Because we're strangers, Wade. Because I don't know shit about your life after the age of eighteen."

"What do you want to know?"

"Come on."

"I'm serious. You've never asked about my life. When did you suddenly get interested in anyone besides yourself?"

"You have no idea what I'm interested in," said Michael, stunned at how suddenly their politeness had turned.

"Because you keep everything a secret. Your delicate little life, so sensitive. You think I'm some big dumb jock."

"You think I'm a depressed drunk."

"You are."

Michael began speed-walking up the middle of the street.

"Aren't you?" Wade yelled. He was a few paces behind Michael. Their loping gait was synchronized, their father's, something to do with those skinny legs and bad knees.

Michael stopped short and turned around. They were standing in the middle of the street, face to face, a foot apart. "At least I feel things, you bloated fucking robot."

They walked fast, heading toward the horizontal ribbons of light at the next big avenue. Tears crept down Michael's long face and Wade's broad one.

"If I'm a bloated robot, then you're a sullen teenager. If you're so unhappy, do something about it. You want to know who I am? Ask! You wait for the world to approach you, and when it doesn't, you pout. You're too old to feel so misunderstood, Mike. Unless you plan to die alone."

They passed a water-damaged apartment building with subtle metallic specks in its stucco façade, probably from the early sixties. On the grass in front, a young Filipino man was giving another young Filipino man—seated on a lawn chair and wearing a white smock—a haircut. It was jarring to see this after midnight, but the men on the lawn behaved as though it was the most natural thing in the world.

"You say I don't feel anything," Wade continued shrilly, wiping the tears from his face with the back of his hand. "You know *why* I'm pissed about my wallet? It's not the damn gas card. I had a picture of mom and dad in there. My favorite picture."

"Which one?" asked Michael, who felt all of a sudden responsible for what had happened, as if by orchestrating their reunion, he himself had taken the wallet from Wade's baggy, faded jeans.

The brothers stopped walking. They were in the middle of the street.

"A picture—from a long time ago. I just liked it."

"What were they doing? Where were they?"

"I think it was in the old backyard. You can't really tell. They're in bathing suits and they look like they're laughing at a dirty joke."

Michael saw Wade just then as a six-year-old wearing Mickey Mouse ears. The guy at Disneyland had mistakenly embroidered "Wayne" onto the hat, but Wade didn't mind. He was a happy child, easygoing even then. He wore his "Wayne" hat for an entire summer.

"What are we doing, Mike? Where are we going?" There was a pleading tone to Wade's questions.

"We're walking it off. I can't go home yet."

"Don't you feel like a target?"

"We're not going to get mugged twice in one night," Michael said. "Oh man, can you imagine?"

"Jesus," said Wade, and they both laughed a little.

At that instant, Michael knew that the mugging had earned the stamp of official memory. He imagined the story they would tell, the pithy paragraph, the recounting. He didn't hear the words but he could feel the shape of them. The moment of the shared chuckle was the moment the mugging had become mutual, an event, another installment in the brothers' soft mythology. This incident, Michael knew with a prescient pang, would assume an unearned weight strictly because it was a memory—a memory for two people who existed for each other only in the world of memory.

They arrived at the honking bustle of a major east-west artery with the four usual corners: giant supermarket, giant bank, giant parking structure, giant hamburger drive-thru. Everything in Los Angeles had grown giant, mom-and-pop shops bulldozed away from high-profile intersections like this one. The garish display blew at the brothers like a gust of wind.

"I should go," said Wade.

"What?"

"I should go," he said. "Mirabelle's waiting up."

"Are you serious?"

"Yeah," he said, reaching up to finger his ear. "It's just starting to hit me. I don't want to be out in all this," he said, looking up and around at the lights and billboards and then down at the sidewalks and the pedestrians that weren't there. "If you want to spend your five dollars on a piece of pie, I'd split it, but I can't just traipse around."

Wade had always been an abrupt leaver, a fact that Michael only remembered during the mildly shocking moment of Wade's goodbye. His goodbyes seemed surprising and inevitable at the same time.

Michael felt a twitching guilt about the night, but he didn't want to eat pie and he didn't want to reminisce. Memories offered little succor for him, perhaps because he and Wade always seemed to remember the same things. Didn't the power of memory lay in its ability to surprise and illuminate? Otherwise, wasn't it just an elaborate brand of small talk, starving the people in question while appearing, briefly, to feed them? Michael knew that a piece of pie with Wade would not feel like progress. Plus, there was nowhere to get pie after midnight, unless you were willing to drive, and what Michael needed was a beer.

"Okay," he said as he leaned in to his brother. They embraced like tin-men with unlubricated joints.

"I'll talk to you," said Wade. "Sorry." He walked back down the darkened street, toward the scene of the crime—or whatever it was—where his car was parked.

Michael sprinted through the blinking intersection and into the supermarket. It was painfully bright and operating-room cold, but it was a familiar shock, and not unpleasant. He yanked a shopping cart out of the corral and began wheeling it through the meat aisle, which was far more populated than the street outside. The bustling aisle gave Michael the sensation of an approaching storm, of citizens stocking up on canned goods and butane, going about their business with the methodical American dread he'd seen on the news. He pushed his empty cart past the various meats. He passed at least three young women ogling lamb chops or pausing to consider a fillet or some other lonely cut. He wheeled past the breakfast meats and into the bread aisle, feeling well-adjusted because, surely, he was the only person there who'd just been mugged and then immediately resumed his quotidian duties. But as he gained momentum down the pillowy aisle of muffins and pita and all the other starches, he felt in his stomach the possibility that he might be wrong. There was the chance, however slight, that others in the market had also just been mugged—or if not mugged, then accosted, attacked, held up, assaulted, shammed, scammed, humiliated, beaten up, shot at, or victimized in some way. It was possible. He checked his watch. It was 12:53 and they were all contained there in the bunker-like supermarket, wherever they'd been before.

He began filling up his cart. He took peanut butter and tomato soup and cans of tuna packed in oil, and he looked long at his late-night shopping companions, who maybe just didn't want to go home.

He pushed the cart, which now also contained a sports drink with electrolytes and some boxes of couscous, into the cereal aisle, where he saw the unmistakable gray rat's nest of a hairdo, simultaneously abject and sophisticated. Simone, still alone and wrapped up in her Euro-scarf, walked quickly down the aisle with a small red basket. There was a furtive grace to her gait, a hurried worry not unlike Alice chasing the White Rabbit. Here was a middle-aged, possibly European woman in a West Coast supermarket at one in the morning, but Michael saw the dewy, distressed heroine of a fairytale. Maybe the night would end well. She—Simone—would be his reward for calling Wade and trying to repair things. This serendipitous detour could alter his life more profoundly than his well-meaning lump of a brother ever could. Maybe he was right to let Wade go, not agreeing to get pie but rather following his instincts.

He began trailing Simone, but he feared he'd make her nervous. He wanted to talk to her without seeming dangerous or desperate. He was too far away to make out the contents of her basket, but from a distance, her knee-length hem revealed a skinny ankle and a strong calf. They were at the edge now, near the verdant maze of produce, when she turned abruptly, a sudden jerk of impatience sending her to the express lane. She fished around in her well-worn leather bag, which looked like a baseball mitt. Michael got in line behind her. She leaned back against the metal railing, staring at something—or nothing—and maybe she sensed the jumbled intentions pulsing in him because she gazed out of her reverie and into his eyes, revealing, maybe, some tiny bit of recognition. And then she began placing her groceries onto the belt.

He grabbed a roll of mints from the display and tossed them into his cart when his stomach—which knew things before he did—turned a lumbering somersault as he remembered that his wallet had been stolen, and that he had no cards and no identification. His pockets were empty—save for the five dollar bill and his car keys—but his cart was full. With his five dollars, he could afford to buy two of the beers in the six-pack in his cart, but he hated that guy, the one who buys two beers and nothing else, after midnight, alone. He scanned an imaginary list, mentally crossing off the things he would not do: he would not meet this brave and mysterious woman; he would not buy provisions for the imaginary storm; he would not call Wade to rehash the details of the mugging. He would excuse himself from the express lane, which had already filled up behind him, and he would leave his cart in the middle of some aisle, which is exactly what he did, and then he slipped a candy bar into his jacket pocket and he went to find his car.

From Uncertain Times

Richard Yates

Richard Yates, born in 1926 in New York, was the author of seven novels and two collections of short stories, including Revolutionary Road, The Easter Parade, *and* Eleven Kinds of Loneliness. *He died in 1992. What follows is the beginning of a novel left unfinished at the time of his death; a longer excerpt originally appeared in* Open City.

WILLIAM GROVE BELIEVED HE COULD AFFORD TO BE almost at peace with the world when the new year of 1963 broke over New York. At an early, tipsy hour of that morning he was walking home down Seventh Avenue with his arm around Nora Harrigan, and they were singing old songs.

"It's incredible," she said, "how many songs you know."

"Yeah, well, I know a few. Do you know 'Mountain Greenery'?"

"I don't think so. I'll try to pick it up, though, if you take it slowly."

She picked it up very well, her light voice trailing only a shade of a beat behind his own hoarse tenor. He knew she would probably laugh when he led her into the first tricky rhyme:

While you love your lover let
Blue skies be your coverlet

And she did laugh, a sweet affectionate sound that made him hug her closer to his overcoat. Things could be an awful lot worse than this. It was four years now since Grove's divorce. It was two years since the publication of his first novel, to generally good reviews, and only a year since his first collection of stories. He had spent six well-paid months in Los Angeles, writing a screenplay based on a famous contemporary novel that he'd always admired—not bad; not bad—and there would be another avalanche of money as soon as the movie went into production in March or April. By then he would be thirty-seven years old, and that seemed a good-enough age for the fuller, more successful, happier part of anybody's life to begin.

He wasn't much to look at—tall and gangling, with lank hair and a face as haunted and sad as the tone of his best work—but having a girl as lovely as Nora Harrigan made significant improvements even in that.

And he did have her; there was no longer any question of it. She was twenty-six and employed as an editorial assistant in his publishing house. In her quiet way she seemed to have read every book in the world, and because she'd been born in Ireland there was a subtle rolling of 'r's in her way of saying "horrible" and "art" and "America." One of the first things Grove learned about her was that she liked to drink as much as he did, and everything he'd learned since then suggested they were made for each other.

"Mountain Greenery" was over by the time they turned the corner onto Barrow Street, and there, five steps down from the sidewalk, they were safe in the warmth and dim light of his basement apartment. He helped her off with her coat and watched the slender, curvy way she stepped out of it; then he hung up both their coats and went on to the kitchen where he made two drinks of bourbon and water, with plenty of ice, and brought them back and put them on the coffee table while he sat close beside her on the daybed.

"Well," he said. "Cheers."

"Oh, yes. And happy New Year, too."

"Know what I've been thinking, though? We'd better not look for a bigger apartment just yet. Be smarter to wait until the movie money's coming in. I'm a little like President Kennedy that way."

"Well, of course. Besides, I like living down here. I think it suits us. But whatever does Kennedy have to do with it?"

"Oh, you know. People say he's going easy on some of the big decisions until he's safely into his second term. He'd rather just sort of coast now, only I guess that'd be a lot easier if he didn't have the Bay of Pigs to live down."

"You're all so funny about the Kennedys in this country, aren't you. Even if you don't like them you talk about them as if they were real, and the point is they're not. They're made up. They're figments of the public imagination, like the British Royal Family. That's what I wanted to tell that dreadfully earnest girl tonight—she kept going on about Jack and Jackie and Bobby and Ethel and Ted, and I wanted to say, How can you be interested in that lot? They're only about as real as salted peanuts and they serve the same purpose, helping people relax in a strange room until the party gets started."

"Salted peanuts," he said. "That's nice."

Nora's lips had such an intriguing, intelligent-looking shape that the only thing to do was kiss them, and then to begin stroking her with his hands.

It did suit them, this odd little place under the street, where you couldn't even tell if it was snowing outside and didn't care. They finished the drinks and made themselves sleepy by making love—it always seemed as fresh and ordained as it had in their first time together—and they slept well into the afternoon.

It wasn't until after breakfast, with their second cups of coffee, that a vague depression began to settle in the room.

"I wish you'd tell me," she said, "what your new book is about."

"Well, it hasn't been going very well. I think I'm sort of blocked on it right now."

"And you can't even say what it's about?"

"Sure I can, sort of. It's about the last part of the war in Europe."

"Yes, I've gathered that, but you weren't in the war really, were you? Except for a very little while?"

"I went into combat in late January of '45. Then I was out with pneumonia for a while, but I got back to the line early in March, and the war didn't end until May 9th. That didn't seem like a very little while at that time. So you see it'll be about some guys in an infantry unit during that— during that period."

She thought it over. "You're making it sound a little like 'The Guts-and-Glory Boys of Company C kind of thing,' she said, "but I know you wouldn't write one of those."

"No. It won't be anything like that."

"Why do you suppose you're blocked, though?"

"If I knew," he told her, "the block wouldn't be there. Look, dear, wonder if we could talk about something else now."

"Certainly. Or we don't have to talk at all, if you'd rather not. We could go out and see what kind of a day it is, and buy the paper. Is that what you'd rather do?"

"Okay. We'll do that."

"Anyway, I'm not really worried about this 'block' of yours. Think of all the time you'll have, when the movie money comes in."

"Yeah."

When Nora left for her job the next morning—she always managed to look crisp and beautifully groomed for the office—he sat slumped at his writing table with several sharpened pencils, and it took him two hours to realize he wasn't working at all.

A stack of finger-wrinkled pages on a far corner of the desk proved there were three chapters in rough-draft form, but they would all need work; and the sketchy opening of Chapter Four kept thinning out into nothing. In another corner of the table lay a few papers marked "Partial Outline" but he hadn't considered them for weeks because he believed that any kind of outline was better kept in his head.

It sure as hell wasn't going to be The Guts-and-Glory Boys of Company C; but then, why were there so very many relishing words like cartridge belt and combat boots and helmet and rifle? And why did the dialogue keep sliding into stilted army phrases like, "Fuck you, Harrison"?

William Grove's first novel had been nominated for the National Book Award, and no reviewer had been unkind about even the earliest of his stories, yet through all the years of work on those books he had saved a good part of his heart for what he thought of as his Army material. So what was the matter now? Why did his nerves keep getting in the way?

He smoked too many cigarettes and went to the bathroom more often than necessary. He lay down on the bed a while—sometimes lying down could help—but before long he was up and pacing the floor, and by three or four o'clock he knew what he was really doing: he was waiting for Nora to come home. That was the way things went through the rest of January.

"I think my brains are still fucked up," he told her once. "Maybe I haven't come out of that second breakdown yet."

"Of course you've 'come out' of it," she said impatiently.

"If you hadn't, don't you think I'd know?"

But he wasn't convinced. Twice, in 1960 and again just after coming back from California, in '62, he had spent a week bewildered in psychiatric wards, and the second time he'd been diagnosed as a manic-depressive. Even now there was a tidy little row of prescription vials in his medicine cabinet, pills with funny pharmaceutical names that he swallowed faithfully every day, and so he always knew he could still be described as a mental case.

"Everybody has moods," Nora said. 'You're just in a bit of a funk, that's all. It'll pass."

Then one February morning, in a characteristically terse phone call from his agent, he learned there would be no more movie money. The project had been "shelved" because it had "fallen apart in the casting."

And it might be years now, if ever, before anybody could get it moving again.

"Oh," Nora Harrigan said when he told her about it that night. "Well, but did you call Paul Cameron?"

"Not yet. There probably isn't anything he can do."

"Call him anyway."

Paul Cameron was a famous writer, author of the book Grove had adapted for the screen. He and his wife were comfortably fixed—they lived on a leafy Connecticut estate, with summers on Cape Cod, and they seemed to have hundreds of friendly connections in the worlds of art and commerce—but against frivolous Hollywood decisions even Paul Cameron was helpless.

"Yeah, I heard it too," he said, and as always in the hours after five o'clock his telephone voice was enriched with bourbon sipped from a heavy, tinkling glass. "Really pisses me off. Not the money part of it so much as the picture. I wanted that picture. Only I guess the money part of it does kind of leave you in the lurch, doesn't it."

"Sure does," Grove said.

"Well, worse things could happen. You still got that great-looking Irish girl?"

"Yes."

"Hang onto her then, and keep punching. I mean you know, keep on with your book. If the work's going well everything else has a way of falling into place around that."

"I know; but it's not going very—yeah, I know."

"You could probably get a Guggenheim."

"Had it already. Two years ago."

"Well, something else'll break for you. Keep in touch, Bill."

"I will, Paul."

There was money in the bank to last through April; then they'd be broke except for Nora's salary, which wouldn't be enough for both of them even if Grove could agree to use it, and he couldn't: he had alimony and child-support payments to meet every month. This was a crisis, and he was suddenly scared.

"Well, let's think," Nora said. "You have friends. Surely one of them might be able to—"

"There's nobody I could borrow from, not in the amount I need. Besides, I don't want to get into anything like that."

"I wasn't thinking of loans. I meant someone who might help you find a kind of freelance public-relations work or something that wouldn't take much time away from your—"

That was when he thought of Henry Wilson, a Negro novelist whose books hadn't yet begun to earn him a living; Wilson had made a profitable sideline for years out of writing about jazz for the album copy, or "liner notes," required by a big recording company. So Grove called Henry Wilson and arranged to have dinner with him one night soon at a neighborhood restaurant called the Blue Mill.

"Oh, good," Nora said over her whiskey on the afternoon of the meeting. "I'm glad we're seeing Henry tonight. I think I like him better than any of your other friends because he's always so down to earth. And he has beautiful manners."

"Well, okay," he told her. "But could you kind of go easy on the booze? I mean you look wonderful but I wouldn't want you getting smashed tonight."

"I have no intention of getting smashed," she said haughtily. "And you're a great one to tell anybody about going easy on the booze, aren't you."

It was sometimes pleasing for Grove to consider how much he and Henry Wilson had in common. They were the same age, both divorced and each the father of two small children. But apart from Wilson's being a Negro there were other important differences: Wilson was short and sturdy, with a handsome thin-lipped face and a voice that always sounded calm. He was "cool," and tonight he was wearing an expensive tweed jacket with his white shirt and dark silk tie.

"So I've been wondering," Grove said in the Blue Mill, "if you think I might be able to pick up some work in the record business. I mean I couldn't write about jazz, but I could do old standards—show tunes, Tin Pan Alley numbers and stuff like that."

"Oh, and he really could, Henry," Nora said. "He knows one thousand songs." But Wilson was already shaking his head. "Nah, that's out," he told them. "No market for it. There's free-lance work in jazz and classical and one or two other categories, but you're talking about middle-of-the-road music, and the record companies use their own in-house people for that. All that kind of writing ever amounts to is nostalgia, you see, and they figure any asshole can write nostalgia."

"Oh. Well then, the hell with it."

"Besides, I thought your line was public relations. Didn't you write some kind of industrial PR for a whole lot of years?"

"I wrote freelance copy for Remington Rand until they decided to hire a PR agency. Don't know how I'd ever get back into that kind of thing now except in a full-time job."

"So take a full-time job for a while. Won't kill you."

Grove had met Henry Wilson at a summer writers' conference where touch football was in fashion, and Wilson had helped him to overcome a lifetime aversion to sports by saying "Sure you can!" when Grove said he didn't think he could go out and catch a long forward pass. Grove went out, the pass came high and fast, and he not only caught it like a real player but ran dizzily with it into the end zone, to the cheers of what seemed at least a hundred people. Now, here in the restaurant, it was as if Wilson were saying "Sure you can" to the question of taking a full-time job. "Do that for six, eight months, maybe a year until you save enough money, then say fuck it and finish up your new book. What the hell you afraid of, man?"

"I don't like the idea of going back, for one thing. Moving backwards."

"Shee-it. Hate to tell you some of the things I've gone back to between books. After my first book I went back to running an elevator. After my second book I went back to selling lettuce in a supermarket. Nothing wrong with going back, long as you know your main plan is to move forward, right?"

"Right," Nora said. "I think that's—I think that's excellent advice."

"Or," Wilson said, stirring his coffee, "You might go into teaching. Your books got good reviews; someplace like Iowa might hire you in a minute. You thought of that?"

"I think it's too late in the year to apply—and besides, the money wouldn't start until September."

"So that leaves the PR business. Make up a good résumé, spread it around town and go to the highest bidder. What's your new book about?"

"It's about the last part of the war in Europe."

"May be a little late in the day for another war novel. Still, you wouldn't be as late as Stephen Crane, and I guess he did all right. I wish you the best of luck with it, my friend."

"Thanks, Henry."

Nora had declined coffee because she said she felt like having another drink instead, and now she was smiling in a way Grove didn't like: the eyes too bright and the upper lip loosened and soft. When the three of them got up to leave she got into her coat soberly enough, and she made it alone past two or three other tables into the open space at the front of the restaurant, but then her knees gave way and she fell full-length on the floor.

A cry of "Oh!" broke over the room and several men sprang from their chairs to come hurrying over but Henry Wilson was already there, crouched at her shoulders and lifting her securely under the arms. Grove arrived too late to be needed, though he got both hands on her in order to appear to help her to her feet, and in pressing against Henry Wilson he felt a heavy shifting of muscle in the tweed. Wilson was no taller than Nora but he was stronger than Grove and he had more presence of mind: he knew just how to disperse the gathering cluster of strangers.

"It's all right," he told them, smiling without embarrassment. "We're in control here. Thanks anyway, gentlemen."

She sagged upright between the two of them, with Grove's arm around her back, as they walked her carefully out to the street. The fresh air revived her at once but she was drunkenly humiliated, trying to fix her hair with her fingers.

"Oh," she said. "Oh, that was horrible. Oh, Henry, you must think I—"

"I think you're a beautiful lady," he said, backing a step away. "And now I think it's time for my good friend to get a cab and take you home."

The rest of February and March were muggy that year— a windless, humid warmth with low skies, with dirty snow still lumped in the street or riding awash down the gutters—and the thawing of winter had never been a stalwart time for William Grove.

Seven public-relations offices turned him down.

"Two published books; very good," one interviewer said.

"Nice piece of luck for you, too, the way the fiction market is today. Still, we do a highly specialized kind of PR here. I'm not sure if you've got the background."

Another man, at another place, said, "Frankly, I'm not very interested in writers who want to set the world on fire with their own 'creative' stuff. I'm kind of a down-home guy myself and I had four years in the army, and my idea of talent is somebody who can come in here and soldier for us every day. You know what I mean by 'soldier'?"

And there was reason now to be concerned about Nora. She wasn't taking care of herself; she was letting her appearance go. On some afternoons after his day of job-hunting, when he met her at a bar near her office, she looked unkempt and bedraggled.

"How'd it go?" she would ask.

"Not so good."

And he'd bring her home in a taxicab. One evening at the beginning of April he could tell there was a quarrel coming.

She was changing her dress, both arms over her head as she unfastened a clasp at the nape of her neck, and he said "Honey, don't you think that dress is about finished?"

She looked startled. "How do you mean? I thought you liked this dress."

"Oh, I do—or at least I did—but the point is it's all sort of rotted through now, in the armpits, and that really doesn't look very—"

"Rotted through?"

"Well, sure. That kind of cloth does rot pretty easily, you see, if you wear it too many times, and it—"

"Oh," she said, and both arms came quickly down as she sank into a chair. "Oh, how hideous. Well, but why didn't you tell me?"

"I did. I've just told you. And listen, it's no big deal. I wouldn't worry about it. Probably just means you ought to throw that particular dress away, is all, and give some of your other clothes a chance. Still, as long as we're on this general subject, there's another matter."

"Oh, God. What?"

"Take a look at your feet."

With a quick movement of her lovely knees she drew her stockinged feet from beneath her and set them primly side by side.

"See?" he said. "See the sort of smudges around the toes?"

"Oh, that's just dye from my shoes. They're cheap shoes, and the black dye rubs off."

"No it doesn't," he explained. "That kind of dirt can only come from the inside. Now, I know it can be hard to bend all the way down and wash your feet in the shower, on mornings when you've got a bad hangover, and the point is you've had bad hangovers every morning lately because you've been drunk every night. So I really don't want to hear about dye from your shoes, Nora. That's dirt, is all. It's what little kids call toe jam."

She had been looking down at her feet, curling the toes under in a cringing, failing effort to hide the smudges, and when she looked up at him again her face was a terrible mixture of anger and chagrin.

"Oh, you can be hateful, can't you," she said. "You can really be loathsome, when you want to."

"I called it toe jam," he said, "because that's what it is. It's toe jam, Nora."

Then the telephone rang.

"Bill? Paul Cameron. So how's it going? You still looking for work?"

"Yes."

"And all you need is kind of a grubstake, right? To tide you over? Because I think I may have something, if you're interested."

Most likely it would be another screenplay, or maybe a temporary teaching job. But it would be something substantial, and Grove felt his lungs beginning to loosen in gratitude and relief.

Across the room Nora Harrigan's face was averted as she crouched at the job of putting her cheap shoes back on. All she had to do now was get up and walk out of here and be gone.

"This may sound a little—bizarre at first," Paul Cameron was saying, "but think about it. How'd you like to write speeches for Bobby Kennedy?"

"Oh Jesus, no. I don't think I'd be right for that, Paul. I don't see how I'd be qualified to—look, can you hold the phone a second? Wait just a second."

He let the receiver fall and dangle from the wall as he hurried back to where she was standing, and he turned her quickly around and took her in his arms. "Oh baby, I'm sorry," he said into her hair. "I can't tell you how sorry I am, but don't go away, okay? Oh, please stay. Just wait until I—"

"I wasn't going anywhere."

"Oh my God, I love you. Just wait for me now, okay?"

And he had her sitting safely on the bed again, ready to forgive him, but the room swayed and tilted as he made his way back to the phone.

"Let me give you the background," Paul Cameron said.

"There's this old college pal of mine named Warren Turner who's become kind of a hotshot Washington lawyer. And the thing is, Warren's gotten himself in very tight with the Kennedys. Called me up just now to ask if I could recommend a writer, so I told him a few good things about you."

"Well, that's awfully—that's really nice of you, Paul, but I don't know anything about politics. I've never been very— I've never been able to get much of a hard-on for politics, if you see what I mean."

"Well, when you put it that way I don't suppose I can either. Still, somebody's got to clean up the mouth on that snarling little bastard, right? And I mean whaddya got to lose?"

Dragons May Be the Way Forward

Leni Zumas

Leni Zumas is the author of the story collection Farewell Navigator *(Open City Books). Her fiction has appeared most recently in* Keyhole, Gigantic, Salt Hill, *and* Columbia. *She has received fellowships from Yaddo, Hedgebrook, the MacDowell Colony, the Lower Manhattan Cultural Council, and the New York Foundation for the Arts. She is collaborating with the artist Luca Dipierro on a full-length animated film called* Until I Find It.

THE YEAR JAMES AGEE DIED, MY MOTHER WAS FIN-ishing high school. She could have read his obituary in the paper but she was probably dropping the needle onto a record instead. All those sock hops—a relentless schedule—meant a girl had to practice. Her legs are so swollen now they couldn't dance if you paid them. While watching her rocket program, she props the knurly white logs on a milk crate. Look, she yells, he's hanging in the blackness from just that tiny cord and what if it snaps?

I say from the next room: It's made of steel. It won't.

James Agee had a drinking problem. He slept around on all three of his wives. He was a socialist obsessed with Jesus. He criticized the government and other writers and his own failed self. By the time he died—of a stopped heart in a taxi, age forty-five—he was in every sense a stray.

And so smart you could hear his brain tick ten blocks away.

And so louche you could lick him off the bottom of your shoe.

It would be better if I didn't think about him. But I do.

My mother is blattering about grace and bravery. They have launched a new rocket and its astronauts are so graceful and brave. Her favorite channel shows their faces, miles above Earth in airless air. That one's a schoolteacher, she says. Far left—see? She's got guts, that teacher. Maybe she'll write a book about her adventures.

I was stretched on a towel in the backyard, fourteen and no friends, when I first read *Let Us Now Praise Famous Men*. When the page said, "And spiders spread ghosts of suns between branches," a nerve I'd never felt before throbbed between my legs.

She shoves her hairdo into my room: Shall I open a can?

It is not soup we are talking about. It is not beer or tuna. Tapioca is the canned good of choice in this house. You wouldn't think it was a great idea to pack pudding in tin, but they do, and my mother eats a few cans a night under the pretense that I am sharing them with her. Two bowls, two spoons, one mouth.

Some speck on the wafer of her brain tells her that this rocket is traveling *now*. It is not, says her brain, a space mission that took place in the early eighties, but in fact an event of today. As we learn about the astronauts, observe their watery movements in the capsule, my mother refers to their moods and personalities in the present tense. When she gets up—slowly, slowly—to make another cup of hot water, I see worms dance on the purpling backs of her knees.

A question from *Famous Men* is burnt onto the skin behind my forehead: "How was it we were caught?" I know a little about caught. I know enough. There is this house. There is my mother. There is until she is dead.

She loves to plump the pillows on her Ku Klux furniture. Each pringly tassel must fall just so. She doesn't sit on the sofa anymore; she will cause too big of a dent. She uses a folding metal chair. I go on the striped wingback, rest the dictionary on my thighs, and read aloud. Her ghouly eyes listen. Sometimes her mouth, on its way to the pudding spoon, says: Read that part again.

The word is *moxa*, I say, and here are your choices: a medieval fortified keep; a small instrument used to brush hair off the South American goose; a preternaturally skilled hoagie maker; or a flammable material obtained from the leaves of Japanese wormwood.

Hoagie is a disturbing word, my mother says.

You have ten seconds.

Well, she says, I don't know what hoagie means so how can I choose?

It means submarine sandwich. In other parts of the land.

Then there's that goose—

Five seconds, I say.

I'll go with flammable material.

Are you sure?

Ha! she says happily, knowing she's right, since on wrong guesses I never ask.

A chewy cackle from the bathroom and I find her crouched near—but not on—the toilet. Massive gray panties swarm at her feet.

What the fucking fuck?

Don't say fuck so much, she says. No wonder you'll die a virgin, filthy mouth like that.

And no wonder she will die beached, left to drown yelling in the tide.

The word is *umbelliferous,* which might mean: excessively warlike; belonging or pertaining to the *belliferae* family of plants, including parsley and carrots; carrying an umbrella; or that which feeds from the underside.

Hard one, she says.

I'll give you an extra five seconds.

Maybe umbrella, she murmurs. Maybe parsley.

Don't forget that which feeds from the underside, I say casually, proud of this phrase. It's one of my best ever. A long belly seamed with nipples and the sucking, splittering mouth—

She guesses umbrella.

Sorry, I say, *belliferae* family of carrots and parsley.

Oh, damn. That was my close second.

Kitchen, late morning, matching yellow bathrobes.

The poison lake is awake!

Stop shouting, I shout.

She says, The wedding announcements page is especially interesting today.

Who?

Two girls from your year at St. Pancreas. It's gotten me thinking—

Do you want more coffee?

About how lonely you must be.

I'm not, actually. Hand me your cup.

Of course you are, beechnut. And it's not your fault. Well, *some* of it is your fault, because if you don't leave the house how can you. . . . But some of it's just plain bad luck. You're unlucky in love.

No, I say, I'm just waiting.

Her mouth makes a sickle of *Go ahead and believe that.* Yes, mother, thank you, I will go ahead. Her haught is terrible, but when she dies, that chin won't jut any longer. Its meat will turn to powder on her collarbone and she'll have no chin at all.

She will die of tapioca. Of tassels. Of watching too much space travel.

Here are your choices: *jipijapa* means a Brazilian hummingbird; a hat made from tender young leaves; Hawaiian bread pudding; or—from the Australian colloquial—to be in high spirits following the beginning of study at a college or university.

She asks, Did you feel *jipijapa* when you started college?

So that's your guess?

Not necessarily. I am pausing to ask you a personal question. Were you in high spirits?

I don't remember, I say.

Sure you do, corn nut.

It was twenty years ago. I don't.

Your father got very excited when he went off to school. He wrote gushing letters.

What is your guess, Mother?

You'd have thought that college was a goddamn cathedral.

Time is up.

I love a good bread pudding.

Wrong, I say.

I know, she says. It's the hat of young goddamn leaves. Are you aware that the sluttish postman has not been bringing our mail?

It's not his fault if we don't get written to, I remind her.

He is a slut, though. I've been watching him. He makes house calls on this very block, if you know what I mean.

I really don't, I say.

Please don't act like the virgin you are so bent on remaining. Anybody with one eye could see what he's up to. Mrs. Poole in the split-level? Mr. Brim in the Oldsmobile? They've been getting their fill of our most venturesome mail carrier.

Who *cares,* I say.

She grunts: It's almost better than television.

On the flickery screen, people in jeans and puffy shirts are learning to waltz. An instructor taps out beats of one-two-three.

I put down the grocery bags and ask, Why are you crying?

I'm not, she says, turning wetly away.

What, do those people all have cancer? Are they dancing to distract themselves?

Isn't it shocking that nobody wants to marry you, with a sunshine attitude like that! Those are just some idiots on public access. I had to switch from my regular channel because (with thumb and forefinger she kneads the loose skin at her throat), because there was an accident.

A crash?

Yes, a crash. The ship crashed. The ship has been lost.

Did the schoolteacher parachute to safety? I ask.

Is this the day your brain decided to stop working? *There are no parachutes in space.* There is cold air and death.

Sorry, I say.

The galaxy is too big out there, my mother says.

The word tonight is *flocculence*—

Don't be coarse, she says.

Your choices are thus: the silence that follows a bad joke; the state of being covered with a soft, woolly substance; the crunch made by teeth on potato chips; the rate of torsion in the flight of seagulls; or an Icelandic sleeping porch built of marble and walrus tusks.

Be nice to have a sleeping porch, she says. You know it's hell on my legs, climbing those stairs every night. Makes them ache to a fare-thee-well. My veins are getting like goddamn garden hoses.

We'll need to install an elevator, I say.

Your dad's insurance won't stretch *that* far.

(It's getting less stretchy all the time.)

You might have to get a job again, sour ball.

I say, Choose or forfeit.

I choose none.

None?

I think they're *all* fake. You've done a trick this time. Whatever I choose will be wrong.

Just choose goddamnit.

I won't, because I don't think it's a real word. I think you made it up—

I ask, Is that your final decision?

She nods. I shut the dictionary. She leans her spoon on the rim of the tapioca bowl, sniffs, tucks her chin. Folds of skin accordion at her neck. James Agee could have described her much better—would have done justice to the weirdness of my mother, her loggishness, her ghouliness, her secret gentleness. He could've spent pages, maybe a whole chapter, doing her justice.

About me, there'd be little to write. *She sits at home of an evening. With mother, with dictionary.* He might have wrung a sentence or two out of my eyes, which are a not-bad shade of blue. He'd have piled adjectives upon this blue, lavished it with taut slippery words until it was unrecognizable as a color and had become—a feeling.

I wonder where the funerals will be, she says.

In the astronauts' hometowns?

Too ordinary.

At the launch pad in Florida?

Too tacky. I'm thinking Arlington Cemetery.

That's for veterans, I say.

And what are they, if not veterans? Soldiers in the space race? Battlers of the galactic elements?

Vomit, I say.

There's that sunshine. There's that charm. Hark!—she cups a hand at the back of her ear—I think I hear the suitors lining up now! Do you hear them? Outside the door? The line is forming *around the block.* Nobody loves a sour ball, sour ball.

James Agee wouldn't have minded; he was sour too. He'd have whispered, We better clean out this mouth of yours! before he kissed it.

Next time I go shopping, I'll be leaving her tapioca off the list. She wants pudding, she can goddamn well figure out how to get it delivered. Or she can put some shoes on for once and hop in the car.

James Agee, please write her into the ground. Tell about the wet earth clumping down onto her coffin. Describe her bone-box with your best, your most precise exaggerations.

In the yellow kitchen, her face is a lump of smile. She has seen the postman getting out of Mr. Brim's car. Dirty deeds, she hoots. Oh, very dirty. She swallows coffee in triumph and I want her to stop smiling, stop watching out the window, stop thinking she *knows.*

Mother, I say.

Daughter?

In case you weren't aware, that rocket ship didn't crash yesterday.

Of course it did, beechnut. I saw it with my own peekers. No survivors.

It crashed in nineteen-*eighty*-something! The teacher has been dead for decades. How can you be so fucking—

Language, she reminds me, and gets up from the table.

Your word tonight is *thole*.

Soul, you say?

Tee-aitch. Here are your choices. To murder someone using brainwaves only; to throw a body into a hole; to sew up a person's face so she can't smile; or to suffer long, to bear, to endure.

What a jolly lineup, my mother says.

I wait. She sips a bite of pudding off the spoon.

I guess I'll pick the most horrible one, then.

Which is?

The long suffer, silly. The endure.

I was a dot in a teenager's egg sac while James Agee was wrecking his looks with smoke and drink and screenwriting. The moment he fell, crumpling on the plastic-taped leather of a taxi seat, I was swinging around in a belly, as yet unfertilized, to sock hop music. He was the man for me and never knew it. He left the planet without being told I was on my way.

My mother has found a new delight to replace her rockets. It is a show about dragons. There is a lot, evidently, to learn about them. They are usually deaf but have excellent eyesight, and it takes a thousand years for a dragon egg to hatch.

She says: I know they aren't real, but maybe they are.

Maybe they are, I agree.

Who can tell for certain?

Not us.

Maybe, she says, they only live beneath the remotest mountains. Or in the deepest pockets of the ocean.

From the porch I watch firstlings of heartsease climb the fence. Tiny green shoots fill the pavement cracks and sunned dirt sends its hot smell into my mouth. It's an hour past mail time. Maybe we have gotten none, or my mother was accidentally right and he's been visiting Mrs. Poole on her carpet.

Then he comes whistling round the corner in his gray-blue shorts. He grins at me with a mustached lip. I want to smile back, but I look down instead.

Beautiful day! is his observation.

I want to answer, but my mouth refuses. It makes a little fist on my face.

I bring you treasure, he continues, our jaunty postman, and holds up an envelope from Eternal Meadow Insurance Company. I start to say Thank you, but he is gone before it can come out.

The money won't last forever. I'll have to get a job again. I will work, and my mother will die, and James Agee will live in the pages under my pillow. I carry the check indoors to my mother, who likes to touch money with both hands before it gets deposited. She lifts her eyes from the blue screen, face sweaty and pleased. She has been waiting.

Listen to this, she says. This is marvelous. Dragons have such peculiar diets! The seafaring ones eat starfish only. The ones in caves eat bats and mold. And the meadow-dwellers are thought to survive entirely on honey bees!

Amazing, I say.

Amazing, she agrees.